# THE POTION WITCH

## THE COVEN: VAMPIRE MAGIC BOOK 2

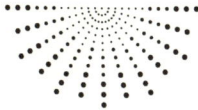

CHANDELLE LAVAUN

# CHANDELLE LaVAUN

# THE POTION WITCH

THE COVEN: VAMPIRE MAGIC BOOK TWO

# CHAPTER ONE

## SAM

THE MARBLE FLOOR was solid black. There was no furniture, no decor, just a few benches carved into the onyx walls surrounding the pedestal holding the orb made of demon-glass.

*Lilith's* orb.

I had no business being in this room. Nothing good came from this room or from that orb. Myself included. Never in my worst nightmares had I ever expected *this* to be my future. When Jackson Lancaster had found me on my boat and escorted me to the secret safe house, I hadn't known what to expect or what role I would play in the upcoming war. I wasn't stupid or naive enough to think I wouldn't have to play a role, not with an actual Coven member locating me. And not just any Coven member either—a *Lancaster*, the first line of arcana. That meant I was somehow important enough to get their attention. I'd always suspected that the safe house was full of special witches with a destiny too honorable to be told outright.

Oh, how foolish I had been.

Finding out that I was Lilith's granddaughter had not been on my bingo card.

*This* was not the role I wanted any part in. Past, present, or future.

Which meant I had no business being in here. Especially without Everest.

Especially with *them.*

Asmodeus chanted with that deep voice of his, and I hated the effect it had on me. He spoke in Lilith's demonic language, and despite being her granddaughter, she hadn't thought me deserving of knowing it. So, I stood there, a pawn in whatever game they were playing without knowing what was happening even while I knew exactly what we were doing. Then again, maybe that ignorance would be my salvation one day. Because I knew what we were doing, and I was terrified it was a crime punishable by death all by itself just for agreeing to participate. I prayed there'd be enough mercy left over for me when this was all over.

Unless *she* won, then I prayed I would not survive the victory.

Asmodeus's chants grew so loud that the marble vibrated beneath my bare feet. Sharp pulses shot up my legs and continued all the way up to my shoulders and down to my hands. Azazel chuckled deep in his throat. He was about to get what he wanted, and he damn well knew it. Green smoke drifted from my palms down to the black marble floor and swirled around the base of the pedestal. When it touched, bright red demonic runes flashed within the marble. My stomach rolled. I bit down on my cheek to stop myself from gagging.

Five of us stood at the points of a pentacle drawn in smoke on the floor. Queen Sweyn stood at the single point on the bottom to my right. But I did not dare glance in her direction. Every moment she looked at me I feared she'd see through my display of loyalty. Nor did I look to my left where Asmodeus and Azazel stood at the top of the inverted star symbol. For Asmodeus, I wanted the ability to feign ignorance. For Azazel, well, anyone who held eye contact with him for more than a few seconds found themselves in his bed . . . and under no circumstances did I want that.

Instead, I focused on the only person in the whole entire kingdom of Avolire who I thought might be stuck in the same hell I was, someone who'd been an innocent human plucked from their lives and thrown into war: *Pierce Fenn.* Something in my gut told me he wanted out of this place as much as I did. Neither of us had asked to be here. Neither of us had asked to be turned into a vampire. Neither of us could stomach Sweyn. I felt bad for Pierce on that part. He was her toy, her handsome British trophy she all but kept on a leash for pleasuring her whenever—and wherever—she pleased. I just prayed he was someone I could trust to help get out of here. Actually, I wanted to take him with me.

Azazel purred.

Pierce's green and red eyes shot over to the fallen Angel of Sin *instantly.* His cheeks flushed. I watched as the tips of his fangs pressed into his bottom lip. I knew he'd been in Azazel's bed, but until this moment, I thought it had also been against his will. He'd *never* looked at Sweyn like that, which meant his days behind closed doors with the fallen angel had been voluntary.

My heart sank. *There goes that idea.* My pulse quickened as panic tried to creep in. I closed my eyes and tried to think happy thoughts, tried to focus on the hope for escape and not the fear threatening to swallow me whole.

I had to get out of this place.

I had to get to The Coven.

But I just wasn't strong enough. There was no way I'd manage to escape on foot by myself. More than that, I didn't know how to keep Lilith out of my head. She'd slide in like the worst kind of intrusive thought. She was literal poison to the brain. Everest knew how to keep her out, but he had not shown me how to do it. He said I was not yet strong enough.

"Is Lilith's little princess not strong enough to do this?" Queen Sweyn said with acid in her voice.

Azazel chuckled so low it sounded like thunder. "She looks strong enough for a lot of sins, my Queen."

"I thought you two were *strong enough* to summon faster than this." I opened my eyes and held my chin high without looking at either of them. "I am just waiting."

*Strong enough.* The words haunted my every thought. There was only one way I would have a chance at getting stronger . . . Lilith had told me so herself. I refused to let myself think about the rituals she had performed on me after Everest stole me from the safe house. But it was impossible to block out my orders. She insisted I would play an important role. For now, though, I had one mission. Once I completed that task, I would get a new one.

That task? To make myself and Everest stronger.

And there was only one way to do that.

"We have already started, little princess. Have no fear," Azazel purred. I felt his gaze slide down my body like the hot rays of summer sunshine.

Pierce cleared his throat. "I thought Everest wanted to wait?"

Sweyn growled. "I thought *I* was Queen."

"My apologies, my Queen," Pierce whispered quickly. "I meant no offense, was merely curious."

"The only curiosity you serve is in my bed," she snapped. I did not miss the threat in her voice. "Angels, summon quicker."

*My bed.* That was my mission. I had to let Everest take me to bed. I had to sleep with him. Lilith demanded it. She'd said something about the mixing of the sins in our blood would give us each more power. More magic. More strength. It made no sense to me, but it wasn't my place to question the why or how of magic. That much I knew for certain. If the only way to get stronger was to consummate this betrothal, then consummate I would.

When I'd first arrived here, I'd thought that wasn't too horrible of an obligation. Everest was gorgeous. And he'd seemed as eager as I was to gain the strength his mother promised it would provide. Except he hadn't touched me. Not once, at least not in private. Everything he'd done in court, or in front of Sweyn and his mother, appeared to be an act. The moment we'd be alone he'd keep his distance. This confused the hell out of me. But worse, it gave me hope that perhaps Everest wasn't on his mother's team after all. Like maybe his heart lay elsewhere.

That witch's face flashed in my mind. The pretty one with pink hair that stared at Everest like he was the oxygen she needed to breathe. The first time I saw him look at her was the first speckle of hope in my soul. If he held the same passion for a mortal witch that she clearly held for him, then perhaps there was a chance. And then there was his fury over Saber hooking up with Azazel . . . Surely, if he was on Lilith's side, he would not have cared. Or at least, that was what I told myself in the sunny hours of the day I was expected to sleep.

Regardless of where Everest's allegiance lay, I knew where mine went: with The Coven. With Heaven. With Earth. I wanted to celebrate in the ashes of Lilith's demise, or at least be part of the reason she lost.

That meant I had to seduce the ancient vampire lord.

And I prayed helping them summon another fallen angel into the realm would get Everest's attention. For good or bad. I would either use sugar or spice to lure him into my bed. I had no other choice. I had no idea how it was going to happen, but my window for getting out was shrinking by the hour. I needed to break through the ice-wall that was Everest. I needed to provoke him. The only times I'd ever seen him lose control were when he was seething with rage. That was my plan, that was why I was in this room in the first place. Because Pierce was right, after all, Everest *had* wanted to wait to summon another fallen angel. All it took was me batting my eyelashes at Asmodeus and then showing a little cleavage when I leaned over in front of Azazel, and I had their attention—and Sweyn's. She loathed when another woman got the angels' lust in front of her. Then it'd only taken a simple question about the other fallen angels and all three of them fell right into my plan.

It was all kinds of wrong, but I was desperate. And if I had to be Lilith's granddaughter, then I would use the evil in my blood for good.

My target was Everest.

Call it women's intuition, but I knew anger was the only way to his bed.

Asmodeus chanted, his voice echoing around the room. Those red demonic runes flashed all around us. I ground my teeth together and stood up straight. *Please, Goddess and Heaven, forgive me for this sin I am about to cause. Help me get out of here, and I shall see her fall forever.*

Asmodeus's chanting in the demonic language grew faster and sharper, the words sending chills down my spine. ". . . *Astaroth.*"

Red smoke burst from the center of the pentacle like a volcanic eruption. I gasped and almost leapt back, but I knew I had to stand my ground. I could never show fear or weakness in front of this group.

The figure of a person with broad shoulders emerged from the red fog. He stood barefoot about the same height as the other angels, but where their hair was dark, his was a dirty blond. And where their eyes were green, his were jet-black. He wore a black leather jacket over what looked like a black toga. Big, black angel wings spread wide as if he was stretching. He threw his arms wide and his head back. Snakes the color of red in Lilith's runes emerged from the angel's shadow. They slithered like smoke around his ankles and hissed.

Azazel quickly chanted the same demonic words Asmodeus just used but ended with "... *Soneillon*."

"*Azazel*," Asmodeus growled, but it was too late.

Lilith's runes flickered like flames all around us.

"Did I ... sin, my brother?" Azazel cackled.

Asmodeus sighed. "Welcome to Earth. Astaroth ..."

A second figure emerged from behind the other.

And it was a *woman*.

Well, not a woman—that suggested she was part-human. This was a female fallen angel. I hadn't known there were any. The only female angel I'd heard of while at the safe house had been Jophiel. Something told me this chick was the opposite of Jophiel. She was the same height as the males and had the same black angel wings as Astaroth, but that was where their similarities ended. Pointed ears the color of midnight stuck out from her long black hair that swayed down by her hips. Large red horns curved backwards almost like a ram's. Her eyes were bright-red. The orbs hanging from her ears glowed like neon lights. Black demonic runes ran down the sides of her arms and legs.

"... *Soneillon*," Asmodeus finished with a growl.

She made a show of closing her eyes and inhaling as she rolled her shoulders. When she opened her eyes, she looked first to Asmodeus and the black runes on her body flashed bright red. He instantly turned to glare and growl at Azazel, the green orbs of his necklace glowing and green lightning shooting from his eyes. Without pausing more than a second, Soneillon turned her gaze to Azazel. They locked eyes, then he turned to snarl at Astaroth. She pressed her palm to the new angel beside her and his red snakes hissed back at Azazel.

Soneillon giggled and those runes flashed brighter. She turned toward Pierce and had barely glanced in his direction when he turned to openly glare at Sweyn, his fangs bared. My jaw dropped. I wasn't quite sure what was happening, but I'd never seen Pierce display such blatant hatred for her. I'd suspected it but this was unfathomable. It was a death sentence for sure. I braced myself for Sweyn's reaction, yet a few seconds passed without one . . . and then I glanced sideways at her. My eyes widened. Sweyn beamed with excitement as she watched the males around us crumble beneath their own rage.

Sweyn giggled like a little schoolgirl.

Soneillon winked at her.

Sweyn gasped, her red eyes widening for a split second before they narrowed into little slits. Like the flip of a switch, the Queen went from excited to seething with rage. She turned to Lilith's orb with her fangs bared and her hands balled into fists at her side. Smoke began to billow from behind Astaroth and Soneillon. Sweyn spun around and growled right at the spot Everest usually stood.

Then she turned and those glowing red eyes aimed their rage right at *me*.

I gasped and took a step back before I caught myself. In sheer desperation, I looked away from Sweyn. I saw it happening in slow motion, my gaze lining up with Soneillon's, except at the last moment, Asmodeus moved behind her and my eyes went to his instead. He arched one eyebrow and smirked at me.

Laughter filled the room like it was being played through a speaker. That smoke covered the floor like fog. A man wearing a black suit stepped out from behind Soneillon's black wings, grinning and clapping his hands. His blue eyes danced with giddiness. The freckles and strawberry blond hair did not match the evil pouring out of his aura.

Asmodeus growled.

Soneillon let out an evil chuckle.

Astaroth shook his head, then shoved her hand off of him.

This new man in the suit spread his arms wide and stretched like a cat. "I can always count on Azazel for his inability to be satisfied in his sins."

Asmodeus cracked his knuckles. "We did not summon you, Mammon."

"You should have kept your greedy little pet on a tighter leash then." Mammon spun in a circle with a wide grin. "For you know better than anyone, the only thing that summons me . . . is greed. And even faster when it's an *angel's* greed."

My stomach sank. *Oh fuck. What have I done? How will I explain this to The Coven?*

Asmodeus put his hands on his hips and turned to Azazel.

If he expected Azazel to feel remorse, he was let down, because he just rubbed his hands together and wagged his eyebrows. "Did you *see* how much fun she is, my brother? Just think of the sins we can stir up together."

*What have I done? Foolish, stupid girl. This is what happens when you play with fire.* My plan to use Everest's rage over *this* to seduce him had a better chance of getting me killed at this point. And if it didn't, there was hardly a reason for The Coven to take me in now. I deserved their justice. I could not be the reason Lilith won. I could not let Heaven think I was their enemy.

I closed my eyes and sent a prayer to the Goddess and Heaven. But not just any prayer. I sent my silent oath of loyalty and just hoped they were listening. *By the Goddess's magic I shall be heard, with mine heart's power I give my word. For in darkness or in light, I pledge myself to Heaven's fight.*

# CHAPTER TWO

## EVEREST

In over a thousand years of life, I'd learned a few things, but the most important was the fact that no plan was invincible. No plan was immune to hiccups. No matter how well-crafted your agenda was, *something* would fuck it up.

This was why all my schemes had contingency plans. Backups for the backups. If I wanted to win, I had to be ready for everything. After all these years of carefully planning my mother's demise, I'd lost count of the detours.

But it'd been five hundred years since something had surprised me.

The count was back to zero.

From the moment Francelina entered that frat house, everything had gone to shit. Every time I blinked she was somewhere she wasn't supposed to be. Any other curveball life threw at me I could roll with, I was quick on my feet and faster in my mind, but with Francelina I was unraveling. It was like nothing was going right, not a single thing was going my way. I was being tested. Fate was calling my bluff, forcing my hand. I had a whole new set of plans and backup strategies, yet I knew they would never see the light of day. If not for Braison, she may never have gotten out of Avolire. Fate had given me an ally unlike any I'd ever had before. I loathed turning him, I felt the pain of his family and Coven-members as I did it, but it was that or let him die.

I'd made the right choice in letting him decide.

And I would be eternally grateful he chose to be my partner in crime.

A thousand years of espionage and sleeping with the enemy, yet I'd never had Coven intel until now. I'd never risked befriending any of them until Salem's prophecy . . . until they'd showed up on our doorstep. It was the single most welcome detour of my life. Braison was an infant in comparison to me, yet his wisdom in war was sharper than Sweyn's or my mother's. He understood that underestimating the enemy was a weakness one could not afford if they wanted to win.

Francelina would never have survived Avolire as a mortal had it not been for him.

Granted, it was Tegan Bishop's bravery and brilliance that got her out. But we would not have gotten to the point of her assistance without Braison. And it was for that reason that I remained with Sweyn for now. The Coven had a plan. For the first time since the One Hundred Years' War with my mother, I was not the one guiding the chess pieces in this game. *They* were. Braison assured me of this. And after that little display between Braison and Tegan, I had to let Heaven's chosen hands lead the way.

However, if they expected me to stay away from Francelina . . . they would have to revise their plans.

So much had changed since the last time I walked through this hospital toward her room. *I* had changed. I hadn't felt like this since I was a teenager. It was an unsettling feeling, a horrible mixture of excitement and dread.

I didn't know what to expect inside her room. I didn't know if she'd be awake or back in her magically induced coma, and for that reason I forced myself to walk through the hospital like a human instead of merely traveling through the shadows of the world like I usually did. If she was awake, I did not want to frighten her. She'd been through too much. Her soul was shaken and fragile. I did not want to be the thing that broke her.

The flowers in my hand . . . I had surprised myself with those. I was not even sure what message I was trying to send with them, especially since I had not written a note. But at least this way my presence in the hospital would look appropriate.

I was not surprised to find her back in the same room. Tegan understood the delicate balance one must maintain when altering a person's mind and memory. I paused just outside of her room and took a deep breath to steady my emotions for whatever I found inside. With my heart lodged in my throat, I opened the door—my breath left me in a rush.

It was the worst kind of deja-vu.

It was autumn all over again, except no bandages. Thank God. I had not the heart to see her like that again. This was bad enough. She just lay there in the bed in that horrible pale-blue gown with her pink hair unbrushed and unruly, almost as if she'd been tossing and turning in her sleep. I knew this was one of Katherine's comas and not regular sleep. I felt her magic in the air around Francelina.

My chest tightened around my erratic pulse. I swallowed through the hot lump in my throat and just stared at her. I saw no sign of me or Avolire on her, which was good, yet a small part of me wanted to leave a permanent mark on her.

I cursed and scrubbed my face with my hand. *Clear her from your mind or you endanger her even more. She cannot afford your heart in this war. Not yet. The risk is too severe.*

With a shaky exhale, I glanced to the dry erase board hanging on the wall with the nurse's name and the date. It was the second of March. *Still.* Francelina had left Avolire just before dawn. Today.

This morning was a lifetime ago.

I tried not to think about the look on her face when I'd handed her over to Braison. Or the pain in her eyes after our trip to the bathroom. More importantly, I tried not to think about the plea for help in her eyes when Sweyn caught her in the Land of the Lore. That look of betrayal on her face would haunt me forever.

Everything I'd done was to keep her safe. I prayed she'd learn to trust me again. I'd tried to stay away, to not go near her in case that had been my error before—as if somehow my attention on her had drawn trouble.

But Sweyn had sent me to locate her.

She wanted revenge on The Coven for outsmarting her.

My stomach tightened into knots. This game I'd been playing was at its highest stakes ever. We were in the endgame now. It was only a matter of strength and strategy to see how long victory would take to claim—for either side. Tegan had told me her plan, or at least part of it. I knew my ignorance and authentic reactions would be required to see it through, which was how I wound up beside Francelina's bed. Sweyn ordered me to locate her. For what purpose, I had not yet been told. And I would have to relay the truth to her.

Which meant it was time for Francelina to wake up. We no longer had the time to let her linger in the safety net of Katherine's magic.

I walked over and sat on the edge of her bed, facing her. For a moment, I could only stare as I gently sat the bouquet of pink flowers on the table beside her bed. I ran my thumb over that small white mark Tegan had placed on her arm to track her location at all times. The Aether Witch's magic was a sharp jolt to the system when touched, but it gave me comfort to know they were watching Francelina.

There were a thousand words I wished to say to her, but I had to hold my tongue for now. Her breath was calm and steady. Waking her from such a peaceful slumber was an injustice. I did not wish to traumatize her any more than I already had, so I leaned forward and brushed her cheek with the backs of my fingers to try and wake her the normal human way.

"*Francelina,*" I whispered, pushing just a smidge of my magic into my voice.

When she did not answer or even stir, I did something entirely stupid and dangerous . . . I leaned forward and pressed my forehead to hers and just breathed her in. Every part of me wanted to kiss her, but I was better than a frat boy, so I resisted. The tendrils of my black smoke magic flickered in my peripheral vision. Any second it would slice through Katherine's magic and wake her. So, for a moment, with my eyes closed and listening to the heavy beating of our hearts, I pretended we were somewhere else.

Somewhere far, far away . . . where the ocean waves rolled softly—

My bare feet sank into powdery white sand. A cool, salty breeze swept over my face. I knew it wasn't real, we were still in the hospital room. The beeping of the machines lingered in the air like birds chirping. My magic had allowed me to slip into the shadows of her unconscious mind and lure her to a place of peace.

When I opened my eyes, I found her standing knee-deep in the aquamarine water. Her long white dress floated away from her body. The waves rolled around her almost like a protective forcefield. In the bright sunshine, her hair looked strawberry blonde as it fell in waves that mimicked the ocean.

I sighed through the pressure in my chest.

She turned to face me with big blue eyes, but the moment her gaze locked with mine, they turned a bright, shimmering pink. My eyes and throat burned. I shoved my hands in my pockets to try and stop myself from reaching out to her.

"Hello," she said with a sharp smile, like she knew I could not be trusted. Her voice was strong and warm.

I tried to smile, but I was sure it failed, so I nodded my head. "Francelina."

She narrowed her eyes like I confused her. "Who are you?"

Sharp pain shot down my spine. This time, I gave her a small smirk. "You don't remember me?"

"Should I?"

I licked my lips. "'Tis an excellent question."

"You know my name." She cocked her head to the side. "And yet I only know your shadow."

"Does it frighten you? My shadow?"

"No," she said without hesitation. She took a few steps forward, closing the distance between us so she could reach out and wave her hands through the black tendrils of my shadow and smoke magic around me. "Sometimes it is easier to cherish the light from the comfort of the shadows."

At that, I smiled. "Do not let that memory leave you."

She looked up at me with those blazing pink eyes. "What is your name?"

I reached up and tucked her hair behind her ear. This close, I could see every freckle covering the bridge of her nose and cheek-bones. I ran my fingertips along her jaw, then tipped her chin up. "Do not try to remember me. Not yet. If you see my face, all you must remember is I shall never hurt you."

"That did not sound as comforting as I think you meant it," she said with a chuckle and a slight furrow of her brow.

"I know." I leaned forward and pressed my lips softly to her cheek as my magic coiled around us, then whispered, "*It is time to wake up now, Francelina.*"

I pulled back and opened my eyes. The bright fluorescent lights of the hospital room stung my eyes. After being in her dream, the stuffy, sterile scent of the hospital burned my senses. The beeping of the machines up and down the hall might as well have been fireworks. I sighed and pushed to my feet. With one last brush of my fingers over her cheek, I took a step backward and then forced myself to turn away from her— and froze.

Her Aunt Kimmy and Uncle Kyle stood in the doorway of her room, their eyes wide and jaws dropped. It was a testament to how off my game I was that I had not registered their arrival. This was a good reminder that I needed to be more careful.

They just stared at me.

Aunt Kimmy's hazel eyes darkened with fear. She pushed her blonde hair back off her face. "You shouldn't be in here. No guests."

Uncle Kyle's silver eyes shot back and forth between me and Francelina in bed behind me. "*What did you do?*" he growled.

"Nothing I am not allowed to do." I shrugged and gave a little smirk. "Nothing she'll remember."

Their eyes widened.

Sharp, electric pulses slid down my spine. I straightened. My sire bond to Sam was burning. Something was wrong. Sam was terrified. I cursed to myself, then met Kimmy and Kyle's wide stares again. "By dawn. Be ready."

They opened their mouths to speak, but I'd already said too much. I pushed my magic out and let the darkness of the realm take me.

# CHAPTER THREE

## EVEREST

TRAVELING through the shadows of the realm was faster than blinking—unless my mother was furious. I was stuck in the darkness of my own magic, present in the room but entirely out of sight from the others. Mother was livid. My vision flashed red, then went back to normal. She was too angry to even speak.

Panic squeezed my throat.

The sight before me was too treacherous to believe.

Inside my mother's tower, with her orb glowing red in the middle, Sweyn, Sam, Pierce, Asmodeus, and Azazel stood at the five points of the inverted pentacle used to summon. The call within my sire bond was too late. The damage had been done. I needed to think quickly to get control of this situation.

Because three fallen angels stood with their black wings around my mother's orb.

Astaroth still wore his toga from ancient times because he was too lazy to change, but the Angel of Laziness caused more damage in the world than anyone gave him credit for. Beside him, Soneillon's red eyes glowed with anticipation. My stomach turned. Her very look stirred an uncontrollable anger within her victim. Wars had been launched by her attention alone, and judging by all the glares in the room, she was already at work. But the last of them . . . he was the real problem, one I had hoped to not be burdened with for some time still.

He spread his arms wide and stretched like a cat. "I can always count on Azazel for his inability to be satisfied in his sins."

Asmodeus cracked his knuckles. "We did not summon you, Mammon."

*Mammon. Fuck.* The walking personification of greed. He would stand in the shadows and whisper desires into your ear in your own voice so you never knew you'd been tampered with.

"You should have kept your greedy little pet on a tighter leash then." Mammon spun in a circle with a wide grin. "For you know better than anyone, the only thing that summons me . . . is greed. And even faster when it's an *angel's* greed."

I cursed in my mind. Any second this hold on my body would snap. I had to be ready to act, and they could never see the panic in my heart. Two fallen angels in the realm were bad enough, now there were *five*.

Asmodeus put his hands on his hips and turned to Azazel.

Azazel just rubbed his hands together and wagged his eyebrows. "Did you *see* how much fun she is, my brother? Just think of the sins we can stir up together."

*She. That's my angle.* I looked to Soneillon and pushed my magic at her until the tendrils of my black smoke coiled around the black strands of her hair and pulled.

She gasped and her eyes flashed with excitement. The black runes on her skin glowed neon-red like the color of her eyes. Her gaze snapped right toward me. I felt the hunger and desire in her attention even before she dragged her teeth over her bottom lip. "Mother taught you how to tease I see," she purred.

I forced myself to look in her eyes as Mother's hold severed. Rage filled my veins, burning like lava through my limbs. I stepped out of my shadows and growled.

Sam gasped and leapt back.

Sweyn narrowed her eyes on Soneillon, then turned her glare to me. "*Everest.*"

"*What the fuck are you doing?*" I shouted, my hands in fists at my sides, my magic coiling up and down my arms. My vision turned red. *Good. Let Mother see this.* I flicked my wrists and light flashed all around us. "*Answer for your sins.*"

Sweyn's eyes widened for the briefest of moments, but long

enough for me to see just how much she feared my mother. I relished in her panic and fear—and stored the information to use against her later. *"My Lady—"*

Mother screamed so loud the marble floor rumbled and the onyx walls cracked.

Sweyn paled.

Asmodeus chuckled like the cocky bastard he was.

Lilith spun to the angels, her favorite followers, and bellowed, *"GET OUT!"*

They vanished instantly, as if they'd never been here at all.

I looked to Sweyn's pet and arched one eyebrow. "Leave, Pierce. Pray I do not see your face for some time."

Pierce whimpered as he bolted for the door and out of sight. *That* I did feel some remorse for. Poor Pierce was as much a victim in this game as anyone else. There was hope for that one yet.

Sweyn stomped her foot like a petulant child and hissed. "How dare you dismiss *my* court in *my* kingdom. Perhaps you forget your place—"

"You're just a half-breed daughter of a slut," I snapped, pouring every ounce of venom in my soul into my words. "I'm the son of Lilith. Perhaps you learn yours finally."

"Excuse you—"

"You're a figurehead. *I* call the shots. Why do you think I can summon Mother and you cannot?" I pointed to the ground where the arrival of the three fallen angels had left burn marks in the black marble floor. "We weren't ready to babysit them yet."

Sweyn growled and her fangs dropped down. I had never feared this spawn and I would not start now. If today was the day I made my allegiance known, then so be it.

*"You!"* Mother growled and turned on Sam. The glowing red runes on the ground lifted up and wrapped around Sam's body, lifting her off the ground. "I gave you *one* task, and you have not managed to complete it, and you think *this*—"

"Tell your son to do his part!" she said through clenched teeth. She turned those gold and red eyes on me. "He knows where to find my bed. It is not me that prevents this."

Mother narrowed her eyes on me. "Why haven't you—"

I sighed, interrupting her scolding as I flicked my wrist to slice through Mother's runes so that Sam stood on her own two feet again. "I've been doing your job for you—"

Mother growled.

"Your insistence on secrecy from the key players on your team are the sole reason things are falling apart. You tell them nothing, refuse their questions, and then explode when they act on their own. Like this." I smirked, just to piss her off. "Did you warn me before bringing Asmodeus and Azazel here? Did you warn me before you drop a bride in my lap? You ask things of me and then blow your own plans to shit because you think in only chaos, and I swear to you that will be your downfall."

Mother crossed her arms over her chest and raised her chin. "Chaos serves a purpose—"

"How does that purpose feel right now?" I screamed at her and gestured around the room. "You have a Queen who thinks she's in charge, a granddaughter whom you refuse to even teach your language, and fallen angels who answer to no one—"

"They are here for a reason—"

"*They fell for a reason!*"

She gasped, her eyes widened.

But the panic in me was growing too strong. I had to disguise it with rage or it all ended right now. "You think yourself better than God and Lucifer? You promised your angels anarchy and sin and yet you expect them to obey your orders. The fallen will always fall."

"Harnessing them limits them. I need them at full power—"

"If I take my eyes off of them for one minute, I'll have new disasters to tend. Disasters that *you* cannot yet handle yourself as you haven't managed to enter this realm again in your own form in centuries." I gestured toward my betrothed. "And you expect me to have time or energy to lie with *that*? Why? So I have yet another set of sins to wrangle?"

Sam flinched but I felt no remorse. Giving her more power was not a task I was excited to complete, especially not in the manner I had to do so, so I growled and spun away from them, all but sprinting for the door.

"Where are you going?" Mother hissed. "I have not released you—"

"Are you going to clean up their mess, Mother?" I stopped and spun to face her. When she just snarled, I nodded. "I thought not. Handle *these two* at least or get out of my hair."

I fled faster than I'd ever moved. Inside, I was a whirling tornado of panic and rage. Too many thoughts raced through my mind at once. I saw nothing until I nearly slammed into Braison outside of my room. I nodded to him and opened the door. Nothing we needed to speak of could be spoken out in the hall. The second we crossed the threshold, I slammed my door shut and threw my magic up to create a barrier around us so we could speak freely.

Braison whistled under his breath. "You really didn't like seeing Saber hook up with Azazel, eh?"

A growl I didn't approve of slipped up my throat. I glanced around my room only to remember I'd torn it to pieces quite literally after Saber went with the Angel of Sin. My stomach rolled so hard I gagged. I couldn't think about what she'd done. It made me violent.

I scrubbed my face with my hands. "Where is she now?"

"Um . . ."

The pause told me more than I wanted to know. Yet still, because I was a glutton for punishment, I glanced over my shoulder at him and arched an eyebrow. "Um?"

Those green and red eyes darted around the remains of my ruined room before landing back on me. "Saber said someone had to monitor what the angels were doing, so she went."

I growled and ripped a chunk of marble off the doorframe of my closet. "I don't want to know . . . I cannot think about . . . you heard of who they summoned?"

"Astaroth, Soneillon, and Mammon." Braison looked sick. His skin turned a grayish-green color. "We have to warn them."

I sighed and stared at the ground. There was no doubt as to who *them* was. The Coven. He meant we needed to let them know they now had *five* fallen angels on Earth. He wasn't wrong.

I looked up at my new friend and grimaced. "We cannot or we risk revealing our allegiance prematurely."

Braison shook his head. "No, YOUR allegiance cannot be risked. Mine has been at risk since you turned me. They are suspicious at best."

"I may need you before I reveal myself," I said softly and slowly. "So you mustn't send message."

He frowned and nodded, then I saw a spark in his eyes like he had an idea. He cocked his head to the side. "What if I went to sleep?"

I stared at him. There were two members of The Coven who had a knack for dreams. The Star Card, Cooper Bishop, was a literal dreamwalker. But their new Devil had mastered the skill, which spoke volumes on Deacon English's power. It was beyond rare for the Devil Card to play within a person's unconscious mind the way he could. It meant he had a strong comfort in dark magic. So, if Braison were to sleep, especially now that Francelina was no longer within Avolire's walls, there was a chance one of his former Coven-mates might be waiting for him.

Sharp, electric pulses slid down my spine. I straightened. My sire bond to Sam was burning. Again. Except this time, I sensed pain. A million images of what my mother could be doing to her flashed through my mind.

Braison just continued to stare at me in silence, unwilling to speak his request out loud but waiting for the answer anyways.

I nodded and headed for my door. "I have to handle something. Take a nap, you look tired."

# CHAPTER FOUR

## EVEREST

UNTIL TODAY, I'd felt nothing but pity for Sam. I'd known she was a victim in all this, entirely unsuspecting of her bloodline and then thrown into the fiery pits of Mother's realm, literally, only to be handed over to Sweyn as a prop. A tool. Had Francelina not shown up before Sam, I would have gotten the required consummation over with. Hell, I'd been numb in that department for centuries. Francelina had changed that. I couldn't bring myself to take another when she was there.

But Francelina did not remember me.

Soon she would again. This was my window to do what I needed to, what I had to do, with a sliver of my self-respect still intact. Mother swore it would give both Sam and I more power . . . power I suspected I'd need to defeat her. So far, Mother had no reason to lie to me. For whatever twisted reason, this was the way it worked.

This anger . . . this fuming rage I felt inside . . . was my life raft in the sea storm of a task that made me sick to my stomach. I was going to capitalize on it. I would shut my mind and heart off and play a role.

*All is fair in love and war.* That was the saying after all.

Before my body even fully took form in Sam's room, I smelled fresh blood. I emerged from my shadows to find Sam standing in the center of her room with a serrated dagger slicing into her forearm. Thick red blood dripped down her white silk gown like a river.

Her gold and red eyes narrowed on me.

"What in God's name are you doing?" I growled through clenched teeth.

"Oh good, you *can* feel that." She lowered her dagger with her blood dripping onto her white carpet. "I was starting to call bullshit on the sire bond."

Rage flushed through my body. "You did *not* harm yourself to call me here."

"I had to get your attention somehow! Apparently pain works better than—"

"Better than—" I gasped as realization hit far too late. "Tell me you did not summon fallen angels just—"

"You don't speak to me!" she bellowed, her voice louder than I'd ever heard it. "You act like I'm the love of your life in court and then nothing—"

"So you unleash three fallen angels onto a world full of innocent people to be slaughtered just to get my attention like some schoolgirl crush? We're in the middle of war, Sam. I'm sorry I'm not showering you with affection and love—"

"*I don't give a flying fuck if you have feelings for me!*" she screeched, blood rushing to her face and turning her cheeks pink. "I grew up human. I'm not in a rush to marry my uncle for fuck's sake."

"THEN WHY?"

"Because I seem to have been bred for the sole purpose of making the great and powerful Lord Everest *stronger.* The only task *grandmother* seeks from me is to bed you and unlock some sinful new magic that I'm sure she'll use to destroy the world and everything beautiful, but I have to do it—"

"WHY?" I stormed up to her, forcing her to stumble back away from me. Intentionally. I wanted to push her buttons, to force a reaction, to force her anger. The only way I was going to be able to do what I needed to was in a fit of rage . . . from both of us. So, I needed to provoke her. "TELL ME WHY—"

"*To get her out of my head!* Because *you* haven't taught me shit. *You* abandoned me. *You* never taught me how to block her from my mind. Every hour I haven't fulfilled my birth's purpose she torments me." She lunged forward and shoved me in the chest with both of her hands with every sentence. "*No one* warned me I was to be turned into a bloodsucker after *you* stole me from the safe house and killed all those innocent witches. *My friends.* And then you handed me over like a trophy and sent me to her realm to be tortured and now I'm supposed to give you my body with no proof or assurance it'll benefit me *at all,* but oh, at least she'll leave me alone—"

I grabbed her arm, spun her around and shoved her against the wall. I fisted her hair and dragged her head back so my mouth pressed to her ear. "She will *never* leave you alone."

*This is it, Everest. Your chance. Do it. Just put you both out of your misery and get it over with.*

But I couldn't. My grip on her hair loosened and the silky blonde strands slipped through my fingers. I couldn't move. Every muscle in my body yearned to flee, to turn and run. My heart screamed and pounded against my chest. Just that sliver of coldness in my mind that only a thousand years of torture could produce kept me in place. It was like my body was at war with itself in absolute desperation. I *had* to do this. I *had* to get more power and magic if we wanted to win this war against my mother. Haven Proctor was the one fated and tasked to kill her, but I wasn't stupid enough to think her own son wasn't going to have to be right beside him. They were going to need me and need me at my strongest.

Yet all I saw was Francelina's face in my mind.

Fate was a twisted, cruel little fuck.

If only Sam had arrived before Francelina, I would have been able to push through as I did all these centuries with Sweyn—a product of survival. It was almost like Heaven was testing me, except I wasn't sure what the right answer was. Did they expect me to fulfill my task with Sam *for the greater good* of the world . . . or did they want me to honor my heart and not touch her?

Then Sam let out a broken sob and I knew my answer.

There was no way I was touching her.

I sighed and stumbled over to the bench at the foot of her bed and sat down, then buried my face in my hands. "I . . . I can't, Sam. I'm sorry."

"You're in love with someone else, aren't you?" She sniffled. "That's why you won't."

"I've been working on a loophole so that we can still attain the additional power without having to do something so incestuous—"

"That doesn't answer my question."

I didn't look up at her, didn't need her to see her answer in my eyes. "Where my heart lies is not your concern."

"Last I checked, I don't need your heart in order to do this—"

"But *I* do," I interrupted her softly. "At least . . . I do now."

"So, I'm just screwed. Fantastic." She sniffled and her breath caught in her throat. When I looked up, she was wiping tears off her cheeks. "She'll just torment me endlessly until she breaks me. That can't possibly take too long with her in my head nonstop—"

"Wait." I frowned as the meaning of her words finally registered. "You can't block her out?"

"*NO!*" she cried and threw her hands up.

I opened my mouth, then shut it. In the back of my mind, I registered that I had dropped the ball on teaching her how to block Mother out of her mind. I just hadn't had to do that since I was younger than Sam currently was. A plan began to take form in my mind, nothing concrete, just images, but I saw the light at the end of the tunnel.

"We might be able to use that."

She flinched. "What?"

"I thought you had blocked her, but if you haven't . . ." I jumped to my feet and rubbed my hands together. "Yes, that might work to our advantage."

"I am not following." She scratched her head. "Now you *do* want to do it?"

"No, neither of us wants to do that—"

"Why does it have to be *that* at all?" She wrapped her arms around her waist and hugged herself. "Why does it have to be sex—"

I held my hand up to stop the questions she was about to ask. "Take a deep breath for me, Sam," I whispered and pushed my magic into my words.

She scowled but did as I asked like she couldn't stop herself from obeying. She couldn't, I'd used a strong dose of mind control that I normally loathed using. But desperate times required desperate measures. As she exhaled that breath, I threw my black smoke magic at her face. It flew like a whip to coil around her head. Her eyes widened.

"It won't hurt you," I said quickly. "It's for protection. From *her.*"

"Oh." Her eyes inspected the smoke halo around her. "Okay?"

"It doesn't have to be intimate, not per se." The plan was growing clearer in my mind now. It was the riskiest angle to play, but it was also the only one. "It's more about committing sins and evilness to invoke the power of Lilith so that she will unlock the rest of our magic."

"Invoke the power of Lilith. Like the Devil. All right. Okay. Well, that's something then." She wrung her hands together. "Your ancient ass surely has to have some brilliant idea on how to do that . . . right?"

My stomach tightened into knots. "I do. But it's very dangerous and requires one hell of a show."

"A show?" She scoffed. "We've been putting on a show since I got here. What's a little more?"

I took a step closer to her to make sure the magical barrier around her thoughts was firmly in place before I spoke my idea out loud. Once I was confident Mother would never have access to this, I spoke slowly and softly, "You need to think carefully and realistically here. Don't tell me you can do this if you don't know with one-hundred-percent certainty that you can do it. Because if you can't deliver the show we need, we will be worse than dead."

Her eyes widened. "What's the show?"

I smirked. "We're going to fake it. We're going to put on a show for her where we are pretending to do the task as she requested of us."

"We pretend to—" She licked her lips and nodded. "Like . . . like . . . like—"

"Yes, like we're actually consummating the way she intended. We'll be fully clothed, so it means your performance will need to be Oscar-worthy."

She grinned, and for the first time since meeting Sam, I saw the glimpse of my mother in her. "I'll give you Best Picture and Best Actress, then top it off with a Tony-Award-worthy performance."

"Are you sure you can do this?"

"I'm not a virgin, Everest." She crossed her arms over her chest. "And this wouldn't be my first time faking it. I can do this. I just need more magic so I can get out of here. I'm desperate and I have nothing to lose—"

"If Mother realizes we're faking it . . . well . . . I do believe you saw her realm firsthand." I arched one eyebrow. "Death would never find us there."

She shuddered and her face turned a little green.

I nodded. "Death is what we have to lose."

She closed her eyes.

"Sam?"

Her eyes met mine. "I will kill myself before she has a chance."

*"No, you won't. She's too fast for that,"* I whispered. Then I sighed. "I tell you this not to frighten you but to make sure you understand what lies in our future if she catches us."

"I understand."

"Do you?" I cocked my head to the side and watched her. "The only way this works is if you can fake it in your thoughts as well."

Her eyes widened. "In my thoughts?"

"When she arrives, she *will* enter your mind, and if you can show her what she needs to see in your mind . . . then the physical show will suffice. That, and only that, is the reason this plan is plausible."

She was quiet a moment, and I let her have the silence to think. Then she looked up at me with her chin held high and her back straightened. "We're in this together, right? If she punishes you, she punishes me."

I nodded.

"And you've been putting on this level of show for centuries?"

"Yes."

She pushed her shoulders back. "Then let's do it. Right now. While I've got all these wild emotions rolling through me. This is it. Get in bed."

"Not in here." I smirked and pointed to the ceiling. "We're going to her tower room—"

She snapped her fingers excitedly. "And I'll sit on your lap on the bench, right?"

I nodded.

"I have an idea." She held one finger up, then sprinted for her closet. In less than thirty seconds, she returned wearing a white chiffon gown with a cinched waist, a plunging neckline that held her chest pinned up high, and a loose-fitting skirt that swirled around her feet as she walked. She stopped in front of me and nodded. "Game time."

I held my hand out and waited for her to take it. When she did, I lowered my voice. "The moment we leave this room, you *must* be in character. Start the show and do not finish it until she gives us our magic. Understand?"

"Yes." She gripped my shirt with her other hand and pulled her body against mine. "If she can play her games, then I can too. I know what awaits us if we fail. I have no interest in risking that. I'm ready."

I hadn't seen this side of her before—this strong, empowered side . . . the driven and fierce side. Perhaps the other half of her bloodline wasn't in vain. Then again, perhaps Mother's blood wasn't too diluted either. With a smirk, I released my magical halo, looked into her eyes— then willed us into the shadows.

Darkness swallowed us.

The moment we emerged into Mother's tower room, Sam dragged me across the black marble floor, then spun us around and shoved me backwards. I went sliding, granted mostly because she'd shocked me, but as my back hit the raw onyx wall, I saw that menacing sparkle in her eyes. She let out a chuckle so evil only my mother could replicate it. I shook my head and beckoned her with both hands. She lunged across the room, then leapt onto my lap, straddling my hips. Her hands gripped the lapels of my blazer as her fangs elongated with excitement.

*Oh, she's good.* That made me smirk.

But I couldn't do this with her looking at me, so I gripped her arms and lifted her up off my lap and then spun her around. She gasped. Her hair whipped me in the face. A sinister giggle filled the room. She squeezed my thighs and arched her back into me.

*Oh, she's very good. We might actually have a chance at this.*

My stomach turned but I reminded myself this was acting. This was the least of all evils for the situation. I gripped her hip, pulling her white dress up on one side. *"What are you waiting for?"* I growled in her ear.

She let out a sexy little laugh, arching into me further while reaching her hands behind her back as if she were unzipping my pants. She wasn't, but damn . . . from the angle I had I almost believed it. Then she sat up straight, yanked her dress all the way up to pool around her hips, and then with quick fingers, she slid a pair of red lace underwear down to her knees.

*Well, I'll be damned. She even brought a prop.*

Before I could say or do anything else, she began her performance.

Most men would have unraveled in my place with a woman as beautiful as Sam gyrating in their lap. But I barely noticed it. I focused on the shadows in the room around us. While she groaned, moaned, and cursed my name in her breathy voice, I scanned the dark corners of Sam's mind and waited for Mother to creep in.

The second I sensed her presence, I pulled out of Sam's mind and dragged her mouth to mine at the same exact time as I flicked my wrist to summon Mother to join us. Sam didn't gasp or startle. She didn't pull back. I hadn't warned her I was going to kiss her, yet she rolled with it like a pro. With a single flick of my tongue against her fang, she threw her head back and sang like Celine Dion.

And then Mother's applause echoed around the tower.

Sam gasped and sat up right, her skin flushed bright-pink. "*Mistress,*" she whispered reverently as she dove for the red lace underwear around her knees.

I lifted her onto her feet in front of me and pretended to adjust my clothing as Sam fixed hers. Our performance was ninety-percent finished. When I stepped around Sam, I found Mother's red eyes blazing like fresh lava. "*Mother.*"

She grinned, still applauding. "Offspring."

I had to give it to Sam, she'd nailed that performance. It was actually somewhat alarming how well she could fake that, but that was a question for another day. "I thought perhaps you might enjoy that."

"You never disappoint." She stepped up and got into Sam's face, then pressed her finger under Sam's chin. "But *you.*"

Sam managed not to flinch. She was impressing me more and more. Even her skin was flushed. "Yes, mistress?"

"I feared the human in your blood had destroyed you. Happy to see you're my granddaughter after all."

Sam bowed her head slightly with a sinister smirk on her face. "Happy to have cleared that up for you—"

*Don't call her grandmother. It's a test.*

"—my lady."

*Good girl.*

Lilith beamed and pressed her palm flat on Sam's chest. A neon-red rune appeared on the back of her hand. It shimmered and glowed for a moment, and when Mother pulled her hand back, that same rune was on Sam's chest. Mother's darkness seeped from within the rune, spreading across Sam's body like little rivers.

Sam closed her eyes and smiled.

Mother turned to me and her eyes flashed. She arched one eyebrow.

I took a deep breath, bracing myself for absolutely anything. I wouldn't know for sure she'd bought our little charade until she gave me the extra magic and then *left*.

"I think you stalled on this task just to ruffle my feathers, offspring . . . To make a point." She grinned a grin that made my stomach turn. "I have never doubted your blood."

I rocked back on my heels and slid my hands into my pockets. "Of course not. You know better."

She giggled and it sounded like glass shattering. And then she was right in front of me. Time seemed to slow down. This moment was the beginning of the end for me. Either she called my bluff or she fell for my lie. Sam would never have been fast enough to escape her, but I had a chance. Either way, this moment marked the change of tides.

Her palm pressed to my chest. The red glow of her demonic rune shined in my peripheral vision. It was brighter and bolder than it had been for Sam. My vision flashed red. My magic pulsed and buzzed with electricity, then rushed to the surface like I was about to set it all loose like a tsunami.

"Time to set you free now, offspring," she purred.

"Thank you, Mother."

Darkness coiled around me, but I was not afraid, for we were old friends.

# CHAPTER FIVE

## SAM

If I had been undecided on which side of the war to place my allegiance . . . what just happened would have given me an answer.

I'd already known which side I fought for.

Now I wanted to be the one to deliver the fatal blow.

I wouldn't get it. There was zero doubt in my mind The Emperor was destined for that honor. Hell, I'd heard Lilith and Sweyn conspiring on ways to kill him. So, if I couldn't be the one to kill Lilith, I would be the one to make sure *no one* laid a finger on Tennessee Wildes. If my entire life's mission was to keep him alive until he ended her, then I would be his bodyguard. His shadow. Even if I were merely that two-second warning he needed to keep himself alive. I wasn't foolish enough to think I was anything in comparison to him, but I'd seen a chess board. There was a row of pawns for a reason.

That would be me.

Because nothing made a woman feel more like discarded trash than being reduced to a piece of meat. It wasn't about *him*. He was my uncle, and every second of the Jerry Springer episode we were just forced to fake would haunt me. His heart lay elsewhere and mine was a pile of ash trapped in my chest. I just wanted to hold my stomach long enough for him to leave my room. He didn't need to see me puking my brains out. I'd earned the right to do so in private.

Because he'd told me our survival had relied entirely on my acting skills, and I'd taken that to heart. I imagined it was the kind of desperate strength they say mothers got when their babies were in danger. I'd let my mind and body be consumed by lust and desire, then gave the performance of a lifetime.

It'd worked. I was happy. I felt magic rushing through my veins unlike before. *This* was magic. This was power. This was electric, an energy unlike I'd never experienced. It was like I suddenly discovered I'd been color blind my whole life and now I saw vivid color.

I still felt sick.

Movement in my peripheral vision made me look over just as Everest walked back to my bed where I'd covered myself up with blankets. I would not cry in front of him. He gave me no reason to think I could rely on him for help or support. For all I knew, he wanted to kill his mother so Earth could be *his*.

He sat on the edge of the bed and faced me.

I licked my lips and shook my head. "You don't need to say anything. We did what we had to. You may leave. I will continue to act the part in court."

He held up a folded piece of paper. "When I leave this room, open this."

I frowned and eyed the paper like it was a snake about to bite me. "What is it?"

"I wrote two spells. They are both written in Mother's demonic language. You will not know what they say." He held his hand up to stop me from speaking. "You will have to trust me and do as I say. Read the first two lines of the first spell. You will see red light like tunnel vision creeping in from the corners. Let it. Then read the last two lines of the spell. Do you understand?"

I nodded. My pulse was racing now. He was helping me. I almost wanted to cry.

"Once your vision clears . . ." he ducked down to meet my eyes and regain my attention. "*Only* once your vision clears, you will read all four lines of the second spell. It will hurt . . . like . . . brain freeze, follow?"

I nodded again. I didn't dare speak in fear he'd stop.

"Repeat the steps so I know you know the order. This is critical."

"Read the first two lines of first spell. Red tunnel vision. Read last two lines." I licked my lips as a rush of adrenaline swept through me. "Once vision clears, I read the second spell."

"Good. Once you complete those steps, you will understand the why of it. But do not speak of this to anyone. What you discover is yours to know only. Once completed, you must burn this paper to dust." He handed me the paper. "Understand?"

"Yes."

He nodded and pushed to his feet. His eyes watched me for a moment. "I am sorry you felt abandoned. It was not my intention. Nor is it my intention now. I am . . . off my game. I believe that's the saying?"

At that, I snorted. "Thank you."

"For what it's worth, and do not dare repeat these words out loud to a single other person or it will get many people killed including ourselves . . ." My eyes widened. He leaned down and whispered, "*I may have delivered a killing spell to your friends at the safe house, but I bet if you think back to right before I arrived, you'll recall a certain visitor who behaved . . . weirdly.*"

I sat up straight. The memory of Tegan and Bentley at the safe house had been forgotten once they were killed and I was stolen. "Do you mean—"

"Perhaps you can ask Mei-Ling."

My eyes filled with tears. Mei-Ling had been Tegan in disguise. He was telling me Tegan had kept my friends safe. I didn't understand the how or even the why—at least the why she knew it was going to happen. But after what I'd seen from Tegan when she escaped with Frankie, I had to trust my friends were secretly okay.

He reached out and brushed a tear off my cheek. "Do not let them see how they hurt you, for it will be used against you. If we are to win, we must be cold, heartless monsters that no one has any reason to *not* trust."

My jaw dropped.

He turned and walked to the door, then paused and glanced back at me. "By the way, that was one hell of a show up there. I'm impressed and proud of you. Try to remember that strength going forward."

I grinned. Butterflies danced in my stomach. "I didn't want to let you down."

"I am sorry I let you down before now." He smiled. "That ends now. So, Lord Braison ought to be on your agenda this evening."

"Th-thank you, Everest."

He nodded. "Be strong of heart, mind, and soul. You will need it."

And then he was gone.

I stared at the door for a long few minutes, trying to compose myself. I'd been through a whirlwind of emotions in such a short time. But I was anxious to see what these spells were, so I finally pushed myself up. It wasn't until I was holding the paper in front of me that I realized the cut on my arm was gone. He must have healed it without me realizing.

I frowned. He'd said he was off his game. I had thought he was just saying that to be nice, but perhaps he meant it. If my guess was right, which was looking more and more like it was, then Everest was as against his mother as I was, which meant he had to be rattled with everything that'd happened the last few days.

And I suspected Frankie played a big role in his game being off. Or Saber. Or both.

I wasn't sure which female had his heart, but it was one of them.

At least he was helping me now.

There were eight lines written in Everest's elegant handwriting on this paper, which honestly was proof enough of his age. *Okay, step one is to read the first two lines.*

I had no idea what they meant, but I read the words out loud to myself. As Everest said, red light crept into my vision from the edges, then slowly slid in until my eyesight was entirely tones of red. It made me feel queasy and panicked. I looked down at the paper and read the last two lines. It took a few seconds but then the red light faded as if it'd never been there at all.

*Okayyyy. Next read the second spell all at once.*

I was halfway through the second line when sharp pain shot through my temples and into my eyes. I hissed and bent over. *Brain freeze, my ass!* It took me longer to get the rest of the spell out, but as soon as I did, the pain vanished. I sagged against the end table beside me. I leaned against it for a minute or so, just breathing and letting my brain put out the fires in my nerves.

But I didn't feel anything different. I frowned and glanced down at the paper—and gasped. The words were in English now. *No, wait. Not English. OH MY GOD.* The spells were very much still in demonic language, but suddenly, like the flip of a switch, I could read them. My jaw dropped. I swayed so hard I had to lay down. Everest had gone full *Matrix* on me and uploaded the language into my brain. And he'd told me not to tell anyone about it, which meant he wanted me to know what was happening while Sweyn and Lilith assumed I wouldn't. My eyes burned with the need to cry.

I had to read the first spell a few times before I realized what it was for. When it clicked, tears ran down my cheeks. It was a spell to block Lilith from my mind so she couldn't just walk in unannounced whenever she wanted. Now, if Lilith wanted to speak with me, she would have to call and my vision would turn red as I'd seen. That was my bat signal now. Then I'd go to the orb and accept the call. Only then could Lilith communicate with me.

I sobbed. Totally and entirely unraveled on my closet floor.

He'd given me privacy from the beast. He'd heard me before, even when I thought for sure he wasn't listening.

Someone knocked on my door.

"Who is it?" I yelled.

"My lady, do you require sustenance?"

*Shit.* It was one of the servants. "No, thank you."

"Very well, my lady."

I cursed and jumped to my feet. Everest was very clear on the instructions to burn the paper, so I ran to the bathroom and tossed it into the sink. *Wait, do I have matches? How do I burn*—green flames billowed from my palms. I gasped and waved my arms only for the flames to stretch out wider.

I felt like Maleficent in Sleeping Beauty.

Before, my green magic had been a smoky fog. Now it was like fire. I felt it rushing to the surface for me to use, and I started to panic. The paper had been consumed by my green flames and was disintegrating before my eyes.

"*Shit, shit, shit. Easy, magic. EASY,*" I hissed at it and held my arms out straight. "Pull back!"

It took a few minutes to calm down, but when it did, I was exhausted as if I'd run a marathon. I sat on the edge of my bathtub just breathing. That wasn't going to work. I wouldn't get far in my escape if that bit of magic drained me so much.

*Wait.*

*Lord Braison. Everest said he ought to be on my agenda tonight. He knew I'd need help with my magic!* All of the mean things I said to Everest or thought about him I instantly regretted. I'd just misunderstood him. I eyed my reflection to make sure I looked normal, then confirmed the paper was gone . . . then I stormed out of my room.

It took me a few minutes to find Lord Braison's room. I was distracted by my emotions and forgot where it was. When I finally found it, I glanced around to make sure no one was watching, then I knocked on the door.

The door swung open, and Lord Braison stood in front of me. His red hair was a little disheveled and his red and green eyes were bloodshot like perhaps he'd been asleep. "Lady Sam, Lord Everest is not here—"

"I know. I was hoping to have a word with you."

"Oh." He frowned and looked me up and down, then stepped back. "Come in."

I walked inside and marched to the far wall where the window was, then I turned to face him. "Are you alone in here?"

He cocked his head to the side. "I am."

I gestured around, then tapped on my ear. "Is it . . . private here?"

"Ah." He crossed the room to stand a few feet away from me and then wiggled his fingers and gray smoke filled the air. "It is now. What may I do for you—"

"I know you're team Coven still, so don't bother denying it."

He opened his mouth, then closed It.

"Just help me," I finished in a rush. "Everest told me to come to you."

"Oh?"

"Well . . . actually, he probably sent me just for this . . ." I held my palms out in front of me and neon-green flames shot up to the ceiling. "Shit, fuck, dammit. Ah, hell—"

He laughed. Gray smoke coiled around my flames and brought them back down to my palms. His laugh deepened. "Shit, fuck, dammit. That's quite a combo, Sam."

My face burned from what had to be a glorious blush. "See? Help?"

He was still laughing as he nodded, but at least he pressed his palms to mine and my magic vanished, then he curled my fingers over my palms and lowered my hands. "I see. You completed your task and now you have more magic . . . and yeah. Help. Right. Let's just keep those cannons at ease for a second, okay?"

I nodded. The idea that Braison knew of *my task* made my skin crawl, and I wanted to vomit all over again, but if that meant I didn't have to explain why I suddenly had more magic, then I was thankful for him knowing.

He smirked. "And the second reason?"

I opened my mouth, then closed it. This was harder to speak out loud, so I had to basically whisper it. "*Like I said, I know you're still team Coven. I know there's no way you'd turn on your family. I need your help to get their help.*"

He narrowed his eyes. All humor gone. "Their help?"

"Please, Braison . . ." Tears filled my eyes. I shook my head. "I may be her granddaughter, but I want her dead. Gone. I am on Heaven's side in this war. I'm with The Coven, and I will do anything to help destroy her. But I have to get out of here. I'm so scared. I'm not asking you to help me escape, I'm sure you have your own plans, but I can't get out of here on my own. I'm from *Florida*."

Braison snorted. "Sorry, sorry. Um, yeah, I'm from Florida too. It's fucking cold out there."

"Please help me. I just need to get a message to them to tell them what happened to me. To get their help out of here. I'll do whatever they say. Even if they want espionage, I can do that. I can spy for them, but I need them to know I'm a good guy, bloodline be damned."

He stared at me for a long moment, then cursed violently. "I can't send a message to them, Sam. Not yet. It's imperative that I remain as seemingly loyal to Avolire as possible right now. If I want to see my family again, then I can't reach out to them."

My heart sank. I nodded. "Okay. All right. I understand. I'll just . . . um—"

"But *you* can."

I gasped. "H-how?"

"How good is your memory?"

My eyes widened. "It's about to be real good."

He smiled. "Get a single piece of paper and a pen, then sit in the window here beneath the light of the moon. Make sure one bare foot is touching the ground. Got that part?"

I ran to his desk on the far wall to where I saw a stack of parchment paper and a pen. With those in hand, I sprinted back to the bench beside the window and kicked one heel off so my bare foot touched the cold marble. Then I looked back up to him. "Now what?"

"I'm going to tell you a spell that you're going to write on that paper. Once you write the spell, the channel is open and you write your message. You're going to want to think about what you want to send to her so you're ready before you start because the channel only stays open for thirty seconds or so, which means your message must be short and sweet. No greetings needed. She'll know who is speaking to her. Concise statements. Got it?"

I nodded. He meant Tegan. He had to mean Tegan. "How will I know if she gets the message?"

"She'll get it. That's a spell only for the—for her." He scratched his jaw, and I saw the worry for them in his eyes. "She may not respond right away, or she may not give you a real answer. Be patient. She has ways of communicating that no one else does. Send your message and then continue on with court as if you are so honored to be here."

I nodded.

He continued. "The spell is three sentences. You will write the first two sentences, then write your message, and then write the last sentence of the spell."

"Like saying *over and out* on a walkie-talkie? Or *ten-four* on a—"

"Yes, exactly. Now, I cannot write this out for you. It's complicated, especially given my Coven magic, so I will recite it once. You must be ready because it would be too dangerous to send more than one message to her at once. And I cannot be in the room when you do it. Got it?"

"Got it. I'm ready." I knew what I was going to say. Short and sweet and to the point. "I understand."

"Okay, here it is. Listen carefully . . ." He leaned closer and whispered, "*For what I speak must not be spoken, send my words to the rainbow token. Bound by Earth beneath the moon, hear my plea in a whispered tune. Silent the night I shall be heard, for her ears only, see my word.*"

I repeated the words in my head a few times, then nodded to him. "Thank you, Braison."

He smiled and headed toward the door. "When you're done, meet me out front so I can teach you how to use that magic."

"Really? Like . . . in open sight?"

He laughed. "Trust me, Sweyn will *love* seeing you with magic. I'll be out there waiting."

"See you in a minute."

I waited until he walked out of the room, then turned my attention to the paper in my lap. I took a deep breath to calm my thoughts. The marble floor was cold against my bare foot and the moonlight streamed in through the window. This was my chance. I couldn't fuck this up.

In quick movements, I wrote the first two lines of the spell: *For what I speak must not be spoken, send my words to the rainbow token. Bound by Earth beneath the moon, hear my plea in a whispered tune.*

Then I added my message: *By the Goddess's magic I shall be heard, with mine heart's power I give my word. For in darkness or in light, I pledge myself to Heaven's fight. SOS. #TeamCoven*

I wrote the final line of the spell: *Silent the night I shall be heard, for her ears only, see my word.*

Then I watched and waited. Surely something had to happen. Braison hadn't instructed me to burn the spell like Everest had, so—rainbow light suddenly covered the entire parchment paper. My eyes widened. I froze. *TEGAN.* I didn't dare move. He said she might not answer. He also said I didn't need to say who I was.

My words vanished . . . and then words written in little rainbow flames appeared on the paper.

*'Put that damn pearl necklace back on, dudette.'*

# CHAPTER SIX

## UNKNOWN

I GLANCED OVER MY SHOULDER, then turned back around. This was exactly how girls got murdered. There were eyes on my back, I had zero doubts on that. There were just some instincts a girl knew not to question. Whoever was following me, they were making sure to stay *just* out of sight . . . lurking in the shadows.

It was my own fault.

Sure, victim blaming was not on brand for my character, but since *I* was about to be the victim, I had no problem admitting to myself that I'd set myself up for this. Patsy Cline may have gone out walking after midnight, but it was not safe for a girl to do in the real world.

Especially in a quiet beach town in . . . actually, I had no idea where I was. Last I knew, we were in the Smoky Mountains somewhere. Now I was walking on a sidewalk parallel to the ocean shore. My boyfriend—now *ex*-boyfriend—and I had been in a hotel room. I'd taken some cold medicine and passed out and then woke up *here*.

*He* didn't think it was kidnapping.

I did.

I'd been so furious with him I dumped him and took off. Like an idiot. It was that moment from *Clueless* movie when Cher got out of the car and the guy ditched her in a bad neighborhood and she was mugged at gunpoint. I'd seen that movie as a small child and always swore I'd never be that stupid. And then I got mad at my boyfriend and just took off alone.

41

He hadn't intended on hurting me. He just wanted us to enjoy spring break with our classmates. I never should have left the hotel. I'd just been in such a state of rage that I hadn't been thinking clearly. Now they were going to be asking my parents to identify my body after whoever was following me got bored with chasing me.

It was too late to turn around and go back to my boyfriend. Not only would that bring me face-to-face with my chaser faster, but I'd been in such a cloud of rage that I couldn't retrace my steps. And, naturally, my phone had no reception. Fate was lining up for me in the worst possible way—

Feminine laughter echoed around me. I gasped. My eyes widened. I didn't slow down. In fact, I picked up my speed. Somewhere close by there was a group of girls laughing. This was promising. Hope flared in my chest.

I pretended to answer my phone, "Hey, I'm almost there."

Silence.

"I can hear y'all laughing, that's how I know."

More silence.

The girls' laughter was closer, and now I heard music playing softly. Golden light spilled into the foggy night sky up ahead about ten feet, so I hurried toward it while carrying on a fake conversation with myself. And then I saw my first true sign of a life raft to grab ahold of. Sitting along the edge of a wooden deck were at least five girls.

"Yes, I see them on the deck. I'm coming up now," I said to myself and my stalker as I hurried up the wooden steps just before the line of girls. "Coming up the steps now. Byeeeee."

I fake hung up the phone and shoved it into my front pocket. When I got to the top of the steps, I gasped. My eyes filled with tears. Like all of the other hotels along the beach, this one's raised deck had a pool right up at the railing so that the ocean would be in perfect view during the daylight. And in this pool right now had to be two-dozen college girls.

They all looked up with shocked, guarded expressions as the wooden planks creaked under my feet. I grimaced and waved but words failed me. I might have actually made it to safety. One creep surely couldn't hurt two-dozen women. *Right? Right.*

Unless of course these girls thought *I* was a creeper and kicked me out.

Just then a girl who looked about my age with hair like midnight and big, pretty blue eyes threw her arm in the air and waved it. "GIRL! There you are! We were worried sick!"

A runaway tear slid down my cheek.

Almost at once, each of the other girls' expressions switched from confusion to ferocious protectors. It was a flash of a second and then all of their faces were bright and smiling. The laughter picked right back up.

The nice girl glanced behind me quickly, then turned back to me with a grin. "Where did you go after dinner?"

Relief rocked me but I managed to clear my throat and then stumbled toward her. "I got lost on my way back."

"Everything looks different here in the dark." She nodded. "Come sit by me. The hot tub will feel amazing on your feet after all that walking."

I practically ran over to her. In less than two seconds, I had my shoes kicked off and my feet submerged in the hot tub as I sat beside her. Goosebumps spread across my skin. I shivered and leaned closer to her, then whispered, *"Thank you."*

She grinned. "We've got to stick together out here, don't we?"

I nodded.

"You all right?"

"Yes, thanks to y'all. Someone was definitely following me."

"Creepy. Well, you stick here with us, and when we're ready for bed, we'll either escort you back to your hotel or you can crash with us until morning. That sound good?"

I smiled up at her. "That's the nicest thing anyone has offered me."

"Like I said, we've got to stick together out here. Hella dangerous. These are my sorority girls. We're here for spring break. You too?" When I nodded, she gave me a friendly wink. "Where *did* you come from?"

So I told her.

When I finished, she just rolled her eyes and laughed. "Men."

"I know. It wasn't smart to bolt. If he's still awake in a bit, I'll call him and have him come get me. Or maybe in the morning." I grinned sheepishly. "I'm just glad I found y'all before I wound up another statistic."

"Well, night's still young. I'm sure we could find a fun statistic for you to become." She chuckled and bumped my shoulder with hers. "I'm Morgan, by the way."

"Hi. I'm—"

"They're here!" Morgan squealed. Her whole face beamed with excitement. She threw her hand up and waved, just like she had when I'd arrived. "Over here, my love!"

*My love?* I frowned and followed her stare—and my jaw dropped. Three grown ass men sauntered towards us with mischief sparkling in their eyes. The one in the middle was by far the sexiest man I'd ever seen. He was some kind of mixture of Antonio Banderas and Luke Evans with his green eyes and long dark hair that curled just under his ears. The smile on his face was sinfully delicious, as was the rest of him.

The guy on the left had black eyes and short, dirty blond hair, and somehow his black toga costume looked hot. The third guy stepped into a patch of light and I saw dark, strawberry blonde hair and matching freckles. The suit was a surprising outfit choice for spring break on the beach, but damn did he look good in it. His blue eyes scanned each of the girls in the pool, and a smirk pulled on his lips.

These three men were . . . celebrity levels of gorgeous.

All of my fear from five minutes ago came rushing back. Something about the beauty of these men freaked me the hell out. They didn't seem to go together. The sexy one in the middle wore black leather pants and a black, silky button-down shirt. But he was dressed normal and casual at least. He could fit in with the party crowd. But to see him walk up with one guy in a suit and the other in a damn toga? My stomach tightened into knots. There was something wrong with this picture.

Then I realized something I'd missed before in my relief of finding people . . . none of the other girls paid any attention to me once I sat down. Not a single one of them even glanced in my direction, let alone smiled or said hello. Only Morgan spoke to me. And now there were three of the most beautiful men I'd ever seen in my life headed right for them and none of them noticed.

Sorority girls hadn't noticed gorgeous men.

Alarms were ringing in my mind. Red flags waving.

I cleared my throat. "Hey, Morgan . . . who are those guys?"

She beamed at them. "That's my boyfriend and his two friends."

My stomach rolled. That somehow made me feel worse. While Morgan swooned over her boyfriend, I took the moment to take a better look at her. She wore a little black wrap dress made of some kind of chiffon-like material. Her black hair hung perfectly straight down her back, not a single strand out of place. No frizz. No evidence of the salty air and humidity. Almost as if she'd just gotten here herself. Even her black-winged eyeliner was perfectly intact.

When I glanced back over to the sorority girls, my heart sank. Something was wrong here. The dozen-ish girls at the far end of the pool all wore matching pink bikinis with their Greek letters written in red. They were all blonde, as in the *exact* same shade of platinum blonde, and their hair was curled to perfection. And they were only talking to each other.

There were three redheaded girls floating on tubes in the water, and while their bathing suits didn't match, their *faces* did. Those were sisters and they seemed oblivious to everyone else around them.

The rest of the girls were randos. As in, they were all in different outfits—bathing suits, sundresses, beach coverups, and some jean cutoffs. None of them seemed to be cohesive, and usually girls liked to coordinate when going out. It was a thing we did, even if we didn't like to admit it. These girls were all talking and laughing but not to each other. It was like they were carrying on their own little conversations.

I imagined this was what an insane asylum might've looked like.

Except we were on a beach.

"Baby, you're late! We've got quite a party going!" Morgan yelled out to the three guys who were only five feet away now. "Come join the fun!"

"Which one is your boyfriend, Morgan?"

She swoon-sighed. Her cheeks flushed. "The one in the middle."

*AKA the sexy one.* I nodded. "What's his name?"

She bit her bottom lip. "Azazel."

*Azazel?* "Like . . . like the fallen angel?" I forced a laugh.

"The ultimate bad boy, *amiright?*"

*What the fuck?* "Um . . . okay. Who are his friends?"

"The toga guy is Astaroth and the other is Mammon."

My jaw dropped. Those were not normal names. Every alarm in my body was going off. This was not right. I couldn't put my finger on what was wrong, but it was *very* wrong. All those instincts that I'd been in danger while walking came back tenfold. I had to get out of this situation. Immediately.

"Actually," I said with a laugh, then pointed to my left, "I think my hotel was down that street."

"But you came from the other way?" Morgan frowned.

I was already on my feet and sliding into my shoes. "Yeah, but I'd made a few random turns. I recognize that building though, so I'm gonna go—"

"Are you sure?" a male's deep voice rumbled right behind me.

I gasped and spun around to find the guy in the toga standing in front of me. His black eyes were entirely soulless this close, like little black holes. He'd been on the other side of the pool. It was impossible for him to be on this side of me.

He placed his massive hand on my shoulder. It was warm to the touch. "Don't you think that's a lot of work?"

"No, it's just—" A wave of fatigue washed over me. My feet and legs felt instantly heavy. The idea of walking sounded horrible. "I mean, it does seem far away—"

"Exactly." He curled a strand of my hair around his fingers. "Wouldn't you rather stay with us and just relax?"

"Yeah. Yeah, I think I would." I let out a deep breath and rolled my shoulders. "I'll just sit for a bit longer."

"I think that's the right decision."

I nodded, kicked my shoes back off, and sat down beside Morgan. But the instant my feet hit the water, I felt like I was jolted out of a brain fog. I didn't want to be here. I was going to leave, to flee as fast as possible. *What just happened? What did he do to me?* I looked up and the guy in the suit, Mammon as she'd called him, was watching me with sharp blue eyes. *No, no, no. Fuck this.* I jumped to my feet and lunged away from Mr. Toga who was still standing behind where I'd been sitting. My shoes were a sacrifice I'd willingly make to get out of this place. Those side stairs were only a few feet away and calling my name.

Azazel slid into my path, and I slid to a stop.

I gasped as heat and desire rushed through me like a tsunami. I licked my lips and stared into his eyes. "I have to . . ."

46

He cocked his head to the side and moved to stand *right* in front of me so there was only an inch between us. "Have to . . . what?"

"Have to . . . have to . . ." I had no idea what I had to do. No idea what I was going to say. All I knew was I had to stay with *him*. He had a girlfriend, but that wasn't my problem. She shouldn't have introduced him to all these girls. I licked my lips and batted my eyelashes at him. "I was hoping you'd tell me, gorgeous."

"What'd I tell you, my brothers? I promised you sin. Welcome back to Earth." He grinned and slid his arm around my waist so he could grab my ass, but I didn't care. I melted in his hands. "Morgan, *my love*, I think we'll start with this one. Keep the others hot. It won't take long."

# CHAPTER SEVEN

## FRANKIE

I⊤ ᴡᴀs one of those nights where dreams evaded me—the kind where you closed your eyes, saw black, then opened them and it was morning. It felt like the beat of a moment even though it'd probably been eight hours or more. The light streaming in through my windows was way, way too damn bright on my eyes. I whined and squeezed them shut and tried to will my brain back to sleep. My body was on board. Every single muscle ached and burned like I'd been running and now couldn't move another inch. My brain, on the other hand, was more like Anna from Frozen: *the sun is awake so I'm awake.*

But worse than that, I felt like I was in the middle of doing something. Like when you forget why you walked into a room or what you were about to say, it was right there on the edge of my memories and yet entirely gone. It made no sense. Even my chest was tight. I felt anxious as hell. I took a deep breath and let it out slowly.

Then I opened my eyes.

What I saw did *not* make sense. While I was lying down in a bed, the ceiling above me was *not* my bedroom. My room had little golden twinkle lights attached to the crown molding, but I was staring at big fluorescent lights. I squeezed my eyes shut again. *Nope, nope, no. Just breathe. You're in your room.* With my vision out of the question, I tuned into my other senses to prove to myself that I was actually in my room, except I didn't smell my laundry detergent on my blankets or the cinnamon incense I usually used right before bed. There was no rush of air over my face from my ceiling fan, no soft rumble of the central air-conditioning. The sheets under my fingers were stiff and nowhere near as soft as mine. There was no snoring from my dogs, nor signs of them dreaming.

But there *was* beeping. Voices seemed to echo from just beyond me. I took a deep breath and cringed at the intense sterile scent, but the movement forced something to stab me inside my nose. I groaned and reached up to see what it was only to realize something was squeezing my middle finger.

"*What is that . . .*"

"*Frankie?*"

"What's on my finger?" I shook my hand. "What is that?"

"Frankie, sweetheart, can you hear us?"

I heard them not answering my question. "Yeah, what is it?"

"What's what—*oh.*" Aunt Kimmy squeezed my right hand. "That's just the oximeter."

*Oximeter? What?*

"Can you open your eyes, kiddo?" Uncle Kyle rested his hand softly on my shoulder.

I frowned and opened my eyes but the bright fluorescent lights overhead stung. "Where am I—"

I gasped. It was a hospital room. I was in the hospital. The oximeter on my finger was that thing that measured my pulse and oxygen level. There was also an IV attached to my left arm and one of those breathing tubes in my nose. I glanced around, trying to remember what I was doing in the hospital, but it wasn't coming to me.

"What happened? Why am I here?"

Aunt Kimmy grimaced and sat back down on the chair beside me. She pushed her blonde hair back with fingers that trembled. "You were in an accident."

Images hit all at once. Raindrops slamming into the windshield. My hands white as snow, gripping the steering wheel. The red and blue flashing lights of police cars in my rearview mirror and the bright white light of the hospital like a beacon up ahead.

There was blood on the backs of my hands.

"On your way here from that party," Uncle Kyle added softly. "Halloween . . ."

The images changed instantly, then changed in the fastest slideshow ever, like my brain was in hyper-speed trying to reset itself. I saw my best friend mostly naked and looking far too pale for a living person in the passenger seat. Then I saw the frat house. The crowd of drunken college kids in costume. The red solo cups everywhere. The ceiling of a bedroom. A baseball bat beneath the bed right by my hand. A tall boy with white-blond hair in an all-white suit bursting through a barricaded door—rainbow light flashed in my eyes and I sat up straight.

"Frankie?"

"Frankie!"

"I remember, I remember." I held my hands out as they both reached for me. My best friend had been with me in that car, yet she wasn't in the room now. It was just the three of us. Yet she should have been here, sitting beside me with her pink hair like before. "Just where's Mei-Ling?"

"*Mei-Ling?*" Uncle Kyle frowned and exchanged a nervous glance with my aunt. "You mean Elizabeth?"

I shook my head. "No, she goes by Mei-Ling now. She told me that when I woke up on Valentine's Day—"

"You didn't wake up, sweetie," Aunt Kimmy whispered.

"Yes, I did. I woke up and she was sitting right here with pink hair. Tai and Malik came—"

"*Malik?*" they both asked with bewildered expressions.

"Yes, Malik . . ."

Aunt Kimmy shook her head and squeezed my hand. "Who is that?"

"Malik, he's the guy—" Colorful light like a rainbow flashed across my vision. I blinked, then found my aunt and uncle scowling at me. "What? What's wrong?"

Uncle Kyle cocked his head to the side. "You were going to tell us who Malik was?"

"Malik? I don't know a Malik." I frowned. "Do I?"

They smiled and eased back in their seats.

Uncle Kyle was still watching me. "You do remember your best friend, right?"

"As if I'd forget Elizabeth."

"You called her Mei-Ling a second ago—"

"*Mei-Ling?* She never goes by her Chinese name—Wait." An image popped into my mind of my best friend sitting beside me with pink hair telling me she'd started using her real name after the incident—a rainbow streaked across the room. I glanced toward the window, but it was nighttime outside. I shook myself. "I've never called her that, at least not since the first time she asked our teacher not to on the first day of school."

"All right, how are we doing in here, Francelina?"

It was a woman who'd spoken, I knew that, but I heard my name whispered in my ear like thunder on the wind. It was a male's voice, a deep sound that sent butterflies dancing in my stomach and goosebumps down my arms.

*"Frankie?"*

I jumped, then shook myself. "Y-yes?"

Aunt Kimmy pressed her hand to my forehead. "Sweetie? Talk to us?"

"I'm fine." I glanced around her to find two women in pink scrubs standing at the foot of my bed. "Who are they?"

"These are your nurses, Jackie and Sarah. They've been looking after you this whole time—"

"What about Katherine?"

Everyone stared at me with their brows furrowed.

"Katherine? The nurse with auburn hair who talks about energies and stuff?" I said. The image of the nurse in question filled my mind instantly. I saw her standing beside me hooking up IV bags with colored liquid in them. "She was here the first time I woke up with all the bandages covering my body—"

"Bandages covering your body?" Aunt Kimmy's voice shot up an octave. "What bandages?"

"This is the first time you've woken up, sweetheart," Uncle Kyle said gently.

"What are you talking about? Katherine told me I'd gotten full body burns from the car exploding and she promised she'd heal me without any scars." I held my arms up as proof. "We had a whole conversation—"

"Frankie," Jackie, the nurse on the left, shook her head, "you were not in the car when it exploded. You would not have survived that, and even if you had been covered in burns, you would have severe scars."

My jaw dropped.

"And there's no Katherine who works in this hospital," Sarah added softly.

"No, no, no." I scrubbed my face roughly with my hands and rainbow light flashed in every direction. When I opened my eyes, I found all four of them staring at me. My eyes widened. "What? Did you say something to me?"

"You're doing just fine, Frankie." Sarah gave me a small smile and slid my chart back onto the table. Then she turned to my aunt. "The brain can do wild things under duress and trauma. She just woke up. Let her ease back into being awake."

"I was awake before though. More than once. I got up and walked around with Tegan—" A kaleidoscope of colors like a neon rainbow swirled around me so intensely that I swayed. "What—"

"Easy, sweetie." Aunt Kimmy took my hand and gently guided me back down to the bed. "Hun, prop her up?"

Uncle Kyle nodded as he reached for the remote attached to my bed. When he pushed it, the back half of my bed rose in an incline so I was sitting up but supported by the bed. "Better?"

"I don't know. I'm confused. I need a drink. My throat hurts." I winced through sharp pain in my eyes. "My eyes hurt too."

Nurse Jackie nodded. "Let me get the doctor so he can take a look at you and we can get you more comfortable. Be right back."

"In the meantime . . ." Sarah put her hand on my leg over the blanket. "How about some water with crushed ice you can munch on?"

I licked my lips and nodded. "That's all I can eat until the doc comes?"

"We need to take it easy on your body, so we'll get you water and ice while we wait for him. Okay, kiddo?"

"Okay." I watched her leave my room, following Jackie out, then scowled. "What don't I know? Y'all are acting weird like I'm super injured but I don't even have any wounds from the accident."

Aunt Kimmy sighed and it sounded like it hurt. "Sweetheart, you've been in a coma since the accident."

My eyes widened. "WHAT?"

"That's why you look uninjured. Your body has been healing while you slept." Uncle Kyle grimaced. "But the good news is you seem uninjured now."

"How long . . ." I shook my head as nausea rolled up my throat. "How long was the coma?"

"That was Halloween night . . . Today is the second of March."

The world spun around me. I closed my eyes and pressed my fingertips to my temples. "That's like five months."

"Yes," they both said at the same time.

Everything was starting to make more sense. The stares, the worried glances, the nervousness. My stomach rolled. "Wait. Hold up. Elizabeth. Where's Elizabeth? I got her out of the house. She was in the car with me. Where is she?"

"She's okay," Uncle Kyle said in a rush. "She healed up nicely within a week or two and has been back to normal since."

"*But where is she?*" I cried. "Why isn't she here? She would be here. This isn't like her. Where Is she?"

Aunt Kimmy gave me a sad smile and squeezed my shoulder. "Sweetheart, you've been in a coma for so long. We weren't sure if you were going to wake from it at all, let alone know when. Elizabeth was here every day. She sat by your side. But after Christmas, her parents . . . well . . . things were really hard for her after the incident, so they went back to China."

My heart stopped. I opened my mouth, but no words came out. I shook my head hard enough to give me a headache.

"They just wanted to give her some peace so she could heal," she continued. "Somewhere no one knew what had happened to her." She tucked my hair behind my ear. "This was very traumatic for her too."

My eyes filled with tears. "No, no, no. She left? Forever?"

Uncle Kyle shook his head. "They insist it's not forever—"

"I wanna talk to her."

They stared at me.

"Give me a phone. Let me FaceTime her. I need to see her face for *my* trauma."

"All right." Aunt Kimmy pulled a phone out of her purse and handed it to me. Only then did I realize it was *my* phone. "I'm taking this back as soon as you hang up. It's too soon to start back socializing and everything."

My fingers were trembling, so I held down the side button and waited for Siri's symbol. "Hey, Siri, call Elizabeth on FaceTime."

"Calling Elizabeth on FaceTime," Siri's robotic voice repeated my command.

It rang a few times before I saw my best friend's face fill the screen. She squealed and tears slid down her cheeks. Her hair was pink. She looked totally and entirely healthy and that somehow broke me. One second I was smiling at her, the next I was sobbing. Aunt Kimmy slid onto the bed beside me and wrapped her arms around me while Uncle Kyle held my other hand tight.

"God, Frankie, I can't believe you're back," she cried and wiped her eyes, which showed the crystal ring on her finger that was identical to mine. "I was so scared."

The memory of that party was burned into my brain. I knew far too well the fear that I was about to lose my best friend forever. I shuddered and wiped my own tears. "I'm okay."

"It's okay to *not* be okay, Frankie, as long as you're alive and awake."

"I am." I forced a shaky smile. "Even if you're in China."

"Mom and Dad swear I'll be home for summer. Tai's going back to college then too." Her face fell and she groaned. "We just have to hang on until then."

My heart sank. Another round of tears burned my eyes and formed a hot lump in my throat. "With you on the other side of the world and like a dozen time zones away."

Her eyes glistened. "I wasn't sure you were going to survive at all. I'll take this as a temporary problem."

I wasn't ready to think about what had happened to us that got me in a coma for almost half a year and my best friend in another world. I blinked and wiped my face with my free hand. For the first time in my life, I just wanted to be alone. I needed to process what had happened and where that left me *now*.

"You look exhausted, Frankie," Elizabeth said softly. "Don't push yourself too fast. Why don't you eat something and watch some TV, then text me in a little while?"

"What time is it there?" My voice was thick and raw.

"I'm twelve hours ahead, so I'll be up all day."

I nodded.

"Get some Krispy Kreme doughnuts and just . . . not overload your brain tonight. Please?"

My stomach growled. "That hot sign better be on."

# CHAPTER EIGHT

## FRANKIE

THE DRIVE HOME WAS WEIRD.

I kept looking over to say something to Mei-Ling only to find the backseat empty. *Why do I keep calling her by her Chinese name? She's Elizabeth, always has been.* My post-coma brain was confused. All I wanted was my phone so I could text her and get a smidge of normalcy back, but Aunt Kimmy was holding it hostage.

Honestly, I couldn't blame her. I'd caught a glimpse at it and all of my apps had at least triple digit notifications. Five months of being away from texts, calls, emails, and *all* my social media accounts. Re-entering society was actually quite intimidating and overwhelming, so I wasn't really fighting her too hard on it. I just wanted to be able to text Mei—*Elizabeth*—like normal.

*Maybe I should just get a new number and delete all my accounts and start fresh? I bet I could ask Mei-Elizabeth to set up all new accounts for me and she'd have it done and ready within a couple of hours.*

"How are we doing back there?"

I jumped and looked to the passenger seat to where Aunt Kimmy was doing her best to pretend she wasn't hovering. I forced a smile. "I'm okay?"

She smirked. "You're not, and that's okay. What were you just thinking about? You were making quite a face."

"Dammit." I sighed and scrubbed my face with my hands. "I was thinking about all those notifications I saw on my phone and wondering if I should delete the accounts and start over."

Her smile turned a little sad. "What if I asked Elizabeth to log in to all of your accounts and go through your notifications? Get everything back to normal and stuff?"

I opened my mouth, then closed it. "That's a good idea. But can I FaceTime her later and ask?"

"You don't need an excuse to call your best friend, love," Uncle Kyle said softly from the driver's seat. He turned into our neighborhood and then looked up at me through the rearview mirror. "I'm sure Elizabeth would love if you called her every ten minutes."

That made me smile. "I just need to feel normal any way I can."

I didn't miss the way they looked at each other or the knot that formed in my stomach, but I chose to ignore all of it. My gut told me the universe wasn't quite done with me yet, that the other shoe was gonna drop any minute now. However, everyone said ignorance was bliss, so I wanted to give that a try. I leaned against the window and focused on the clear blue sky over our heads. It was March in Florida, so it was gorgeous. Birds flew overhead, chirping and carrying on with their normal day-to-day life. The windows were closed, but I knew it was a lovely seventy-five degrees with that spring crispness in the air, still months before the torture of humidity returned to haunt us. Despite the five months in a coma, my neighborhood looked exactly the same. Every palm tree, every mailbox, even the cars in the driveways . . . all the same as if Halloween was yesterday.

I'd never thought Florida's lack of typical seasonal changes would be a good thing.

It was actually helping a little.

Just as my chest was loosening and I started to breathe easier, we took a left turn onto our street and I spotted my neighbor walking her dog . . . her golden retriever that had been a quarter of the size it was now the last I saw it. Two houses down, my neighbor Marissa's daughter was walking down the sidewalk with her. *Walking*. Little Daphne was *not* walking back at Halloween. And Marissa did not have that pregnant belly either. I gripped the edge of the leather seats and clenched my teeth.

*It's okay. This is normal life stuff. This doesn't affect my life at all.* I closed my eyes and took deep breaths. *This is all fine. Everything will be fine.*

But then the car slowed and my eyes flew open. *We're home.* I looked out the window and gasped. There were people in Elizabeth's driveway, walking from a car I didn't recognize to the front door. They unlocked the door and let themselves in. A whole family of like six people that were definitely not related to my best friend.

"*Who are they?*" I screeched. "*What are they doing—*"

"They live there now—"

"WHAT?"

"They're in China, love. You know this," Aunt Kimmy said softly. "They're just renting the house out for a bit while they're gone."

I pressed my face to the glass to get a better look as our car turned into our driveway. The second it stopped moving, I yanked my seatbelt off and leapt out of the car, fully expecting to charge across the street and find my best friend hiding in a closet or something. But when I crossed from the driveway to the front sidewalk, I slid to a stop. My body turned to ice. I opened my mouth, but a whimper came out.

There, in my front yard, was a *For Sale* sign.

With a *SOLD* sticker on it.

The other shoe had dropped. My stomach rolled, sending my entire breakfast shooting up my esophagus like a rocket. I clenched my teeth to keep it in. The world spun around me. I staggered a few steps, then found myself sprinting to the sign as if getting closer would change the outcome.

SOLD.

SOLD.

SOLD.

*No, no, no, no, no.* In the back of my mind, I registered my aunt and uncle speaking to me, but my ears were ringing too loud to hear anything. Uncle Kyle unlocked the front door and pushed it open, then turned back and yelled something. I sprinted across our front lawn, through the front door, and then slid to a stop on the shiny hardwood floors.

The walls of our foyer and living room were lined with cardboard boxes. They were all taped shut and labeled with words like *books, dishes, living room*—I squeezed my eyes shut. My chest tightened like a vise on my heart, squeezing the life out of me. I forced deep breaths.

*This is a dream. This has to be a dream. I'm going to open my eyes and be back in that hospital bed.* A few breaths later, I reopened my eyes and whimpered. Nothing had changed.

The only furniture still out and unpacked was a black sectional sofa that I had no memory of. No rugs. No end tables or coffee table. No lamps or charging cords. I stumbled forward and looked to the left only to find the kitchen table was gone. Our kitchen counters were completely vacant of everything. It looked as if we'd just bought the house and hadn't moved in yet.

I pushed my hands through my hair and shook my head. "No, no, no."

"Frankie, we can explain."

I spun to face her, fully prepared to lose my shit when I realized belatedly that my three dogs had not greeted me yet. My heart stopped. Panic like I'd never felt consumed me. "Where are the boys? BOYS? *BOYS!*"

Howling erupted from across the house. I recognized Bo's higher-pitched howl, Houdini's rapid barks, and Bubba's deep howl. Relief washed through me. Not that I expected my aunt and uncle to have them packed away, too, but logic had gone out of the window.

"They're in your room," Uncle Kyle said from the hallway right outside my bedroom door. He smiled and nodded. "Brace yourself for impact."

I nodded. He pushed the door open, and it was a stampede with all three of them trying to get through the doorway at the same time.

Tears filled my eyes. "BOYS!"

Bubba got to me first, still howling, and started throwing punches at me with his fat paws. Bo leapt forward like a jungle cat and landed gracefully into a sprint, then slammed nearly full speed into my leg. Houdini wiggled so hard he could barely walk. He sneezed and licked the air rapidly, then pushed between Bo, still perched on my leg, and Bubba, who was still attacking my other leg. I giggled and dropped to the ground so they could tackle me. I wrapped my arms around them, trying to pet them as fast as I could. For a moment, all was right in the world. As they punched, licked, and climbed all over me, I felt something settle inside of me.

But that moment was shattered the second I looked up and spotted the boxes labeled *master bed, master bath,* and *library.* There were dozens and dozens of boxes all looking ready to board a moving truck. My aunt and uncle hovered in the foyer as if the boxes didn't exist at all.

"What's going on?" I glanced back and forth between them. "Someone start talking."

Aunt Kimmy's face fell. She gnawed on her bottom lip and spun a ring around her finger. "Your uncle lost his job—"

"But I found a new one!" he added with a smile, as if that somehow answered anything.

"*But* it's in Tampa." Aunt Kimmy shrugged. "We don't have a choice but to move there."

I opened my mouth, then closed it. The idea that I'd be moving across the state, hours away from my home and school and friends . . . that was almost too much for my mind to handle in the moment. I couldn't seem to process the emotions I was definitely feeling, like perhaps my brain was merely ignoring them. I had too many questions to ask before I dealt with feelings.

"You didn't know when I was waking up." I gestured to all the boxes. "Yet we're all packed and the house is sold? What about me? Were you just gonna leave and visit on the weekends—"

"NO!" they both practically screamed.

"I was going by myself so your aunt could stay with you until you woke."

"We've barely been in this house since Halloween anyway, so I was just going to stay in the hospital room with you."

"What about the boys?"

"I was taking them with me to Tampa."

I shook my head. "How could . . . I don't understand . . . you expect me to just leave *now*?"

"Well . . ." Aunt Kimmy shrugged one shoulder, her blonde brow furrowed. "Elizabeth won't be back until summer at the earliest, and you've missed a lot of school, so we thought starting over somewhere new would be best for you."

"Somewhere no one knows what happened—"

"*People know what happened?*" I shrieked as a cold chill slid down my spine.

Their faces fell.

"Who knows? WHO? How? What do they know?"

Uncle Kyle held his hands up. "*We* never told anyone but . . . Franks, it was huge. That entire party in the frat house saw you two making your escape. You stole a car from someone. There were so many witnesses."

My stomach rolled as the memories threatened to come back.

"The . . . monsters who did this to you two . . . they went to jail," Aunt Kimmy's voice was rough and raw. "All of those kids at that party came out and testified. It was all over the news. There was nothing we could do to conceal it."

Uncle Kyle nodded. "The nice young man who carried Elizabeth and helped you get into the car—"

"Malik—"

"What?"

"That's his name, Malik—" Streaks of neon color like a rainbow flashed in my eyes. I shook my head and blinked. "What was his name?"

Uncle Kyle frowned. "I . . . I don't remember. But he was under investigation until they were able to prove his innocence. The school suspended him and cut him from the team—"

"*WHAT*? That's horrible. He saved our lives—"

"He did. And luckily, another university saw his character and welcomed him to their school. Outside of Florida, far from the drama." Uncle Kyle ran his hand through his black hair. "Naturally, your entire high school knows. It's the reason Elizabeth's parents took her back to China. To get away from all of it, to heal."

"So, you're doing the same thing as them, making me move for my own benefit without my opinion."

"No." His silver eyes darkened. "I had to find work where I could and that led to Tampa. It's entirely unrelated. I just thought . . . I just feel like it's the universe looking out for you."

"Maybe fate knows this is what you need and forced our hand to give it to you?" my aunt added.

I shook my head and ignored the tears brimming on my lashes. It wasn't adding up. This wasn't like them. My entire life they'd made a point of asking my opinions on things that involved me. Never before would they have just up and moved us to another city. In fact, to make it easier for me, they'd given up their whole lives when my parents died so that I wouldn't have to relocate. *This* made no sense for them.

The idea that the *only* job my uncle could get was all the way in Tampa was suspicious as fuck. "None of this makes any sense. There's something you're not telling me, and I want the truth."

"Frankie, we just told—"

"Bullshit. You told me *bullshit*." I climbed back to my feet and pointed right at them. "I think I've been through enough, and for that matter, so have you. We all deserve honesty with each other, so stop acting like robots I've never met before and tell me the truth. What's going on?"

Uncle Kyle looked pointedly at my aunt and arched one eyebrow. "We tried."

My eyes widened. "Tried *what?*"

Aunt Kimmy sighed and it sounded like it hurt. "The truth isn't always the easiest to hear, my love. You've been through a lot. We were just trying to take it easy on you—"

"Screw that. Rip the damn Band-Aid off. *Please.*"

They stared at each other like they were communicating telepathically.

"Guys. Please!" I looked back and forth between them. "I'm begging you. Just tell me the truth. I don't care if it's harder to hear. I'm already not okay. I'd rather have the truth than live a lie just to break again later." I gestured wildly to myself. "The trauma healing hasn't even started yet, so I'm basically still in shock. That means you have nothing to lose."

Uncle Kyle smirked. "We raised her with honesty and respect, we knew a coma wouldn't change that. If she hadn't sniffed it out, then I would've gone along with it, but . . ."

"I know, I know." Aunt Kimmy smiled at me, but it was a sad smile. "In the name of honesty, you're not going to handle the truth very well. At least not at first."

"Well, I'm not handling the lie all that well either, so . . ."

"It's a hard pill to swallow." He pointed to the couch. "Want to sit?"

"I've been sedentary for five months. I need to feel my muscles working while I'm freaking out. Just start talking."

She opened her mouth then shut it and frowned. "I've been waiting fourteen years to tell you this, and I still don't know *how* to say it."

Uncle Kyle cleared his throat. "See, the thing is . . . some people aren't like other peo—"

"For the love of God, just rip the Band-Aid off and SAY IT."

She nodded. "You're a witch, Frankie."

I gasped and jerked back. "Excuse me?"

Uncle Kyle grinned. "You heard her, Franks. You're a witch."

Aunt Kimmy sighed again. "Band-Aids serve a purpose, ya know."

I stared at them. Of all the things they could have said just now, *that* was not one I'd expected.

"I don't think she heard us." Uncle Kyle leaned down into my line of sight and grinned. "We said you're a witch, Franks."

I had no idea what face I'd made, but she nodded and brushed her blonde hair over her shoulder. "She heard us."

"What . . . I don't . . ." I pinched the bridge of my nose. "Okay, I get it. You say something outlandish to trigger an extreme reaction so that when you tell me the truth it lacks a punch. Right?"

Uncle Kyle chuckled. "That would've been brilliant. What could we have led with? Maybe, *sorry, Franks, you really shift into a dragon and play with your pet kraken.* That would've softened it a bit."

Aunt Kimmy narrowed her eyes. "That's quite the visual."

"Or maybe *you're actually a werewolf and the next full moon you'll shift and—*"

"GUYS." I stomped my foot. "This isn't funny."

"Humor is a wonderful coping mechanism, Franks."

"Good, I'll have somewhere to start with my future therapist." I snapped my fingers. "Joke is over. Ha ha, you got me. What's the truth?"

Uncle Kyle opened his mouth, but Aunt Kimmy held her hand over it. "Love, more jokes aren't going to help her right now."

"Correct."

She turned her hazel eyes to me and the edge in them made me stand straighter. With a grimace, she said, "The truth is that you are a witch. As wild and crazy as it sounds, it's true."

I blinked like I was shaking an Etch A Sketch. "I don't know what you expect me to say to this."

"We know. We expected *that*. You are a witch. Your uncle and I are witches." Her smile turned sad. "Your parents too."

"My parents. Right. So, if I'm a witch, then where's my magic?

Hmm?" I waved my arms around. "If I'm a witch, why did you wait until I'm eighteen to tell me? Is it like that movie where I get my powers at this age—"

"You had magic. You lost it."

A strangled sound left my lips. I pressed my fingers to my temples. "I lost it?"

"You lost it when you were little. The trauma buried it, so we let you heal without it and live as a human." Aunt Kimmy's voice was soft and thick with emotion. "We hoped you'd never have to know. We hoped you'd live a happy, ignorantly blissful *human* life."

"Because once you start using your magic, you become a target for demons." Uncle Kyle's whole face darkened. "The world is at war right now, and it's only going to get worse—"

"*War?* What war? With who?"

"Lilith and her demons."

"*What?* What does that even mean? What are you saying to me right now? Is this some kind of sick joke?" I shook my head and gestured to the boxes. "This is a weird lie to run with—"

"We're not lying."

"Right, because I should believe that right now—"

"We were protecting you—"

"*From what?!*" Tears filled my eyes, and they felt like lava pooling on my lashes. "My whole world has flipped inside out and you wanna tell me this crazy shit? I can't handle this—"

"Which is exactly why we weren't going to tell you until we got to Tampa." Aunt Kimmy cocked her head to the side and arched one blonde eyebrow. She put her hands on her hips. "*We* know how wild this sounds. How impossible and crazy. We knew it would be too much today, so we wanted to wait a few days until you'd settled into the new house."

Uncle Kyle walked over and wrapped his arm around my shoulder, then gently led me over to the couch. With a soft push, he sat me down in the corner seat and sat to my left. "Lying to you is the hardest thing we've ever had to do. It *kills* us to keep secrets from you."

Aunt Kimmy sat on my right side. "We can explain everything and answer all your questions, but you have to let us. You don't have to pretend you're not freaked out."

"Oh my God. You're serious about this?"

They nodded.

Witches. *Witches.* I was starting to think they were legit, that this was somehow the truth, because it was unlike them to be intentionally cruel. They never lied to me. They never made jokes when I was hurting until *I* made jokes. My stomach tightened into knots. I wrung my hands together.

"Franks." Uncle Kyle put his hand over both of mine and held tight. "We're right here. We are gonna walk you through this. We're taking this slow. But you *are* a witch, like we are, and it is the reason for many, many things."

"I don't know how you expect me to believe this."

"We—"

"Prove it." I leaned back and wrapped my arms around myself. "Prove we're witches."

They looked to each other, then nodded. At the same time, they both pulled out wooden sticks about a foot long that looked straight out of the Harry Potter universe. Nothing fancy, just wood with etchings carved into them, but I couldn't see what those were.

Aunt Kimmy held hers up. "This is my wand. And this is your proof . . ."

She did a swish and flick with her wand and white light shimmered from the tip. The boxes straight across from us popped open at once. Stacks of our blue plates lifted into the air and then shot into the kitchen and began *putting themselves away.*

I gasped and sat up straight. "What the . . . Did you just . . . Did you just—"

All of our fuzzy blankets rose from another box and flew toward us. They shook themselves out, refolded, then draped themselves over the cushions. Three other boxes opened and sent out a rapid-fire release of books, one after another shooting across the living room toward the library behind us.

My jaw dropped as I gripped the edge of the couch for support. "What did —did you— you just—*bibbidi bobbidi boo?*"

"Sure." Uncle Kyle cackled. He grabbed my wrist and pulled me to my feet, then swished his wand at me. *"Bibbidi bobbidi boo!"*

Light flashed and swirled all around me. In the blink of an eye, my leggings and oversized shirt turned into a full satin ballgown with lace embroidery and rhinestones. The socks and sneakers on my feet changed to strappy stilettos.

I whined and swayed on my feet. All three of my dogs rushed toward me barking as if I'd been attacked.

"Now . . ." he pursed his lips and eyed my dogs, "which one of them should be Gus-Gus?"

"NO!" I sank to the floor and pulled all three of them to my lap. "Oh my God. Oh my God!"

Aunt Kimmy shook her head and chuckled. There was a flash of light and then I was back in *my* clothes. My breath left me in a rush. I pulled my dogs all the way into my lap so we were one big cuddle puddle. They were my emotional support.

"Truth is, we started packing this morning." Aunt Kimmy grinned and flicked her wand, and all of the stuff went flying back into their boxes. "While you slept, we took turns packing up so we'd be ready to move."

I stared at the boxes, waiting for them to open back up again. "I don't understand. How do these things connect? I'm so confused. Let's assume I believe the whole witch thing, let's assume I don't expect to wake up any second, I'm still lost. Why do we have to go *now*?"

"Because of this." Aunt Kimmy pointed the tip of her wand at my arm. There was a cold tickle and then neon-blue flames wrapped around my body.

I screamed and swatted at it—except it didn't hurt. My jaw dropped.

"That's *your* magic, Frankie," she said. She sat down on the ground beside me and covered my blue flames with her hand, putting them out entirely. "I did that to prove that *you* have magic as well. If you're ready to hear more, we're beyond ready to tell you."

I stared at my arm and nodded.

"We know this is a lot. And because you're so smart, we can't just give you the bullet point notes. We have to tell you as much as we can. To do so, we need to back up a little bit."

I nodded again. Words were too hard for me in the moment.

"The real name for our kind is *arcana,* but along the way *witch* became the slang term and we've all rolled with it. Now, you remember the story of the Garden of Eden a certain way, the way all humans do, but the truth is much different. Lucifer was never evil. He never fell from Heaven, and while he *is* the King of Hell, he is also *the* most powerful angel. He is God's right hand. His favorite. And because he is so kind and wonderful, so entirely selfless, he took the blame for the dawn of evil in our world. Lilith is darkness incarnate, the meaning of evil. She caused the fall, she caused demons to enter, and she caused darkness in the souls of humans and angels alike. There are a number of angels who did truly fall and turn to her side."

"But Lucifer is not one of them." Uncle Kyle nodded. "It is important you remember that."

I blinked and licked my lips. I tried to summon words, but none came, so I nodded.

"Heaven has been at war with Lilith since. The humans were not capable of fighting off her demons, so the species of arcana were born to serve as guardians of the realm. There's a long, long list of details and stories about the lineage of witches that we can tell you about later. The important thing right now is to understand that witches were born to protect this world against Lilith, and that is why we have magic." She took a deep breath and rubbed Bubba's belly. "If you look back in human history at all of the dark times of war and treachery, Lilith is behind all of it."

That caught my attention. "Like what? An example please?"

"The Salem witch trials." Uncle Kyle's whole face darkened. "In an effort to protect our realm from Lilith, two twin witches accidentally ripped a hole in the dimensional wall around us, letting evil waltz in without even a speed bump. *That* caused the witch trials, because it caused the humans to lose their minds a little with what they saw happening around them. That hole was only permanently closed . . . on Halloween night."

My eyes widened. "The night of my accident."

They nodded.

"Continue," I whispered.

"Another example is the One Hundred Years' War that happened in the fourteenth century. King Henry the Sixth was actually the ruler of all witches at the time. He led us to victory against Lilith. That's when witches stepped out of human politics forever."

I shook my head. "That's the war you referred to before—"

"No," they both grumbled.

Uncle Kyle pulled Houdini into his lap. "When that war ended, Lilith was not killed. She was just blocked from returning temporarily. She's been trying to rebuild strength and return since. We've officially been at war with her since last summer, even if none of us realized it."

Aunt Kimmy shuddered. "She has not returned here herself. She's just been acting through others. But she is coming, of that The Coven has been abundantly clear."

"The Coven?"

"The twenty-two witches who are Marked by Heaven to be the rulers of the species. Anything that isn't human, actually, report to them and follow their laws."

"Oh. Oh, okay." I scrubbed my face with my hands. "Okay, so . . . but like . . . why not tell me?"

"Because witches are being hunted now more than they ever have been."

"Demons can smell our magic. They sense it. And once you encounter one, it will only get worse and worse—"

"Like Percy Jackson and the monsters," I heard myself whisper. "Once he knew the truth, the mist no longer protected him."

"Yeah, kind of like that." Uncle Kyle chuckled. "I love fantasy books. They really help explain shit to new witches."

"But why now? Why do I have magic *now*?" I held my hands up to inspect them as if I could still see the magic on my skin. "Did the coma trigger it?"

"The accident did."

I gasped.

"This is not going to be easy to hear, my love, but you had magic as a toddler. We have photos and even videos of you using my wand. But . . ." she licked her lips and closed her eyes. "Your parents were killed my demons."

A broken cry slipped up my throat.

"You almost died with them." She took my hand and squeezed. "Your mother had gone out to try and . . . well, she was trying to prevent you all from dying. You were with your father. At the last moment, he managed to hide you in a safe place using magic. That magic he used on you . . . forced your own magic to go dormant, like it was in a deep, deep sleep."

"He sent us a fire message and we came as fast as we could, but it was too late." Uncle Kyle shuddered. "We thought your magic would return when it was ready. It didn't."

"And when you'd seen us using our magic, you were terrified. You'd scream and shake . . . So we stopped using it in front of you."

"PTSD?"

They nodded.

I scrubbed my face with my hands that were shaking. "Keep going, please."

Aunt Kimmy took my hand in hers. "Your Uncle did not lose his job. That was a white lie. The truth is we have to move because your magic has awakened."

I scowled. "I don't understand."

"There's a huge community of witches in Tampa, a neighborhood bigger than ours full of families with kids and such."

Uncle Kyle grabbed my hand and flipped it over. "Let me show you something."

He dropped his wand in my palm. The second it touched my skin, blue flames shot out of my hand. I cursed and threw his wand back at him, but my magic just *followed*. It was like throwing gas on a fire, everything I did just made it worse and worse.

Uncle Kyle just chuckled. "See? All I did was put my magical wand in your hand and *boom*."

"*Kyle.*" Aunt Kimmy huffed and shook her head. She pointed her wand at my raging magic, and it vanished. "Not that he's wrong. And this right here is why we have to move you to Tampa. There, you'll be able to learn and practice your magic in a safe space. There are teens your age. Here, you'd have to hide. Here, if your magic was provoked at school, it would be . . . really bad. But in Tampa, at Gulf Shores High School, you'll be surrounded by witches."

"I'll be safe from demons there?" They both grimaced. "That's not the reaction I wanted."

"Demons can find you almost anywhere, but at least in Tampa the other witches can help protect you."

Uncle Kyle bumped my shoulder with his. "We had not planned any kind of move until you woke up last night. We sold the house to a friend who had been looking. All of what you see happened this morning once we knew you were being discharged."

I took a deep breath and sighed. "Because living here is dangerous?"

They nodded.

"I'm a little . . . overwhelmed by all of this." I looked to them and waited until they nodded. "Imma have a ton of questions. Like, I need a lot more information."

"We're prepared. And we'll get on the magic lessons."

"If Elizabeth were still here, I would *not* be okay with this."

"We know." Aunt Kimmy held her hands up. "And we're not against using magic to get the Chen family to move to Tampa once they return."

My eyes widened. "Humans live in the same town?"

They smiled and nodded. "She won't be across the street, but she can be around the corner."

I pointed to them. "I'm gonna hold y'all to that."

They laughed.

"When do we have to leave?" I asked.

"We wanted you to have one last night here. We leave in the morning."

I glanced around our living room at all of the packed-up boxes with my entire life in them. It would only take a few minutes for them to get the rest ready to leave. There hadn't been a moving truck out front, but my gut told me they could have one here in minutes. They said they wanted me to have one last night at home . . . but I wasn't sure I needed it. Or wanted it. This already didn't feel like home. The furniture wasn't even the same as I remembered it. Everything else was packed in boxes. There was no way I would be able to relax knowing what I did now and knowing I was moving hours away in the morning.

*What's the point in staying?* My chest tightened. Elizabeth wasn't across the street. I had no interest in answering a million questions from my other friends. Dragging out the inevitable just sucked. I licked my lips. "Let's just leave now. The trauma won't care where I am."

# CHAPTER NINE

## FRANKIE

I WASN'T ALLOWED to tell Elizabeth about the whole witch thing.

I told them that wasn't going to work for me.

They told me to be patient and they'd let me talk to The Coven about it.

I then informed them they had until Elizabeth returned to Florida and then I was telling her, permission from The Coven or not. Demons or no demons. My best friend and I had been through too much. If she had been across the street when I got home, I would've told her already but it wasn't exactly something to say over FaceTime with a person on the other side of the world.

My phone vibrated in my hand. When I looked down, I found text messages from Elizabeth.

'I can't believe one night changed so much.'

'Let's just not think about it that way,' I sent back. 'We just have to find our new normal.'

'Yeah, which means you have until June to find a house for us to move to within a mile from your new house.'

I grinned. 'A mile, eh? I'll see what I can do.'

She sent the fingers crossed emoji. 'FaceTime me once you get in your new room?'

'Will do. Should be soon.'

I took a deep breath as I slid my iPhone back into my pocket. The GPS said ten minutes until arrival, which meant this was my new town, so I wanted to pay attention. My independence was important to me, now more than ever. I needed to start learning my way around, learning the street names and what stores were around. The *Publix* sign up ahead made me sigh with relief. There was no grocery store equivalent to *Publix*. But in all fairness, so far this part of Tampa didn't look much different than Tallahassee. More palm trees though. This definitely wasn't the Tampa Bay most people thought of when Tampa was mentioned. It had to be some small-town subset of it with a name I hadn't learned yet.

So far, it looked like a normal Florida suburban town with stop-lights every other second and Corporate America in surround sound. We sat at a red light in the middle lane just watching a screaming match between the guy selling bouquets of roses and the homeless guy whose handwritten sign was being used to swat at the flower guy as if it were a bat. While the two were arguing, a woman wearing a trash bag as a hat scurried over, stole the bucket of cash, then fled faster than I would've thought those legs could move. The two guys had just noticed what happened when the light turned green and Uncle Kyle drove through the intersection. I cursed and spun in my seat to look out the back window as the homeless man took off in pursuit. The flower guy was still screaming at him.

I grinned and sat forward. Florida was so bat shit crazy. I loved it. Something told me this move a few hours south was going to be much more entertaining. I kept waiting for fear or sadness over this move to kick in, but it hadn't happened yet. Instead, I found myself growing more and more excited the closer we got. Something about what happened in the frat house made me *want* to move away and reinvent myself, to not be that girl everyone talked about. What happened to us was not our fault, but I knew lots of people who would claim otherwise. My aunt and uncle had made the right call in moving us. I couldn't even blame Elizabeth's parents.

We slowed at the next intersection and made a right turn. I glanced down at the GPS and butterflies danced in my stomach. We were less than a mile away now. I pressed pause on my *Halestorm* playlist and tossed my headphones back in my open bag. This was it: my new neighborhood. The anticipation was killing me. I slid to the middle seat to get a better view. The road we were now on was lined with huge oak trees that stretched over the two-lane road to make a sort of tunnel. The sunlight streaming in between the leaves made for a gorgeous sight. Between the two lanes was a grassy median that looked perfect for walking the dogs along. I glanced over the backseat to check on the boys, but they were all cuddled up in a pile, sound asleep.

When I turned back around, I caught a quick glimpse at a short brick wall with the words 'GULF SHORES' written on it. The O had a five-pointed star inside of it. I frowned and tried to get a better look, but we went by it too fast. The lane into the neighborhood ended at a stop sign, leaving us only the option to go left or right. A car to our right was crawling through the stop sign in a pathetic attempt to turn left, but it was okay, it gave me a chance to look around.

"So, to the left is the human side of the neighborhood," Uncle Kyle said as he pointed to the left. "To the right is our zone."

I frowned. "How do you know the difference?"

"If you're human, you don't. But our magic subconsciously keeps them away." Then he pointed to the right. "However, those guys are usually a good indication."

Aunt Kimmy laughed.

I slid back over to the window on the right side to see what they saw—and my jaw dropped. In the grass, on both sides of the road, had to be three dozen iguanas. Huge, massive, mini-dinosaur looking iguanas with big spikes running down their backs and tails as long as their bodies. At least a dozen of them were in various shades of neon-orange and had to be about six feet long. They were basically alligators at that point.

"What in the Jumanji kind of shit is this?"

They both laughed as we turned onto the road, letting the jungle beasts surround us.

"Animals know they're safe with us, so they hang around where we can protect them." Aunt Kimmy pointed behind us. "The humans kill them if they go over there . . . so they don't."

"Why would they kill them?"

"Technically, they're an invasive species." Uncle Kyle looked up at me through the rear-view mirror. "But so are humans."

*Humans.* I rolled my eyes and shook my head. I wasn't quite ready to accept this whole witch notion, but I hadn't woken up yet, so it had to be true. Also, I'd stubbed my toe really bad at one of the gas stations and saw stars for a few seconds . . . so I was definitely awake, as the theory went. But the idea that I wasn't a human was a hard pill to swallow.

The neighborhood looked totally and entirely *human* as we drove through it. Just a bunch of ranch-style one-story homes in various colors with bright-green grass and lots of colorful flowers. I saw palm trees, oak trees, and a bunch of other trees I didn't know the name of. The neighborhood was cute. I liked how each house had its own individual flair. This was no cookie-cutter development. I'd never seen a home with a black front door, and yet I'd seen at least two dozen. If that wasn't interesting on its own, the rest of the doors we'd passed were the exact same shade of green—a hue somewhere between emerald and hunter. It was pretty but . . . that many houses?

I frowned and paid closer attention to the next few houses. The entire street of houses had either black or green front doors, except every single one of them had that same five-pointed star on them or in the windows.

"I see a lot of . . . are those pentagrams?"

"Those are pentacles," Aunt Kimmy said from the front seat while texting someone. "The five-pointed star by itself is a pentagram, but with the circle around it, it's called a pentacle."

I nodded. Seemed like good information to know. "It represents the five elements, right?"

"Yes, it does." Aunt Kimmy smiled at me, which I only saw in the side-view mirror. "Also, protection and balance. It's the chosen symbol for arcana. We invented it long ago, but societies throughout history have adopted it and used it for their own meanings."

I frowned. "And the witches aren't mad about that?"

"Absolutely not. They are protecting themselves more than they realize, and that's what we want. It's our job to protect the humans."

I was about to ask about the black and green doors when we passed a pale-green house with a purple door. A vibrant plum purple. The pentacle hanging on it had little pink flowers on it. The next house on the corner also had a plum purple door with a pentacle made of sunflowers. We stopped at the stop sign, and while we waited for the three other cars to make their move, I glanced around at the houses. More specifically, their front doors. Across the street to the left, the three houses closest to me were that same purple. Up ahead, the two corner houses had purple doors as well. We made a right turn, then drove three streets down and made a left. All the doors lining the street had been purple, but in the distance to the right on the streets we'd passed, the doors had been black or green.

The first house on the left after our turn had an aquamarine-colored door and its pentacle was made of seashells. There were a handful more purple doors before I saw three aquamarine doors in a row.

"Okay . . . what's up with the doors?" I pointed as we drove by yet another purple door with a giant pentacle made of twigs hanging like a wreath. "There's a pattern. This means something."

Uncle Kyle grinned. "They indicate the type of witch that lives in the house. Purple is for Wands—"

"Wands? Like in Harry Potter?"

"Yes . . . and no." Aunt Kimmy grimaced and half-turned in the passenger seat. "While in a more literal sense, the wands used are very much the same as in Harry Potter, their function is slightly different."

"That did not clarify things as you might think."

She chuckled. "Let's back up. So, there are four types of witches—or as we call them, Suits. Each and every witch, including the members of The Coven, belong to one of these four Suits. Those four types are Wands, Cups, Pentacles, and Swords."

"Like in a tarot deck?" I wasn't an experienced tarot card reader, but I'd seen them before, not that that helped me understand the meaning any better.

"Exactly. The Suit you are indicates the type of magic you are strongest in. Not saying that a Cup can't use a wand, but it wouldn't be their best fit." She pursed her lips. "Kind of like you *could* play catcher or first base, but your best fit on the field is the pitcher's mound."

"*Oh.*" I nodded as I glanced out the window at the four moms pushing strollers down the middle of the street with little umbrellas floating above the strollers—entirely untethered to anything. I shook my head. "Okay, that helps. Continue?"

"Swords are the warriors, the soldiers. They go on to become Knights. You can think of them as witch military. They get stationed around the world to fight demons for a living. The Cups are healers. They're potion masters. Their magic is calm and grounding, meant to support the others. They go on to work in infirmaries around the world."

"And you're both Wands," I said as pieces started to click in my mind. "I saw your wands."

"You did. We are. Wands are spellcasters. We're the most like Harry Potter witches. We use wands to do all kinds of things. Some of us go on to be Pages who work with the Knights to protect people."

"The Pentacles are the hardest to explain," Uncle Kyle said as he stopped the car to let a kid and his dog cross. "They're like the ambassadors to the human world. They tend to be in leadership roles, the responsible ones who rein the rest of us in. *Their circus, their monkeys* kind of thing."

"Right, right, right. So then I'm assuming the four Suits have one specific color assigned to each?"

"Yup. Can you guess which is which?" Uncle Kyle wagged his eyebrows at me through the rearview mirror.

I pursed my lips. "Black is for the Swords. Has to be. And the green gives responsible vibes so I'm guessing Pentacles?"

"Two for two." He laughed and slowed the car in front of a pale, sand-colored one-story house. "Can you get all four?"

"Well, potions are liquid and aquamarine is the color of the ocean so . . . that must be Cups?" When they nodded, I continued, "Which means purple is for Wands."

"Four for four. Good job, Franks." He cheered and pulled into a red-brick driveway. He put the car in park, then looked over his shoulder at me. "We're here."

My breath caught in my throat. All of a sudden, nerves crashed down around me.

Aunt Kimmy smiled. "You ready?"

"Sure. In theory."

"Fake it 'til you make it?"

I grinned. "You know how I roll."

"Come on, kiddo. Let's get inside and get settled, then we'll order some delivery and relax."

"Right. On the count of three, we get out." I took a deep breath. "Three . . . two—"

"ONE!" Uncle Kyle threw his door open and jumped out.

Aunt Kimmy chuckled and slowly pushed her door open. "Come on, you know he can only contain himself for so long."

*You got this, Frankie. No big deal.* I leaned over the backseat to my dogs. "Boys! Ready to get out?"

All three of their little heads popped up. Uncle Kyle yelled hello to somebody, probably a stranger walking by, and it made all three dogs jump to their feet. I smiled, got out of the car, and turned to shut the door—and froze. My jaw dropped. The sunset painted in the sky was more vibrant than I'd ever seen. And I was born in Florida. I assumed I'd seen the extent of the colors of the sunset, but evidently I was wrong. "Whoa."

"Frankie?"

I pointed to the sky. "Where was this back home?"

Uncle Kyle chuckled from the other side of the car in my peripheral vision. "It's the magic in the air, the presence of arcana, that makes those colors that much more vibrant."

I took a deep breath, then sniffed a few times. "Do I smell the beach? The air is salty—"

"The beach is five minutes away. Just follow the sunset."

I gasped. "Y'all should've led with that this morning. It's like you don't know me at all."

"Dammit. She's right, love."

"Can we go there now? First?"

Aunt Kimmy's face fell. "Sorry, not right now. Vanessa wasn't expecting us until lunch tomorrow, so she scrambled to clear up her schedule to meet us tonight. She's inside waiting for us."

"Can we go after?"

She arched one eyebrow at me and pursed her lips. "You start school tomorrow morning, and we have to unpack everything—"

"Using your magic wand—"

"So, let's see how quickly we can get all settled in and then we'll see about going to the beach. Deal?"

"I see what you're doing. It's working." I sighed and turned back to the sunset. "Fine, deal. Wait, who is Vanessa?"

Aunt Kimmy walked by me to the back of the SUV, then opened the trunk, so I followed her. "Vanessa is an old friend of mine who is renting this house to us."

"She just has spare houses?" I asked with a frown as I hooked the boys' leashes into place. "Why does that feel weird to me?"

She just chuckled. "The Coven lived here for a while. This town became a miniature homeland for our kind. People wanted to live near them—"

Houdini licked the side of my face. "Why? That sounds dangerous."

"Well, we're drawn to them. To their power. It's a subconscious thing. If they were still in town you'd feel it—Bubba, don't jump! You're gonna hurt yourself." She scooped him up and gently sat him on the ground. "We have a hotel in town for visiting witches, but whenever someone moves out of town, their house is bought up by other witches to prevent humans from accidentally buying in, then they either sell to known witches or rent out to witches who want to live here temporarily."

Bo barked impatiently so I helped him down and then lowered Houdini down after him. Once all three dogs were out, I took Bubba's leash from Aunt Kimmy and led them into the front yard.

"Are you okay, Frankie?" Aunt Kimmy asked softly, following me into the grass. "You seem to be handling this in stride but . . . it's a lot, I know."

"I think I'm okay? Honestly, after what happened, I think anything would've been *a lot,* so might as well go with the new."

Uncle Kyle tugged my hair playfully. "She's a trooper."

I smiled and watched my boys sniff every piece of grass near us. This was our new home, and while I had no idea how long we'd be living here, I knew it was going to be a little bit. Especially if I had to learn how to control my magic and then learn to use it. Part of me still struggled with the whole concept, especially as I glanced left and right at this residential street and found nothing spectacular. Not that it wasn't a cute neighborhood. It just looked so *human.* I was waiting for the reality of the magic to become overwhelmingly obvious, but perhaps that would happen once I went to school.

My stomach turned. School. I hadn't started a new school in forever, and I'd never done it without Elizabeth. Not that I was shy, but my whole life had been flipped upside down and now I wasn't sure what was what. I needed to unpack and at least make my new room feel comfortable.

I cleared my throat. "So when will our stuff arrive?"

"Oh, it's already here." Aunt Kimmy grinned and headed toward the house, waving us along with her.

"What? How? C'mon, boys." I tugged on the leashes so I could keep up.

Aunt Kimmy marched for the front door of the yellow house with a cute porch out front. "We shipped it—"

"But how? That was just hours ago—"

"Magic, Franks." Uncle Kyle held his wand out.

I frowned. "The moving company guys weren't human?"

He grinned like the Cheshire Cat. "Nope."

I blinked and stopped beside him on the sidewalk just before the porch. "Explain?"

"Remember we explained about the different Suits? And how the Pentacles help arcana assimilate with human culture?" When I nodded, he shrugged. "Well, many centuries ago, one of the Pentacles families realized The Coven needed easier ways to communicate with the civilians, but also the humans kept going into war with each other and we needed ways to hide magical belongings quickly . . . so they basically started a magical shipping service. They designed the whole premise, then hired some Wands to do the magic part."

My eyebrows rose. "One family did this?"

"The English family, yes."

"Bo, leave it," I snapped to stop him from chasing a large curly-tailed lizard, then turned my attention back to my uncle. "As in, they're from England?"

"What?" He frowned down at me, then he smiled. "*Ohh,* no. Their surname is English."

"They're one of the founding twenty families." Aunt Kimmy was typing on her cellphone. Then she looked up and made a funny face. "Actually, their name was really Heinglitz, but as with many names and words throughout history, over time it was changed to English. It's been *English* for a few centuries now, and since they have quite a legacy by it, they don't care to change it."

I blinked and shook my head. "I love how you drop the words *twenty founding families* and then just roll on like it's no big deal. Later I'm gonna need more info on this but for now . . . this English family must be wealthy?"

Uncle Kyle wagged his eyebrows and grinned as he pointed his wand at the lock on the front door, even though we were like ten feet away still. "No one richer."

Light sparkled within the gold lock and then the purple door popped open an inch.

"Hey, our door is purple."

"Franks, I just used a wand to open it. We talked about it in the car."

"Right. Duh. I knew that. I'm fine." I rolled my eyes but then a thought occurred to me, something I hadn't yet paused to consider. "What were my parents?"

"Wands," they both answered softly.

I nodded. "So I'm probably a Wand?"

"Probably." Uncle Kyle cleared his throat and fidgeted with his wand. "Shall we go in? It's hot as hell out here."

The front door swung wide open and a woman with black hair stepped out. Well, more like she slid into the open doorway with her arms wide and a huge grin plastered on her face. It was like that GIF Elizabeth and I used a lot. "Kimmy! Kyle!"

Aunt Kimmy let out a soft sigh, like the sight of her was a relief. "Vanessa."

I watched with my dogs sitting at my feet as Vanessa hugged both my aunt and uncle like their lives depended on it. I'd never heard this woman's name before, and yet they seemed super close. *The plot thickens.*

Then her bright-green eyes focused on me and they seemed to twinkle a little. "*Francelina.*"

"Frankie, please." I smiled and nodded but didn't wave as I was holding Bubba and Bo on a tight leash since they sometimes were unpredictable with new people. "Nice to meet you—"

She tackled me. This Vanessa woman tackled me in a hug and actually lifted me off my feet a few Inches. All three boys were now barking and jumping up on me. "Um, Vanessa, the boys don't like strangers—"

"OH!" Vanessa sat me back on my feet, then leapt back. She pulled three dog cookies in the shape of a bone from her pocket and knelt down in front of them despite them still barking at her. "May I? They're the same kind you give them—Kimmy gave me the list."

"Oh. Yeah, thanks for asking. Go ahead."

"Sorry, puppos, I'm friend." She held those treats up and smiled. "Now, who wants to sit down and be a good boy for his cookie?"

All at once they sat. I blinked and shook my head. "Wow."

Vanessa handed the cookies out one at a time, then smiled up at me as she stood. "I'm a dog person, they know it. I just got them a little excited. Sorry. I just haven't seen you in so long."

My eyes widened. "I, um—Sorry, we've met?"

"You were practically a baby the last I saw you. I knew your parents." I must've made a face because she winked and waved her hand through the air. "But let me stop being weird. Come inside. It's too hot out here. I just got here a few moments before you all did, so I still have a few things to do, but your stuff was already inside."

"From the English family's magic moving company," I grumbled but none of them heard me.

"Okay, three keys are on the hook here right inside the door. They work all the locks." Vanessa pointed to her left as she entered the foyer. "The clicker for the garage is on the kitchen counter, in case I forget."

The moment the boys and I were inside, the front door closed softly behind us. Golden sparks flickered from the lock. The ice-cold air-conditioning slammed into me, and I sighed. It was glorious. I wondered if a witch invented air conditioners because they were definitely magic in this Florida heat. Once my eyes adjusted to the dim indoor lighting, I realized we stood in a small foyer with key hooks on the left wall and a little section on the right with raincoats and rain boots lined up ready for us. Three pairs. I'd never seen them before, and they were definitely too small to fit anyone in this family.

"Frankie?"

I jumped at my aunt's voice but pointed to the rain gear. "Whose stuff is that?"

"Oh." She giggled and pointed her wand at the items. Light sparkled like pixie dust, then the raincoats and boots changed to be our sizes—or at least they looked right. "There."

"What just happened here?"

She just laughed and then pointed her wand at the wall beside the raincoats. Three big, golden hooks appeared out of nowhere. I opened my mouth to ask what they were for when suddenly my dogs' harnesses and leashes flew between us and landed on the hooks. I looked down to my dogs and my jaw dropped.

"They're naked."

"Well, yeah, we're home now." She winked and waved for me to follow her around the corner. "The boys won't really need those much now that we're here."

"Why?" I frowned as we rounded the corner and came out into the open floor plan living space. The all-white kitchen was nestled into the corner on my right with a huge eat-at island that bridged the space between the living room. The back wall of the house was made of glass and showed off a gorgeous patio out back with bright-green grass beyond it. The brand-new black sectional sofa my aunt and uncle had purchased during my coma sat perfectly in the middle of the living room with our television on the opposite wall. It looked like we'd already moved in.

"Because every house in the neighborhood has spells to keep dogs within the yard unless they're hooked on a leash that a person is holding. We don't like lost dogs, or dogs getting hit by cars. That way if a dog somehow does get out but wanders into another yard, they'll be trapped there until someone comes to get them." Vanessa smiled at me as she flicked her wand and the sliding glass doors opened, letting fresh air in. "Go ahead, puppos, go play."

They took off running for the backyard, already barking and playfully biting each other on the way out. My stomach tightened into knots. I wanted to trust her, but I couldn't, so I chased after them, except when I got to the open door I watched as Bo slid to a stop about a foot from the wooden fence. He cocked his head to the side for a moment, then threw his snout in the air and howled. Houdini and Bubba copied without hesitation.

I grimaced. "I probably should warn our neighbors about the howl fests."

Vanessa chuckled. "No worries. The houses here have spells to keep noise contained. You'll only ever hear noise from your neighbors if there's danger. Those are the only sounds permitted through."

"No way."

Vanessa arched her eyebrow, then pointed her wand out the open door toward the house to our right. The blue sky sparkled and then *Silver Springs* by Stevie Nicks blared over the six-foot-tall wooden fence as if I was playing it from a speaker right in front of me. My eyes widened. Vanessa chuckled and flicked her wand again and the yard went silent.

"Holy fuck."

She threw her head back and cackled. "Trust the magic, Frankie. Your boys are safe in the yard. Let them play while you get settled."

I spun around and froze. It was like that scene in *Beauty and the Beast* when all the pieces of houseware were singing *Be our Guest* and everything was flying around. My aunt and uncle were hard at work with their wands, sorting through the boxes of our stuff that had beat us here.

"Vanessa, where should we get takeout from?"

"*Kyle. No,*" Aunt Kimmy hissed and tossed hand towels right at his face. "We've been eating take out at the hospital for months. This is our first night here. Let's have something home-cooked."

He threw his hands up. "Fine. Cook. Knock your socks off."

"Why do I have to cook? I'm putting everything away—"

"What's it look like I'm doing, love?"

"You're the better cook—"

"And you're the better driver, and yet you made me drive here." Uncle Kyle wagged his eyebrows. "That means it's your turn to do the heavy lifting."

Aunt Kimmy narrowed her eyes at him. "Really? You're going to organize every single room and put everything away in its new designated spot that we haven't even established yet? I mean, we haven't even looked at the drawer situation in our bathroom. How big is our closet? Which side is mine? Where do we want the cups in the kitchen?"

He opened his mouth and pointed at her, then said in a loud voice, "Pasta or potatoes?"

Aunt Kimmy gave him a little smile and kissed his cheek. "Love you, hun. Whichever meal you'd like to make we'll be happy with."

He pursed his lips and nodded. His eyes locked on our new kitchen. "How about baked ziti? Yeah, that'll be good. A nice heavy meal before Frank's first day."

Three boxes labeled '*KITCHEN*' floated over and landed on the island. "I put your speaker in the big one."

"All right." He cracked his knuckles, then dug into the boxes with his bare hands. "I'm thinking our neighbor had it right, a little Stevie Nicks to welcome us home."

Aunt Kimmy walked over to me and Vanessa and rolled her eyes, but she was smiling. She leaned forward and whispered, "He's going to avoid using magic just so he won't have to try and help me put stuff away. And then I won't have to be nice and let him help when I really just wanna do it myself."

I snorted. "I'm not entirely sure if that's healthy or not."

"Tough to tell, kiddo." She winked, then pointed over her left shoulder. "Sweetie, why don't you go set up your room? I put all your boxes in there already. Take your time. Relax. Settle in. We'll call you when dinner is ready?"

I took a deep breath, then sighed. "Right. And the boys?"

"Door will stay open so they can come and go." She used her wand to send about a dozen boxes flying through a doorway on our left. "I'll be in and out. The boys will find you. Go ahead."

"Come on. I'll show you." Vanessa took my hand and dragged me to the right into a small hallway with three closed doors. "Right, so this first one is the laundry room. The one in the middle is the bathroom, and the door on the left is your new room."

"Cool." I opened the door to my room and peeked inside. The room was nothing special. White walls with the same light hardwood floors as in the rest of the house. The window on the far wall over-looked the front yard, which I did like. It would allow me to spy on the neighborhood discreetly. The entire left wall was a closet with those accordion doors. The wall to my right had my bookshelves. They were empty, but that was okay. I loved setting up my library. My bed was nestled in the far corner, which I also liked. My boxes of all my stuff were sitting in the middle of the room.

"You okay?"

I turned back to Vanessa and found her green eyes watching me. With a smile, I nodded. "Yeah, just . . . adjusting. Thank you for hooking us up here."

"You're welcome." She squeezed my shoulder. "You've got this, Frankie. Just breathe in that salty ocean air and everything will be fine."

And then she was gone.

I turned to face my new room, and for the first time felt a little bit empty. But it was weird. I didn't wish I was back home. Sure, I loved my softball team and I had other friends, but none of them were like Elizabeth. Honestly, my best friend being on the other side of the world was the main reason I didn't want to stay. I didn't want to face my school and be treated like a freak. Or a victim. This move was going to be easier. And if I was being honest with myself, the whole being a witch thing was kind of epic. It was getting harder to deny its realness, and that wasn't a bad thing. If this was somehow a dream, then I figured I ought to enjoy it while I could.

The boxes were going to wait though. I walked around them toward my bed and discovered the window on the right wall was a bay window. With a grin, I climbed up and settled in. All I wanted was to talk to Elizabeth, so I pulled my phone out and FaceTimed her, but after a few rings I gave up. I sat my phone down and looked out the window—and frowned. I could see clear through to our neighbor's yard to where a boy with dark-red hair sat on the step of their wooden deck. He looked young, or at least small, like perhaps he wasn't more than my height.

Purple light flashed in front of him, and we both jumped.

He leapt off the deck, but his foot caught on something and he stumbled forward, crashing down to his knees before his momentum sent him face-first into the gravel walkway. I cursed and opened the window to call out and see if he was okay, then froze with my face sticking out the window. The poor guy was already flipping onto his back. There was no blood or anything, so he was most likely fine. And then he started to laugh. Like full belly, body-shaking laugh.

I leaned back but I left the window open. I was captivated by this new neighbor of mine for some reason. He rolled onto his stomach, then staggered onto all fours. I was an athlete, always had been, which meant I was usually surrounded by other athletes . . . and this guy . . . was not one. His arms and legs shook a little as he climbed back to his feet. He even stumbled on his way back to sit on the steps. I suspected this dude was gifted in clumsiness.

He was also older than I originally assumed. His face definitely belonged to a teenager. He was just short. With a dimpled smirk, he brushed his hands off on his jeans, then picked up a stick off the ground—*no, wait. That's a wand.* Excitement rushed through me. He was about to use magic. I'd seen my aunt and uncle use their wands, and now their friend Vanessa, but somehow witnessing a perfect stranger perform magic was different. Maybe because he didn't know I was watching. Maybe that made it more real. I leaned forward to try and listen.

His voice wasn't carrying, probably because of that spell Vanessa talked about, but by the way his mouth moved, almost like he was singing, I imagined he was saying a spell. Granted, I was working only with my minimal knowledge of Harry Potter. Actually, he reminded me of Ron Weasley in class waving his wand like it was a saltshaker. In my head I heard Hermione's voice warning him he was going to poke someone's eye out before correcting his enunciation.

I had no idea what he was trying to do, but magic kept sparkling and flashing from the end of his wand. He kept dropping it and cursing. His left sneaker changed to a ski boot, then a bright-red rain boot, and then a black boot before returning to the white sneaker. His blue jeans suddenly had pink spots all over them. He ran his hands through his dark-red hair and stomped his foot. I tried not to laugh, but when he held the wand up and seemed to threaten it, I lost my composure.

Just as I was closing my window so he wouldn't hear me laughing, a woman with the same dark-red hair color stepped out onto the deck. She was even smaller than the kid. She waved her hand and shouted in a beautiful British accent, "Time for dinner, love."

"Coming, Ma," he shouted back in the same accent.

*The plot thickens a little more.*

My phone vibrated against the glass. I cursed and dove for it, finding Elizabeth calling me back on FaceTime. I hit the button and held my phone up and smiled. "Hi."

"Oh no, what's wrong?"

I frowned. "Nothing—"

"That's your fake smile." She held the phone closer to her face. "Don't bullshit me. Talk to me."

"I'm just doing my best right now, trying to adapt." I sighed and leaned back. "Distract me. Show me China."

# CHAPTER TEN

## FRANKIE

I JUMPED out of the car and took my first deep breath since arriving in this town. Something about the crisp, salty ocean air just hit a reset button for me. Talking to Elizabeth had helped re-center me, and her staying on the phone while I set up my room really helped me get it done. But getting to see the beach before I started school was crucial for my well-being. If there was anything good that came out of this move, it was the closeness to the ocean. Back home the drive to the beach was a much bigger commitment.

"I need my toes in the sand."

Uncle Kyle turned to face me, but there was no smile on his face, and his silver eyes lacked their playful sparkle. "Before we go out there, we need to go over something."

My pulse skipped. "What is it?"

Aunt Kimmy walked up to stand beside him. Her face was grim. "Listen, we've mentioned demons before but you've yet to see one. This is not a joking matter. We need your undivided attention before we go onto that sand."

I swallowed roughly. "Well, you've definitely got it now."

"Good. Most witches don't know that there are demons in the ocean." I must've made a face because she nodded. "They're drawn to magic and power, so The Coven living here for twelve years had its effect. The demons linger because of it."

My heart pounded in my chest. I leaned to the side to eye the shoreline behind them. "So, there are demons in that water? Now?"

"No. And yes." Aunt Kimmy grimaced as she tied her blonde hair up in a ponytail. "They're not just sitting there, but any little bit of magic can summon them, so you need to be careful and very, very observant."

I nodded and wrung my hands together. "Okay. Um . . ."

"Breathe, Franks. We're not trying to scare you. We just want you to know the truth of the world so you're not caught by surprise." Uncle Kyle squeezed my shoulder. "You're going to learn what to do, and what not to do, but for tonight we just need you paying attention to *us*."

"If we say to do something, you have to listen. Not because you're a child, but because you're untrained. Got it?"

"Yes, coach. Got it." I gave them two thumbs-up. "You just say how high, and I jump."

Uncle Kyle narrowed his silver eyes on me. "Maybe we should give her a bat, just in case?"

"I left one in the trunk—"

"On it." He did a swish and flick with his wand, and by the time I glanced over my shoulder, I saw my Louisville Slugger flying straight toward us. "Good thinking, love."

I reached out and caught the bat, the grip against my palm instantly calming my nerves. "Okay, but like . . . am I supposed to carry my bat around with me everywhere? It's a bit big and can I actually kill a demon with it?"

Uncle Kyle's silver eyes sparkled. "Actually, I have a great idea. Let me see that bat?"

I handed it to him and arched my eyebrow. "Gonna wrap some chains around it like in The Walking Dead?"

He grinned and wagged his eyebrows. I was about to ask questions when he pulled his wand out and pointed it at my bat. Silvery light sparkled around my bat for a few seconds before it shrank down to about two inches tall. Another flick of the wand and a silver key ring dangled from the handle. "There, now it's a keychain so you'll always have it."

I chuckled and reached for it. "Whoa."

"Hold that thought." Aunt Kimmy took my miniature bat turned keychain and then grabbed my hand and pressed it to my palm. "Close your hand around it."

It tingled against my fingers as I squeezed it in my closed hand. "Now what?"

"Picture a dagger," she said softly. "Any dagger."

I stammered and my mind went blank. "Uh . . ."

Silvery magic hit my arm, causing little neon-blue flames to dance along my skin. I gasped and an image of a dagger filled the dark canvas of my mind. I saw it clear as day, as if I were holding it. Those blue flames shot down to my hand and then crawled between my fingers. Warmth filled my palm. The keychain vibrated against my skin for a second, then a long silver blade popped out the bottom of my hand. It was about six inches long and curved slightly halfway down. My eyes widened. The hilt poked out the top of my clasped fist. It was crystal-clear and curved in the opposite direction of the blade with intricate gold inlay at the top. I opened my palm and found more of that gold inlay around the base of the hilt and along the sides of the blade.

I blinked a few times, just staring down at this gorgeous weapon in my hand. "I . . . I saw this on Pinterest . . ."

Uncle Kyle pursed his lips and nodded. "Well done, Franks."

"Now what?" My voice came out a little too squeaky for my liking.

"You're going to recite a spell that will change this dagger into your baseball bat and vice versa. Once you learn how to use your magic, you might not need to say the words, but for now, the words will suffice. All you have to do is take a deep breath and recite the spell in your mind, no need to say it out loud. So do it with me . . ." She took a deep breath, exhaled slowly, then waited for me to copy. With a nod, she softly chanted four lines in perfect poetic verse.

I licked my lips, then recited the words she'd said. *"Take this image in my mind, transform my weapon now in kind. By way of water, strength in might, hold thy magic for my echoed rite."*

Blue flames spread across the dagger, swallowing it whole in the blink of an eye. No sooner did the magic cover it did it change back into a full-sized baseball bat. I frowned. The bat had been two inches long a minute ago—the bat vibrated in my hand, then shrank back down to the keychain size Uncle Kyle had given me. My eyes widened.

"Now, where's your phone?"

I pulled my iPhone out of my pocket and held it up to her. "Why?"

"Repeat after me . . . *In Aether's name, I call to me . . .*"

"In Aether's name, I call to me."

*"Deceive the mind for all to see."*

"Deceive the mind for all to see," I repeated. The bat keychain turned cold instantly. When I looked down, I found it had turned into a two-dimensional sticker of a bat. "What am—"

"Put the sticker on the back of your phone case."

At this point, I was beyond questioning why, so I just peeled the back off the sticker and stuck it to my phone case. Once I ran my finger over the sticker to ensure it was flat, I looked back up to my aunt. "Now what?"

"Now, when you need a weapon, you'll always have it, since you teenagers never go anywhere without your phones." She winked playfully, then tapped on the sticker. "Just press your finger to the sticker and recite the spell you just used."

"Go ahead. Try it, Franks."

I shrugged. *"In Aether's name, I call to me, deceive the mind for all to see."*

Sure enough, the sticker instantly popped off my phone case and landed in my palm in the form of the miniature baseball bat. I shook my head. *"Take this image in my mind, transform my weapon now in kind. By way of water, strength in might, hold thy magic for my echoed rite."*

Right as those blue flames appeared, I pictured the dagger in my mind and the bat changed into it immediately. I grinned and recited the spell again, this time picturing a full-sized bat. For a good minute I practiced these spells over and over, changing the weapon into a sticker and back again.

Uncle Kyle chuckled. "Show off."

"I call it teamwork, love." Aunt Kimmy nudged him with her shoulder. "Feel better about it now? The demons?"

I barked a sarcastic laugh. "Hardly. Can you give me an idea what the demons might look like?"

"They're black. Darker than night itself." She tapped on her cheek just below her eyes. "And their eyes are bright, glowing red."

Uncle Kyle snapped his fingers. "And they smell like maple syrup."

My eyes widened. "Seriously?"

"That's usually a good warning sign, but if they're in the water, you won't smell them." He gave me two thumbs-up and grinned. "All right, sandy toes time. Let's go."

I changed my weapon back into a full-sized bat because that was my comfort zone. This whole talk about demons had me on edge, so I wanted to be ready. Aunt Kimmy hooked her arm around mine, leaving my right hand free to swing that bat if I needed to. Together we followed my uncle over the small dune and onto the open beach. I kicked my flip-flops off immediately and didn't bother to pick them up. I'd grab them on my way back to the car. The feel of the powdery soft sand squishing between my toes felt like coming home. I smiled as a chunk of pressure eased off my chest. It was a gorgeous, crystal-clear night without a cloud in sight. Nothing but diamonds twinkling in the midnight-black sky. The waning crescent moon was a tiny sliver of gold in the dark, barely illuminating anything yet painfully beautiful all the same.

The Gulf of Mexico was a soft lullaby, waves gently rolling onto the shore. The three of us walked until our toes sank in the wet sand and the next wave washed over our bare feet. We all sighed. For a moment we just stood there in silence, letting the ocean heal the trauma in our hearts. The beach had always been a special place for us. We always made time for it. But we'd never lived this close, and now I was kind of mad we hadn't.

*We're here now, Frankie. Just enjoy it.*

"*This was a good decision,*" Uncle Kyle whispered from my right side.

Aunt Kimmy chuckled softly. "*I can't believe we were going to not come tonight.*"

I smiled and pulled both of them tighter to me. "Can we sit for a few minutes? I know it's late but . . ."

"But?" they both asked in perfect unison.

I shrugged. "I'd like to know more about this witch society of ours before I go to a school with witches in attendance. Ya know, to reduce the risk of embarrassing myself?"

They laughed and nodded, then led me back a few feet to sit on the dry, powdery sand. We sat in a line, with them on either side of me like a protective bubble. I wasn't mad about that. Frat boys were one thing, demons were totally different. We sat in silence for a few minutes, just enjoying the salty cool breeze sweeping across our faces. I silently willed my bat to return to its sticker form on the back of my phone, then shoved my phone into my pocket.

Eventually, Aunt Kimmy cleared her throat. "So, is there something specific you wanted to know?"

I frowned. "Well . . . you said witches live here in this town. Why here? You might have told me but it's a lot to remember."

"Fair. I can't remember if I told you or not." She chuckled. "So to make a very long story short, in 1692 two members of The Coven accidentally ripped a hole in the barrier protecting our realm from the other dangerous ones—like Lilith's or the Fae. This hole let any monster or demon from other realms walk right in. It was very dangerous. They patched the hole temporarily, but in doing so the pressure caused smaller holes to burst open around the world. These were referred to as Gaps. The largest Gap in the whole world was right here in Tampa, so for the last decade, The Coven has been stationed here to monitor and maintain demon activity."

"That Gap was closed in October, by the way." Uncle Kyle sighed heavily. "Won't lie, I had no interest in living here while it was open."

"And where The Coven lives, civilians will follow . . . like a moth to a flame. We can't help it."

I nodded and rubbed my hands together. "Right. I guess I get that. So, where else do civilians live?"

"Everywhere. Anywhere." Uncle Kyle ran his hands through his black hair. "There are arcana headquarters in most of the major cities around the world: New York, Boston, LA, Miami to name a few. The Coven appoints witches to run them and sort of be in charge of the cities, along with Knights who will fight any demons who roll into town."

"Right. Makes sense." I spun the crystal ring around my finger and watched the waves. "Here I was expecting you to say there was our own version of Hogwarts somewhere."

"Oh," they both said at the same time.

I glanced back and forth. "What?"

"There are two schools."

My eyes widened. "What? Where? Why didn't we go there?"

Uncle Kyle grimaced. "See, the thing is, there's a place called Eden that is witch home country. Humans cannot enter Eden, and there's a magical barrier wall to keep demons out. It's our safe place, or it is supposed to be."

"Where is this home country?"

"It moves. Throughout the history of the world, Eden has been in different locations. In Ancient Greece, the Greek humans thought Eden was Mount Olympus . . . The Romans saw us the same. For a few centuries, Eden was in Europe. But it's been in the United States since the late 17th century. It was first in Salem, but in 1692 it moved to the Appalachian Mountains down in the Tennessee and Carolinas area."

"I'm going to have a lot of questions about how that works later, though that doesn't answer why we didn't move there instead."

"We thought about it back before the accident. There's a school there called Edenburg for all witches . . ." he shook his head, "but with Lilith's new war looming, things are a mess. The Coven had to evacuate all of Eden in December. They just had a massive mini-war there last week, so we figured maybe Eden wasn't the best decision just yet."

"Edenburg must be epic."

They nodded.

Aunt Kimmy cleared her throat. "In the fall, The Coven opened up a magic school in Manhattan. Everyone is pretty excited about it. But we figured you'd prefer *this* to the big city."

*This* was the ocean. I nodded. "You're probably right about that."

"We know this is a hell of a lot to take in at once." Uncle Kyle bumped my shoulder with his. "We wanted this to be as stress-free and easy as possible."

"There are witches here your age. Well, of all ages. From diapers to dentures." She giggled at her own joke. "But the teens at the high school have all grown up with magic, and they'll be great mentors for you to start learning, which is why we wanted you to start school immediately so you can meet them."

Butterflies danced in my stomach at the mention of school. I was suddenly nervous. I wrung my hands together to hide the shaking. "Do you think they'll know I'm a witch too? How will I spot them?"

She pursed her lips. "You should feel the difference between human and arcana, but don't worry, they'll spot you."

"They'll spot me? Why? Do I look different? Do I look non-human?"

They shook their heads, but Aunt Kimmy was the one who answered. "You're new to your magic, but once you get comfortable, you'll realize you can feel magic in other people. They're not rookies, so they'll feel your magic right away."

"And then they'll hear your name." Uncle Kyle leaned into me. "You're a Proctor, like me. That's a big deal in our community."

I scowled. "Being a Proctor is a big deal? Then why did you change your name?"

His cheeks flushed. "Because the Proctor name was being carried on by your parents, so I decided to take my wife's name when we married so *her* name would not die off."

"That's sweet of you." I smiled. "But why are we a big deal?"

He took a deep breath, then slowly exhaled. "Right. Long story short again, when arcana were created, there were one hundred bloodlines, but only twenty of those founding bloodlines survived. One of those founding family bloodlines was the Proctor line. *Our* line."

"Wow." A cold chill slid down my spine, so I shivered. "We're a founding family. That's intense. What are the other nineteen lines?"

"The Lancasters were the first, birthed from the angel Jophiel. They are the keepers of the light. Most of them live in England, except for Jackson Lancaster who is in The Coven." He frowned. "Though I did hear rumor that the entire Lancaster bloodline just moved to Eden. So that'll be interesting, and more reason to steer clear of there for now."

"Okay . . . so Lancaster and Proctor . . ." I waved them on. "Who else? Who was next?"

Aunt Kimmy pursed her lips and narrowed her eyes like she was thinking really hard. "The order is a little fuzzy. It was a long, *long* time ago. But what's important are the bloodlines that survived. Lancaster was first of all of the one hundred, and they survived. The second of the one hundred was the Bishop line. They also survived. They're one of the most important lines because they are and always have been the strongest with magic."

"So, the first line are the *keepers of the light* and the second line are the most powerful? Did I get that right?" When they nodded, I continued, "Are there any Bishops in The Coven now? You said there's a Lancaster."

They both laughed.

I scowled. "What's funny?"

"Like half of The Coven are Bishops." Uncle Kyle snorted as he scooped a handful of sand and let it slide between his fingers.

Aunt Kimmy rolled her hazel eyes. "Not half, but a good chunk. There's Tegan Bishop who is one of The Coven leaders, and her twin sister, Emersyn, and two brothers, Cooper and Bentley. Hunter and Devon are their parents, and they have an uncle named Kessler."

"That *is* a lot. Are there Proctors like us?"

Uncle Kyle grinned. "Oh yeah. The other Coven Leader is Haven Proctor, but everyone calls him Tennessee. His sister, Bettina, is in The Coven. Kenneth and Saraphina Proctor used to be, but they've retired from The Coven now."

I frowned. "Wait, so then I'm related to The Coven leader and his sister?"

He wagged his eyebrows. "See why I said your name would stick out? Literally every witch in the world knows Haven Proctor's name, even if they refer to him as Tennessee. He's basically worshipped like a god by civilians, and rightfully so. His sister is quite a badass too. And while that might feel like big shoes to fill, remember that they'll *want* to help you."

"Why?"

"Because no one—and I mean *no one*—wants to be on Tennessee's bad side."

# CHAPTER ELEVEN

## FRANKIE

"This suddenly feels like a terrible idea."

"You're gonna do great, Franks."

I groaned and rested my forehead on the steering wheel. "How do you know that?"

"You're a warrior, kiddo. You have been since the day you were born," he said softly. I felt his hand squeeze my shoulder gently, easing some of the tension in my back. "And when you and Elizabeth were in trouble, you pulled it together and got you two out of there. In the face of the most heinous, intense trauma, you could have collapsed, but you fought your way out over and over until you won."

I sat up and looked over at him with my heart lodged in my throat. There were words trapped inside of me, but I couldn't hear them myself. The emotions were too much, ranging from terrified to heart-broken. I'd been charging through every moment since I woke up in the hospital, and I knew I was intentionally avoiding the healing part of my trauma. But there were moments when it slid in and crept up on me. This was one of those moments. When I woke up and realized I was starting a brand-new school in a brand new city, I had a full blown panic attack. My aunt had found me sitting on the floor in my shower. Anxiety was a bitch like that. Aunt Kimmy promised I didn't have to arrive at the same time as everyone else, where everyone would be staring at me.

But that grace period was up, so my aunt and uncle drove with me to school for moral support and were going to walk home, leaving my car with me. They didn't want me to feel trapped without a getaway car. Aunt Kimmy went inside to get my schedule while I clung to my steering wheel. Uncle Kyle was a beacon of calm energy. He always calmed me down just by being around.

"Deep breaths, in and out."

I leaned back against the seat and just breathed. "I haven't had to do this in a long time."

"And you had Elizabeth last time. I know." He sighed and turned toward me in the passenger seat. "I know you are new to our world, and your aunt and I take responsibility for some of that, but witches aren't like humans. We stick together. We look out for one another. We're like one big extended family, especially in this town. So while this is daunting, they're going to welcome you in with open arms. The sooner you get in there and meet some of them, the sooner the anxiety will subside."

I arched my eyebrow at him. "Somehow I doubt this."

"Your aunt is coming. Time's up." He shrugged and turned back to face forward. "Come on, Franks. Just wait until they start showing you magic . . . you'll forget all about this stress."

With a curse, I flipped the visor down and checked my reflection. My blue eyes were bright and clear, no visual sign of panic, though my cheeks were flushed and my bottom lip looked puffy from all the gnawing on it I'd done. My hair wasn't my normal vibrant hot-pink, it'd faded to a cotton candy pink. "Yeah, well, can you use magic to re-dye my hair?"

He froze with his hand on the handle. A playful smirk spread across his face. "As a matter of fact . . ." He reached into Aunt Kimmy's purse on the floor at his feet and pulled his wand out. With a quick flick, a pink cloud wrapped around my head.

I jumped and glanced up to the mirror. My jaw dropped. My hair was now back to its vibrant hot-pink color. A chuckle slipped out of my mouth.

"See?" He winked, then pushed his door open and climbed out.

I took one last glance at myself in the mirror, then forced myself to jump out of the car. I took in my reflection in the windows of my navy-blue Volkswagen Jetta. The great part about moving from a northern Florida town to a more central Florida town was that the culture wasn't much different. Florida was Florida. It was hot as fuck and the humidity made the air wet and sticky, so clothing wasn't expected to consist of much. Today, my outfit was my standard cut-off jean shorts, white tank top, and my all-white Adidas sneakers. I had a super thin, soft, white cotton button-down shirt to cover up if I was cold inside or if a teacher went on a dress code rampage.

"All right, you're all set up and ready to go."

I looked up as Aunt Kimmy approached. "That feels like a threat."

She stopped in front of me and handed me my black backpack and two pieces of paper. One was pink while the other was white. "There are papers and stuff inside but also your class schedule and a map."

"How do my classes look?" I grumbled as I slid my backpack onto one shoulder. My gaze slid over the schedule printed on paper as pink as my hair. "Compared to home?"

"Well, she put you in honors classes since we're halfway through second semester. Your guidance counselor is a witch, so we were able to fudge your school records. Next year we can get you back into AP classes if you're feeling up to it. Let's think of the rest of this semester as a warm-up?"

I sighed. "Okay. That sounds fair. Still, kind of nervous to look."

"I got you into PE for home room, which means you'll have it every single day and then you'll go straight to lunch." She wagged her blonde eyebrows. "Rather proud of myself for that one."

That made me laugh. "As you should be. I bet you got a funny look when you asked for it."

"You have no idea." She snickered. "First period is about to end any second now. You ought to get moving so you're not late to third period."

"Block scheduling. Cool. At least that'll be familiar—"

"Do you have your phone?"

"Yes, Uncle Kyle." I held it up to show him the sticker of my baseball bat on the back. "I'm ready."

"Okay, humor me and show me." He waved his hands. "I need to see you do it before we leave."

Aunt Kimmy smiled and nodded. "All of it."

I rolled my eyes and pressed my thumb to the bat sticker on the case, then softly whispered, *"In Aether's name, I call to me, deceive the mind for all to see."*

Just like last night at the beach, the sticker instantly popped off my phone case and landed in my palm in the form of the miniature baseball bat. I held it up for them to see, then lowered my hand and recited the next spell. *"Take this image in my mind, transform my weapon now in kind. By way of water, strength in might, hold thy magic for my echoed rite."*

Right as those blue flames appeared, I pictured the dagger in my mind and the bat changed into it immediately. I looked pointedly at them and recited the spell again, this time picturing a full-sized bat. Then to drive my point home, I did not recite the next spell out loud. I merely thought it, and once again the bat shrank down to the small sticker. With a smile I pressed the sticker back to my phone and nodded.

"See, Franks? You've got this." He tugged playfully on my hair. "But I'd try to save the dagger for a last resort with the humans and human-passing."

"Human . . . passing." I snorted. "That's a new one."

Aunt Kimmy gave me a hug. "Don't hesitate to call or text if you need anything. We're right here."

"I will." I hugged her back, then gave Uncle Kyle a high five. "Good luck with your first day in town."

Behind me, the bell to signal the change of classes rang so loud all three of us flinched.

My stomach tightened into knots. "That's my cue."

With that, I hit the lock button on my car remote and waved, then spun on my toes and marched toward the buildings. Doors flew open, letting a stampede of students pour out into the sunshine. I held my head high as I walked inside the main doors my aunt had just come from. It felt a little like swimming upstream, dodging students left and right. None of them seemed to pay attention to me, like they didn't care if I was new there or not. A few of them glanced at my pink hair and nodded. One girl actually said she loved it. Another girl frowned at it and then lifted the long strands of her blonde hair. I could've sworn I saw the wheels turning in her mind. I tried to memorize her face to see if she wound up dying hers.

When I walked inside, I held my schedule up, outside was too damn bright to read a thing. I scanned over my class list and spotted some familiar words: chemistry, geometry, English, world history, and of course, PE. But the art class and art history *were* surprising, pleasant surprises yet surprises nonetheless. I nodded and pulled out the map to see how to get to PE class when I felt a weird tingle in the air. It was like electricity, a little pulse that tickled my spine. I stopped short and looked up . . . and spotted my neighbor about ten feet ahead of me.

He wasn't looking at me, hell, he wasn't looking up at all. His eyes were locked on the floor like he was trying to hide while walking. His dark-red hair was disheveled like he'd run his hands through it a lot. As he got closer, that energy grew stronger. There was nothing outwardly spectacular about this kid, he wore a white shirt and blue jeans with white sneakers not dissimilar to mine. He looked entirely normal. And yet, I felt drawn to him.

My phone vibrated in my hand, so I glanced down to see a text message from my aunt that said, *'By the way, you'll FEEL a difference between witch and human. The witches will carry with them an electric sort of energy. You'll feel it before you see them. So don't freak out if that happens.'*

I chuckled and sent back, *'Sometimes you are psychic.'*

She sent back a wink face emoji. *'Remember, if you can feel them, they can feel you.'*

*'Okay. Gonna try and make a friend. Wish me luck.'*

I let out a deep breath and shoved my phone into my back pocket. When I looked back up, I found my neighbor was only about ten feet ahead. He was looking at his phone so he hadn't seen me yet, but I was determined to introduce myself. I wasn't shy, and I didn't want to wait around for some witch teenager to approach me, especially since I didn't exactly have the kind of face that said *please come talk to me.* So, I cleared my throat and put a smile on my face and took a step forward—

"HE'S OPEN!" some guy shouted and his voice echoed down the tiled hallway, bouncing off the maroon lockers.

And then I saw a football soaring above students' heads. A guy with long brown hair and a nice tan leapt out from behind a group of girls. He jumped in the air and snatched the football. But when he landed, he slammed right into my neighbor and the two crashed to the floor. Mr. Long Hair was back on his feet in a split second, laughing and cheering. He turned to face my neighbor, then spiked the ball into his stomach.

My vision went red with rage. Every part of me wanted to summon my baseball bat from its sticker form on my phone and show this prick a taste of his own medicine. I clenched my teeth and balled my hands into fists.

"How'd that taste, French fry?" He threw his head back and laughed.

My neighbor pushed up onto all fours just as a guy with a short blond buzz-cut rushed up beside Mr. Long Hair. Buzz-cut grabbed my neighbor by his shirt with both hands, lifted him in the air, then threw him into the burgundy lockers like he weighed no more than a pillow. Both bullies cackled and high-fived.

*I think the fuck not.* I dug my heels into the ground like I was about to steal home base and sprinted right for the bullies. With both hands, I shoved Mr. Long Hair so hard he flew over and crashed into his friend. Both of them staggered back so I stepped in front of my neighbor who was sitting on his ass against the lockers with his legs spread wide.

Mr. Long Hair charged at me with blazing brown eyes, but I didn't flinch or step aside. No, I knew how to fight. My uncle made sure I took martial arts from a young age. So when he dove for me, I expertly took a step forward and slammed my hand into his throat while I swept his legs out from under him. His eyes bugged out wide as he choked and slammed into the ground *hard* with a thud. The hallway full of students froze in place, their eyes watching us like a bomb about to go off.

Mr. Buzz-cut snarled and charged for me with the same idiotic gusto as his friend. I just waited until he was right in front of me, then grabbed a fistful of his shirt and yanked, throwing him into the same lockers he'd just thrown my neighbor into. He cursed and pushed right back toward me, turning on me with flushed cheeks and blood on his nose.

"*HEY!*" a male teacher screamed from a classroom door about ten feet down the hall. "*Move it or lose it, boys. MOVE. NOW.*"

The rest of the students in the hall scurried like roaches when you turned on the light.

Mr. Long Hair staggered back to his feet, still coughing and holding his throat. "*You . . . little—*"

"Mr. Jordan, move it or it's detention," that same male teacher shouted from his open classroom doorway. "You too, Mr. Burke."

I winked just to piss them off.

Mr. Buzz-cut pointed his meaty finger in my face. "Go fuck yourself."

"Fuck me yourself, coward," I snarled back.

"BOYS!"

Mr. Long Hair grabbed his friend's elbow and dragged him back in the direction they'd come from. I glared at their backs in case they decided to turn around. Fighting at school was never my goal. I only ever did it in defense of others. Bullies deserved it.

That teacher turned and narrowed his eyes at me. "You new here?"

I nodded. "First day. Sorry. I hate bullies."

He smirked and pushed his silver glasses higher up his nose. "I can't encourage any fighting . . . just be careful?"

"Will do. Thank you." I smiled and eased my posture so I didn't looked like a junkyard dog waiting to charge. Once the teacher disappeared back into his room, I turned and looked down at my neighbor. "You all right?"

He was still sprawled on the floor . . . laughing. "Meh. I've had worse."

"I bet. Guys are dicks." I held my hand out to help him up. "Hope you didn't mind my interference?"

His grin turned crooked, and his hazel eyes sparkled. "I was thinking if they dented the locker with my face, I might get out of class this week . . . but something tells me I'll get another chance. So, thank you." Then he took my hand and let me lift him back to his feet.

"You're welcome. I'm Francelina Proctor, but everyone calls me Frankie."

He pushed his dark-red hair off his forehead. "I'm Archibald Mann. Everyone calls *me* Archie. Nice to meet you."

I adjusted my backpack into place. "You're my new neighbor."

"Yeah, I saw you arrive." He tugged on his button-down shirt. "I thought about saying hello, but you seemed to have your hands full with the dogs and stuff."

"I saw you trying to use a wand," I said before I could stop myself. Then I slammed my hand over my mouth and glanced around. "Oops, said that loud."

"Don't worry about it. I've noticed they don't seem phased by us. It's like their ears just don't hear those words." He chuckled as he picked his backpack off the ground. "And . . . I'm just not a Wands Suit, but I'm trying. You probably saw how well that's going so far."

I grinned. "I don't even know which Suit I am. I'm new to all . . . *this*."

Archie took my schedule out of my hand and looked at it. "I'm also new here. Well, new to Tampa, not this lifestyle."

"I'm new to both. Where you from?"

"Cool. We both have PE next. C'mon, I'll show you where it's at." He handed my schedule back to me. "Eden. You?"

"Oh sweet. Lead the way." Together we walked down the hall and out the doors on the far end of the building. "So, Archibald, eh? That's your name?"

"I bet you thought Francelina was bad." He chuckled. "It's a family name."

"I like Archibald, actually, but Archie is still better. Family names are nice, or at least I think so." I smiled and bumped his shoulder with mine playfully. "So, curious, if you're not a Wands Suit, then why were you trying to use a wand?"

He grimaced. "Pentacles aren't going to be on the front lines of the war, but I'm not foolish enough to think we won't all be in danger, so I'm trying to . . . I don't know . . . have a backup plan. Though I'm now dying to try that hand to the throat move."

I threw my head back and laughed. "Tell ya what, I'll show you some fight moves and you help me learn this whole witch thing?"

He grinned. "Deal. So, you never said where you're from."

"Shit, you're right. Sorry. I'm from Tallahassee."

"A Floridian already. Nice. That probably will make the move easier." He pointed to a bricked pathway to our right. "Eden is very different from here."

"What's it like? I only just learned about Eden last night and not much. My aunt and uncle said it's home country for us? Like demons and humans can't get in?"

"Yep. It's a small town. Most people don't live there unless they're students at Edenburg or they have children who attend. But it's safe, for the most part—"

"For the most part? That's ominous."

He shrugged and pointed to the left for us to turn onto an uncovered walkway with the sun attacking us. "Have you heard about Lilith?"

"Yeah. War is coming and all that jazz."

"Yeah, so The Coven had to evacuate Eden recently because of Lilith. It's a long story. They resolved the issue and made Eden safe again, but that's why I'm not there. Mom didn't want to go back."

I frowned. "Are you bummed about this?"

He stopped at the entrance to the gymnasium, pausing with his hand on the handle and pursing his lips. "I don't know."

I giggled. "Ya know, that's fair. Sorry, I didn't mean to get all heavy on you. We just met."

"So you don't want to know my mother's middle name and her favorite brand of cereal?" He pulled the door open. "I had a pet squirrel once—"

"And by pet do you mean you just went full Snow White sitting in your backyard?"

"To-may-dough, to-mah-dough." He gestured for me to enter first.

I stepped through the open doors, but the change from bright sunshine to fluorescent lighting caused my vision to go dark for a second. I stopped walking and just blinked until my vision cleared. "Did you go full song and dance with your squirrel?"

"I did name him Thumper, which I realized belatedly in the movie was a rabbit not a squirrel." He stopped beside me, frowning at the ground. "I used to get so annoyed no one got the name reference and then I learned it's because I'm a dumbass."

"At least you know it." One of the bullies from before was suddenly right behind us. Mr. Buzz-cut swooped in fast, shoving Archie into the wall. "Eat paint—"

"Oh, is that what happened to you?"

Mr. Buzz-cut spun around with a snarl. "You've got a big mouth—"

"And I can back it up, princess, so keep talking." I took a step forward without taking my eyes off him. "Touch me or him. I dare you—"

"*Mr. Burke!*" a woman hissed from down the hall. "Locker room. Now."

He looked down his previously broken nose at me with blazing hazel eyes. "Saved by a teacher yet again—"

"Lucky for you."

"Mr. Burke, I have not forgotten the terms of our arrangement," that same woman yelled with a growl. Her light-brown hair was slicked back in a high ponytail and she wore a whistle on a neon-yellow rope around her neck. "Touch one of my students and you're suspended."

"Go on. Get." I shooed him with my hands. "Bad dog."

He spun and lumbered down the hall toward the woman, who I assumed was our PE teacher.

"What's his problem?" I sighed. "You're new here."

Archie nodded. "He's definitely worried I'm gonna steal the girls away from him."

I snort laughed. "There's probably a spell for that, right? Wands and shit?"

"He's one of us though, so retaliation would be swift and painful." He gestured as if he held his wand in hand in that moment. "I mean, you saw me with a wand."

"And I've never used magic." I cursed dramatically, throwing my arms in the air. "What to do?"

"You two, get in there. Now." We jumped at the sound of the teacher's voice. She didn't watch us running to catch up. She just reviewed her keyboard. When we got close, she snatched my schedule but didn't look at me. "Archie, you'll be on the away team. Get changed and out to the field."

"Yes, ma'am." He winked at me, then slipped through the doors.

"Another new student this late in the year? Ludicrous." She handed me my schedule. "I'm Coach Andrews. Come with me to get a uniform, then we'll hit the field."

# CHAPTER TWELVE

## FRANKIE

As far as PE uniforms went, these weren't bad. My old school made us wear black, and the *short* sleeves were so short that they were basically to everyone's elbows. We were always melting, even those of us on varsity sports teams who were used to being outside in the heat. But Gulf Shores High School's colors were evidently white, red, and burgundy, and they took the smart path in giving us white T-shirts. And the sleeves were proper length. We all had a choice between burgundy or red athletic shorts, so I grabbed the burgundy. Apparently our mascot was a dragon, because there was a giant red dragon on the front of my shirt. All in all, not too shabby.

By the time I got changed and onto the baseball field out behind the gym, the rest of the class had already taken the field, which meant *everyone* noticed me walking out there. Not that I ever thought my pink hair would allow me to blend in, but still. The dugout on the left was empty, as that team had taken the field, which meant the dugout I had to walk by was filled with students. All of whom were staring at me. I kept my eyes focused on our teacher, Coach Andrews, standing on the pitcher's mound, but that didn't mean my peripheral vision didn't see them looking. Nor did my ears miss the whispers. I didn't blame them. What kind of parent made their child start a brand-new high school in March? It was uncommon, and therefore a bit of a spectacle. It was fine. I could handle it. I'd rather *these* whispers and stares from curious strangers than the ones I would've gotten had I returned to my old school.

I shuddered internally at the mere thought of that.

And then I spotted tweedle-dee and tweedle-dum at the front of the dugout. They looked the same as before, just in their PE uniform. It was such a shame they were such dickheads because they weren't unattractive—*on the outside.* Not that I was interested in anything romantic. I'd been through a lot. I just wanted to figure out this whole magic thing and do a little self-discovery.

"Take the field, little bitch, so I can run you over," Mr. Long Hair snarled at me as I approached the open gate beside the dugout that led to the field.

A few students gasped and looked at me.

I looked over and met his beady stare, then rubbed my throat and faked a cough. I smiled. "That worked so well last time."

His buddy, Mr. Buzz-cut, slammed his glove into the chain-link fence around the dugout and growled like a junkyard dog. "Go fuck yourself—"

"Again, *we've been over this.*" I stopped just in front of him so I could hold his stare when I said, "Fuck me yourself, coward."

There were gasps and snickers in the dugout, but I ignored them.

"You have no idea who you're messing with." Mr. Buzz-cut leaned forward. "You don't know who we are."

"Really? The bruised throat and busted nose suggest otherwise." I turned to walk backwards. "But it was so nice meeting you."

I honestly had no idea what had come over me. Bullies were the worst, I never buckled to them, but I never antagonized them from the jump. I'd been in detention many times for a fistfight in school because they chose to pick on someone in front of me. My aunt usually lectured me about how learning martial arts wasn't so I could get in fights at school . . . but Uncle Kyle always defended me. Bullies deserved what they got, and if my training kept one kid from getting beat up and humiliated, then it was worth it. Actually, that was the only thing my aunt and uncle ever really argued about. She preferred verbal confrontations while my uncle insisted knuckles had to get bloody sometimes. I liked to dance on the line between both.

If these two dipshits were as aggressively violent as they appeared —to a new guy in town who was half their size—then I had no problem with my attitude. Or perhaps what happened in that frat house changed me a little. Perhaps a little aggressive, preemptive self-defense was just who I was now, because maybe a small part of me wondered if I could have prevented that night from happening. *Don't think about that right now, Frankie. That's the past. Focus on now.*

"Ah, Miss Proctor, come on out here," Coach Andrews shouted from the mound. "You're with the away team on the field."

*Is that a good thing or bad thing?* Because my two new besties were definitely going to want my head after my mouth just now. But I held my head high and my shoulders back as I marched out to the pitcher's mound. I took a quick glance around the field and noticed every other position on the field was taken. Butterflies danced in my stomach as hope flared. I was a pitcher ever since I was in little league. Sure, once I went to high school I switched mostly to softball because *that's what girls play,* but the pitcher's mound was a comfort zone for me.

*Wait, where's Archie? She said he was on the away team.*

"All right everyone, this is Frankie Proctor. She's new to town and therefore new to our school, but we're not gonna make a big deal about this. She's just going to jump in right where we are." Coach Andrews looked to me, though her mirror red sunglasses meant I couldn't see her eyes. But I had to give her props for the head-to-toe outfit coordination. Even her *New Balance* sneakers were white and red. She cleared her throat and lowered her voice so she was only talking to me. "Sorry to drop you in the deep end, kid—"

"Nah, I prefer it this way. No fuss. Just tell me where you want me and stuff."

She nodded. "Cool. So, we're playing baseball this week and next. We started last week. Rotating everyone around to different positions. Have you ever played baseball? Or softball?"

I smirked. "Varsity softball team. State champs last two years."

Her eyebrows shot up over her sunglasses. "No shit? Look at that. What position do you play?"

"I've been a pitcher since I was five in little league." I held my hand out for the baseball. "Obviously, I pitch underhand for softball, but I can throw overhand like the boys. Which would you prefer?"

She shrugged and placed the ball in my hand, then held the glove out for me. "Whichever. Have fun with it. But try to take it easy on most of them. They're not athletes like you."

I arched one eyebrow. "Except for two of them, right?"

"Gee, I don't know who you might be talking about." She grinned and backed away with a wink. "Let's play ball."

I grinned and tossed the ball up in the air a few times. My chest felt suddenly lighter. I hadn't even realized I'd been feeling as much pressure as I had been, but at least for now, I was in a comfort zone on the mound. When I looked up to the catcher, I found Archie crouched behind the plate. The catcher's gear overpowered him a little, but he didn't seem to mind. He waved at me, so I waved back. As I put the glove on, I glanced around the field behind me with a smile and a wave.

"All right, first up to bat," Coach Andrews called out. "Tomás, let's go."

I turned to face the plate. "You good, Archie?"

Through the cage of his helmet, I saw him grin. "I can take it. Don't hold back!"

The dude—Tomás, as she called him—glanced back and forth between me and Archie, then just shook his head. With a smirk, but not an asshole one, he nodded to me. His dark eyes sparkled like he hadn't a worry in the world. "You heard him, Pink. Don't hold back."

After one strike and two balls, he crushed my fourth pitch straight into left field. He smiled and gave me a thumbs-up as he ran to first base. By the time the shortstop had the ball, Tomás had made it to second base. He winked at me.

"Claire, you're up." Coach sighed. "Y'all, I shouldn't have to call out each name. Know your order and be on deck for your turn at bat."

The entire dugout grumbled.

A brunette with a face full of freckles skipped up to the plate. "You can hold back," she said with a sheepish smile.

I chuckled and gave her two easy, slow pitches in a row. She swung and hit the second. The ball hit the ground and rolled to the second baseman—who looked to first base, then shrugged and tossed the ball back to me. I was taking it easy with my pitches. No one wanted me to show up here and strike everyone out. This was PE, and most of these students didn't want to be out here at all. I'd already made an aggressive first impression on tweedle-dee and tweedle-dum, and anyone else who was listening in the dugout, so I wanted to try and be nice. I *was* the new girl, after all.

"Jacob, you're on deck," Coach Andrews yelled out as a pretty blonde girl stepped up to the plate. "Quit talking and be ready."

I glanced over to the dugout as Mr. Long Hair walked out with a bat in his hand. *Ah, so your name is Jacob.* He narrowed those beady brown eyes at me. I just chuckled and turned back to the plate as the next batter got ready. She wore her platinum blonde hair in pigtail, fishtail braids. Despite the color of her hair, her eyebrows were pitch-black, and the right one had gold stud piercings that matched the gold hoop on her nostril. She adjusted her helmet, and my gaze landed on her long coffin-shaped nails that were painted a matte black. Then she gripped the bat and held it up and my jaw dropped. She had the coolest tattoo made of swirling black lines all the way down her right arm and covered even her fingers. On the back of her right hand was a yellow crystal tattoo. I wanted to get a closer look, but now was not the time.

"C'mon, Jo, crush it!" another girl yelled from the dugout, unknowingly pulling me out of my girl-crush moment.

Jo looked cool as fuck. I already wanted to be her friend, and I found myself secretly hoping she was a witch. I got in position and met her stare. When she nodded, I nodded back and then pitched a nice, straight and easy fastball. Nothing *too* fast. This was still a warm-up for someone who'd been in a coma for months and hadn't thrown a single baseball until today. Jo narrowed her dark eyes that were almost solid black, then swung her bat, crushing the pitch and grounding the ball toward the third baseman. The red-haired girl playing third base caught it, touched the base to send Tomás back to the dugout, then threw the ball to second base. Unfortunately, that dude missed the catch. When he finally tossed it back to me, we had the brunette girl on second base, and Jo on first.

Jacob didn't waste any time getting up to the plate or running his mouth. His long hair wasn't tied back or anything. For some reason, that always bothered me. Teachers always made a big deal about us girls having to tie our hair back for PE, but boys with long hair never got the same harassment. It didn't help me feel less antagonistic toward Jacob.

"Like what you see?"

I gagged dramatically. "I was just wondering if you needed a scrunchie for that rat's nest you call hair."

It was kind of a dirty move, but I didn't wait for him to be ready, I just pitched the ball as fast as I could. It shot straight into Archie's glove with a thud while Jacob just watched. He never got a chance to swing.

"Strike one," I said with a chuckle.

"You bitch. I wasn't ready—"

"If you're at the plate, you're ready to bat," Coach yelled out. "We've been over this. Eyes on the ball at all times."

"*Are you ready, princess?*" I said in a high-pitched voice. "I'm going to throw it now. Try to swing this time."

"Eat paint," he snapped.

My second pitch was just as fast and just as clean. He swung, but the ball was already in Archie's catcher's mitt before the bat swept over the plate. I held two fingers up.

"That means strike two," Archie whisper-shouted. "Not a peace sign."

Jacob kicked red clay at Archie, which earned him a scolding from coach. Again. He snarled at me, so I simply rubbed my throat. His whole face turned as red as his shorts. I could've struck him out. He was so enraged it wouldn't have taken that tricky of a pitch for him to miss, but I decided on a different method of aggression for him, especially as he was mumbling vulgar insults in my direction.

"Jacob, *language*," Coach Andrews snapped.

"Were those too fast, princess?" I grinned at him. "Here, maybe you can hit this one."

I changed my position and gave him a mediocre speed underhanded softball pitch. It was practically *walking* to the plate it was so slow. I could've run up and hit it. I just grinned and wagged my eyebrows as he cursed me out. The bat made a pretty *ding* sound when he finally hit the ball. Naturally, it flew way out into the outfield where the boy with glasses was not even paying attention.

Jacob made a big show of tossing his bat toward the dugout as he gloated. "See that?"

"Everyone saw that little league pitch." I clapped my hands really slowly. "Too bad you're about to be out."

"What?" He looked toward first base and cursed before he had to full-out face-first dive to touch it before the player caught the ball.

"You deserved that, Jacob. Keep your head in the game," Coach Andrews shouted, then blew her whistle. "Madge, batter up."

I looked up, then did a double take. Madge was a girl who looked like she jumped off the front cover of Vogue magazine. She had to be five-foot-nine with legs for days that were on full display as she'd rolled up her burgundy shorts practically to her ass. She had short black hair that hung straight to her jaw with a sharp edge to them. Her bold red lipstick was as flawless as the fashionista glam red eyeshadow. This girl was flawless. I had to shake myself back into focus. It wasn't until she stepped up to the plate that I realized she had the same exact tattoo covering her right arm as Jo had, yellow crystal and all. But that made sense. Those two cool girls had to be besties.

*Note to self: When Elizabeth gets back, get badass bestie tattoos.*

Madge raised one red, stiletto-shaped nail in the air. "Question for clarification, Coach—"

"You just have to hit the damn ball, Madge." Coach laughed and shook her head. "I don't even care if you get on base. Hust hit the ball this time, okay?"

Madge gave her a glorious grin, then popped her helmet on. She turned hazel eyes on me. "Hey, Pink, gimme something I can hit so I can go back to the shade, 'kay?"

I chuckled. "What would you like?"

She pursed those red lips. "One of those slow underhand easy pitches you gave princess."

Jacob shouted another obscenity.

*Good, so the other students had noticed my pettiness.* I nodded. "Coming right up."

I gave her the exact pitch I gave Jacob, but she just missed it. She groaned. "I'll get it, Coach. I'll hit the damn ball."

"Hey, Madge?"

"Just give it to me again. I can do this."

"Yeah, just lower your grip on the bat. Your hands are too high. That's why you missed." I waited as she did as I said and then looked back to me. "Perfect. Hold on tight and swing like that ball is Jacob."

Coach Andrews snorted. "*Frankie.*"

Madge was grinning like a madwoman. I loved it. I now needed to be friends with her *and* Jo. Just like she asked, I gave her the exact same pitch, except this time she got a piece of it. The ball flew over my head, then bounced right where the second baseman was supposed to be. That guy hobbled over to the ball, but just as he caught it, Jacob shoved him out of the way.

Coach Andrews blew her whistle. "Jacob, *one more* and you're going to the Dean's office. Hear me?"

Jacob snarled and stayed on second base. He glared at me. I winked. That brunette girl jogged across home plate, then hurried toward the dugout . . . right past Madge who was walking to first base.

"Oh, I hope no one gets me out," she yelled dramatically and slowed her pace.

The second baseman tossed the ball to the first baseman. Madge was out. She gave a dramatic bow, then giggled and bounced off to the dugout. "Sorry, Jo, slay for both of us!"

"Aaron, let's go." Coach was still shaking her head at Madge. "Behave yourself."

*Ah, the cowardly lion is named Aaron. What an insult to the name Aaron.* But I kept my mouth shut because I always matched energies. So if Aaron wanted to be a dickwad, then I'd be one right back. It was up to him. I merely stood ready to pitch.

And then Aaron sauntered straight up to the plate and pushed Archie. "Back up, Tinkerbell."

I rolled my eyes at the exact same time Archie did. Archie was tough. That much was already obvious. It made my heart sick to wonder why he was so tough. He was probably bullied relentlessly. Guys seemed to get some sick joy out of picking on the short guys, as if their height was their fault. Then again, the mind of a bully was a vapid wasteland. I took a deep breath to calm myself, but then Aaron took a practice swing and the wooden bat smacked Archie in the back of the helmet.

"Oops, accident." Aaron laughed. He turned those hazel eyes on me. "Don't break a nail."

I wound up and delivered. He swung about six inches too high, and he'd swung so hard that when he missed the ball, he spun all the way around and stumbled into Archie.

"Strike one!" Archie shouted.

Aaron turned and slammed his bat into Archie's chest, who lifted off his feet and then slammed into the clay on his back with a crunch. He leaned over him. "Say it again, Tinkerbell—"

"Strike one." Archie chuckled.

"You son of a—"

"Aaron, you'll go to the Dean with Jacob. Don't push it."

Jacob was behind me on second. Jo was on Third. Archie met my stare and nodded. I grinned. There were some instances when showing off was just the appropriate thing to do. *This* was one of those instances. Bullies deserved no mercy. I had one hell of a fast pitch in softball, but it was even faster in baseball. Not that I was anything compared to the shit in the pros, but neither was this jackass. I held Aaron's glare and took a deep breath, then with every ounce of strength I had inside of me, I aimed that ball right at him. It tingled against my fingertips as it left my hand. It was by far the fastest pitch I'd thrown today, but right before it got to the plate, little blue flames wrapped around the ball and it curved. That wasn't supposed to happen. That was *definitely* magic. I tried to keep my expression blank. That'd never happened to me before. I was going to have to be careful with it.

"Strike two!" Archie grinned.

"Frankie, maybe give him something he can hit? Quarterback queen here ain't used to hitting things." Coach chuckled. "Though that was beautiful."

Aaron's face was redder than a stoplight.

I gave him a straight, right down the lane pitch any rookie with athletic skill could hit. I watched it fly right toward the plate, and I rolled to the balls of my feet, ready to move if his hit came anywhere near me. Just as expected, he whacked the shit out of the ball and sent it soaring right for the shortstop. A cocky grin spread across his face. But I wasn't a rookie either. One easy little jump to the right and I snagged the ball right out of the air. Without missing a beat, I spun on my toes and looked to the second baseman. Jacob had started running to third and was sprinting back for second, just a few steps away. I could've easily thrown the ball to my own teammate and got Jacob out, but I was feeling too petty.

Instead, I chucked the ball right into the side of Jacob's foot.

He screamed out as he flew forward.

The second baseman plucked the ball off the ground and tagged the base a split second before Jacob's face crashed into the red clay and his feet hit the back of his own head like a scorpion's tail.

"You're out!" Coach shouted from across the field. "Nice play—"

"You little bitch!"

I turned just in time to watch Aaron charging the pitcher's mound. Everything slipped into slow motion, yet it happened so fast. In my peripheral vision I watched Jacob leap to his feet and charge for me like a raging bull. A plan formed in my mind. I kept Jacob in my peripheral view but focused my attention on Aaron. Coach sprinted for us, but she'd never make it. His entire team was running to empty from the dugout and rush to the field. My own teammates hurried over. *Archie* ran like a little tank for the mound.

"Come on, coward," I shouted and slowly took a step back, right into Jacob's oncoming path. "Put your money where your mouth is!"

Aaron pushed off the ground and dove in the air to tackle me. I waited until the last second, then jumped backwards—*and the two bullies collided mid-air.* There was a crunch, then they hit the ground in a tangle of limbs.

"OH!" the entire class yelled.

Aaron and Jacob cursed as they rolled in the grass, shoving at each other to try and get up. Coach Andrews was approaching fast, blowing her whistle like a freight train. Her face was red with rage.

I cackled and bounced on my toes, then leaned down to pour salt to the wound. *"You done messed up, Ay-ay-ron!"*

He lunged from the ground and tackled me. We crashed onto the grass with him bellowing like a deranged lunatic. This six-foot-tall guy just tackled a five-foot-four female half his body weight. It wasn't a good look for him, and *that* made me laugh. I pushed at his shoulders. Blue flames flickered beneath my palms and then he flew head over heels onto the grass. Jacob charged for me, so I swung my leg up and kicked him in the chest. He staggered backwards a few feet and then a small person dressed in catcher's gear tackled him from the side, taking him down to the ground. *Archie! Hell yes!*

I jumped up. "C'mon, princess, you can do better than—" I cut myself off with a fake choke.

Aaron grabbed Archie by the back of his shirt and lifted him off the ground. But Archie was a fighter. He threw his leg back and kicked Aaron in the side of the knee. Aaron shrieked and both of them went down with Aaron pinning Archie's small body beneath him. Jacob lunged for me again, so I thrust my arm out, slamming the bottom of my palm right into his nose. He screeched and dropped to his knees, gripping his nose as blood was already gushing.

"ENOUGH!" Coach Andrews screamed. She pulled Aaron off of Archie, then spun on all four of us with wild blue eyes that were no longer hidden behind sunglasses. "THE OFFICE! NOW! ALL FOUR OF YOU!"

I sighed. There were worse ways to start at a new school. At least I'd have something to tell my aunt and uncle when I got home. I cleared my throat. "Sorry, Coach, they had it coming—"

"Save it for the Dean, Miss Proctor," she snapped. "And Archie, what were you doing?"

He threw his helmet off and grinned up at her. "Couldn't let her be in that fight alone."

Coach screamed in frustration. "NO TALKING! JUST MOVE!"

Both of the bullies did, in fact, run their mouths. They were bitching and complaining, literally pointing fingers at me. Coach was basically pushing them off the baseball field.

I helped Archie back onto his feet. "Thanks for the backup."

"Figured I owed you one." He shrugged. "C'mon, let's go before we get in more trouble."

When I looked up, most of the class was laughing or openly gawking. But not all of them. There were about a dozen, give or take, who all huddled together and watched me with narrowed eyes. Not *us*. Me. They watched *me*. I felt that tingle in the air like when I'd first seen Archie walking in the hall. Those kids were witches, and I wasn't so sure they were happy with me fighting with two of their friends. My aunt and uncle insisted arcana watched out for each other, but I wondered belatedly if that would instantly extend to the new girl, especially when I'd just accidentally used magic on Aaron, which had probably looked intentional.

"CLASS DISMISSED!" Coach shouted. "FRANKIE. ARCHIE. NOW."

We raced after her, pausing inside the gym only to get the catcher's gear off of Archie. Coach Andrews stood at the glass doors with her hands on her hips and her glare laser-focused on Aaron and Jacob.

"Maybe my first day will be a short one," I said with a chuckle.

"I've never been suspended," Archie said with a frown. Then he shrugged. "Could be fun."

"NOW!"

We scurried to catch up with Coach, but as soon as we got close, she spun on her toes and marched forward. Aaron and Jacob leapt into a brisk pace, like they wanted to remain out of her reach. Archie and I were silent as we followed them up the sidewalk and back inside that main building where the four of us had previously been acquainted. Except this time, we made a sharp left turn the second we passed through the doors. We stomped down the quiet hall to a little cul-de-sac of offices.

"Miss Proctor. Mr. Mann. Sit. Now." Coach pushed open the first door on the left and gestured inside. "Stay here until he gets back."

She didn't wait for us to sit before she turned and all but shoved Aaron and Jacob through the glass door opposite of us. They dropped into the chairs that sat across from a woman with cat-eye glasses and a sharp navy-blue suit. Coach walked over and stood between both of the bullies like she did not trust them for one second.

"Who's that lady?"

"Principal." Archie frowned. "I forgot her name. We call her Mrs. O though. She's cool . . . most of the time."

I nodded. "And who's office are we in?"

"Mr. Barrett. The Dean." He sighed and leaned back in his chair. "Not cool most of the time."

"This should be fun."

Movement in my peripheral vision made me jump, but it was just a skinny, frail-looking middle-aged man with silver hair and matching glasses perched on his narrow nose. He glanced into the Principal's office as he shut the office door behind him. With a heavy sigh and a shake of his head, he walked over and sat in his chair across from us. He cleared his throat and pushed his sleeves up to his elbows. "I just love Mondays. My two new students have gotten in an all-out brawl on the baseball field."

I licked my lips. "Mr. Barrett, if I may, I can explain—"

"You may not," he snapped. "You were in a fight in the hall between classes and then another not even an hour later? We do not accept this kind of behavior at Gulf Shores High School."

"But, Mr. Barrett, she was just defending me—"

"From the pitcher's mound, Archibald?"

The door swung open behind us, making all three of us jump. I frowned as three girls walked in with their heads held high. At first, I was too busy reveling in that electric tingle in the air that meant they were witches. It was such a new sensation. It reminded me of the first time I saw snow and just wanted to stand outside to feel the coldness on my skin. The girl on the far left had beautiful brown skin and big yellow eyes . . . *and my backpack.* I frowned and looked to the other girl with gray eyes and curly black hair and found her also holding a backpack.

The girl in the middle with shoulder-length wavy brown hair and light-brown eyes stepped forward and held her hand up. A gold chain dropped from her palm. At the bottom was a gold circle with a five-pointed star inside of it—a pentacle, as I'd learned. "We're here for *them.*"

# CHAPTER THIRTEEN

## FRANKIE

"EXCUSE ME, young lady, but you cannot just march in here," Mr. Barrett snapped. "And these two are suspended."

The girl with curly black hair pulled a wand out of her back pocket and tapped the tip against the glass door behind her. The air pulsed and shimmered. Something sparkled. When I looked, I found the other girl had also pulled a wand out and was using it to shred papers, except the papers were shredding into speckles of dust that evaporated.

"Now, now, Mr. Barrett . . ." the girl in the middle flicked her wrist and the pentacle hanging at the end of her gold chain began to swing left to right and back again. She smiled sweetly. "You're not going to suspend these two students from school."

Mr. Barrett's face went blank. His eyes seemed to glaze over. "I'm not going to suspend these two students from school."

"They're new here and are therefore prey for the predatory bullies," she chanted softly. Her cheeks flushed a faint pink. "And you don't blame them for defending themselves in the face of danger. You're going to let them off with a warning and ten community service hours."

Mr. Barrett blinked, then looked to us. "Miss Proctor and Mr. Mann, I understand that you're new here and the other students have been bullying you relentlessly, and while I cannot condone violence, I must say I don't blame you for defending yourselves."

My eyes widened. This dude was literally about to suspend us and now he wasn't. I eyed the three girls. They were calm and steady. The two with wands were doing *something*. Light twinkled from the tips of their wands as they moved them around. The girl with the cool pentacle charm seemed to be hypnotizing the Dean, except not quite because he wasn't repeating her word for word. It was strange. I wanted to ask about it.

Archie smiled at the ground. His dark-red hair was sticking out in every direction.

Mr. Barrett sighed. "But I cannot just let this slide without any repercussions. So, I'm giving you ten community service hours to be completed by the end of the month. Each. If you fail to provide the required proof, you will then get detention for a week. Understood?"

I glanced up to the three girls, then back to him. "Yes?"

Archie jumped to his feet. "Thank you for being so understanding, Mr. Barrett."

"Please try to stay out of any more fights, or I will be forced to be much stricter."

I stood and nodded. "Understood."

He gestured for the door. "Go ahead, get to lunch."

"Thanks, Mr. Barrett." The girl with the pentacle charm winked at me, then spun and walked out the door of the Dean's office. "C'mon, guys."

Archie and I followed the three of them out into the main hallway, which was still empty and eerily quiet.

The girl with pretty brown skin handed me my backpack, then pointed behind her. "Get changed in there."

"Okay." I looked over to Archie only to find him hurrying into the guy's bathroom with his backpack. I gave the girls a tentative smile. "Be right out."

I practically flew through the bathroom door and into the first stall. It wasn't until I opened my backpack and found my regular clothes folded neatly inside that I remembered I hadn't put them in there. Coach Andrews had given me a locker in the locker room *with a lock*. My clothes had been folded on the shelf inside and my backpack sat below. With a scowl, I peeled my gym clothes off and put my jean shorts and white tank top back on. My button-down shirt was tied around my hips. I shoved my gym clothes in my bag and sprinted back into the hall to find Archie and the three girls waiting for me.

The girl with curly black hair and gray eyes looked me up and down and then nodded. "Let's get to lunch." She led our little group out the main door and onto the sidewalk.

"Hey, um, how'd you get my stuff out of my locker?"

Ms. Curls gave me a smirk over her shoulder and held her wand up. "Magic."

"Oh. Right." That didn't entirely clear things up for me, but since they just got me out of a school suspension, I was going to let it slide.

She chuckled. "It *was* a bit of an invasion of your space and all, but I figured you wouldn't want to go back into the locker room and be ambushed by the other students. And who wants to eat lunch in their PE uniform?"

"Especially covered in clay," Ms. Yellow Eyes wagged her eyebrows. Her dark hair was buzzed short on the sides, basically blending in with her dark skin. But the long strands on top had caramel-colored streaks in them. "*And* a little blood."

The girl with the pentacle charm threw her head back and laughed. "*You done messed up, Ay-ay-ron.* Goddess, I haven't heard anyone say that to him in years. It did not disappoint."

"Wait." I stopped short and the others stopped with me. "You're not mad?"

They all frowned, even Archie.

"I mean . . . I used magic on Aaron—"

"That wasn't intentional—"

"How do you know?"

Ms. Curls scowled. Her gray eyes were sharp. "Gut feeling?"

"Oh." I chuckled. "Good call. I have no idea how that happened."

"Yeah, your face pretty much told us that." She grinned. "Why would you think we're mad?"

I threw my hands up. "I don't know. I'm new to this world of magic. Guess I thought you were gonna rough me up or something . . . or threaten me? I mean, I was getting some nasty glares on the field."

She shook her head. "Pink, those were *not* for you."

"We were glaring at the jackasses who attacked you," Ms. Yellow Eyes gestured toward the office, "because their behavior was abominable."

"Yeah, you were amazing." She gestured for me to keep walking. "C'mon, word will spread fast about this, so let's get to lunch before the bell rings."

"Right, sorry." I fell into step with them. "Not that I dislike the nickname Pink or anything, but my name is Frankie—"

"Proctor. We heard," Ms. Curls said with a wide smile. She reached over to shake my hand while we walked. "I'm Esther Goldstein. Welcome to Tampa."

The girl with the dark-brown skin stepped up beside me and held her hand out. "And I'm Ava Miller."

"Hi, Ava. Did you intentionally match the caramel in your hair to your eyes?"

"Pink gets it. We're gonna be friends, I can tell." She cackled. Then she pointed to the third girl. "This here is Birdie Buckley. She's the quiet type, but when we need her to pull her tricks with that talisman of hers, she slays."

*Talisman?* I made a mental note to ask about that later, because I definitely had questions.

"Well, thanks for bailing us out." I cleared my throat. "Community service was a nice touch—"

"Oh, you won't have to do that." Esther waved her hand. "My mom will sign off on it, especially once she hears *why* you got in trouble and how you kicked their asses. No big deal."

"Well, again, thank you. I appreciate it . . . since you don't even know me."

Ava wrapped her arm around my shoulders. "We don't have to know you, Pink. Arcana protects arcana. We have to have each others' backs out there or we'll never survive."

"Ava, personal space?" Birdie gestured wildly in my direction. "She's a Proctor, and you're looking like a chaser right now."

Ava gasped. "*Birdie.*"

Esther snickered under her breath. Birdie shrugged.

"What's a chaser?"

Archie chuckled. "A chaser is a civilian who clout-chases after founding families or anyone in a seat of power or importance."

"The Proctors were a founding family, which means you're important *and* powerful." Birdie pointed to Esther. "She's also from a founding family on her mom's side."

Esther smirked. "Which means I get to hide among the crowd like I have an alias."

"This is weird. My last name never had so much importance before now." I shivered at the weirdness of this information. "Still not sure I grasp what a founding family fully is."

"Don't worry. We'll help you." Archie smiled up at me. "I mean, I owe you."

I grimaced as we turned onto a covered sidewalk. "I really hate bullies. Those guys are a piece of work. What's their problem?"

Esther rolled her eyes. "Aaron and Jacob have always been cocky assholes."

"Yeah, but they got worse," Ava grumbled.

I frowned. "Why did they get worse? And when? Was it me?"

Birdie scoffed. "No. Sadly."

Archie nodded. "It was me. They're very threatened."

Everyone laughed.

Esther shook her head and almost growled. "It's a power trip."

I bit my bottom lip. "I feel like I'm missing something?"

She sighed. "I know you're new here, but do you know about The Coven?"

"Big, scary, powerful witches who are in charge?"

They all nodded.

"Okay, so what? They part of The Coven or something?"

Esther laughed in a short burst. "They wish."

"Oh." I scowled.

"See, thing is, Frankie . . . The Coven lived here." Esther paused as we rounded another corner. "They went to school here with us. They lived in our neighborhood. They're our age. We grew up with them. Sure, we didn't hang out a ton with them, but that's not their fault. Hard to have something in common with civilian teenagers discussing parties and prom when you're fighting demons and trying to keep the rest of the world alive, ya know?"

I nodded. "Shit. Yeah, I imagine that had to be hard for them."

"It was. I'm sure. Not that they would've ever admitted it. Now, some of them were cool as shit and super chill. *They* hung out with us from time to time."

"Oh, like who?" I wanted to make a mental note of the easy, chill Coven-members in case I ever met them.

"Henley and Royce Redd, for sure." Ava nodded thoughtfully. "They're siblings."

"Easton . . . especially when he was a slut." Birdie blushed.

The girls all giggled.

"Now he's with Lily, who is mad chill and also in The Coven, but you can't blame the girl for giving the rest of us the cold shoulder when a lot of us used to hook up with her boyfriend." Birdie grinned. "Some of us more than others."

Ava shrugged. "No regrets. Whenever and whatever he wanted. Besides, I'm taken now too."

Archie scowled. "You used to hook up with Easton?"

"I mean, like twice right before he finally convinced Lily to be exclusive with him." Ava shook her head. "I never expected monogamy to last for him."

I looked to Archie. "Do you know them too?"

"They left town before the great Archibald Mann arrived." He grinned.

"Everyone in our world knows who they are, Frankie. They're like famous for us." Esther looked to me with a smile. "You'll know all their names in no time—"

"Oh, Willow and Chutney were nice." Ava snapped her fingers. "But shy and a little suspicious of everything that moved, so they tended to stay in the middle of their Coven-mates."

Esther reached up and pinned her black curls on top of her head with a clip. "Point I was trying to make is that when The Coven lived here—for the last twelve years—no one tried anything. No one fucked around because no one wanted to find out . . . from *him*."

"Who?"

"Tennessee," all three of them said in perfect unison.

Archie flinched, which was apparently the appropriate response because the girls nodded.

I narrowed my eyes. "And which one is he again? I know my aunt and uncle said that name and it's not one you forget hearing, but I've learned so much information in a matter of hours that it's not all sticking."

"That's super understandable. And Tennessee is the Emperor." Esther squeezed my arm. "And while he wasn't Coven Leader until after they left Tampa, everyone treated him as such because, historically, the Emperor is *always* one of the Leaders. Dude may be drop dead gorgeous, but he's the single most terrifying person I have ever met."

Ava and Birdie nodded, then shuddered.

"So, he's an asshole?"

"Not even a little bit," Esther answered immediately. "He's actually a super nice guy. Very respectful. Like everything you wouldn't expect from the Emperor. But he is."

"He really is," Birdie echoed.

"Like we could go on and on with examples of just how good of a person he is—but it's a long list. Trust us." Esther made a funny face. "But he's also equally terrifying."

"But he's nice?"

"*So nice,*" all three of them said.

"And scary?"

"*So scary,*" they said in unison again.

I nodded. "And beautiful."

All three of the girls swooned. "*So beautiful.*"

"It's the eyes," Birdie said softly. "One is green, the other is blue."

"It's also the hair." Ava tugged on Esther's. "It's a lot like hers."

I looked Archie. "And what do you think of this Tennessee?"

"Oh, I don't know him the way they do." He blushed. "But when I see him in Eden he just seems stressed to me."

"Okay, so I get that this Emperor dude is nice, gorgeous, and terrifying—*and stressed*—but what does this have to do with tweedle-dee and tweedle-dum?"

Esther chuckled at their new nickname, then sobered. "All jokes aside, Tenn would *never, ever* let behavior like that slide. No one, including those asswads, would've dared try."

"Even if he wasn't nearby, his presence in this town was enough to keep everyone in line." Ava shuddered. "And I mean everyone. Even the adults were afraid to piss him off."

Esther pointed to her. "Exactly. So, while Tennessee Wildes was a resident of our town, Aaron and Jacob were on their best behavior."

Birdie scoffed. "Which meant they ran their mouths and gave attitude but never went too far to warrant Tenn's attention."

"But Tenn and The Coven left for Salem in October, and I guess they saw it as their window to lay claim to some stake of power, figuratively speaking."

"Ah, so like a power vacuum?"

They nodded.

Archie frowned. "Have you not informed him, or The Coven, about this?"

Esther shrugged as we slowed to a stop outside the cafeteria. "Honestly, I think we all hoped they'd calm down after a bit. But it's been getting bad, so we might have to report them, especially after what happened today with you."

"Whoa, hey now." I held both hands up. "I don't want the first thing they hear about me to be in the form of tattling. Snitches get stitches."

Esther scowled. "This kind of violence shouldn't be allowed—"

"I agree. I just . . . Let's not rush into it, okay? Let's see what happens."

She pursed her lips, then nodded. "Okay, but I can't promise someone else won't tattle."

"What will be, will be—"

"Heyyyy there, Pink!"

I turned toward the sound of my new nickname and found Tomás from PE strolling up to us with a wide grin that dimpled his cheeks. "Hi, Tomás—"

"*Oh mi Diosa. Recuerda mi nombre.*" He pressed his hand to his chest and wagged his dark eyebrows at me. Then he reached out with his other hand and took mine, lifting it to kiss my knuckles. His brown eyes sparkled in the sunlight. "*Hola, señorita, eres un hermosa rayo de sol. Eres tan hermosa como un cielo al atardecer.*"

"*Gracias?* I think?" I smiled and pulled my hand back. "My Spanish is a little slow, something about the sun?"

"He said you're as beautiful as a sunset sky—or something like that." Esther smacked his shoulder. "Stop being gross. Introduce yourself."

"My apologies. I am Tomás Hernandez. It's nice to meet you."

"Frankie Proctor. Nice to meet you too."

"Let me get your food—"

"Oh, that's not necessary—"

"*Diosa,* yes, it is. You will be ambushed, the school already knows

what you did to them, and they'll want to trample you in affection."
Tomás grinned. "Please, really, give me your money if you want, and let me grab it for you from the line. Your first day has been intense enough already."

Esther sighed. "I'd let him, Frankie. Today at least."

"What about you guys?"

"My boyfriend is getting our food. He likes to help but he's a Cup, so he doesn't get as many chances." Ava hooked her arm around mine. "C'mon, let's sit."

Tomás stepped in front of us. "What would you like to eat? Pizza? Chicken nuggets? Burger?"

"Um . . ." I looked to Archie. "What do you like here?"

"The pizza is delivered."

"Pizza it is then. And a coke if they have it? Thank you, Tomás. How much do I owe you?"

He frowned, then gave me a big smile. "I don't remember. I use my card. I will let you know. Promise. Archie, you want the same?"

"I can get my own—"

"No way, mi amigo. I got you too." He gave us two thumbs-up, then skipped through the cafeteria doors.

Esther chuckled. "I think you've got an admirer already, Franks."

I grinned. "Did you just call me Franks?"

She pursed her lips. "I think I did. Is that weird?"

"Nah. My uncle calls me Franks. I like it."

Birdie's stomach growled so loud we all jumped. She grimaced. "I dropped my breakfast burrito this morning. I'm starving."

"Look, Seamus is already there with our food. C'mon." Ava tugged me into a skip.

Together, we all crossed the grassy area over to a small section of picnic tables that were nestled beneath some sprawling oak trees. It was shady and looked cool. As we approached the table, a golden retriever puppy popped up from the ground to greet us.

I gasped. "PUPPY!"

The dog lunged for me, taking me down to my knees in a split second. He licked my face and wagged his tail a mile a minute.

"Rootbeer!" Ava dragged the puppy off of me. "Crazy girl, what has gotten into you?"

I giggled and ran my hands through her golden fur. "Dogs tend to react like that to me. I don't know why—wait. Hold up, is she a service dog?" I tapped on the harness with the words 'SERVICE DOG' written on it in bold letters.

Ava sighed. "Yes, she is, but—"

"She's friendly," a deep male voice said from close by. When I stood up, I found a tall boy with ginger red hair, matching freckles, and big blue eyes staring down at me. He held his hand out. "I'm Seamus O'Brien."

I shook his hand. "Frankie Proctor. Sorry, I didn't know she was a service dog—"

"No, it's okay. She knows when she gets out here to these tables that she's allowed to be her silly puppy self. She's so friendly. I have to give her friend breaks." He turned his head to the side and tapped on a little skin-colored device strapped to his ear. "I'm mostly deaf. Rootbeer is my second set of ears, because if it's not in front of me, I am not going to hear it."

"His hearing aids work really well most days *and* he reads lips." Ava stepped up and kissed him on the lips, then turned back to me. "And he's my boyfriend."

"OH. Cool. So, do you know ASL?" I asked while signing with my hands.

His smile spread wider until it crinkled his eyes. He lifted his hands and signed back, *"Yes I do! Most people don't around here so I stopped asking."*

That was sad. *"Well I do."*

*"That is awesome."*

"Where's my baby?" Ava frowned and walked around Seamus, then squealed. She bent over and picked up a big, fluffy white bunny. "Frankie, this is my girl Float."

I opened my mouth, then shut it. "Float? As in she floats?"

"YES!" Ava giggled.

Archie chuckled and sat down at the table beside Esther. "Rootbeer float."

I moved to take the seat next to Archie. "There's a story there."

Seamus turned to Ava. *"Go ahead, my love. Tell them,"* he signed.

She blew him a kiss, then sat across from me with her bunny still cuddled up in her chest. "So, Seamus and I both moved here like two years ago. We both already had our pets. I named her Float because she floats. He named her Rootbeer because when he first got her as a baby, she kept bringing him cans of root beer."

I snort-laughed.

"When we met and discovered their names, we made a joke that we had to be best friends." Ava swooned. "And then our girls became inseparable so we decided we'd just have to get married because we cannot separate them."

"*It's science*," Seamus signed to me.

"That's amazing," I said while also signing it.

Birdie snatched a burger off the tray in front of Seamus, then sat cross-legged on the tabletop next to us. "This burger is amazing right now."

"Hey, Pink!"

I jumped and glanced over my shoulder—and had to stifle a gasp. Those two cool girls were walking up to us, and they looked even cooler than before now that they weren't in PE uniforms. Madge looked sharp and chic in an all-black crop top and miniskirt ensemble with red strappy sandals. She looked expensive. Beside her, Jo wore a black knit beanie with a sweater vest made of the same black material. She wasn't wearing anything under the sweater so both of their matching tattoos were on full display—and I noticed they each had another yellow crystal inked on the center of their chests. Jo was putting on a pair of pentacle-shaped earrings that were a few inches long. I wasn't an earring girl, I tended to rip them out on accident, but I was a huge fan of the curved bone charm hanging from her leather necklace.

"Welcome to our little gang, Pink," Madge said with a smirk. She held her hand out for me to shake. "And nice work with those dickbags today."

"Thank you. I'm Frankie." I shook her hand.

"Madge Sullivan." She gestured toward her bestie. "This is my soulmate, Jo—"

"*Bonjour, chérie.*" Jo leaned forward and kissed each of my cheeks, then sat down across from Esther. "*Je m'appelle Joséphine Côté. Mais vous pouvez m'appeler Jo.*"

I opened my mouth, but nothing came out. For a second, I just stared. "Shit, was that French?"

"*Merde, désolé. Oui, je suis français. Je viens de Paris.*" She grimaced. "*Je ne parle pas bien l'anglais.*"

"I got the *shit, sorry* part." I grinned. "And okay, the *from Paris* part too. Did you say to call you Jo?"

"*Oui.*"

"But you understand English?"

"Oui, je comprends l'anglais."

Madge tugged on one of Jo's braids gently. "Luckily, *I* speak French, so I translate."

Jo arched one eyebrow. "Tu mens."

"I do *not* lie." She scoffed. "I didn't say I speak French as beautifully and fluently as *you*, but I do speak it enough to translate what you're saying."

Jo just sighed.

I leaned forward. "I can understand most Spanish when it's spoken to me, but getting my own words out in Spanish is a nightmare."

Jo gasped. She slammed her hands on the table. "*Merci! Il est tellement plus difficile de dire les mots!*"

Madge squeezed Jo's hand. "She is agreeing with you, Pink."

Tomás returned then with our food. He gave me a flirty wink and slid onto the bench at the table across from us. "What did I miss?"

"What did *you* miss?" Seamus cursed. "I want to hear what *I* missed."

The others launched into the story of what went down in PE class. It was weird to hear it from someone else's point of view, let alone a whole group. They all laughed and joked around. For a moment, I forgot these were witches. They seemed like regular teenagers to me. No one hesitated to welcome me into their group, and they didn't make it weird either. They acted like I'd always been here. It was nice.

"You okay over there, Franks?" Esther leaned forward to get my attention. "That face screams existential crisis."

I chuckled. "I'm just . . . adjusting still. Y'all seem so . . . human?"

Madge licked her lips. "We have to be. It's a survival thing."

"*Lorsque nous sommes en public, nous devons cacher notre magie.*"

"*When we're in public, we have to hide our magic,* that's what she said." Madge gestured to the school behind me. "There are a lot of us in this school so it's easy to forget and start using magic—so we kind of have a rule not to."

"And by *we have a rule,* she means Tennessee has a rule and no one wants to get caught breaking it." Tomás chuckled. "Though, that is still survival mode, isn't it?"

They all laughed.

I smiled. "I just . . . I wasn't sure what you'd all think after what happened in PE. But you just accepted me in like I'd always been here and that . . . that's really cool."

Esther smiled back. "Arcana stick together. Especially lately. Dangerous times. Also, humans are nice enough, but they tend to not understand us."

"So we've got to have each other's backs." Madge nodded as she pulled her lipstick out of her designer purse that I didn't know the name of but recognized the logo. "Because we've seen what a witch hunt looks like in history."

We all shuddered.

"And humans get uncomfortable around our magic." Seamus scooped Rootbeer into his lap to cradle her despite her being a full-grown golden retriever who probably weighed at least seventy-five pounds. Then again, Seamus's muscular arms were on full display in his muscle tank so I shouldn't have been surprised to find him strong. I'd been more distracted by the intricate tattoos because I couldn't quite tell from over here what they were of. "They feel very anxious around us."

Ava's bunny, Float, lunged for Rootbeer, leaping right out of Ava's arms and onto the pup's belly. "Traitor."

"You'll notice it soon enough, then you'll never be able to unsee it." Esther glanced over her shoulder. "It's nice to not have to mask ourselves all the time."

I gestured around the group. "Aside from my two biggest admirers, is this it for witches our age here?"

"No," they all said at once. Then laughed.

"*Oh la la.*" Jo snapped her fingers excitedly. "We should have party tonight? For Frankie? À la plage? *Avec un feu de joie?*"

"Plage! That means beach!" I high-fived myself when Jo nodded. "I'm in. I don't know what else she said, but she had me at beach. That's my happy place."

"She said with a bonfire," Madge added with a chuckle. "And hell yes, I'm in. I'll tell everyone?"

Everyone nodded.

Esther leaned forward again. "This is good. You'll get to meet the rest of the witch kids in town. It'll be fun."

"Awesome." I tapped on the wooden picnic table. "So . . . uh . . . why don't they eat out here with you guys?"

Archie smiled. "It *is* a great spot."

"Well, for starters, we didn't used to sit out here." Esther blushed. "This was The Coven's spot. We *never* ate out here with them. This was THEIRS."

"And you didn't just sit with The Coven," Ava said with a terrified kind of laugh.

I glanced around. "So why are we out here?"

Esther shrugged. "They don't live here anymore. We kept thinking they were coming back any day and didn't wanna get caught in their spot . . . but they're not. I mean, they left in October and haven't been back. So, we're gonna claim it. Babysit it for them."

Archie laughed. "Babysit it?"

"Well, yeah, I mean . . ." Esther looked around at the others. "If they come back and want it, then obviously we let them have it."

Birdie let out a deep breath. "I like to think they'd like that we sit here now."

Madge snorted. "We call that a coping mechanism."

# CHAPTER FOURTEEN

## FRANKIE

THE REST of the day went pretty smoothly. Aaron and Jacob had gotten a three-day suspension because it was their third trip to the Principal's office. I didn't feel too guilty about my part. With them not on campus, I didn't feel the need to watch over my shoulder for a threat. I'd sensed about a dozen other witches in the halls between classes, though only a few acknowledged me. I was holding out hope for the others.

My classes had been great too. Apparently I'd missed geometry this morning, and I'd discovered during lunch that Archie and I had that class together as well as second period together in chemistry. So every morning we had the same class, which meant we already had a plan to carpool to school. It made me happy. He wasn't Elizabeth, but he was really cool. Subtly hilarious too. Fifth period, which was right after lunch thanks to block scheduling, was English and I didn't have Archie, but I did have Seamus and Tomás. My last class of the odd days was seventh period art history, and I was obsessed. Jo and Madge were in that class with me. I was bummed I'd missed the whole school year in there but texted my aunt that I wanted to take it again next year. On even class number days, I'd have art class with Jo and Ava after lunch and then history with Archie and Birdie.

All in all, things were looking good. Which naturally made me nervous. I had no reason to feel that way, but I just kept feeling like the other shoe was gonna drop. It was a nagging, horrible feeling. *Just ignore it, Frankie.*

I threw my backpack in my trunk, then leaned inside to turn it on and get the AC pumping while I waited for Archie. He didn't have a car, so I promised to be his ride to and from school. It was nice to have the company, and we were neighbors, so it was logical. It was somewhat alarming how much comfort I found in having at least one witch friend in my classes, even though I'd just met them. They passed the vibe check, though, and my gut told me they were good peoples. I was trying not to overthink it and ruin perfectly good opportunities to make friends, which was the only reason I hadn't sped off campus already, I *wanted* to be friends with Archie. So, I was waiting. My teacher let me out a few minutes early so I could run down to the office to get myself a locker. That'd taken about two minutes.

The bell rang so loud I actually jumped. Even my heart skipped a beat. Light flashed out of the corner of my eye, so I looked down and then gasped. Those little blue flames were dancing around my fingers. I cursed and shook my hands, but that only made the flames grow bigger and brighter. The doors to the buildings opened to let students rush out, which meant any second I'd be spotted. I spun around to face my car, then called my aunt and held my phone to my ear with my shoulder. *Pick up, pick up, pick up.*

"Hey, honey—"

"*How do I make the flames go away?*" I whispered in a rush, then glanced around to make sure I was still alone.

My aunt cleared her throat, then I heard a door click. "Do you mean your magic?"

"*Yes,*" I whisper-shouted. I kept wiggling my fingers, but it was gas to the flame. "It's just getting worse."

"Okay, love, just breathe," she said in that calm voice of hers. "Close your eyes for me, then cross your arms across your chest so your hands are buried beneath your arms."

I did as she asked. The flames tingled against my bare skin. "Right. Now what?"

"Take a deep breath, then another and another. Breathing steady is key here. Then think about the ocean. Picture it in your mind. Really go there."

With my eyes closed and my hands buried in my armpits, I took a big, deep breath and let it out slowly. I pictured my beach back home, the one I used to go to with Elizabeth on the weekends. The sun was high and bright, shining warm onto our skin. The air was crisp and salty, and each deep breath chased away some of the tension.

"Feel the sand between your toes," my aunt said softly, her voice like a lullaby. "Listen to the waves washing onto the shore."

I scrunched my toes, feeling the crunch of the powdery sand as if I was actually there. The waves were slow and low, rolling onto the shore in a gentle caress. I watched the water rush up to my feet and then slide away, dragging shells and sand with it. Little air bubbles popped up in the sand from where crabs buried themselves. The sunlight danced along the surface of the water, making the colors sparkle.

"Now open your eyes and look at your hands."

When I looked, I wasn't even surprised to find my magic had faded. The beach had always been my happy place where I felt the most peace. "Thank you."

"Any time you feel your magic rushing to the surface, just close your eyes and go to the beach." Her voice was low and soft. "It's an extension of ourselves, so if you feel startled, it will too."

I sighed. "Thanks, Aunt Kimmy."

"Anytime, love. You heading home from school?"

"Yeah, giving my new friend—and our neighbor, Archie—a ride home."

"Look at you making friends already." She chuckled. "Well, your uncle and I can't wait to hear about your first day."

"Hey, my friends are gonna have a little beach party tonight so I can meet everyone. Is it cool if I go?"

"Sounds like it would be rude if you didn't." She giggled again. "Of course it's all right. How about I pick up a pizza on my way home, and we can eat together before you go?"

"Pizza is definitely what I need."

"See you soon."

I hung up and shoved my phone in my pocket as I turned back to face campus. The sidewalks in every direction were crowded with students. Most of them were headed to my right where school busses were waiting. I kept my eyes on the building I knew Archie was in, which was straight ahead. About another minute or so later, the door flew open like someone shoved their whole body into it. A familiar head of dark-red hair came flying out with his hand somehow caught on the handle. I stood up straight like I could somehow stop Archie from being thrown into the railing with the door. He yanked his hand back, but gravity grabbed ahold of him, and he rolled down the flight of stairs, taking a few kids down with him.

"Oh, shit." I stopped short as Archie got up.

He was laughing. This kid had one hell of a sense of humor. He didn't seem injured. He just chuckled and apologized to the students he'd crashed into. He wiped his hands off on his jeans and took a step forward but collided with another student who shoved him to the side. It took his little legs a few feet to catch his balance, and by now he was in the grass between the building and the sidewalk. I nodded in approval. That fifteen-foot-wide space was probably the safest option for him.

Just as I was relaxing back against my car, Archie's toe caught on a tree root raised about an inch off the grass and he stumbled forward like he'd just stepped on ice. I covered my face with my hand and tried not to chuckle. At that moment, he looked up and spotted me. Except he didn't blush or get embarrassed, he just laughed and waved. I waved back. He held one finger up, then slowly and carefully tiptoed his way across the grass, making sure to use big steps over the tree roots.

But he was so busy watching the ground that he missed that he was headed right for the pole on the sidewalk that held up the covering. I opened my mouth to call out to him when he suddenly looked up and stopped short, except the laws of physics propelled him backwards where he slammed into *that* pole. The *ding* his head made on the metal was so loud I heard it from where I stood. He stopped and stared at the ground, just shaking his head and chuckling. After a few seconds, he took a deep breath and marched toward me. This time he managed to make it all the way across the lot to me without tripping or falling.

I must've made some kind of face because he just held his hands up and sighed. "You just got a crash course in who I am as a person. Pun intended."

I snort-laughed. "You okay?"

He narrowed his light-hazel eyes and nodded. "Tricky route."

"C'mon, Fred Astaire, let me drive you home." I opened the passenger door for him, then walked around and climbed into the driver's seat. "You'll be safe in here at least."

"I'm afraid to attempt driving at this point." He clicked his seat-belt into the buckle and looked up at me. "I'd hate to be the first person to trip a car."

We both cackled like comic book villains as I backed out of my parking spot and beelined for the school exit. I was just turning right onto the main street when a thick bolt of lightning cracked across the sky followed by immediate thunder. We both jumped a little and then leaned forward to look at the sky through the windshield. Somehow, I hadn't noticed how gray the sky was or how thick the clouds moving in were.

I whistled and shook my head as I rolled to a stop at the red light. "That storm is *close*."

He frowned over at me. "What do you mean?"

"Thunder is the sound lightning makes as it streaks across the sky—"

"Right, I know that."

"So, you can tell how close to the ground the storm is by how fast you hear the thunder."

His jaw dropped. He leaned forward just as another lightning shot across the sky. "Well, that's—"

Thunder rolled like a freight train.

He pursed his lips. "Yeah, I'd say that's close."

I chuckled as the light turned green. "I love when there's thunder but no rain. It's like nature is fighting with itself."

"She'd be a doll if she could keep that fight inside until we get home." He leaned against the window, looking out with a pensive expression. "I've been beat up enough today."

He meant it as a joke, but we'd just met, so I wasn't comfortable enough with letting it go entirely. "You okay? I mean, those guys could really hurt you."

"I'm okay. Honest. I've seen worse—" He gasped and pointed to the sidewalk. "OH, can we pull over? Let's pick them up."

"Who are they? Which people?" There was a steady flow of students walking off campus.

"Those two guys up there, the one has a short brown mohawk?" He pointed out the windshield. "The other has curly blond hair?"

"Right. I see them. Who are they?"

"Atley Carrier and Peabo Mason. They're arcana and younger than us, so they're not dicks. Peabo lives at the end of our street, but Atley lives next door to me." He pointed to them again as I slowed down. "Do you mind giving them a ride?"

"Of course not." I pulled over just in front of them. "Go ahead, call 'em in."

He rolled the window down and stuck his head out—or tried to but the seatbelt yanked him back inside. He yelled out, then giggled. "Ouch."

"*That's* ouch? You didn't even say ouch when they threw you into the lockers—"

"Yeah, but I was mentally prepared for that contact." He tugged on the seatbelt. "This was just foul play."

I laughed and honked my horn as the two boys walked by us. "HEY!" I yelled through the open window.

They both jumped and spun toward us with guarded expressions. Now that I saw their faces, I knew they were definitely younger, maybe even middle school age—then again, they were leaving the high school, so they were probably freshmen with baby faces. Their eyes narrowed on us, and their entire body language was preparing for a fight. But then Archie leaned back out the window and they relaxed.

"Want a ride?" Archie pointed to the sky. "Storm's a bit close to walk home, yeah?"

"Yeah?" The kid with the mohawk leaned down to look through the window. "Oh, hi. Who are you?"

Lightning lit up the whole sky despite it being mid-afternoon.

I frowned. "Introductions in the car. Get on in."

They climbed in. I spun in my seat as they buckled up. "That was far too easy to kidnap you."

They laughed.

"This one with the mohawk is Atley." Archie pointed to the kid behind him with blond curls. "This is Peabo. They're freshmen."

They may have been young with younger faces, but there was some age in their eyes I couldn't put my finger on. Not to mention the biceps. They weren't huge, but they were chiseled. These kids were not normal freshman. I cleared my throat. "Hi. I'm Frankie Proctor—"

"OH," They both said in a rush, their eyes snappinf up to me.

"Oh?" My stomach tightened into knots. "You heard about me?"

Atley cocked his head to the side, eyeing me closely with sharp gray eyes. "You're Tenn's cousin?"

"Tenn?" Then it clicked. "Oh, that Tennessee guy? The Emperor."

"Yeah, him. You're a Proctor, so you must be related?"

I opened my mouth, then shut it. "Isn't his last name Wildes? Or is he a Proctor on his mom's side? Shit, I think I've been told this already."

"His real name is Haven Proctor," Peabo said sheepishly, his face turning pink like he realized maybe he wasn't supposed to say anything. His pretty emerald-green eyes wouldn't linger on me for more than a second. "It's a whole story, pretty sad too. Best not to ask and just accept it."

I nodded. "Fair."

"Peabo and Atley are close with The Coven." Archie turned back in his seat with a proud nod. "They trained with them and helped out when they lived here. Right, guys?"

"Yeah, they're cool." Peabo pushed his dirty blond curls out of his face. "We're like the middle children of this community, so they took us in."

"You lost me." I pulled back onto the street and started driving.

"Well, there's like two dozen teenagers here—not including The Coven, which made it three dozen?" Peabo shrugged. "Then there's four younger kids, like in elementary school still . . . then there's us. Right in the middle."

"And Lesleigh Buckley. She's twelve. We're thirteen."

I frowned over to Archie. "Buckley? Did I meet someone today with the last name Buckley? Sounds familiar?"

Archie chuckled. "Birdie Buckley. They're sisters."

"Yeah, so Lesleigh hangs with her sister and her friends a lot."

"Lesleigh is cool though." Peabo blushed. "She's been hanging with us more lately."

There was a story in that blush, but I just met him, so I wasn't going to call him out on it. "What about the four younger kids?"

"Well . . ." Atley sighed. He reached up and scratched his jaw and that was when I noticed he had tattoos. Some kind of black bands around his wrists. I was driving so I could only get glimpses in the rearview mirror. "All four of them are younger siblings to Coven-members, so they just kind of stick to each other."

"I have heard so much about this Coven, and I've never even met them." I chuckled. "Which ones have little siblings?"

"Sean Burroughs is Chutney's brother. And Ryan Walcot is Willow's brother. They're all cousins too."

Atley nodded. "And Kaelynn Corey, Easton's little sister—"

"Is Easton the former slut?" I looked to Archie. "Do I have the facts right?"

Archie laughed. "So I've heard."

The boys cackled in the backseat.

Atley leaned forward while we drove. "Don't let Lily hear you call him that."

Over his head, Peabo's face scrunched up in confused concentration. "I don't know. I think she low-key gets some kind of twisted pleasure out of knowing she took the sluttiest guy in school and made him monogamous."

That made me giggle. "I wanna meet this Lily now."

"She's cool." Atley leaned back against his seat.

"Who's the fourth little Coven sibling?" I glanced back through the mirror.

"Aspen," they both whispered and stared at the ground.

I looked to Archie, but he just shook his head, but he was also new to town.

"We don't like Aspen?"

Atley's face fell. "Aspen used to be great. I mean, I'm sure she still is, but . . . her sister Libby was in The Coven . . . and she died in the fall."

"Oh my God." I shuddered. "How old is Aspen?"

"Ten." Atley's eyes were sad as he stared out the window. "It's been really hard on her. Then last month she tried to use a Ouija Board to talk to Libby but somehow managed to summon this shadow-demon thing instead . . ."

Peabo shuddered. "The Coven was furious with her. Which was fair, because that demon hurt a lot of people."

"They were only mad for a few minutes, but I know Aspen feels awful."

Archie scowled. "That's heavy for someone so young."

"I told them she needed some help, but I don't know if they have time to come down and see her or not." Atley shrugged. His voice was so worn and raw for someone so young. "So Lesleigh and the rest of us, we've been trying to get her to hang with *us* instead of the younger kids."

"Trauma has a way of aging us," I said softly.

We were quiet a moment or two while I drove home. I glanced in the rearview mirror and caught the two boys exchanging nervous glances. Archie looked out the passenger window like he was a puppy with his tongue hanging out. Dude had the lockdown on happiness, and I needed the recipe. But the two guys in the back were stressed. I cleared my throat.

"Is it weird for me to be asking so many questions?" I frowned. "Like rude and invasive?"

Atley shrugged again. "Arcana communities are close-knit and pretty open."

"And honestly, everyone has just been really forthcoming with the tea today." Archie turned to me and wagged his eyebrows. "That ain't your fault."

We all laughed.

I parked in the driveway at my house. "What's that say about me?"

Atley leaned forward again. "Honestly, there's an interesting calmness to your energy. It's almost . . . disarming? But in a good way? That's what I was just thinking about. Like you've got an aura that's peaceful."

"Yeah, like super chill and relaxing." Peabo nodded. "Makes people want to talk to you, tell you stuff. You asked questions and words just came out. I bet you're used to it."

I opened my mouth, then shut it. "How old are you guys? That was one hell of an answer."

"We're thirteen, but we've been hanging with The Coven since we were like eight? So, I guess we've kind of matured a little quicker than most kids our age."

Atley nodded and looked down to the black tattoo bands on his wrists that I was dying to ask about. "Yeah, we've seen some shit."

I snort-laughed. "Same, dude. Same."

"OH shit!" Peabo sat up straight as a grin spread across his face. His green eyes were locked on the sideview mirror for a second, then he half-turned in his seat. "They came! I didn't think they would—"

"Whoa, really? Who is it?" Archie unbuckled his seatbelt and spun around. "*Interesting.*"

"What is? Who is it?"

Archie leaned forward to look. "Those are Coven-members, I think?"

"That's Royce Redd and his new boyfriend, Thiago Diaz." Atley threw his door open. "Both Coven-members."

Butterflies danced in my stomach. I was about to actually *see* Coven-members with my own eyes. I jumped out and looked across the street to where two dark-haired guys stood, and my breath caught in my throat. Even from across the street I could tell these two guys were very attractive. The one on the left had wavy brown hair that fell to his shoulders and a sexy five o'clock shadow scruff on his jaw, and I could see his eyes were a light blue, which meant that up close they were probably to die for. In the Florida sun, his skin was a gorgeous bronze color. The other one wore suspenders and pristine platform white sneakers, so I was already obsessed. His hair was jet-black and cut short on the sides with the strands on top left long so they could be swept back. It was very modern Elvis Prestley, and something told me this guy would take that as a compliment. His skin was a pretty porcelain color, a stark contrast to his boyfriend's for sure. He was also a little leaner. The cotton sleeves of his T-shirt didn't quite strain the same way they did on Thiago. But he was a couple inches taller— without the platform sneakers. He looked smooth as hell, especially with the black sunglasses.

They looked fantastic. But they felt *powerful.* With every step I took toward them, that tingle in the air that signified witches felt like it'd been supercharged. I finally understood the *moth to the flame* reference for civilians following Coven-members. That magic was like a fireplace on a winter night that I wanted to cuddle up in front of, which made no sense.

"ROYCE!" Atley shouted from behind me and jumped up and down.

The Elvis-looking one on the right looked up and grinned. "MY DUDES! Come here!"

*Okay, so Royce is Elvis. That means the other one is Thiago.*

Atley and Peabo sprinted across the street, beelining straight for Royce who gave them each a hug and a million-dollar smile. They definitely were close with The Coven if that was how they were greeted. That had to be really cool for them. The boys turned to Thiago and got high fives and a wild grin that dimpled his cheeks. *What a pair those two make.*

Archie cursed behind me. I turned to look and found his backpack half-empty with the rest on the street. He hurried to collect everything, shoving stuff back in his bag. "Go ahead. I'll be right there."

He'd had a rough day, so I let him have a moment to collect himself . . . and his stuff. I turned and hurried across the street, anxious and excited to meet Coven-members, even if it was only two of them. The shakiness in my voice when I introduced myself was not a flattering moment, but they didn't seem to notice.

"Frankie. Great name." Royce looked down at me, sliding his black sunglasses down to reveal a devastating pair of sapphire-blue eyes—that were looking at me sharply. "A Proctor, eh? I'll have to let Tenn and Bettina know they've got a cousin—or . . . shit I don't know how you're related."

"*Francelina* is such a pretty name, but I will call you Frankie if you prefer." Thiago winked to me. Then he turned to Royce. "You're better off asking Myrtle and Saffie. Or Kenneth."

"You're right." Royce snapped his fingers, and I saw the wheels turning in his head. But then he shook himself and gave me a smile. "Well, I'll let them know they'll have to come down and meet you."

My face flushed with heat, so I knew I was blushing. "Thank you."

"Tell me, what's your favorite flower?"

"Umm . . . cherry blossoms?"

Royce's eyes sparkled. He held his hand out to the side and wiggled his fingers and green mist swirled between them like a snake. He pursed his lips, then flicked his hand toward my house. "How about that?"

I frowned and glanced over my shoulder, then did a double take.

A large, willowy cherry blossom tree sat in the middle of my front yard. My breath left me in a rush. "What in the—"

"It's his Coven magic. They all have elemental power," Atley whispered helpfully in my ear. "Royce's is plants and flowers and shit."

Royce pursed his lips. "Shit *is* part of nature."

Thiago rolled his eyes. "Great, now he's going to be throwing literal shit at demons."

Royce gasped. "*I am now!*"

We all laughed.

Thiago shook his head, then frowned and pointed across the street. "Your friend okay?"

We all looked to my driveway just as Archie slammed my car door and started to walk forward, but the strap to his bag was caught inside the door, so he was yanked backwards. His feet slid out from under him, sending him flat on his ass on the cement with his arm still caught in the strap. He staggered back to his feet, pulled his arm loose, then gripped the strap and pulled as hard as he could. But his hand slipped and that fist shot up and punched himself in the face.

"*Oh, shit,*" Royce whispered with a giggle.

Finally, Archie just gave up and abandoned his backpack to dangle from my car door.

Thiago nodded. "That's the look of defeat."

"He's had a rough day." I grimaced.

Archie looked up to us and waved, then sprinted down my driveway and across the street. As he got to us, he stepped up onto the sidewalk, but his leg didn't go high enough. His toes caught on the edge of the curb, and he flew face forward with all that momentum from his sprinting and face-planted right on the sidewalk. Hard.

Royce snort-laughed so hard he spit on himself. He laughed so hard he had to bend over at the knees. His face turned red and his eyes teared. Thiago was covering his mouth to hide his chuckle, but Royce's giggles sent all of us into giggle-land. Thiago bent over and held his hand out to help him up, but when Archie took his hand, Thiago pulled and Archie slammed into Thiago's chest. The two of them staggered back a step.

Royce wheezed and started to bounce. "I can't—I can't—gonna

pee! I'm sorry—" He turned and high-tailed it inside the house behind him.

Archie laughed and smoothed the front of his shirt down. "If he pisses himself, do I owe him a new pair of pants?"

Thiago ran his hand through his long hair. "Sorry, he's been through a lot lately. I haven't seen him laugh like that . . . ever, actually."

Archie brushed his shoulders off. "See? I'm good for something."

Thiago laughed. "Are you okay?"

"I've had worse."

I patted him on the back. "You might have to stop saying that or I'm going to get concerned."

Archie grinned.

Atley shook his head but turned his gaze back to Thiago. "So, what brings you guys here?"

Thiago pointed to the house behind him. "Royce wanted to check on a girl named Aspen? He said—Oh, *you* called?"

Atley's whole face lit up. "Yeah, I did. I wasn't expecting such a fast arrival."

"I'm new to The Coven, but apparently they feel pretty bad for how things went down for Aspen, so your call hit hard, I think? Anyway, Royce . . . he thought I might be able to . . . commiserate with her in a way that helps her heal."

I had no idea what that meant, but given that Aspen was struggling with grief from the death of her sister, I had a pretty bad feeling I could guess. And for that reason, I did not inquire more.

"Can I come in and talk . . . before you go see her?"

Thiago squeezed Atley's shoulder, then stepped aside and gestured to the house. "Please do. I'd like to know what I can before I go to her. It's a delicate thing."

Atley turned to me and Archie. "Sorry, guys, you probably shouldn't join us for this—"

"Of course not. I hope you all can help find some peace for Aspen." I smiled to the powerful man in front of me, then held my hand out. "It was nice to meet—"

"*Left hand,*" Peabo hissed. "Coven introduces with their left hands only."

"Oh shit. Sorry?" I switched hands, then looked up to him. "It was nice to meet you, Thiago. Tell Royce I said the same?"

He shook my hand, and I noticed on the inside of his left forearm was a tattoo of the Roman numerals *XII*. That meant something. An image flashed in my mind of the same thing on another arm but the numerals *XVI*—my vision flashed with color like I'd stepped inside a kaleidoscope. I frowned and shook my head to clear my vision.

"It was lovely to meet you too, Miss Frankie." Thiago gestured for Atley and Peabo to head inside the house. "Hope we aren't forced to meet again under such dire circumstances, but alas, such is the nature of The Coven."

"That's ominous as fuck, Thiago."

"I know." He giggled. "Archie, take care of yourself. I'd invite you in—"

"Nah, nah. What she said." He waved him off. "Besides, I clearly need a nap or something."

Lightning streaked across the sky, and this time rain dropped onto us in buckets. Thiago cursed and only some of it was in Spanish, the rest almost sounded Portuguese. Archie and I waved to Thiago one last time, then spun on our toes and sprinted back to my car. A quick click of my button and his backpack was loose for him to grab.

"Remember, Esther is gonna ride with us to the beach tonight!" Archie yelled out as he headed for his house. "I'll text you!"

"Okay! See you in a bit!" I hurried through my front door and sank to my knees a split second before all three of my dogs tackled me. "Boys, boys, boys, have I had a wild day . . ."

# CHAPTER FIFTEEN

## FRANKIE

"TRUST ME, we want to be fashionably late." Esther chuckled as she buckled her seatbelt in the passenger seat. "This way everyone else has settled in and will be chillin' by the time we get there. Then we can slip in unnoticed, and I can give you the tea on everyone before you meet them."

Archie leaned forward between the front seats. "Yeah, the last thing you want is everyone to arrive and see the new girl standing there. It'll be like a stream of awkward introductions."

We all shuddered.

*Great, now I AM nervous.* I wasn't before, not really.

"Archie sit back. It's not safe like this." Esther playfully swatted at him. "We're small, we have to be buckled in so we don't fly out if some jackass hits us."

"I appreciate that your default is to assume someone else would be hitting us and not that I'd be a bad driver." I winked at her as we rolled to a stop sign.

"Please, only someone with fast as fuck reflexes could handle Aaron and Jacob the way you did on the field. I'm not worried about you. Archie, on the other hand—"

"I just want to hear what you're saying."

"I'll turn, see? This better?" Esther turned sideways in her seat. "Now we're all buckled and secure."

Archie chuckled and shook his head, but in the rearview I saw the sparkle in his eyes. "You're the mother of the group, you know that, right?"

"Someone has to be." She stuck her tongue out at him. "Also, I'm glad you're both introverts like me and shudder at the idea of a processional line of introductions."

I shuddered again at the mere idea of it. "So how late are we?"

"About fifteen minutes, but Birdie is gonna tell me when everyone else is there so we can arrive." Esther pointed to a gas station on our right. "Stop there?"

"Did we forget something? Were we supposed to bring stuff?"

"No, Jo and Madge are hosting this party, figuratively of course."

Esther wrinkled her nose. "Jo isn't always the most willing to bring junk food. And while I appreciate her European viewpoint on diet, at a beach bonfire, I want to eat like a toddler."

I laughed and pulled into the station. "Well, I'll go ahead and fill up while we're here if you guys wanna grab the snacks?"

"Sounds good."

My gas tank was on the passenger side, so I pulled up to the back-side of the front pumps with a straight shot view of the store so I could keep an eye on them and they could watch for me. I frowned. *Why am I so worried about this right now?* I shook those intrusive thoughts away and looked up to the store. "Oh, it's a 7-Eleven? Noice. I need a big, giant Slurpee the size of my head."

Archie was already out of the car. "Shit, now I do too. Coke flavor, Franks?"

I smiled. *Franks.* Now three people called me that. But Archie and Esther were my favorites already in Tampa. There was just something about their energy that made me feel welcome and comfortable. "With a splash of cherry on top, if they have it."

"That sounds delicious," Esther grumbled. "Screw it, I need one too. Let's raid 'em, Archibald."

"Ya know, the name is growing me lately," Archie mumbled as he walked away with Esther.

I chuckled and climbed out of the car with my credit card in hand. The tank was only half empty, but it made sense to go ahead and fill up while I was here. I locked my car behind me, then walked around to the pump. I was barely paying attention to the machine as I typed in my zip code because some creepy white dude with serial killer style aviator glasses from the '70s was headed right for me. His mustache was black but definitely had crumbs in his hair from the bag of Cheetos in his hand. I wasn't sure what was greasier: the sweat on his bald head or the few strands of black hair clinging to the side of his temples. He wore cargo pants and a white tank top with neon-orange fingerprint stains from where he'd rubbed his Cheeto fingers.

His bloodshot eyes were locked on me. When he licked his lips, my stomach rolled. I knew he was watching me. I knew he was going to approach me and say something. There was something about his aura that made me pull my cellphone out of my back pocket. That bat sticker was right there for me if I needed it. Creepy men were like wild big cats in the forest, make too quick of a movement and they were prone to strike. So, with quick but steady movements, I pulled the pump out of my tank and sat it back on the hook where it went. I didn't take my eyes off the creep, not even as I hit *no receipt* on the machine. I glanced quickly over to the store doors and spotted Esther and Archie hurrying toward me, both of their gazes locked on the creep, and despite the unease in my gut, this almost made me smile.

"Hey there, blue eyes." The creep stopped at the front of my car and leaned against it. A cold chill slid down my spine. There was no way I was moving closer to him to get into my car. I'd climb in the backseat if I had to. He ran his tongue over his top teeth, and his thoughts were practically written on his forehead. "You by yourself, pretty lady?"

"No, my boyfriend is here," I said without hesitation.

It was always my immediate answer. My fake boyfriend. I'd created a whole fake backstory and everything and practiced it so it felt natural. And *that* spoke volumes as to what it was like being a woman. I never felt safe. And after what happened on Halloween, I knew most *friends* couldn't be trusted either.

The creep gave me a sideways grin that sent a cold chill down my spine. "Where is he?"

I looked him dead in the eye and arched one eyebrow. "In the trunk," I said with my coldest voice possible, then stared at him like I wanted *him* to be my next victim.

The creep looked to the trunk, then back to me. I didn't take my eyes off of his. I stared without blinking. He frowned and looked to my trunk again, then back to me.

I tapped my fingers on my car. *"Wanna see?"* I whispered.

He scowled and then scurried away, glancing back at me like he wanted to make sure I wasn't following him. I kept my eyes on him until he got in his beat-up truck and sped off. Behind me, Esther and Archie cracked up laughing.

"Franks, that was iconic." Esther clapped her hands slowly, the bags of snacks hanging from her arms. "Impressive."

Archie held all three of our Slurpees so he just nodded with a grin. "That worked surprisingly well."

I pointed to my face "You've gotta have that crazy, deranged, raging bitch face that makes them think you might actually have a person in the trunk. Go full serial killer mode, scares the creeps away."

We all laughed and climbed back in the car to head to the beach. Esther flipped the mirror down and started practicing her serial killer faces. Archie was laughing so hard at her failed attempts that his whole face was red and his body shook.

"Oh, you think it's so funny?" Esther wiped tears out of her eyes and turned around to look at him. "Let's see *your* murder face, Arch?"

He was still trying to stop laughing long enough to make a serious face when I pulled into the beach parking lot. They were both laughing so hard they made no sound except for the occasional hiss or snort, so I parked and took the moment with them distracted to survey the situation in front of me. The parking lot was full, and I took relief in the fact that I recognized most of them from the school parking lot. I'd parked in the last spot on the front row so the only thing between us and the party were the dunes, and that was both good *and* bad. Good, because it meant no one on the beach could easily see the look of panic I knew was on my face. Bad, because it meant *I* couldn't easily see the faces of everyone on the beach. I turned the car off immediately and shut off the lights, but I knew our arrival hadn't gone unnoticed. Two beams of light streaking across a beach were gonna stand out. *Shit, why did I park in the front?*

"Hey, existential crisis girl." Esther snapped her fingers in front of my face. "Breathe dude."

I took a deep breath, then let it out. "I'm fine. It's fine. We're all fine."

"You see the bonfire? Well, on the right side of that, sitting on a purple blanket, is our group. The people you met at lunch today. So, strap on a slightly less murderous expression than you gave that gas station creep and head straight for them. You'll see Rootbeer. She lays upside down on the sand and refuses to move unless Seamus calls her."

I frowned. "Is the beach another off-work zone for her?"

Archie snort-laughed. "Rootbeer is never *off* work. She's always listening. Always."

"Don't mistake her closed eyes and belly-up pose as distracted." Esther grinned and threw her door open. "Come on, you've got this. Everyone else is harmless, except for Aaron and Jacob."

I jumped out of the car and hurried over to Esther. She stepped over the foot-high wooden fence and headed into the valley of the dunes, then stopped to wait for us. I stopped beside her and turned just in time to watch Archie close my car door on his button-down shirt and then try to walk forward only to be yanked backwards. He didn't curse or yell out in pain as his spine hit the doorframe. He just sighed and hung his head. With a roll of his eyes, he pulled the door open and it slammed into his knees. He grimaced and grabbed his shirt, then slammed my car door closed.

Esther didn't laugh at him. Neither did I. Actually, I was starting to worry about just how clumsy he was. Perhaps he needed to ask a doctor about his equilibrium or something. He looked up at us and smirked as he shrugged his shoulder and stepped over the fence—his right foot caught the edge of the wood and he face-planted into the sand with a *thud*.

We both cursed and leapt toward him.

"I'm okay," he said with a laugh. "I've had worse."

I scowled. "I *am* worried about what happened to you in Eden, Archie. You keep saying *I've had worse*."

He got to his feet, then brushed sand off his clothes. "I'm durable."

"Come on," Esther said with a chuckle. "Archie, take her other side so we're a barrier, and maybe they'll assume you're Madge or Jo."

"I'd be flattered." But I didn't resist when they flanked my sides, I appreciated the show of support, especially once we walked onto the beach and away from the privacy of the dunes. I didn't count but there seemed to be about two dozen people on the beach, which wasn't a lot, but it wasn't nothing either. I cleared my throat but kept my chin held high. "Okay, gimme the tea. Who's who?"

"Right. Where should I start," Esther mumbled to herself.

Just then a girl about fifteen feet ahead looked up and gave me a snarl. Her hair was light-blonde and pinned up on top of her head. Those dark eyes were downright glaring at me. I nudged Esther's arm. "How about her? She seems less than friendly."

"Oh, she's the Pits, man. Just taking her misery and trauma out on everyone else." Esther sighed. "Aside from dirty looks and occasionally snark remarks, she's harmless."

"Why's she miserable?"

"Her parents moved her out of Edenburg a couple years ago," Archie whispered back. "Her name is Lauren Pitts, hence the nickname."

"Yeah, and then Tennessee straight up told her he wasn't attracted to her and she needed to back off." Esther shrugged. "The cherry on top of her misery milkshake."

"That seems harsh," Archie whispered. "He said it like that?"

"Who knows? She was rather insistent. Like a gnat. So, he probably snapped."

I smiled. "He's human. I'm sure he has his moments."

"Actually, I'm not so sure how human that boy is." Esther snickered. "But that's a discussion for another time. We're talking about *our* crew."

"Right. Yes. So those four girls huddled together are the *Ah'*-Queens, nicknamed as such because all their names end in *ah*. Hanna, Amanda, Sierra, and Kara. They're into makeup, like *really* into it. And *really* good at it. If you make eye contact for too long, they will beg you to let them do your makeup. Which sounds fun but . . . it feels more like punishment once they're done." I must've made a face because she grimaced. "Or maybe I'm just insecure and always feel worse about myself after they're done."

I smiled. "That's relatable. I'll heed your warning and treat them like bears—avoid eye contact. Is that bears you're supposed to do that with? Screw it, you know what I mean."

Although, as I watched them closer, I kind of wanted to get their advice. I'd never been a makeup girl. Elizabeth and I always struggled with it. Aunt Kimmy wasn't much help nor was Elizabeth's mom. These four girls looked magazine-ready. And they were all different skin tones and complexions, so there was a wealth of knowledge and how-to there.

"And the guy they're all ogling is Brody." Archie pointed to a guy with dark hair buzzed so short he was almost bald. He wore no shirt or shoes, and his cargo shorts were stained, ripped, and potentially sprinkled with blood. "He's an art kid. He likes to make weapons, but he also makes everyone's talismans. Truly giftedi."

My eyes widened. "Whoa, that's badass. What's he making now?"

"Me nervous," Esther grumbled. "Like, okay, we don't need to be welding at the beach *at a party*. Where are the safety goggles? Where's the—"

"It's okay, Esther," Archie said in a calm voice as he reached over me to grab her hand. "He knows what he's doing, and the ocean is right there to put out any runaway flames. Right?"

She nodded as we kept walking. "Right, so the two playing hacky sack? That's Lucas and Marina. They're a couple. Both upperclassmen. She's a soccer player who's being recruited by the University of Florida—"

"Oh hell yeah. Get it, girl," I said before I could stop myself. "And him? He seems coordinated."

"Varsity basketball. He's graduating this year, going to UF as well."

"That's so cute, they're going to college together—*oh*. Those are kids." I nodded my head toward the three kids who couldn't have been more than eight or nine. "Wait, you said Coven-members had younger siblings, right?"

"Yep. That's Kaelynn, Ryan, and Sean. But they like to not be known as the little siblings." Archie grimaced. "Where's Aspen?"

"She's up there with the boys." Esther pointed up ahead to where Peabo and Atley were playing with glowing lightsabers with two girls. "The little one with the side braid is Aspen. The other is Lesleigh—"

"Birdie's younger sister?"

Esther grinned. "Look at you. That's some memory. Yes, exactly."

I looked around to see if we'd missed anybody besides our group of friends on that purple blanket in front of us when I spotted Rootbeer, the golden retriever, lying belly-up in the sand just beside Seamus. She was the same color as the sand, so without the purple harness, she was damn near camouflaged. I giggled and shook my head—and Rootbeer's tail wagged, whipping sand onto everyone on the blanket.

"*Rootbeer, no! Stop!*" Seamus cackled and pinned her tail to the sand. "Can you at least turn your butt away from us?"

She jumped up and sat on her haunches, then put her paw on his arm.

"Oh." Seamus turned around with a guarded expression, then smiled. "Good girl, Rootbeer. Our friends are here. Go ahead, go say hi."

That was all the warning I had. The next thing I knew, I had a full-grown golden retriever covered in sand in my face. I laughed and caught her in my arms. "Hi, pretty girl."

"*Rootbeer!*" Seamus scrambled to his feet, then took her from me but was careful not to sit her back down. "Sorry, Frankie. She never acts like this."

"I'm not mad about it." I laughed and waved to the group. "Though next time I'll have to bring my boys with me."

"What kind of dogs do you have?" Seamus moved the big bowl of fruit over so I could sit.

I took the empty seat and sat down. "Three beagles. They wanted to come tonight, but I wanted to meet everyone first."

"That's fair."

"What's fair is that you move over." Tomás pushed Seamus to the side, then slid in between us. "Since he has a girlfriend and I . . . *do not.*"

"Hi, Tomás."

"*Buenas noches, guapa,*" he said with a dimpled grin and wag of his eyebrows. "It's nice to see you again."

"Tomás!" Birdie smacked him on the back of the head as she walked by to sit across from me. "Behave yourself or I will call your grandmother."

Tomás gasped. "*¿Mi abuela?*"

"*Sí, tu abuela.*" She then slid her hand in front of her throat without breaking eye contact. "Your choice."

Tomás made the cross motion with his hands with a frown. Then he turned to me and smiled. "I fear no one more than mi abuela. I will move to a safe distance away from you, because I am a good boy."

I patted the top of his head like he was a dog. "That's a very good boy."

And then he jumped up and moved to sit next to Birdie. I laughed and looked around at the group. Archie had sat down on the other side of Seamus so that he could pull both Rootbeer *and* Float into his lap. All three of them looked stupid content with this. Ava was taking pictures of it.

"*Mais c'est très mauvais pour toi!*" I looked toward the sound of Jo's French and found her looking down at Esther's haul of snacks with disgust. "*C'est de la malbouffe. Ce sont des déchets.*"

Madge rolled her eyes and tucked her black hair behind her ears. "Yes, they know it's junk food, love. That's kind of the point."

Esther sat down with a grin. "You don't have to eat it, Jo. Promise."

She narrowed her eyes at the bags of chips, then nodded. "*D'accord.*"

Madge wagged her eyebrows. "*C'est dommage—*"

"Hey, I know that one," I blurted before I could stop myself. "Means *that's too bad*, right?"

Jo's dark eyes sparkled with delight. "Yes! *Très bien.*"

Madge took Jo's face in her hands and kissed her lips. "You are adorable. I love you."

"You guys are a couple." I shook my head. "That makes sense. You look so good together."

Madge frowned. "I told you she was my soulmate?"

"Yeah, but like I thought maybe—"

"Soulmates are a real thing," Esther said softly. "The marks on their arms, with the crystals, those are not tattoos. It's the physical manifestation that they're soulmates."

My eyes widened. "Wait . . . what?"

Archie looked down at his bare hand that had no markings. "It's really something amazing to be marked like that. To know you've met your other half."

"For arcana, two people who are soulmates were originally one soul split into two. So, it's not a figurative statement." Esther beamed at her friends. "It's why they look so damn perfect together, because they are."

Jo blushed and leaned into Madge who kissed her forehead.

I opened my mouth to ask more about this whole *soulmates* thing when I spotted four girls sitting in a circle with books open in their laps. They sat between the bonfire and the ocean, and they were so serious I thought they might've been doing a ritual or seance or something.

Esther followed my stare. "Oh, those are our little nerds. We love them."

"They're not doing witchcraft?"

"Pretty sure they're doing chemistry." Esther chuckled, then popped a chip into her mouth. "The one facing the bonfire with her back to the water? That's Caitlin. She's a senior and valedictorian of her class. Also, she's a Pentacle."

"*Also,* she's going to an Ivy League university next year up north." Madge grabbed the bag of Tostitos and frowned. She looked over her shoulder and shouted, "Yo, Cunningham."

Caitlin looked up from her book. "What?"

"Where you going next year?"

Caitlin rolled her eyes. "You ask me this every other day, Madge. I'm going to Brown in Rhode Island."

Madge snapped her fingers and nodded. "Right, right, right. Different color. Thanks, boo. We're so proud of you."

Caitlin smirked. "Shut up, butthead."

"The other three girls are Barb Angstrom, Ruby Nam, and Patti Leek." Ava crawled into Seamus's lap so she was the little spoon. "They wanna go to the New York next school year, so they're parents said they had to get straight A's and all kinds of other shit to prove they can handle living on their own."

"Are they seniors?"

"Nah, they're freshmen."

I frowned. "I'm missing something. What's in New York?"

"The School of Magical Arts," they all said in perfect unison, then laughed.

Archie leaned over Rootbeer's head to meet my eyes. "There's always only been one magic school for witches to attend. That's Edenburg in Eden. It's a prep school kind of thing where students live on campus like college."

"But Tennessee opened up the first magic school outside of Eden *ever.* It's located right in the heart of Manhattan." Ava reached up and ran her hands through Seamus's red hair. "They also welcome shifters there, which I personally think would be so cool to see."

Seamus rested his chin on top of Ava's head. They were quite adorable all cuddled up together, looking like complete opposites. "It's cool because you're still living in New York among the humans and the normal world."

"That's true, Eden gets a little . . ." Archie frowned. "Lost in their own heads sometimes?"

"That makes sense."

"So, Frankie . . ." Birdie leaned forward, her gold pentacle talisman dangling from her wrist. "What do you think of our little community so far?"

"I'm basically obsessed?" I laughed and gestured around us. "I mean, It's a Monday night and I'm at a party on the beach. Can't beat that. I actually came here last night with my aunt and uncle. I didn't know this was your hangout spot."

Esther grimaced. "It's actually The Coven's spot but we use it now—"

"Kinda like their lunch spot?" I arched one eyebrow.

Archie chuckled. "Babysitting this spot too?"

"Well . . . yeah. I don't know how to explain it, it's just . . ." Esther pursed her lips and looked around like she was searching for her words.

Birdie frowned and nodded along with her. "You haven't met them yet, but . . . their magic and their aura . . . it leaves like an effect in the air. It's . . . it's . . ."

"Home." Esther smiled softly, her cheeks flushing. She tried to hide her blush beneath the curtain of black curls, but I saw it. Her gray eyes sparkled like lightning in a thundercloud. "It feels like home."

Everyone was silent.

"Is that what it is?" Archie whispered.

"*Oui*," Jo whispered back. "*Voilà ce que c'est.*"

"That's what it is." Madge nodded her head to her soulmate. "I've never been able to find the right word but leave it to an Irit to find it."

Esther tucked her curls behind her ears. She opened her mouth to say something when Rootbeer jumped to attention. She barked once, then sat in front of Seamus and put her paw on him. She was alerting

161

him, though to what I didn't know. Seamus sighed and seemed to brace himself.

"You shouldn't be here," a voice I recognized too well said from behind me. "Leave."

I looked over my shoulder to find Aaron and Jacob behind us. *Ah. She was warning him they were coming.* I jumped to my feet because under zero circumstances was I knowingly going to give them the upper hand. They'd given me no reason to doubt they'd attack me. The others also all got up, and that told me more about these two bullies than anything else. But I faced them anyways.

"I said leave," Jacob snapped again.

"No?"

Aaron balled his hands into fists at his sides. "You don't belong here. This is a private beach."

"First of all, it's literally a public beach." I pointed to the signs up by the parking lot. "And funny enough, it doesn't say your name anywhere up there."

"This is *our* beach—"

"Please, they just told me this was The Coven's spot before they left. You gotta be better with your lies."

They lunged forward but Esther moved in front of me with her wand out. "Let's not do this."

Aaron pulled out his wand from his back pocket and twirled it around. There was a wild, manic sort of expression in those hazel eyes. "Really, Esther? *You* are gonna challenge literally anyone with a Wand?"

Jacob laughed. "Yeah, what are *you* gonna do with it? Get us out of class? Fix our grades? Please."

I frowned. There was something I definitely didn't know about Esther, but I already knew these dicks deserved to get a taste of their own medicine.

Tomás jumped between us. "Stop. C'mon. *Mis amigos, relájate, por favor.* We're on the same team—"

Aaron leaned closer to Tomás. "Listen, pretty boy, just because you're sweet on the new bitch in town doesn't mean she's one of *us*, so stay out of this before I wreck that pretty smile of yours."

"Careful, all those muscles from the volleyball team are going to hurt us." Jacob flapped his arms like they were chicken wings. "Don't be ridiculous, *amigo*. You're a Pentacle. What are you gonna do? Birdie's the one who does all the heavy lifting in that department anyways, so move or we rearrange your teeth, chicken legs."

Seamus gripped Tomás by the back of the shirt and pulled him backwards, then slid into that spot. He didn't speak. He just stepped forward until his chest was pressed against Aaron's. I hadn't realized just how big Seamus was until that moment. He was about two inches taller than Aaron, another inch or two taller than Jacob, and he had to be at least fifty pounds heavier than both of them. His biceps were so much bigger than I'd realized at school. Granted, tonight he wore a tank top that left little to the imagination when it came to his muscular frame.

Aaron's upper lip curled back. "There's still two of us—"

"And two of *us*," Atley slid in between them as if he was six-foot-seven instead five-foot-seven. All four of the guys were taller and bigger. Hell, they'd all finished puberty. Atley was only thirteen. His voice still had some deepening to do.

Peabo walked up beside him all nonchalant like they were discussing breakfast. He pulled a curved dagger out of nowhere and flipped it in his hand. "I'd love to demonstrate how much size doesn't matter."

Aaron and Jacob paled a little and took a step back with their hands raised as if the two young teens held them at gunpoint.

Atley reached down to his left leg to where a blood-red serrated dagger sat snug in a holster thing. *Oh, Peabo probably had one of those too.* He pulled the dagger out, then scratched the side of his jaw with the tip of his blade. It was such a badass ballsy move and something about those bands on his wrists told me he could back it up.

"What? No threats for us?" Atley pointed to Peabo with his dagger, then back to himself. "'Cause we sure as shit aren't as big or as tall as you two dumb fucks. Let's hear your mouths run now. Really, let's have it."

When they said nothing, Peabo chuckled, and I had to give him credit for how menacing it sounded coming from such a young kid. "Do you wanna see who goes down first? Us with our blades or you with your precious little wands that you use to pick your noses with?"

Archie snort-laughed.

Aaron snarled in his direction. "Who you think you're laughing at, strawberry shortcake?"

Seamus's golden retriever Rootbeer jumped in front of Archie and growled, the fur on her back standing tall. Aaron narrowed his eyes at the dog and lowered his wand as if he was going to do something to her when Seamus fisted Aaron's shirt and hauled him up to his own chest.

*"Threaten my dog one more time, and I will pour poison down your throat in your sleep and peel your bones from your flesh for her to chew on,"* Seamus said with a growl.

Jacob grabbed Aaron's arm and yanked him backwards to stand beside him. "No one's going to hurt your dog, O'Brien. Take a deep breath and listen."

*He did not just take a jab at him being hard of hearing.*

Jacob pointed to Archie with one hand and me with the other. "What have these two done to warrant such loyalty?"

"What did Archie do to warrant such betrayal?" Esther snarled. "Frankie defended him, a perfect stranger, when you two were throwing him into the lockers. And that stunt on the baseball field? You're heathens."

"You little mouse—"

"Did you know Royce is in town?" Peabo cocked his head to the side and flipped his curved dagger in his hand, catching the hilt with ease. "Thiago is here with him too. Two Cards right around the corner . . . Shall I call them?"

Aaron and Jacob scowled and exchanged nervous glances.

"We're all a little sick of your shit," Seamus said with a snarl. "We've let it go on too long."

"We *should* have reported you to The Coven months ago." Tomás sighed and shook his head. "We kept hoping you'd calm down. But this is too much."

"You're right, it is." Atley pulled his cellphone out of his pocket and held it out for everyone to see. "Hey, Siri. Call Tennessee Wildes on speakerphone."

It rang *once*. Not even a full ring, really, before a deep, velvety voice answered with a growl. "Are you in immediate danger?"

"No."

"Good, hold on so I can kill this spider-demon."

The line went quiet.

No one on the beach made a sound for at least ten seconds but then Esther stepped up between Atley and Peabo and pointed to the phone in Atley's hand. "Ever since *he* left, you two have been picking on everyone here. Verbally, emotionally, mentally, and physically. You've even been bullying humans. We've all been letting it slide."

"You're lucky The Coven has been busy with the war and Lilith." Peabo lowered his dagger and shook his head. "Everyone else in town may have been too nervous to call and pester them about something so pathetic as two jackasses on a power trip, but *we* have no problem calling."

"Tenn kills demons fast." Atley held his phone higher. "He'll be back any second now."

"Aaron, Jacob?" Esther cleared her throat and crossed her arms over her chest. "What will it be, boys? Are we telling Tennessee what you've been up to, or are you gonna cut the shit and behave? Choice is yours."

I was starting to realize Esther was somewhat of a leader of this little community, and it left me with more questions. She had a commanding presence, but it was somehow still subtle. When she spoke, the others listened. Yet these guys openly mocked her as weak with a wand in front of everyone, and no one responded as if it weren't true. Which suggested that it was such a ridiculous thought that no one felt they needed to justify it . . . *or* it was true. I had questions.

"Sorry, Atley," Tennessee's deep, velvety voice rumbled through the phone. "I'm back."

Aaron and Jacob held their hands up in surrender and backed away. Quickly. They grumbled, then spun and basically sprinted off the beach.

"Sorry, Tenn." Atley cleared his throat. "We, uh, well—"

"What did they decide?"

Atley flinched ever so slightly. "W-what?"

"Aaron and Jacob."

Everyone gasped.

"I . . ." Atley scowled. "I thought you put me on hold?"

"That is not the answer to my question," Tennessee growled.

Atley sighed. "Yeah, they left. But listen, I, uh, I wasn't actually gonna snitch on them."

"You just wanted to use me as intimidation?"

He chuckled nervously. "Yeah?"

Silence.

He chuckled *very* softly. "Let me know if you get to the stitches part."

"Thanks, Tenn."

The line went dead.

Atley shoved his phone in his pocket, then sheathed his dagger. "He said *hold on*, didn't he?"

Peabo chuckled. "Knowing Tenn, he just forgot to hit the hold button and accidentally heard everything. Ya know how he forgets to put shirts and shoes on all the time?"

This seemed to calm Atley's nerves as he smiled and nodded. It was only at that moment I realized everyone else had come closer to watch the confrontation. Everyone looked to each other with nods and unspoken understanding, then turned and went back to what they were doing.

A warm arm wrapped around my shoulders. "You all right, Frankie?"

"Yeah." I looked up into Tomás's eyes and smiled. "I just hate that I'm new here and already have enemies. I hate what they've made me into."

"They're not worthy of your sympathy." He squeezed my shoulder, then dropped his arm and stepped back, holding his hand out to me. "Come, let us put our toes in the water and wash away the bad vibes."

With a grin, I kicked off my flip-flops and put my hand in his. The smile he gave me was truly beautiful in the way it lit up his face. I wanted to like him, wanted to feel the butterflies of attraction, but nothing came. It was just frustrating like that. Granted, I couldn't remember the last boy I actually had a crush on.

But as the ocean swept over my bare feet, I took my first deep breath since arriving at the beach. The breeze sliding off the water was crisp and cool, carrying that scent of salt in the air that I loved. My mind wandered to Elizabeth. I wondered what she was doing in China, *how* she was doing in China. Had she made any new friends like I was? Would it bother me if she had? What would I tell her about all this when she got back?

"Tomás, I do think you were warned."

I frowned and looked over my shoulder to find Esther standing right behind us. "What's that?"

"Your abuela is still awake at this time of night."

"I was behaving!" Tomás threw his hands up in surrender and backed away from me. "We were just chatting. Being friendly."

Esther arched one eyebrow and crossed her arms over her chest. "Give her some breathing room."

He turned to me, pressed his hand to his stomach, and bowed dramatically. "I shall be with the others."

I watched him run away from us back to the blanket and sit beside Ava and Seamus. "Thanks? I think? He seems harmless."

"He's a total sweetheart." Esther sat down on the sand, then patted the spot next to her. Once I sat down, she chuckled softly. "I only came over because I knew you'd totally zoned out on him and hadn't heard a word he was saying."

My eyes widened. "He was talking that whole time?"

She threw her head back and laughed, then covered her mouth with her hand.

"Fucking hell. I feel awful. I didn't mean to space out."

"I know, I know." She wiped her eyes and sighed. "That's why I decided to play it off like he was being too forward with his flirting. That way he wouldn't know you weren't actually listening."

I bit my bottom lip and knew I was blushing. "Thank you. I'm trying to keep up."

"It's a lot, I know." She glanced over her shoulder to the group. "We may not be *The* Coven, but we're our own little coven. We look out for each other. We help each other."

"Are you like . . . the leader of the group? It seems like everyone follows your lead."

"Ah, the perks of being a member of a founding family." She laughed humorlessly. "You'll see. Why do you think they're all *so* protective of you?"

"Because my last name is Proctor?" I frowned. "That's weird, dude."

"You're not wrong. I've always been grateful for my dad's last name of Goldstein. People have to actually get to know me to know I'm an Irit."

"Right, and Irit is one of the founding families?" When she nodded, I just shook my head. "What are the others?"

She frowned. "I don't know all of them, and that's intentional from The Coven. They try to protect them from all this pressure we live with."

"Why aren't they all protected?"

"Well, the Lancasters were the *first* arcana, birthed from the angel Jophiel's womb. The Bishop family has the most magical power and strength. Proctors have always been the best warriors. The Irits have always had the best intuition. Many of us have been Hierophants in The Coven because psychic abilities are prevalent in our blood."

I had no idea what Hierophant meant, but I was going to circle back to that question.

"Then there are families like the Putnams who had been success-fully hidden, but the first set of twins were born from the Putnam line and that made the whole family infamous. Most of them went into hiding after Salem and never came out, though Paulina Putnam was Death for years and lived her in Tampa. She told me once the Putnam line had always had a close connection with darkness." Esther shiv-ered. "Which makes sense considering the twins."

*Death? Another word I don't know the meaning of here.*

"And of course the English family—"

"OH, I've heard of them. They started the shipping company and are like the richest witches ever."

"I'm not surprised you've heard of them." She laughed. "Deacon English is the Devil now. He lived in Tampa briefly before the whole Coven left for Salem. They're stupid, stupid rich, but Deacon doesn't show it."

*Devil? Okay, these words definitely connect to each other and this Coven. But how?*

"The other founding families . . . I'm not sure. I've heard a few names be rumored but nothing concrete. If I ever have a chance to talk to Tegan Bishop, the High Priestess, I definitely want to ask. It'd be nice to know if you and I are the only ones out here from these lines that *aren't* in The Coven."

*Make that four words.*

"It's weird to me to be told two Proctors are in The Coven and not know them, to never have known them."

"There's more than just you three too." She held two fingers up, then lifted another finger as she counted. "There's also Kenneth Proctor, who retired from The Coven recently. Then Saraphina Proctor, also used to be Coven, and her mother, Myrtle Proctor, who is the Lead Crone."

"Yeah, that helps reduce some pressure."

She snickered. "Sorry. But I get it . . . more than you do actually. I want to say you get used to it, the pressure from the others, but you don't. It's actually getting worse with the war. I have this sinking, gnawing suspicion those of us from the twenty lines aren't going to get to remain on the sidelines for the main event."

"You mean like fight in the war?" My stomach turned.

"Yes." Her voice was low and uneven. "Which . . . fine. Fair. It's just, can't they bring us in now so we have time to train and prepare? Every time my phone rings I'm waiting for it to be *them*. It's why my parents live in Tampa, because *they* do. Mom also is expecting to be dragged into the war."

"You think it's inevitable." I glanced back to the group to make sure no one was close, then asked what I'd wanted to earlier. "What did the dickwads mean about your magic?"

"You caught that, eh? I'm not surprised. You're quick." She wrung her hands together. "My family, the Irit line I mean, used to be majorly involved. We used to always be members of The Coven or work alongside them. Half of Crone Island are Irits. But my magic is weak. I can't do most spells and things other Wands can do. It's frustrating."

"Why not? Did something happen to cause it?"

She nodded. "Centuries ago, an angel entrusted my grandmother —obviously many times removed—with an object. This angel told her to protect it with her life, to keep it safe until the right person came to reclaim it. It's been passed down from mother to daughter since."

"Do you have it?"

She nodded. "Yeah."

"Who are you holding it for?"

"Absolutely no idea." She chuckled. "But when the Hierophant was living here in the fall, I asked him for guidance. That's when he told me that the reason the Irit bloodline has had such weak magic is because our magic is too busy protecting what the angel gave us. He says we'll know the person when it happens and to trust our intuition."

I shivered. "That's intense."

"Very." She cleared her throat. "Anyhoo, that's why it seems like I'm the leader of this group. Fair warning, it's probably going to be *you* they look to soon."

"Oh, something to look forward to."

"C'mon, let's rejoin the group and relax. Have some fun. We're gonna read tarot cards and play with our pendulums." I must've made a face because she chuckled and shook her head. "Don't worry. You can just watch."

"Thank God," I mumbled as we both stood back up and walked over to the group.

Tomás looked up at me with a grin far too wide for comfort. "Frankie, we have made a decision."

"Oh boy. I'm scared." I sat back down beside Archie.

Birdie gave me a wicked smirk. "We're going to figure out which Suit you are by having you try all of them."

My eyes widened. I froze with my hand on the bag of Skittles. "What does *that* mean?"

"You'll see."

# CHAPTER SIXTEEN

## FRANKIE

*T*HE SUN SAT *high in the sky, yet the barest hint of its light reached my face. The air was thick with dark-gray smoke that billowed from the ruins and rubble around me. Ash rained down, landing on my skin. I took deep, labored breaths, but each one sent sharp pains into my ribs and down my spine. My chest burned. I was bound to spit fire any minute now. I pressed my palm to my side and found my clothes wet and sticky. When I lifted my hand, I tried to ignore the way my fingers trembled.*

*Blood stained every crack and crevice of my palm, running like rivers through a valley down my wrist as I held it up to my face. I licked my lips and tasted the metallic twinge of blood. My stomach rolled.*

*It was not my blood.*

*And for that, I would have theirs.*

*"Wake up, Francelina."*

I woke with a gasp so hard I choked on it. My heart pounded against my chest like it was trying to break out of its cage. I rolled onto my side and felt sweat drip down the side of my neck. My hair was wet and plastered to my skin. My pillowcase was soaked. With a groan, I kicked my blankets off of me, then patted myself down only to find sweat covered every inch of my body. I sat up and spotted all three of my dogs sleeping in a cuddle puddle on the fuzzy rug on my floor. Given how much sweat was on me, I didn't blame them for abandoning me.

171

That dream was . . . intense.

Never in my life had I had such a visceral dream. It'd felt so real, like I was there. A cold chill slid down my spine and I shivered. The air conditioner clicked back on and cold air washed over me, causing goosebumps to cover my skin. I was a sweaty, disgusting mess. I climbed out of bed and tiptoed across to my closet to change into some dry clothing. When I reemerged from my closet, however, I found all three of them sitting in a row waiting for me. They looked up with big eyes and their tails wagging.

The clock on my nightstand said it was three in the morning, which meant the boys and I had only been asleep for about two and a half hours. But the looks on their faces told me they wanted to be up and moving. I glanced to my bed and the sweat-soaked sheets and cringed. There was no chance I was getting back in there without changing the sheets, except the closet with all the clean spare sheets was on the other side of the house next to my aunt and uncle's room. I didn't like my odds of not waking them up and having to answer a million questions. They'd always cared, a lot, but the coma just sent them into hyperactive mode. I didn't blame them. I just didn't want to talk about that dream yet.

I sighed and looked down at my boys. "Wanna go for a walk?"

They jumped and spun in circles, bouncing up and down.

"I'll take that as a yes." I waved for the door. "But be quiet."

The four of us crept down the hallway toward the front door where I stashed their leashes and stuff. It took me just a few seconds to get their harnesses on and then we were slipping out the front door. The night was warm and stagnant. There wasn't a breeze to be felt, none of the trees swayed or rustled. Everything was just silent. It was a little eerie, but I couldn't put my finger on why.

The boys trotted down the sidewalk like this was the best night ever, their tails wagging a mile a minute. They had their snouts to the ground like vacuum cleaners as we walked. I chuckled and pulled out my phone to call Elizabeth because that was habit. If she wasn't walking the dogs with me, then I called her while I did it. But it was three in the morning—*wait, no. She's in China.* I could have called but the street was so damn quiet the idea of speaking out loud felt wrong. Instead, I sent her a picture text of me and the boys out on our stroll with a caption quoting Patsy Cline's *Walking after Midnight* song.

My phone vibrated immediately. When I opened the screen, her response was there. 'WHY ARE YOU OUT ON A WALK AT 3AM FRANKIE?'

'They had to go potty?' I lied.

'BULLSHIT, YOU HAVE A BACKYARD AT THAT HOUSE.'

I grimaced. She always called me on my bluffs. 'Well . . .'

'DON'T LIE TO ME.'

'FINE. I had a bad dream. It was just really intense and I was sweaty and gross and I just needed fresh air to shake it off, okay? Is that better?'

She sent me emojis with the crying face. 'I still don't like you being out there by yourself—and the boys don't count.'

I ran my finger over the magical sticker on the back of my case and smirked. 'I have a weapon?'

The eye-rolling emojis were sent so they filled my entire screen.

'Look, I've met my neighbors. They're cool af. If trouble comes for me, I'll knock on their door.'

'I don't like it, Frankie.'

I sighed. 'I don't like a lot of things. Like you being in China, for starters.'

'TELL ME ABOUT IT.'

'I'd love for YOU to tell ME about it. What's it like? What are you doing every day?'

First, she sent a gif of a girl sitting at a window, watching the rain and crying. 'I'm working on my homeschooling. Learned some new video games. I don't really know. I'm finding things to fill my time. I'm not really allowed out.'

'What do you mean? Your parents won't let you leave?'

'I can . . . but I can't. It's tricky. And I'm not sure who's more overbearing, my parents or Tai.'

I grinned. 'How is Tai?'

'He's Tai.'

I rolled my eyes. 'Speaking of boys, meet any in China?'

'Did you already forget the part where I'm not really allowed out?'

'So then you're not playing video games online with people?'

'Oh . . . that doesn't count.' She sent the emojis of a person hiding. 'I'm not into dating right now, not yet. Too soon.'

My stomach turned at that. 'But you're okay?'

*'Yeah, I'm okay. What about you?'*

*'I'm cool.'*

*'I meant are there any cute boys? What about this Archie kid that's your neighbor?'*

'OH. Well . . .' I bit my lip and shrugged even though she couldn't see me. *'Archie is super cool. I like hanging with him. But we're just friends.'*

*'Is he not cute?'*

*'He's cute but like . . .'*

*'Isn't he really short?'*

I scowled. *'That's not why—I mean, yes, he is short. But it's not that . . . It's like . . . it's like . . . it's like the idea of me dating Tai.'*

*'GROSS,'* she sent with the vomiting emoji.

*'He's not MY brother, dude.'*

*'Might as well be at this point.'*

I chuckled. *'Fair. Anyhoo, there is a cute boy named Tomás. I haven't figured out where his family is from yet, but he's got a sexy accent and speaks Spanish. And these adorable dimples.'*

*'So you're into him!!!'*

*'I wouldn't go that far. But I'm trying to be into him?'*

A cold chill slid down my spine like someone had reached out and ran their fingers down it. I shivered and glanced around, but there wasn't a person in sight. The dogs had their noses to the ground—they flinched and looked behind us to our left. Their ears perked up and their tails curled towards their backs. My heart stopped. I glanced back in that direction, yet there was nothing but shadows.

My phone vibrated and made me jump. I cursed and looked down to find a text from Elizabeth.

*'That's fair. Are you back home yet?'*

I peeked over my shoulder to the shadows beneath those oak trees. *'No, but we're heading back that way.'*

The boys were on high alert now. The fur on their backs stood tall. There was nothing back there, but I felt what they did. It was like eyes watching us. *Someone* was watching us. I hurried my steps, half-dragging the boys along with me, but they kept turning to look behind us, which naturally just sent my pulse into hyperdrive. *Just keep walking, Franks.*

I made it about another two houses down when I felt something poke me from inside my pocket. Without slowing my pace, I reached into my pocket and found something cold and solid. When I pulled it out, I found the rose quartz crystal Esther had given me earlier at the beach. More specifically, it was a pendulum. I held it up, letting the crystal dangle from the silver chain. The rose quartz seemed to glow despite the bare sliver of a crescent moon up in the sky. It was almost like it was lit from within.

That tingling sensation slithered down my spine again. I stood up straight and glanced over my shoulder. There was nothing. No one. But I *felt* someone. I stared into the shadows between the houses waiting for something to step into the light. It was probably nothing, probably a figment of my imagination, yet I still found myself reaching for my phone so I could get my finger on that sticker. If I needed it, I could have a dagger in my hand in seconds. A bat even faster.

"*You shouldn't be out here,*" a deep male voice whispered in my ear.

I spun around with my heart in my throat and gasped. But it was just Archie.

My breath left me in a rush. "*ARCHIE.*"

"Sorry, didn't mean to scare you." He gave me a nervous chuckle and pointed to his left. "I was sitting on my side steps and saw you walk by, so I came over."

I looked up and realized I was home. I was literally standing on the sidewalk in front of my house. "I . . . scared the shit out of myself for a second there."

"I noticed." He crouched down and ruffled the boys' ears. "You okay?"

"Yeah. Yeah, I'm fine. Weird dreams, ya know? So, I went for a walk." I glanced around our street. "What are *you* doing out here?"

He looked up at me sheepishly, then stood up straight. "I was just trying to practice with my wand without anyone watching."

"Oh." I nodded. "How's that going?"

He grimaced and pointed to the wooden fence on the side of his house that was in shambles. "I might need help fixing that."

I snort laughed. "I'm not much help there."

"Mom will fix it in the morning. Or she'll call someone who can." He looked up at me with a smile, then frowned at my hand. "Whatch'ya got in your hand? Is that a pendulum?"

"Yeah, I found It in my pocket. Esther gave it to me at the beach earlier but I was too nervous to try with them watching. I guess we have that in common."

"Hopefully not *that* in common too." He laughed and pointed back to the busted fence. "Wanna go in your backyard? I can show you how to use that."

"You know pendulums?"

"Hey, I may suck with a wand, but pendulums are more my wheelhouse."

"Cool. Because I'm confused." I tugged on my dogs' leashes and led them to the side gate for the backyard. "So, Archie, what's coming for me with this challenge the group has taken upon themselves?"

"With the talismans?"

"Yep. Should I be scared?"

He shrugged as we went through the side gate. "Can't be worse than me with a wand."

"But what do they want me to *do?*" I reached down and unhooked the boys' leashes so they could run free. "It's all very ominous, Archie."

"Nah, nah. As we told you, each Suit has a designated style of talisman that they use for their brand of magic."

"Is that how they do it at the schools? Just have everyone trying them all out—"

"Goddess, no. There's a crystal ball that tells you, not much different than the sorting hat in Harry Potter except it doesn't talk." He grinned and gestured to sit on the stone steps in my backyard. "Because of their close proximity to The Coven all these years, the parents here took their kids to get sorted into their Suits and helped them get talismans so they'd have something to work with. That's how they know what they are—"

"And you went to Edenburg?"

"I did, yes. But I think they're all assuming you're not gonna run up to Eden just so you can get sorted right away."

"No, definitely not. That'd be overwhelming as fuck."

"So, they wanna play this little game where they try and guess which Suit you are." He pet Bubba as he ran by with a stick. "It just means they're gonna have you try our talismans out. No big deal, really."

"Oh." I nodded. "That doesn't sound too bad."

"Exactly. And neither is a pendulum." He rubbed his hands together, then reached into his pocket and pulled out his own pendulum. His was a tiger's eye on a silver chain. He held it up in front of him so only his thumb and middle finger touched the chain, allowing it to hang straight down. "Pendulums tap into the energies of the world around us."

I held mine up like he was. "How do I make it move?"

"You talk to it. Now, you don't have to speak out loud, but when you're first learning, it's a bit easier to actually say it. You wanna make sure your arm is rested, and like your shoulder isn't lifted or anything, and you wanna be calm. Breathe. Keep yourself steady."

"Okay. Like this?"

He looked at me and nodded. Then he lowered his pendulum. "You're gonna do this by yourself so the crystals don't get mixed signals. What you wanna do is establish a baseline. Once you get comfortable with your pendulum—like that *specific* one—you might not have to do this every time you use it. But you'll have to feel it out. Now, you're going to take a deep breath, then say to your pendulum, *show me yes*."

I took a deep breath as he instructed with my pendulum hanging from my hand, then said, "Show me yes."

The rose quartz crystal instantly swung to the left, then back to the right.

"Then you say, *stop*."

I nodded. "Stop." The pendulum stopped short and hung straight down again.

"Now you say, *show me no*."

I licked my lips. "Show me no."

Yet again, the crystal moved on its own. I could've sworn I felt a tingle through the chain. This time it swung toward me, then away from me, swinging back and forth that way. I told it to stop again, *and it did*. My jaw dropped. This was some kind of magic, that was for sure.

"Now you can say, *show me maybe*."

I stared at my pendulum. "Show me maybe."

The pendulum swung diagonally.

I shook my head. "This is wild. How many things can it do? Can I say, *show me I don't know?*"

To my shock, the pendulum changed course mid-swing and began circling in the air. I giggled. "This is cool. So now what?"

He shrugged. "Now you ask it questions and remember which swing meant which answer."

"Okay. Okay. Let me try." I cleared my throat. "Are my aunt and uncle going to catch us out here tonight?"

The pendulum swung toward me, then away.

"Nice. All right, um, is Archie's mom going to be mad at him for wrecking their fence?"

The pendulum flew to the left.

"Ah, c'mon!" He laughed and hung his head. "Dammit."

"This is fun. And naturally, I have no idea what to ask it now that I'm here."

"That's okay. It's best if you practice and get connected to your pendulum when you're alone, so it can focus on just you."

"Thanks for showing me that. I didn't want to ask in front of everyone, felt like their eyes were all on me."

"Anything else you want to ask about?"

"Yeah, what are all those words everyone's been using? Hierophant, Death, Devil, High Priestess . . .?"

"Oh." He frowned. "Those are the Cards of The Coven."

"Cards?"

"Right. New here. Got it. Okay, so you know how the four Suits are from tarot cards? Wands, Pentacles, Swords, and Cups?" When I nodded, he continued, "Those are all the minor arcana cards. In a tarot deck, those range from ace, page, knight, queen, king, and then one through ten. But there are twenty-two major arcana cards and each of those has a specific name—"

"Are you about to tell me that tarot cards are based on witches and not the other way around?"

He grinned. "See how quick you are? Yes, The Coven has the original tarot deck. Over time, the humans copied it and made their own versions. They don't know that's where it's from, our magic erases the *us* part of their memory, but it's par for the course with humans and witches. Actually, give me your phone?"

I handed it to him. "So, the words Hierophant, Death, Devil, High Priestess . . . they're part of the twenty-two?"

"Yep." He was downloading an app, but I couldn't see what it was. "This is a free tarot card app. Open it up and read through all the cards, and you'll get like a cheat sheet on the foundation of our society."

"That's really cool. I'm going to study this because I hate being confused."

"Ask me anything, anytime. There are no stupid questions." He smiled. "Go ahead, hit me with it."

"What's their magic like? I mean, it must be special."

"The Coven? It's elemental magic." He shrugged. "And that's not always literal. So, like, the Empress has control of fire, smoke, and metal. Oh, Royce is the Wheel of Fortune. He has power over plants and nature."

"What about his boyfriend, Thiago?"

"He's the Hanged Man. His powers are interesting. It's like light and shadows. Really tricky stuff but important." He pursed his lips as he thought about all their magic. "The Sun has the sun. The Moon has the moon. The Star can go into dreams. Death can summon the dead and communicate with them. High Priestess has water, air, and spirit—which includes wisdom and intuition."

"What about this Tennessee I've heard so much about?"

"Uh, the Emperor has the power of water, wind, and earth."

"Damn. That's so cool. All of that is so cool. I wanna see that in person."

"It's a crazy thing to watch. For sure."

"So, if you could pick . . . which Card in The Coven would you want to be?"

"The Fool, probably," he said quickly like he'd thought about it before.

"Why? What can they do?"

"Because The Fool can speak to animals, and that just seems like it'd be really special."

I stared at my dogs for a long minute as they ran around the yard chasing bugs. "Well, shit, now I have to change my answer."

He threw his head back and laughed. "What were you gonna say?"

"I was thinking Death. I'd love to be able to talk to my parents. They died when I was four."

Archie cursed. "Now *I* have to change my answer."

I bumped him with my shoulder and smiled, because I didn't feel like taking this conversation to dark places. "The High Priestess feels like a badass Card."

"Or the Magician." His eyes were distant. "I've seen Willow in action in Eden. It's pretty epic what she can do—what?"

I fixed my face. "Sorry. I was just . . . guess I'm surprised you didn't say Emperor. Figured most guys would want that one."

He scowled and shook his head. "I bet most guys would. But no, I wouldn't ask for that. Sure, I'm sure the magic power part is cool, but the rest of it is way too much."

"That's fair. Do you wish you were marked for The Coven?"

"No. I don't wish that at all." He grinned and stretched his arms and legs. "I've seen what they're up against, and it's a living nightmare."

"The grin doesn't fit that sentence."

"*What the hell happened to the fence?*" Archie's mom yelled out from their porch. "ARCHIE!"

"Oh, shit." He jumped up and stumbled down the steps. "I can explain!"

# CHAPTER SEVENTEEN

## FRANKIE

"When do Aaron and Jacob come back to school?"

"Too soon," Archie grumbled.

Tomás pushed the gym door open, then held it for us. "They had a three-day suspension, so they'll be back in school Friday."

I slid my sunglasses off the top of my head onto my face. "I don't *want* to fight them. I'm just not afraid to. There's a difference. Everyone else sees this, right? I'm not a hothead."

Archie made a face.

I gasped dramatically and pressed my hand to my chest. "I'm not!"

He chuckled and shrugged one shoulder. "You're not. But you're like a bomb that's fully ready to explode at all times. All someone has to do is push the button and *boom*."

"Yeah, I know." I grabbed Archie's arm and yanked him toward me just before he tripped over a student who'd stopped to tie their shoes. "My therapist back home was working on that. I probably need to find a new one here. I just . . . I'm just . . . It's like . . ."

"Like you have some vendetta against the world but no targets to use that aggression on?"

"Yes. That." I chuckled nervously. "But I'm not a jerk to my friends—"

"No," Archie and Tomás said at the same time.

"Honestly, I think it was your magic." Tomás gave me a soft smile, the one he used when he *wasn't* trying to flirt with me. "You said your

181

magic had been lost since you were four? I bet all that magic trapped inside of you with no outlet festered like a wound."

I stopped so fast Archie crashed into my back. He cursed and leapt back only to collide with the person behind him. It was just limbs flying in every direction and a lot of cursing. I grabbed his arm and yanked him back to his feet. The girl he'd crashed into was already on her feet and running away from us with a glare.

"Sorry, Archie," I said with a grimace and tried to fix his denim jacket.

"I'm good, I'm good." He held his hands up and nodded. "I'm just lightweight and fly easily. Please continue, Tomás."

"I was just thinking maybe that's why she feels angry all the time. Repressed magic."

"Do you think that's it? Really?"

Archie snatched his backpack off the ground. "That makes a lot of sense."

Tomás nodded. "I had the same problem when I was a kid. A witch therapist actually pointed it out."

"You're good now though. What did you do to fix it?"

Tomás reached into the pocket of his black jeans and pulled out a bright royal blue crystal with swirls of lighter blue and gold. "Take this."

The stone was about the size of my palm. It was a fat little oval that wasn't even as thick as my pinky finger. It had a slightly curved indention on one side that helped it fit snug to the curve of my palm. Instinctively, I wrapped my fingers around it and squeezed.

"That's a lapis lazuli palm stone. This stone has quite a history with lots of different meanings, but among those are harmony, clarity, spiritual growth, inner power . . . stuff like that. It's often used as an aura tool to unlock your intuition and purify your energy." He tapped on my fingers wrapped around it. "It's said if you hold this stone in the palm of your hand, it'll bring about deep inner knowledge, clarity of the mind, and relief from chaos."

"This helped you not react so . . . explosively?"

He chuckled. "Well, I was never quite like you, but yes, it helped me."

"If it's too much, you can tone it down by holding amethyst with it."

We both looked to Archie.

He shrugged. "I know stuff too."

"I need to get me one of these—"

"You can have that one."

"No, it's yours. It was in your pocket—"

"So I'd have it to give away." Tomás cheeks flushed pink. "Esther's mom told me a stone like this must be passed on from one witch to another, to help my fellow arcana in a time of need. She said I'd know when . . . and here you are. Needing it. So, it's for you, for now, then you can pass it along."

I smiled up at him as we made a shortcut across the grass. "Thank you. Really. This is so sweet. I never knew crystals had so much meaning."

"So your ring is a coincidence then?"

I held my right hand up to look at my crystal ring. Elizabeth wore a matching one. We both wore them on our middle fingers because the stone was so huge we thought it needed the balance. "My bestie and I bought matching ones years ago. We always wear them. I don't even know the name of this stone—"

"Clear quartz." Tomás frowned. "I'll be honest, crystals aren't really my thing. I only knew the other one because I was told. Archie?"

"Clear quartz is kind of like a powerhouse stone. It's for all chakras. It's like the mega stone, definitely the most versatile healing stone." He was inspecting my ring with sharp concentration. "It's also an amplifier so you can put it with another stone to give it a power boost. A lot of people will use it for cleansing, like for their tarot decks and stuff."

I shook my head. "Do you have a book on this shit?"

"Yeah, we can get—" his words cut off as his toe caught the edge of the sidewalk from the grass. In slow motion, he flew straight into me at just the right angle that I toppled over and crashed into Tomás before all three of us tumbled to the sidewalk. "We can get you a few books."

We laughed and lay there on the cement in defeat.

"Archie, my man, we've got to work on your coordination before you hurt yourself," Tomás said between laughs. "Or *us*."

"Crystals or some shit." I pursed my lips and nodded. "Maybe we oughta ask Esther."

Archie was the first to get back to his feet. He ran his hands through his dark-red hair to brush strands of grass out. "I don't know. Keeps me tough."

"TOMÁS!"

We all jumped and spun around until we spotted Seamus hobbling toward us carrying Rootbeer in his arms. The golden retriever was panting and looking a little distressed, which meant Seamus was super distraught. His blue eyes were wide and panicked.

"Seamus? What's wrong?" Tomás hurried over to them. "What happened to her?"

He sighed. "She's a little overheated. She's just a baby—"

"She's almost two years old—"

"*She's just a baby, Tomás.*"

"Right. Right, she's a baby." Tomás rubbed her ears. "Where's her bag with her fan and stuff?"

"I forgot it. I was running late for my test, and I just forgot it." Seamus's eyes glistened like he was going to cry. "I don't have a car—"

"Come on, I'll drive you home so you can both cool off." We were close enough to the parking lot that Tomás was able to unlock his car and have the *beep beep* be audible.

"Oh, Archie, can you tell Ava for me?" Seamus yelled back to us.

"I'll find Ava. No worries." Archie gave him a salute. "Frankie, I'll catch up with you at the picnic tables, 'kay?"

"Yeah, of course. Go get Ava." I sighed and headed into the cafeteria *alone.* All of my anxiousness came rushing back tenfold. But the lapis lazuli crystal felt nice in my palm, so I squeezed it tight and focused on the cold air-conditioning hitting me and not the weird looks from students. *"Where are you, Esther?"*

When I didn't see her or anyone in our group, I shot her a quick text. '*I'm getting in the cafeteria food line, want anything?*'

By the time I actually got into the line, Esther had responded. '*Grab me some chicken nuggets plz? Meet you in the line.*'

I nodded and shoved my phone back in my pocket as my thoughts drifted to what they guys had taught me about repressed magic. I needed to learn more about this and see if that was actually my problem. Naturally, a human therapist wouldn't have any knowledge of it, so it would've gone undiagnosed.

"Cool Stones shirt."

I looked up and found a dude in a white polo shirt leaning against the wall in front of me. It took me a second to remember I'd put on my old Rolling Stones graphic T-shirt this morning, the one with the logo in neon colors. "Oh. Thanks."

"Name three songs."

I exhaled through my nose and squeezed my palm stone. *Don't react. Don't explode on him. Not worth it.* "Pardon me?"

"I said . . ." he grinned and pointed to my t-shirt, ". . . name three songs by them."

*Just give him a chance to realize he's being a dick. Don't react.* "Name three songs by the Rolling Stones?"

"Yeah."

He wasn't getting it. I crossed my arms over my chest and power gripped my palm stone. "Why do you do that?"

He frowned. "What?"

"I said . . . why do that?" I gestured to my shirt. Out of the corner of my eye, I saw the other students in line looking at us. The palm stone was still gripped tight in my hand but didn't seem to be doing much good yet. "Do you get some sick satisfaction out of belittling people in public and embarrassing them? Does it fill a void in your little heart? Get you off a little?"

He glanced around at the other students and laughed nervously. "No, of course not."

I nodded. *Keep your voice calm and low. You can correct his behavior without snapping.* "Then allow me to repeat myself. Why do you do that?"

"Why do chicks wear shirts for bands they don't know?"

That bomb just went off. Some subconscious part of my brain was watching this moment from the outside and knew that I wasn't that easily offended yet I couldn't keep it in anymore. This was the bomb Archie meant. "Would it make you feel good if I can't name them? Would you feel better making me look stupid? Because you look like an asshole. In fact, you look like an asshole either way. If I can name three songs, then I've put you in your place and beat you at your own game. Now *you* look stupid. If I can't name them, then you celebrate your victory and look like an asshole. So, I really don't see what's in it for you to ask such a thing."

He just stared at me with his jaw hanging open.

"I mean, what if I'm one of those people who can sing every lyric but can't ever remember the title of songs? What if I'm new to the band and like their work and wanted to support them by wearing their shirt but I haven't learned their song titles? What if the shirt was a gift from someone I care about and I didn't want to offend them by returning it? What if it was my boyfriend's shirt and I wanted to wear it because it smelled like him? What if I spilled orange juice all over my shirt and a friend loaned this to me? What if I'm poor and the only clothes I can afford are from a thrift shop and this was all they had that fit me?"

"Okay, okay, look—"

"No, let's keep going. After all, you're the one who started this. *You* called me out when I was just standing here quietly. So, what about those contexts for me wearing this? Or, how about this, what if I saw it on the rack at Forever 21 and just thought it was fucking pretty so I bought it?" I arched one eyebrow. "Because that's allowed too."

"I know that."

"Do you?" I cocked my head to the side. "Then why did you ask? We've circled back to that question."

"People just wear shit they don't know all the time and it's weird!"

"People . . . or women?" I crossed my arms. "Because there are four guys in my line of sight right now all wearing different band shirts, and you did not ask a single one of them to name three songs. In fact, you just previously said *chicks* not people. Did you think I missed that?"

His jaw dropped. Around us, other students snickered and laughed.

"Listen, I don't entirely disagree. People wearing merch for things they don't know is a little odd to me. Like when my aunt wears Star Wars shirts despite refusing to watch any of the movies. I may tease her about it at home, in private, but I'd never belittle her by commenting on it in public. Just like I haven't asked those four guys to name songs from their band shirts. Or how I haven't asked you to give me three quotes from any character from *The Office* that isn't Michael, Dwight, or Jim—ya know, since you're wearing that *Dunder Mifflin* shirt." I shrugged one shoulder. "See how easy it is to not be a dick?"

"I wasn't trying to be a dick—"

"Are you sure?" I narrowed my eyes on him. "By the way, it's my dead father's shirt. His older brother bought it for him at the concert he took him to as a teenager. My uncle gave it to me."

The kid looked green and sick to his stomach.

"So, like I said, do you feel better now?"

"I didn't know that," he said softly.

"No, you didn't. How could you? That's the whole fucking point. And for the record, no I don't feel better calling you out right now. It feels shitty. But over my dead body am I going to let you belittle me over a fucking band shirt. Be more creative."

"I'm sorry."

"But ya know what? Just for you: Satisfaction. Start me Up. Jumping Jack flash. Paint it Black. Sympathy for the Devil. Honkey Tonk women. Or my personal favorite, Beast of Burden. Just to name a few." I smiled big. "There, feel better?"

"Franks?" Esther hissed my name a second before she grabbed my elbow and dragged me away. "C'mon, let's go."

I let her drag me away, but as we walked back outside, I realized we hadn't gotten food. "Wait, food—"

"Ava told us to the lunches she'd already gotten." Esther grimaced. "She took off home after Archie told her."

"I hope she's okay—"

"Me too. Ava said she'd update us when she got to them. Seamus . . . well, he panics a little with his fur baby."

That made me smile. "I do, too. So is Archie out here?"

"Nah, Peabo, and Atley dragged him away for something. I don't know." She hooked her arm around my elbow. "So, are *you* okay?"

I scowled. "Why do you ask?"

"You were just telling a teenager off for asking about your shirt."

I rolled my eyes. "I loathe when men do that, quiz me on what I'm wearing. It's disgusting."

"You're gripping that palm stone like it's an oxygen tank—"

"Oh." I uncurled my fingers to show it to her. "Tomás gave it to me. He and Archie think it might help me. They think my repressed magic might be what makes me so angry at the world and one blink away from exploding on some pathetic teenager in a lunch line being a dick about my band shirt."

She didn't laugh or scoff, she just nodded. "They may have a point. So, it's definitely worth looking into. Repressed magic is *danger-ous*. We can ask my mom what she thinks. For now hang on to Tomás's palm stone. It's an old powerful one that's been passed down for generations from South America."

"I don't feel bad for calling that guy out. Or the creep at the gas station. *Or* Aaron and Jacob. But it'd be nice to feel a little more in control of my emotions." Then I really looked at my new friend and found slight bags under her gray eyes that were a little bloodshot and dark. "Esther, are *you* okay? You weren't in gym class today."

"I had a migraine so I went to the nurse to lie down. She's one of us, so she gets it." She let out a deep breath. "But I didn't really sleep last night, I had like three weird dreams about you."

"I had a weird dream about me too." But then her words really sank in, and I remembered what she'd told me the night before. "Wait, what did you see? What's your intuition trying to tell you?"

"I'm not sure. That's also weird. Normally I can put words to what I'm feeling, but with you I can't."

I looked up and spotted Birdie, Madge, and Jo sitting at the main table in the middle. And then I noticed a smaller version of Birdie at the edge of the table. Across from her was an even younger girl with bright silver eyes and dirty blonde hair worn in a side braid.

Birdie followed my gaze, then smiled. "Frankie, this is my little sister, Lesleigh."

The girl looked up from whatever she was doodling in a notebook and grinned. "Hi. This is my friend Aspen Tarbell."

Aspen's face lacked the same happiness as Lesleigh's. Sure, those silver eyes were bright and sparkling, but that had everything to do with the sunlight and not the emotion pouring out of her. She managed a small, toothless smile. "Nice to meet you."

I waved at them. "Nice to meet you too. Thanks for joining us for lunch. I like meeting people in small groups."

Aspen's smile widened ever so slightly. "Yeah, I don't like big groups either if I'm expected to talk. If I'm not, then big groups are cool so I can hide in them."

I opened my mouth, then shut it. "Well . . . shit, kid. That's true."

We all laughed, which seemed to make Aspen's aura a little lighter if only for a second.

"So, Esther, what's wrong?" Birdie leaned across the table and dangled her talisman charm. "Spill or I'll use this against you."

Esther rolled her eyes. "Nothing. I was just telling Frankie I had some weird dreams about her last night."

"How weird?" Jo asked with her pretty but thick accent. Her platinum blonde hair was rocking an 80's style wave today. "*Est-ce que quelque chose de grave va lui arriver?*"

Madge scowled so hard it wrinkled that space between her eyebrows. "Yeah, what Jo said. Is something bad gonna happen for her? Like that kind of weird dream—"

"No, no, no, no, no." Esther waved her hands in front of her, then reached for a chicken nugget. "More like . . . more like . . . usually, I pick up on things about arcana, ya know?"

"It's true, you read us all so well." Madge used a napkin to wipe off her purple lipstick before picking up her burger off the plate. "But you can't see Pink?"

Esther looked at me with gray eyes that looked like a thunderstorm before a hurricane. "No. It's . . . it's like there's too much to see that I can't see anything specific. Her aura is insane—"

"Is it the repressed magic?" I held up the palm stone.

When the other girls frowned, I filled them in on what the boys told me. They frowned even harder.

"*Te sens-tu tout le temps en colère?*"

"Um . . . Madge?"

Madge flinched, then realized what I needed and covered her mouth with her hand. "She asked if you feel angry all the time."

"Oh. I mean, yes and no? Like, I'm good and fine and happy, but the slightest little thing and I'm pissed off." I pointed to my shirt. "Just now some random kid was being an ass and demanded I name three Rolling Stones songs as if I needed to prove I was allowed to wear the shirt. I could've just ignored him or rolled my eyes, or named three songs and let it go. But no, I had to confront him on his shit."

"I don't see the problem with this." Madge licked her lips and waved her burger toward the building. "Prick deserved it."

"Yeah, but it's not in the details here." I frowned and tried to find my words. "It's like . . . I look forward to when people give me a reason to tell them off. I shouldn't want a reason to be a bitch."

They all nodded, their gazes distant like they were thinking.

189

Jo blew a big hot-pink bubble with her gum, then popped it. She pointed her coffin-shaped nail at me. *"Pendant combien de temps a-t-elle été réprimée?"*

"Good question, love." Madge leaned forward like she was looking for something. "You look normal and feel normal . . . How long was it repressed?"

"Since I was four, evidently."

"So twelve years—"

"Fourteen, actually." When they all frowned, I smirked. "I'm eighteen. My aunt and uncle held me back after my parents died so I started kindergarten two years late."

*"Merde."*

I snorted-laughed. *"Merde* indeed, Jo."

Madge used her burger to point at me. "Fourteen years is a long time. I bet it's the reason for your unease and need for an outlet. Your magic has been screaming to get out."

Birdie tapped on the table in front of her. "Esther? What are you thinking? You've been really quiet. I know you don't like to play the family card, but fact is fact, you're different than us. So, think out loud, that way we can help."

That made me smile. These girls knew that Esther's family was special, and while they made lighthearted jokes about it, when it came down to serious stuff, they respected it. They knew the magic in Esther's bloodline made *her* magic more potent than theirs, and they relied on it in moments of stress. Their hearts were in the right place. It just made me worry more about Esther.

"I'd like to read Frankie's tarot cards," she answered without looking at me. Finally, she turned her gaze to me. "I wanna see what we can find. At least start with those before I dive deeper. Repressed magic can be tricky to unload."

I shoved three fries in my mouth, then rubbed my hands together. "Okay, do I have to do anything for that, and can we do it now?"

"Nope, and yes, we can." She reached into her backpack and pulled out a purple velvet bag with a silk drawstring. "So have you ever had a tarot card reading?"

"Never. I know nothing."

"Right. So, tarot cards are sort of like a vessel that taps into the magical essence of our world and serves as a tool for us to use to try and get guidance and deeper understanding of what's going on in our lives."

I blinked. "That was eloquent as fuck."

She snort-laughed, then hung her hand and giggled. "I needed that laugh. Thank you."

"So how does it *work*?"

"I think about what I need to know while I shuffle the cards and then I lay them out and interpret the meanings based on the images."

I leaned forward to look as she pulled a huge duck of cards out of that velvet bag. They were taller than normal playing cards and looked a bit wider too. The edges of them were like a neon-hot-pink not too far off from my hair color. The cards themselves were painted in shades of pink, purple, and blue like clouds in a sunset. As she held the deck up, I saw the back of them had something that was metallic gold that shimmered as she moved, and they reflected the sunlight. I watched closely as she split the deck into three piles and then shuffled them back together.

"I don't do spreads like most people do." Esther shuffled the deck quicker than I'd ever seen someone shuffle. "You'll see."

"Those cards are gorgeous."

"Thank you." She beamed up at me as she shuffled. "Okay, let's get started. Frankie, while I shuffle, I just need you to breathe and try to give me your energy, throw it into the cards, 'kay?"

*Throw my energy into the cards. Right. Whatever that means. No big deal.*

*Focus, Frankie.*

I took a deep breath, then let it out. The movement of the cards between her hands was almost hypnotic. I focused my eyes on them and imagined my energy flowing out of me like waves rolling onto the beach.

"*Goddess, show me what I need to see for Frankie,*" Esther whispered as she continued to shuffle.

After a few seconds, she sat the deck down on the picnic table and flipped the top card. She cringed. Birdie, Madge, and Jo shuddered.

"What?" I leaned forward and picked up the card lying face up.

The card was a pale pink with metallic gold markings that looked kind of like shooting stars emerging from a pillar. *Oh wait, are those supposed to be like fireballs?* At the bottom of the card it said, '*XVI*

*THE TOWER'*. I frowned. I remembered them telling me The Coven was represented by the major arcana, but I wasn't sure if this was one of them.

I cleared my throat and sat the card back down. "What does this mean? The Tower? Is that one of The Coven's Cards?"

"When doing tarot readings like this, pulling a major arcana does not symbolize Coven-members," Birdie said softly, her eyes locked on the card like it was a snake about to bite. "The cards all have their own meanings."

"Okay, what does this one mean?"

Esther exhaled and tapped her fingers on it. "The tower—"

"*Merde,*" Jo whispered.

"Why shit? Esther?"

"The tower is the most dreaded card in a reading." Esther grimaced. "It represents swift change, like disaster and upheaval. It's like your life is imploding or is about to. It's abrupt change in the most aggressive ways."

"Pull a clarifier." Madge shuddered and sat her burger down in disgust. "Or several."

Esther flipped another card, then scowled. She flipped a third card and shook her head.

"What are those?"

"Death, Justice, and Judgement."

Jo spit her bubblegum out on a napkin. "*Non? C'est vrai? Ce n'est pas possible. As-tu mélangé les cartes?*"

"I shuffled," Esther hissed.

My pulse quickened. "Okay, do those cards mean how they sound?"

"Death means change, not actual death, but change in the way of evolution. Not as violent as the tower." Esther pointed to the other two. "Those sound about right. Let me reshuffle. I wanna do something different."

Before I could say another word, she scooped all the cards back up and began shuffling. "*Goddess, send to me the Hermit so I may see within her soul.*"

She sat the deck down but held her palm on top. Gold and navy-blue glitter sparkled beneath her fingers for a split second. I jumped, but the others did not. When she moved her hand, we all groaned.

The tower card stared up at us.

Esther squeezed her eyes shut and shook her head sadly. "Your soul is changing, Frankie. This is why I cannot read you the way I normally can."

"*Tire plus. Maintenant.*" Jo waved her hand, then she hissed and flipped the next card. "*Oh, ce n'est pas mal.*"

"Bad? No. The Ace of Pentacles signifies having the means to manifest your goals. *Madge?*"

Madge had flipped another card. "King of Swords."

"A calm, powerful ruler led by intellectual power." Esther tapped her nails on the table. "So, again, it says your soul is changing, but . . . maybe you're the one intentionally trying to change? Let's see if we can get some advice for you on that."

She collected the cards again and reshuffled at an impressive speed. "*Goddess, send to me the World for advice on these changes.*" Gold and navy-blue glitter sparkled beneath her fingers again.

I wasn't surprised to find The World Card sitting face-up on the table. She was somehow asking for the card she wanted to see on top. It was magic, that I knew, but it was incredible. I was captivated, even while my stomach sank with every flip of a card. The first card she flipped read *The World*, which I was expecting, but when the next card was yet again The Tower, my breath left me in a rush. That card was haunting me.

"Really? The advice for the Tower is the Tower? C'mon." Esther aggressively flipped another card. "Four *and* Five of Pentacles? No. Nope. You're not taking this seriously."

I flinched. "Me?"

"The cards." Esther groaned and scooped them back up. "Seven of Wands!? Okay, now you're just being sassy."

I looked to the girls. "Is it normal for her to talk to her cards like this?"

"Yes," they said in unison.

"Okay, you know what? I'm not going to shuffle see if we can get some deeper insight. We're gonna take matters into our own hands." Esther flipped the deck over and spread the cards out in a straight line, then began looking through them. "When I'm nervous about a situation, I like to find the Fool for guidance. Ah, ok there she is . . . and our guidance is . . . *Four of Cups.*"

"Introspection and withdrawal?" Birdie scratched her head. "That doesn't clarify anything. Why is this not helping? This always helps-"

"High Priestess, what is holding her back?" She began diving through the cards again. "Three of Cups? How does celebration and friendship hold her back? You want her to be alone? Fine then, what does she need to move past this—*what?*"

"*The World?*" Birdie scrubbed her face with her hands. "Do we need to purify your cards?"

Esther cursed. "I don't know. I'm not . . . I'm still blocked. I can't *see*. Let's try something different—"

"Stop." I threw my hand on top of the cards. "I may be new here, but I know all this tense energy ain't helping anything. The cards tell me change is afoot. Cool. That's enough for me right now. We can try this whole thing again in a few days, 'kay?"

"*Oh, merci mon Dieu.*"

Madge jumped and looked to her soulmate. "Thank God what?"

Jo held her phone up to show us the screen. "Rootbeer is okay. Just hot."

We all sighed and nodded.

I grabbed a chicken nugget off the plate in front of me. "Well, at least we've got that happy news."

# CHAPTER EIGHTEEN

## FRANKIE

I WOKE WITH A GASP, my heart pounding in my throat. My mouth was dry and thick. I rolled onto my right side and reached for my glass of water, but my hand slid over a cold, hard surface. My eyes were thick with sleep so I couldn't get them open, but my other senses kicked into gear. Beneath me should've been my bed with soft sheets, except this felt unmistakably like hardwood floor. Cold air swept over my body, making me tremble from head to toe. I curled my arms and legs in and reached for my blanket, yet found none. My fingers grazed over the bare skin of my thigh. My arms were bare. The goosebumps spreading across my body made my skin tingle.

My eyes flew open.

The room was dark, definitely no lights were on, but there was a flickering orange glow all around me. I had to blink a few times before I was able to see clearly. The hardwood floor was directly beneath my face, I was definitely lying on the ground. It took me a second to summon the energy, but I finally managed to sit up—and choked on a gasp.

I was on the floor wearing nothing but my underwear.

The orange glow came from white candles sitting dangerously on the floor without even a plate or bowl to secure them. Wax dripped down and puddled at the bottom of the candles. My pulse quickened. There were two candles at my feet, one on each side by my shoulders, and then one over my head almost like—I looked above me to the candle by my head that flickered with its flame. Two lines stretched in opposite directions from the candle. The lines were dark in color and too thick to be a liquid. I ran my fingertip through one of the lines and it came up *red*.

It was blood.

There was no confusing that metallic scent in the air. My stomach rolled. I pushed to my knees and glanced around me. My heart caught in my throat. I reached down to the floor to stabilize myself as my body began to shake like a leaf in a hurricane.

Because drawn in blood on the floor . . . was a pentacle.

A hot lump formed in my throat and my eyes burned. I wrapped my arms around my waist and sank back onto my heels with my knees still digging into the hardwood floor. At each of the five points of the pentacle, a white candle was lit and flickering.

There was no noise but for the beating of my heart and the ragged breath escaping my mouth. I didn't understand what was happening or why. Or *how*? *What does this mean? Did I do this? How could I do this and not know?* I thought about screaming for my aunt and uncle, yet somehow the idea of them seeing this shook me to my core.

*"Get in bed, Francelina,"* a male voice whispered in my mind. *"Get in bed and this will all go away."*

I was now hearing things, imaginary things, but getting in bed sounded like the best idea anyway. My body trembled and quaked with every step I took toward the bed. I looked down at my hands to find blood dripping from all ten fingertips. I tried to move faster but my body was frozen down to the bone. My legs screamed in agony. Each breath felt like I'd swallowed shards of glass.

This had to be a dream. Nothing made sense otherwise. Fear gripped my spine, but I tried to push it away. My bed was a beacon of hope. If I could just get there, all of this would go away. I knew that in my soul. By the time I climbed into my bed, my muscles gave out, turning to mush and puddle. I collapsed against the sheets, using the sliver of strength I had left to pull those covers up and over my shoulders.

*"Close your eyes,"* that voice whispered again.

I squeezed them shut without hesitation. I wanted this to end. I wanted to wake up. Light flashed in my face. I cringed and lifted my hand up to block the light and the blood on my hand was gone. I frowned and looked down at myself and a little whimper left my lips. I was in my pajamas, in my bed, by myself.

*No, no, no, no, no. This isn't right.* I whined and looked around my room, using the glow of the television to light the path. My heart stopped. That pentacle was *gone*. No blood. No candles. *What the hell is happening to me?* I lifted my hands to run them through my hair and screamed. Those little blue flames covered every inch of my hands and starting to crawl up my arms. *Think, Frankie. Think. What did Aunt Kimmy say to do?* I squirmed and blew on the flames, but that wasn't doing anything. I didn't even know if they were real fire or if real water would put them out.

*Water. She said think of the ocean.*

I closed my eyes and thought about the ocean. I heard the waves rolling onto the shore, sweeping over my bare toes as I scrunched the powdery white sand between them. The air brushing across my skin was warm and soothing. I took a deep breath and let the imaginary salty air carry me off to sleep.

# CHAPTER NINETEEN

## FRANKIE

"It's talisman night, Pink. You ready?"

I glanced over my shoulder and found Esther walking out the back door. Her black curly hair was pinned up by her wand and it looked super adorable. "That sounds more like a threat than anything else."

She chuckled as she sat down on the top step with me. "What are you doing out here? Freaking out?"

I frowned and gestured to my new backyard to where my three beagles were hunting something in the bushes but could only be seen by the white tips of their tails. "No, I'm supervising the hounds. Letting them play. Wait, *should* I be freaking out?"

"Oh, I didn't even see them in there." She giggled. "And not at all. It's gonna be fun, you'll see."

The gang were sticking to their plan to have me try out all of their talismans and try to guess which Suit I was. They said I could make a trip up to Edenburg whenever I wanted and they'd let me touch the crystal ball, but that seemed like a lot of work. So I was secretly thrilled they wanted to have me test it out, even if I was pretending to be shy.

I had no idea what to expect at lunch when they all insisted on this. I texted my aunt and uncle. They needed to know about this plan, mostly because I wanted them there in case I blew something up. I'd already seen the destruction Archie made by using a talisman that wasn't his Suit. My friends were more than happy to come over for a dinner playdate.

"*Rootbeer, wait!*"

We both turned around just as Seamus unhooked Rootbeer's leash, but she was half-dragging him across my patio. He grunted and grumbled, then she was free. The golden retriever barked once, and it was like a scene from Jurassic Park with my little raptors moving within the bushes with only their curved tails visible. My dogs *loved* other dogs, so I wasn't normally worried about new dogs coming up to them, but Rootbeer was charging like Usain Bolt for an Olympic medal. She barked over and over. My boys emerged from the bushes with their ears perked up, tails curled at the ready, and one paw lifted off the ground. It was moments like this when them being siblings really showed. Houdini was the first to move. He lunged forward with his rapid tongue-licking of the air and his tail wagging. Bo needed to howl in a high-pitched note so the whole neighborhood knew he was about to make a new friend. Bubba was basically bouncing in place he was so excited.

Rootbeer swerved around Houdini and ran around Bo and Bubba. She just literally ran circles around them until they realized they could join her. Then the game was afoot. The four of them chased each other and played. It was actually adorable. I wasn't sure who was more excited about this impromptu playdate.

"SEAMUS!" Ava yelled from somewhere behind us. "Did you ask first!?"

Seamus just strolled over and sat down next to Esther without reacting to Ava at all. Esther tapped his left softly. When his big blue eyes looked up, I signed, "*Ava is talking to you.*" I pointed. He spun around and smiled.

The frustration on Ava's face instantly faded. She cringed and then signed, "*Sorry,*" to me. She turned to Seamus. "Did you ask Frankie first before you released her?"

Seamus frowned. "Yes?"

"He texted me like half an hour ago asking if Rootbeer could come." I smiled and gave him a wink. "I said of course. But she's your service dog, you don't have to ask."

His face fell and he shrugged.

Ava looked angry again with the way her brow scrunched together. "A lot of people don't think that way."

"Where's Float?"

She leaned against the door frame. "I left her at home with my parents. You have hunting dogs and she's a rabbit. I figured this wasn't the right time to introduce them, with all the people here. Plus, Rootbeer doesn't get to just be a dog with other dogs. I wanted her to have a night to just play."

Seamus's smile widened and his cheeks flushed pink. "I know everyone here tonight will have my back, so I can let her have fun. Not many other dogs in the neighborhood."

Esther chuckled. "I wanna be offended that pop culture associates witches with cats but . . . dammit, it's just so accurate."

"I want a dog."

Ava screeched and jumped three feet over. She pressed her hand to her chest. "Archie! Dammit, don't sneak up on people like that."

"You do move surprisingly quietly."

"Esther, I'm little. That's not hard to do." He winked and walked toward us, but when he got to the step, his foot slid off and he landed in Seamus's lap. "And then there's that."

We all laughed. Seamus helped him up.

"I'm thinking of lining my jeans with Bubble Wrap."

"But then once they pop, they won't protect you." I frowned. "Maybe you should just wear knee pads?"

"Or line your clothes with padding." Seamus cocked his head to the side. "You are very durable though."

Tomás skipped out the back door with his arms spread wide and a huge smile on his face. "¡Hola, amigos míos! ¡Ya estoy aquí y estoy lista para la fiesta!"

Ava rolled her yellow eyes. "This is not a party, Tomás."

"I don't know." I pursed my lips. "There's a bunch of us and my uncle is cooking. This might be my ideal form of a party."

"See! She gets it." Tomás skipped over and sat *right* next to me, like his thigh was touching mine. He leaned over and kissed my cheek, then wagged his eyebrows. "Es guapa e inteligente."

"Bonsoir—oh, la, la." Jo cringed and waved her hands without stepping foot out the back door. "Non, non, il y a des bugs. Moustiques. Non."

Madge sighed from right behind her. "She's right. It's mosquito hour. Get your asses inside, heathens."

Then they were gone, closing the back door with them. We all stared at the door for a moment before we got up and headed inside. I whistled for the boys. They came running with Rootbeer hot on their heels and Seamus skipping behind them.

Birdie was walking in the front door with her little sister Lesleigh as we walked in. The two were just bigger and smaller versions of each other in their matching olive-green T-shirts and jean shorts with frayed hems. Their brown hair and brown eyes were identical. Even their mannerisms were the same, and it made me smile. I didn't have siblings. I'd always wondered what that would've been like.

"Aspen!" Lesleigh cheered and sprinted across my living room.

That was when I realized we *did* have quite the little party happening in my house. Tomás was on to something. Luckily, Esther had given me the run-down of the witches in town, complete with pictures in her phone so that I could recognize people when I saw them. It was a lot like that scene in *Devil Wears Prada* when Anne Hathaway's character had to study the pictures of people going to that event. Most of the people were a blur, but a few I'd made sure to remember.

Of those few, Monica and Edward Tarbell were included. Their daughter, Libby, was a Coven member until she died in the fall. Monica was a super gifted Wand that was well respected and renowned in the community. Edward was a super loving, fun dad—so I'd been told. And seeing as he was currently wearing an oversized chef's hat and an apron over his button-down floral shirt, I had to say the reputation fit. He and Esther's dad, Elijah, were helping Uncle Kyle cook, though I wasn't sure why it took three of them, but they were having fun. Elijah kept having to take his glasses off because the steam from the pot kept fogging them over. He thought it was hilarious.

Monica was leaning against the island next to Aunt Kimmy and Archie's mom, Agnes, who I hadn't actually met until tonight. She was even smaller than Archie. I wasn't sure if she was over five feet tall. She did have the same dark-red hair and hazel eyes like her son.

Leah emerged from the hall where the guest bathroom was and

stopped beside us. "I beg you all, don't ask him to do any magic tricks tonight?"

My eyes widened. "Say what now?"

My friends laughed.

Esther groaned but she smiled. "Dad used to work as a clown and a magician. He's really good at magic tricks and card tricks, but like, once he starts, he will not stop, and next thing you know you're three hours into a routine. And while you'll enjoy it, you will realize you had other plans for your evening."

"Don't threaten me with a good time. Why is this bad?"

Leah snorted. "Because he wants to be besties with Edward—like for years now—but he's awkward and shy without his costumes on, and so this is a really good step for him. Look at him telling normal jokes and not punchlines."

"There's a bromance there. Edward just hasn't realized it yet."

"I am so here for this support." I looked to the others. "No one interrupts. But Leah, you better warn my uncle. He's . . . he's . . ."

"I know. Your aunt told me." She laughed and walked toward the kitchen.

Monica's silver eyes that matched her daughters lit up when Lesleigh hugged Aspen. "Hi, Buckley girls."

The doorbell rang, and Aunt Kimmy just flicked her wand. "Come in!"

Atley and Peabo walked in like they were on a mission.

I waved. "Hi, you joining us?"

Atley frowned. "Oh, um . . . no, sorry, I didn't know there was a party happening?"

"See! ¡Es una fiesta!"

"It's not a party. At least not intentionally. The others are insisting I try all the Suits' talismans, so they brought theirs over—everyone else is here for damage control and to watch."

Atley nodded, his sharp gaze sweeping across the living room. "We can join you . . . but we were gonna go to Hidden Kingdom with some of our human friends. Ricky's older sister is coming here to pick us up."

"Yeah, go have fun." I waved my hands. "No need to sit here and watch me fumble."

Peabo chuckled. "We also came here to see if Lesleigh wanted to come with us."

Lesleigh's eyes widened. She turned to her sister with a fully mastered beg. "Birdie, can I?"

Birdie narrowed her eyes on Peabo. "Yes. Turn on your locations so I can track you, and no fucking around with anything non-human. Got it?"

Peabo gave her thumbs-up. "Our locations are always on."

"Aspen, you're here." Atley smiled. "You wanna come too?"

She gasped and sat up a little straighter on her barstool. "Mom?"

Monica's silver eyes glistened like she wanted to cry. She tucked her blonde hair behind her ears to act casual. "Of course. Go have fun. Stay with Atley."

"Even in the bathroom?" Aspen arched one eyebrow at her mother.

Monica rolled her eyes. "Smart ass. Stay together, all four of you. No one goes anywhere alone or I'll send Birdie after you."

Birdie made a show of cracking her knuckles.

The boys gave them a salute, then laughed and waved for the girls to follow them.

Monica sighed. "I'm gonna owe that boy a nice birthday present. He's been so good to her . . . after . . . everything . . ."

Leah wrapped her arm around Monica's shoulders and squeezed. "His aura is pure. I think he's a good apple."

"Esther?" A girl walked in with a wand in her hand. "Am I in the wrong house?"

"In here, Whitney!"

Whitney stopped short when she saw Esther's parents. "Oh, I mean, unless now's a bad time?"

Esther looked to her parents. "Mom, Dad, do you care if Whitney gives me a temporary tattoo?"

Elijah looked to his wife. "I mean, it's like a henna, right? That's no big deal."

"I wouldn't care if she got a real one." Leah winked to Esther. "But, Whitney, I wanna see how you do it so I can do Esther's from now on."

Elijah wiped the fog from his glassed again. "Yeah, my parents will be much more understanding if Leah does it."

I looked back and forth between them. "What's this about magic tattoos?"

"Whitney is giving me a temp tattoo for anxiety." Esther held her arm out and pointed to her wrist. "I'm not allowed to have real tattoos because I'm Jewish . . . and this is one of those things my dad's very human parents are strict on. So, we respect their wishes, especially since Whitney is gifted."

My eyes widened. "Can I have one too?"

Archie snort-laughed. "A little bomb prevention?"

I smacked his arm playfully. "But yes."

Whitney nodded and tied her black hair behind her head. "Wicked. Yeah. I'll do yours after hers. Esther, have a sit?"

Esther sat on the couch and held her arm on the armchair while Whitney pulled a chair over to sit across from her. As Whitney pulled a fancy black wand out of her combat boot, I hurried over and sat next to Esther to watch. Leah leaned over the couch to watch from the other side.

I meant to watch the tattoo magic, but Aunt Kimmy, Agnes, and Monica dropped four leather-bound notebooks on the coffee table, then they opened them up and started flipping pages. My friends instantly moved to take seats around us. I must've made a face because Esther giggled.

"These are our grimoires. Our own books of shadows, so to speak." Esther pointed to them while Whitney drew with sparkly light coming off her wand and onto Esther's skin. "Since we can't have access to The Coven's, for obvious reasons, we have come together to make our own for us all to refer to."

"Like your own little coven." Archie smiled. "That's cool."

I cocked my head to the side. "Does The Coven know?"

Monica looked up from the pages. "Kessler knew. He checked it *constantly* to make sure nothing dangerous was in there. But he thought it was important for us to have guidance on things so we wouldn't hurt ourselves trying it on our own. Ya know?"

"The Coven should make a library for everyone."

"There is one in Eden. It's massive." Archie frowned, then pursed his lips. "But maybe that's not sufficient?"

"Humans have free public libraries online. They're huge."

Monica's eyes widened. "Imagine if every witch in the world had access to spell books and stuff online like that?"

Agnes blinked then shook herself. "That would be . . . That would've been life-changing for me as a kid."

Leah walked over and eyed the books in front of her. "The Coven could oversee it to ensure everything is safe. There's so much that could make life easier for us."

"Someone who knows The Coven should tell them." Archie smiled and looked to Monica.

"I will. I definitely will." She lifted a book. "I want to . . . have an example to give him when I present the idea. Kessler . . . he likes people to come with full plans."

"Atley called Tennessee on the phone at the beach. He could just call him—"

"No." Monica shook her head. "No. Tennessee is . . . How do I say this?"

"Am I about to hear the first bad thing about this guy?"

Everyone chuckled but nervously. It was crazy to see the effect this one guy had on everyone even when he was a thousand miles away.

"No, I have nothing *bad* to say about Tennessee Wildes. He's done incredible things as Coven Leader in such a brief amount of time. He's going to revolutionize our society. And with Tegan Bishop as his soulmate and co-Leader? Our world won't look the same when they're done with it."

"But?"

"But they're teenagers." Monica sighed. "Tenn is eighteen. There's still so much of the world an eighteen-year-old cannot know, especially about the day-to-day lives of adult civilian witches. I can't imagine the amount of pressure he's under with this war against Lilith . . . and for that reason, I don't want to burden him with something like this. I will present an idea to Kessler, a longtime friend of mine, and then let him present the idea to his son."

"I think that's a wonderful way to look at it." Agnes smiled down at the pages while she read.

Uncle Kyle cleared his throat. "Right, so Frankie excels in stalling. She knows dinner is almost ready and she's just going to sit here and get y'all to keep talking until it's time to eat. Then she'll be too tired to play with your toys."

I gasped dramatically for show. "I am appalled."

"Go ahead then . . . Try a wand." He wagged his eyebrows. "I triple dog dare you."

"Fine." I reached over and plucked the wand in Esther's hair out, causing her black curls to bounce around her shoulders. "See, I'm not scared. I've got a wand. No big de—"

Gold and navy-blue glitter exploded from the wand, like it was seeping from the pores of the wood and spilling onto my hands. I cursed and tossed the wand back to Esther, but my hands were splattered with glitter.

"Uhh . . . oops?"

She laughed and caught her wand. But I didn't want to let that slow me down or intimidate me, so I leaned to my left and plucked Ava's wand from her lap. Except when I touched it, every light in the house exploded and we were drenched in darkness.

Everyone cursed.

"Sorry, sorry!" I yelled.

Lights came back on, and Aunt Kimmy stood with her wand up in the air. "Well, that was fun."

"All right, let's try an actual spell." Monica moved an unlit candle in front of me. "We're gonna make this candle bigger—"

"Here, Franks. Catch."

I looked up as Uncle Kyle's wand flew through the air toward me.

"Third time's a charm," I said as I caught it easily, but the second my hand touched it, little blue flames shot out of the tip.

That candle exploded into small pieces.

Everyone stared at me.

Monica scowled and snatched the wand from my hand. "How about we move away from wands?"

I grimaced. "So does this mean I'm not a Wand?"

"Yes," everyone said in perfect unison.

Aunt Kimmy sighed and held her wand out. "Let's clean this up—"

"*Non! Attends!*" Jo held her hand up. "*Laisse-la nettoyer. Voici ce que nous faisons.*"

Madge's eyes widened with excitement. "She is right. This is what

Pentacles do. We're the clean-up team. We go in and fix magic gone wrong."

"Here. Use mine." Tomás held a shiny gold object out to me. "Go ahead. *Our* talismans are controlled by *us*."

Ava rolled her eyes. "And the wand controls us?"

"No, but they're different. Wands have a magical essence within them, especially your talisman wand. So, you and the wand work together," Tomás held his talisman up, "while Pentacles are the only magical essence in this combo. Our talismans are trained and treated to react to us. We're bonded in a different way. The magic only comes from *us*."

"Not that you think that makes you superior or anything."

His dark eyes shot to me and widened. His face fell. "No. No, I don't."

"I'm just kidding." I held my palm out. "I'd love to try yours."

His talisman looked basically like an old school corkscrew with the solid gold bar with a swirly sticky thing sticking out the bottom about three inches. "Is this a corkscrew? You're messing with me, right?"

"I would never mislead you, *mi amor*."

I took his talisman, wrapping my fingers around the gold bar, then I pointed it at the pile of candle rubble. Light flashed, something crackled, and the wax rubble exploded into white dust.

Aunt Kimmy coughed and waved her hand in the air. "Nope. Not it."

"Try *mine*." Birdie walked over and held her arm out. The gold pentacle charm dangled from a gold chain. "Tomás chose his because it's also a corkscrew. Do not let him fool you."

He threw his arms out wide and grinned. "Magical wine night?"

Birdie rolled her eyes. "It also takes training to do clean-up as Jo suggested. Let's try something smaller, easier. You saw me use a form of hypnosis to get the Dean to change his mind, right?"

I nodded. "Yeah, I did. So you want me to try and make you do something?"

"Not me. It's my talisman so it won't work." She pursed her lips. "Who wants to volunteer?"

"I'll do it." Tomás jumped up and then sat on the coffee table in front of me so we were face to face. "Make me do anything you want."

"Gross," Uncle Kyle grumbled.

"Okay, so you're gonna hold this like you would a pendulum." Birdie held her talisman out to me. "When you touch it, it's going to seek out your magic. It'll connect with you, imagine it like plugging in your phone to your car to play your music through the stereo."

"Think about what you'd like him to do or say." I must've made a face because Madge slid to stand behind him and then flapped her arms like a chicken. Then she winked. "Imagine it in your mind, then push with your magic."

"*Sens-le dans tes doigts.*" Jo tapped her temple, then wiggled her fingers. "In your fingers."

I took Birdie's talisman between my thumb and middle finger like would a pendulum. Hot, sharp energy shot through my fingers and up my arm. I hissed. It hurt a little bit, but I didn't want to look weak or scared, so I held on to it. The muscles in my arm ached and burned. Something definitely wasn't right. But then Madge started the chicken dance again, so I had to try. I looked into Tomás's eyes and held the talisman up. *Dance like a chicken.*

His eyes lit up for a split second, but then there was a pop and smoke exploded between us. I dropped the talisman on the ground and reached out, but there was so much smoke I couldn't see him. My heart caught in my throat. Everyone else dove forward, but it was Aunt Kimmy's wand that swept the smoke away.

Tomás's eyes were wide. His skin was covered in black dust and his hair was sticking out in every direction. "I'm okay. Right? Right? I'm good?"

The adults swarmed him, but after a second, they stepped away and nodded.

"I'm sorry, I'm sorry." I snatched Birdie's talisman off the ground and hissed as it burned again. "Here."

"I think we can rule out Pentacles as well." Birdie chuckled and wrapped her gold chain around her wrist.

Esther and Archie were watching me with curious expressions. I felt like they were making mental notes of things to look into and discuss later when the whole group wasn't around. It made me a little bit nervous. While Archie struggled with wands, and with simply just walking without tripping, he did know a lot about magic and the way it worked. And Esther *definitely* knew magic, even if her own was a little weakened on the outside. They definitely had thoughts on what all just went down.

"Okay, Cups time!" Seamus announced as he bounced over to where I sat. "Cups are *much* safer. The talisman itself cannot harm anyone—unless you throw it hard enough."

I snort-laughed. "This is why we're friends, Seamus."

He grinned and his eyes sparkled. "You can use my chalice."

He sat a silver chalice on the coffee table. It was far more intricate than I expected it to be. And surprisingly pretty. It was entirely silver with olive branches engraved in the stem and up around the glass.

Aunt Kimmy cleared her throat pointedly. "Agnes, I believe you're up to bat here."

Archie's mom, Agnes, used to be a potions instructor at Edenburg, so I wasn't surprised my aunt was asking for her to help me out. I'd made quite the mess of the wands and amulets. I didn't know who Archie's dad was, but I was wondering if he was as uncoordinated as Archie, because Agnes was sure on her feet. She picked up a long tray full of supplies off the kitchen counter and carried it over to the coffee table without tripping or spilling anything.

Seamus dropped to his knees beside the tray with an excited smile on his face. "Which potion do you want her to try first?"

"I think we'll go with something easy." Agnes began arranging objects on the tray.

"What did you say?" Seamus ducked his head down.

Agnes glanced at him, then did a double take. She blushed and looked him straight in the eye. "Sorry, Seamus. I said, I think we'll go with something easy."

I frowned and then realized she'd been looking away from him so he couldn't read her lips, and the sound of her voice must have traveled in the wrong direction. Seamus did so well that it was easy to forget he was hard of hearing.

"I was thinking of a tea. Nice and simple but effective." She made sure she was talking straight to him. "But something we'll know if it works."

Seamus nodded, then snapped his fingers. "Headache tea."

Agnes smiled. "Good idea. We'll do that."

"We'll do what? Headache tea?" I leaned forward and tapped on

Seamus's shoulder to get his attention. Once he looked at me, I said, "What is headache tea?"

"It's a potion to heal a headache." He licked his lips and pointed to the tray. "What you do is—"

"No, don't tell her." Agnes held her hand out. She smirked. "I want to see how she does without instruction."

"Throwing me into the deep end, eh?"

"Call it a gut feeling." She grinned and crouched down on her knees across from me. "What I want you to do is just look at all the ingredients on the tray. Forget what they're called or their intended purpose. Just see what happens."

"That is frustratingly vague." I bit my lip. "How do I start?"

"Take the chalice into your hands. See if your magic steps up to the plate and shows you the way." She waved her hands over the tray. "Just focus on your intention of healing my headache."

"Agnes, your style of teaching is interesting. But okay, let's give it a go." I wrapped my fingers around the stem of Seamus's chalice and lifted it into my hand. The silver was cold to the touch but didn't tingle or hurt. Nothing outright happened just from holding it, so that was a good sign. "All right. I am going to heal Agnes' headache."

At first nothing happened. I was just staring at this tray full of random objects. I saw rose petals and what looked like thorns from a rose stem. There were far too many little jars of herbs that looked the same while looking slightly different at the same time. If I stared at those too long, I was going to go crazy. There were cloves and garlic, and a stack of cinnamon sticks. I saw mint leaves, chives, rosemary, thyme, arugula, and like two dozen other things, including some small vials of different color liquids. It was a lot. Too much, in fact. I didn't know where to start.

"Just give it a try. No pressure." Seamus smiled and gave me two thumbs-up.

I took a deep breath, then sat the chalice on the coffee table next to the tray, practically under Seamus's nose. Then I rested my fingertips on the edge of the chalice with my left hand and on the edge of the tray with my right. *Okay, magic, show me what to use to make this potion. Please.* And then I exhaled and tried to push with my mind. I had no idea if I was doing this right or not. This was one hell of a crash course into witchcraft. I was about to give up when neon-blue flames billowed from beneath a little potion bottle in the center of the tray.

My eyes widened. I sat up straight. Those blue flames . . . I knew those. That was *my* magic. I stared at them for a moment, then picked up the bottle, removed the lid, and poured the contents into the chalice. Those blue flames vanished as if they'd never been there. With a frown, I sat the potion bottle down—and the flames reappeared. I gasped as excitement rushed through me like adrenaline. This time the flames were dancing along the edge of a little white bowl filled with bluish-purple flower petals. I picked up the bowl and the word *lavender* bounced around my head. I definitely hadn't known this was lavender. With my left hand, I pinched some of the petals from the bowl into the chalice now filled with the clear liquid.

The blue flames jumped from the bowl to a leafy green branch, then onto a stack of tiny dried-out yellow flowers, and then onto the little brown balls. *Rosemary, chamomile, nutmeg.* My magic filled in the name of the ingredients as I touched them. Forget following the yellow brick road, I was following the blue flames. The last two ingredients I knew before I touched them. Mint and cinnamon. Once I put all of those into the chalice, the blue flames covered my hand and the top edge of the chalice. I frowned and covered the chalice with my hand, and instantly those blue flames swirled within the cup. Blue smoke of the same color billowed from between my fingers.

Once the flames and smoke vanished, I pulled my hand back and just stared at it. "Did y'all see that?"

"The smoke is normal," Seamus said with a nod.

"Good to know." I glanced around the room to the whole group, but no one seemed alarmed or confused. Something in my gut told me I was the only one who'd just seen the blue flames. And then I looked to Esther who had a little smirk but wouldn't meet my eyes. Archie just nodded.

"All right. Let's see if you're about to heal my headache." Agnes lifted the chalice to her lips and drank a big sip. She licked her lips and set the chalice back down. "Tastes delicious—*oooh.*"

I reached for her like I could fix whatever happened that made her close her eyes mid-sentence like that. "What? What happened? Does it hurt?"

She exhaled, slow and steady, then opened her eyes. "That is the gentlest headache healing I've ever felt. Impressive, Frankie."

Seamus grabbed his chalice and drank from it. He licked his lips as if he were taste testing wine at some winery. Then he blinked and nodded his head. "The nutmeg and cinnamon were a surprise choice for me but . . ."

"I think we have to add them to the potion's ingredients from now on." Agnes chuckled.

"What does that mean?"

Agnes grinned. "Congratulations, Frankie, it's a Cup!"

Ava sighed loudly. She leaned against the kitchen counter, running her fingers through Float's white fur. "Thank the Goddess. I was *not* looking forward to seeing her test out Swords."

Everyone laughed, including me.

"And perfect timing." Uncle Kyle clapped his hands. "Dinner is ready."

# CHAPTER TWENTY

## FRANKIE

She was going to catch me.

I stared down the hallway to my right, willing him to appear. But he hadn't yet, and with every passing second, my window for escape closed more and more. "C'mon, where are you?"

Light flashed through the open, arched windows down the length of the hall and then an explosion rocked the entire castle. I dropped to my knees and ducked down, clinging to the wall as the world shook. The stone walls trembled, sending little pulses through the stones into my bare feet. Dust spilled from the cracks in the ceiling. A second explosion was so much closer that the force broke chunks of stone from the walls. Bright orange flames shot across the ceiling.

And then I heard her scream.

I couldn't wait any longer. I had to make my run for it, or I'd be her prey.

My chest was on fire with every breath I took. I licked my lips and winced at the metallic taste of fresh blood. I pulled the hood of my cloak over to cover my face, then gripped the hem of my dress and sprinted in the direction he'd said was our exit.

Another explosion rattled the walls. Heat from fire filled the air. I cursed and dug my heels in harder. The hall made a sharp left turn and, when I rounded it, I found myself in an open corridor made of that same gray stone. I slid to a stop. My heart stopped. The left side of the corridor was window after window, separated only by columns. On the right side, it was open to a small courtyard. There was nothing to hide behind, no coverage at all. If she was watching, she'd see me without a doubt. I could crawl but that would slow me down too much.

A sharp whistle pierced through the sky.

I gasped and dropped to my stomach as a cannonball crashed through the column beside me. Stone crumbled and rained down on me. The cannonball slammed into the statue in the middle of the court-yard. I took a deep breath and craned my neck back to look up at my path and butterflies danced in my stomach. That archway up ahead was filled with bright sunlight. That was safety. If I could just get there, I could get out of here.

He said he would be here. He said he was coming. But I had to move. I pushed up onto my toes, then I counted to three. If he wasn't here at zero, I was making my escape.

Three.

Two.

One.

"Just run," I whispered to myself and lunged into the air.

The rubble sliced into my bare skin as I ran. My shins ached. I didn't slow down.

"THERE!" she bellowed, her voice rattling the stones on the wall. "GET HER!"

Her voice carried through the wind like thunder. A cold chill slid down my spine. She was so much closer than I realized, but not close enough. My gaze locked on that archway. Goddess, watch over me. I leapt through the archway and into the mid-day sunlight—and landed on all fours on my bedroom floor.

Pain shot up my thighs, into my hips, and through my spine. My hands and wrists burned. I hung my head and exhaled. It was just a dream. Only a dream. My pulse hadn't yet caught that memo. *Wait, why am I on the floor?*

I pushed off my hands and leaned back to sit on my heels—and gasped.

*Not again.*

I sat in the middle of a pentacle drawn on my floor in sand and seashells. *No, no, no.* I fell back and landed on my ass. My hands slid across the lines drawn in beach sand. Shells of every shape and color were mixed in. The lights in my room were off, yet there was a soft blue glow from between the floorboards. My heartbeat thundered in my veins, slamming against my chest like a hammer. My ears began to ring. My muscles tightened and locked down. Even my throat felt tight like I couldn't get enough oxygen in.

Darkness crept into my vision from the outside, creating a little tunnel in my eyes.

That blue light shot up through the floorboards until its beams looked like towers around me. For a moment, time stood still. I was afraid to move, afraid to *breathe*. And then I blinked. The blue glowing towers of light swirled exploded into little blue particles. I sucked in a deep breath and held it. I was frozen.

And then those glowing blue embers began to *move*. I squeezed my eyes shut. *This isn't real. This is not happening.* But when I opened my eyes, those glowing blue embers were swirling around me like waves in the ocean.

"*No, no, no. Stop. STOP!*" I swatted at the glowing blue waves as tears burned my eyes. "*Make it stop! STOP!*"

With every slice of my hand, the waves rolled away from me and began to stick together and take form. The glowing blue embers swirled into the shape of humans with pointed ears and long swords in their hands. I scrambled backwards until my shoulders crashed into my bed frame. My hands trembled. I tried to stand but my legs gave out from under me.

"*They are coming,*" a deep voice whispered in my ear.

I gasped and dove away from my bed, swatting at my ears, but no one was there. "Who said that?"

"*They are coming.*"

"*They are coming.*"

It echoed around my room over and over and over. The words picked up speed until they blurred together into a low hum in my ears. The blue glowing embers slammed into my face and the world turned black.

"*Breathe, Francelina,*" a deep male voice growled.

I gasped and sat up, throwing my hands up to stop the glowing embers, but they were *gone*. It was all gone. There were no shells or sand on the floor. No pentacle. No chanting voices echoing around me. The lamp on my nightstand was actually still on, casting my room in a soft golden glow. I exhaled so hard I swayed and fell back. My head hit my pillow. Relief washed through me, even as my heart pounded. I lifted my shaking hands and scrubbed my face. I was in bed. *My* bed. I pulled my knees up, wrapped my arms around my shins, and rolled onto my side.

My whole body shook. Sweat dripped down the side of my face and down my spine.

But through the cracks in my curtains, sunrise was lighting up the sky.

# CHAPTER TWENTY-ONE

## FRANKIE

My head felt like it was a balloon barely tethered to a string that was gripped in a toddler's hand at Disney World. The world kept spinning and bouncing. I ran my hand along the line of burgundy lockers to anchor myself as I tried to walk down the hallway. My first class of the day had already started, so there was no one out here to witness me stumbling. I wasn't even sure how I got to school in the first place. I didn't remember driving here, and that terrified me. My stomach rolled like I was going to be sick, and I crashed into the wall. Sweat dripped down my back and coated my arms. My skin was hot and clammy. I needed to sit down.

It was like I was acting on autopilot. My body was doing things, but my mind wasn't actively present. Subconsciously, I knew I was stumbling down the hall, but it was like I was watching a movie of it in my head. I watched my own arm reach out and turn a door handle, then push it open so I could slip into the stairwell. The world spun again. I cursed and threw my arms out to steady myself and then I was on the floor. I had no idea how I'd gotten there, if I'd sat down or fallen, but my back was pressed to the wall at least. I pulled my knees to my chest and wrapped my arms around my legs.

I closed my eyes and counted to ten while I focused on breathing in and out through my nose.

Then I opened my eyes and choked on a scream.

The stairwell was *gone*. I sat crouched on my knees on a cold, gray, stone floor in a room with walls made of the same stone. There was no furniture or windows. No statues. I didn't even see a door. The room was tall and circular. The ceiling was vaulted at least fifty feet above my head. I had to get out of this place as fast as possible. It was too cold. My body was covered in goosebumps and trembling. My hands were so cold they burned. I lifted my shaking fingers up to my mouth to blow hot air on them when my gaze landed on the blood coating my fingers.

My breath caught in my throat.

The blood was so fresh it was still dripping down my palms and wrists in little rivers. Tears burned the backs of my eyes. I looked down but there was no blood in sight. *But I'm in the middle of the room.* A cold chill slid down my spine. I turned and my heart stopped. My eyes went so wide they could've popped out of my skull.

Sitting in the middle of the room was a black orb a little bigger than a basketball. Darkness swirled within it like it was alive. It felt like someone was watching me through the orb. The black pedestal it sat on was covered in strange red symbols. I frowned and followed the stream of symbols down to the floor—the world spun around me. The entire stone floor stretching the five feet between me and that orb was covered in those symbols in red. *No. Not red. BLOOD.* Those symbols had been drawn in fresh blood . . . the same blood coating my fingers.

A whimper slipped through my closed teeth. My breath left my mouth in a cloud of white smoke. The temperature plummeted. It was suddenly so cold that my bones rattled against each other. A voice whispered in the air loud enough for me to hear it but too quiet to make any of the words out. But the sound made every muscle in my body tense and tight. My stomach was a ball of rocks.

A pair of red eyes beamed from within the orb.

I gasped and pressed my fingers to the stone floor. My body had taken over again, acting on its own. In my mind, I saw a different rune than the ones on the floor, but it was similar. My fingers traced this symbol on the stone. Words slipped through my teeth that I heard myself chanting in a whisper, though I had no idea what I was saying. A sharp, high-pitched whistle shrieked from inside the orb. It sounded like a train whistle right on top of me. Those red eyes were shaking now.

"*YOU,*" that voice in the orb screeched, its voice cracking.

I felt my lips curl into a smile as I met those eyes head-on. Power filled my lungs and burned down my arms. I wrote that last symbol again, but this time it glowed a hot pink like my hair. "*ME.*"

Light exploded, and for a moment everything was pure, solid white.

"*FRANKIE!*"

I gasped and jumped, throwing my arms and legs out in every direction. My legs slammed into some kid's legs and sent him tumbling to the ground. Someone's arms wrapped around my body and yanked me backwards. Gold and navy-blue glitter sparkled from everywhere this person touched me, and it was the only thing that cut through the fog in my mind.

"*Esther?*" I whispered.

"It's me. It's me. I've got you," she whispered back, her breath rushing over my ear.

I collapsed in her arms and fell apart. Tears I hadn't cried for all the things that had happened to me came rushing from the well.

"Frankie, are you hurt?" It was Archie. That was who I'd knocked over. He leaned over me with a crinkle between his dark-red eyebrows. His hazel eyes were sharp and focused on me. "Are you okay?"

"No. I'm not okay," I said between sobs, still gripped tight in Esther's arms. "I think I'm losing my mind."

"Okay, just breathe. We've got you." Esther squeezed me tighter. "No one is going to hurt you."

I wanted to believe her, but I was having a hard time breathing between sobs.

"Right. We're done with school for today." Esther exhaled and started to rock me like a baby. "Archie, tell everyone to meet us at the beach."

"I'm on it." Archie crouched down and pressed his palm to my back. I felt magic tingle along my spine, and the air I was choking on went smoothly in and out of my lungs. "Just breathe. We've got you."

I couldn't have explained how I got from the stairwell at school to the beach, but the next thing I knew, I was standing calf-deep in the water with the sand squished between my toes. The sun shined down on my shoulders and the water, making the ripples look like little diamonds. For all I knew, I'd passed out, that was how stressed my body had been. Even standing on the beach I wanted to take a nap. The waves gently caressing my feet was my favorite lullaby. If someone put a beach chair behind me, I'd happily sit and fall asleep.

It wasn't even mid-day yet, so the sun wasn't all the way up above me and its rays weren't quite as sharp and aggressive as they would be by noon. Someone had made sure to put my polarized sunglasses on my face, and for that I was grateful. Watching the little fish swim around my feet was therapeutic somehow. Behind me, I heard my friends talking and I knew they were discussing me and what had happened. Esther's voice was calm and steady, and she filled them in on what she knew, which wasn't much. I needed to tell them everything. They were witches. These dreams couldn't possibly be a human thing.

A shadow slid over my head. I frowned and looked up, expecting an umbrella or something, but instead I found a midnight-blue sky with stars twinkling and a golden crescent moon shining down on me. *What the . . . How'd it get dark so fast?*

When I looked back to the beach, I gasped and jumped back. Glowing blue objects moved along the horizon. They had to be cruise ships or something. The light was soothing, like I just wanted to close my eyes and sleep. I blinked slowly, and then I was standing on top of the water surrounded by the glowing objects. I spun around and my stomach sank. The objects were *people*—rows and rows of people glowing a pale turquoise-blue and walking toward the horizon. A warm breeze swept over my back. I wanted to go with them. I'd be at peace if I just went with them. I shivered and took a step—

"Frankie?"

My body was gently jostled. I jumped and looked down to find Archie's hand gripping my elbow. I blinked up at him. "What's wrong?"

He waved his hand in front of my face. "Come back to us."

It was only then that I realized a strange mist had clouded my vision. I exhaled in a rush. "I don't like this."

He frowned and nodded but didn't let go of me. "C'mon, come sit with us and tell us everything so we can help you."

"I hope you can," I heard myself mumble.

Archie's smile was unwavering. "We can. Promise."

The rest of our little group was sitting on that same purple blanket they'd had out at the bonfire Monday night. Ava had a little harness on Float with a long leash so the rabbit could hop around the blanket freely. Madge sat between Jo's legs so her soulmate could braid her hair into pigtail French braids. Jo's hair looked almost white in the sunlight. It wasn't until I got closer that I saw it was braided into a fishtail mohawk braid. I just wished one day I could achieve half of their effortless coolness. Tomás was stretching while Birdie was whispering with Esther. Seamus had an umbrella set up for him and Rootbeer to sit under.

Archie cleared his throat. "Look, don't be embarrassed or shy about all this. You're new to magic but we're not, so as honest as you can be with us, the better our odds at helping you. 'Kay?"

"Thank you, Archie. Easier said than done sometimes, but I'll do my best." I smiled and sat next to Rootbeer under the umbrella. Animals had a way of calming me. I ran my fingers through her fur. "How's she doing? Heat still a problem?"

Seamus grimaced. "She's okay, but I don't want to push it."

Ava closed her yellow eyes and shook her head. Float was stretching out in her lap, and in the sunshine, the contrast of her white fur with Ava's brown skin was beautiful. "I think I have to become a veterinarian. If we're gonna stay together, I have to be able to put his mind at ease about her."

I cocked my head to the side. "Are there a lot of witch vets?"

She opened her mouth, then shut it. "I only know of the one. Shit, I may have just stumbled onto something."

"See? She helps." Seamus pulled a battery-operated fan out of a bag and propped it up in front of his dog. "She's a good girl."

I chuckled and kept combing my nails through her fur. It was better than those sandpit Zen gardens people used to buy.

Esther cleared her throat. "Um, Birdie, would you mind helping me out?"

I looked up and found everyone staring at me. I sat up straighter. "What?"

Archie's face fell. "We've been talking to you for like ten minutes."

My jaw and heart dropped. *What?*

"No worries, Pink." Birdie crawled over to kneel in front of me, then she held her hand up and let that gold pentacle dangle. "I'm not hypnotizing you, so don't worry. But sometimes when our magic

223

locks up our minds like this, we need to just help *unlock it.* Understand?"

I sighed. "Honestly? Not sure. But I trust y'all, so whatever you say."

She started speaking but the words were not registering in my mind, so either that wasn't English or I needed to be more worried about my mental state. None of the others seemed concerned in any way. And then suddenly there was silence. I scowled. My ears had been ringing. I hadn't noticed until it stopped.

"Better?"

I looked up into Birdie's warm brown eyes and smiled. "Thank you."

"*Parle-nous, Frankie. Qu'est-ce qui s'est passé?*"

Madge hissed. "Love, give her a second. She'll tell us when she's ready."

Jo narrowed her eyes on her soulmate, then pointed to me. "She is tough. Give her a break," she said in her thick French accent.

That made me smile. "I *am* tough. Thank you, Jo."

Madge rolled her eyes. "You got lucky," she mumbled to Jo.

Seamus leaned towards me and signed, "*What did Madge say?*"

"*She told Jo she got lucky,*" I signed back.

Seamus chuckled.

Tomás pulled a bag of Doritos out of his backpack and opened them. "I agree with Jo. Tell us what happened. Chip?"

I reached into the bag and pulled out a handful of chips. "Thanks. And . . . I just . . . It sounds crazy."

Esther leaned forward and took my hands in hers. "Don't hold back. Give us all the details and let us decide if it sounds crazy."

I nodded and took a deep breath . . . then I told them everything. Even going back to waking up in the hospital and feeling the weirdest deja-vu. All of my dreams layered on dreams. The voices. Those red eyes in that orb. I even talked about Aaron and Jacob. Lastly, I told them about what I saw on the beach. When I finished, everyone was quiet.

"So, yeah." I cleared my throat. "What do you think?"

Birdie frowned at the ocean. "Esther?"

"I need to see a deeper look at what's going on in your magic."

Esther sighed and pushed her long black curls off her face. "I need to get a read."

"Like another tarot card reading?"

She shook her head. "No, and not pendulum either."

Madge held her hands out in front of her. "Read her palms."

Everyone else nodded enthusiastically.

"Is that all right, Frankie?" Esther tied her hair up on top of her head, battling against her curls. "It doesn't hurt."

I copied Madge and held both of my hands out in front of me. "Whatever you need to do. I trust you."

She crawled closer so my hands rested comfortably in her lap. Her gray eyes were sharp and focused on my hands for a moment before she took my left hand in hers and lifted it up to her face. Her pale fingers traced the lines in my palm and nodded. She whispered to herself like she was taking notes.

I was a bit too fragile to ask for a play-by-play, so I looked to the ocean instead. At this point, I wasn't expecting to know the answer for my issues, nor did I really need to know the cause. I just needed Esther, or anyone else, to find an answer for me. That wasn't my normal motto, usually I was a hands-on kind of gal, but I knew that whatever this was, it was above my pay grade.

"Interesting." Esther dropped my hand into my own lap. "I want to do an aura reading. Birdie, can you reach my wand?"

"How do you do an aura reading?"

Esther smiled as Birdie sat her wand in her outstretched hand. "Actually, your magic feels a little . . . defensive right now. I'd like if you just closed your eyes and let me do my thing."

I squeezed my eyes shut. "Do your thing."

She chuckled. I felt a tingle in my skin and light flashed against my closed eyelids. Gold and navy-blue glitter swirled in the darkness like her magic wanted to say hi. A bright white light crept into the corner of my vision. A soft, soothing warmth filled my muscles. My body buzzed. I felt weightless, like I was hovering in the air.

"Okay, you can open your eyes."

My eyes flew open, but everything looked the same, looked normal. Whatever she'd done, she'd only done it to me. The others were all looking to Esther expectedly, except for Tomás who held the bag of chips out for me to take some.

"I'm thinking," Esther whispered, holding her hands up to ward off questions.

"Palm reading is her specialty." Madge nodded toward Esther. "The Irit family line is known for their intuition."

Tomás pointed at her with a chip. "The Irits are also known for aura reading."

Esther groaned. "You can't still be upset about that."

Seamus snickered. "Don't tempt him with a good time."

"So . . ." Archie rubbed his hands together. "What did you find?"

"I'm afraid to say this, because admittedly it doesn't make much sense, but . . ." Esther put her hand on mine. "But I think you're experiencing clairvoyance."

Ava gasped. "As in psychic visions?"

"It's the only answer that makes sense for what I'm reading in her palm and her aura. There's turbulence on the horizon and I've only seen this kind of . . . kind of . . ." Esther waved her hands around like she was searching for the words. "Acceptance? For most witches with strong intuition, myself included, the feelings and unconscious dreams speak of things that *could* come, but it's not so literal. It's like feelings and stuff. It makes our magic tense. It's basically like my magic has anxiety because it's constantly trying to guess what's coming. But people with psychic abilities, with actual clairvoyance, their magic is not worried—"

"How do you know so much about actual psychics? Are any of you one?"

"Bentley Bishop is the Hierophant in The Coven. He's been blessed with psychic powers in more than one way." Esther was staring at her bag. "And before they left town, he and I had a lot of conversations, which I'm suddenly realizing weren't as casual and nonchalant as I thought. He must've seen you coming."

"Her magic doesn't have anxiety?"

"Her magic is a warrior ready for battle. It knows it's coming and it's ready to fight. Which would explain Frankie's ticking time bomb personality where she explodes on people. I'm not sure we're looking at repressed magic at all . . . I think we're looking at evolving magic."

Tomás cursed.

Archie glanced back and forth between us. "So what are you saying? About her dreams?"

"Well, *if* I'm right and these are psychic visions, it would explain how they seem to attack her out of nowhere. Also explains why they're so visceral for her, because she's actually experiencing them." Esther scrubbed her face with her hands. "I need to talk with my mother . . . We need to get you a healer."

"*A healer?*"

"Yes. But the right one, because they are not all the same."

"Katherine." Madge snapped her fingers. "Katherine would know."

*Katherine? Why does that name sound familiar?* An image filled my mind of a woman with auburn hair standing next to my hospital bed. She was hooking up colored IV bags—rainbow light flashed in my eyes. I gasped and my balance faltered but Archie caught me.

"What just happened? Did you have another vision?" he asked softly.

"No." I frowned. "I don't know what that was."

Seamus put his hand on my shoulder. "You need to let your magic rest."

"You need . . . you need . . . Where is it?" Esther dug through her bag, looking for something, then huffed and dumped everything onto the sand. She dug through the stuff until she pulled out two gold necklaces: One had an amethyst crystal and the other had a white-ish stone with black spots. Before I could object, she had both of the necklaces hanging from my neck. "Amethyst and black tourmaline. Good for protection."

"Okay . . ."

As she grabbed her now empty backpack and began shoving her stuff back inside, she accidentally grabbed the corner of a blue velvet bag. At first I thought it was her tarot cards, but that had been purple not blue. She lifted her hands and a couple dozen blue crystals poured out and into the sand. Esther cursed violently and scrambled to put them back in her bag.

I scowled. "What were those?"

"*Rune stones*," Jo whispered in her French accent.

"Oh, like from the Nordic tribes?" I frowned. "Or was it Vikings? I don't know. That part of history confuses me sometimes."

"*Pas les Vikings. Les Anges.*"

"Angels? *Les Anges* is angels?"

Jo grinned and nodded. She pointed to the bag gripped tight in Esther's hands. "*Runes Angéliques.*"

"The runes on them are not in the Nordic language. They're Angelic runes," Birdie said softly, almost reverently. "The language of Heaven and Angels."

My eyebrows rose. "How do you know that?"

"The Angel said so." Tomás pressed his hand to his chest over his heart. His normal bubbly, flirty personality was nowhere in sight.

I shook my head. "How . . . how old are these?"

"Ancient." Esther glanced around to the others, then back to me. "So, as you know, my mother and I are part of the Irit founding bloodline. We used to be super powerful. Magic in our line passes from mother to daughter. Centuries ago, an angel went to my grandmother —many times removed, of course—and bestowed an honor upon our family—"

"*Honor* is used loosely here." Ava snort-laughed.

"Honor means something different to Heaven." Esther shrugged. "This angel gave these rune stones to my grandmother for safekeeping. The angel told my grandmother that one day in the future someone would cross her path and the stones would sort of . . . come to life. No idea what that literally means, but we're told we'll know it when we see it. And once that happens, we'll know that was the person the stones were fated for, and they are to inherit them forevermore."

I shivered but I wasn't cold. "Why? What are the stones? What do they *do?*"

"No idea, honestly. But that angel insisted these would be a tool used to defeat Lilith." She took a deep breath, her eyes looking almost wistfully at the bag. "The story says once these stones are passed on and our job is done, our magic will restrengthen to its former glory."

"That's incredible. We gotta find this person for you." I leaned closer to the bag. "Can I see them?"

She hesitated, then cursed. With a quick flick of her wrist, she dumped the bag of rune stones back onto the sand. They were various shades of blue and were entirely transparent. On one side, there were runes engraved in gold glitter, but I'd never seen the symbols before. They were breathtakingly beautiful. There was an aura coming off them in waves. It was warm and made my body feel light weight. My fingers tingled. It was a feeling I'd never experienced.

"What do the runes mean?" I whispered, unable to raise my voice.

Archie leaned forward to get a closer look, his hazel eyes wide and in awe. "People don't speak the Angelic language."

I pursed my lips and tried to think. "Aren't the Nordic rune stones supposed to be kind of like tarot cards or oracle cards? I think I saw that in a movie once. Maybe these are too?"

I reached out to touch the one closest to me and neon-blue flames shot out of my hand and swallowed Esther's stones whole. I screamed and swatted at it, but it was too late. My magic swirled and billowed around the rune stones. The gold glitter-engraved symbols glowed a neon-pink and then lifted into the air. The others all dove back, but I was frozen, locked in place. The rune stones themselves shimmered with light from within until that light was as bright of a blue as my magic. The stones moved together and the runes on them vanished. For a moment, it looked like we were staring at a miniature ocean.

And then a single symbol appeared stretched across the surface of all the stones. The rune looked kind of like a capital C with a five-pointed star in the middle of it. Or like a pentacle whose circle was broken. That meant something and my magic *knew* it. I felt my pulse flutter as butterflies danced in my stomach. An image filled my mind of me driving that car I'd stolen on Halloween toward the hospital with my best friend dying in the passenger seat. Even with my eyes open, the bright sunlight reflecting off the sand, and the glowing pink rune in front of me, I saw the streetlights shining through the rain-drops on the windshield. I saw my arm glowing with little pink flames and then when the flames faded away, there was a tattoo on my skin in black of the letters *XVI*—

Rainbow light flashed across my vision.

I stared at the stones with my heart in my throat. I'd just forgotten something. I knew it with every fiber of my being that I'd just been thinking about something, something that happened to me, and then it was just . . . gone.

And then the symbol vanished. The rune stones went back to being shades of transparent blue with glittery gold runes engraved in them. Like nothing had happened at all.

"*Frankie. It's you.* You're the one," Esther whispered as my neon-blue magic rolled back onto my fingers. Her eyes were wide as she stared at me. "You're the one the angel wanted me to wait for. It's *you.*"

# CHAPTER TWENTY-TWO

## FRANKIE

"Okay, where do you want all these paper lanterns?"

Madge looked up from her clipboard to Seamus, then pointed to her left. "Bring those over to Ava. She's going to fill them with these little twinkle lights."

As Seamus lugged two big boxes across the gym, I glanced around. I'd been helping him carry boxes of decorations in since neither of us were gifted with a wand. Seamus said they used magic to decorate, but so far everything looked perfectly human.

"Why are you frowning?" Madge lightly tapped on my forehead with her pen. "What's wrong?"

"I was just wondering where the magic is?" I gestured around the gym. "Also, if you can use magic to decorate, then why didn't you just use magic to create decorations?"

"That would be nice, wouldn't it?" Madge shrugged one shoulder, then glanced over and yelled, "Jo, please, remove Tomás from the flower walls. He will break them before he gets them hung up."

Jo swatted at Tomás's hands, forcing him to drop the curtain covered in fake flowers of every color. She shooed him away. He looked up and spotted me watching them and his smile widened. My stomach tightened into knots. I needed to find an opening to let him down gently. I just wasn't interested in him that way. It was unfortunate but still true.

"Only a Wand could create decorations, and while Ava is brilliant at using her Wand to put up these decorations, she does not have the skill to create. And Esther, well, her magic is weak—*wait!*" Madge scowled and spun around until she spotted Esther on the far side of the gym with Birdie. "Esther! Come here!"

Esther hurried over, and the closer she got, the more that electricity in the air tingled. It didn't usually feel like that with her. Those gray eyes of hers really sparkled today. They were almost a light blue now. Even her skin held more color than before.

"Why are you guys looking at me like that?" She glanced back and forth between us. "What?"

I looked to Madge, but the fashionista was just staring at our friend pensively. "Madge?"

She cursed. "Where's your wand?"

Esther pointed to her hair where the wand was sticking through her messy bun. "Why?"

"Has your magic come back stronger yet?" I prayed I wasn't overstepping but those rune stones had been for me, or so she said. I reached into my backpack that was sitting on the table next to Madge and pulled out that blue velvet drawstring bag. The second my hands touched it, blue flames billowed from within it. I held them up. "We haven't talked about these much, admittedly because I'm a little freaked out by it, but you said once your job was complete, your magic would restrengthen . . . So has it?"

She opened her mouth, then shut it. Her eyes were wide. She reached up with hands that trembled ever so slightly and plucked her wand from her hair. "I've been too afraid to hope it was stronger now, because what if it isn't?"

"What if it is?" Madge cleared her throat. When I looked up to her, she had a shimmer in her eyes. "*Try it now,*" she whispered.

"What . . ." Esther looked around the gym, then back to her wand. "What should I try?"

"Try the stars," Whitney said from suddenly behind us. When we all looked to her, she shrugged. "What? Those chiffon strips we drape across the ceiling with the twinkle lights are a pain in the ass to put up —even with magic. Ava and I have skill but that's a bit beyond us."

"Okay. Right. I can try that." Esther licked her lips and stared at her wand. "I know how to use this. I know how magic works. I just have to . . ."

She spun away from us toward the center of the gym and waved her wand like that dude in an orchestra leading everyone. Instantly, white sheer curtains lifted off the ground and shot straight to the ceiling. Gasps echoed around the gym and then I heard footsteps hurrying toward us. I glanced around to find all of Esther's friends with tears in their eyes and flushes in their cheeks. They watched silently as she expertly draped the fabric, then lifted strings with golden lights within them. When she lowered her wand, the ceiling looked like a galaxy of stars twinkling down at us.

Her magic was back.

Esther choked on a sob and the group pounced on her with the most violent group hug I'd ever seen. They were aggressively happy for her. I meant to get in there, to celebrate with her, but I was taken aback by the emotional power of the moment. This was friendship. For all the jokes and light-heartedness, they all cared so damn much for each other.

"What happened?"

I jumped and spun to find Atley standing there with a horrified expression on his face. Behind him Peabo, Brody, and Danny looked more concerned than scared. I smiled. "Esther's magic is strong again."

Their eyes all widened and then they tackled her in a hug.

Madge was the first to break from the hug. She wiped at her eyes, smearing her purple eyeliner, and held up her clipboard. "Okay, okay, I think we can re-evaluate our decorating plan. What should we have Esther try next?"

Ideas were thrown at her in rapid-fire. I couldn't discern one from the other, so I just backed away. Magic was still so new to me, and I wasn't a Wand, which meant I wasn't going to be much help. I was feeling some type of way, but I couldn't put my finger on it. Obviously, I was so happy for Esther. I knew her magic being so weak while having such prestige to her family name bothered her more than she let on . . . Seeing that dark period end in front of me was surreal and . . . *magical*. But it was also a reminder of *why* this happened.

And the *why* kept me up all night.

Esther's mother had come over to talk to me and my aunt and uncle about the rune stones, but she didn't know much more information than Esther had. She did, however, have a little blue leather notebook with a cool lock that apparently their family had been keeping notes in since they got the stones. That notebook was currently in my aunt's possession. She wanted to read and research as much she could before I tapped into them. Since I was so new to all this, I was grateful for it.

"You all right, Miss Existential Crisis over there?"

I jumped and looked to Archie who stood beside me. "What?"

He pointed to his own face, then to mine. "That's an alarming face to be making. Wanna share with the class?"

I bit my bottom lip and shook my head.

"Okay, wanna share just with *me* since I'm the only one standing within earshot?"

I frowned and looked up and my breath left me in a rush. The others had all followed Esther to the other side of the gym where she was creating glow-in-the-dark butterflies that hung on strings from the ceiling.

"Yeah, the shock at you finding out they all left is part of the alarming thing."

I closed my eyes and smiled. "Archie . . ."

"Why don't you loosen your grip . . ." When I looked, I found my left hand gripping the bag of rune stones so tight my muscles were straining. He tapped my hand softly. "Yeah, that's *your* arm. Very good. We're making progress. Let's uncurl one finger at a time, shall we?"

A little nervous chuckle came out. I took a deep breath, then slowly uncurled my fingers, but my muscles were so tight they didn't want to relax. Archie caught the bag of stones and put them in my other hand. I exhaled and shook my left hand out. "Thanks."

"No problem."

I groaned. "What does this mean, Archie? Why did some angel leave these *for me* centuries ago? Why me? And what do these runes mean? What do these stones do?"

"I don't know what this means or what the stones do, though I know you'll find out soon enough." He pulled the bag from my hand and opened it. "I also know that you're a Proctor. You come from the line of Edward Proctor, the son of angel Uriel, who was given Archangel Michael's Heavenly sword to fight Lilith in the last war. That is not a coincidence, of that I am positive."

I stared at him. I didn't know what to say. Archie was quiet and unassuming, yet when you got him alone, he really knew and understood a lot about magic, the world, and the history of arcana. He was an old soul who saw too much.

"While I cannot read the Angelic language, I do know what that symbol you saw last night was. The big one in pink..." He gestured with his hands to make the shape of it. "That rune meant The Coven."

I gasped. "*Really?*"

He shrugged and dug through the bag of stones. "You see things in Eden, and if you listen closely, you'll hear them here too." He held the one stone with that same symbol on it.

"It was a message, wasn't it? That's what it felt like. The stones were telling me to seek The Coven, weren't they?"

He smiled. "I think that is a safe bet."

"But why?"

"For help." He frowned. "They're not just brutal warriors. They're experts in magic and this world we live in. That's why there's so many of them. We're supposed to go to them for help, whatever help we need. People just forget that in times of fear and war."

"Dude, how old are you?" I blurted before I could stop myself. "Sorry. Just, you say some of the deepest shit."

"I get that a lot." He cleared his throat and shifted his weight around, then handed the bag of stones back to me. "When you're ready, you should seek them out for help with these. Also, I could be wrong, but I'm pretty sure I overheard that the High Priestess can speak the Angelic language, so she'd be your first stop . . . and then probably your extended family members. Until then, just keep those safe and near you at all times."

"And the notebook Esther's mom gave me." I nodded. "Thanks, Archie. Not to get all touchy feely on ya here, but I don't know what I would've done without you here. You and Esther."

He smiled and his cheeks flushed. "You're a pretty stand-up friend too. I bet Elizabeth would agree."

My heart hurt. "Thanks."

"Right." He cleared his throat. "Well, we've made us both uncomfortable, so I'm gonna take a bathroom break. When I get back, we'll forget this happened."

I was still laughing as I watched him walk through the door that led out to the hallway where the bathrooms were. With a sigh, I turned and shoved my bag of scary angel stones back into my back-pack. Esther and her family had kept these stones safe for centuries. I needed to at least keep them safe for a day.

"You okay, Frankie?"

I spun to find Tomás standing there with a sheepish smile on his face. "I think I'd have to ask you the same thing . . ."

He wrung his hands together and shifted his weight around. The nervous chuckle made *me* nervous. "Yeah, um, well . . . I wanted to ask you something, but it's hard to find you alone."

*Oh boy. Here we go.* I took a deep breath and nodded. "Well, ask me then."

His face turned bright-red. He glanced over his shoulder like he wanted to make sure we were alone, then looked back to me with puppy dog eyes. "I was wondering if you'd like to be my date for the dance tomorrow?"

*Whomp, there it is. Shit. Okay, Frankie, you wanted a way to start this conversation, so have it.* I smiled. "I'm not the type to beat around the bush, so I'm just going to be blunt . . . I don't have romantic or physical feelings for you. I've been trying, because you're so adorable. It's just not there."

His face fell and it hurt my heart. He looked to the ground and nodded. "I understand."

I reached out and put my hand on his shoulder. "I do really like you, as a friend, and I would've loved to go as your date for fun, but I don't want to be inconsiderate of your feelings. I don't want to lead you on."

At that, he peeked up at me through his dark eyelashes and gave me a small smile. "You haven't, which is why I was so nervous to ask because I was pretty sure you were going to say no."

I groaned. "I'm sorry, Tomás."

"It's okay. Thanks for being nice about it." He sighed and glanced over his shoulder to the group. "If I'm being honest, I wasn't sure I liked you that way either. You're really pretty and super awesome, but I wasn't sure. I was hoping though, I mean, you're the first new girl in town in a while so I had to try. Because, man, it's hard being single with them. Ava and Seamus are still in that puppy love stage and then there are literal soulmates."

"What about Esther or Birdie?"

"Esther and I dated two years ago. I wasn't good for her. She's . . . she's got all this pressure on her with her bloodline being what it is. I wasn't the right match for *that*. And now that her magic is free? I don't expect her to get to stay with us. Something tells me The Coven will claim her as one of their pets soon." He frowned. "And Birdie? We both feel like I'm her little brother, so that just wouldn't work."

"I get that. My best friend has an older brother who is gorgeous but . . . he's my brother and that's gross."

"See!?" He threw his arms up. "You get it."

We both laughed.

"Well, what about the other girls?"

"Barb, Patti, and Ruby are heading to SOMA next year for sure. Caitlin is going Ivy League and will be living among humans, which is not where I wanna be. Pitts is miserable, so no thanks. Marina only cares about soccer. Sierra's my cousin, like for real. The other three makeup girls, I don't know—"

"Whitney seems really cool." I pointed to her. "I mean, she does magical tattoos. That's epic."

He pursed his lips. "She does make really cool art too. I don't know why she doesn't hang with us more."

"Maybe she's shy? Maybe she's uncertain if she's welcome to be in the group? Y'all are a very tight knit circle." I shrugged. "Why don't you go talk to her?"

"Just ask her to be my date for the dance?"

"Why not? Best case, y'all fall madly in love. Worst case, you have fun at the dance together and keep it platonic."

He snapped his fingers. "Fuck it. Why not? It'd be nice to not go to a dance alone *again*. Okay, Imma do it."

"Good luck!"

He spun on his toes, then skipped across the gym toward Whitney. I smiled and shook my head. *Dodged that bullet.* It was a damn shame I wasn't attracted to Tomás. He was such a great guy and would probably be a fun boyfriend. Dating was not an area of my life I excelled in.

"Did anyone lose their chihuahua?"

*Jacob.* I knew that grating voice anywhere. I spun and rage filled my veins. Jacob and Aaron were carrying Archie by the back of hoodie, his feet dangling about a foot in the air between them. Archie looked entertained, and that was the only reason I hadn't already pulled out my bat. Because the look in *their* eyes was pure antagonization. They wanted to piss me off, to instigate a fight to retaliate. They wanted me to get in trouble.

"We'd be happy to take this one to the shelter—"

"Put him down," I snapped. My hands were already in fists at my side. "Now."

Archie smirked at me. "At least I got to pee first."

Only Archie would be making jokes when being carried by the scruff like a kitten. He just let himself dangle. He didn't try to get free or defend himself. I genuinely thought Archie found this to be hilarious, and it made no sense to me.

Aaron looked around, then gave me a sickening smile. "No cameras in here right now so they can use magic. How convenient that is for us."

"No one will have proof of what we do." Jacob smacked Archie's cheek with the back of his hand. "Shall we break something on him first?"

"Nah, how far can he get from us? Let's take the bitch down first." Aaron wagged his eyebrows. "Her friends are too busy over there to notice. I bet we could break a few bones first."

I sighed. Bullies were exhausting. "Do you really wanna do this? You really want a fight? Haven't you had enough?"

"You got us suspended from school," Jacob snarled.

"No. *You* got you suspended from school for having a brawl on a baseball field." I gestured between them. "Do you not remember you both charging the pitcher's mound unprovoked?"

"*Unprovoked?* You little—"

A shrill scream ripped through the gym.

I spun toward the sound with my heart in my throat. Rootbeer barked and tackled Seamus like she wanted to shield his body with hers. The glass windows at the top of the gym walls exploded and shards of glass rained down on us. Dark objects shot across the ceiling.

"*DEMON!*" Archie yelled.

*Demons? OH MY GOD. What? Those?!* They were so small, about the size of a basketball, and had little wings that fluttered so fast you could barely see them. They swarmed like gnats trying to find a way around the fabric hanging from the ceiling.

A black object bounced off the ground, soared over Rootbeer's body, and slammed into Esther's chest. She screamed and flew backward, her back sliding across the gym floor. Atley pounced on Esther with his sword drawn. He grabbed the demon by the wing, pulling it off of her so he could stab it with his blade. Black liquid splashed onto the ground.

And then chaos reigned around us.

"Aaron—"

"Drop him! GO!"

I glanced back just as Archie's feet hit the ground and his legs buckled beneath him, sending him crashing onto his knees. Aaron and Jacob were already out the door. Those cowards just ran away.

"Franks, get that bat out!" Archie yanked on my arm. "Get it out!"

*SHIT.* I pulled my phone out of my pocket, then pressed my finger to the sticker of the baseball bat. In a flash of blue magic, my Louisville Slugger sat perfectly in my grip. I adjusted my grip and swung it around out of pure habit just as one of those demons dropped down right in front of us. There was a flash of red eyes. I screamed and swung my bat as hard as I could. The demon shot straight into the wall with a splatter.

"*What the hell are these?*" Peabo shouted. He was chasing one across the gym, but his swings were missing like the demon was dodging him. "Atley!"

"I don't know! These are new!" Atley dove in the air and tackled a demon, wrapping his arms around it. "Catch and kill!"

Something moved in my peripheral vision. I spun and screamed with all the rage in my body. Five demon gnats were hovering around my backpack. I went full Hulk-smash mode and whacked the shit out of whatever I could hit.

"The stones!" Archie grabbed my backpack, then sprinted away. "HOME RUN DERBY!"

*Home run derby?* I gasped. *OH!* The demon gnats were chasing him. *They must be drawn to the magic in the stones!* I cursed and sprinted after them, hitting each of them with my bat as we ran. Once they were gone, we ducked behind a table. I looked out to our friends and my stomach sank. There were demons *everywhere.* It was a swarm. I tried to keep track of my friends, but they were running and dodging demons.

Ava leapt to her feet and screamed as she whipped her wand back and forth. She bolted across the gym, shooting spells at the demons. Whitney had her back pressed to a wall, but she was also throwing magic at the demons with her wand. I had no idea what they were doing. ll I saw were flashes of light.

Gold and navy-blue glitter shot like a firework through the chaos. Demons hissed and shrieked when Esther's magic hit them. I scanned the gym for her, but I couldn't find her. I just saw her magic going everywhere. Peabo and Atley were *fierce*. I suddenly understood what the rest of this community knew about these two young teens. But they couldn't do this on their own.

"We have to kill them, right?"

"Yeah. They're not gonna just leave." Archie cursed. "These things are annoying."

"Are they drawn to the stones in my bag?"

He nodded.

"Fun. Stay here with them."

I didn't give him a chance to argue. Archie was great but he was too clumsy for this. He tripped on air on a daily basis. He needed to just stay down and stay hidden. *I* had to get in there and help the boys.

"ATLEY!" I planted my feet and swung my bat into a demon gnat. "KILL!"

He jumped up and sliced his sword through the demon's body. As black demon blood splashed onto him, he looked to me with wide eyes. "AGAIN! PEABO!"

"I SMASH. YOU KILL!" And then I charged into the fight with a battle cry.

I ran around the gym like a headless chicken just swatting at anything that moved. My body found a rhythm. I thanked my years as an athlete for that. But in my head, it was just a steady stream of screaming. I tried to keep an eye on my friends, but it was impossible. Every other second there was magic shooting by me. The lights in the ceiling flickered like in a horror film.

A demon dropped in front of me. It bounced off the ground, then flew right toward me like a baseball from the pitcher's mound. I slid to a stop with a curse, jumped into position, then slammed the demon into left field. I watched in horrified slow motion as that demon soared right for Archie who was no longer hiding behind the table. I screamed his name, but it was too late. It crashed into his face and sent them both flying into the shadows.

"I'm fine!" Archie shouted from out of sight.

I took a deep breath and cringed at the scent of maple syrup clinging to the air.

The doors to the gym opened. I braced myself for more demons, only to find my aunt and uncle standing in the open doorway. Uncle Kyle held a stack of three pizza boxes. Aunt Kimmy held a bag with what looked like bottles of soda. Their eyes widened.

"Well, this is a fun surprise." Uncle Kyle chuckled. He actually *chuckled*.

Aunt Kimmy pulled her wand out and swirled it in the air while whispering words I couldn't make out. Light sparkled over my head. I turned to watch as my aunt's spell disintegrated three demons at once. I gasped and looked back at her, but she just kept going without pausing.

Uncle Kyle was still holding pizza boxes, but he hurried into the gym. "Franks, send 'em here!"

I lunged toward a demon and swung. It soared right for my uncle who calmly just lifted the pizza boxes and drop kicked the demon to the ground. Then he stomped it with his foot, causing black demon blood to splatter across his jeans.

He laughed. "AGAIN!"

We did this five more times before I turned and found no more demons. I spun in circles, scanning the gym for more. There had to be more.

"Okay. Demons are dead," Aunt Kimmy yelled out. "Take a deep breath, kids."

I exhaled in a rush and dropped my bat onto the floor so I could rest my hands on my knees. My chest and lungs were on fire. The oxygen I sucked in burned a path down my throat. Sweat dripped down my temples and my spine.

"Right. Let's get the lights back at least." Aunt Kimmy flicked her wand, and the lights came right back on over our heads. She nodded. "That's better."

"Well, we know you're hungry now." Uncle Kyle chuckled and finally sat the three boxes on a table. "Come and get a slice while it's still hot."

Atley was breathing heavy and still gripping his sword like he was waiting for more. "Don't we need to clean up?"

"In a minute. Everyone over here. Now." Aunt Kimmy waved for everyone to follow her. Once we were all together around the pizza boxes, Aunt Kimmy pointed her wand like a flashlight at us, walking one by one. "Let me assess any injuries first. The clean-up can wait. But grab a slice while it's hot. It's important to eat."

Tomás, Brody, Whitney, and Danny went straight for the pizza without hesitation.

Birdie held her hand up. "Um, I'd like to warn the rest of the community. Just in case."

"Thank you. Yes. Go ahead. You'll have to step outside for your phone to work but don't go far." Aunt Kimmy turned to Atley. "Can you go with her?"

Atley gave her a salute, then followed Birdie for the door.

Peabo cleared his throat. "Can I do a little perimeter check? I'd feel better if I knew there weren't more lurking in the shadows. The Coven always does a perimeter check after an attack—ever since Cassandra."

"Yes, but not alone. Brody, would you go with him?"

Brody grabbed another slice of pizza, then unsheathed his dagger. "We got this."

Once they took off, Aunt Kimmy turned back to the rest of us. "Okay, who's hurt?"

"Seamus is." Ava pointed to her boyfriend beside her. "He was protecting Rootbeer and they sliced him up pretty good."

I gasped and turned toward him. "Is Rootbeer okay?"

Seamus didn't respond. He was just sitting on the ground next to his dog, running his blood-splattered hands through her fur. He turned his head to the side, and I saw a little river of blood running down his neck from right behind his ear. I cursed and moved closer. Rootbeer barked and put her paw on Seamus's arm.

He jumped and looked up with wide, panicked eyes. "What?" he yelled so loud we all flinched.

Ava scowled and dropped down in front of him. She cupped his face and turned it from side to side, then she reached up and pulled not one but *two* shattered hearing aids off. They were covered in both black demon blood and Seamus's red blood. His face fell as he stared at them in her hands.

She kissed his forehead, then stood and looked to my aunt. "He's not gonna be able to hear a single thing without these. Um, his parents have extras—"

"Why don't you go get those and come back?"

"I can bring him to the infirmary. I know sign language," I offered.

Ava's yellow eyes filled with unshed tears. She nodded. "I'll meet you there?"

"Yep. Don't worry. I've got him." I tapped his shoulder to get his attention, then I signed, *"Ava is going to your house to get your other hearing aids. She's going to meet us at the infirmary. Okay?"*

"Yeah." He looked up at his girlfriend and smiled. His voice was much louder than it needed to be, but without his hearing aids, he'd have trouble knowing how loud he was so no one flinched or said a thing. "I'm okay. Just little cuts. Rootbeer is not hurt. I'll go with Frankie."

Ava started to sign, but she was struggling. "Dammit, I have to get better at ASL faster. Um, ask him if he wants to take Rootbeer with him or should I bring her home?"

He was watching us with a frown, and I saw his frustration in his eyes, so I signed, *"Do you want Rootbeer to go with you or home?"*

He looked to his dog. "Rootbeer, you want to go home—"

She jumped in his lap, which gave us all the chuckle we needed in that moment.

Ava sighed. "Okay, I'll go now. I'll meet you at the infirmary."

Uncle Kyle cocked his head to the side. "Madge, Jo, are you okay? You hurt?"

Jo tapped on her chest. *"Je serai marqué à jamais."*

Madge laughed. "She'll be scarred forever."

*"Je suis blessée émotionnellement."* Jo shuddered and specks of black demon blood fell off of her blonde hair. *"Je ne serai plus jamais la même."*

"You're right. We'll never be the same." Madge scrubbed her face with her hands. Her stiletto-pointed nails were stained with black demon blood. When she pulled her hands away, she smeared her eyeliner down her cheeks. She huffed. "We got too comfortable with them here. We *can't* be the same. Give me pizza."

"But are you hurt?"

"No, Uncle Kyle. I am not physically injured. Unless I find a wound after a shower. Can I just have pizza now?" Madge pouted her bottom lip at my uncle. I loved that they all referred to them as aunt and uncle because I did.

He chuckled and handed her the whole box. "Feed your other half too please."

I wiped my face, then gagged as the maple syrup scent invaded my senses. "Where's Esther? That first demon got her—"

"I'm here," she said softly from where she was sprawled out on her back on the floor. "I'm alive. That's all I know."

"Right. Okay." I grabbed my bat, then walked over to her. "Let's get you and Seamus to the infirmary."

"Um . . ." Archie waddled out of the shadows with my backpack hanging from his chest. Half of his face and upper body were covered in both his own blood and black demon blood. "Add me to that list."

# CHAPTER TWENTY-THREE

## FRANKIE

"MAYBE YOU GUYS should call your parents?" I glanced over my shoulder to Esther in the passenger seat, then to Archie behind her. Both of them had a little too much of their own blood on them for my comfort. "Just not on FaceTime, because . . . we don't need a panic."

They laughed.

The door behind me opened and Rootbeer leapt inside. She snuggled right into Archie's lap before Seamus was even in the car. She was rather obsessed with Archie. I watched in the rearview mirror as our second redhead buckled his seatbelt. It was actually hard to tell which of the speckles on his face were blood and which were freckles. He looked up with bright-blue eyes and met my stare in the mirror.

"*Ready?*" I signed.

He nodded and signed back, "*Yes. Let's go.*"

I put the car in drive and drove off. "But really, please call your parents?"

"I've been texting mine. They're gonna meet us there." Esther glanced back to Seamus, then looked to me. "How do I sign *phone* and *mom?*"

I showed her because Seamus was staring out the window. Esther nodded, then reached back and tapped on Seamus's knee to get his attention. The angle she was turned gave me a grisly view of the wound on her chest. She signed the two words. I looked into the mirror to watch his reaction.

He frowned and patted his pockets, then grimaced. "I don't have my phone. Can you call her?" he yelled.

Esther gave him a thumbs-up, then turned back around, already dialing her phone. "Hi, Mrs. O'Brien—what? . . . Oh, you heard. Yeah, no, it's okay. They're all dead. But listen, Seamus got a little scratched up . . . No, he's okay. Really. But both his hearing aids broke. Ava is on her way to get his backups, but Frankie is driving a few of us to the infirmary. Seamus cannot find his phone, so it's probably in the gym still . . . Yeah . . . Of course . . . Okay. See you soon."

She turned and gave him another thumbs-up.

"Okay, your turn, Archie."

"Oh. Right." He pulled his phone out of his pocket and dialed, then held it to his ear. "Hey, so . . . I think I swallowed a demon. Or part of one."

"*Archie,*" I hissed and shook my head.

"So, what had happened was these demon gnats attacked us, and Frankie was smashing 'em like baseballs in the home run derby, and I did not move fast enough."

I snort-laughed so hard my sinuses burned.

Esther spun sideways in her seat to look back at him. Black demon blood dripped from her black curls onto my center console. "For someone so small, you really are a danger to yourself. I mean, how'd you get a demon in your face? Twice?"

"I'm an over-achiever?"

We all laughed. Even Seamus, which told me he was reading lips now. I was always impressed with how well he could do that.

Archie frowned. "Actually, I believe I ducked *into* the demon baseball."

"I didn't see that I hit you twice—"

"Look, I just wasn't prepared for how slow these little legs would move."

I sighed. He was just so nonchalant about it. "Let me guess, you've had worse?"

Archie pursed his lips and narrowed his eyes like he was thinking about it. "I think that might depend on if I did in fact swallow the demon."

Esther grimaced in disgust. "I am not checking your poop."

He looked down at his stomach, then back up. "I think I'd rather puke it back up rather than have it go out the proper exit."

I giggled. "Hey, at least now you have a good pickup line. *Baby, wait 'til you meet the demon on my tongue.*"

They cackled.

"Well, thanks, Frankie, I don't think I'll ever be able to do that again." Archie shuddered. "Then again, some people eat pineapples to get a better taste . . . and all things said, maple syrup isn't the worst—"

"ARCHIE!"

Esther was laughing so hard she couldn't breathe.

"I didn't catch all of that, but I think I don't want to," Seamus yelled. He was smirking.

Esther shook her head and mouthed *he's being nasty.*

Tears slid down my cheeks from how hard I laughed. I pulled up in front of the infirmary and parallel parked. "Archie, I say this in the spirit of friendship, but you have the most fucked up sense of humor I've ever seen."

Archie grinned. "Thank you."

Esther choked on the oxygen she was trying to suck in. "Wait, are you on the phone with your mother this whole time? She heard you say all that?"

"She's heard worse." He shrugged. "Anyhoo, we just got to the infirmary. I'm gonna go get my face fixed . . . Okay . . . Yeah . . . Right, I love you, bye."

"You tell your mom *I love you* on the phone, like every time?"

He unbuckled his seatbelt, then scowled up at Esther. "Each time you speak to someone you love it could be your last, and you won't know until after. Trust me, I'd go back in time to say it more often to the people I've lost."

My chest tightened as his words hit hard. For a moment, we all just sat there in silence in my car, undoubtedly as we all thought about the people we didn't want to lose. A hot lump formed in my throat.

Seamus cleared his throat. "Thanks for lightening the mood, dude," he yelled with a smirk.

Archie cackled and jumped out of the car. The rest of us climbed out after him. I let Esther and Archie lead the way through the opening in the white picket fence and up the red brick pathway. I wanted to make sure I was next to Seamus until Ava or his parents got here in case someone tried to talk to him. Rootbeer trotted between her owner and me with a happy, sloppy smile on her face.

I looked up to the colonial-style home with gray wooden siding, a white roof, and black shutters with pentagrams etched into them. There were nine French windows on the front wall, and I loved the candles flickering with orange light. The front door was painted black, and they had a pentacle made of twigs on it. The outside looked nothing like a medical facility, so I was curious to see the inside.

Esther opened the door and led the way inside. Archie was hot on her heels. I had to admit seeing them walking with such ease despite their injuries made me feel better about this whole situation. Seamus gestured for me to go in ahead, so I leapt over the threshold. Inside was a whole lot of *not what I expected*. It basically looked like the inside of a residential home, complete with a grand wooden staircase that led to an open-air hallway on the second floor.

"Oh boy," a young girl said from out of nowhere. "Guess the rumor is true, eh?"

"If you mean, were we unexpectedly attacked by demon gnats the size of basketballs, then yes." Esther chuckled and pointed to her own chest. "I'm not entirely sure what's beneath all this blood, but I do know it hurts."

I stepped out from behind her and spotted a girl who couldn't have been much older than us. She had a wild mane of red hair that I was low-key jealous of. Her amber eyes were wide and staring at us.

I waved. "Hi, who are you?"

"I'm Gin. I'm one of the junior healers here." She grimaced. "You don't look hurt, but you two guys do . . ."

"Right, Archie here had a little face action with the demons.,"

"Which I might've swallowed." Archie grinned like this was the highlight of his day.

I gestured to Seamus beside me. "This is Seamus. He's deaf and both of his hearing aids have broken. New ones are on their way here."

"Oh, we know Seamus here." She smiled and looked to Seamus, then signed, "*Hi, friend! You and Rootbeer take the room upstairs with the bay window? She'll like that one.*"

"*Thank you! Will you be healing me?*" Seamus signed back. When she nodded, he waved to us and then led Rootbeer up the stairs.

Gin then looked back to us and bit her bottom lip. "Right. So, demon gnats are a nuisance. Um—"

"I'll take care of them, Gin," a smooth, deep voice said from the hallway to our left. "Tend to Seamus upstairs, please."

"Perfect." She waved to us, then hurried up the stairs.

But I wasn't watching her. My gaze landed on the guy walking into the foyer. My breath caught in my throat. My heart did weird little jumps in my chest. I swallowed roughly and tried to keep my cool. He was tall and gorgeous. His hair was the color of freshly fallen snow, though his eyebrows were jet black. Somehow it didn't clash with the paleness of his skin or the all-white outfit. It was giving Billy Idol vibes but *prettier*—dangerously pretty, in fact, with that sharp jawline and the wicked sparkle in his blue eyes.

"Good evening." He gave us a tight-lipped smile and pressed a palm to his stomach. "I'm Everest. Katherine sent me here to help out with some of the nastier ailments while she's with The Coven, so I will be tending to your wounds tonight."

*Everest.* A million images flipped through my mind—rainbow light flashed in my eyes. I blinked and shook my head. Sharp pain lanced through my temples, so I pushed on them with my fingertips. I hissed through clenched teeth loud enough to trigger both Esther *and* Everest to look at me. I tried to give them a reassuring smile, but neither of them fell for it.

"Archibald, your mother beat you here and is in the middle room just behind me." Everest smiled and half-turned. "Go ahead in there and I shall be with you in a moment. Try not to eat anything you shouldn't."

Archie cackled and walked off, pausing only to give us two thumbs-up.

Everest watched to make sure Archie went into the correct room, then turned his attention back to us. The intensity in his blue eyes made me inhale sharply. He arched one eyebrow at me and his lips curved into a little smirk—and then the expression was gone. *His* face was a mask of professionalism, while *my* face was hot and definitely as pink as my hair.

"Esther and Francelina, follow me—"

"You know our names?" Esther cocked her head to the side.

He gave her a small smile and my pulse skipped beats. "Francelina's aunt called as soon as you left to warn us."

And then his gaze shot back to me, and I swallowed roughly. *Seriously, body, what is wrong with you? Get a grip. He's just a boy. A really stupidly, dangerously pretty boy.* I wasn't used to having this kind of reaction to anyone. Normally I reacted to boys the same way I did to Tomás: I acknowledged they were cute and maybe liked their personality but felt absolutely numb and apathetic in every other way.

But not with Everest.

I couldn't even breathe normally in front of him, and we'd just met. My body was locked in place and in the process of overheating.

"Francelina?"

I jumped and looked around to find Esther was already ten feet away while Everest just watched me with a sparkle in his eyes like I was entertaining him immensely. *Wait, he said my name. But like my whole government name.* I cleared my throat and opened my mouth, but no words came out, just a squeak.

His one eyebrow twitched like he was trying really hard not to react. "Are you all right, Francelina?"

Butterflies danced in my stomach. I licked my lips and nodded, or I thought I did. There was a chance I just stared at him. I didn't know what was wrong with me. I felt like I'd stepped into a sauna and now couldn't find the door to get out.

Esther was suddenly in my face. "Did you have another vision? What'd you see?"

That lock on my body snapped and air rushed through my lungs. I blinked and shook myself. "What? No? I don't know?" I looked over Esther's shoulder and my eyes locked with his. Words dried on my tongue.

"Visions?"

I opened my mouth to answer him, but no words came out.

"Yeah, she's had some issues. I was actually going to call Katherine today." Esther wrapped her arm around my shoulders and squeezed. "Maybe you can help both of us in a room together? She's been through a lot."

"Of course, you and Francelina can take the room in the back—"

"It's Frankie. You can call her Frankie."

"Come, let us see to your needs in private." Everest nodded once and then turned and gestured for us to follow him.

If it wasn't for Esther dragging me by the elbow, I couldn't have said if I would've been able to move. But we were catching up to Everest and my muscles were already trying to lock down, so I squeezed my eyes shut. Esther wouldn't let me walk into a wall. The temperature in the foyer and hallway was a little on the cold side, so I knew the moment we'd crossed into the room because the air was cozy warm and smelled like vanilla.

"Make yourselves comfortable. I shall be right back," Everest said softly from right behind me, his breath sweeping over the back of my head.

The door clicked shut.

Esther snorted. "Are you holding your eyes closed?"

I nodded.

"We're alone. You can open them now."

When I did, I found her standing in front of me with her hands on her hips and her eyebrow arched. "What the hell is going on with you?"

I cleared my throat and shook my head. "Nothing?" But I couldn't stand there with her watching me like that, so I walked around her and sat on the chair next to the bed.

"Oh my Goddess."

"What?" I fidgeted with my crystal ring.

She gasped. "*Frankie. You like him!*"

I sighed and collapsed against the back of the chair, then scrubbed my face with my hands. "Make it stop."

She giggled excitedly. "So this is Frankie with a crush—"

"Oh my God, *shhhh,*" I said with a groan. "I can't have a crush on a person I just met for two whole seconds—"

The door swung open, and Everest sauntered in with one of his hands in his pocket. "Sorry to keep you waiting."

"—*Or maybe you can,*" I heard myself whisper.

"What was that, Francelina?" His voice was smooth and silky.

My face was on fire. All I could do was shake my head.

He nodded and gave me a smirk but turned his attention back to Esther. "Why don't we start with your wounds. Please lie down on your back."

I couldn't take my eyes off of him. I watched as he carried a tray of vials and gauze over to the bed and got to work. A strange chill swept through my body. I shivered and wrapped my arms around myself as a light filled my eyes. One second I was watching the speed of Everest's hands as he treated Esther's wounds . . . the next I was walking through a garden covered in ice.

Everything was covered in snow. Every flower petal had a layer of ice on it. I walked with my head held high but only because I had to. There were too many eyes on me. I saw them in my peripheral vision, men and women dressed in formal white gowns and tuxes. I stole a glance down at myself only to find I was wearing *red*.

I was *freezing*.

But then something hot pressed to my forehead and I was back in the infirmary.

I gasped and threw my hands out to grab the armrests and hold on tight. That warmth still pressed to my head, and it was calming my runaway heartrate. It took me several blinks before my vision cleared enough to actually *see* around me.

And then I wanted to die.

That heat on my forehead was Everest's hand. He had his palm resting against my skin. And the armrest I held was actually his knees. My stomach sank like I was on a roller coaster. I wanted to scream, run away, and throw up a little. I had his soft white pants fisted in my grip. Both hands. My mouth was dry, but it didn't matter because no words were coming to me. Judging by the tightness in my chest, I wasn't breathing either.

"*Come back to me, Francelina*," Everest whispered.

Like the flip of a switch, my body kicked into gear. My lungs breathed the oxygen I was swallowing, though my cheeks were still burning. "*You can call me Frankie*," I heard myself whisper back.

He chuckled and pulled his hand off my face. "There you are. Welcome back."

I started to smile except his hands covered both of mine and my brain short-circuited.

"You see what I mean?" Esther sat up in the bed. I saw her over Everest's shoulder. Except she now had all this gauze and cream spread over her chest. "She'll be just fine, then *boom*, lost to a vision."

I scowled. "*What?*"

"Your friend explained everything you've been experiencing. She is worried about you, and I have to agree." He uncurled my fingers from his pants, then stood up. Without dropping my hands, he gently pulled me onto my feet. "Come over and lie on this other bed, please."

My mind was not registering the words coming out of his mouth, all I knew was the softness of his skin, the feel of his bare hands on mine, and the way his fingers curled to let mine hook around his. He walked backwards like he didn't want to spook me. It took me far too long to put the words together. He wanted me to lie in the bed. I licked my lips and nodded, then forced my way around the foot of Esther's bed to the side of the room with the other bed.

I stopped at the side of the bed and frowned. "Wait, why? What's wrong with me?" I turned and choked on a gasp.

Everest waved his hand in front of my face, and I saw a cloud of black—and then my body acted without my approval. I hopped onto the bed with my legs dangling off the edge. He stepped up so close that our bodies touched from my knees down to my ankles. Heat radiated off his body. I was falling apart with every second he looked at me, and it was so unlike me.

"Your magic and your mind have muddied the water, so to speak, so we just need to clear it up and this shouldn't keep happening." His finger tipped my chin up, forcing me to look him in the eye. "Do you understand?"

My eyes widened. This close to him, I realized his eyes were not normal. Instead of black pupils, his were royal blue. Where there normally would've been a color like blue, green, or brown was a nearly solid white iris except for the rim, which was the same royal blue as his pupils.

My breath left me in a rush.

"Francelina?"

"Your eyes are beautiful," I heard myself whisper.

"Thank you." He smiled softly. "On that note, I'm going to keep you overnight so we can settle your soul back to where it should be. Lie down, rest, and I will return shortly."

# CHAPTER TWENTY-FOUR

## FRANKIE

I'D BEGGED my aunt and uncle to go home to sleep.

Them sleeping in chairs beside me in a bed made me go into a full panic attack. It was too soon. I hadn't realized how much trauma I had from that coma, but it was surely a rude awakening. I needed them to leave me alone in this infirmary so I could remember I wasn't just waking from a coma. Everest had to give me a potion to calm me down.

But I was so calm that I couldn't seem to fall asleep. It was like I didn't *need* sleep. So I'd just been lying in bed staring at the floating candles up on the ceiling for a long time. I had my phone, so I could've called Elizabeth, especially since it was the middle of the day for her. Or I could've watched YouTube or listened to music . . . and yet, I just lay there. My body was warm and cozy. I was comfortable.

Blue light glowed from my right, making me look over with a frown. It was coming out of my backpack that was sitting in the chair next to the bed. I stared at it for a long moment before my brain put the pieces together. It must have been those rune stones. Curiosity was the only thing that made me lean out of bed to reach for my bag. It took me a few moments to actually get my bag open. It was like my body was too Zen-'d out to move quickly.

When I finally got to the navy-blue velvet drawstring bag, I knew I'd been right. That blue light was billowing from within it. They hadn't done this before, at least not since when I first touched them. I yanked the drawstring, then tipped the bag and dumped them into my palm. They started to pour over, so I held both hands side-by-side. The two dozen-ish stones filled both palms, tingling against my skin wherever they touched me. The blue glowing light grew brighter and brighter until it was like holding a neon sign. My pulse quickened. Something was happening. I'd yet to learn what these did so this was exciting.

The gold-glittered runes engraved in each stone changed to blue like they weren't even there . . . and then a symbol appeared. It was stretched out across all of the stones. This symbol glowed bright neon-pink, brighter than the stones had just been. It was like a beacon. The symbol seemed to pulse right along with the heavy pounding of my heart. My breath caught in my throat. My chest tightened. I was supposed to do something with this. The symbol *meant* something. I cursed and looked over at my phone, considering calling Atley to do me a huge favor and call The Coven. But that would've been horribly rude.

I exhaled and closed my eyes. *Come on, stones. Just tell me what you mean. Or show me. Just SHOW ME what I have to do. I don't speak your language yet. Give me some kind of clue. Just take me there. Take me where I need to be, and I'll go.* With a groan, I opened my eyes—and choked on a scream.

I was not in my bed in the infirmary anymore. I had no idea where I was. I'd never been here before. It looked like some European village. It didn't make any sense. I'd been in the infirmary. I had no idea how I suddenly appeared—*ohhh. I'm not awake, am I?* I started retracing my thoughts back to when I was lying in bed. I assumed I was awake, but I should've known better. That potion Everest gave me was *strong*. When Esther had first told him I was having psychic visions, her words not mine, he'd asked if I'd been lucid dreaming. Then he'd explained to me what that even was . . . and I wondered if he unlocked some skill I didn't know I had. My magic was so new to me.

*Okay, Frankie. You're lucid dreaming. Everest said it was a thing. You just need to watch what's happening until you wake up. Just stay calm. That's what he said.* I opened my eyes and looked around with new intention. The stones still sat in my palms like they were in my bed, so I had a feeling this dream was about them somehow.

I stood before a grand, elaborate fountain that had to be thirty feet tall. It had fairies carved into it like they were climbing to the top. I had to crane my neck back in order to see the top. It looked like something I'd expect to see in Europe. The pool beneath it had to be fifty feet in diameter, at least. It had little spotlights inside the pool of water at the base that pointed up toward the fountain and made it shimmer like solid gold.

Someone was watching me. A blue glow radiated up from my palms. From the stones. I looked down and exhaled roughly. They were glowing again, and that same glowing pink symbol flashed from the surface of them. My stomach tightened into knots.

"*What do you want?*" I whispered to them.

The wind swept across my back, carrying an odd floral scent and an unusual chill. It sent my paranoia into hyper-speed. I turned in a slow circle, eyeing the area around me for anything suspicious, but nothing looked out of place. This quaint little village was dark and quiet. Empty of everyone but me. Yet the feeling inside me, the sense of alarm and dread, intensified. It was like my body knew something I didn't. *Something isn't right here.* A chill ran down my spine and I shivered. It felt like fingertips tracing down my back.

I took a deep breath, and it left my mouth in a cloud of smoke. In Florida. In March. Then I felt it . . . eyes on my back. I knew it with every fiber of my being. With my heart pounding in my throat, I spun on my toes—and gasped. In front of me, standing silently and unmoving, were dozens of people. Except they weren't real people . . . They were ghosts, transparent and glowing a bright yellowish color. They had pointed ears and narrow faces full of stone-cold rage. The ghosts stood in perfectly formed lines, like an army straight out of Hell itself.

My pulse quickened and my fingers trembled. I swallowed and it echoed in my ears. It was my dream. These figures were the same ones I'd seen in that other dream except those were blue instead of yellow. But they had the same pointed ears and swords.

"*They are coming,*" that voice had warned me.

They were here.

I didn't move. I couldn't. This couldn't be a coincidence, yet I had no idea what to do. I glanced left and right without moving my head. There was no one else around. There was no sign of life at all, not even a mosquito or cockroach. There wasn't even a clue for me to use to know what to do. I just stood there in a standoff with this fairy ghost army. We were in some kind of staring contest. Running wasn't my style, especially not this fast, but I wasn't going to stand here all night.

In the movie *The Sixth Sense,* the kid learned he just had to talk to the ghosts. That was the only idea I had.

"What do you want?" I cried in frustration. "Just tell me!"

They lunged for me all at once. I gasped and stepped back, but my legs hit the wall of the fountain's pool, stopping me in place. Not that it mattered, the fairy ghosts ambushed me in the blink of an eye. They surrounded me entirely with their arms stretched out toward me. I didn't have time to react. One second they were in those rows staring, the next there were a dozen glowing yellow hands resting on top of my rune stones.

"Well, this is interesting."

I jumped at the sound of an unfamiliar male voice, but the spirits lunged away from me and landed on their knees like they were bowing to the person. I looked up and my eyes widened. There were *two* people standing about twenty feet away from me. The male had long, wild red hair with metallic beads wrapped around some of the strands. He had glowing orange eyes with an energy that felt like pure wildness. He had the sharpest facial features in his jaw and cheekbones, but it was the pointed ears poking out through all that hair that sent a chill down my spine. He wore a crown made of tree branches with dark-pink flowers on it and strings of turquoise leaves and glowing twinkle lights. His outfit was strange: an olive-green tunic lined with gold grommets and a trench coat seemingly made entirely out of bright-green vines.

The female was painfully beautiful. Everything about her was mesmerizing. All I could do was stare. She had wild hair that varied in shades of blue, purple, and turquoise. Her skin was lusciously tan. Her eyes met mine, and I heard myself gasp. They were unlike anything I'd ever seen. Her eyes held a galaxy of colors that glittered just like the Milky Way. Her outfit was basically giant green leaves that covered her lady bits and were connected by flowered vines, which were strapped all around her torso, chest, and limbs.

The male crossed his arms over his chest and cocked his head to the side like I was the most fascinating toy. "I thought you did that?"

*HUH?*

"No," the female scowled without taking her eyes off me. "I thought you did?"

"Huh." He pursed his lips and glanced down at the ghosts still bowed before him. "Really, Sage? This is normally your thing—"

"She's your daughter, Thorne." This *Sage* threw her hands up and rolled those pretty eyes of hers. "Your daughter. Your responsibility. Your words, not mine."

"She has a point, Father."

Thorne jumped with a curse. "God, you're tiny."

A petite little redhead with vibrant lavender eyes and pointed ears hopped out from behind the man she'd called her father. "That's more your fault, not mine." She grinned and walked forward to stand right in front of the ghosts.

"That's two for two for you, Brother." Sage giggled. "You're on a roll. Please, don't stop."

Thorne rolled his orange eyes at his sister. "My Saraphina, your arrival—"

"The same as yours, I'm sure." His daughter smiled.

"Alone?"

"Me, alone in Hidden Kingdom? How unheard of." Saraphina's smile turned crooked. "I do believe that was *also* your fault."

Sage threw her head back and cackled like a movie villain. She held three fingers up.

Thorne sighed and it sounded pained. "These are not the same times as those—"

"I am three and a half centuries old, Father. I am well aware of the danger we're in." She held her hand up and counted down with her fingers from five. As she held up her last finger, her smile warmed. "And I am not alone."

A massive wolf lunged from within the shadows behind these people. It was the biggest wolf I'd ever seen. It was blacker than night itself and seemed to be made of smoke and shadow, and its paws and tail weren't solid in form. But the eyes were the creepiest part. One was glowing gold, the other sparkling red. The wolf pounced on the front row of ghosts, yet none of them even flinched, which seemed to please the animal as it began trotting up and down their lines.

"SPOT," a deep male voice shouted. A split second later, a gorgeous man with short dirty blond hair and gold eyes stood between

Thorne and Sage. He shook his head. "It's like we have to start your training all over again."

The wolf stopped and turned toward the pretty guy with his tail whipping back and forth.

"We all have to have our fun *somehow*, Brother," another guy said suddenly from beside the pretty guy, though this one was equally as beautiful. They had nearly the same face, with glowing gold eyes and blond hair, but this one had *long* locks. "Raziel, perhaps Spot needs to take a sweep through the park before we leave?"

*Raziel* sighed and put his hands on his hips. "You enable him, Zabkiel. But fine. Spot, make sure the park is clear. Go ahead."

Spot howled at the moon, then vanished into smoke and shadow.

"See, Father? I am not alone. Riah was right behind me."

Riah, who seemed to also be referred to as Zabkiel and that confused me, spoke in a language I'd never heard. But Raziel, Thorne, and Sage all nodded.

"My brother was just going to finish the job he was supposed to—"

"Yes, yes. We've been busy, Sage." Thorne looked to the ghosts and pressed his hand to his chest. "I am sorry for my delay."

I frowned. He was apologizing to the ghosts.

Saraphina pressed both hands to her chest and her eyes glistened. She spoke to them in that same language I'd never heard that definitely didn't sound like a human language.

Thorne chuckled at whatever she'd said to the ghosts. "Fair. But now that we're here, Daughter, you're so much more qualified to—"

Saraphina chanted words in a language I'd never heard. I tried to listen and watch, to follow what was happening since there had to be a reason I was lucid dreaming this, when suddenly the two gorgeous blond guys stood in front of me. At first, I assumed I was just getting a front row view of whatever they were doing, but then both pairs of golden eyes locked on *me*.

I gasped and jumped back, but I was already up against the fountain's pool, so my legs were swept out from under me and I went flying toward the water—a tan hand grabbed my wrist faster than a person should've been able to move. I was yanked back upright onto my feet and found the one with long hair holding onto me. His skin was warm against mine. I felt it. I didn't think lucid dreams worked *like that*. Panic began to surge inside of me.

"Easy," he said in a soft, calm voice. "Step away from the fountain, *lita toah.*"

*Lita toah? What does that mean?*

The other one bent over and scooped something up off the ground. When he stood, his palm was glowing neon-blue. "You need to keep better care of these, *lita toah.*"

My jaw dropped. My stones. I'd been so startled I'd dropped my stones. I cupped my hands and held them out for him to dump them back in my palms. Words just weren't coming out. I had no idea what was happening or how.

Riah, or Zabkiel, gave me a small smile. "You shouldn't be here, *lita toah.*"

"You need to keep better care of yourself in times like these." Raziel's smile was warm, but the sharpness in his eyes was not. "Now more than ever."

"Malachi!" Saraphina yelled from fifteen feet back. "Check?"

*Malachi?* But then the Raziel one bowed his head and hurried back over to Saraphina. Sage started to come to me, but Thorne yanked her back with a shake of his head. She pouted and stomped her foot.

A large tan hand landed on top of mine, making me jump and look up at him. It was the long-haired guy. He pressed his fingertip to the space between my eyebrows. Glittery silver mist coiled around my head. "Worry not. Help is on the way."

I tried to speak but only a whimper left my lips.

He smiled. "Try not to use those until you speak with Tegan."

*Tegan?*

"Francelina."

I gasped at the sound of Everest's voice in my ear. My body spun to face him without hesitation, like I was tethered to him. He stood there *right* behind me with those incredible blue and white eyes that watched me carefully. I licked my lips. "I was just talking to them."

Everest arched one eyebrow in question.

I glanced over my shoulder to Riah but there was no one there. My eyes widened. I turned fully but *no one* was there. No Thorne and Sage. No Raziel and Spot. No Saraphina. No ghosts. It was just *me.*

*What the hell? No. No, they were just there.*

"Everest . . ." I shook my head and turned toward him. "Everest, I—"

I choked on a gasp. Everest still stood in front of me, but we were in the foyer of the infirmary. I was still in my pajamas that my aunt brought for me. When I looked to my hands to check for the stones . . . they weren't there. My hands were empty.

A cry slipped out of my mouth. "*Everest*—"

"*It's all right,*" he whispered and moved to stand right in front of me.

I knew I barely knew him. I knew it would make me look crazy. I knew I was falling apart. But I fell into Everest's chest and sobbed.

He wrapped his arms tightly around me and just held on. "It's going to be okay."

# CHAPTER TWENTY-FIVE

## FRANKIE

"So basically I've missed all the fun this weekend?"

Tomás grinned and nodded as he grabbed his fifth slice of pizza. "Atley and Peabo have kicked our asses all weekend."

"If any more demons come for us, we'll be ready." Seamus wiped his face off with his napkin.

Ava rolled her golden eyes as she took a sip of her lemonade. "Y'all are feeling bold after four demon-fighting lessons."

Both boys blushed.

Jo held up her hands to show me her coffin-shaped black fingernails and how two of them were broken down to the start of her finger. *"Ils ne comprennent pas à quel point cela leur fait mal."*

"Only a fool doesn't understand how much breaking your nail all the way like that hurts." Madge shuddered and pushed her soulmate's hands down into her lap beneath the table. "My knee is killing me. I'm gonna have to wear flats to the dance Friday and I'm pissed."

"You're pissed?" Birdie's eyebrows rose. "I look like I've been dragged by a train. I'll have to wear pants to the dance to cover all the bruises on my legs."

I frowned. "Wait, I don't have a dress."

Esther cursed. "We were supposed to go Saturday morning. Okay, we'll go tomorrow after school because I also don't have one."

"Don't worry, Frankie, Atley and Peabo are great teachers at demon-fighting." Tomás leaned his elbows on the table and grinned.

"And you're starting from a higher athletic skill than the rest of us, so you'll catch up to us tonight."

*Tonight.* I leaned back in my seat and exhaled. I'd been in the infirmary all weekend so Everest could feed me potion after potion to help settle my magic. It wasn't exactly the way I wanted to spend my weekend, but two full days of staring at Everest was not a bad thing. Apparently, my friends had been learning fight moves while I was healing. While I'd done a decent job with my bat Friday night, I wanted to learn how to use the dagger a bit. Or more importantly, how to kill them. If I'd learned anything from video games and movies, it was that monsters had a specific way they had to be killed. We'd gone out for pizza first though, since I hadn't gotten to hang for days. We were just finishing up, then were headed to the beach to train.

"I'm gonna hit the restroom before we go to the beach." Archie threw some cash on the table, then jumped up, but his knees slammed into the tabletop. He hissed and cursed. "I'm fine. Be right back."

"Actually, hold up Archie. I'll go too." I stood while reaching in my pocket for cash. I followed Archie's lead and placed it on the table, then joined Archie over by the door back inside the restaurant from the patio. Once I caught up to him, I whispered, *"You know, for witches, I'm really surprised no one has built a magical toilet on the beach."*

Archie snort-laughed, and that somehow messed up his footwork because he tripped and crashed into a family of five waiting by the hostess stand. He cursed and apologized as I lifted him back onto his feet. I'd never met someone as clumsy as him, and yet he healed faster than anyone else. There was no sign of that demon attack on his face.

"Your mother must worry about you every time you leave the house," I said with a laugh as we approached the bathrooms.

He chuckled. "You have no idea."

"Are you gonna be okay in there?" I pointed to the men's room, then winked. "Maybe hold on to the wall?"

He paused outside the door and glanced over his shoulder at me. "How long should I wait before I send in reinforcements to see if you've blacked out again? Maybe you should use a urinal so you can't drown in the tank."

I threw my head back and laughed. "Meet you at the table."

"Beat you to the table!"

Archie had a twisted sense of humor, and I loved it. He was teasing as much as I was. Luckily, I hadn't had a blackout or vision since Friday night. Everest had upped my potions after my little trip to that fountain in my head. It'd only been three days, but so far that was a record for me.

It wasn't until the lady standing next to me at the sinks gave me a dirty look that I realized I was grinning. Which made me laugh because I definitely looked crazy. She practically ran out of the bathroom. Granted, me following right behind her probably didn't help.

"Francelina?"

I gasped and stopped short. I froze like a deer in headlights at the sound of his voice. My eyes widened. Without moving, I glanced left and right but I didn't see him. And then the scent of cinnamon swept over me and my pulse quickened. *Everest.*

"Did I frighten you?" he whispered in my ear.

My breath grew tight and short. Slowly, I spun to face him, and my heart skipped. He was so close. *Too* close. My brain short-circuited with him this close. Every muscle in my body screamed to just crash into his chest like I did Friday night after that dream. I craved the way he held me. All I could do was stare. This close I could see the vibrant shades of blue within his pupils and on the outer rim of his white irises. They were the most incredible eyes I'd ever seen.

He reached up and gently tucked my hair behind my ear. My eyes closed as his fingertips grazed my cheekbone. My traitorous body was out to embarrass me, especially as I leaned *into* him until my face rested in his palm.

"Are you okay, Francelina?" His breath swept across my face.

I opened my eyes and looked up at him. "You tell me."

"Did you have any visions at school today?"

"Umm . . ." I bit my bottom lip, and his eyes tracked the movement, which only sent my pulse into a tailspin. "That depends."

He arched one black eyebrow. "On?"

"If I say yes, will you drag me back to the infirmary and make me stay overnight again?"

"My, my, Francelina. Are you looking for an excuse to skip school?"

"Not to skip school, no."

His nostrils flared.

"Everest?"

We both jumped at the sound of his name being called by a woman. He dropped my face and turned just as a waitress walked around the bar and held out two brown bags with handles. She said something to him that sounded a lot like a list of food, but my heart was pounding so loud in my ears I couldn't hear.

Over his shoulder, I watched Esther walk inside the restaurant with sharp gray eyes until she spotted me, then she stopped and waved. I nodded and held one finger up. But Esther wasn't stupid or blind. She looked over and spotted Everest standing just to the side speaking to the waitress. Esther's eyes lit up. I had to look away from her or I'd embarrass myself even more than I probably just had.

"Thank you," Everest's deep voice sliced through my mental spiral. He gave the waitress a friendly smile and a nod, then turned back to face me. His lips curved into a smirk. "Francelina."

I looked up and met his stare with a wide smile. "Better save something in those bags for me."

His smirk vanished, and his eyebrows sank low over his eyes. "*Why?*" he growled.

I shrugged one shoulder. "My friends are going to give me demon-fighting lessons—"

"You will not be harmed—"

"I don't know. You never know. Archie's pretty clumsy." I stepped up closer to him. "So, save me a snack just in case?"

He bent down and whispered. "You will *not* allow yourself to be injured—"

"Accidents happen—"

"*Francelina.*"

I smiled. "Fine."

"Fine what?" He ducked his head down. "Say it."

"*Vampire,*" I whispered because I couldn't help myself. Twi-hard habits died hard.

He looked to the ceiling. "Fucking Twilight," he mumbled to himself.

I giggled, which brought his laser-sharp gaze back to me. When he just stared, waiting expectedly, I sighed. "I will not intentionally allow myself to be injured just so I can see you. Happy?"

"Perhaps if I believed you." He shook his head in defeat with a little smirk fighting its way back. He nodded his head toward the door. "Go. Your friends are waiting."

"Have a nice night, Everest. I hope you enjoy whatever's in that bag." I turned and started to walk backwards. "Wish me luck."

"Be careful, Francelina."

# CHAPTER TWENTY-SIX

## FRANKIE

"SHIT. I LIKE THE PURPLE TOO."

Esther giggled. "Come out, let me see."

I opened the fitting room door and spotted Esther standing in front of the trifold mirrors at the end of the bank of fitting rooms. She stood barefoot on the raised dais, and when she spotted me, she spun around to face me and struck a pose, then her gray eyes widened with excitement and her jaw dropped. "Frankie."

"Let's forget me for a second." I gestured to her dress. "Oh my God. Esther, that dress is incredible on you."

She wore a cocktail dress with a high neck, long sleeves, and a cut tight to her body. But the entire thing was made entirely of embroidered flowers. The bottom layer was a nude-colored mesh but there were so many flowers attached that the mesh wasn't visible. The flowers were a combination of colors that were giving wildflower vibes. They looked gorgeous with her wild mane of black curls.

"Yeah?" She twirled in front of the trifold mirrors. "I think this might be the one."

"Absolutely."

She cheered and clapped her hands while doing a little penguin happy dance. "Okay, now we just need to narrow one down for you."

I grimaced and stepped up to the mirrors as she jumped down. This was my tenth dress I'd tried on, and so far only the third one I liked. It was a soft lilac material that hugged my body like a glove all the way down past my knees except for the slit on the left. Little white and pink flowers were printed all over the material with white lace running along the neckline and hem. The dress was basically strapless except for the thin ribbon-like straps that tied on each shoulder. It was hands down the sexiest thing I'd ever worn.

"This one is just so . . ."

"Hot." She stood behind me and wagged her eyebrows. Then she licked the tip of her finger and touched the air while making a sizzle sound. "As in *hawt*."

"Yeah, that's the problem. Who am I wearing this for?" I shrugged, then to demonstrate my point, I stuck my leg out to showcase the slit that went almost all the way to my hip. "I'm not interested in any guy I've seen at school. This dress is asking for unwanted attention."

"It's not unwanted with Everest."

I rolled my eyes. "He doesn't go to our school."

"You can bring a date that's high school aged. It's allowed."

"I'm too young for him, Esther."

She scowled. "You're eighteen."

"Yes, but I'm only a sophomore in high school. It's weird for a full-grown adult to be talking to a high school student."

She shook her head. "He's eighteen. I thought you heard that whole conversation with him Friday night."

My eyes widened. "WHAT?"

Esther giggled. "I knew you liked him!"

"Wait, wait." I shook my head and held my hands up. "Is he really only eighteen? How did I miss that?"

"Yep. He graduated in December, which means you're the same age. Which means, if you hadn't been held back from starting school on time, you two would've been in the same grade."

My jaw dropped.

Esther grinned. "*Which means* he's literally your age and not a full-grown adult and actually the most appropriately aged person for you to date. Because you dating Tomás might've actually been illegal."

I gasped and smacked her arm.

"I think you should ask Everest to be your date to the dance."

I bit my bottom lip as butterflies danced in my stomach. All three mirrors showed just how pink my face turned as I blushed. "If I had known that, I might've been a little more bold last night at the restaurant. Dammit. I haven't seen him since, and trust me, I've been looking."

"Didn't he give you his phone number so you could text him if you had any problems?"

I arched one eyebrow at her. "My infatuation is not a problem for him to solve."

"Isn't it though?" She shimmied and stuck her tongue out. "Don't make that face. Just text him and ask."

"That's abusing the trust with my healer."

She sighed and threw her hands up. "Fine. I guess you just have to go the infirmary and ask him."

"You can't just walk into the infirmary without needing medical attention." I scrubbed my face with my hands. "I'd need a legit reason to go in there. I haven't had a new vision since everything he gave me, and he basically scolded me last night for even joking that I'd let myself get injured just to see him."

"So I'll give you a fake rash that he can fix," she whispered in my ear.

I gasped and dropped my hands. She was right behind me, but I looked at her through the mirror. "That would work . . ."

"Yes, it would." She chuckled and jumped back. "Okay, get your clothes on. Let's head there."

"I didn't pick a dress yet." I pointed to my dressing room where a white dress, a red dress, and a pink dress hung on hangers. "I need to narrow it down."

"You *need* to find out if you're gonna have a date with a certain gorgeous healer." She walked into her dressing room and closed the door. "We have pics of each. Once we know if he's going, we'll be able to pick the dress for you."

"Right. Okay." I hurried into the fitting room and slipped out of the lilac dress. "I can't believe I'm going to do this."

Esther was giggling from her dressing room. Then I heard the door open and close. "All right, hand me all four dresses. I'm gonna ask the lady to hold all of these for us. Then we can swing back by once we get your answer."

I grabbed all four hangers, cracked the door open, then stuck them out for her. By the time I got my jean shorts and tank top back on and started to walk out, Esther rushed inside the room with me. She had a wild, mischievous look in her eyes as she locked the door and then pulled her wand out. My eyes widened.

She held one finger up over her lips to tell me to be quiet. I barely had time to blink before she did a swish and flick with her wand. Gold and navy-blue glitter slammed into my face. I coughed and swatted my hands through it. Every inch of my exposed skin tingled and turned warm.

"Yeah, that'll do it."

I coughed a few more times, then looked up into the mirror and gagged. My entire body was covered in a rash. My skin was red and blotchy like I lived in a house made of poison ivy. A whimper left my lips. "*Esther. My FACE?*"

"Yeah?"

I held my arms out to inspect her work, then bent over to see the rash even reached to my toes. I stood upright and spun to face her. "*My whole body?* What the hell? Why?"

She shrugged with a glint in her gray eyes. "So he has to touch you . . . all of you."

I opened my mouth, then shut it. Heat radiated out of my face.

"You're welcome." She winked and shoved her wand back into her purse. "Now, let's hurry to the car because while you and I can see this, my spell has a two-minute buffer before it'll be visible to the human eye—"

"*Esther!*" I hissed and grabbed my crossbody, then sprinted out of the fitting room and out the store doors. Esther's car was parked on the curb right out front, so I was at the passenger door and yanking on the handle in seconds. "*Come on!*"

Esther strolled out of the store laughing. She clicked the button on her key fob so I could climb in. When she finally slid inside the driver's seat and locked the car, she looked up to me and grinned. "Just kidding. Humans will never be able to see what I just did."

I gasped. "ESTHER."

She cackled and turned the car on. "I was afraid you'd chicken out once you saw my handiwork. I'm the ultimate wingman, Franks."

"I hate you." I exhaled and pressed my hands to my chest. My pulse pounded against my ribs. "The panic attack you just gave me. I look diseased, like someone needs to alert the CDC."

"Thank you!" We were already driving to the infirmary, so she didn't look at me, but she did a happy dance and grinned. "Having full strength magic is *unreal*, Frankie. I finally get it."

I frowned. "Get what?"

"Why everyone is so obsessed with the founding families. My mom and I are the only ones from one of those lines I'd ever met who weren't also in The Coven, so I just never realized the difference between us and other civilians. And then I meet you, a civilian Proctor with this insane aura and magic that is *not* normal. I was really alarmed by that before, but I get it now."

I sat up straight and looked to her. "What do you mean my magic is not normal? What do you mean you were really alarmed?"

"Well, I wasn't gonna tell you I was alarmed by it. You were too new to this world. It would've been cruel to tell you without having any new information." She flicked on her left turn signal and checked her mirrors. Her energy was pulsing with electricity. "I mean, now that I feel the full strength of my *actual* magic, I'm not so alarmed by yours. Because you're a Proctor, and that's so much more important than me being an Irit. Edward Proctor fought Lilith herself with Archangel Michael's sword in the war, so your line is far from normal."

"There's that word again, Esther." I shook my head. "Why is my magic not normal?"

She looked at me, then did a double take. Then she frowned. "Really? Frankie, have you not noticed no one else has magic that comes out of their hands?"

I just stared at her profile.

"Civilian witches don't have neon-blue flames that pop out of their hands. Witches only have magic when it comes from a wand or an amulet, or a chalice if they're Cups, or if they perform spells a higher-powered witch created—"

"What are you saying, Esther? Why can I?"

She shrugged. "Honestly? I have no idea. Now, I may not have known Tennessee was a Proctor when he lived here because *he* didn't know—that's a whole story for another day—but the only Proctor I knew of that was still alive was Kenneth Proctor and he was a Coven-member. Proctors are like the Bishops, they're *always* in The Coven."

"I'm not in The Coven—"

"Yet." She glanced over at me and had the grace to grimace. "Look,

I don't mean to freak you out, but those rune stones being fated for you can't be a coincidence. Coven-members are in life-threatening danger on a daily basis now, so while I hope no one else dies, I wouldn't be surprised if they did . . . and I have a guess of who might get Marked to replace them."

My stomach turned. I gripped the edge of my seat and exhaled.

"Okay. We're here."

I jumped and looked up to find we were parked out front of the infirmary. My face fell. "Oh my God, I forgot. Why would you drop that bomb on me right now?"

"So that you look distressed and Gin will panic into getting Everest to tend to you." She giggled. "The whole plan is ruined if you don't make it *to* Everest."

"Esther."

"Also, you look ill and contagious, so Everest will put you in a private room instead of the open beds room in the back—"

*"How am I supposed to do this now?"* I groaned. "You just told me you think I'm fated to join The Coven the next time one of them dies!"

"SO?" She leaned down to catch my gaze. "Frankie, I've seen you fight bullies. I've seen you hit demons with baseball bats. More importantly, I saw the way you weren't even the slightest bit phased by being attacked by demons when you've only known they exist for a few days. My friends have known about them their whole lives, and have seen demon attacks because of The Coven living here, yet they fucking panicked when shit hit the fan."

"What . . . what are you . . . what are you . . ." I shook my head.

"I'm saying your fate didn't bring you to Tampa to leave you here permanently. I'm saying when the war starts, you're going to be on the front lines and you're not actually that freaked out about this statement because somewhere deep down inside of you . . . you already knew this." She reached over and squeezed my shoulder. "Because now that I have *this much* magic, I have no intention of sitting on the bench, so the sooner I get you mentally prepared for *our* destiny, the better for both of us."

I stared at her for a moment then shook my head. "You're bat shit crazy."

"And yet I'm the one you gravitated toward other than Archie.

Birds of a feather and all that jazz." She reached over and unbuckled my seatbelt. "Now, go in there and get you a date."

I froze with my hands on the door handle, the nasty rash covering the backs of my hands. "What? You're not coming in?"

She scowled. "To watch you ask a guy on a date? Def not."

I whined. "Why did I let you talk me into this?"

"Because Everest is gorgeous and," she paused to wag her eyebrows, "I believe your words were, *I'd risk death to climb that mountain, so the name fits.*"

My face burned. "Right. I said that out loud. Not my fault. He'd given me a potion."

"Go get your mountain, Frankie."

"Is it weird to ask him out?"

"Why? Guys do it, so why can't we?"

I cursed. "Fine. I can't waste the art that is this spell. Or sitting in here any longer with your truth bombs."

"That's the spirit." She shooed me with both hands, her gray eyes bright and sparkling. "Just remember, nutmeg's Nutella. That's the spell name I did."

"Right, that makes no sense at all." I exhaled and opened the door. "Wish me luck."

I didn't look back at Esther as I hurried up the brick pathway to the front door because I might've lost my nerve. Esther was right. I did like Everest. I'd never in my life had a crush on a boy like I did with Everest. Ever. Elizabeth would've been flabbergasted. Had it not been the middle of the night for her, I would've called her for support, but I wasn't going to wake her up for this. I'd tell her when she woke up because there was no way I was going to be able to sleep after this. Whether he said yes or no, I was going to lie awake thinking about what I was about to do.

*Just do it, Frankie. Esther isn't going to reverse this spell unless you at least try.*

*What's the worst that could happen?*

I held my chin high and walked inside. I'd only just met the guy Friday night, and it was only Tuesday now, but he'd been on my mind since. He was a song stuck in my head on repeat over and over and over without relief. Seeing him at the restaurant made it so much worse. I lay in bed all night reviewing every moment of that interaction.

"Frankie?"

I looked up and tried to smile at Gin, but the horrified expression on her face caught me off guard. "Hi, Gin."

She froze halfway down the stairs. "Um . . . what happened to you?"

I grimaced. "No idea. This just suddenly happened. Could it be a reaction to one of those potions Everest gave me?"

"I doubt it, but go into that room you were in this weekend, and I'll send him in there."

"Okay, thanks, Gin." I hurried into the room in the back before I could chicken out.

I slipped inside and shut the door behind me, then hopped onto the bed. I'd been here all weekend, so it felt fairly natural to recline against the back and wait. Except this time my legs were restless and bouncing and my fingers trembled. For the first time in my life, I was going to ask a guy out on a date. The only reason I wasn't totally freaking out was because of that interaction at the restaurant. The looks, the whispers, the *growls*. The way he tucked my hair behind my ear, then held my face in his palm. If he didn't feel *something* for me, he wouldn't have picked up on my hints about hurting myself just so I could see him. My gut told me I wasn't alone in this infatuation, so instead of obsessing over the *what if* scenarios, I was just going to find out and be done. I'd rather know if the feelings weren't mutual before I let them run even farther away from me.

The door opened. I grabbed the blanket and pulled it over me in hopes he'd actually have to make it closer to me before he bolted. My pulse quickened. I felt instantly frozen and overheated at the same time. My stomach turned. *Here we go. It's okay. It's fine. Just do it.*

Everest stepped inside the room, and I knew the moment he realized it was me on the bed because that professional smile turned into a deep scowl. It was the same face he made when I made my little joke last night. "I thought we had an understanding last night, Francelina—WHAT *happened to your face?*"

I smiled. "You tell me."

He sighed and shut the door, pausing only to lock it behind him before crossing the room to me. His blue and white gaze narrowed on my face, then lowered to my body under the blanket. "We agreed you wouldn't hurt yourself."

"I didn't do this." I hadn't.

He narrowed his eyes on my face for a long moment, then cursed. "Show me."

I threw the blanket off and stretched my legs out flat on the bed. "This is a genuine need for you."

He pursed his lips and nodded, his gaze sliding over every inch of my exposed skin. His attention on my body chased away every last chill. He reached over my right leg and gripped my left ankle, then spun me to face him without taking his hand off me. I gasped and looked up into his eyes, but he wasn't looking at my face. He slid his hand up the side of my calf until he got to my knee then dragged my body to the edge of the bed.

I inhaled a shaky breath. My body trembled. I watched his face, but I felt all five of his fingertips slide a burning path up my outer thigh. Heat radiated out of my skin. I had to hold on to the edge of the bed to stop myself from reaching for him. I licked my lips. "So, what's the prognosis?"

He sighed and shook his head. "I'll have to notify The Coven that this has spread again. We'll have to quarantine you until they can get here. So, no school. No spring dance on Friday night—"

"What? No. Wait, why?" I shook my head to clear all the infatuated thoughts. "Wait, can't you just heal me? Fix this?"

"No, I cannot." He cocked his head to the side and arched one eyebrow. "Or you can just tell me what spell Esther used to do this."

My jaw dropped. "You knew. How?"

He let out a little chuckle that made me weak at the knees despite the fact I was sitting. His left hand slid a path back up my thigh and then *under* the hem of my denim shorts. I squirmed as his fingers pressed into the skin on my hip. "No rash under here . . . or here." Without taking his hand out from under my shorts, he reached up and carefully pulled one strap of my tank top off my shoulder to reveal perfectly clear skin.

"*Everest . . .*"

"You either used a spell to create this or this is an infection The Coven eradicated from our societies a century ago." He traced one fingertip down the side of my arm. "So, which is it? The Coven or the spell?"

I licked my lips and swallowed roughly. "*Spell,*" I whispered.

He nodded and pulled his hands off me, which made me whine. "Why?"

"I had my reasons—"

"*Francelina,*" he growled, and the sound unraveled me a little.

"Fine." I took a deep breath and let it out. *Here's your chance, Franks. Just rip the Band-Aid off and ASK.* "I'll tell you what spell I used if you agree to be my date for the spring dance on Friday night."

He cursed violently in another language. Before I could ask what he'd said, he took my face in his hands and dragged my mouth up to his. Our mouths crashed together in a frenzy of lips and tongues. I sighed and reached for his shirt, pulling him between my legs so he was closer. My pulse thundered in my veins, my body on fire. There was nothing sweet or tender about it. He kissed me like he was starved for it, like I was the oxygen he needed to live. His fingers dug into my jaw as he held me. I'd never known a kiss could feel like this. My ears started to ring, and my head got a little fuzzy. I knew I was in desperate need of breathing. I needed to pull away, but my hands dragged him even closer.

And then he was gone.

I gasped for air and reached for him. I wasn't done. "Everest—"

"We can't—That's not what this is—"

"Bullshit. You don't kiss someone like that if you don't mean it."

He ran his hand over his face. "Francelina—"

"Be my date for the dance?"

His face fell. He closed his eyes and licked his lips . . . then nodded.

I squealed in my head, but on the outside, I kept it cool so I didn't spook him. "Nutmeg's Nutella."

His eyes flew open, his expression incredulous. But he let out a little smirk, then turned to a cabinet behind him. I couldn't see what he was doing, but when he turned back, he held three vials in his hands. "Esther's good. Drink these."

I took one at a time, tossing them back quickly and reaching for the next. Once I swallowed the last one, I licked my lips and held the empty vial out to him. A quick glance at my body proved my skin was clear again. No sign of a rash anywhere. "Thank you."

"Don't do that again, Francelina."

"Do what?" I batted my eyelashes at him.

He arched one eyebrow. "Do not harm yourself as an excuse to come here to me, even by spell. We went over this last night."

"I won't need to. We have a date." I hopped off the bed and closed the distance between us. I pushed up on my tiptoes and tugged him against me by his shirt. Then I pressed my lips to his. I kissed him just long enough to remind him that he wanted this too. Then I pulled back and whispered against his mouth, "The dance is at eight in the school's gym. Meet me out front. My aunt and uncle don't need to know about this."

# CHAPTER TWENTY-SEVEN

## FRANKIE

I HADN'T BEEN BACK to the infirmary since Tuesday's rash adventure. Everest was a flight risk. If I went in for any genuine reason, he would've assumed it was a ploy to see him, so I was a good girl and stayed away. He'd texted me a few times since but only to check if I'd had any more visions, and each time I confirmed I hadn't he'd stopped responding.

"He's gonna show," Esther said softly as I pulled into a parking spot at school near the gym. "His response was proof he likes you."

"You mean kissing someone when they ask you on a date isn't the normal way to answer?" Archie leaned forward between the front seats. "Guess that's why I'm single."

I snort-laughed. "I love that that could mean that you kiss everyone or that you don't. Could go either way."

"I've heard that about me before." He sighed. "But alas, I only go one way."

Esther half-turned in her seat and narrowed her eyes on him. "And which way *is* that, Archie?"

"One of my best friends back home is gay. We've been friends since we were kids. He's stupid pretty too." He leaned in closer. "Like *stupid* pretty. And like, all around a wonderful person. If I can't get my body to want *him*, then I just don't think guys are it for me."

"Yeah, but did you try?" Esther waved her hands. "With your friend?"

"Have you seen a rom-com before? I didn't wanna confuse him or make it weird just to confirm what I already suspected."

The dance had already started, and there was a chance Everest was waiting for me up by the door, but this tea was too interesting to walk away from. I turned to face both of them. "Have you tried girls?"

"Oh yeah. A female friend of ours was very interested in me and she was awesome. Super fun and pretty. One of my favorite people. And while I discovered I didn't have romantic feelings for her, I assure you my body had no issues with it."

Esther gasped dramatically. "*Archie.*"

"This tea keeps getting better. Please continue. What happened with this girl?"

He shrugged. "We went back to being friends pretty quickly because I didn't wanna lead her on. And we stayed friends after."

"That doesn't mean you're not bisexual. I mean, I've known really pretty guys that I haven't wanted to hook up with."

"I don't know." Esther frowned. "I would've smashed Tennessee if given the chance. He's that pretty."

"He's definitely heard that before." Archie laughed and shook his head.

"Then again . . ." Esther tapped her chin with her finger. "Tenn's girlfriend is also hot, and I probably would've smashed *that* too if given the chance."

I nodded. "Well, if they're ever in the market for a third, we'll let them know."

She fanned herself. "Now *that's* a sandwich."

"Great. Now I'm hungry." Archie giggled, then jumped out of the car. "C'mon, let's go find food."

"He's got a point. Besides, Everest is probably up there waiting to quench your thirst."

She was out of the car before my mind could conjure up a response. My thoughts had gone back to that kiss and short-circuited the rest of my brainwaves. By the time I was out of the car and shutting the door, my face was on fire. I checked my reflection in the windows of my car, smoothing my hands down my dress.

"You look fantastic, Franks." Esther leaned against the car beside me. "The sexy lilac dress was the right choice."

"Thanks. I feel awkward as hell." I sighed and shook my arms and legs to try and relax. "I'm leaving my phone in the car. Can you hold my key in your purse?"

"Yeah, for sure." She held her hand out for it.

I leaned inside my car and started to put my phone in the center console when it vibrated in my hand. I frowned and looked down—and gasped. "Everest just texted me."

"What did he say?"

I opened his text message and read out loud, "*Gin tripped down the stairs and broke her nose. I need to heal her real quick so I can leave.*"

Archie laughed. "She sounds like me."

"Do we believe him—"

"He sent a picture." I climbed back out of my car and held my screen out for them to see the picture he sent of Gin sprawled on the stairs with blood all over her face. "So I'd say yes."

Archie reached over my arm and zoomed in on Gin's face. "She's laughing. She's had worse."

Esther laughed and pushed him back.

I shot a response back. '*Oh, Poor Gin! I hope it heals easy for her.*'

My phone vibrated again. I looked down to find another text from him. '*Please go inside with your friends and have fun.*'

Esther cleared her throat. "He sent you a pic. I think it's fair to send one back."

"Yeah, show him what he's missing." Archie gestured to my dress.

My jaw dropped. "*Archie.*"

"I may not wanna smash—to put it in Esther's words—but I'm a guy and I'm not blind."

"Archie makes very good points, especially since Everest *does* wanna smash." She pushed my arm up above my head with the selfie camera mode on. "Take the pic."

I quickly snapped a selfie before I had a chance to really think about it, then I sent the picture to Everest with the caption, '*You better be here. Who else am I wearing this dress for?*'

'*That is body paint, not a dress, Francelina,*' he responded immediately. Before I could answer, he sent, '*I'll be there.*'

Esther leaned over my shoulder. "See? He wants to smash. Now let's go get a snack before he arrives and you're too nervous to eat anything."

I groaned. It was too late. I was already too nervous, but I wasn't going to tell her that. My bravado needed to stay in place or I'd crack. I threw my phone into the center console, then shut my door and locked the car. I was just handing Esther my key when I felt the tingle of a witch approaching.

"Look, Aaron, I found a bouquet!"

*Oh no.* I spun around just as Jacob lifted Archie up in the air like he was a bouquet of flowers. Bullying was not acceptable in any way, but at least this joke made sense. Archie's button-down shirt and pants were a matching pale-pink with flowers printed all over them, so he actually *did* look like a bouquet. It wasn't funny, but at least they were getting smarter about it.

"Put him down," I growled. My phone with my bat sticker was in the car already, but I could do damage with the sharp end of my car key.

"I'd like to see you try in that slutty dress." Aaron looked me up and down, and it was definitely disgusting. He licked his lips and let his gaze linger on my body. "I could help you get it off first—"

"Back off, asshole." Esther jumped in front of me with her wand held up between her and them. "Put him down now or you'll get a firsthand experience with my full magic."

Jacob scoffed. "Please, you hung up some decorations. I'm so scared—"

"Okay." Esther flicked her wand and sent streams of gold and navy-blue glitter shooting right at both of them.

They cursed and jumped back, trying to dodge whatever spell she'd just lodged at them. Jacob threw Archie to the ground, but it was too late. One second both of them wore khakis and pastel-colored button-down shirts, the next they wore *tighty whities*. They shrieked and tried to cover themselves with their hands while cursing at Esther.

Archie and I cackled.

Esther just shrugged with a wicked smile. "Gee, boys, guess you'll have to go home and change."

They bolted.

"Fuck, that felt good."

I gave Esther a high-five. "As it should. How'd you do that?"

"No idea." She grinned like a maniac. "I just thought *tighty whities*, and it happened."

Archie adjusted his bowtie. "It's really not fair I wasn't a Wand."

"Right?" I handed Esther my car key. "Let's get a snack?"

We hadn't decorated this time. We were all too afraid we'd attract demons. So, the humans took over, and as we walked through the front doors of the gym, I had to admit they did a great job. Without magic. Granted, they used all of my friends' decorations, but it still was done well. There were flowers and twinkling lights *everywhere*. It was like walking into a fairy garden in full bloom. The DJ had the dance floor jammin', fully packed and loaded with students. All along the sides of the gym were tables with rose gold tablecloths and flowery center-pieces. It wasn't fancy in a formal way, but it was just really pretty.

Apparently, the dress code was pretty strict. Everyone had to wear either floral-printed clothes or pastel colors. I appreciated the effort to build an aesthetic. No one back at my old school did that. As someone with pink hair, I liked the touch of detail. I was so distracted by all the details that I didn't realize we'd joined our group until Rootbeer barked right in front of me.

I jumped with a little gasp, then looked down at her and smiled as I pet her. "I'm so sorry, pretty girl. It's nice to see you too."

"It's so strange, she only acts like this with you." Ava chuckled. She looked like a pure ray of sunshine in her yellow floral dress that did incredible things to the tone of her dark skin, especially with her eyes and caramel-highlighted hair. "Everyone else, it's all business until Seamus gives her the command she can relax. You? She's a rebel with a cause."

That made me grin. "I have that effect on animals, especially pretty girls who wear flower collars."

"*Oh la la. Mon Dieu.*" Jo fanned herself and gestured to my dress. "*Très sexy. C'est magnifique.*"

I felt myself blush. "*Merci beaucoup.*"

Then Madge walked up, and my jaw dropped. "Are your dresses color inversions of each other?"

The two soulmates struck a dramatic pose, and I loved it. They both wore flat sandals that strapped all the way up to their knees in metallic gold. Madge's cocktail dress was a dark-turquoise silk with cream-colored flowers while Jo's was a cream silk with turquoise flow-ers. They literally completed each other, and for some reason, that brought tears to my eyes. Knowing those cool black swirls covering their right arms with the glowing yellow crystals meant they were soulmates was just so damn special.

"I love your love. I am obsessed."

They blushed and held on to each other. I looked away to give them their moment. My gaze landed on Seamus who wore a full suit that was printed in grass. As in, the design someone chose was to make fabric out of a picture of grass—like zoomed in on the blades of grass up close like we were in the Ants movie. His shirt was brown, and I knew without asking it represented the dirt.

"Seamus's suit?" Ava sighed and closed her eyes.

"I gotta say, I love it." I laughed. "I mean, I wouldn't wear it to literally any other event, but this one . . . It's perfect. I love the confidence you have to wear it."

His smile was beaming. "Thank you!"

"Go ahead. Show her." Ava smiled and gestured to his jacket. "She'll love it. She's like you."

He let out a giddy chuckle, then hurried over so he was close to me. Then he glanced around to make sure no one was looking . . . then pulled one side of his jacket open to show Ava's pet bunny, Float, was in a baby sling wrapped around his waist. He snort-laughed.

A sound I'd never heard left my lips. It was part-gasp, part-scream. "*You smuggled a bunny into the spring dance,*" I whispered. "I adore this so much. Oh my God."

"Oh great. Someone else to encourage him."

I spun around to find Birdie sitting at the table with her legs propped up on the chair beside her. She wore a pale sky-blue pant suit. That was when I realized they'd done what they said. Madge wore flats because her knee hurt, and Birdie wore pants to cover her bruises. "Why didn't y'all just get healed?"

Birdie narrowed her eyes on Archie. "He said we needed to learn how to heal from injuries so we're not taken down so much by them."

"Hey, do you see me getting healed every time I get hurt?"

"Where's Tomás?" Esther frowned and looked around. "Peabo and Atley? Or your sister—"

"Tomás and Whitney went to raid the food situation. Peabo and my sister are dancing on the dance floor and I'm playing it cool by leaving them be." Birdie rolled her eyes, but she smiled. "Atley was with Aspen, but I don't know where they went."

The others frowned. There was a beat of silence, then they all jumped to attention and began discussing whether or not they needed to be worried about them. Finally, Seamus suggested they take a stroll around the gym and see if they could see them.

"Cool, but we're making a pit stop for a snack," Archie said as the group headed off.

I started to follow them when a warm tingle slid down my spine like someone was watching me. My pulse quickened. I glanced over my shoulder but there was nothing behind me except for the shadows of the gym where the lights didn't touch. Yet the feeling only grew stronger. My feet carried me into the shadows on their own, like something had put a spell on me and was dragging me toward them. It felt like the shadows themselves were grabbing hold of me.

And then I saw him.

*Everest.*

My breath caught in my throat at the sight of him. He was leaning against a pillar drenched in darkness, yet his eyes glowed like an animal's at night. My skin flushed as butterflies danced in my stomach. I smiled and hurried over to him.

His heated gaze looked me up and down. Slowly. "I didn't think you'd see me in the dark."

"*I'd see you anywhere,*" I whispered before I could stop myself. "I have never been afraid of the dark."

"Perhaps you should be," he whispered back.

I stepped up flush against his body and pushed up on my tiptoes, which in these little heels brought my mouth perfectly in line with his. "No shadow is going to keep me from you."

And then his lips were on mine. He took my face in both of his hands and tipped my head back to deepen our kiss. I wrapped my arms around his waist and pulled him tight against me, needing to feel the heat of his skin through his clothes. One of his hands pushed through the waves of my hair, sending goosebumps across my whole body. When he fisted my hair on the back of my head, I gasped against his mouth.

He groaned and dropped his hands, then backed away from me with a curse.

"Everest," I said between breath. "Wait—"

"We're at a school dance." His voice was soft and rough all at the same time. He reached down and took my hand in his, then pulled me toward the lights of the dance still happening all around us. "Let us join your friends *and dance.*"

The only reason I didn't groan and protest was my hand gripped in his. It was the only tether to sanity I had left, otherwise I would've run off into the sunset with him without looking back. I had no idea what this boy did to my brain when he was near me. When he wasn't, I could use my rational, logical brain and know I'd just met him. I didn't even know his last name or where he moved here from. Or how he knew Katherine. I knew nothing about him personally.

But all of that vanished when he was in front of me.

It was alarming, really.

Yet with my hand in his, I didn't have the ability to care.

We stepped out of the shadows together, and my whole friend group gasped in perfect unison. Apparently I'd kissed him in the shadows for longer than I realized, long enough for my friends to circle all the way back to our spot. Archie grinned and nodded in approval. Esther bit her bottom lip to try and hide her giggle, but I saw it. The others openly gawked. They all knew who Everest was at this point, but they hadn't seen him with me. And I may have forgotten to tell the others I'd asked him to be my date.

I cleared my throat. "Guys, this is Everest . . . and these are my friends."

He nodded and gave them a small smile, but his eyes shot down to me. There was an interesting sparkle in them, like he wanted to ask me something. Instead, he glanced away at something, then back to me with a subtle arch of his eyebrow. I frowned and followed his glance only to find Tomás standing about ten feet away with wide eyes and a dropped jaw. His gaze was locked on our intertwined hands. My face flushed. *Well, this is awkward.*

Esther subtly held her wand up and flicked it, causing the song to change from a dance pop song to *Perfect* by Ed Sheeran. "Come on, Archibald. Dance with me."

Archie held his hand out. "Fine, but you have to lead, or we'll just look silly."

"You got it, princess." She took his hand and led him onto the dance floor, glancing back over her shoulder. "Come on, y'all."

"You heard her, Tomás." Whitney looked up at him with a blush on her cheeks. "Let's dance."

He bowed adorably, then took her hand and followed Esther. Madge and Jo skipped after them, already tangled up in each other. Rootbeer lunged onto the dance floor, then spun in a circle and barked at Seamus. He and Ava hurried out to her, then Seamus tapped on his chest and she jumped up with her paws on him so they were all dancing together.

Brody walked by me with a smile, then stopped and looked behind me. "Hi, Birdie, wanna dance?"

"Oh." Birdie blushed and tucked her hair behind her ears. "Yeah. Yeah, that'd be cool."

I watched them go onto the dance floor, leaving me standing on the side alone with Everest. Something told me he wasn't a guy who danced often, but I was riding a high from just him showing up that I felt no fear in asking. So, I turned and smiled up at him.

He sighed and shook his head, but a little smirk pulled at the corner of his lips. "Would you like to dance, Francelina?"

"I thought you'd never ask."

He led me out to the middle of the dance floor until we were surrounded by other couples. When he wrapped his arm around my waist, my knees might have buckled a little. But he didn't seem to notice. He just took my hand back in his and laced our fingers.

"Is there a story between you and that Tomás?"

I reached up with my free hand and ran my fingers through his white-blond hair. "What makes you think there is?"

"I saw his reaction to seeing us together," he said softly so no one else heard. "It seemed to . . . unsettle him."

"Does that bother you?" I licked my lips and reveled in the way his eyes tracked the movement. "That he and I were . . . something?"

A little rumble vibrated his chest. "*No.*"

I chuckled. "Liar."

"You are free to bind yourself to whomever you'd like."

My pulse quickened. "Tomás has a little thing for me. He's been flirty since I arrived. He asked me to be his date for the dance last week before the attack, but I told him I only had a platonic friendship to offer him. He was gracious about it. I met you maybe an hour later?"

He nodded but gave me a little smirk. "And your feelings for me are strictly platonic of course."

"As platonic as your answer when I asked you to be my date."

He chuckled. "Forgive me, my self-control ceases to exist when you're near."

Warmth spread through my body. "I'm glad."

We moved to the melody of the music without taking our eyes off of each other. With all the golden twinkling lights surrounding us, I felt like I was in a fairytale. With every sway of our bodies, he leaned in closer until I felt his breath sweep across my forehead. I pushed up on my tiptoes to kiss him when the song ended and switched to a Drake song I'd never heard of.

Everest stepped back and whispered, *"I'm not the biggest fan of public displays of affection, Francelina."*

*Noted.* I took his hand and dragged him off the dance floor to the door in the dark corner. He didn't ask questions. He just let me lead him out into the hall and around the corner, then through another door. The halls were dimly lit because the school didn't want anyone walking around, but I didn't care. We passed the girls' and guys' locker rooms, then pushed through an unmarked door at the end of the hall. I'd only been in the room once, but I knew Coach Andrews' office had a couch and no one else would be ballsy enough to come in. I opened the door and stepped inside.

I didn't flick on the lights even as Everest shut the door behind him. The only light in the entire office came from a neon-red sign that hung on the wall above the glass window that overlooked the hallway, the same hallway we'd just walked down. I looked up at him cast entirely in a red glow and my heart skipped beats. I closed the distance between us and pressed my hands to his chest.

"Francelina, this is not—"

"Public display." I pressed my lips to his.

He groaned and leaned into me, digging his fingers into my waist.

I gripped the lapels of his white blazer and pulled him down to me. We stumbled across the room until my ass slammed into Coach's desk. In the back of my mind I heard things crash and fall but Everest reached down and grabbed my thighs, lifting me up to sit on the desk. The slit in my dress parted and I felt his fingers dig into my bare skin as he shoved my legs apart. I moaned against his mouth and wrapped my legs around his hips, pulling him flush against my body between my legs.

Goosebumps spread down each of my limbs like electric shocks that made my nipples harden and press into his chest. Warmth spread through my veins as heat bloomed inside of me. I slid my tongue over the tip of his then licked the back of his teeth—

He leapt backwards, then stumbled even farther from me.

But I wasn't done. He couldn't wind me up like that then just leave me hanging. I jumped off the desk and charged for him then shoved both of my hands into his chest. He gasped and flew backwards until he crashed onto the little leather couch under the window. I didn't give him a chance to move, I pounced. I leapt right into his lap, straddling his hips as far as the material of my dress would let me. He sat up straight and sucked my bottom lip into his mouth. My whole body trembled. I fisted his silky hair in my hands and slid my tongue against his.

His hands gripped my knees— he flipped me around faster than I knew my body could move. I gasped and arched into him, pushing my ass right into him. His hands gripped my hips, pulling me against him so close I felt every inch of him. Unable to stop myself, I rolled my hips against him and felt his body stir beneath me. My toes curled. Little whimpers escaped my closed mouth. I shook in his arms. I wanted him. Never in my life had I felt desire like this.

He fisted my hair and yanked my head back then nibbled on that soft spot behind my ear and it unraveled me. My breaths were ragged and gaspy. I gripped his thighs and rolled my hips over and over until I felt the hard proof that he wanted this as bad as I did. He growled and dragged his teeth down the side of my neck. My nipples hurt from how tight they were.

One of his hands slid up my body and cupped my breast. He must have felt my hardened nipples against his palms because he groaned and then his hands moved up to the thin ribbon-like straps of my dress tied on top of my shoulders. I felt the tug of material and then the top of my dress dropped and cold air swept across my bare breasts. When his hands cupped my breasts and I felt the heat of his palms against my skin a little moan slipped out of my mouth.

My body trembled. I rolled my hips again, grinding myself on him. He groaned against my skin and rolled his hips with me so we were both working for that release. I closed my eyes, threw my head back onto his shoulder, and lost myself to the sensation the friction of his pants caused. But then one of his hands slid down the front of my body to my hip, to where the slit in my dress was stretched. His fingers burned a trail up my inner thigh then *under* the thin lacy material of my thong. He pressed his lips to my throat and bit me at the exact moment his fingertip found that one sweet spot between my legs.

To my horror, I screamed his name.

He expertly moved his finger in quick circles without relent. I was coming undone beneath his touch. My entire body was on fire. I moaned and began to shake. He turned my face with his other hand then took my mouth with his. His tongue flicked at mine in sync with his finger. I moaned against his lips. He was unravelling me but I wanted him lost *with* me. I wanted him squirming in pleasure so I reached between us and gripped him through his pants.

He hissed against my mouth.

And then we were falling sideways onto the couch. The cold leather against my bare breasts made me shiver which made him moan. He tipped my head back and deepened our kiss. I would have been lost to his tongue in my mouth had he not pulled back to meet my eyes and *licked his fingers* before pushing them back onto my body. I moaned his name before he reclaimed my mouth with his.

The new angle we were in on the couch gave me the space I needed to unzip his pants and pull him out. He hissed until I wrapped my hands around him and squeezed the tip of him. He growled and his body trembled. And then we were lost to each other. To his fingers rubbing me in circles, to my hand sliding up and down him, to our tongue licking at each other.

Heat exploded inside of me. I threw my head back and screamed but his hand covered my mouth to drown out the sound. The pleasure was so swift and strong my whole body spasmed. He rocked his hips, using my hand still holding him to bring himself to climax right after me.

And then the world went dark.

"*Francelina,*" he whispered in my ear.

I moaned and turned to face him, pressing my lips to his. He cupped my jaw and kissed me in abandon. He kissed me like he was hungry enough to devour every inch of me. I wrapped my arms around his neck and hooked one leg around his hips – and felt fabric. I whined and broke our kiss to look down.

"*What?*" My dress was tied back in place. His pants were zipped with his shirt tucked in like nothing ever happened. I sat up and he sat up with me. We were still in Coach's office under the red glowing sign but there was no evidence of the pleasure we'd just given each other on this couch. "Did I just . . . did I just . . . was that vision—"

He chuckled. "Do you dream of me pleasuring you often?" he asked against my throat.

I looked down into his eyes. "That will depend on whether or not that just happened."

He squeezed my legs together causing a warm tingle to spread through my body, a crying plea for more of what he'd just given me. "Can you still feel my fingers on you?"

I moaned and sank my teeth into his bottom lip.

He pulled back and laughed. "We are in your teacher's office, Francelina. We cannot do this here. I had to clean us up."

"I don't care." I took his mouth back in mine—

My phone rang loud and shrill from my Apple Watch. We both gasped and broke apart. I cursed and looked down at my watch to find Esther's name in bold letters.

"You better answer that."

*Dammit.* I hit the answer button. "Hey!"

"Hi, um, where'd you go?"

"Oh, uh, we went for a walk since it's so nice out."

Everest arched one eyebrow at me, which looked extra dashing in the red glow of the sign.

Esther exhaled roughly. "Well, you better get back."

"Why? What's wrong?" There was something wrong with the tone of her voice.

"A fistfight broke out after Aaron and Jacob decided to throw Archie around like a bouquet at a wedding, so Tomás and Seamus pounced, then the other guys jumped in. And like other human guys too. On both sides. Some of them actually *helped* those assholes. The

Dean has canceled the dance effective immediately . . . and we can't fix this with magic."

I cursed. "Right. So we have to flee the premises."

"Unfortunately."

"I'll meet you at the car in five."

# CHAPTER TWENTY-EIGHT

## FRANKIE

I LET myself into the infirmary as usual but at least this trip was legit. There were no fake rashes and no real injuries. I'd decided to not have Esther's mom just sign off on my volunteer hours without actually volunteering. I wanted to do my part, so I'd called Gin to see if I could do some hours with them for the weekend. Sure, I hoped to see Everest, but the infirmary had been so good to me and my mental disaster that I wanted to give back.

There must have been some kind of alarm or bell that went off when someone entered that only the healers could hear because someone always appeared within sixty seconds of me walking in. I waved.

Gin spotted me and smiled wide. "Frankie! I'm so happy you've volunteered for the weekend. It's the perfect timing."

I frowned. "Perfect timing for what?"

"The Spring Equinox Ritual on Tuesday!" She waved for me to follow her up the stairs. "Did you not know about that?"

"Never heard of it—the ritual, I mean. Obviously I've heard of the equinox."

She led the way to the room at the back of the hall, then opened the door and gestured for me to enter. "After you."

I hurried in, then slowed to a stop. The room looked nothing like the others I'd been in. This room was made of white wooden beams on the floor and walls, almost like the contractor never finished it up.

There was no furniture at all, but in the far corner on the left was some kind of long cushion with a few big pillows and blankets on it, like that was the designated spot for people to sit. I glanced around in confusion. The room was full of natural light, but the only windows were in the ceiling.

But the part of the room that really made me nervous, and I wasn't sure why, were the mountains of flowers all separated by color. And then there were big glass bowls that were empty and just sitting in the circles of sunlight on the floor caused by the windows in the ceiling.

"This is our prep room."

"What does that mean?" I gestured around. "Because it looks like the start of a horror film."

She giggled. "I said the same thing when I first started. But no, this is where we perform special kinds of magic and rituals to give us the ingredients we need to heal people with. It's complicated to explain unless you're a healer or a Cup."

"My friends think I'm a Cup."

"I know. I heard. It's why I'm so excited to have you help us out today because you can handle this." She shuddered. "A lot of other people can't."

"That's ominous." I nodded. "And feels like a lot of pressure already."

"Nah, you can't mess up."

"Sure. I believe that." I chuckled. "Okay, so lay it out for me. What's this ritual and what is all this for? And what am I gonna be doing here?"

"Right, so the Spring Equinox Ritual is when all the witches in our community come together to celebrate entering spring from winter. It's about new life, new beginnings, and balance. It's like the day we honor the Earth and give back." She gestured to all the flowers. "This is one part of many tasks, so don't freak out. But these flowers have been selected and will be used in the ritual. All we need you to do is to treat them in the bowls."

I frowned. "The bowls are empty though."

"Well yeah, but they won't be." She giggled and pointed to a line of bottles and vials lined up along the back wall on the ground next to that cushion. "You're going to fill the bowls with different combinations to create potions. Once those are right, you'll dump the flowers into the bowls so they can soak."

"And then what?"

"Someone else's job. They'll take the flowers and mold them into flower crowns and wreaths and such for us all to use on Tuesday." She put her hand on my shoulder. "But really, your job is just to make the potions and put the flowers in."

"Okay, how do I make the potions?" I glanced around. "Is there a guidebook or labels or something? I mean, what's in the bottles?"

"Oh, different things. But from what Leah Irit and Agnes Mann tell me, you have quite the natural skill for potions." She pointed to the wall again. "I want you to shut your brain off and go with your gut. Don't think about it. Just pick some and roll with it."

My eyes widened. "Surely you're kidding."

"I'm not, and don't call me Shirley." She winked and turned for the door. "Remember, don't think about it! Just grab and pour."

"Gin—"

"I'll be right downstairs if you need me." She waved and then slipped out the door, leaving me alone.

"Don't think about it. Shut your brain off. Don't think about it." I groaned and scrubbed my face. "I don't think they know who they're talking to."

*And I'm talking to myself. Or the flowers. I'm not sure which is worse.* I cursed. I prayed for the day when all of this magic stuff didn't feel as overwhelming as walking into the *SAT* testing room to take the exam without having studied a single thing for it. *Screw it, Frankie. She said I can't mess up, so just go for it.*

I walked around the mountains of flowers and empty glass bowls to the back wall where the bottles were all lined up. There were bottles of every shape, size, and color in front of me. Doubt crept in. They sure were expecting a lot from me with this. But standing here panicking wasn't going to make it any better, so I dropped down to sit on the edge of the cushion.

*Trust your gut.* Whatever that meant. I just started picking bottles up and smelling them. Some had intense scents that belonged in gardens or kitchen spice cabinets. Some were fragrant-free but rich in vibrant color. I looked over to the piles of flowers and an idea came to mind. There were bottles to match the flower colors. She said not to overthink it, so I was going to treat those flowers with the liquids from their matching bottles.

"Come here, reds." I jumped to my feet and grabbed all four bottles that were either red in color or held red liquid inside. "Hello, my little pretties."

Then I carried them over to the bowls in the farthest sun circle. I pretended I was some expert chef who knew exactly what they were doing as they dramatically poured liquids into bowls. Once the reds were set, I swapped out those empty bottles for the three green bottles. Next came the pink, then yellow, and blue. I had just filled my arms with at least eight bottles for the white flowers when the door to the room flew open.

I froze like it was a T-Rex.

But it was *Everest.*

I gasped. His eyes met mine in an instant. We both stood silent and still just staring at each other. He held a tray full of vials, and between those and the ones I held, it was the only reason I hadn't rushed to kiss him. Plus, I needed to calm down this insane lustful reaction to him.

He cleared his throat. "Francelina."

I smiled but it came out all wobbly. "I'm helping Gin prepare for the ritual."

His eyes widened for a second, then went back to normal. He nodded. "I see."

"Yeah. I'm making potions." I had to busy myself, so I turned to the left and began filling the glass bowls for the white flowers— without looking at him. "What are you doing in here with those?"

"Same thing. I've made these special for the ritual." He walked along the edge of the room, staying within my peripheral vision the whole time. "To help restrengthen and rebuild. There's been a lot of death and damage here, and I want to make sure it's purified."

At that, I looked up and met his stare from the other side of the room. "That's really kind of you, especially since you're not from here."

"You're not from here either," he said softly as he bent down to pour one of the vials into an empty glass bowl. "But your kindness does not surprise me."

I blushed and refocused on the white-painted bottles only to realize I'd emptied them all already, so I carried them back over to the wall. I'd gone through all the bottles and vials that matched flower colors, but I was out of those. The flowers that didn't have matching bottles needed some of them, so I had to pick which to grab, except there was nothing obvious about it. And with Everest in the room, I couldn't even read my gut instincts because even those were focused on him. I had to turn away from him entirely so I wouldn't be tempted.

My thoughts just kept going back to Coach's dark office.

"I am sorry your dance got cancelled," he said suddenly as if he were reading my mind.

"I'm sorry I answered my phone—" I slammed my mouth shut. Heat exploded in my face. "I mean, you know, so we could've continued our date. At the dance."

*Nice save, dumbass.* The floorboards creaked beneath his weight a split second before a warm tingle slid down my spine. He crouched down beside me, sitting his tray down with all the other vials. He was so close to me that I could lean forward and pick this back up where he left off in Coach's office.

We stared at each other in a silence so loud we were probably disturbing other guests.

Every nerve ending in my body was overwhelmingly aware of just how close he was. That cinnamon scent of his invaded my senses, unraveling me with every second he didn't touch me. My skin was starting to burn with the need to drag his body down on mine right there on that cushion behind me. I'd been suffocating in my need to touch him since last night. I dreamt of his fingers on my skin, of his teeth grazing my throat, of his lips on mine.

I let out a shaky breath and my gaze dropped to his mouth. I wanted to taste him.

His fingers brushed through my hair, and I gasped like I'd been electrocuted. Hot energy raced through my entire body. My pulse skipped beats, then pounded like a jackhammer. He twirled my hair around his fingers. My whole body trembled.

Then he growled, fisted my hair, and dragged my body into his. To my absolute horror a little whimper slipped through our lips. I gripped the back of his head and pushed off my feet, pulling him down onto the cushion with me. He didn't fight me. He braced his hands on the cushion above my head and rolled his body along mine, our hips gliding together perfectly like they did on that couch mere hours before. I moaned and wrapped my arms around his neck. The cinnamon scent surrounded me.

My self-control snapped. I tangled my fingers through his silky hair. I melted into him, pressing every inch of my body flush against his. He angled my head back to deepen our kiss and ground himself against me just right to make me moan. When I slid my tongue into his mouth, he growled and flipped onto his back then cupped my face in his hands as he kissed me senseless. The warmth of our breaths swirled and mixed together. My body was on fire, and I would let it burn. I wanted more. I couldn't get close enough.

We had too much clothing on today. I'd stupidly worn long jean pants and a t-shirt because I'd dressed to work not to be worked over by Everest. *Stupid, stupid, stupid.* I rolled onto my side, pulling him with me so I could reach down and slip my hands under his shirt. My fingers traced every ridge of his chiseled abs but his hands were still in my hair and on my face. I wanted them on my body. On my skin. I wanted to leave our hands out of this entirely and give us what we both so desperately wanted. I slid my hands around to his back and dragged my nails down his skin.

He growled deep in his throat and then I was on my back again, his body pressing into mine. His body twitched and trembled. I lifted my head and took his bottom lip between my teeth, dragging his mouth back down to—he gasped and rolled off of me so fast he vanished into the shadows across the room.

He cursed and jumped to his feet, wiping his face with his hands before turning and all but sprinting for the door. "I'm sorry—"

"Everest, wait—"

"That's not why I'm here, Francelina," he said in a rush.

"Here in this room right now or in Tampa?"

He paused outside the door and just sighed. Those gorgeous eyes bored into me. "*Both.*"

"So? Why can't I—*we*—just be a happy accident?" I pressed my hands to my chest. "Why can't we just focus on whatever this is between us? This is not normal for me. This . . . this . . . intensity."

He closed his eyes like my words hurt him. "The *happily ever after* you want cannot happen here."

"Here as in *this room* or here as in *between us?*"

"Both," he whispered.

"Well, why don't you like *me* decide if I need the *happily ever after* right now—"

"Francelina—"

"Or if I just need you in this room right now."

He hissed through clenched teeth. "*Francelina.*"

"Everest—"

"I can't." He groaned and gripped the door handle. "I'm trying to protect you—"

"From what?"

"From *me.*"

I blinked through the hot tears stinging the backs of my eyes and swallowed through the hot lump in my throat. "I don't understand."

He opened the door, then looked over at me with a broken expression in his eyes. "I know."

"Explain it to me then. What am I missing? Tell me what I don't know."

"Not here." He nodded his head. "When you're done, just leave my tray of vials here. I will return for them later."

And then he was gone. The door clicking shut behind him echoed in my heart.

# CHAPTER TWENTY-NINE

## FRANKIE

"So LET me get this straight . . . this entire theme park is a cover-up?"

Seamus grinned and looked up at me as he scooped dark-gray dirt into mason jars. "Yep. The Gap in Salem caused other Gaps to open up, but this was the largest of those. Once the humans moved into the area, they had to build something to explain some of the shit that happens here, and I guess a theme park to rival Disney world and Busch gardens was what they thought blended into Floridian culture the most."

I nodded. "Ya know, I can't say I blame that thought process."

"Gotta love Florida, right?"

"For better or for worse." I glanced around. "I cannot believe y'all haven't brought me here yet."

He stood up and loaded the six mason jars of soil onto his rolling cart. "Old habits die hard."

"What do you mean?" We walked down a pathway through the shadows of what they called fantasy forest until we got to an opening between two oak trees where we took our walk off trail. "Y'all don't come here?"

"We do, and we don't." He stepped out into the moonlight at the edge of the forest along a black iron fence that bordered a huge lake. The theme park stood as dark shadows all around us. "The Gap here used to allow demons and spirits in from other realms, like there were a bunch of Seelie fae spirits that used to march around the park at night. The Gap just attracted a lot of activity. If either of us had the ability to see spirits, we'd probably see them around us right now."

That made me glance around. "Creepy."

He chuckled. "You get used to creepy things once you're in our world long enough. The spirits here are just stuck for one reason or another and can't pass on. Paulina used to come here almost daily to try and help them move on. I used to help sometimes. The spirits find my aura calming . . . and Rootbeer's."

"That's quite flattering."

His cheeks flushed, even in the moonlight it was obvious. "Thank you."

"Wait, who's Paulina? I think I forgot who that is."

"Paulina Putnam. She used to be the Death Card in The Coven, but she was nearly killed and lost her Mark in the process. The Death Card can see spirits and talk to them like we're talking right now." His face fell. "After Paulina was Saffie, but the Goddess took her Mark because immortals aren't allowed to be in The Coven permanently."

"Is there some newsletter that goes out to civilians to update everyone on their roster?"

He grinned then reached into his cargo pocket and pulled out a dog bone. Rootbeer perked up instantly. She licked her lips and watched until he tossed it three feet away, then she pounced. He looked back to me. "I don't know about the rest of the civilians, but *we* have Atley and Peabo to actively keep us updated. We also have the family members of the Cards, so they also keep us in the loop."

"That makes sense. Don't let me hold up the job. I'm watching and learning." I gestured around us because I wasn't sure what we were doing. When he knelt down, I cleared my throat. "Wait, did you say this Saffie is immortal? There are immortal people?"

"*People* might not be the right word for them, but yes. There are species that are immortal. Vampires, the royals of Seelie fae, and angels, of course. Saffie is a half-breed. Half-witch, half-Seelie. *But* her father is Prince Thorne, so she's actually Seelie royalty."

I opened my mouth, then shut it. That was a lot to unpack. I thought about asking more questions, then decided better of it. There were some things I just didn't need to know yet. "Right, so Saffie is out. Who is the new spirit speaker?"

"Spirit speaker. That's cute. Um, I don't know her. She's not from here. Her name is Savannah Grace. Can you push the cart over here?" He waited for me to push it over, then he smiled and opened the drawer on the bottom that was full of bags of seeds. He reached in and grabbed one of the bags and tossed it to me. Then he pulled another for himself. "Savannah is originally from Eden, apparently, but lived most of her life in Salem. So, we're just gonna bury these seeds anywhere in here. Dig, place, bury. 'K?"

"Got it." I dug a hole and placed a few seeds spread out in a line, then buried them again. "Good?"

"Good. So, yeah, Savannah only became Death at the end of last month, I think. Not sure the specific date because they were in a war with the Seelie King, and from what I hear it was awful." He was focused on planting the seeds but kept glancing over to Rootbeer to make sure she was good. "Anyway, things are a bit hectic and scary for them these days, but as soon as I get the chance, I'm going to ask Savannah to come down and put these spirits at rest."

I smiled, but he was too busy working to notice. "So, you don't come here because of the spirits?"

"Demons." He shuddered and grabbed a new bag of seeds. "If you were a witch here at night, you encountered a demon. The Coven did nightly rotations to kill them, and they didn't want us here after hours because then they had to worry we'd get hurt, and they needed to focus on the kill. Which is fair. So most of us didn't wanna be anywhere near here close to nightfall, and during the school year it's hard to come during the day. In the summer no one *wants* to here during the day. You're a Floridian. I don't have to explain that."

I laughed. "Fucking fair."

"But there were always certain occasions when we did come at night, like tonight and tomorrow night." He reached in the drawer to find it was empty. He brushed his hands off and pushed to his feet. "Or any night Tennessee is on rotation."

I buried my last seeds, then jumped up, brushing my hands off. "Why his night?"

"Because that dude can kill anything and everything all by himself." He closed the drawer, then waved for me to follow him about twenty feet away to a section of flowers sprouting beneath a canopy of oak trees. "Tennessee is the only one who wasn't distracted by us being here. He knew where we were even if he was on the other

CHANDELLE LAVAUN

side of the park. He'd just sit in a tree like Spiderman waiting for the creepy crawlies to show, then he'd kill 'em."

"I can't wait to meet this dude so I can finally see why everyone worships him."

Seamus stopped and stared at the ground. "He's the grandchild of the Archangel Michael."

I gasped. "What? Like *the* angel?"

"The one and only. We only learned that back in December, but it gave us the explanation for *why* he is the way he is. He's basically an angel walking the streets of Earth. Like no matter what's happening around him or how people act, he's just . . . good."

"That's really something. Angels. That's wild." I gestured to the flowers in front of us. "We just staring at them?"

He chuckled. "Shut up."

"So, tonight you come here and collect ingredients for the ritual on the equinox, right?" I waited until he nodded, then I nodded. "So why tomorrow?"

"But we always come the night before the equinox ritual. It's tradition. It's like the night we get to just have fun and connect with the humans here. It's important to go into the equinox with that balance." He crouched down and plucked some flowers but said a prayer to the goddess before he ripped them from the ground and thanked the flowers for the help they'd provide. "We have to honor what we use. Go ahead, you can pick them now. I made our tribute for both of us."

I smiled and nodded then dropped to my knees to help pick flowers. "What's the deal with the equinox ritual?"

His face paled. "No one told you?"

"They did but it was a lot of *you'll love it, it's so fun, don't stress about it.*" I shrugged. "I volunteered at the infirmary on Saturday, helping them make potions to soak all the flowers in, but I didn't get much more info than that. Got a lot of *trust your gut* and *don't think about it* there too."

"That doesn't help someone with anxiety." He shook his head. "Everyone in our community gathers at the park in our neighborhood. Monica usually puts a spell up that makes humans not want to be there so we can be comfortable. There's always a ton of food and stuff, like any good cookout."

"And?"

He scowled. "You know, I think I know why everyone has been vague with you. It's so common knowledge for us, since we've been doing it our whole lives, that I'm somehow struggling to think of specifics."

I laughed. "Yeah, that's fair."

"But there is a ceremonial part of the ritual where we all go into the lake—no, don't make that face. There are no gators in that lake." I must've made another face because he shook his head and shrugged. "I know, every Floridian knows that if there's water, there's a gator . . . but this lake has *magic*."

"If you say so."

"There are *lots* of ducks though. Chutney's ducks are always eager to help in the water."

I cocked my head to the side. "Chutney's ducks? Is that code for something?"

He snickered. "All right, that's enough flowers. And no, Chutney is the Fool Card—"

"The animal whisperer!" I threw my hands up. "I still say that's the best power out of them all."

"I one-hundred-percent agree."

"The stuff we're collecting right now we'll use in the ritual like I did with the flowers?"

"Yeah, everyone arrives at the equinox ritual with their part. Since we're Cups, *this* is us prepping our part. What you did at the infirmary is *their* part. They create amulets for healing that we give back to the Earth. It's similar but different."

"That's cool." I pointed to the cart. "What else do we have to get? And also, why are we getting all this from here?"

"Because the Gap was here, this area has been infused with magic, so the stuff we collect has already been charged with the energy we need to help us." He rocked back on his heels and started counting with his fingers. "Well, we got leaves, tree roots, soil, and flowers. And we replanted flower seeds to replace what we've taken. By the way, we come back the day after the equinox to plant more. The only thing we need now is moon water."

I jumped to my feet. "Okay. Moon water. Lead the way and maybe explain what that is?"

He chuckled, then turned to Rootbeer and whistled. She grabbed her bone and raced over to us. When Seamus held his palm out, she dropped her bone into it without hesitation. He put it back in his cargo pocket, then rubbed her ears. "Good girl. Tell Frankie not to look at me like that. I always give your bone back when we get home."

I laughed. "I seem to have lost my ability to not show my thoughts on my face."

"It's probably more about your aura. Humans can't feel it, but we can." He waved for me to follow him as he pushed the cart back through the forest and onto that walkway. "Moon water is water that has been charged by the moon's energy overnight. The moon's effect on tides creates this energy connection between the moon and water. It's like a purifying and amplifying force. It's used for a lot of stuff like spells, rituals, intuition, enhancing intentions . . . all kinds of stuff. I love to use moon water in all my potions, makes me feel grounded and humble"

"I love that. I want moon water for myself. How do we make it?"

"Oh, it's super easy. You just take a jar—we tend to use mason jars —and sit them outside at night in direct moonlight. You sit there and have a little chat with the moon about what you need help with and then you leave it out all night." He reached down and pet Rootbeer's head as she trotted beside us. "You can put stuff in the water too, like crystals, talismans, amulets, jewelry—anything you want."

"Can you drink it?"

He grimaced. "They say you can . . . but when I was a kid, I found mosquito larva In a cup of water I'd left outside for a weekend, and there are just some things you can't forget."

I snort-laughed so hard it echoed around the trees. "That's the most Floridian thing I've ever heard. Mosquitos are the true evil in the world."

"I bet they're from Lilith. They gotta be."

I pushed him playfully. "What about the other Suits? What are they doing for the ritual?"

"They're doing what we are, just catered to their brand of magic." He leaned closer and whispered, "And I have no idea what that is."

We both laughed. Seamus was so easy to be around, I was actually kind of glad there weren't other Cups here. But it also made me sad to think he usually did this alone. He was in a good mood, so I didn't want to ask and rain on his parade. These thoughts led me to think about Aaron and Jacob. I hadn't seen them at the dance after Esther's underwear prank, and the Dean had already pulled them aside after the fight. But I did wonder what would come of this.

I cleared my throat. "So what happened with Aaron and Jacob?"

He grunted. "Bunch of dicks. They've been expelled from Gulf Shores High School. Right now they've been put on house arrest inside their homes until The Coven can be called to let the Coven Leaders decide how to handle it. The Leaders are in charge of everything and everyone. Even the shifters and fae report to Coven Leaders."

"And the Leaders are Tennessee and his soulmate, Tegan Bishop?"

"Very good, yes. They're both fair people, but this is bad. These guys need real discipline now before they become a threat to humans. Or worse, a threat to exposing us to the humans." He shook his head. "I don't know what Tenn will do, but I guess we'll see."

"Have they been called yet?"

"I don't know. We're not quite used to them not being here, so I'm not sure who's been appointed as the liaison. Maybe one of their parents who live here?" He shrugged. "We'll find out."

"True that." I cleared my throat. I'd tanked the mood a bit talking about them. "So where are we getting our moon water from? Or are we sitting jars out?"

He pointed straight ahead to where an orange glow lit up the end of the tunnel. "I do this a little differently than other people. You'll see."

I opened my mouth to ask more questions when we walked into that orange glow and I saw something that made my heart stop. My breath caught in my throat. Up ahead, there was a quaint little village that looked straight out of Europe. In the center of the courtyard sat a massive fountain.

I recognized it in an instant.

From my dream.

Seamus was talking beside me, telling me all about how he uses the fountain's pool as his moon water and why . . . but I couldn't hear his words over the pounding of my pulse in my ears. It was my dream. My *vision*. It didn't make sense. That whole time I'd assumed I'd taken an adventure into the Europe, not down the damn street.

The closer we got to the fountain, the clearer my memory of that vision became. I needed to tell someone about this. I needed to tell *Everest* about this. Of all my so-called visions so far, this was the first one that happened in a setting from real life. By the time we stopped in front of the fountain, my hands were trembling. It was identical to my vision.

I glanced over my shoulder, waiting for those spirits with the pointed ears and swords—the ones I'd seen in my blue in a previous dream that were yellow in the second. But they didn't show. The courtyard was quiet. Eerily quiet. The wind rustled through the leaves of the trees, bringing a sharpness to the air that I was trying to pretend was just me psyching myself out.

*They are coming,* that voice had warned me. It had been right. They had come.

I knew that vision wasn't happening in real time, but my mind was too overwhelmed by being here that it had to replay it in my head. I remembered every detail. I'd been holding my rune stones, and the spirits had touched them and then those people appeared, the really pretty ones with gardens as clothing and they had nature-themed names. *Thorne and Sage.* Surely I wouldn't have made that up myself. They felt oddly familiar though but I'd learned so much information since arriving in Tampa that I kept forgetting things they told me only to learn it again like it was brand-new information. Like the other names in my vision, there had been far too many. The only other one I remembered was the wolf made of shadow and smoke named Spot.

*"Step away from the fountain, lita toah."*

*"You need to keep better care of these, lita toah."*

*"You shouldn't be here, lita toah."*

Their words echoed like pinballs in my mind.

*"Try not to use those until you speak with Tegan,"* the one had said.

That couldn't have been a coincidence. Tegan Bishop was High Priestess and Coven Leader. I didn't know if I knew that before the vision though. If I did, then perhaps it was my subconscious trying to help me. Archie had also said I needed to contact The Coven about my rune stones, and that conversation happened before the vision.

*"Francelina."*

I gasped at the sound of Everest's voice and spun around to look for him, but he wasn't there. Because this was real life and not my vision. But dammit it felt real. I needed to talk to him about this. Soon. But in the meantime, I wondered what would happen if I took the stones out, so I reached into my crossbody bag and pulled the drawstring velvet pouch out, then dumped them into my palm. They immediately began to glow neon-blue, the color of my magic, but as I crouched down to lay them out on the pool's ledge, the gold runes vanished. I froze in a half-squat.

A new symbol took shape, but this time it glowed neon-*red*.

It had never turned red before. Hadn't turned a color other than pink. I frowned and started to ask Seamus if he knew the symbol when the wind carried a scent through the courtyard. I sniffed the air a few times. A cold chill slid down my spine that made me shiver.

Seamus was hard at work scooping water from the pool into empty jars. When I tapped on his shoulder, he looked up at me. "Yeah?"

"Do you smell that?" I pointed to the air and sniffed for show. "It smells like . . . like . . ."

"*Maple syrup,*" he whispered. His face fell. "Demons."

I looked up to the black night sky just as red eyes dusted the sky like twinkling stars from a horror film. Seamus cursed and dove for Rootbeer a split second before the demons dive-bombed us. Something slammed into my chest and sent me flying backwards and landing in the pool with a splash. My rune stones scattered across the pool floor, mixing in with the coins humans threw in to make wishes on. I knew they were important, but I couldn't care about that yet. I had to get to Seamus and Rootbeer who were surrounded by demons and trying to fight them off. But these demons were like seagulls hunting for food off beach goers' plates. There were dozens of them.

I scrambled to my feet just as the runes on my stones began to glow pink. *What?* But then I saw neon-blue flash in my peripheral vision. When I looked up, I found the ingredients on the cart Seamus and I just collected all *glowing*. It was a sign, and I wasn't going to ignore it. I dove out of the pool and raced for the cart. We didn't have time to be fancy, so I just started throwing everything into the water.

*Moon, please hear me,* I prayed silently to the moon sitting pretty with a waxing gibbous glow that made it nearly full. *I'll learn how to fight demons, I promise, just help me get my friends to safety. Please.*

I yanked the drawers open and tossed seeds and leaves into the water. As each one sank beneath the surface, blue mist billowed from the surface like steam. I looked up, then did a double take. The pool had turned into a cauldron. I grinned and threw my hands out toward the water, my neon-blue flames shooting like rivers from my palms to the pool. *Moon and tide, give me death.*

The water in the pool surged high into the air and then rolled out of the fountain like a tidal wave. It crashed into demon after demon, turning them to dust without slowing down. *Poof, poof, poof.* The demons were destroyed one by one until the night fell still and quiet.

I was panting. My chest was tight and my throat raw like I'd been screaming. Hot tears formed in the back of my eyes and a lump sat in my throat. But I looked to the sky and sank to my knees at the edge of the pool. I pressed my hands to my chest. The moon had answered my prayer. "Thank you, thank you, thank you."

"Seamus, are you okay? Rootbeer?"

She barked so I looked over and almost cried. She looked perfectly fine and normal, not even wet from the water. She sat between Seamus's legs with him propped up against the pool.

Seamus nodded and rubbed her back. "I agree, Rootbeer. We're gonna have to start over with our ingredients."

I snorted and then burst into laughter. Seamus chuckled and shook his head.

I scrubbed my face with my hands, then held my palms out to start collecting my rune stones from beneath the surface when they shot into the air all at once. It was like a meteor shower to watch them float over to the pool ledge right in front of me. I pulled the navy-blue velvet bag out and held it open while I scooped them back where they belonged.

"Well . . . that was interesting."

"*What the fuck just happened?*" I whispered. "Where'd they come from? I thought the Gap was closed?

He looked over at me with incredulous blue eyes. "You're new here, but I assure you the demons were not the shocking or unsettling part of what just happened."

# CHAPTER THIRTY

## FRANKIE

I FLEW through the front door of the infirmary with one thing on my mind.

Everest.

I didn't care that I'd just met him. I didn't care that we hadn't even taken the time to get to know each other. I still didn't know his last name or anything about him. But the one thing I'd been told over and over since I arrived in Tampa was to trust my gut. To not question my intuition and to *listen* to it like a compass. And my gut was telling me Everest was in my life for a reason. Something told me he was here *for me*. It was ridiculous and silly and so naïve of me to think, but I felt it in my bones.

It wasn't until I saw that fountain from my vision standing before me that I realized the one single thing that overlapped in all of my visions . . . *Everest*. That voice I'd heard telling me to get back in bed and reminding me to breathe. That had been *his* voice. I knew it with every fiber of my being. While I couldn't explain these visions or what the one in Hidden Kingdom was about, I knew that Everest had been in there with me. When I'd first seen him, he was in the park with me. It was only when I looked back that we were in the infirmary.

That meant something.

I had no idea what, but I was going to find out.

Except not tonight.

Tonight I had other needs.

One of the other healers I didn't know very well stepped out of the kitchen on the left, undoubtedly triggered by my entrance, but she wasn't alarmed to see me. She just smiled and looked me up and down. "Do I smell demon blood?"

I nodded.

"Are you injured?"

I shook my head. "Where's Everest? I need . . . to discuss my visions he'd been treating." It wasn't a total lie. I did but I wasn't going to do that just yet.

She nodded and pointed upstairs. "Check the spell room. That's where I last saw him."

"Thank you."

I sprinted up the stairs, but when I glanced over my shoulder, the healer had already retreated back to the kitchen, so I didn't bother slowing down. I raced down the hall and threw the spell room door open. Moonlight streamed in through the windows in the ceiling, but it wasn't much. Most of the room was cast in darkness.

But no amount of shadow or darkness blinded me from him.

Everest was sprawled on that cushion in the far corner of the room with one leg bent at the knee and the other stretched out to where his bare foot dangled off the edge. He had one arm propping his head up atop the pillows that were pushed against the wall. In his other hand he held a book. Those white and blue eyes were wide . . . and locked on *me*.

I didn't speak.

He just stared at me without moving, frozen like a statue. Until I locked the door.

His eyes widened. "Francelina—"

"Shut up." I grabbed the hem of my demon blood splattered shirt and pulled it up and over my head and tossed it aside. Then I kicked off Vans and felt the energy tingling through the hardwood floors of all the magic left over in the room. "I'm not here to talk."

That was all the warning I gave him before I sprinted across the room and dove on top of him. When I heard his book hit the ground I chuckled and lunged for him at the same time as he gripped my jaw. Our lips crashed like those raging tidal waves. He gripped my thighs and pulled as he sat up so that I was suddenly straddling his lap and it reminded me of that couch in coach's office. I reached for the hem of his white shirt and yanked it off of him, breaking our kiss only long enough to pull it over his head.

His tongue slid over mine and I moaned. And then he flipped me onto my back and sat up on his knees looking down at me. I thought he was going to run again, I thought he was going to cut us off, so when he unbuttoned his jeans I moaned a string of obscenities that earned me a cocky, sexy smirk. I bit my bottom lip and reached for my own zipper but he beat me to it, his long fingers worked quick to unbutton them. He gripped the waistband of my denim shorts and pulled, sliding them off my legs in one smooth move.

He just stared at me lying in front of him in only my underwear. His gaze traveled every inch of me like he was committing my body to memory. His attention was so heated and intense I was squirming. I felt like I was going to explode if he didn't touch me. Now. So I jumped up onto my knees in front of him so we were nearly face-to-face. My chest was tight and pounding, sending little pulses through every limb like the ticking of a bomb before it detonated.

Without taking my eyes off his, I slid my hands up his silky-smooth chest and gripped his neck then pulled his mouth to mine. He held my jaw tight in his hand, his long fingers digging into my skin. His thumb slid down to my chin then pushed my head back. He deepened our kiss, devouring me with every flick of his tongue and brush of his lips.

When I had him right where I wanted him, breathing my breath as his own, I slid my hands down and gripped him with both hands. He threw his head back and hissed through clenched teeth. I slid my hands up and down his cock and his eyes closed like nothing had ever felt so good.

He hissed again "...celina..."

I leaned forward and licked the side of his throat where his pulse was pounding. "Good boy," I whispered.

He growled like jungle cat and it was all the warning I had. He reached down and gripped my thighs under my ass and lifted me up until his face was buried in my cleavage then he pulled me down right onto his cock. I felt every hot inch of him as he slid all the way inside of me in one fluid motion. I threw my head back and screamed, digging my nails into his shoulders to hold on. He hooked my legs over his arms and thrust in and out of me. This position had him hitting that sweet spot with every roll of his hips. I wasn't going to last long but I didn't want it to end.

I wrapped my arms around his neck and claimed his mouth with mine. I licked the roof of his mouth and he moaned around my tongue. His arms trembled with every thrust of his hips. I'd never been held and fucked at the same time but I knew I'd think of this forever.

And then I was on my back. His body was hot and heavy, pushing me into the cushion and forcing him deeper inside of me. I moaned his name so loud my voice cracked. He unhooked my legs from his arms so I wrapped them tight around his hips. He planted his hands on the cushion beside my head, buried his face in my cleavage and rolled his hips. I choked on the whimper that came out of me. He rolled his hips back, pulling almost all the way out of me then slammed back in so hard my eyes rolled. I reached up and gripped his back, sinking my nails into his skin.

His hand gripped my waist then slid up my side to my bra. I felt the material tighten on my skin and then it was ripped off of me. Cold air rushed over my skin for a split second before his body covered mine. The feel of his smooth, warm skin against my bare breasts was a sensation that sent me over the edge and my climax hit me hard. My legs tightened around his hips and I screamed.

He lifted his head and covered my mouth with his hand to muffle the sound of my ecstasy. Except it sent my orgasm rolling into round two. He groaned and pressed his forehead to mine as his hips bucked and his own release followed.

*Knock.*

*Knock.*

*Knock.*

Someone was at the door. Everest's hand was still pressed tight to my mouth as we both froze. That door was locked, but a witch probably knew how to open it with magic. If they came in they'd find a whole lot of naked sinning in here.

The person tried the handle but the door didn't open. "Everest? Are you in there?"

It was Gin. She hadn't seen me come in so she shouldn't have known I was there. My pulse quickened. We were both panting and shaking, our bodies covered in sweat. He pulled out of me and I whimpered against his palm.

"*Everest?* Are you okay?"

He arched one eyebrow at me and made a *tsk tsk* sound, then gave me a little smirk. "Yeah, I'm in here. I'm fine. I dropped something."

"Oh. Okay. It's late, you shouldn't stay up working. Katherine wouldn't like it."

"It's all right, Katherine knows what I'm working on." He flipped me onto my stomach and slammed inside of me from behind.

My eyes widened and a raw scream burned a path up my throat so I bit the pillow to muffle the sound. I fisted the sheets with both hands. He gripped my hips, digging his fingers into my skin hard enough to leave a mark. *Good.* I wanted him to. I wanted to see the evidence of our passion on my skin tomorrow. He pulled his hips back, sliding all the way out of me until I felt the tip of his cock press against that sweet little spot he'd played with last night. It was a tease, he wanted to torture me. He wanted a puddle in his hands and he was going to get one.

"We're not work all night healers here. It's not healthy, Everest."

He chuckled just loud enough for me to hear. "I assure you she'd insist I finish." He thrust back inside of me hard, his hips slammed into my body.

I bit the pillow and gripped the edge of the cushion as he rocked his hips into me again and pushed my body further up on the cushion. My body trembled as he pulled back.

"Fine. Do you need any help?"

His grip on my hips tightened as he angled my hips back and slammed back into me but this sent him even deeper and we both grunted. "I think I've got it handled."

His speed picked up and the new tempo made my vision tunnel. I wasn't breathing enough but I couldn't risk a breath and make a sound to reveal that he was fucking me senseless with Gin right outside that door.

"All right, well, if you need it I just made a fresh batch of Katherine's coffee for Nora—"

He pushed my legs apart with his knees and I gasped. But then he slid his hands up to my waist and pushed down with his weight. His hips swiveled faster and harder. His cock so deep I could taste it in my throat.

"—so don't hesitate to steal some."

"Nora needs the caffeine for the night shift," Everest said with a deceptively smooth voice despite the speed of his hips slamming into my body. His cock twitched like his release was almost here. "I shall be fine."

Gin somehow was oblivious to the rapture on the other side of that door but I wasn't and somehow knowing she was *right there* was making my body hotter and hotter. Sweat dripped down my spine. This position unraveled me. Each thrust of his hips sent him pushing even deeper inside. My eyes rolled with every thrust. My whole body trembled.

"Just wake me if y'all need more coffee, please? I hate feeling like the only one not working."

"Go to bed, Gin." Everest slid his body over mine, pushing me into the cushion. With one hand he gripped both of mine, pinning me down. "My work is mostly for personal reasons and do not require your guilt."

With his other hand he reached between the cushion and my body to rub circles on that sweet spot. I gasped and inhaled some of the pillowcase into my mouth. But my eyes rolled into the back of my head. He was everywhere at once. I felt his body on every inch of me and *deep* inside of me. His hips rolled like the tide in a hurricane while his finger drove me into a frantic frenzy in quick circles. My orgasm sent me into orbit. I couldn't breathe. Couldn't see. My body trembled from skull to toes. This was mind numbing, soul cleansing ecstasy and it was going to traumatize me in the best and worst of ways.

"Okay. Goodnight, Everest."

Just when my muscles began to loosen and oxygen burned a path down my throat, Everest wrapped his body around mine, his hands gripping mine and the cushion. The weight of him pressing into me seemed to send him deeper. There was something about the combination of his ragged breath in my ear and his lips on my throat that unraveled me in a way that made me want to write my name on every inch of his skin to claim my territory. The way our bodies slid together, our sweat mixing and blending as we became one rewired my senses. All I knew was *him*.

Turned out he was right earlier when he'd run from me. He was trying to protect me from him. Because as his orgasm pushed me into another I knew I was never going to be the same.

# CHAPTER THIRTY-ONE

## FRANKIE

"There is a limit for how many roller coasters I can ride back-to-back in one evening." I pushed off the cold metal railing and wiped my hands on my little sundress because they felt sticky. "We've exceeded that already. I'm going to get a snack."

Esther wagged her eyebrows. "And by *snack* you mean Everest is here?"

I rolled my eyes "I want to watch the fireworks and that starts soon. So imma get me a snack and then watch."

She narrowed her eyes. "That wasn't a no."

Our friends laughed and started teasing me about him. I knew I was blushing, but I didn't care. We were in line for yet another roller coaster—one we'd already ridden three times since the sun went down because the park wasn't super busy. My stomach was already in knots. I hadn't been able to calm myself down after my night with Everest. My aunt and uncle had panicked when they woke to find I wasn't in my bed and I had a voicemail from Seamus's parents checking in on me after the demon attack at the park.

Unluckily, they'd tracked my phone down to the infirmary and went looking for me. Luckily, Everest lied smoothly through his teeth while looking them straight in the eye. It was just enough to get me off the hook for not going home or calling, but not enough to worry them. But they'd dragged me out of there before I could really talk to him. I felt like a different person this morning. Something had happened between us, something monumental that was way too big for two teenagers who just met, but I needed to talk to him about it. My emotions were just too intense, and it was freaking me out a little bit.

"She *did* wear that dress for him tonight—"

"I did not." I rolled my eyes and gestured to my little light-pink sundress with ruffles. "I bought two dress options for the dance but wore the other. Esther told me I should wear this tonight, so I did. It's pretty. Shut up."

They snickered.

"Ignore them. You look gorgeous." Madge aimed daggers with her eyes at the others. "That dress is perfect on you."

Tomás cleared his throat and looked over at me but didn't quite meet my eyes. "So is Everest coming to join us tonight?"

"His shift has like five more hours, so no, I don't think so."

Ava pouted her lips. "Then why are you bailing on us?"

"I'm not!" I held my hands up in surrender. "Y'all have lived here your whole lives. You've seen this fireworks show a million times. I haven't."

Birdie scowled and looked at her watch. "Yeah, but—"

"But nothing. Please, I'm totally good. I'm gonna just chill like a proper tourist."

Jo pursed her lips. "We don't want you to go alone."

"No, I'm fine to watch myself. Have fun. Ride your rides." I climbed over the railing and into the exit lane. Then I pointed at them. "Stay."

"Text us after the fireworks, okay?" Esther yelled as I walked backwards. "Also, Archie is out there somewhere."

"I'll look for him." I gave her a salute. "Enjoy the ride!"

They were all pouting and waving, but I knew as soon as I was out of sight they'd recover just fine. After all, I was the new girl to the friend group. They'd been surviving without me just fine. I'd been on rides with them since we ditched seventh period. The back-to-back roller coasters for the last two hours or so was a bit much, which was as much a surprise to me as them. But those butterflies just danced around in my stomach. It was excitement but also nervousness. It made no sense. I just wanted to get a snack and sit down for a few minutes while I disconnected and watched shit blow up in the sky.

A classic American past time.

But as I rounded the corner of the creepy clown zone into the fantasy forest-themed section, I found Archie and Aspen crouched between trees off the path. I frowned and skipped over to them only to find them picking through leaves that had fallen to the ground and selecting which ones to put in a big plastic bag they'd gotten from one of the stores.

Archie looked up and smiled at me before I was even within ten feet. Dude had some sensitive senses. "Hi, Frankie."

"Hey, Arch." I leaned against one of the oak trees to act casual while they were being strange. "Hi, Aspen."

"Hi." She smiled up at me for a split second before scowling in concentration while picking up leaves.

I watched them for a moment before curiosity got the better of me. "Okay, I can't resist. What are ya doing?"

Aspen sighed and stared with a broken sadness in her eyes. "The Spring Equinox Ritual was Libby's favorite of the year. The Devil can sense peoples' desires but also their hopes and dreams. Libby was really good at that. She loved the ritual because she could feel what everyone was wishing for. It made her happy."

"The ritual is about growth and rebirth as we enter spring." Archie grabbed a handful of leaves and gently placed them in the bag.

"Archie's helping me honor her tomorrow." Her eyes were red like she'd been crying or trying really hard not to. "I think she would like it."

"I think so too."

"Do you know what we're doing?"

"I don't, but it's the intention that matters."

She smiled. "That's what Archie said."

Archie didn't stop collecting leaves, but he did glance up at me and wink. This boy was unlike anyone else I'd ever met. He'd just moved to town shortly before me, and yet there he was helping a heartbroken ten-year-old little girl mourn and honor her sister who'd died when he could have been riding roller coasters with his friends.

"So, what *are* you doing?"

She took a deep breath, then let it out. "Well, Libby liked the ritual because she liked feeling their hope and excitement but also their needs so she could try to help them if she could. She may not be here now, but I know now that she's watching, and so I want to give her the moment she loved. Archie said if we collect leaves from the park, we can have everyone write their goals and hopes on them. Then when they walk into the lake, we can send them to her."

"You should soak them in moon water first," I said before I could stop myself. I didn't even know where the idea came from. "Sorry, your thing. Ignore me—"

"No, no. I like that idea. Archie, what do you think?"

He frowned. "We'd need a lot of moon water."

"Seamus uses the fountain's pool as moon water."

Archie's jaw dropped. "That's brilliant. We'll bring some home with us tonight and soak our leaves in them overnight, then take them out at dawn so they have time to dry out."

"And maybe you can borrow some of the coins in the pool too."

Aspen gasped, her silver eyes widening. "Archie, can we?"

"As long as we pay tribute to them when we take them and put the coins back tomorrow, I don't think it'll be a problem." Archie narrowed his eyes on me. "What else you think?"

"I have no idea. I don't even know where these ideas are coming from—oh, maybe her favorite flowers?"

"Okay, I can do that—"

"Did she wear a perfume? Like one that was super specific to her?"

Aspen's bottom lip trembled. She nodded.

"Put a few drops of that into the moon water. The more you have the better." The words just kept coming. I felt like I'd been possessed and someone was speaking through me. "Then have a fire near the water so everyone can light their leaves so the smoke will smell like her. I'm sure one of your mothers can think of something to help the leaves not burn so fast."

Tears spilled over Aspen's eyelashes. She dove for me and wrapped her arms around my waist. I hugged her back, holding on tight until she pulled away. Archie's eyes glistened, but he looked away.

Aspen sniffled and wiped at her eyes. "Thank you. I'll try to remember that."

"Call me if you need help." I pulled my phone out. "What's your number?"

She blinked up at me as she recited her number. I typed it into my phone, then saved her name. "Okay, I'm texting you now so you have mine. Text me any time, 'kay? For anything."

She grinned. "Thanks, Frankie."

"We have to stick together, right?" I winked, then started to back away. "I'll let y'all get back to it, but text me if you need anything."

They both waved. I turned and walked through the tunnel made by the canopy of oak trees. My thoughts went immediately to Everest. Or, more specifically, the way he affected me. When I was with him, nothing else mattered. Like a moth to a flame, I just lost myself in the intensity between us. It was an all-consuming kind of thing. The logic didn't matter. When I wasn't with him, I could think clearly. On my own I kept going over every detail of every conversation to try and make sense of it.

He was a stranger when he was away.

I'd known him forever when he was near.

I sighed and tried to shake my thoughts of him away. The fireworks show was starting soon, so if I wanted a good spot to watch, I needed to get my snacks and get moving. When I emerged from the forest into the village surrounding the big courtyard, I tried not to look at the fountain. It was getting ignored tonight. Instead, I marched over to the snack cart to my left and got in line. There were far too many people in line ahead of me for how little time I had left, but at least if the show started, I could watch from the line, which was better than nothing.

My Apple watch vibrated against my wrist. I turned my hand to read the notification and found a text from my Aunt Kimmy. 'Hey, hon. How are you doing?'

I reached down to my little crossbody purse and pulled my phone out, then I opened her text and sent her a selfie of me in the food line. 'I'm good. No visions or demons. About to watch fireworks show.'

"Are you ladies here with anyone?" a deep male voice purred in front of me.

A soft feminine laughter answered. "That depends on if that's an invitation."

My phone buzzed and a picture from my aunt popped up. It was her and my uncle sitting around the table on Archie's deck with bottles of wine, bowls of pasta, and a few board games. Around them I spotted Esther's parents and Aspen's parents, along with Agnes and a handful of other adults I'd seen before but didn't know the names of. My uncle wore a chef hat like that guy in the *Ratatouille* movie, and he was loving it. I chuckled. It was nice to see them enjoying themselves after they spent months sitting by my hospital bed.

"So, what's your name, gorgeous?"

"I'm Azazel," that same deep voice purred. "This is my brother, Asmodeus."

I frowned and my fingers froze on the keyboard of my phone. Those were not normal names. Those sounded like villains from a Marvel movie. I peeked up at them discreetly, and my eyes widened. Both of these guys were well over six feet tall, with long dark hair, mischievous green eyes, and smiles that sent a chill down my spine. I cringed. But their attention was focused on the two platinum blondes drooling over them.

My phone buzzed again, giving me the reprieve from the soap opera unfolding in front of me. It was from my aunt again. *'Bromance game is strong tonight.'*

I grinned. *'Good. He needs it.'*

*'We're gonna be hanging here at Agnes's for a while if this bromance is any indication. So don't wait up for us. We'll sneak in like naughty teenagers so we don't wake you.'*

I chuckled and shook my head. *'Please do not elaborate.'*

She sent winking emojis. *'Please relax and have fun with your friends.'*

"Azazel, if you're going to invite the ladies back to the hotel with us, then can we just get to that part?" Asmodeus sighed.

Azazel chuckled deep in his throat and the two blondes giggled. "Let's take this party elsewhere, ladies."

*WOW. These two are bold.* I was about to roll my eyes in disgust when the girls swooned and draped themselves around the guys.

A new text notification flashed across the top of my screen. It showed only one word: *Everest.* My pulse quickened. I tapped the bar with his name to open up our text thread.

*'What are you doing?'* he asked.

I sent him the picture I'd sent my aunt, because it explained the answer but also because I looked good in it. *'Bout to get a snacky snack.'*

My phone rang. His name spread across my screen. I hit the

button and held the phone to my ear. "Hey, you," I said in an effort to sound casual and not like a stage-five clinger.

"Hey, you." He chuckled and it made my heart do weird things because it wasn't a sound I heard much. "Do you know where Lookout Tower is?"

"*Yes,*" I breathed.

"Meet me there. Now." His voice was warm and chasing away the nervous butterflies in my stomach.

The line went dead. I giggled and jumped out of line, then basically sprinted back into the forest area. Esther and the gang had shown me Lookout Tower first. It was yet another Coven hotspot that they were *babysitting* for them since they left town. I'd just made it to the wooden stairs I had to climb up when I realized I needed to update Esther before I lost my mind to the aura that was Everest.

I pulled my phone out and sent her a message. '*So Everest just showed up . . . I'm gonna hang with him.*'

'*Lookout Tower has the best view of the fireworks for couples . . . Just sayin.*'

I bit my bottom lip. '*He's already up there.*'

'*Damn. He's smooth. Go get a mountain tour,*' Esther texted back with a winky face. '*If you wanna meet up with us tonight LMK. Otherwise we will assume you'll be . . . busy ;)*'

Before I could respond, she sent a *GIF* of Mount Everest. I snort-laughed and then shoved my phone back into my little purse and started my climb up the ladder. I was halfway up when I started wondering why this group of superheroes with magic hadn't come up with a better way to get in and out of the tower. By the time I got to the top, I wanted to take a nap and maybe move in so I'd never have to climb back down.

A pale hand popped into my view and all my frustration popped like a balloon. With a grin and a blush in my cheeks, I put my hand in his. The warmth of his skin sent flutters of electricity through my body. He lifted me up until I stood on my own feet in front of him. And just like every time I saw him, I forgot who and where I was. I leaned into him, pushing up on my tiptoes so I could press my lips to his. He sighed against my mouth, and it sent a shiver down my spine. I gripped his white shirt, pinning him in place. He cupped my face with his hands and kissed me slowly. Reverently. Like he was memorizing every moment.

When he pulled back, there was a sparkle in his eyes, a softness that hadn't ever been there before when he looked at me. "The view of the fireworks is breathtaking from up here."

I smiled. "The view is already pretty perfect." *Ew, gross. Frankie, really? Who ARE you right now?*

He chuckled softly under his breath, then took my hands in his, tugging me through the doorway and into the tower. We hadn't actually come up here before because no one wanted unnecessary physical activity with that ladder, myself included, so as he pulled me inside, a part of me wanted to look around and check it out. But Everest's eyes were locked on me, so I was helpless to look anywhere else.

We stopped beside a leather couch. To my surprise, he kicked his shoes off, then slid his hand over my waist. His fingers squeezed but not enough to hurt, just enough to let me feel him there. "Let me hold you while we watch the show."

My breath caught on the hot lump that formed in my throat. I nodded and tried to rein in the emotions that had my eyes burning like I was going to cry. He sat down on the edge of the couch, dragging his hand down the side of my body until he got to my feet where he quickly pulled my shoes off and sat them next to his. I watched in silent fascination. He wasn't behaving like the person I'd known the last week . . . and yet this felt like the most real version of him.

He smiled up at me, and it sent butterflies attacking my senses again. Then he turned sideways and leaned back, propping his head on a couch cushion. One of his legs was bent over the side of the couch and touching the ground. He was the picture of calm and collected. I liked this comfortable side of him. I slid over his lap to lie on my side between his body and the back of the couch with my face propped on his chest. I wrapped my arms around his waist and tangled both of my legs with his. He reached over me and pulled the blanket hanging on the back of the couch to drape it over my body.

I sighed and nestled into him. Just beyond our feet, the spires of the castle cut across the midnight-blue sky. For a few moments, we just lay there in silence holding on to each other . . . and then I realized something was wrong. I couldn't put my finger on what or why, or how I even knew, I just felt it in my bones. My heart felt heavy and slow. Dread clawed up my spine.

"Everest?"

"Yes, Francelina?"

I closed my eyes and cringed because I loved the feel of his voice rumbling through his chest and into my face. "Just tell me what's wrong."

It was his turn to sigh. "You feel it."

It wasn't a question, but I answered anyways, whispering, "*Yes.*"

He ran his fingers through my hair with one hand, but the other landed on top of mine where it rested on his chest. "I have to leave," he said softly.

"This tower or this town?"

"*Both,*" he whispered.

I whimpered but it sounded more like a groan or a growl. I pushed up and propped my chin on his chest so I could see his face. "Why?"

The haunted expression in his eyes made my stomach turn. "My boss needs me elsewhere."

I wanted to cry, scream, and throw up all at the same time. "Katherine?"

"Katherine is a good woman." He brushed the backs of his fingers across my cheekbone.

I squeezed my eyes shut and asked the most important question. "When?"

"Before dawn."

My heart sank to the bottom of the sea like that necklace in the Titanic movie. Tears burned the backs of my eyes now. My bottom lip trembled. "But you'll miss the Spring Equinox Ritual."

"I am sad to miss it, but I must." Then he took my chin between his fingers and forced my gaze to him. "I *will* see you again, that I promise."

"And it won't be soon enough," I cried, then buried my face in his chest so he couldn't see just how much I was falling apart from this news. "It's just not fair—"

"What isn't?"

"To meet you and feel all these things I feel for you even when I shouldn't yet . . ." I huffed. "And then to have you stolen right out from under me. It sucks."

"It is but a cruel, twisted trick to be given such a short time with you when it hits as hard as it does."

I pressed my ear to his chest to listen to his heart beating beneath the surface. "You must go before dawn?"

He nodded.

"Then let's enjoy our last night—" I started.

"This will not be our last night, Francelina—"

"Our last for now," I added. "Our last *for now*."

Those blue and white eyes watched me with heat blazing inside of them. There was something else in his expression, something that caused sharp pains in my heart. It was an old, soul-deep kind of pain that I did not understand. And for the first time since learning my magic, I did not want to figure it out. At least not tonight.

He swore this would not be our last night, but I knew we both suspected he was lying—or that life would take the possibility away from us.

The fireworks shot into the night sky, exploding into colorful sparkles. Esther had been right. The view from Lookout Tower was spectacular, but as the colors filled the open doorway, I knew the only view I wanted was the one beside me, cuddled on this couch.

"*What are you thinking right now?*" he whispered and ran his fingers down the side of my face as I looked up at him. "*Tell me.*"

"*I'm thinking that I don't even truly know you, and yet I miss you already . . . and you haven't even left yet.*" Tears burned the backs of my eyes. I was getting emotional, and I didn't understand why. I'd only known him for a little more than a week, yet this impending goodbye felt like I was losing what I'd been searching forever for. It was a pain that hurt deeper than made sense. "*I'm thinking that these emotions are scaring me, and now I'm losing before I get to even know you.*"

He cupped my face in both of his hands, tipping my head back to force my eyes to meet his. "*You have known every part of me from the very moment you saw me. No distance will ever take that from us.*"

A rebel, traitorous tear I hadn't approved of slid down my cheek, and I watched the sight of it shatter something inside his eyes. He cringed and swiped it away with his thumb and then his lips were on mine.

His kiss wasn't panicked or frenzied. He wasn't lost to the hunger inside of him and devouring me. This kiss was from the heart. This kiss was slow and sweet, like he planned to take his time. His hands weren't gripping me hard enough to bruise, they were soft and tender. He rolled me onto my back and let his body press into me. Last night had been raw passion where we couldn't get close enough to each other but that wasn't where we were now.

There was a lightness in his touch as he slid his hand up the side of my thigh, under the hem of my little sundress, and up to my hip. I took his face in my hands so he couldn't break our kiss. I didn't need his mouth anywhere other than on mine. My whole body was warm and mushy, my skin tingled and burned like I was cozied up to a bonfire on a winter night. His fingers slid beneath the waist band of my underwear – and then they were ripped clean off of me.

I chuckled against his lips and whispered, "*good boy.*"

His return laughter was low and deep and almost sound like the rumble of thunder. His lips found mine again and everything else disappeared. All I knew was the heat of his skin burning through his clothes and the feel of his tongue sliding against mine. My chest burned. My fingers trembled as I held on to his face. My body *ached*. He rolled his hips and thrust all the way inside of me. I gasped against his lips. He'd taken me before, but never like *this*.

Over his shoulders I saw the bright lights of the fireworks flashing one after another. I'd never watch another fireworks show the same ever again. Not after this moment with Everest.

I needed him more than the air I breathed. My feelings for him had claimed me swiftly and without warning. It was a flip of a switch, like there wasn't a moment where I knew him that I didn't feel *this* for him. I wasn't even sure what *this* was. There were no words in my mind or heart for it, but it was all consuming. My pulse was a runaway freight train and he was the conductor.

He rolled his hips and hissed. I moaned and nibbled at his lips with my teeth. He cupped my face with both hands, deepening our kiss with every stroke of his tongue. I wrapped my legs around his hips and fisted the material of his shirt stretched tight across his back as he thrust into me slow and steady.

The pleasure each roll of his hips sent rushing through me was so warm and sweet it was almost a lullaby. I closed my eyes, lost to the sensation of his body inside of me and all around me. I reached up and fisted my hands in his hair as a little cry slipped out of my mouth. His hips moved faster. My back arched. My toes curled and pointed. My knees pulled up higher like he was melting me into a ball but the new angle of my hips made the slide of his cock hit all the best spots.

He lifted up, planting his hands on the leather couch to give him leverage to swing his hips back and forth until I was on fire and melting with every thrust. My whole body spasmed. I felt myself tighten around his cock and then he moaned, following me closer to our ecstasy. I heard myself whispering his name over and over like a scratched record but he was all my mind knew.

One of his hands pushed into my lower stomach like he wanted to weld us together from the outside. He buried his face in the crook of my neck. I heard the rasp of his hand gripping the leather couch beneath my ear. I cried out and whimpered but it felt so incredible. I felt every millimeter of him inside of me, every ridge, every vein as he slid in and out without pause. The way he pushed down on my stomach was some kind of cheat code to pleasure.

And then his thumb pressed into that sweet spot and I screamed. My senses pulsed and my body throbbed. My body convulsed. Sweat covered every inch of our skin. His muscles twitched and tightened. He lifted his head from the crook of my neck and looked into my eyes so I gripped his jaw and pulled him close just as the grand finale of the fireworks show exploded in the night sky outside. He squeezed his eyes shut and let out a shaky moan. My body tightened, my stomach spasming.

My orgasm was rolling in but it was too much. I felt *too much*. I was about to be ruined forever. Tears pooled in my eyes and my vision blurred. *"Everest—"*

His body trembled. *"Fr—celina—"*

His lips crashed into mine as we both hit that climax together. He kissed me through the wave, wreaking havoc on my heart with every brush of his lips. As the lights of the fireworks filled the night sky I closed my eyes and let my senses feel every second of this bliss before everything went dark.

# CHAPTER THIRTY-TWO

## FRANKIE

EVEREST WAS ALL I could think about.

My mind was a whirlpool just circling the drain. I had more questions than ever and now he was gone. The only answers I'd gotten were the ones that questioned if he had feelings for me, too. After last night in the tower, I knew he did. Yet somehow that just made it so much worse. Both for the pain and the confusion. In the infirmary and even on our date at the dance, he'd been a certain amount of detached. Even in our passionate moments alone I'd only been confident in the fact that he wanted me physically. But he was different last night. From the moment he *called* me instead of texting to when he teased me and chuckled to the softness in his eyes and his entire demeanor. It was like he was a different person all together.

That different person felt like home.

And that made absolutely no sense.

I knew that. I knew if my aunt and uncle heard the thoughts swirling in my mind, they'd send me straight to therapy. They'd blame themselves for giving me space to try and heal my trauma by being as normal of a teenager as possible, given the whole witch revelation. A therapist would have a field day with my infatuation with Everest. I refused to call it love, that was far too dangerous, but no matter which label I used, it had the same outcome. They'd probably blame the trauma and the coma. I'd probably end up on a grippy sock vacation to a padded cell or back in a hospital bed with IVs and machines attached to me.

Granted, right now even I would've been curious to see what my brain scans looked like. I wondered if psychologists used MRIs and CAT scans to determine mental health. Seemed like they would but I had no idea. I pulled out my phone and felt a sharp, intense pain through my chest at not finding a single notification from Everest. There *was* one from Elizabeth, but I'd had an epiphany this morning and realized I was avoiding my best friend. I'd basically ghosted her since I met Everest, and deep down in my subconscious mind, I'd done it intentionally . . . because I didn't want her to see the mess I had become.

Over a *boy*.

*Gross.*

But it was the truth. No one knew me like she did. No one would see through the mask like her. She would've called me on my bullshit. She would've pointed out all the glaring red flags over this boy and scolded me for being stupid. She would've recognized the fragile cracks in my sanity and launched an intervention *from China.* There would've been a therapist, psychiatrist, *and* psychologist at my doorstep the next day. I wasn't even sure the difference between those three professions, but they would've all been there.

If only I had let her *see* the mess I had become.

I wouldn't hurt so much right now.

*I can't fix the Everest issue, but I CAN fix Elizabeth.*

I went looking for our text thread, the one we'd never deleted and was definitely hogging most of the memory on my phone and MacBook. I wanted to cry at how far I had to scroll to find it. My heart sank. The last thing I'd texted her was that I'd call her when I got home from Esther's house—and then I hadn't. Actually, as I scrolled through our conversations since I'd arrived in Tampa, all we'd talked about were my new friends. *Dammit.*

My pride had to take this hit. *'I'm sorry I've been ignoring you.'*

Those three bubbles popped up immediately, which made me feel worse. *'Ignoring or avoiding?'*

I cursed myself out at that one. I'd just proved myself right. She knew. She'd known. She wasn't even looking at me and she knew. It didn't make me feel better. *'Does it help if I didn't consciously realize I was doing it until just now?'*

*'. . . that's a good question,'* she sent back with a GIF of a person thinking hard, then a laughing emoji.

My stomach rolled. *'Don't joke right now. I'm being serious.'*

*'Frankie, it's been like a week. You were in a coma. You moved to a new city. Give yourself a break because I know I did.'*

I exhaled. *'Why does that make me feel worse?'*

Those bubbles appeared. *'LOL.'*

*'Elizabeth!'* I sent with a frown face emoji.

*'So . . .'* she sent, followed immediately by, *'What's his name?'*

*'Everest,'* I said, and suddenly I wanted to tell her everything right then and there.

*'Like the mountain?'*

I rolled my eyes. *'Yes, like the mountain. And yes, those jokes were made though not to his face.'*

*'That's too bad. You should change that.'*

*'I wish I could.'*

*'Ah, there it is. The disturbance in the Force that I felt.'* Before I could respond to that, she sent another text. *'Why does your location show you in a lake?'*

I smiled and held my phone up to snap a picture of the lake in front of me. We were still a good twenty feet from where the celebration was happening, but right after I hit send, I realized how strange the image looked. Everyone here was wearing all-white, myself included. And there were little bonfires surrounding the lakeshore.

*'I have A LOT of questions about that pic, dude.'* She sent with laughing emojis. *'But it looks like you're at some kind of an event. You should go enjoy it.'*

*'Can I call you when I get home tonight? It should still be before dinner for you.'*

*'Of course, but can you do me a favor first?'*

I frowned. *'Of course?'*

Those bubbles hovered on my screen for an eternity while I held my breath. *'Send me a selfie with you, Archie, and Esther. I need a visual. OH and I wanna see the dog and bunny best friends—you know what, just photo dump me.'*

I chuckled. *'Okay, I will send pics as I can take them. But I'll call when I get home.'*

*'I'll be here.'*

"Who are you talking to?" a male voice asked.

I glanced down at Archie and Esther and smiled. "My best friend. I've been neglecting her a bit. She wants pics of tonight —I didn't tell her what it was or anything."

"Don't worry about that. The magic in the air handles that for us. And don't ask me to explain the how of that." Esther laughed. She took my phone and stopped walking, then held it up to take a selfie of the three of us as she was on the far left. We smiled for the picture, then she handed my phone back. "There you go. That one was so cute."

"Thanks." I sent that one over, then went into my photo album and started sending pictures of my new friends that were taken before tonight. The less photos I took of this cult-looking event, the better.

Esther cleared her throat. "I thought you were texting *him*."

I groaned. "I wish."

"He left this morning. It hasn't even been twenty-four hours." Esther bumped my shoulder with hers as we walked toward our friends. "If he's even at his destination, because we don't know where we went, then he's probably just getting settled in. Give him time."

I nodded. Esther had quickly become one of my favorite people, but it was too soon to show her my crazy. "Yeah, I know."

"Right, well, unless you want the rest of the gang to dissect your emotions, you might wanna take a second and reel 'em back in." She smiled softly. "I say that with love, not judgement. Just take a few deep breaths and push all that out of your mind for the next hour. Maybe turn your phone off."

I nodded. "Good idea."

"I'll go get them rolling on another topic before you come over." And then she bounced over to our friend group that was standing with her parents, Archie's mom, and my aunt and uncle.

"Wait." I frowned. "Do they all know something?"

Archie blushed. "Well . . . you did stay in Lookout Tower *all* night and never met up with us after Everest showed up."

My jaw dropped.

"Meh, don't stress it. Actually . . ." He scowled and pursed his lips, then he laughed. "Your cousin, Tennessee, has spent an entire evening on that couch with his girlfriend. Maybe it's a family thing?"

I buried my face in my hands and groaned. A chuckle slipped out. "How do you even know about that?"

He shrugged. "Haven't you noticed how much they talk about him? And The Coven?"

"Touché." I shook my head and laughed more. "So, me and my cousin have hooked up on that couch. I don't know what that says about us."

"Well, if you word it *like that*, other people will have things to say about it."

I snorted and smacked his arm. "Thanks, I needed that laugh."

"I know." He looked over at me with eyes that saw way too much. "You have doubts. About *him*."

I nodded. "It's just a gut feeling."

"Well, where do your doubts lie?"

"He didn't even tell me where he was going. Is that not suspicious? Or at the very least a red flag?" I scrubbed my face with my hands. "And I didn't even *ask*."

"Why didn't you?"

"Because . . . because . . . I don't know what happens to me when I'm around him." I rubbed my chest that was tight and burning. "It's stupid, I know—"

"No." he grabbed my arm and pulled me to a stop in the shadow of an oak tree. "It's not stupid. Tell me."

"I can't even verbally explain it sufficiently. I just . . . get consumed by him. It's like nothing else exists. It's like . . . hypnotic."

"Well, maybe tonight you can focus your intentions on getting some clarity there." He gestured to the lake. "This is the night we plant the seeds to grow for tomorrow."

"You are the most interesting person I've ever met."

He smirked. "I'll take that as a compliment."

"You should."

"HEY!!" Ava yelled from up ahead. "GET OVER HERE!"

We cursed and hurried over to the group.

Ava held out a bowl full of big leaves and in her other hand a Sharpie. "Here, take your leaf—"

"I've got mine." Archie held his up, all three of his. "What? There was no limit."

I grinned as I took both a leaf and the Sharpie. "Thanks, Ava."

She winked, then turned around.

"I can't think of one thing to write, and you wrote three." I shook my head. "This feels like a pop quiz on the first day of school."

Archie snort-laughed. "There's no wrong answer. Just write one thing that you want this year, but not a material thing. Doesn't even have to be a full sentence."

I took a deep breath, then exhaled. *Write one thing.* I tried to think about what my hopes and dreams were for the year, but the truth was I had no idea. All the plans I had died on Halloween. Witch or not, I didn't come out of that incident the same person, and while I hadn't done a proper job of healing from that trauma, I knew I would always be somewhat changed from it. Eventually I'd have to start working on my own healing adventure. I just wasn't sure how to start that while also entering the whole new world of arcana, of magic and war and demons.

In the end, there was only one word that came to mind. So, I uncapped the Sharpie and wrote *mental & emotional peace* on the leaf. Then I handed the marker back to Ava. When I looked up, I found most of the community had already walked to the bonfires with their leaves and were waiting for the signal. Esther led our little group to the closest one and the rest of the people lingering finally got into gear.

Monica, Libby's mother, walked over to our bonfire with tears glistening in her eyes. She looked to Archie. "*Thank you,*" she choked up.

Aspen held her leaf to the fire. When she pulled it back, it had a little flame on it. Archie had filled me in that Monica had done some spells on the leaves to protect everyone from getting burned. Monica and her husband Edward lit their leaves next. Then, at the same time, the three of them walked to the edge of the lake and sat the leaves on the surface of the water.

That was our cue to start. They were going first, then the rest could follow. Archie was hot on their heels. He didn't even know Libby, from what I understood, yet he was just as connected to this moment. It made me wonder who he'd lost that he was grieving in place of Libby. I followed after him with our friends behind me.

One after another we sat our leaves on the water and then backed away.

It was such a sweet gesture.

Once everyone's leaves were floating at the edge of the lake, the moon that was nearly full sank lower in the sky and morphed into a glowing golden crescent. My jaw dropped. There were gasps all around us.

"*The Goddess's moon,*" Archie whispered. "*She's listening.*"

And then all at once, a gentle wave carried the leaves toward the center of the lake. White smoke billowed into the sky from all the little miniature flames. The air smelled sweet like a bakery.

Monica cried out, then covered her mouth with her hand. Edward wrapped his arm around his wife's shoulder then pulled Aspen into him with his other hand. All three of them just stood there holding on to each other with tears in their eyes.

"Warm vanilla sugar from Bath and Body Works." Aspen sniffled. "Libby's favorite."

The silence that followed was thick enough to cut.

I'd never met the girl we were honoring, but it made me want to protect this community from all harm. The love and support they had for The Coven was profound and heartwarming. I wanted to be a part of a community that cared for each other *like this.*

The smoke billowing off the leaves turned bright red.

Everyone gasped.

"What's that mean?" Aspen hissed.

Archie shook his head. "I don't know."

All of the red smoke swirled together until it was one plume shooting into the sky . . . and then it swirled and moved, then formed into an arrow pointing toward the pier to our right. The red smoke arrow was *flashing.*

"*Move,*" Archie whispered. Then he cleared his throat and yelled out, "*Get away from the pier!* Move! Everyone, move!"

Without hesitation, each and every one of us lunged to the left at a dead sprint. We had no idea why, but none of us wanted to be near the pier. A few seconds later, red mist billowed from beneath it. Within the red mist a black hole grew bigger and bigger.

There was a moment where the world seemed to stand still.

And then a sea of black poured onto the dark soil of the lakeshore.

"DEMONS!" Archie screamed.

The demons charged for us, trampling the benches and picnic tables into shreds without slowing. Some of them ran through the bonfire but kept going. I heard screaming all around me. We were trapped. The park opening was now blocked by the demons. I felt everyone's panic as if it were my own. My stomach rolled. If that red arrow hadn't pointed to the pier, a few dozen people would've been standing right next to it. The demons would've barreled right into them like a tsunami. They wouldn't have had time to fight. That arrow saved their lives.

*Libby. That was Libby.* I knew it with every fiber of my soul. Aspen said she knew Libby was watching after that incident with the Ouija Board last month, and now Libby had just saved lives from beyond the grave.

And then chaos descended upon us. The demons looked like big wolves with glowing red eyes and yellow venom oozing from their mouths. I pulled my phone out and pressed my thumb to my sticker. I had my bat full-sized and changed into the dagger in the beat of a second. I hadn't had any demon-fighting training but instincts took over. I sliced my blade through the air left and right, cutting anything within reach.

"*Aspen!*" Archie sprinted away from us and ran toward Aspen who was surrounded by demons. "*Down!*"

Except they weren't attacking her. It was like they wanted to take her with them, which was so much worse. Archie tripped over something and crashed into a couple of the wolf demons. He staggered to his feet and tried to fight them off, but his arms and legs were sluggish and not connected with enough power to do damage. It looked more like a pillow fight. With a curse, I dug my heels into the ground and ran for them.

"Atley! To the left!" Agnes yelled out orders from behind me. "Peabo, push 'em to the lake!"

The ground in front of me erupted like a bomb went off. I flew into the air and rolled, then crashed to the ground. Dirt and fallen leaves flew into the air like fireworks. Bright neon-yellow light pierced through the ground and shot into the sky. Everything happened in the flash of a second. I didn't have a chance to react. Three men dressed in all-white jumped straight up and out of the valley and into the air.

They seemed to hover before landing in a perfect crouch. They were *not* human. No human moved like they did. Nor did they have glowing red eyes. I crawled across the dirt on my forearms because the demons zoomed right by me. I wasn't trying to be a coward, I was trying to get to Esther. She had to have a plan or info about these demons. Someone had to.

"ARCHIE!" Agnes yelled.

The ground rumbled, and a loud war cry ripped through the park. Three dozen figures jumped out from the crack in the ground. They all had pointed ears, long hair with tiny little braids, and a bow and arrow strapped to their backs. They wore silver armor that was barely visible against their nearly silver skin that shimmered like abalone shells in the ocean.

And then I saw their eyes.

Their *black* eyes. From eyelid to eyelid, they were solid black.

Agnes choked on a gasp. "*Unseelie . . . Unseelie . . . HOW . . . Unseelie?*"

I crouched beside her. "Unseelie? What does that mean?"

Her face was snow-white. She peeled her eyes off these *Unseelie* people and screamed, "ARCHIE!"

His face snapped toward us, then paled. He swayed on his feet.

"UNSEELIE!" Agnes screamed again and her voice cracked. She spun to me and dragged me down behind a bush and practically lay on top of me. "*Hide.*"

My friends dove forward and huddled around us. Agnes had me pinned down on my knees, but I had to find my aunt and uncle. I craned my neck around until I spotted them standing shoulder-deep in the lake *Why are they in the lake?* Panic gripped me like cold hands around my throat. There was no way for me to get to them. The demons were a stampede and I'd seen *Lion King*. The roar echoing off the demons sounded like a freight train or a tornado. It was so loud I couldn't hear myself think. All around the park our community was thick in battle with them, and my heart was lodged in my throat.

"*ARCHIE!*"

"What is he doing?" Tomás shook his head, his eyes full of fear. He held his hands up and pumped them. "Slow down!"

I turned to follow their wide stares to see Archie in his little scrawny frame sprinting right for us. He pumped his arms and legs.

His face was straining like this took a lot of effort. His hazel eyes shot to the sky and blazed with rage. He was going to get himself killed.

"He's gonna hurt himself—*get behind a tree!*" Ava pointed to a huge oak tree.

Someone shrieked to my right. I jumped and looked over as one of those Unseelie plucked a woman off the ground and flew away with her. Screams ripped through the roar of the demons. I looked left and right and wanted to scream, cry, and vomit all together. The Unseelie were grabbing people one after another. Just snatching them without slowing down.

"Grab him!" Birdie yelled.

I turned back and rolled to the balls of my feet, ready to jump to catch him when Archie leapt into the air like Michael Jordan going for a dunk. The world seemed to slide into slow motion. Warm golden light like sunshine flashed all around him. My heart stopped. My friends screamed in panic. I couldn't take my eyes off of him even as I heard the desperate, panicked cries all around us. That golden light softened, and I watched as Archie's little body stretched until his legs were almost as long as his whole body had been. White linen pants turned into black ripped jeans tucked into beat-up combat boots. His arms flew out wide and quadrupled in size as chiseled muscle stretched tan skin. His entire right arm was covered in a black swirling tattoo.

On his left forearm was the Roman numeral *IV* between two glowing gold bands.

Archie landed ten feet in front of us in a perfect crouch with long black hair flapping in the breeze. Blue and green magic fired from his palms, shooting right into the chests of every Unseelie carrying a person. They bellowed and dropped their prey, who plummeted into the lake.

The Unseelies all froze mid-air. I couldn't even see their wings they were so dark. They stared at him with wide, black eyes.

"TENN!" Atley screamed so loud his voice broke. I looked over and found literal tears in his eyes, even as he held two daggers and sliced demons' heads off without missing a beat. "TENN!"

Peabo swayed into a tree and had to brace himself. "TENN?!"

"TENN!" The whole park seemed to be screaming his name at once. "TENN!"

*"Tenn?"* My breath left me in a rush. *"That's* Tennessee?"

"Oh my GOD!" Esther had her hands on her head in shock. She sank to her knees. "Archie was Tennessee."

I turned back to look at Tenn just as he spun to face the shore and held his right hand out in the air to the side. The air pulsed and then a long black sword slammed into his palm. The second it touched his skin, he threw it into the air like a boomerang into the night. Demons burst into ashes as his sword ripped through them.

That must have triggered the Unseelies, because all at once they charged for him with blinding speed. But Tenn just threw his hands up and pushed hurricane-force winds at them, pushing them back so fast they flipped backwards.

"Agnes!" Seamus shrieked.

I glanced back, then did a double take as rainbow mist slid over Agnes's body. Her long, dark-red hair was now straight white-blonde cut into a sharp angle like the edge of a dagger. The freckles vanished. She looked to us with purple eyes and earrings wrapped around both her ears. She pulled a dagger from the combat boot she suddenly wore, and I realized she had a similar tattoo sleeve on her right arm.

*"Agnes?"* Seamus squeaked.

A demon lunged over the bush in front of me, but Agnes jumped up and slammed her dagger into the demon's stomach and flicked it to the side. Black demon blood splashed down the side of her body, but she didn't seem to notice. She stood and my jaw dropped. Gone was the teeny, barely five-foot-tall woman. Now she had to be at least five-foot-nine with muscles sharpened like a fighter's. "I'm Mona. Stay down, stay together. Stay here."

Without another word, she charged into battle just as more demons rushed in through that black hole beneath the pier. Mona cursed. "TENN!"

"HOLD ON!" He pressed one hand to the ground and the whole world shook like an earthquake.

We gripped the ground and tried to hold on. I felt hands on my arms as my friends crashed to the dirt. Demons couldn't stay on their feet. They rolled like tumbleweeds.

Tenn's mismatched eyes blazed with power and fury as he forced the demons to fall over. "NOW!"

He released his hand, then fired blue and green lightning over our heads. Mona, Peabo, and Atley lunged back into battle. The scent of maple syrup filled the air. But those winds faded a second later, and the Unseelies swooped down—except they didn't go for Tenn.

They went for *people.*

Tenn cursed a string of obscenities that almost made me giggle. *Almost.* But then he tapped those gold bands on his left arm and a six-foot-long sword landed in his open palm. Massive white angel wings popped out of Tenn's back, and I choked on a gasp. He shot straight up into the sky, spinning in circles as he fired magic and wind in every direction with rapid speed. A gold breastplate covered his chest, and now his shins and forearms were strapped with golden armor. I had no idea what that was about, but I remembered someone telling me he was the grandson of the Archangel Michael, and it made perfect sense. That sword was glowing a white so pure it was almost purple. White magic flickered and coiled all around it as if it had electricity running through it.

I was frozen in place, not from fear but in *awe.* Tennessee darted across the park faster than my eyes could track. The Unseelies were scrambling and growing desperate. They kept grabbing new victims only to have Tenn light their asses up with that white fire.

"What's he doing? Kill them!"

"He can't!" I yelled back. "He's focusing on saving everyone they grab!"

"He's just one person!" Esther hissed—then she gasped and pointed to our right. "The portal thing is closing!"

I looked over to where that black hole was and found that rainbow mist filling the entire hole and sparkling.

Esther screamed and lifted into the air in the hands of an Unseelie.

"Fuck that." I charged after her.

The Unseelie was heading for that golden crevice in the ground, and over my dead body was it taking my friend with it. Esther's gold and navy-blue glitter kept hitting the Unseelie in the face. Each hit made him drop lower in the sky. I dug my toes into the ground and pushed as hard as I could, then I dove . . . and tackled both of them to the ground. Dirt flew up all around us. But I didn't hesitate. I flipped the Unseelie onto its back and slammed my dagger into his throat.

Purple blood splashed in my face.

Esther's magic shot over my head, but when I looked up, four men in white suits surrounded me. They snarled and long, pearly fangs dropped from their other teeth. *Fangs.* I yanked my dagger out of the Unseelie's throat and jumped into fighting stance, ready to pounce, when Esther hit two of the vampires with magic. I swung my dagger through the air and sliced a gnarly gash across the one's face. He screamed and red blood splattered into the fourth vampire's eyes, which gave me the chance to embed my dagger into his gut. I yanked it out and jumped back, grabbing Esther to run back to our friends.

The vampire with the face-gash leapt into our path, but he just vanished into that golden crevice.

The other two vampires charged for us. Black smoke shot up from the ground and threw them backwards, but our path was still blocked. They jumped back up and charged again—then suddenly they were *convulsing.* Their bodies were locked tight, every muscle spasming and twitching. Blood poured from their eyes, nose, mouths, and ears. Their creepy red eyes were trembling.

I looked over for help and spotted Tennessee with one hand stretched in our direction, his fingers flexed. He turned his wrist and the vampires shrieked and dropped to their knees. Blood burst through the pores in their skin. I grabbed Esther and scurried backward just as all three vampires exploded like bloody glitter bombs.

My breath left me in a rush. Tennessee narrowed his eyes on the puddles of vampire in front of us, but with his other hand that glowing six-foot-long sword was sending lightning across the lakeshore, blocking the Unseelie from swooping in.

People screamed, but I couldn't see from *where.*

Tenn cursed violently. The rage in his eyes grew brighter. He threw his hands up and water shot up from the lake to entomb each Unseelie. They all gripped their throats and banged their fists against the water holding them, but they didn't pop. He was *drowning* them.

My eyes widened.

Tenn wasn't even facing them. His mismatched eyes were on his own people. His power was so intense and strong that he didn't need to watch. Nothing was going to get around those massive white angel wings either. He glanced left and right, up and down, like he was checking every angle for victims. The muscles in his arms strained as he dragged all three dozen Unseelie to the lakeshore. Dirt shot up and coiled around their legs, pinning them in place as he slowly drowned them.

Tenn wasn't even breathing hard as one by one the Unseelie suffocated in the water bubbles of his making.

They were all dead.

He lowered his arms, nodded his head to the side, and those glowing crevices closed right up. We were alone in the park again.

Silence echoed around us as we all just openly gawked at him.

"*Fuck me.*" A girl with black and purple hair suddenly appeared *right* beside me. "You're so hot."

# CHAPTER THIRTY-THREE

## FRANKIE

TENNESSEE'S MISMATCHED GAZE SHOT RIGHT to her, and instantly his eyes went from cold-blooded assassin to lovesick puppy dog. His lips curved up on one side to a dazzling sideways grin. He straightened his stance and tapped on the golden bands on his left forearm—his sword vanished. The angel wings and golden armor disappeared.

The girl giggled. "That feel good, babe?"

*Babe? OH. This must be his soulmate, Tegan Bishop, the High Priestess.*

"That felt *so* good." He rolled his shoulders and stretched his arms out. "I needed that."

"Hey, Tegan?" Mona shouted from over to the left. She pointed to the sky and made a circular motion. "We clear?"

"Oh yeah, we're good." She snapped her fingers and a white box appeared in the sky over by the pier. "I mean, they're gone for now."

People walked through the white box like they'd been standing there waiting for it to open. There had to be two dozen of them. Each and every one of them had a Roman numeral inked in black on their left forearms.

My eyes widened. I leaned closer to Esther. "Is that—"

"*The Coven,*" she whispered and crouched down. "*They're here.*"

Everyone else in the park slowly began to move toward us, their eyes all wide and excited. I eyed this Coven I'd heard so much about, but there were so many it was hard to see details on any of them. Or perhaps I was a little overstimulated. But I did see Royce and Thiago near the front of the group.

A gorgeous girl with long Rapunzel-like platinum blonde hair was at the front of the group. Her gold eyes looked like pure sunshine. She threw her arms out wide, and I didn't know where to look first: the swirling black lines covering her right arm or the *III* Mark on her left forearm. "*Suuuure*, when Tenn tortures and suffocates to kill, it's hot . . . but when Emersyn does it, it's a fucking concern."

A boy that looked exactly like Royce but with blond hair and purple eyes gave her a crooked grin. "Butterberry, when you sprout white angel wings, you can suffocate any monster you want."

Tennessee shrugged and nodded. "That feels fair." He held his left hand out and flexed his fingers. The air pulsed, and just like before, a long black sword flew toward him.

But a tall girl with a split-dye hairstyle jumped out from the crowd and lifted her hand up—*and Tenn's sword slammed into her palm.* She grinned over at him. "Thanks."

Tenn arched one black eyebrow at her. "Excuse me. That's mine."

"Look, some little sisters steal sweatshirts." She strolled toward him and I realized how identical they were with their mismatching green and blue eyes. Half of her head was platinum blonde, but the other side was as black as Tenn's. "*Your* little sister steals your sword. That's just who we are."

Tenn chuckled and shook his head. "I missed you too, Hope."

She didn't drop his sword or hand it over, but she did hug him. "Thanks for not dying, bro."

Tegan giggled and leapt forward—and evaporated into *rainbow bubbles.* I cursed and jumped to the side just as she re-formed right in front of Tennessee. When he stepped back from his sister, his smirk turned into a full grin. Pink light flashed from the center of his chest where a pink crystal poked out the top of his V-neck shirt. He wrapped his arms around her and lifted her off her feet. They held each other for just a second before they broke apart.

They were talking to each other, yet I couldn't hear what they were saying. I frowned. "Did someone hit the mute button?"

Esther snickered. "Knowing Tegan, I think that's exactly what she did."

*"They're talking about the Unseelie,"* Seamus whispered. *"They don't know how they got in, and they don't want us to know that."*

Ava shuddered. "Seamus, we've been over this. Stop reading The Coven's lips when they're going to lengths to prevent us from hearing them. There's a reason for it, love."

The others grumbled and nodded.

"Hey, Frankie—"

I spun back and cursed, throwing my arms out in self-defense. Tegan was *right* in front of me. But my magic hadn't realized it was her, and it moved faster than I knew it could. Blue flames shot out of my hands and flew right at her face. "No!"

She held her hand up and my flames coiled around her fingers like they were long lost friends. "Sorry, I did that on purpose." She giggled.

I exhaled and fell back onto my ass, then pushed my hair back. "What? Why? Why do you know my name?"

She sank to her knees in front of me, close enough that I saw every speckle of color in her pale-green eyes. This close, I realized her hair was entirely purple but like in an ombre where the top was super dark and then faded to a lighter purple at the tips. The combo with her green eyes was insanely cool. *You're staring, Frankie.*

I closed my eyes and shook myself. "Sorry—"

"Don't be."

When I opened my eyes, I found her right hand up in front of my face. Those black lines covered every inch of her skin all the way to her fingertips.

"Take a deep breath, Frankie."

My body listened to her order, sucking in a gasp of air—and then rainbow-colored mist slammed into my face. I flinched and scurried backwards. Sharp pain shot through my temples and into my sinuses. Images flashed like a flip-book in my mind. I hissed and pressed my fingers to my temples.

"Yeah, I had a feeling." Tegan chuckled, but I didn't know why my pain was funny.

I squeezed my eyes shut, but the images grew brighter and clearer. People's faces flew by one after another, but I couldn't place names. It was going too fast. The world spun and I swayed. It felt like I was having a stroke or seizure or something.

"Hey there, Frankie," another woman's voice broke through the chaos that was raging through my mind.

I opened my eyes with a cringe—and gasped. I knew her face. Images with her in them slid into my mind. I saw her standing beside my bed with colored IV bags. "*Katherine . . . you're Katherine?*"

"I sure am. Good to see you again." She held out a vial in front of me. "Drink this for me."

It was probably a horribly bad sign for my sanity, but I didn't hesitate to trust her. I grabbed the vial and chugged the liquid that tasted like apple juice. It slid down my throat, easing my pulse with every second. The pain vanished. I blinked and rubbed my eyes.

"Yeah, that should help." Katherine smiled and shook her head. She nodded her head in Tegan's direction. "That's my chill pill potion. Tegan's magic packs a punch, especially this kind. This will help your mind settle while the magic leaves your system. Think of it like you're downloading a file. Give it a second and you won't feel so crazy."

"Thank you," I breathed.

"You're welcome." She stood up but held her hands out. "Stay seated for a minute."

I nodded.

Tegan crouched in front of me again. "Tell me, Frankie, what's your best friend's name?"

"It's Elizabeth—" I gasped. All at once the images made sense. I knew what was happening. My memories were coming back. My memories from before. It wasn't all there yet, it was still chaotic, but at least I knew what was happening. "It's Mei-Ling. She goes by Mei-Ling now."

Tegan's grin was every bit the Cheshire Cat. "What day was it when you woke up from your coma?"

Emotions I wasn't prepared to feel hit me like a brick wall. "Valentine's Day."

"Very good. Chill for a hot sec." She winked, then stood up and walked over to stand beside Tennessee. "Good to go, Babe."

My friends stared at me with a million questions in their eyes, but I couldn't answer them. Not yet.

Tennessee cleared his throat, bringing all of our attention back to him. "All right, everyone move in close. I wanna make sure you can all hear me."

The Coven moved to stand behind him and Tegan. Their faces were masks of intensity. They weren't relaxed at all. They were all business. I glanced around but no one seemed concerned about their expressions. Actually, they all seemed overwhelmingly relieved they were there. Everyone hurried to huddle in as close to them as possible, then sat down on the ground or leaned against trees.

Tennessee smiled. "Hey, guys, before we talk . . . is anyone hurt? Like a real injury that needs attention right now?"

A guy in the back raised his hand. There was blood on it. "I think I need stitches on my head."

A few other hands raised in the air, but I couldn't see who they belonged to.

Tenn nodded. "Right. If you need medical attention, please walk to everyone's favorite oak tree and have a sit. Katherine will be right there. Ma, can you help?"

Mona's cheeks flushed but she nodded. "You betcha."

As Katherine and Mona walked toward a huge oak tree behind me, I noticed quite a few people headed in their direction. Everyone else kept their gazes locked on Tennessee, hanging on his every breath.

"Right." Tenn put his hands on his hips and sighed. "As I'm sure you've deduced at this point, for the last two weeks or so I was here disguised as a guy named Archie. I'm sorry for deceiving you. I assure you I did not do so to spy on you or anything. The truth is I was here undercover so that I could protect you, so that I would be here the very moment shit went down."

Atley held his hand up in the air. "If you were Archie, then who did I call on the phone that night? We all heard your voice."

All of the teenagers nodded and pointed to him like he'd asked the question they were thinking. And it was a good question. Archie had been standing right there when Atley spoke to Tennessee on the phone.

Tegan grinned and pressed her finger to her throat. "Yeah, that was me," she said *in Tennessee's voice.* When everyone gasped, she just shrugged. "I'm a master schemer, what can I say?"

"Yeah, I almost blew my own cover when *I* answered that call." Tenn chuckled but then he sobered and turned back to the group. "Okay, here's the deal . . . You all know me. This town was home for most of us for a long time and you were good to us. Some of you are our literal family. For that, I'm going to be honest with you. The truth is the war with Lilith has already started. Each time we thwart one of her schemes, she delivers a new one, a significantly worse one. First, she almost single-handedly prevented the twins from closing the Gap in Salem. Next, she attacked us with enemies made from our own kind, warped and poisoned by her magic. We've fought the Seelie King and his knights. We've fought fallen angels. We managed to kill Leviathan, but Asmodeus and Azazel are very much at large, and they were here last night—"

Everyone gasped and looked around.

"They're not here right now." Tenn held his hands up. "I saw them at Hidden Kingdom last night. That's why I knew something was going to happen tonight and had my Coven-mates lurking in the shadows, ready for a fight."

Esther raised her hand. "Tenn . . . why? Why did they attack us? Who was that?"

The crowd grumbled and nodded in agreement.

Tenn sighed. "On Samhain we lost a family member. Larissa. And while her loss was devastating, her Mark was passed on to the next person worthy of the Card. That's how Coven life works. That person Marked as our new Tower suffered a horrible accident the night she was Marked and Katherine was forced to put her in a magically induced coma to help her heal, a coma she only woke from in February."

"Who?" someone yelled from the other side.

I stood up and everyone's eyes shot to me. The memories were still loading, but I knew the truth enough to know he meant me. I raised my left arm out and there it was, the Mark of The Tower. *XVI.* Everyone gasped, but the gasps from my friends made me the most nervous. "Me. It's me."

Tenn smiled. "Frankie is our Tower. When she first woke last month, she wound up kidnapped by vampires and taken to the kingdom of Avolire, along with two of her friends, one of whom was turned into a vampire against his will."

The aura in the park grew thick and terrified. Their faces were pale with worry.

"I know. We did not know the vampires were so boldly breaking Coven Law. We didn't know that Queen Sweyn had given her unwavering loyalty to Lilith. Fortunately, Sweyn underestimated our own Queen of Darkness and Tegan was able to rescue Frankie and her friend. But in doing so, it made us an active target."

"Queen Sweyn wants us dead. She wants to kill us on behalf of Lilith." Tegan glanced around the group. "But after outsmarting her the way I did, she wants revenge. She wants payback for what I did, so we set her up for failure. We set her up to show her hand."

"We needed proof that she wanted to hurt us. We needed undeniable proof that she broke laws so that we could provide her with the proper, aggressive consequences. We got that tonight." He looked to the ground and shook his head. "We didn't expect it to go quite like that."

"Sweyn had plans for me," I heard myself say. I looked to Tegan. "That's why you asked if I wanted to be bait, because you knew she was butthurt and would come after *me*."

"Yes. And we had a feeling she would retaliate against this community because she knows most of The Coven lived here. We have family here . . . People that mean a lot to us." Tegan looked around the park at all the faces watching her. "I took Frankie's memories of everything that happened since she woke up so she wouldn't remember a single detail . . . so that she was the perfect bait. I sent her *here* because I knew y'all would welcome her in, but also . . . two birds one stone. We could focus our energy here."

"Those men in white." Esther pointed to the spot where the blood still stained the grass. "They had fangs. Those were vampires."

"Yes. *They* were here for Frankie. The Unseelie were here to snatch and grab. The demons were a distraction."

"One of them got away." Esther wrapped her arms around my shoulders. "He left—"

"I know. I let him go."

I smiled because I knew *why*. Tegan wanted to send a message. She was one ballsy motherfucker.

"*Why?*" Esther whispered.

"Because dead men tell no tales," Tenn's sister said with a grin.

"*MA'AM, speak for your damn self,*" a girl with a *thick* southern accent yelled from the far side of the Coven's huddle. She had blue hair with white pieces framing her face. Her makeup was professional-level good and dramatic. Madge and Jo nodded in approval beside me. The girl pointed to the *XIII* Mark on her forearm that was perfectly blended in with all of her other tattoos. "I assure you these som' bitches have shit to say."

The entire Coven chuckled.

Tegan shook her head. "Yes, but *Sweyn* can't talk to them like you can, Savannah."

Savannah grumbled and crossed her arms over her chest. I couldn't hear her, but her Coven-mates giggled and patted her on the back.

"Look, I wanted Queen Sweyn to know I beat her. Again. Fuck around and find out." Tegan shrugged. "She needs to know what bear she's poking."

Everyone in the park shook their heads. There wasn't surprise in their response, which was a good indication Tegan had been pulling shit since day one.

"Thanks, babe. They'll all sleep better tonight now." Tenn rolled his eyes, but he was smiling. He licked his lips and sobered again. "You're not going to like this, so brace yourselves . . . but I'm evacuating Tampa. Effective immediately, and it *is* mandatory."

Everyone gasped and sat up straight. People glanced around to each other like they wanted to make sure they'd heard him right. Whispers echoed between the trees as panic began to rise.

"All right. Everyone, stay with me." Tenn raised both hands in the air. "Hunter, you here?"

A big guy with blond hair and golden eyes like Emersyn stepped forward with a smile as he lifted his hands and pushed golden mist through the crowd. I watched as the moment it touched people they instantly calmed and settled back in place. "We know how you're feeling, but let Tenn finish, and I'm sure you'll feel a little better."

"The evacuation is mandatory because our town here is no longer safe, so we're moving all of you to Eden. Tonight. I cannot and will not knowingly put my own people at risk. If you don't want to go to Eden, you can go somewhere else, but you won't be allowed to stay here. And if you've been paying attention to arcana life outside of Tampa, then you know how much danger the rest of our fellow witches have been in. If you decide to evacuate to a different city, that is up to you, but while I've been here, my Coven-mates have been prepping for your arrival in Eden."

Monica stood. "How long is the evacuation for?"

"I'm not sure. I want to be honest with you. So long as Queen Sweyn and the vampire kingdom breathes, this town remains in danger." Tenn grimaced. "I don't want to sound cruel, but I've seen your demon-fighting abilities without us around. Vampires are lethal and smart. You. Are. Not. Safe. Here. Nod if you understand this."

He waited as the whole crowd nodded.

"All children will be enrolled in Edenburg starting tomorrow. I'm going to hold an assembly at the school in the morning so we can discuss more in detail. For now you just need to know that it is happening."

"Shit," Madge mumbled.

Jo nodded. "*Merde.*"

"*Mierda,*" Tomás echoed.

Birdie exhaled in a rush. "Fucking hell."

Tenn ran his hand through his messy long black hair. "I cannot promise Sweyn won't return and destroy everything here in spite. So, if it is important to you, you'll need to bring it with you. Sebastien English will be here with the English family moving company—I think we're all familiar with them."

Everyone chuckled, including Royce and the pretty blond boy that looked a lot like him. I looked around until I spotted my aunt and uncle who'd gotten stuck standing on the other side of the park. They met my stare and nodded, so I smiled back. They'd told me about the English family's moving company when we got here. It was nice to know something ahead of time and not feel lost by everything they were saying. My memories may have been returning but I still didn't know anything about Edenburg or Eden that wasn't surface level info.

Ava cleared her throat. "What about our pets?"

"I swear to the Goddess if a single one of you abandons your pet in this evacuation, I will personally have your magic stripped. Permanently." A short girl with brown ringlets glared her pretty blue eyes at everyone, her cheeks flushed. Yellow smoke swirled around her hands. "Did I stutter?"

Everyone shook their heads.

Ava grinned. "That settles that then."

Tegan chuckled. "Thank you, Chutney. And she has the support of her Coven Leaders on that threat. Bring your pets—"

"What about our plants?"

Tegan's eyebrows rose. "You mean like your gardens?"

"The ones inside."

"Yeah, I have my friends in pots inside."

"They have to be taken care of too."

"I love witches. Y'all treat your plants like your children." Tegan shook her head. "Yes, bring them. You're not going to jail. We have accommodations for all of you. Y'all, this is not a hurricane evacuation where you only grab what you can carry. We have portals and magic. We got you. We will help you get moved. I promise."

"So, take a moment, take a deep breath, and let's do it. I may suck at a wand—" Tenn paused as everyone laughed again. "But I have people who are good at them coming to help make this process quick."

Tegan held her hand up and a white box appeared off to the side. People dressed in black gear and strapped with weapons poured in looking every bit like an army. Then at the end of the squadron were about a dozen people wearing purple blazers. I frowned. The purple color meant they were Wands.

"See these lovely Pages wearing purple blazers? I've brought them in to help y'all get packed up. They'll be going around assisting the movers and anyone who needs it." Tegan turned to that blond boy who looked like Royce. "Deacon, can you call your father and see if they're ready for me?"

"On it." He pulled a cellphone out of his pocket, then jumped through the white portal box.

"These guys in black are the Knights of New York. They're here to watch your backs and kill anything that tries to hurt you." Tenn's eyes sharpened on something to his right. "Except for Aaron Burke and Jacob Jordan, who despite their intention to in fact hurt people, I've instructed the Knights not to harm."

Everyone gasped and looked to them.

Aaron and Jacob stared at Tenn with eyes and skin that looked a little green. Two sets of adults standing behind the bullies closed their eyes and cringed. They were visibly terrified of Tenn and wildly disappointed in their sons. Both of those things I understood.

Tenn glared at the bullies, and watching him torment them like this, in such a professional *I'm just better than you* way was so therapeutic. "You two and your parents will report to Coven Headquarters in Eden the moment you arrive there. You will see me first before your accommodations or I assure you your punishments will be worse than I'm currently planning. Understood?"

They nodded.

"Good." He turned his gaze to the rest of the crowd and his eyes softened. "Now, I'm going to let you have your ritual you've all been planning since we were so rudely interrupted. I know we did our tribute for Libby already, but I think we owe her a little of our gratitude. In case you didn't realize it, *she* sent us that arrow warning us, and everyone over near the pier is alive right now because of it. And that's pretty damn special, so we're going to thank her properly. Any of my Coven-mates who'd like to join us for that, please see stick around."

He winked at Aspen and tears filled her eyes. Her bottom lip trembled.

Tenn cleared his throat. "The rest of my Coven-mates, please get back to Eden. And someone, for the love of God, get Thorne and Sage there before I return. And call Cassandra and her brothers and—"

"Already on top of that, babe." Tegan tapped her temple, then kissed his cheek. "Stay, honor Libby, then call me and I'll come back for you. We'll be ready to get to work."

That girl Savannah with the cool blue hair and tattoos and the XIII on her arm stepped up. "Tenn, may I stay?"

"Yes. Thank you." He waved for her to follow him over to Aspen, then he smiled down at the young girl. "This is Savannah Grace, our new Death Card."

"Aspen Tarbell. I know," Savannah said with a smile when Tenn opened his mouth to introduce her. Savannah crouched down in front of her. "Hey, kiddo. Gimme your hand. I have something for you, little ma'am."

Aspen frowned. "What do you have?" But she held her hand out like Savannah asked.

Savannah didn't answer. She just reached out and slid a red silk scrunchie onto Aspen's wrist. Aspen choked on a sob, tears instantly pouring down her face. She tackled Savannah who immediately wrapped her in her arms and held on tight. She whispered in her ear.

Esther leaned in close and whispered in my ear, "*That was Libby's scrunchie she ALWAYS wore.*"

I blinked and felt a tear on my eyelashes. *Fucking hell.* I wiped my eyes. There were sniffles and cleared throats all around us.

Tenn turned back to his Coven-mates with glistening eyes and nodded his head. "Go ahead, go to your families."

They charged into the crowd like they'd been dying for him to release them. One girl with long black hair only made it about fifteen feet before a couple tackled her in a hug that was a little violent. There was definitely a story. Especially given they were all crying. Two toddlers hugged the girl's legs, so she dropped down and pulled them into her arms. A pretty blond boy with a wild smile walked up behind them with glistening eyes.

One of the little girls my friends had introduced me to, the pretty little blonde one, sprinted for him with her arms out wide. "EASTON!"

He lunged forward and scooped her into the air, and she squealed.

Between us and them, I saw that Chutney girl hug a little boy and two adults in a big group hug. Another girl with strawberry blonde hair hugged her parents and little brother. And then both girls turned and tackled the couple next to them. A massive blond dude the same height as Tennessee went over to Libby's family, but he kept glancing over to where Mona was treating injuries with Katherine. Royce was talking to his parents. There was no doubting that genetic pool. They were practically triplets. Yet not a single one of them were smiling. Their sapphire eyes were all tense and sad.

The rest of The Coven slipped through Tegan's white box and out of sight, except for Tegan who was standing beside it but watching the lake.

Tenn sighed and rubbed the back of his neck. "Tegan, please take Frankie to Headquarters now. And her aunt and uncle."

I flinched. "Wait, what? I can't stay?"

He shook his head and moved closer to me so that no one else besides my friends could hear us when he whispered, "*She came here for you. I'm sorry, but no. If she knows you're still here—*"

"No, you're right." My heart sank. "I can't endanger anyone else any more than I already have."

"Thanks, Franks. I'll be right behind you." Then he turned away and headed for Libby's family without another word.

I looked to Esther. "Call me when you get to Eden?"

She nodded and gave me a small smile. "Will do. We'll see you soon."

The others waved, and I waved back with a rock in my stomach. I couldn't tell why I was feeling this dread, but I was. Or perhaps it was nerves. The sooner I got through that portal and could ask all the questions I needed to ask, the better.

When I got over to Tegan, I shook my head. "*You.*"

Tegan grinned. "How's my little baitfish feeling?"

I laughed. "Overwhelmed. I have questions."

She hugged me. "I have some answers. But not here. C'mon."

"I figured." I started after her, then glanced back at Esther. "She's important. You know that, right?"

Tegan smiled mischievously. "I've known that since October, yes."

I jumped. "Really?"

Tegan shrugged. "She was waiting for you to set her free. Now that she is, I'll bring her into our group. Tenn has been talking to me about her while he was here. He wants to keep her close for many reasons. The Coven collects pets, especially founding family lines."

# CHAPTER THIRTY-FOUR

## FRANKIE

TEGAN'S PORTALS were the coolest piece of magic I'd seen yet.

One second we were on the lakeshore in Tampa, the next I stood on the front lawn of a massive old Victorian-style wooden house with a wraparound porch. It wasn't quite dark yet here, so I could still see the outline of the mountains around us. This was definitely *not* Florida, but I could not remember where Eden was.

"Welcome to Eden," Tegan said from beside me.

"Where is Eden exactly?"

"Buried deep in the Appalachian Mountains of Tennessee-ish." She frowned. "I also got here from North Carolina. It's not quite so literal. Magic is weird like that."

"*Magic is weird* is the explanation for a lot of things, isn't it?"

She chuckled. "Indeed."

"So everything that happened before with being kidnapped and going to Avolire and then almost being fed to demon cats—that was all real?"

"For good and for bad, yes."

I wasn't so sure where the *for good* part came in from that adventure, but I wasn't going to argue that point right now. My memories were heavy in my mind, like super sluggish. I needed to give them time to settle in.

"Where's Mei-Ling?" I looked to her and arched an eyebrow. "Don't think I still believe that China story. Where is she? Tennessee said you were hiding her from Sweyn because you knew she was gonna come for us."

"Good, your memory is returning quickly. That'll help." Tegan flicked her wrist. "We had to say she was in China so you wouldn't demand seeing her."

I frowned and glanced up at the house, then did a double take.

My best friend stood there with wide, dark eyes and pale-pink hair. "FRANKIE!"

My eyes stung. "MEI-LING!"

Then we were charging for each other. I hadn't seen her since—well, I wasn't quite sure when Tegan took her place. But I'd thought my best friend had been turned into a vampire for too long, and I hadn't seen her since I found out she hadn't. Sure, I saw her on Face-Time, but that wasn't the same at all. We tackled each other in a hug, holding on tight enough to hurt. But the warmth in her skin was a relief. Everyone in Avolire had felt so damn cold. Not like Twilight where their bodies were cold though. It was just a different feeling that I couldn't quite put my finger on.

After a moment we both stepped back and wiped tears out of our eyes.

I held my finger up with our matching crystal ring on it. "Tegan gave me a heart attack back there. I watched you get turned into a vampire."

She held her ring up and pressed it to mine. It was very *Captain Planet* of us, but we'd been doing it since we were kids. "I hope I looked hot as a bloodsucker."

"Yeah, that's the biggest concern."

I gasped and looked over her shoulder at the sound of a familiar voice I hadn't heard in forever. "TAI!"

Mei-Ling's older brother, who was basically *my* older brother, strolled up to us with a wide smile on his handsome face. "*Frankie.*" My name was a relieved sigh.

I threw my arms open and hugged him. He was warm and familiar and smelled like snickerdoodle cookies. "You smell like my cookies."

He laughed and pulled back. "We made some for you."

I spun around to face Tegan. "Did you know tonight was gonna happen?"

"Yes and no." She shrugged. "Don't stress yourself out with these questions. Get to know me and my brother for a bit first."

I narrowed my eyes. "What's your brother's name?"

"Bentley—"

"The orange lightning dude? From when I was paralyzed?"

"That's him. Our psychic Hierophant."

"Yeah, I'm gonna not ask questions right now." I laughed and pressed my hands to my temples. "What are you two doing in Eden? I thought this was witch home country?"

"It is." Tegan strolled over so we were standing in a circle. "But I have my tricks and Mei-Ling is a target for Sweyn, so we have to keep her safe—and removing her memories from Avolire would break her mind. I refused to do that. So, she's been hanging with us, being a stowaway until we figure shit out."

"And Tai is a peace offering." Tai laughed. "It's a long story."

"Where are your parents? Where's Granny Ling?"

"China," they said at the same time.

"Tegan says she's got that shit covered, and our human brains shouldn't try to understand that." Tai arched an eyebrow at her. "Tegan says they should be safe."

Tegan shrugged.

I opened my mouth to ask more about that when I heard a dog howl that I recognized in an instant. When I turned toward the sound, I found all three of my boys racing toward me from an open portal. I dropped to my knees and cuddled them as they licked my face and hands.

"I wanted you to have your emotional support floofs right away." Tegan nodded. "But they'll like living here."

I looked around. "So is this my aunt and uncle's new house here? It's huge—"

"This is Coven Headquarters."

"Oh." I frowned and looked around. "Where will I live? Those brick buildings apartments or something?"

"That's the campus of Edenburg. You'll live here. The Coven lives together here in this house." Tegan gestured toward the school. "Your aunt and uncle will be close by though, just beyond the school in the town."

I ran my hands over Houdini's fur. "And my dogs?"

"Here with you if that's where you want them."

Mei-Ling reached down and fluffed Bubba's ears. "There are other dogs here. And Savannah's cats. The boys will love it."

"And once Chutney returns, you may not see your dogs again." Tai shoved his hands in his pockets and rocked back on his heels. "As all the pets seem to migrate to her room or by her side all the time."

I chuckled. "She's the one who talks to animals?"

They all nodded.

"She seems fun." I grinned and climbed back to my feet. "So where have you two been staying?"

"In your new room." Mei-Ling blushed. "I've started decorating for you so you'd feel more comfy."

"Well, let's go inside then." I gestured to the big house and knots formed in my stomach. "Because if I stop moving for too long, my mind might start processing everything Tegan made me forget these last two weeks."

Tegan cackled. "C'mon."

We walked up to the house together with my boys trotting happily at my feet. I was more than a little bit nervous about this. My memories were still settling in, but I already felt different than I had when the day started. For starters, I knew I was a Coven-member. It made me want to text Esther about just how much she'd nailed her guess. I'd learned a lot these last two weeks about arcana culture and society, and yet what I experienced in Avolire made me much more aware than any of my friends had been.

*Oh God. Asmodeus. Azazel.*

"Frankie? You okay?" Tegan appeared in front of me.

"Asmodeus." My stomach rolled. "Azazel. They were standing in line in front of me in Hidden Kingdom—"

"Yes, and Tenn saw them too. But they were up to their own shenanigans and left. More importantly, they're not here now." She put her hand on my shoulder. "Tenn can talk to me telepathically. We were literally talking all day, every day. He told me everything. So, while it may have seemed like you were there on your own, I promise you weren't. Not at all. I was there even when you couldn't see me. Okay?"

The pressure in my chest lightened. "Okay. Right. I think the nightmares from Avolire are going to fuck me up hard."

Her face fell. "We have ways to help you with that too. Just breathe. The Coven is one big family. Your problems are our problems. We will be right here with you every step of the way."

"Thanks, Tegan."

"You're welcome." Tegan pushed the door open and stepped inside. "Welcome home, Frankie."

I glanced over my shoulder to Mei-Ling and Tai, but they smiled and gave me two thumbs-up. Then I looked forward and took a step inside—something black landed on my shoulder. I froze. A second later, something landed on my other shoulder that was also black. My eyes widened.

And then two small cat faces leaned down to look at me. *Meow*.

"Meet Freya and Luna." Tegan moved to stand in front of me. "Savannah's cats. They sit on the stairs and stare at the door until she returns. They've developed a new way of greeting people."

"Oh. Hi, kitty . . . kitties." I reached up and tickled under their chins, and they purred in my ears.

"Come on, girls. Come here." Tegan held her arms out and both cats leapt into her chest. Something about Tegan holding two black cats just felt so right. "Brace yourself, boys. Olli is about to let the house know you're here. And he likes to lick. In three . . . two . . . one . . ."

A loud howl ripped through the silent house. My boys froze in place, their ears perked up. A white-tipped tail similar to my boys' tails swished back and forth in the kitchen doorway. I heard the sound of nails on hardwood floor and then a brown and white basset hound appeared around the edge of the dining room table. *That must be Olli.* He stopped howling and stared at my boys, his tail swishing back and forth at a rapid speed. My boys were doing the same. They were beagles, but they definitely were more basset hound than plain beagle because they weren't much taller than Olli and their ears only a little shorter.

This house was about to be bad for everyone's knees.

And then Olli leapt forward into a pounce. All three of my boys took off running for him. But Olli jumped up and spun around, then sprinted in the opposite direction. The chase was on. We'd just walked in the house and already the four of them were playing chase around the furniture. I smiled and started forward when a giant dog bigger than a Great Dane flew around the corner up ahead. He stopped short but the fluffy fur between his toes made him slide.

Flames danced along the top of his fur.

"OH MY GOD! THAT DOG—"

"Is made of fire." Tai chuckled as he walked around me to lean against the wall. "It's been a really weird couple of weeks for us here, adjusting to animals being made of fire and lava."

"His name is Squishy. He's Bentley's fire doggo. Apparently he's from the Seelie realm? I don't know, dude. It's intense as fuck." Mei-Ling pointed to the basset hound leading the game of chase right under Squishy's belly and then back around to the dining room. "That basset is Olli. He's Saffie's dog . . . *from 1692*. She went back in time and brought him here. Time travel, dude."

I nodded. "So everything is totally normal. Got it."

Tai shuddered. "Wait until you meet Spot."

A large black mastiff rushed down the stairs, then slid to a stop in front of me. He sniffed me all over, looked me in the eye, and cocked his head to the side and sat down. The concentration in his stare was unnerving.

"What did I do?" I asked him softly.

Tegan crouched down and pet him with the one hand not holding cats. "I know, Albert. You smell him on her. We're gonna get him home to you as soon as possible, okay, bud?"

Little Olli rushed over and licked Albert's face, activating him in the chase game.

I blinked at the sudden change of emotion in Albert. "What was that? What just happened?"

Tegan cringed, and I felt it in the air around her. *"Braison's dog,"* she whispered.

*OHHH.* My heart hurt. I rubbed my chest. Lord Braison. That memory hadn't yet returned until she said his name. Now I couldn't unsee his face when he spoke about his family. And he had a dog. That made me want to cry. I knew how much my own dogs were upset with my absence all those months of my coma, and how when I was around, they hovered at my side. This poor dog had to be so sad.

"He's just a puppy," Tegan said softly. "But Olli is his new best friend, which is why Olli is here instead of with Saffie. Olli helps Albert be a happy boy. Olli's kind of the ringleader."

"That's so adorable. Look at them." I gestured to my dogs as they flew by me hot on Squishy's flame tail. "That fire won't hurt the non-fire doggos, right?"

"Nope." Tegan chuckled. She turned to the stairs and lifted the cats onto the rail. "Savannah will be back soon. I'd hate for you to miss the chance to pounce on her face."

Now that I didn't have cats in my face or dogs stealing my attention, I was able to look around at the place. My jaw dropped. It looked like a regular house. *Coven Headquarters* sounded like it'd be a fancy, high-tech, CIA-level office. But this was a *home*. The warm brown hardwood floors reminded me of my floors back home. The foyer was small and mostly open to the rest of the house. There were stairs on my right, and the wall on the side of the stairs had two doors in it. To my left was a massive living room with the largest fireplace made of stone that I'd ever seen. It looked more like an old-time hearth. It had a ledge in front of it with fuzzy blankets folded and a few pillows in the corner, like perhaps people sat there. The window on the front wall to my left was floor-to-ceiling, but there were two big cozy chairs in front of it. There was actually a lot of furniture. A few big recliners and a couple sofas. A giant cream-colored fuzzy rug sat in front of the fireplace.

The room was an open floor plan, so I had a perfect view of a wooden dinner table to rival Da Vinci's *Last Supper*. Beyond the table was a doorway into a kitchen and then on the right it opened up into another room, though I couldn't tell what was in there from where I stood. The energy in the house was cozy and warm and super comfortable. It *felt* like home, which was really quite bizarre. But the weirdest part was how quiet and empty it was.

I cleared my throat. "So, where'd everyone go?"

Tegan made a funny face. "Well . . . see . . . I didn't want you to feel bombarded the moment you walked in, so . . ." She snapped her fingers and rainbow list flashed all around.

I gasped.

The living room was full of people that had not just been there.

"Whoa . . ." I took a step back. "Holy shit. They were there this whole time?"

"Yup."

I sighed. "Magic is so cool."

Everyone laughed.

Tenn's sister nodded. "See? I told you she'd handle it well. She's a Proctor."

Tegan wrapped her arm around my shoulder and led me over to the stone bench in front of the fireplace where a big blond dude with a tense face sat with his elbows on his knees. "This here is my dad, Hunter Bishop. He's the Temperance Card, and his magic is emotional manipulation. Which means, you're gonna sit right here next to him so he can keep you chill as fuck while you are introduced to the chaos that is this Coven family. Cool?"

"Cool." I held my hand out. "Hi, I'm Frankie."

He smiled and it made his golden eyes sparkle. Then he shook his head and held out his left hand, revealing his Mark on his arm as we shook hands. "Coven shakes with our left hand to show our Marks. You'll get used to it. I'm Hunter. Have a sit and chill with me, kiddo." He patted the stone beside him.

I smiled and sat down. Instantly a golden glow wrapped around me and every ounce of tension in my body just vanished. I exhaled. "Shittttt, that's good stuff."

Hunter hung his head and chuckled. "Did we just become best friends, Frankie?"

"Hell yeah." I grinned. It was wild to me that Tegan's energy was so electric and intense when her father's was the calmest feeling I'd ever experienced. I patted the stone bench beside me. "Mei-Ling? Tai?"

They hurried over to sit beside me.

"Imma run through some introductions fast, but don't worry, no one expects the info to stick the first time." Tegan cleared her throat and backed up to the first chair closest to the foyer where the gorgeous blonde girl sat in the lap of a blond boy. "This here is—"

"Hey! You're the one who looks like Royce!" I blurted, then slammed my hand over my mouth. "Sorry, I think I'm a little comfortable."

Hunter grinned.

Royce's blond doppelganger grinned. "Well, Royce *is* my cousin, so that tracks. But I'm older, so technically he looks like me."

Tegan rolled her eyes. "This is Deacon English. He's our Devil, which doesn't suit him at all."

I waved. "English. Right. The filthy rich founding family that started the magic moving company."

"Filthy rich, eh?"

I blushed. "My aunt and uncle said no family was richer than yours."

The blonde in his lap held her left hand out. "I better start doing more arm workouts then."

Everyone cackled.

"Yeah, that's us. Stupid filthy rich and we can't help it. Let me know if you want a shopping spree, and I'll have the plane come get us." He grinned and scratched his jaw which is when I noticed the black lines covering his right hand. On the back of his palm was a lavender crystal. "Though I better make sure Claudia puts those anti-demon spells on ours like we did Walter's."

"Nope. She don't wanna know about that yet, D." The blonde in his lap rolled her golden eyes and smacked Deacon's leg playfully. She looked to me and waved with a tatted hand that matched D's. In her glorious southern accent, she said, "I'm Emersyn Bishop. Empress. Crazy one's twin."

I nodded. "Who I'm guessing has tortured demons to death and was scolded for it?"

She shrugged. "I plead the Fifth."

Tegan rolled her green eyes. "Right, moving on. Big guy here in the flannel is Timothy, Tenn and Bettina's uncle. Former Coven Leader. Now he's much happier as our Hermit Card."

Tim shook his head, but he looked to me with warm, kind brown eyes and salt-and-pepper hair. He scratched his five-o-clock shadow. "Trouble, your introductions need tweaking."

"Whatever. I'm giving the highlights." She walked away from him and over to the first couch where a blonde woman sat watching us silently. "This is Constance. Also a former Coven Leader who is now our Justice Card and preggo. So, we don't let her do much."

"Hi, Frankie. Welcome home." Constance smiled, her cheeks a rosy pink. "My soulmate, Daniel, is at the school prepping for all the Tampa kids to arrive. He's a professor there who used to be the Head-master. Now Kenneth Proctor is the Headmaster."

"Right. One of my relatives that I still need to figure out how we're related." I pressed my hand to my stomach. "Congrats on the baby."

"Thank you." She beamed. "You'll see two young blonde girls return with my husband. Those are my adopted daughters, Kenny and Kiki."

"They're sweethearts. Their aunt Nadia was our Sun Card for a little while, but she passed, so her nieces are our family now." Tegan gestured to the next person on the couch. "I think you met Thiago?"

I waved. "Yes! Hi!"

"Hello again!"

"And *this* is my best friend, Bettina. She's Judgement Card." Tegan leaned against the chair where the girl with the split hair dye sat next to a very handsome guy whose hair looked bronze. "Her real name is Hope Proctor. She's Tenn's sister. We all call her Bettina. It's a whole sad story that's a real buzzkill so I won't tell you yet."

Tim cackled.

"Bloody hell, Tegan. Don't be a wanker."

I gasped. "You're British. Wait, you must be the Lancaster!"

The guy with bronze hair and eyes the color of the Caribbean Ocean gave me a small smile. "Jackson Lancaster, yes. I'm The World Card. And Bettina's soulmate."

I whistled. "Lots of soulmates here, eh?"

"How many do we have now?" Tegan sat on the edge of the coffee table and started counting with her fingers. "Me and Tenn. Em and D. Bettina and Lancaster. Mom and Dad. Kessler and Mona. Connie and Daniel. Kenneth and Landreia. Easton and Lily. Saffie and Riah. Malachi and Chloe. Thorne and Myrtle. That's eleven so far."

"Wow." I shook my head. "Here I thought Madge and Jo being soulmates was impressive."

Constance chuckled. "It *is* impressive for civilians to be soulmates. The Coven tends to be full of them."

"Oh cool," I said as one of the doors under the stairs opened and two people walked out. "Oops, Tegan, two new intros are needed."

She craned her neck back. "Hey weirdo and Waldo, come here."

The girl had indigo-colored hair that was rocking that shag style. She had the coolest yellow-green eyes, and her entire body was covered in tattoos. I wanted to be her friend instantly. And by the way her eyes lit up when she saw me, I had a good feeling about that. "Pinky! Hi! I love the hair. I'm weirdo, but everyone calls me Lennox."

Lennox was one of those gorgeous people where it was impossible to pinpoint her race or heritage because she was definitely a mix of more than one. Her skin was the most incredible light-brown shade that made her tatts pop. The guy who walked in right behind her looked like he should be her boyfriend, but I wasn't sure if they were together or not. He had short dark hair that was shaved on the sides. He was tall and physically fit with toned muscle. His skin was a few shades darker than Lennox's but also looked incredible with all those tattoos.

"I guess that makes me Waldo?" He narrowed his hazel eyes. Then he shrugged and waved to me. "I'm Warner. Lennox and I are high-quality Coven pets."

She nodded. "But we're always happy to collect more, so thanks for providing Mei-Ling and Tai for us."

I laughed. "Happy to be of service."

The front door opened, and the rest of The Coven walked through wearing sad smiles and tense auras.

Tegan held her hand up and they froze. "We're gonna do this runway style. Ready, Frankie?"

"Pop quiz me tomorrow just for fun." I waved them on. "Bring it."

Tegan curled her fingers. Two people stepped forward together. "The blond pretty boy is Easton. And that's his soulmate, Lily. They're the Lovers and Sun. Next."

The next person up was Royce. He did a fancy bow to me and grinned and hurried over to sit next to Thiago. "We've met."

"Yes, we have." I waved, then spotted the girl who spoke to animals. "Chutney. The animal defender."

"That's me." She giggled and dragged the strawberry blonde with her who just waved. "This is my cousin Willow. The Magician."

The black cats hissed and meowed, then lunged off the stairs. I couldn't see her face, but I recognized her by her tattoos and blue hair. *"Little ma'ams, this ain't how we doin' this."*

I chuckled. "That's Savannah, right?"

"Yep. Give her a minute. Her cats have been stressed. And this big guy is Kessler Bishop, *my* uncle who just so happens to be my soulmate's adoptive father. But I assure you I am not related to my soulmate biologically." Tegan pursed her lips. "*His* soulmate is Mona, whom you met as Agnes."

Kessler waved. "Mona and Katherine said to tell you they're helping pack up the infirmary there, then they'll come with them."

Tegan nodded. "Fine by me."

"So is this everyone then?" I gestured around the room as the ones who just arrived settled into seats."

"Nah, we've got a couple stragglers not here at the moment." Tegan shrugged. "Both of the Coven variety and pet variety."

The front door flew open and slammed into the wall so hard it fell off the hinges. Tennessee cursed and tried to catch it but it just left him holding a door in both hands. Then he sighed in defeat and sat the door on the ground. "Babe?"

Tegan just chuckled. "I'll fix it."

Tenn nodded and walked into the room. "Hey—"

Easton threw his hands up and shouted. "BOSS!"

"ARCHIE!" Royce cackled.

And then they tackled him all at once in a group hug, which I was positive he both loved and hated.

Then Tegan flicked her wrist, and they all flew away. "*Mine.* Damn." She held her hand out to him.

He crossed the room to her to take her hand with a goofy grin on his face. "*Mine.*" He bent over and kissed her.

"Where's Cooper to yell *gross*?" Deacon chuckled.

Tenn broke away from Tegan with a scowl. "What do you mean *where's Cooper*?"

"Oh, Bentley needed to handle something, so he brought Coop. You know, Bentley kind of shit."

Royce pointed at her. "Which you're pretending you don't know anything about."

Tegan grinned. "Correct."

"I don't wanna know yet. Grace period." Tenn laughed and ran his hand through his hair. "Okay, let's talk about what the fuck just happened. We have everyone else? Where's Henley?"

Royce frowned. "Downstairs, boss?"

Tenn nodded. "Tell her to come up."

Royce flinched. "I've been trying, yet she's still in that coma."

"No, no, I saw her. She's up."

Royce paled and gripped the armrest of the couch. "Boss, I was just been down there with her. She's very much still out."

Tenn shook his head. "She was in The Coven meeting Tegan called when she told us her crazy plan to swap places with Mei-Ling—"

"WHAT?" Royce and Deacon shrieked.

Tenn pointed to the couch right where Thiago sat. "She was sitting right there on the couch right between you and Em."

"No, Tenn, she wasn't," Em said softly.

Tenn scratched his head. "She even asked Tegan a question and Tegan answered it. Babe, tell them."

Tegan grimaced. "You're all right."

"WHAT?" everyone yelled in perfect unison.

Tegan sighed. "She was at that meeting, just not in physical form—"

"*Ma'am.* There weren't no spirits in this room for that meeting." Royce whimpered.

"Whoa, hold on, Savannah." Deacon leaned forward and held his hands up. "Hold on, Tegan, your desires here are freaking me out."

Jackson cursed. "But they're not lying."

Tenn looked to Tegan. "What is happening here, babe?"

"While Mom can do things with astral projection others can't, the Chariot is not the only Card who can do it." Tegan held her hands up to stop people from talking. "The Moon, The Star, and Death can astral project if they know how and are willing. Cooper was afraid to until Savannah's spell. He's only done it a few times— and one of those times he witnessed Savannah's first accidental attempt. But Henley has always known how and is no stranger to it."

"*What are you saying, Tegan?*" Royce whined.

"Henley attended that meeting through astral projection." Tegan's face fell. "I saw her, though I was not aware that Tenn saw her as well or I would have said something to him to avoid this conversation. To avoid the pain."

Royce groaned and buried his face in his hands. "This is too much."

Tenn hung his head and put his hands on his hips. "Royce, I'm so sorry. I genuinely thought she was back—"

"Not your fault, boss. Not your fault." Royce pinched the bridge of his nose. "I just need her to wake up before I break."

Thiago pulled his boyfriend into his lap. "We're all working on it, and we're here for you. Both of you."

"I take it there's been no change?" Tenn asked softly. When everyone shook their heads, he just cringed. "And what about Devon? How's she doing?"

That calm golden energy around me turned ice-cold for a split second before Hunter caught himself. "Her body has healed perfectly. Riah says we have to be patient. For both of them. He says their ailments were too severe to recover fast. But I'm with Royce, I'm about to break here."

Tegan jumped up and over to the stone ledge where she sat next to her father and hugged him. "I'm working on it. For both of them, I promise."

Tenn cursed violently. Dude had a real skill for his swear word combos. He sat on the coffee table where Tegan had just been. "And what about our Seelie friends? And the angels?"

"They're all together. They took Henry and Millie Anne with them." Tegan closed her eyes. She looked exhausted. "They're trying to find out how the fuck the Unseelies got back in and the fact that none of them know is more unsettling than anything else right now."

Everyone nodded.

Tenn stood and stretched his arms out. "Fantastic. Okay, well, let's get out back and do Frankie's initiation. We need her at full power. Now."

My eyes widened. "Excuse me, what? My *what*?"

# CHAPTER THIRTY-FIVE

## FRANKIE

When I first learned about The Coven, I hadn't understood the importance or the honor of being Marked for it. Granted, I was fighting for my life in Avolire surrounded by vampires who wanted to consume every ounce of blood in my body—*after they bred me*. I shuddered. That memory was not one I needed back.

But re-entering the world of magic through the lens of an innocent teenager made a huge difference, one I was still processing. My friends in Tampa worshipped The Coven. I'd heard about them nonstop. I knew the honor it was to be one of them because of the love the others had for them. Seeing their emotional relief when Archie turned out to be Tennessee in disguise had blown my mind. None of them had been angry with him for the deception. They instead saw it as a sign of admiration and respect that he'd gone to such great lengths to protect them. When the entire Coven walked through Tegan's portal having clearly watched what happened, the relief in the park was overwhelming.

I just wished I felt it more.

I wished this felt like the blessing it apparently was. Sure, I was honored. I had no idea what I'd done to deserve it, but I was flattered. And after the demon attacks and then that ambush from vampires *and* Unseelie tonight, I was glad to be Marked for The Coven. But not for the honor, not for the prestige, not even for the power.

It was for the fight.

For as long as I could remember, I had this rage boiling inside of me with nothing to do with it. Esther thought it was from my magic being trapped. Archie had suggested it was my parents' death that fueled my fire. And maybe it was both of those things. Or maybe it was for something *more*. I didn't know. I was just relieved to finally be in the place to do something good. To fight. Esther had called it: I was destined to be in this war against Lilith. To be on the front lines. That should have scared me. Should have kept me awake at night. Yet I was fired up and ready to go.

I felt like one of those wind-up toys that'd been wound to the max and was just waiting for someone to sit me down so I could fly.

As I looked at my own reflection in the mirror, I stared at the white ceremonial sheath dress I'd been given. Apparently all rituals done by The Coven that were important like this had to be done in these sleeveless dresses. Even the guys. No one told me why. Then again, it didn't really matter. The one I wore had belonged to Larissa Willard, the former Tower Card who died minutes before my Mark arrived. Chutney and Willow, Larissa's cousins, had given this to me. They said Larissa would be honored, and me being the same size as their cousin was fate. That honor was one that touched my heart. I couldn't imagine the pain they felt losing their cousin and then having to watch her role be replaced.

I pressed my hands to my chest and felt my heart pounding against my fingers. "I hope I wear your white proud, Larissa. And I hope you found peace."

I took one last deep breath, then turned and opened the bathroom door into my bedroom. Mei-Ling and Tai sat on the couch waiting. It was still strange to me that my room was big enough to have a full-sized couch and a queen-sized bed and still have room to move around.

"How do I look?"

Mei-Ling scoffed. "You know you look good in white."

Tai shook his head. "You look like I'm gonna be worried about you a lot."

I grinned and tackled them in a group hug. Mei-Ling and Tai were the siblings I never had. Having them here meant a lot. After a moment, I stepped back. "I'm sorry you can't watch, but I'll describe it for you after. And I want y'all to know that I'm happy you're both here."

Tai gestured to the door. "Go on. Go get initiated. It sounds terrifying."

"Shut up, Tai. Frankie's tough." Mei-Ling rolled her eyes, but she did walk over and yank the door open. "But they did say dinner was after, so hurry it up. We're hungry."

"All right, okay, I'm going."

I hurried out the door and down the stairs. They'd given me a room on the third floor. I wasn't sure how I felt about that, but Mei-Ling insisted it was the more fun floor as it was full of the more rebellious Coven-members and none of the adults. Apparently Tegan and Tenn had the penthouse because it was designated for Coven Leaders. I tried to imagine my aunt and uncle being cool with me sharing a room with a boy, but Hunter was the chillest person I'd ever been near. Also, I didn't have a soulmate, so it definitely wasn't the same.

When I got to the bottom of the stairs, I found Tegan waiting for me. "Ready?"

I nodded. "At least I think so."

"Yeah, you're gonna be fine with this. Don't worry." She glanced over my shoulder and smiled. "I'm gonna go out back and get everyone in position so we can do this fast. Em's fried chicken will be done any minute, and no one wants to linger. Say hello, then come on out."

"Okay—wait. Say hello? To who?"

"Heya, Franks."

I gasped and spun around. My aunt and uncle were sitting in the chairs by the front window. I grinned and rushed over. They jumped up and hugged me a little tighter than they normally did. I hadn't seen them since I got to the park for the ritual. That attack had separated us and then Tegan whisked me away.

Aunt Kimmy had tears in her eyes but a smile on her face as she tucked my hair behind my ears. "My little niece . . . in The Coven. I'm so proud of you."

Uncle Kyle ruffled my hair that she'd just fixed. "A perfect fit for you. Can't wait to hear about your potion bombs—"

"*Honey.*" Aunt Kimmy hissed and swatted at him, but he just grinned. She rolled her eyes. "Are you nervous? How are you feeling?"

"Did you know where I went before? When I woke in February. Do you remember all that?"

Uncle Kyle's face fell. He nodded. "We did, yes. We do remember."

"Tegan told us what happened. She *almost* caught you before you were in that van, but she was breaths away from Witch's Shock after that run-in with Lilith's magic. She felt horrible but promised to get you back." Aunt Kimmy grimaced. "When she returned to the hospital with you, she explained the situation, though I'm sure we don't know a fraction of the horror you went through. But she told us we had to play the part."

My breath left me in a rush. "So you knew this whole time? That's why we moved so fast. You knew."

They nodded.

"I'm sorry we had to lie to you—"

"No, don't be." I shook my head. "I'm glad I got to forget about Avolire for a couple weeks. I'm glad I got to learn about being a witch the way I did, and I made new friends. So, it's good. It was the right call by Tegan."

"She offered to take our memories too," Uncle Kyle said softly, "so we wouldn't be lying to you, but we wanted *someone* to know the truth."

I hugged them again, then wiped my face of runaway tears I didn't have time to shed. "Did you get set up in a house here in Eden?"

Uncle Kyle grinned. "We're staying in the hotel. Our room has a huge balcony, and they have a gym and room service—"

"He hates it, clearly." Aunt Kimmy rolled her eyes again but in that loving way she always did with him. "Don't worry about us. We're safe. Just know we're close by if you need us for anything. And we're so incredibly proud of you."

"Now get out there because that fried chicken smells so damn good." He eyed the kitchen. "Maybe I should check and see if it's done. Taste test."

I laughed. "Okay. Stay for dinner?"

They nodded.

I started for the back door, then stopped. "Oh, Mei-Ling and Tai are upstairs. Call them down if you want. Be right back!"

When I went out the back door, I found The Coven standing in a circle, waiting for me in the massive backyard. It was dark out, but it looked like this house sat along the edge of a forest. I wanted to stop and look around, but they were all watching me, standing there barefoot in their sleeveless sheath dresses waiting patiently. The guys all looked lethal in their white sheaths. It was impressive. As I walked up the pathway toward the opening in the circle, I went around the circle trying to remember everyone's name.

Tegan materialized in front of me, her dark-purple hair blowing in the breeze. "All right. Go stand in the center of the pentagram. All you gotta do is open your magic up, and we'll do the rest."

I narrowed my eyes on her. "That's it? No other instructions?"

"Ma'am, that's exactly what I said!" Savannah threw her hands up. "What a thing to say to someone with anxiety!"

"Right, so . . ." Deacon cleared his throat and rubbed his hands together. "It has become my role to warn all new Coven-members that this shit will hurt. It'll only last for a second or two, but it's intense. These other weirdos fail to remember this."

Thiago frowned at me. "Frankie has seen some shit, from what I've heard. I do not think she needs this warning," he said softly in that gorgeous accent of his.

Jackson turned to me and smiled. "Also, your senses are going to go bloody wild after. The weirdos also fail to warn new Coven-members that while you've been Marked, you do not yet have full power. You're about to be plugged into an electrical socket and it's going to be different on the other side."

I nodded. "I feel like this is the origin story of every Marvel movie. Both for the superhero and the villain."

Bettina threw her head back and cackled. "She ain't wrong."

"I mean, if that's what happens, then Deacon should revise his warnings." I shrugged. "You're about to go from Steve Rogers to Captain America. Much better verbiage."

Tennessee shook his head. "See, guys? I told you she was gonna fit in with us."

"It's the trauma," Hunter said with a laugh, which made everyone else cackle.

Tegan waved for me to follow her, so I smiled and stepped inside the circle with her. Black lines shot across the field in the shape of a pentacle and a circle around it. *Oh. Okay.* I hurried over to the center like Tegan had instructed. Once there, everyone else began to move into place. Tegan reappeared at the top point. Emersyn was on my left. Behind me, Tennessee stood at the bottom point to my left and his sister Bettina took the right. My cousins. I needed to figure out *how* we were related.

"Ah shit, Bentley isn't here." Tegan pursed her lips as she gripped her crystal necklace. Light flashed so fast that if I hadn't been watching I would've missed it. The crystal turned into a leather-bound book. "Dad. Yeah, Dad, can you take the open point?"

Hunter walked over to take the point of the pentacle directly to my right.

"*Ma'am.*" Savannah shuddered from her spot in the circle behind Tegan. "Don't think we missed that you picked Mr. Chill Pill for the point. Act all nonchalant you want, but we call bullshit."

Thiago grinned. "It's a little nerve-wracking to be a spectator the first time after your initiation, isn't it?"

Savannah closed her eyes. "I don't think we should talk about what I saw."

"Wait. What you *saw?*" I glanced around the circle to everyone. "What exactly is about to happen here?"

Everyone snickered.

I turned to face Tennessee. "Archie?"

He grimaced and shrugged one shoulder. It was weird to see Archie's mannerisms in a six-foot-five muscular dude. "Look, real talk? When we initiate a Card, it unlocks their full magic and the gift that comes with it. And said gift usually puts on a little show for everyone during initiation. We can't predict what that's gonna look like for everyone. Some Cards' gifts are a little more unsettling than others."

Everyone looked to Savannah.

"Oh, were *you* unsettled by what I saw?" She shook her head. "Give me that face one more time and I swear I'll tell each and every one of you what I saw."

"Dammit, Savannah. You can't say that like that." Deacon shook his head. "Now I *really* want to know."

"Wait, wait." I waved my hands to get their attention. "No one has said what gift the Tower has. What can I do?"

"The Tower is the potion master." Tenn smirked. "Which is why you did so well with the Cups."

"So I'm not a Cup?"

He frowned. "There's a good chance of it, yeah."

"Right. Okay. So, potions. Well, that shouldn't be too bad." I nodded and turned to our High Priestess. "Ready, Tegan."

"What did your initiation look like, babe?" She leaned around me to look at her soulmate. "I mean, *I* almost drowned everyone on Crone Island—"

"Yes, let's relive that. Thanks," Emersyn grumbled.

But Tegan continued, "Tenn's got water, wind, and earth. I'm just curious what that looked like from a five-year-old."

"Actually, that's a good question, bro. I wanna know."

"No, Bettina, you don't wanna know." Willow wrapped her arms around herself. "I still have nightmares from it."

"*Really?*" Deacon's purple eyes sparkled. "That's cool."

"How are we related?" Royce rolled his eyes. "It was not cool. We were kids. It was horrible."

"I don't remember most of it." Easton pursed his lips. "It was just really wet."

"Of course that's what you remember." Lily rolled her eyes, and it reminded me of my aunt and uncle.

"You see what you do, babe?" Tenn gestured around the group. "Chaos. You are a chaos demon."

Bettina giggled. "But this only makes me want to know *more*, so someone start talking."

"Cooper actually wouldn't let us talk about it when we were kids." Chutney said softly. "But it took me *days* to calm all the sharks down."

"*Sharks?*" Bettina squealed.

"We're on land, Moonshine." Jackson reached out and squeezed her shoulder with his hand that had a red rose tattoo on it. "No sharks can get you here."

"Yeah, that's what we thought." Timothy snickered.

"I think we handled it pretty well, given that most of the Coven were younger than him."

"Imagine if you had listened to Constance when Constance said *maybe the kids should sit this one out.*" Constance arched one blonde eyebrow. "After all, Constance is the one who said we needed to wait a couple years before we unlocked all of that."

Emersyn's eyes widened. "You didn't get initiated right away?"

"No, we were all terrified of what that would look like." Timothy was still chuckling. "We were right to be, as it turned out."

Hunter grinned. "I had to leave Tegan at Bettina's parents' house so I could come down for it. That's how worried we were."

Tegan groaned. "But what *happened*? Uncle Kessler? Babe?"

Tenn pursed his lips. "Easton's description was pretty apt. Though I missed a lot of it."

"Yeah, we found you five miles down the road an hour later." Timothy was turning pink from how much he laughed. "What were you doing that whole time?"

"I was chasing it?"

"Chasing *what*?" Tegan was growing impatient. "What happened?"

Kessler sighed and shook his head. "He started a hurricane."

Tegan gasped. "*No.*"

Tenn shrugged. "Twister *was* my favorite movie."

"Wait, how did that happen?"

"Well, Frankie, we thought given his gifts, that the safest option for timing would be during hurricane season." Kessler grimaced. "More specifically, during a hurricane watch."

Timothy snort-laughed and covered his mouth.

"We *had* waited for the town to be evacuated and boarded up for the storm." Hunter was trying not to laugh. "We thought they were prepared."

"I'll never forget the moment when in the middle of it Devon said, *uh oh, we messed up.*" Constance joined Timothy in giggling.

"You did his initiation during a hurricane?" I looked back to Tenn. "Were you scared?"

"I was basically the cow in that scene in *Twister*." He shrugged again. "I had a lot of fun."

I glanced over to his sister to find her laughing so hard no noise came out. She bent over and put her hands on her knees and shook her head. That did it. We all just burst into laughter. There was just something about the humble admittance of failure from the adults combined with the visual of young Tenn just flying through the air in a real-life hurricane that was just hilarious.

Tegan cursed and wiped tears from her eyes. "Right. I think we all needed that."

"Hey, Tegan, remember that trick you did by the river when you did the hologram of what happened to us?" Bettina pointed to her brother. "I think we need to do that so we can see this little moo cow flying around a hurricane."

Tenn nodded. "Yeah, let's just watch all my traumatic moments in life."

"And y'all are worried about *my* crazy." Savannah shook her head. "Ma'am, that was a whole lot of nope."

Emersyn sighed. "My fried chicken's gonna be done and we haven't even started—"

"Oh shit."

"Dammit, woman."

"Ma'am, you waited this long to rein them in?"

"Did you hear my stomach growl just now?"

"*Your* stomach? Mine and the baby's growled."

Tegan held her hand up in the air to silence everyone. "Okay, okay. My bad. Let's get this done for Frankie. It's been a long ass day."

My pulse fluttered. Butterflies danced in my stomach. I hadn't been nervous before, but after hearing all of that, I realized I had no idea what I was getting into. I raised my hand. "So I just stand here?"

Tegan smiled. "Yep. I'm going to read some shit in the ancient language that unlocks everything. You just chill."

"And brace for impact," Deacon grumbled.

"You're really butthurt about the pain, aren't you?"

"Royce, I think I died a little on that beach. Or did you forget?"

Tenn chuckled. "Oh yeah. I did forget."

Deacon turned wild eyes to him. "Seriously?"

"I just remember being mad you had the audacity to look dead after I'd said horrible things about you to Tegan when I was being jealous." Tenn grinned. "Like, how dare you."

"I also was mad at you for having the audacity to look dead," Emersyn said sheepishly. "Boy, did I get my karma for that one."

Deacon shook his head, then looked to me. "You should get out of here while you can, before you have a soulmate in this Coven and can't leave."

"Noted." I smiled. "Go ahead, Tegan. You better just start or this ship will never leave the dock. I'm ready for whatever happens, pain or not."

"In three . . . two . . . one . . ." Tegan threw her hands up in the air and rainbow mist rose up from the ground around the outside of the circle, then shot up into the air to the tips of the trees far above our heads. That leather book floated in front of her.

"*Lily?*" Tegan grinned. "Goddess, I'm still not over that yet."

Lily's eyes twinkled. She grinned so wide her cheeks dimpled. She raised her left hand up, and I saw her *XIX* Mark, the Sun Card, as perfectly bold as everyone else's. Bright yellow light shot out of her palm. A second later, the sun lifted from behind the tree line where it had been setting and the sky turned shades of pink like my hair.

Easton sniffled, his eyes brimming with tears. She blew him a kiss.

There was a story there I didn't know.

Tegan chanted words in a language I didn't know and waved her hands and rainbow magic flashed. A sea of flowers filled every inch of space between the lines of the pentacle. My eyes widened. They were all my favorite flowers. *Beach* flowers, the ones that grew along the coast and on the sand. They were in shades of pink, white, and lavender. My breath caught in my throat. I'd never told anyone here about them.

Emersyn flicked her wrists and two balls of fire appeared in her palms. She flung her hands and shot her fire to the ground just outside the circle. Flames flickered all around us. She sighed. Thiago frowned and leaned *away* from the flames. Bettina dropped to one knee and pressed her palm flat to the dirt. A cloud of pink mist billowed out from under her fingers and then bright white light flashed. Ice slithered out from her hand, covering every inch of the black lines of the pentagram.

Just then Tegan's shouting grew louder, and sharp pain shot down my spine. *OH SHIT.* I sucked in air, and it made a hissing sound. Every single muscle in my body tightened. My pulse hammered in my veins. *Oh shit. Oh, that burns.* Clouds that hadn't been there slid over our heads and roared. They flashed, then lightning sliced through the sky and slammed right into my chest. Electricity shot through my muscles. I clenched my teeth and groaned. Sharp pressure pierced through my heart and down my spine.

Magic sparkled along the ground like light shining through tree branches. The pentacle drawn on the ground turned bloodred. My heart stopped. A gust of wind swept sand across the field that felt like little shards of glass when they hit my skin. The sand caught in the blood of the pentacle. Seashells sprouted from within like flowers growing in a garden. My eyes widened. It was like my dreams. Those visions. My pulse thundered in my veins. My ears began to ring. My muscles tightened and locked down. Even my throat felt tight like I couldn't get enough oxygen in.

I was afraid to move, afraid to *breathe*. It was happening again.

My body rumbled and shook like I was on a roller coaster. I felt my magic rushing to the surface, but I was helpless to stop it. My arms flew up and my magic shot out of me like a broken dam, like those trees in Lord of the Rings releasing the river. Except it wasn't water, it was neon-blue flames. They flowed in every direction, rolling away from me in waves and heading right for my Coven-mates. They all frowned and watched them get closer, but they didn't move.

It hit Tennessee first, crashing into his chest. His magic flashed bright green and blue everywhere my flames touched. Except for those gold bands on his arms, those glowed so bright I had to look away just as my magic hit Bettina and burst in a cloud of pink smoke. One by one all around me my neon-blue waves crashed into the others and forced *their* magic out. Tegan's whole body glowed as white as the sun.

I glanced around with my heart in my throat. As their magic began to subside, little pink flames flashed over their heads. They swirled around, then morphed into symbols. I gasped. Each and every one of them had different symbols. My fingers twitched with the need to write them down, to draw them in the dirt. They were potion ingredients. I knew that somehow. My magic was telling me what potions each of them needed, but I didn't know what all the symbols were. I didn't even have a pen or a camera.

*Remember these. Remember the symbols.*

*I have to make them these potions.*

Just as I was trying to burn the images to memory, my blue flames rose up off the ground. My Coven-mates cursed and shouted as my magic swept their legs out from under them, tossing them left and right like buoys in the ocean. The moon sank super low in the sky like it wanted to illuminate the chaos I'd created.

Bright white light flashed in the sky and then lowered toward the ground. My blue flames rushed to the ball of light like it was a vacuum until they were gone entirely, then the white ball shot into the sky and vanished.

My body was burning and twitching. My muscles convulsed. I gripped the ground, but my vision was tunneling and turning dark. My chest was too tight. There was too much pressure on it.

"*Breathe, Francelina*," a deep male voice growled.

My knees slammed into the ground. I coughed and choked. The ground rumbled beneath me and the air pulsed.

"*BREATHE, FRANCELINA!*"

I gasped and flipped onto my back, my legs twitching like a fish out of water. Air rushed into my lungs. That was Everest's voice. The one I always heard in my mind, in my dreams. I didn't understand why or if it was even really him talking to me. It could've just been my subconscious mind taking on that voice. Either way, it was only the sound of his voice that made me realize I had been holding my breath. For a few moments I just lay there breathing in and out.

Tennessee leaned into my line of vision with a lopsided smile. "You dead?"

"Uh huh." I coughed, then went back to breathing.

Tegan appeared beside him, looking down at me. "Those pink symbols above our heads, were those potions we need?"

I nodded.

"Do you know what the symbols mean?"

I shook my head.

"Figured. Okay, well, I magically drew them in the Book of Shadows when you're ready for them."

"Thanks." I blinked a few times, then realized I still saw pink flames in my peripheral vision. I gestured around us. "Do you see those too?"

"We all do." Tenn nodded. "I'm gonna help you up, 'kay?"

I tried to lift my hand for him to grab when suddenly my body just sat up on its own. Tenn nodded. Tegan crouched down in front of me. I glanced around to the others and let out a huge sigh of relief when I found them all unharmed. Pink flames still danced along the ground, so I held my hands out and wiggled my fingers and they shot right to me, disappearing from sight.

"I haven't seen the pink since Avolire."

"Yeah, that's me." Tegan shrugged. "I put a spell on you to try and contain your magic as much as possible since we'd dropped you in with civilians."

"It did sneak out a few times." Tenn chuckled. "But I was prepared to handle it."

"Is that what happened to your fence?"

He grinned. "I really can't be trusted with a wand."

"Noted." I laughed and scrubbed my face. "Okay, is that it? Is it over? Am I initiated?"

"You're all done. Ripe and ready to go—"

"Don't, Easton." Lily covered his mouth with her hand.

"Is anyone hurt?"

"I'll let you know tomorrow," Willow groaned and climbed to her feet. "Drowned by neon fire waves is a new one."

"It was the symbols for me." Chutney shuddered.

Tenn stood up and gestured behind me. "All right, everyone. Let's give Frankie a minute to breathe. Go on in and get out of your whites so we can let Emersyn's chicken destroy us properly."

Everyone laughed.

"Welcome to The Coven, cousin." Tenn winked to me, then walked away.

Tegan squeezed my shoulder. "Just take some deep breaths. Let the crazies get in the house first. Adjust to the new sensations for a minute, then we'll go in."

It was weird to suddenly *feel* everything around me. Without looking I could pinpoint where each of them were just by sensing their auras. Jackson's warning made a lot more sense now. It was kind of like being able to see lights through my closed eyes. It was fascinating. I found myself really focusing on them. I wanted to learn what my Coven-mates felt like so I'd always be able to identify them without my eyes. But as all of their auras blinked out as they went inside, my thoughts went to one thing and one thing only.

Everest.

*Breathe, Francelina.* That was what he'd said. His voice was unmistakable. It would likely haunt me the rest of my life. I didn't know if he was somehow telepathically communicating with me or if it was a figment of my imagination—and I didn't know which of those options scared me more. From the moment I laid eyes on him in

Tampa, my heart had run away with me. It had confused the hell out of me to feel so strongly for a perfect stranger.

But he wasn't much of a perfect stranger in reality. Not after those days and nights in Avolire. I reached up and pressed my fingers to my throat, remembering the collar he'd made me wear to play the part of his pet. Or the night he'd bitten me in front of everyone and those black lines showed up on my skin. My eyes had turned as pink as my hair.

"What's happening in that head of yours?"

I jumped at the sound of Tegan's voice. "The wrong things."

Tegan sat down beside me and nodded. "Everest is not the wrong thing."

I groaned. "How'd you know?"

Tegan smiled. "I was there, Frankie. In Avolire. I saw you two."

I shook my head.

Tegan's face turned serious as she stared at the same nothing I had been. "I also saw him that day in the hospital when you woke up in the middle of the night and I saved you. And again when you went for your first walkabout and he talked to you."

I gasped. "I knew you saw him. I knew I wasn't crazy."

Tegan looked to me and the sharpness in her eyes sent a chill down her spine. It was like I could *see* her brain working, trying to figure something out. She licked her lips and looked away from me. "For reasons I have not yet figured out, but I'm working on, you mean something to Everest."

"How lucky for me," I grumbled.

"I think so, actually." Her voice was soft, which I suspected wasn't her normal. "You know all those dreams you've had that were terrifying? Everest pulled you out of them. That night you were lured to the park by Asmodeus? Everest saved us. I was not ready to battle Lilith myself, and we would not have survived that night without him. We wouldn't have gotten out of Avolire without Everest. I know he's behaving in a confusing as fuck way, and we have so many questions for him, but he is on our side. He saved us when we were nearly trapped and almost killed by Sweyn in October. He saved a lot of us by killing demons on Samhain in Salem with us. He even once saved Saffie when she accidentally wound up in Avolire."

"I just don't understand."

"Honestly, I don't either fully. But that man is old. He might even be the same age as Sweyn—and that's one of my first questions I have for him." She smirked. "But I know he was in the last war with Lilith. There are stories in the Book of Shadows about a strange vampire with blue and white eyes saving arcana from demons. He's been lurking in the shadows of our world for centuries, never coming out unless Sweyn sends him out because he hasn't wanted to risk revealing his allegiance . . . and yet . . ."

"And yet what?"

She looked at me. "And yet he's risked everything he's worked for . . . for you . . . *Repeatedly*."

Tears filled my eyes.

"When those vampires attacked you tonight, you saw that black smoke hit them, right?" Tegan narrowed her eyes on me. When I nodded, she nodded. "That was Everest. I don't know where he was, but he was watching *you*."

# CHAPTER THIRTY-SIX

## EVEREST

I BENT over the sink and splashed cold water on my face.

Again.

It wasn't working. I still wanted to bury my face in the toilet bowl and vomit everything inside of me. My hands trembled. My stomach was in knots. My pulse was racing so damn fast I couldn't determine one beat from the next.

I couldn't seem to catch a break. It was Murphy's Law. Everything that could go wrong would go wrong. At least when it came to all things Francelina. Fate was calling my bluff, forcing my hand. But I had to hold on a little longer. It was too soon. I'd waited this long, surely I could wait a little longer to make my exit at the right time.

Sweyn sent me to find her.

She wanted revenge.

But that hadn't meant I had to interact with her. I was damn good at lurking in the darkness of shadows where no one could see me. Sweyn wasn't checking up on me. She trusted me blindly and unconditionally. I should have kept my distance and just watched Francelina until Sweyn made her move. I'd been there for days watching without her knowing. I'd even seen Tennessee there disguised as that little stumbling Archie. It was a brilliant move to have him there. She was safe with him. I could have kept my distance, but then that demon attack happened.

I hadn't been able to resist the urge to see her with my own eyes up close. The look on her face when she'd seen me . . . I wasn't strong enough to ignore it. Not when she left Avolire the way she had. Not when I knew the moment her memories returned she would hate me. So, I succumbed to my weakness, to my desires for her. I let myself have those stolen moments that would make her hate me even more later. By now she was back with The Coven, her memories returned and all the happenings of Avolire fresh in her mind.

Last night in that tower had broken something inside of me. I didn't know if I would be able to keep my emotions in check much longer. I didn't know how long I could play this game. A thousand years down the drain . . . because of one tender stolen night.

I groaned as my stomach rolled.

Movement behind me caught my eye. Not many could sneak up on me, but she was rather gifted at it. I looked up and met her stare through the mirror. There were things I needed to say to her, to tell her . . . to ask her. Yet I feared if I opened my mouth, the bile sitting high in my throat would unleash.

"I warned you," she all but growled.

I exhaled through my nose and nodded.

"I told you to stay away. I told you not to let her see you. I begged you to let me go in your place."

"*No*," was all I managed to get out, but it was barely more than a whisper. *I couldn't ask that of you.*

She tucked her black hair behind her diamond-studded ears, then crossed her arms over her chest and leaned against the bathroom door-frame. When she was furious like this, the red rims in her eyes nearly drowned out the hazel-gold color of her irises. She glared at me through the mirror, looking fierce in her pristine, tailored white pantsuit.

"No? No. Right. Perfect." She shook her head and pursed her red-painted lips. "You're going to get all of us an eternity of torture in *her* realm because you won't let me help you."

I snarled and clenched my teeth.

"Go ahead. Snarl. Might I remind you I'm the only one who is not afraid of you." She stepped closer and put her hands on her hips. "Might I remind you *why* I don't fear you?"

"*Saber*," I growled. "Stop."

"Stop? *Stop?*" She threw her hands up and began pacing the bathroom of the cabin we were in. "When are you going to let me help you? Can't you see what this is doing to you?"

I hung my head and gripped the sink harder as my stomach rolled again.

"You have to stay away from her," she snapped, bringing my eyes back up to hers through the mirror. "Being near her is killing you."

All I could do was stare. She wasn't wrong, and we both knew it.

"You've waited too long to not survive this." She shook her head. "I warned you not to let yourself go too numb, and now look at you."

I rolled my eyes.

"Don't. Don't do that." She pointed to my reflection. "We need you alive."

"Saber . . ."

"*I need you alive, dammit.*" She stomped her foot as her emotions began to unravel. Her cheeks flushed. "We're so close to being free. Don't do that to me."

My heart sank and my chest grew tight. "I'm trying—"

"*Try harder.*" She grabbed my arm and spun me around to face her for real. "I don't want to survive this war without you, do you understand me? Forget Sam, forget Francelina. I'm the one who has been here this whole time. Me. Right here with you every step of the way. I don't care what you feel for them, for *her.*"

I cringed.

"*I love you,*" she whispered just loud enough for me to hear. She shook her head and her hair came loose. "*You made me a promise a long time ago. Don't make me lose you now that we're at the finish line.*"

"*You won't,*" I whispered back and tucked her hair back behind her ear. "I've got this under control."

"Do you? Really? Because I wasn't aware the Unseelie attacking The Coven was part of the plan yet."

I groaned.

"And then you attacked the sentinels? You've lost your mind. You risked *everything* with that stupid move . . . for her." She licked her lips and shook her head again, this time looking away from me. "You're breaking your promises and that scares me. If you love me as much as you say you do, then you'll stop risking us to protect her."

I opened my mouth to argue when my vision turned red. Saber

dove out of the bathroom and out of sight. I spun back to the mirror as my vision pulsed in shades of red. Mother was livid. I took a deep breath and forced myself to stand upright. I had to play the part Mother needed to see. Once I felt in control, I flicked my wrist and sent my black magic into the mirror.

"*Offspring,*" she growled, and it echoed off the bathroom walls. Her face appeared in the mirror, blocking out my reflection. Her red eyes blazed with rage.

"Mother."

"*Where are you? We have things to do—*"

"Like breaking yet another one of our strategies on a whim?" I arched one eyebrow at her and forced my voice to sound calm. "The Unseelie were not part of our plan at *this* stage."

"I want them dead."

I gripped the edge of the sink, leaned in closer, and growled. "And how did that go, Mother?"

She snarled and flicked her white hair over her shoulder. "I want Haven Proctor's head—"

"Everest, what's taking so long?" Saber stepped into the doorway of the bathroom wearing the tiniest red lingerie I'd ever seen. She knew Lilith was speaking to me through the mirror, though she couldn't see her. But Saber knew how to play the game better than even I did. She gripped the doorframe and struck a seductive pose, then batted her eyelashes at me. "Come to bed. Now."

Then she licked the tip of her fang and sashayed into the bedroom where she was just visible enough to watch her lay herself out like a dish I was about to devour.

"*Offspring,*" Mother growled. "We have battle strategies to form this night. You do not have time to play with your toys. Get back to Avolire to your bride so we can proceed."

I glanced over my shoulder and eyed Saber in that bed, then turned my attention back to my mother and snarled. "Unlike you, Mother, I know how to stick to a plan. And tonight, as you can see, I have plans of my own."

# CHAPTER THIRTY-SEVEN

## SAM

EVEREST HAD BEEN AWAY for too long.

I was losing my mind. Over two weeks without Everest as an anchor in this depravity. Sweyn had sent him to hunt down the pink-haired witch and I had not heard from him since. Braison checked on me daily, but we did not get many chances to openly talk as Sweyn had taken to watching our magic-training sessions.

Saber just snarled in everyone's direction, especially mine. Though, I was her lover's betrothed, so I should not have been surprised by her open hostility. Malik barely spoke, and when he did, he was too nervous to even speak of anything that could've been over-heard as us conspiring against Lilith. So far he was only interested in talking about our humanity and how we'd lost it forever. Pierce was either in Sweyn's bed or Azazel's.

None of the female vampires would speak to me. They hated me for my rank and bloodline.

Every male vampire looked at me with lust. If Everest didn't hurry up and return, they were going to take me. None of them feared me. Me being a witch prior to being turned made them loathe me, and it seemed they wanted to punish Braison by taking it out on me because they *were* afraid of him. Braison wouldn't hesitate to attack them, he'd even killed a few who'd provoked him, but he had a whole lifetime of experience with war and being desensitized to killing things.

I was known to flip cockroaches back onto their feet because I hated watching them suffer.

I sighed and scrubbed my face with my hands. Lilith being my grandmother made no sense to me. But if I wanted to survive, then I needed to learn how to be a terrifying menace with my magic the way Braison was so no one would mess with me. At least then they'd have legitimate reasons to hate me . . . and then men wouldn't touch me when I walked by them.

All of this had made me desperate for . . . anything.

Then last night I'd gotten a break. I'd been walking down the hall when I'd heard Astaroth and Mammon approaching. In a panic, I'd jumped inside the closest bedroom only to discover it was Asmodeus's chamber. Luckily he hadn't been there. He'd been off playing with Azazel. But while I'd been waiting for my window to escape, I'd discovered an ancient-looking journal. Inside it were all kinds of spells and rituals for things, but more specifically, I'd found one for summoning an angel.

Apparently summoning a fallen angel was difficult work as the power of Heaven protected the realm from it. However, summoning an angel could be done if a person knew how. As I sat crouched in front of a pentacle drawn on the floor of my bedroom in my own blood, I prayed I'd remembered the instructions properly. I'd drawn it all out to fit the diagram. I'd said the words written on the paper.

The show Everest and I had performed for Lilith had worked. She'd fallen for it hook, line, and sinker. Her faith in us was almost as foolish as what I was doing, but I had to try something. Sweyn had unleashed Unseelies on the witch community in Tampa, and I knew we needed help.

Lilith had given me more magic. She'd made me stronger. It seemed like I should be able to do this. I was a witch too. That magic ran deep in my veins. But when I lifted my hands after reciting the spell, green smoke drifted from my palms down to the black marble floor and swirled around the base of the pedestal.

Just like before, when it touched, bright red demonic runes flashed within the marble. Green smoke billowed from the ground in a circle. A figure emerged within the center. A figure with *black* wings. *NO. No, no, no. Please Goddess and Heaven, forgive me.* It was too late. I'd done it wrong. I'd messed up somewhere. Tears pooled in my eyes. My breath caught in my throat. I froze in panic. My body went ice-cold and numb.

Then my green smoke faded away and I looked up to find a petite, pretty little fallen angel staring down at me. Her wings were black, but the long hair was navy-blue. She had golden topaz eyes and matching little horns of the same color, but they seemed to be made of the crystal itself. In the center of her forehead was a gold metal symbol that seemed to be stuck to her skin or was part of her body. She was beautiful, and it was no doubt part of her sin, to lure victims in with her body. She was the ultimate predator without a doubt, and I had just unleashed her.

"Well, hello little one." She reached out and tipped my chin up, forcing me to look into her topaz eyes. All ten of her fingers wore these like gold metal cages around them and each one was stiletto-sharp. "Did you summon me?"

I swallowed roughly and nodded. "Yes."

"Why?" She put her hands on her hips, highlighting the skin-tight black sleeveless leather bodysuit worthy of a Marvel superhero she wore. "What is your name?"

"I am Sam—"

"Lilith's granddaughter?"

I nodded. "I was trying to summon an angel—"

"Whatever would you do that for?"

*Lie, Sam. Lie well.* "As a gift for Sweyn and her fallen angel boys. Something to play with."

"I am no angel, child." She ran her gold pointed rings over the dark navy-blue swirling tattoos covering her arms. "I am judgement and vengeance."

My whole body trembled in fear. *Just kill me. Kill me now so I don't spend eternity with Lilith. Just take me out.*

She crouched down and met my stare. "And you summoned *me* because you are no better than Azazel. Or did you not learn with Soneillon and Mammon?"

My bedroom door flew open and slammed into the wall so hard it broke off the hinges. Asmodeus charged in with rage blazing in his eyes. "*What were you doing in my chamber—*"

He gasped and slid to a stop. His green eyes were wide and glowing. "Reuelle."

She stood and stretched her arms and wings out. "Asmodeus."

"You're early," he growled.

She shrugged and her topaz eyes sparkled. "I saw an opening and I took it. I've been away from you long enough."

And then she dove for him. In the blink of an eye, she was across my room with her arms wrapped tight around his neck. His fingers dug into her body he held her so tight. They kissed and stumbled across my room.

I cursed and sprinted out of my room—and slammed right into Azazel's chest.

"What a shame your betrothed still has not returned for you," Azazel purred in my ear. When I squirmed and pushed him away from me, he dragged me against his body and let out a sick, evil little chuckle. "You have two choices: stop pretending you don't want me in your bed, or I'll make you want me. Either way, we're both going to enjoy you in my bed tonight."

# CHAPTER THIRTY-EIGHT

## UNKNOWN

"You can put the pizzas right here," I shouted over the music, but the two frat boys stood there gawking with drool practically dripping from their mouths. I waved my hands in front of their faces to break their trance, then pointed to the kitchen island behind them. "Right behind you, boys."

They cursed and spun around to gently sit the six pizza boxes each they carried onto the table. Their wide eyes kept glancing around to all my sorority sisters dancing along to the DJs handiwork. The party was in full swing, we'd just run out of food. Fast.

"What kind of party is this?" Joey asked as he leaned around me to get a better look.

Rob nodded and licked his lips. "And how do we get invited?"

I rolled my eyes. "It's a girls-only party. No boys allowed."

Rob whined. "Why would you do such a thing?"

"When you all look so good . . ." Joey couldn't keep his eyes to himself. "What's the theme? Heaven?"

"It's Angel's eighteenth birthday, so this is our angel party for Angel." I reached into my bra and pulled out a wad of cash, then held it out to them. "Because she's a good girl. Now take your money and run or you'll be banned from all of our future parties."

Their eyes widened. Rob grabbed the cash and Joey's shirt and dragged him away. Their heads snapped left and right and back again as they beelined out the front door. I giggled and followed after them to make sure they left. Alone. Once they were in their car, I turned to the DJ and nodded to the island.

"Ladies, fresh pizza is in the kitchen!" Morgan yelled over the Nicki Minaj song she was playing. "Get it while it's hot!"

I did good. This party was going perfectly so far. As the president of the sorority, I took my role very seriously. I always made sure each sister's birthday was celebrated the way she wanted. Angel had graduated high school a year early and spent her entire freshman year here at State as a minor. That meant every frat boy on campus had a countdown until Angel was legal. Literally. So, Angel wanted a *no boys allowed* party. She wanted a night with just her sisters, good music, and a hell of a good time.

The theme wasn't technically Heaven, but it *was* angels. Each and every one of my sisters had donned white angel wings from the party store and put on their pretty white dresses. We knew the second we told a single one of the frats they could come over, they'd all be here in minutes. My sisters were enjoying torturing them with every post on social media.

The birthday girl walked by me holding a slice of pizza in each hand. I didn't blame the guys for wanting her. She was a perfect blonde Barbie doll with big doe-eyed blue eyes and tan skin. She was on the dance team, so her body was perfectly toned. And she was always smiling.

I slid in beside her and yelled over the music. "How's my birthday Angel doing?"

"Oh my GOD! Becca!" She spun and hugged me. "This is the best birthday EVER!"

"Well, I still have a surprise coming for you—"

She gasped in my ear, then stepped back with wide, excited eyes. "Is it BOYS?"

"Mayyyyybe." I winked, then spun her around. "Go dance. You'll see soon!"

She giggled and skipped away with her pizzas. My name was called, and when I looked, I found the DJ waving for me to come over, so I made my way over to the DJ booth where our very pretty new friend, Morgan, was playing music only by female artists—to fit the theme.

She looked over at me with bright-blue eyes as I walked up. The black headphones nearly blended in with her black hair. "Hey, Becca! How we doing?"

"Amazing." I slid in closer and waved for her to lean in. "Is her gift here?"

Morgan's answering smile was wicked. "Waiting out front for my cue—"

"Oh my God! Bring them in! Yes!" I clapped my hands and nodded. "You're gonna announce them, right?"

"I got this. Don't worry." She winked as she picked up her microphone and turned down the music. "How we doing, ladies!?"

My sisters threw their arms up and cheered.

Morgan cheered with them. "Where's my birthday girl at?"

"I'm here!" Angel pushed to the front of the crowd with her hands still raised to the ceiling, her pizza slices gone. "I'm here!"

"So, birthday girl, I have a question for you . . . See, I know this is an angel party, but . . ." Morgan paused for dramatic effect, "how would you feel about letting in a few hot *fallen* angel boys?"

The girls cheered and clapped their hands. I giggled and got my phone out to record. When I hired Morgan to be our DJ, I told her our theme and the occasion and then she told me about her three super-hot guy friends who worked as exotic dancers and *loved* to do private parties. Morgan promised they'd dress for the theme, wings and all. I hadn't believed that part.

Then the girls all looked toward me, and their eyes widened. Their jaws dropped. I glanced over my shoulder, then did a double take. My breath left me in a rush. Three men sauntered through the crowd like they owned the place. They moved in perfect unison, each step in time with the others. The flashing pink and purple lights blocked their faces, but I knew by the wide set of their shoulders that these were not boys, they were *men*.

Each of them wore black-feathered angel wings.

I grinned. They were so earning that five-star review already. But then they stepped into the light of the dance floor, and we all gasped. Angel fanned herself. All three of them were tall and *gorgeous*. The one in front was sin incarnate with dark-green eyes and that long black hair that curled at the ends around his ears. On the left was a blond with eyes the color of night itself. But the one on the right had strawberry blond hair, blue eyes, and freckles that just made him even prettier.

Morgan played a song with a heavy beat, one that would be ideal for putting on a show. The girls knew it too. They screamed and cheered, then started chanting *"DANCE, DANCE, DANCE!"* There was so much giggling and swooning over these guys that I knew we wouldn't need to call in the frat boys.

I had a bad feeling these three weren't expecting to get paid in cash.

The one in front with the long hair and the sinfully perfect plush lips moved forward, sliding across the dance floor like he was floating on air. He went straight to Angel and ran his fingers over the white wings she wore. "You must be the birthday girl," he purred.

She nodded and squirmed, her cheeks flushed with excitement. "I'm Angel."

"I'm Azazel." He lifted her hand up to kiss her knuckles without breaking eye contact. All around the room, the girls giggled and grew more excited. He stood upright, then slowly began unbuttoning the buttons on his black shirt, revealing perfectly toned tan skin. "And these are my friends, Astaroth and Mammon. I believe we're here to make this party a little more *wicked.*"

# CHAPTER THIRTY-NINE

## FRANKIE

MY HANDS WERE COVERED in blood.

My blood.

I reached up and pressed my fingers over the holes in the side of my neck to put pressure on the vein, but it was no use. My heart was pounding, pumping blood through my body like a rushing river rapid. Each beat sent a wave of my blood pouring over my fingertips and sliding down my throat. The front of my white dress was scarlet red and soaking wet. But I had to keep running.

She was coming.

Queen Sweyn wanted my blood, my witch blood. I had to get out before she caught me. Because she would either drink the magic in my blood for her own use or she would chain me down and breed me like she'd wanted to before.

I had to get out. But everything in this damn place was white. Every hallway looked the same. I slid to a stop at the end of the hall, but each direction was more of the same. My other senses were all I had to try to guide me to freedom, so I closed my eyes and took a deep breath. The air sweeping over my left hand was colder than the air on the right. I turned my head to the left and breathed it in . . . and caught the faint scent of crisp mountain air and a garden.

With a curse, I turned left and sprinted as fast as I could down the hall using my nose as my guide like a dog. With each step I took, that *mountain air grew stronger and sharper. I smelled pine trees and smoke. Hope flared in my chest as I rounded yet another corner, following my scent trail. I glanced over my shoulder and choked on a gasp.*

*I'd left a blood trail.*

*It was Hansel and Gretel's breadcrumb trail fit for a horror film.*

*I was getting lightheaded. My hands and feet were numb. But up ahead the hallway ended with open air. The midnight-blue sky beckoned me, the sparkling stars cheering me on like fans in the bleachers egging me to steal home plate. I was so close. I just had to make it. I dug my heels in and pushed my legs as hard as I could, then lunged into the open air*—my feet hit cold, wet grass. My legs buckled on contact, and I stumbled a few feet before my balance gave out and I crashed onto my knees. My lungs were burning. I held my hands up and wanted to scream.

No blood.

A quick scan of my body showed my sweatpants and hoodie I'd fallen asleep in were still on and there wasn't a single drop of blood in sight. No white gown. No puncture wounds in my throat from fangs. I groaned and braced my hands on the dirt for a few seconds to try to catch my breath. After a few seconds, I sat up and leaned back on my heels, then looked around. I was outside Coven Headquarters, but not out back where we'd done my initiation and not on the side closest to the school campus. I was on the *other* side, right along the edge of a dense forest and a little too far from the house than I was comfortable with.

Apparently I'd been sleepwalking. That was new for me.

The trees in front of me rustled. I sucked in a breath and jumped to my feet just as Queen Sweyn emerged from within the shadows.

My breath left me in a rush.

She looked exactly like I remembered. Tall, thin, and with skin as white as snow. Her hair still fell straight down past her hips like someone dumped white paint on her head. Those eyes though . . . There was no forgetting her glowing red eyes.

"My, my, that was easy, little witchling." She let out a husky laugh and licked her lips and took a step forward, stepping out from the line of trees.

Glowing blue forms shot up from the ground, forming a line between Sweyn and me. They were *people*. Translucent people. My eyes widened as it clicked. These were spirits. Two more popped up on either side of me. They gripped my elbows and dragged me backwards so I was out of arm's reach for her. Then they kept going.

Sweyn snarled and lunged after us, but a light-gray dragon shot out of the tree line to my left and landed right in between me and *her*. Sweyn flinched and jumped back, but she aimed lasers with her eyes at the dragon. My brain was trying to wrap around the fact that a dragon stood in front of me, but I needed to pay attention to the threat.

Movement in my peripheral vision made me jump, but it was just Savannah, Thiago, Willow, Chutney, Lily, and Easton.

Savannah wiggled her fingers and black smoke curled between them. "Time for you to go, ma'am."

Sweyn growled. "I do not fear you infants, nor your rodent. Do you really think I'm here alone? What's a few of you against me and my vampires?"

Rainbow mist swirled right beside me, then Tegan appeared in its spot. Beside her, the other Bishop family members stood tall and terrible and ready to fight. Sweyn's glare faltered for a split second. She stepped back without taking her eyes off the Bishops, like she was afraid of them.

Tegan made that *tsk* sound. "Didn't think it'd be that easy, did you?"

Sweyn's face was an ice-cold mask of hatred. "Well, she came out here."

"Because I let her." Tegan looked down her nose at the Vampire Queen in disgust. "I left her unprotected and you showed your hand. You're too old to be this foolish."

Sweyn snarled and lunged for her, but Tegan was faster than I expected. She opened a white portal box right behind Sweyn, then summoned a gust of wind to slam into her chest and throw her into the portal. We still heard her growl echoing between the trees as the portal vanished.

"Get Frankie back inside," Tegan said in a rush.

I opened my mouth to disagree when the bright white light of Tegan's portal washed over me. The other Coven members were right beside me. The last thing I saw was rainbow mist flying straight up into the air. When the light faded, I stood in the living room of Coven Headquarters.

"What the fuck just happened?" I said to no one specific.

"You went for a walk," Tenn answered.

I looked over and found him sitting at the dining room table next to Deacon. "You're up."

Tenn shrugged one shoulder. "You'll find I don't sleep much."

Deacon grinned. "Let's just say we all watched you go running out the front door in your sleep."

"That's great news," I grumbled and waddled over to the table to sit. I cursed. "But what the fuck just *happened*? I do *not* sleepwalk—"

Tegan reappeared in the seat right next to Tenn so abruptly I actually flinched. "I'm not sure you don't. At least not now that your magic woke up."

I stared at her.

"Look, some people—and I use that word lightly—have the ability to go into people's dreams or subconscious minds." Tegan leaned forward and steepled her hands in front of her face. "I won't pretend I knew Sweyn could do this. And I won't pretend it doesn't unsettle me a bit."

Tenn laughed.

Deacon covered his mouth and snort-laughed.

"*Ma'am,* what is wrong with you—you know what? No." Savannah shook her head and her hands as she stomped for the stairs. "I'm going back to bed. Holler if you need me."

"Good night, Savannah," Tenn and Deacon yelled together.

Tegan smirked. "Thanks for your help!"

She stomped up the stairs, grumbling something about her cats on her pillow again.

"They're singing a song about being on her pillow. They think it's funny." Chutney giggled, but then she yawned. "I'm gonna let that be what I remember from tonight."

"What about Silas?" Thiago pointed to the front door.

Chutney stopped on the first step. "He's sleeping on the porch like the good guard dog he is."

Willow looked up the stairs and sighed. "Hey Tegan, could you—" she vanished into a white box.

Thiago held his hand up. "My turn?"

Tegan giggled and flicked her wrist and Thiago was gone. "Anyone else?"

"And miss the view?" Easton scoffed and gestured for Lily to go up the stairs in front of him in her little loose pajama shorts. He grinned. "See? Night, y'all."

Hunter tapped Kessler's shoulder, then opened the door on the side of the stairs. "I'm going to stay with Devon—"

"Dad, you need a bed—"

"I gave him one." Tegan looked to her father. "Please don't stay awake. If you can't fall asleep, let me know and I'll get something for you. Please?"

He just nodded, then disappeared down the stairs.

Kessler stared after him for a moment and then pinched the bridge of his nose and cursed. "I'll go talk to him."

Emersyn walked to the stairs before pausing. "Deacon, come to bed."

"I was going to go down and check on Henley—" He stopped and narrowed his eyes. He smirked. "It can wait."

And then it was just me, Tenn, and Tegan.

"This almost feels nostalgic," I said with a chuckle.

Tenn grinned that mischievous grin I used to see on Archie every day. "I feel like you shouldn't have said that."

I looked to Tegan. "Are you about to suggest I be bait again?"

"Not bait." She pursed her lips like she was thinking. "Let's say I have an idea to protect you, but it's crazy and unconventional and might not last?"

I shook my head and chuckled. "I'd say your last scheme worked well, so go for it."

Tenn arched one black eyebrow. "Do you want to know what her idea is?"

"Do you have a planned-out strategy you think will work? Like you did these last two times?"

Tegan's eyes sparkled. "Yes."

I nodded. "Well, I didn't know *those* plans until after, so why change our style now?"

Tegan grinned. "So you're cool with whatever?"

"I trust you." I leaned back in my seat. "Just let me know when it's over, okay?"

"You got it." Tegan stretched her hands and rolled her neck. Then she recited a spell in the ancient language and threw her rainbow magic right into my face. "There, that should do it."

# CHAPTER FORTY

## FRANKIE

SILENCE.

"I'm done talking now. It's your turn to speak."

My friends just stared at me with wide eyes and dropped jaws, their food forgotten and getting cold. I glanced over my shoulder but no one else had reacted. Everything had been so crazy since we left Tampa that I hadn't gotten to talk to them. So much had changed. My memories made me feel like an entirely new person. Sure, the version of me these friends met in Tampa was authentically *me*, but things had happened to me in Avolire that would affect my personality forevermore.

I needed these friends to know the entirety of me. It was important if our friendship was going to last, and I desperately wanted it to. Mei-Ling would always be my best friend, but she was a human. While she was hiding out among The Coven, she wasn't able to go everywhere I went. I needed witch friends too. This group of teens had taken me in without hesitation or question and really saved my mental health when I arrived in Tampa. I didn't want to lose them.

So I'd told them everything. The whole truth of it all from waking up to Tegan's reveal. Except I didn't tell them the spicier parts of my time there. I wasn't ready to talk about Everest, not about that. Actually, I hadn't told them about the vampires I thought were on The Coven's side. I was afraid to betray their secret and get them hurt, so they got the watered-down version of the story.

I hadn't wanted to tell them anything out in the public like this, in the middle of the Great Hall where all the students of Edenburg were having lunch. Together. And it wasn't like Gulf Shores High or my school back home, every single student here was a witch. Luckily one of the tricks Esther knew how to do was create a sound barrier so we could talk without anyone hearing us.

And now that I had, they were just gawking. At me.

"Dude . . . *vampires?*" Tomás shuddered. "I didn't know they were real. That's so creepy."

Birdie leaned forward and whispered, *"Did any of them drink from you?"*

*"Everest did,"* I whispered back and felt my face warm like I was blushing. "But only because he had to."

Jo's dark gaze swept the base of my throat like she was looking for signs. *"Ça t'a fait mal?"*

"Yeah, did it hurt?" Madge wagged her eyebrows.

"No, it didn't hurt." It actually had felt pretty good, but I didn't think that was a safe thing to tell people.

Seamus was staring at his plate of food. "I can't believe Braison is a vampire now. Poor Albert."

Ava ran her hands through her boyfriend's hair. "Rootbeer and Albert used to have play dates."

"Oh. Well, Albert is at Coven Headquarters. He's been staying with Chutney. Also, there's a few other dogs in the house and now mine, so he's got friends." My heart broke a little remembering the mastiff smelling his owner on me after weeks of not being around him. "I hope they see each other soon."

Esther rolled her wand between her fingers. "What are they doing with your human friend and her brother?"

"Keeping them in Headquarters. Apparently they have to stay hidden until Sweyn, and the threat to their safety, is dead."

They cursed.

Esther shook her head. "I feel like this is a lot to process and I need to sleep on it and then ask questions tomorrow."

"Honestly, that's fair." I took a sip of my soda, then licked my lips. "Okay, your turn. What did I miss at the assembly?"

Esther scowled. "Tenn didn't tell you?"

"Yeah, *Archie* didn't tell?"

"I haven't seen him yet. Or Tegan." I looked out the window to the clouds in the sky. "Katherine gave me a *strong* sleeping potion after what happened last night."

"What happened last night?"

"Oh . . . right . . ."

Esther hissed. "*Frankie . . .*"

"So, I had this dream I was being chased through Avolire by Queen Sweyn and then when I woke up, I was outside at the border of Eden by the forest and then she, like, suddenly . . . appeared."

They gasped.

"The Coven was there, or a good chunk of them. Tegan was playing Sweyn *again* and she fell for it *again*." I shuddered. "Then Tegan threw her through a portal and put up some spells and shit."

"So you got good sleep after that courtesy of Katherine." Esther chuckled. "Sounds about right."

"Yeah, and when I woke, I found a note from Tenn saying to skip the assembly." I tapped my nails on the table. "So what did he say?"

"He explained the new training plan for students."

"Basically, fuck math, hit the mats." Tomás chuckled. "No, seriously, he's scrapped academic classes for the rest of the school year."

I blinked in surprise. "Seriously?"

"Yeah, pretty much." Birdie swung her talisman amulet in circles. After my initiation, I could now identify just how anxious she was. "All of our classes are now geared toward war."

"Rootbeer's getting a special vest." Seamus fed her a piece of grilled chicken off his plate. "It's gonna light up if demons are near."

Tomás nodded. "Like that hobbit's knife in the movie, so I'm sticking with them."

Esther rolled her eyes and popped a grape into her mouth. "He wants everyone to learn how to defend themselves if attacked, so the non-Swords students have to spend their afternoons learning how to fight. And as a person who was recently attacked by demons, I am grateful he's enforcing it."

Ava cringed and pulled Float up into her arms, running her fingers over her white fur. "It's crazy to think back to that night now . . . knowing we had *two* Coven members there. And one was Tenn."

"*Nous aurions pu mourir.*"

"Yeah, I'm actively trying to *not* think about all the ways we could have died that night." Madge kissed Jo's cheek. "But thanks, love."

"What about the Swords students?" I pointed across the hall to where Peabo and Atley were sitting with some boys and comparing daggers. "They're already doing that?"

They all frowned.

"You know . . . I don't know." Birdie scowled. "I don't think he said—"

"He said he had plans for the Swords and they'd discuss with their Sword Leader in class." Esther looked over her shoulder to our two friends, then back to us. "Which probably means he didn't want to say and risk terrifying everyone else."

They all nodded and stared at their plates of mostly untouched food.

"Are y'all okay?" I gestured around the group. "Because Coven magic is *insane,* and I can legit sense your auras like flashing lights. This evacuation was sudden and huge. How are you?"

Madge snorted. "Girl, we've all secretly been wishing we could go to school here. The only thing we've lost is the beach, but we're about to learn so much more magic that it's worth it. I'm excited. Nervous but excited."

"It's not the being moved to a new town and school that's bothering us—and I think I speak for everyone at this table here—it's the reason it happened that has us a little uneasy."

"War," Jo said softly as she untied her braids and started over. *"Tu ne peux jamais vraiment être prêt pour la guerre."*

Esther leaned forward until her chest pressed against the edge of the table. Her gray eyes looked like storm clouds. "You're in The Coven. You know war is in your future. You know you'll be in the battle on the front lines. You can prepare for that. The rest of us? We have no idea if we're gonna have to fight, and that unknown is unnerving."

Tomás nodded. "Shit just got real."

"So then prepare for war. Prepare as if you know you'll get called up—"

A little boy went flying in the air about a table length away from us. His food flew everywhere like a tidal wave. He landed with a *thud* and his beans splashed into his face. My heart stopped. *Oh no.*

"You shouldn't wear skates in school, kid," Aaron yelled with a sinister chuckle. "How do your beans taste with dirt in them?"

Jacob leaned out from behind him holding his cellphone out, and I knew by the flash that he was filming the whole thing. "Tomorrow we should try to catch this in slow motion."

"Maybe Shaun White can give us a one-eighty."

The kid tried to stand but his knees slid in the Jell-O and he belly-flopped back into his spilled food.

Jacob cackled.

Aaron shook his head. "That'll never get you on the medal podium."

Tenn emerged from the shadows behind a column at the front of the hall.

Everyone gasped and sat up straight.

Aaron and Jacob stammered and backed up like they were actually considering running.

Tenn marched up the aisle, his mismatched eyes locked on tweedle-dee and tweedle-dum with a glare that even made me cringe. He stopped right in front of them, so close their bodies might've been touching. He didn't speak a single word, just glared down his nose at them. He towered over them by at least six inches. They didn't even reach his shoulders. Tenn's nostrils flared. He flicked his wrist and the poor kid lifted up onto his feet, then he slid the boy behind him.

He held his hand out to Jacob who had the brains to place his phone in Tenn's palm. The second he let go, Tenn curled his long fingers around it and crushed it with his bare hands. He dumped the pieces back into Jacob's hand.

Jacob's face paled. Aaron cringed like he was bracing himself.

"Do not misjudge my leniency for cowardice. I will strip every ounce of magic from your veins and send you into the human world to suffer a mundane life." Tenn's voice was calm and steady, but barely more than a growl. The air around him pulsed. "I am your Coven Leader, and there is no mortal in this world who outranks me. So go ahead. Try me. Your magic is the least of your worries. I can take your voice so you can never speak another word. I can rob you of your senses. I can *break you* any way I want to, and there's no one who can stop me."

Chills ran down my spine.

Tomás cursed under his breath beside me.

"Do *not* mistake my compassion, empathy, and kindness for my own people as weakness. I would re-open the dungeons from three centuries ago with barbaric punishments before I see one of my own causing any harm to my people. Do you understand me?"

They nodded. I was pretty sure they'd shat themselves by now.

"We're being hunted by demons, vampires, Unseelie fae, fallen angels, and Lilith—and whatever new monster she creates to torment us. We have to stick together. We, as a community of arcana, must be able to trust that the witch beside us will have our back whether we've been attacked or if we trip in the lunchroom." He leaned forward. "And do not think I missed the pencil Aaron slid onto the floor to make someone trip."

They blanched.

My eyes widened. I *had* missed that Aaron put a pencil on the floor.

Tenn crossed his arms over his chest and eyed the mess. "Clean up this mess."

"We don't have wands anymore."

Tenn smirked. "I know. *I* took them, remember?"

They paled.

He nodded to the mess. "Guess this is your first glimpse at life as a human. Clean it. Now."

They scrambled to get napkins, running into the line.

Tenn shook his head and turned to the kid who couldn't have been more than ten and looked ready to sob. His whole face and demeanor instantly softened. "You all right?"

The kid sniffled and nodded.

Tenn crouched down. "Are you hurt?"

"*I don't think so,*" he whispered.

"That's a lot of food. Did you just get that?" When the kid nodded, Tenn turned to glare at the boys who were rushing back with cleaning supplies. "Did you get to eat any of it?"

The poor kid shook his head.

Tenn stood back to his full height and yelled, "Hey, Gloria, you back there?"

The lunch lady stuck her head out and smiled. "Yes, sir—oh boy, got a spill? Well, come on back, sugar. I'll get you a new plate."

When the kid froze like a deer in headlights, Tenn crouched back down. But this time he whispered, "*Where are your friends sitting?*"

The kid bit his lip and shook his head. "*I'm new here this semester. I haven't made any yet. I'm shy.*"

"We're new here too." When I looked over, I recognized the boy as Chutney's little brother, but I'd forgotten his name. He grinned. "Today's my first day. I'm Sean."

"I'm Alex," he said timidly.

Sean pointed to two other kids about their age that I recognized as Willow's brother and Easton's sister. "Come sit with us. We're kinda shy too."

The other little boy cleared his throat and whispered, "*Tenn, his clothes are wet now.*"

Tenn frowned and looked down. He held his palm up and the boy's clothes dried instantly. They were still stained from food, but at least they were dry. "Now they're not. Good lookin' out, Ryan."

Easton's little sister jumped up and walked over, her blonde curls bouncing with every step. "I was going for seconds, so I'll grab your food from Gloria."

Alex relaxed and hurried over to sit next to Sean and across from Ryan, his back to the lunchroom, which was probably a good idea as everyone was still watching. Myself included. But seeing the difference in Tenn's entire aura between the bullies and the bullied was hypnotizing to watch.

Tenn smiled down at Easton's sister and held his fist out, which she bumped with her own immediately. "Thanks, Kaelynn."

"Now you should probably do something about the fear of God you put into everyone else or you'll have an even bigger mess to clean than these two buttheads." She gestured to the lunchroom. "I'm not sure they're all breathing."

Then she was gone, skipping back into the lunch line toward Gloria. I snickered.

Tenn looked around the room and sighed. He threw his hands up. "Don't be dicks and I don't have to be a dick. 'Kay?"

Everyone nodded.

"Show's over now." Then he walked a few feet over and sat on the bench right next to me, leaning against the table with his long ass legs stretched into the walkway. He glared at the bullies, which made them spill the beans they'd just scooped up.

"Feel better?"

He grimaced. "Not really. I hate being a dick."

"I love that all the little kids in here are gonna go home today and tell their parents The Emperor said the word dick. Twice."

His face fell. "Shit."

I giggled. "Your dad's gonna love that phone call."

He threw his head back and sighed dramatically. "This is why I didn't want to take the role from Uncle Tim. He was so much better at this."

"I don't know, crushing the iPhone into pieces with your bare hand was epic."

Tenn looked over to Seamus and grinned. "Felt good too."

Birdie leaned over and whispered, "Did you really suspend their magic?"

"Except for in self-defense, it'll only work for that. Can't have them murdered by demons just because they're a couple asshats." He arched one eyebrow at Aaron who was trying to pretend there wasn't food under the table. "I genuinely hope they just start being better people."

"And if they just aren't?"

I smiled. "I bet Tegan has ideas for you already."

"I'm afraid to ask." He closed his eyes and shook his head. "I have to tread carefully though. Lilith likes to prey on the slighted and give them a reason to turn on us. We've already suffered that fate and it hurt."

It was hard to remember that he was Archie when you looked at him, but when he said stuff like that, I realized why Archie had seemed so unique. Because he wasn't just some civilian. He'd seen some horrible things, That changed a person's outlook on life . . . and bullies.

Aaron and Jacob finally finished cleaning. They bowed to Tenn, then scrambled out of sight.

Tenn sighed. "Well, that was a tangent I wasn't prepared for."

"What do you mean?"

"I came to get you to pay a visit to the crystal ball, to get sorted into your Suit officially."

My friends gasped.

"Can we come? I wanna see—"

"Tomás, no. We can't go." Esther shook her head at him. "People already are gonna think we get special treatment. We don't need to make that worse."

Jo nodded, her eyes watching the rest of the lunchroom. "*Oui.* They are watching."

Tomás sighed. "Fine. I hadn't thought about that. Sorry."

"We'll catch up with you guys soon." Tenn stood and stretched his arms. "We're going right into a meeting anyway."

I jumped up and smiled at my friends. "I'll text you the results."

They waved and yelled words of encouragement as we walked out of the Great Hall. I looked up to make casual conversation, but he seemed to instantly tense up. Either that or he'd let his mask drop once we left the public setting. His eyes were sharp and tired at the same time. His muscles were tight. Magic kept flickering around his fingers.

"There you are." Bettina stepped out in front of us on the sidewalk. She punched him in the arm but smiled and waved to me. "Hey, Franks."

"Hey, Bettina. We're going to see the crystal ball to get me Sorted."

"What are you doing here?" His pace slowed as she turned to walk with us. "Where's Tegan? Why aren't you two together? Should I be worried?"

"Your soulmate is in bed right where you left her, passed the fuck out."

His grin said he was proud of himself. "Well, I was gone for a couple weeks—"

"Gross. We had a deal." Bettina cringed. "I'm not mature enough yet for that."

"I didn't say anything." He laughed and stepped aside to hold a door open for us.

Bettina slid in beside me as we walked through. "Your best friend dating your brother is all fun and games until she wants to talk about their sex life."

"You're so dramatic."

"Am I? *Am I, Haven?*" She turned to walk backwards down the hall as he followed. "Tegan likes to FaceTime me from bed, and she's really bad at making sure your body parts are covered."

Tenn snort-laughed and stopped in front of a door. "I'm sorry. That's terrible. Please don't retaliate."

"I won't." She shrugged and opened the door. "But Jackson might."

"Nah, he's a good lad. He wouldn't do that to me." Tenn led the way inside what appeared to be a normal-looking office, complete with a desk and filing cabinets. The only oddities were the weird columns on either side of the desk that were about hip height. Tenn went right up to one and waved his hand over the top, but nothing happened. "What the hell? Where is it?"

Bettina walked over and held her hand the same exact way he did.

He rolled his eyes and shoved her aside playfully. "Really? I just tried that."

She made a face at him. Tenn held his other hand out, then a giant crystal ball slid up from within the other column on the other side of the desk.

"*Oh*," they both said at the same time.

"You're an idiot." Bettina snickered.

"Maybe if you weren't being such a gnat I could concentrate."

"Maybe if you actually ate lunch instead of having a lunchtime shag, you'd be able to concentrate—"

"Well—"

She covered his mouth with ice. "Don't be gross. Who are you . . . Easton?"

He tried to get the ice off but it wasn't budging. She walked away. He tried to grab her, but she wrestled away from him, then he flexed his hand and her hand flew up and slammed into his mouth. The ice vanished.

"This is so entertaining." I sat in the chair in front of the desk and crossed my legs. "I need popcorn."

"Why are you so batty today?" He pressed his palm to Bettina's forehead and pushed her back enough where her swings missed his body. "Maybe if *you* had a lunchtime shag, you'd calm down."

"Maybe if *you* hadn't sent Jackson to teach the teachers how to train students to fight, I could have a shag."

Tenn's face fell. He dropped his hand. "This is retaliation."

She grinned and reached for the ball. He swatted her hand away. She hip-checked him. He shoved her. They may have both been super tall and terrifying with magic, but in this moment, they were typical siblings shoving at each other.

He palmed the crystal ball, but nothing happened. He shook it like a snow globe, still nothing. She stole it from his hands, but nothing happened, it just remained gray. She shook it the same way he just had, and again nothing happened.

He stared at her with a deadpan expression. "Right, I didn't just try that."

He stole it back. She snatched it with both hands. He used his wind magic to fly the ball back to his hands. She turned the ball to ice and yanked it back.

"Would you stop—"

"Just let me try," she hissed. "I'm better with this kind of magic anyway."

"It's my office."

"Well, technically it was mine." We all jumped and turned to find Timothy leaning against the doorframe. His dark eyes glanced around the office. "And since you haven't touched a single thing, I'd say it's still mine."

They both froze. Tim just shook his head, walked to the wall, then pressed his hand to it. A panel slid up and a crystal ball floated out. It landed in his palm and turned jet-black.

Tenn threw his hands up. "Why do we have a decoy ball?"

"Because, nephew, students used to try and put spells on it," Tim grinned and tossed it to him. "To get the Suit they wanted."

The ball was white in the air, but it turned black again before Tenn even touched it. He grimaced. "There needs to be a Coven Leader manual."

"I actually started making one for you last year, but then I died—"

"HEY!" Bettina shuddered.

"No!" Tenn cringed.

They threw ice and water at him. He laughed and brushed himself off.

Bettina reached for the ball, but Tenn held it way above her head. She hissed. "Haven!"

"Hope." He stuck his tongue out at her. "Tell me what you want—"

"I wanna touch the ball."

"You touched it in August."

"Yes, but I need to see it again."

"Why? It doesn't change."

"Really? Are you sure? Because it wanted to be purple."

"But you got Swords—"

"And Uncle Tim said I could pay the ball another visit—"

"What? When?"

"Before I died—"

"HEY" Bettina full body shuddered.

"NO!" Tenn's cringe looked painful.

Timothy laughed. "Hope, I only said I'd let you touch it again because I needed to give you an incentive to try. You were too busy insisting it was wrong to actually let it prove it was right. Your Suit does not chang.-"

"See?" Tenn made a face at her.

"Maybe I'm both? It flashed purple. Uncle Tim, you saw it."

"I did. And it did consider Wands—"

"*See?*" She stuck her tongue out at Tenn and elbowed him in the ribs to try and steal the ball from his hands.

"But you are Swords, if the elbow in the ribs wasn't an indication."

"See? Now go wake up Tegan and bother her—"

"No, she needs to sleep. She rarely sleeps anymore. It's actually growing more and more difficult for her to be able to sleep."

"Yeah, hence the shag." Tenn rolled his eyes.

Timothy looked to me and shook his head. "I'm sorry."

"What is wrong with you today? Seriously, what is happening?" Tenn held the ball up in the air. "Answer me honestly, and I'll let you touch it."

"Listen, look, we've been killing demons all day, every day since you left—and before you left If you recall—but Bentley benched us two days ago, and if I don't kill something soon, I'm going to break something." She squirmed. "I have all this . . . this . . . it's like rage in my body and I have to do something with it—"

"Hey, that's what I always say." I chuckled. "It's like restless leg syndrome but my whole body and I just need to hit something."

"She gets it!"

Timothy shook his head again. "What Michael was thinking when he chose a Proctor, I'll never know."

"Why?" all three of us said.

"Bishops may be the most powerful and Irits the most intuitive . . ." Tim held his hand out for the crystal ball. "Proctors are the warriors, which is why Uriel had Edward so that he could handle Michael's sword. So why Michael then chose the line with Proctors to procreate with really confuses me. Give your sister the ball, Nephew."

Tenn handed it to her. It flashed purple for a split second, then turned jet-black.

"I'm just saying Tegan got all the colors, all the Suits. Maybe I'm both."

"You're not both, the Wand influence comes from your mother's inherited gifts from Heaven." Tim held his other hand up as she started to speak. "We'll get you a talisman wand and see how that goes—"

"Tenn blew shit up." I grinned when all three of them looked to me. "Him touching a wand was dangerous."

"Yeah, it's not fair."

"Mona told me all about it." Tim laughed and took the ball from Bettina. He turned to me with it. "Well, Ms. Proctor, let's see what it says for you."

"We think she's Cups," I said as I stared at it. "Remember?"

Tenn grimaced. "I knew you were the Tower already. That Card has the gift of potions. And the way you're able to create potions is indicative of your Coven rank. Normal Cups can't do what you do, which I believe should be obvious after what happened in Hidden Kingdom that night."

I frowned. "Did I tell you about that night?"

"I was there. Watching." He shrugged and pointed up. "I was in the trees, waiting to step in if you needed it."

"You saw what I did?"

"I did. I couldn't see whatever you saw, but I know a normal Cup doesn't see that."

"Are there any Cups in The Coven?"

"Hunter and Bentley and Chutney."

"So if that's why I'm good with potions, then you're saying I might not be a Cup?" I scowled. "But you saw me with a wand . . . and the amulet did nothing . . ."

The ball floated into my palms and instantly turned black.

"YESSSS!" Bettina cheered and clapped her hands.

Tenn grinned. "Look at that! Another Proctor is a Sword."

"Next time you see Michael, you should ask him why—"

"It's probably petty." When they looked to me, I shrugged. "He's probably pissed and just wanted to know that someone who was going to cause the utmost carnage would have his sword."

Tenn looked to his sister. "That feels like a you kind of answer."

"Yeah, it does. I'm so glad she's a Proctor."

The bell rang and it made the siblings jump. Both of them pulled daggers.

"Easy, easy. Whoa now." Timothy laughed and held his hands up. "Weapons down, you three. Goddess almighty."

*Three?* Tenn and Bettina looked to me with the same frown I had on, and we all realized together that I also had pulled out my weapon without knowing.

"Proctors. Bat shit crazy." Tim walked to the door and yanked it open. "It's the bell for class. C'mon, let's get back to Headquarters. Bentley and Cooper are back and looking for you."

"Right. I'm a little nervous about where Bentley went and why."

They grumbled something about Bentley being Bentley as we headed out of the building and across the courtyard. It amazed me how much these two siblings were like me, which shouldn't have since we were related, but I didn't have much experience in the sibling or big family thing. After watching these two bickering in the office, I knew they were scary similar and I felt like they had a lot in common with me. Then again, I felt a kinship with Timothy too.

"Tim, you're not a Proctor, right?"

"Nope. My sister's husband was."

"So you're both Proctors but neither of you use the name?" I scowled. "You're Wildes and—"

"Blair." Bettina sighed, and it sounded a little sad. "It's a long story but from age four until December I thought my name was Bettina Blair, so that became my identity. Before that only my parents, Haven, and Uncle Tim called me Hope. I'm still trying to figure out how to handle the name thing."

"Because she's not a big fan of the name Hope—"

"I never said that!"

"Out loud." Tim laughed. "It's okay, I didn't pick those names."

"Yeah, I don't know how to not be Tennessee. I'd like to carry on the Proctor name though."

"I thought you and Trouble didn't want kids?" Tim looked concerned.

"We're just low-key terrified, that's all." He shuddered. "And definitely not something we want to even consider until we're older."

"I think Cooper would have an aneurysm." Bettina grinned as she pulled her split-dyed hair up into a ponytail. "But it is a predicament because . . . Tegan's a Bishop. The Bishops are a massive name for us."

"Well, why can't you be Tennessee Haven Proctor and Bettina Hope Proctor?" I shrugged. "Or you could just become a Bishop."

"I'm scary enough to people now. If my name was Bishop . . .?" Tenn whistled. "Besides, Bentley *and* Cooper are Bishops."

"I think Deacon would be thrilled to leave the English surname behind."

"Deacon Bishop." I snorted. "That's amazing."

Tenn looked to me. "Yeah, once Deacon hears *that,* there's no turning back."

"You know, the Irit surname is passed on through Esther's middle name . . . and her mom's too." I gestured to them. "You could let Proctor be a middle name if you have children."

"That's a good point. Because Jackson worked so damn hard to get the Lancaster line back that I can't not take his name."

"OR you just scramble the letters in all your names and just make new ones." I held my hand up to block the sun from shining in my face. "Names are just words someone made up at one point."

Bettina stopped short. "What's Katherine's last name?"

"It's . . ." Tenn stopped and stared at the ground. "Shit, I don't know."

"Katherine the healer? Why?" When they both looked to their uncle with twinkles in their eyes, I gasped. "Wait, Tim, are you and Katherine a couple?"

"Yeah, Uncle Tim, *are you?*" Bettina wagged her eyebrows.

He rolled his eyes, then started walking again. "Yeah, we are."

"But what's her last name?" Tenn whispered as he followed. "I can't believe I forgot it."

"Maybe Tim can give her a new one."

He stopped on the steps to Headquarters and gasped, turning on me with wide brown eyes. "You're as bad as these two. What am I gonna do with *three* Proctors? Anarchy."

We laughed and walked across the porch to the front door.

"You're gonna train us is what. Well, maybe not Haven, Mr. Angel boy, but me and Franks, yeah." Bettina held her hand up to me for a high-five. "We're so gonna spar. I can't wait."

I gave her five and chuckled. "It's gonna be so nice to not have to hold back like I have to in class."

"Oh, that's right. Haven says you're a trained martial artist. Fuck yeah. I'm ready."

"Ready for what?" Easton said from somewhere out of sight.

Bettina bounced inside with a wide grin. "Frankie's a Sword."

There was a chorus of cheering and applause before I even got all the way in the house. Once I did it was high-fives in every direction. The entire Coven seemed to be in the living room waiting on something. It was a bit overwhelming, so I slid over to sit on the stone ledge in front of the fireplace to be out of the way a bit.

"Hey, boss, is this a lunch meeting or like . . ." Royce paused in the doorway to the kitchen. "Or is it like a meeting I can eat during?"

"Just bring me something back with you." Tenn cleared his throat and sat down on the big chair near the fireplace. He glanced around the room. "I thought you said Coop and Bentley were back?"

A white light flashed and then Tegan appeared in the middle of the living room with two guys. One of them I recognized instantly as Bentley. He looked the same as I remembered: a few inches shorter than Tenn with long brown hair and eyes the color of champagne. The black *V* on his left forearm looked less sinister when his skin wasn't doing the lightning and lava show.

"See, Coop? He's right there." Tegan pointed straight ahead to Tenn. "Just like I said he would be."

Tenn jumped up and gave Bentley one of those halfway dude hugs. But when Bentley stepped aside, Tenn threw his arms wide open. "C'mere, big guy."

"I need to put a microchip on you or something," Coop mumbled as he crossed the room to him. "Or like a GPS tracking device would be better."

Tenn gave Coop a proper hug. "Next time just come with me. It was fun—"

"Don't encourage her, Tenn." Coop sighed and gestured to Tegan with his thumb. "You're the only thing controlling her at this point."

"Challenge accepted." Tegan went over and wrapped herself around Tenn's body.

"Now look what you did," Willow said with a grin from the couch.

I watched this Coop with curiosity. He was Tegan's older brother, and after everything I'd heard about the Bishop family, I was intrigued by them. Cooper's whole aura was a little firmer feeling than his siblings. Tegan, Emersyn, and Bentley were wild cards. That much was obvious. Hunter was chill but also nothing like Cooper's energy. Something told me Cooper felt like he was everyone's big brother and took on a lot of responsibility for himself.

Cooper sighed. "Did I miss anything?"

Bettina flopped down on a couch next to Willow. "Frankie got sorted into Swords, so the Proctor versus Bishop battle is starting to shape up."

"Yep, now I want to see that." Easton pretended to write in a note-book. "Let's not forget that idea."

Deacon waved his hand. "Actually, I think we already saw that battle back in October—"

"Yeah, yeah, yeah." Cooper grabbed a throw pillow off the couch and chucked it right at Deacon's face, but they were both laughing. "So where is this Frankie? Or did you scare her off with your crazy already?"

I laughed and stood, brushing my hand off on my jeans so I could shake his hand. "Crazy is about the only thing that makes me feel at home."

Cooper spun around with a smile on his handsome face. White light flashed from our chests. I froze. His pale-green eyes that were the same shade as Tegan's widened. Everyone in the room jumped up in shock. Their wide stares went back and forth between me and Cooper. He reached up and rubbed his chest. My skin felt warm and tingly all of a sudden.

Royce stumbled forward, then gripped Cooper's shirt and yanked the collar down. "WHAT?"

Everyone just stared at his chest.

I did too. Because I was trying to wrap my head around what I was seeing. There, on his chest, was a white, heart-shaped crystal with little black lines about an inch long sticking out from one side. I opened my mouth, then closed it.

Emersyn scowled and hurried over to me. She tapped her finger to my chest. "Can we see?"

"Does this . . . Is this . . ." I pulled just the top of my shirt down enough to see the same crystal on my chest. As we were watching, they both turned emerald-green. "Is this what I think it is?"

I knew it was. I'd seen too many of them now to not know.

But I needed someone to say it out loud.

"*Soulmates,*" Savannah whispered from the front door. "You're . . . soulmates."

# CHAPTER FORTY-ONE

## FRANKIE

"ALL RIGHT, one of us has to break this silence."

I jumped and looked over to my left to where Cooper Bishop stood a few feet away. He wasn't looking at me. He was staring at the little wooden shack in front of us. Well, not a shack. More like a small wooden cabin-like building that sat nestled between some massive oak trees that made the building look tiny. I'd been staring at it, too, though I hadn't really seen it at all yet.

My thoughts were spiraling around the fact that Cooper Bishop was my soulmate.

*Soulmate.*

I was struggling to wrap my head around this. A soulmate was not something I was mentally prepared for. Sure, I'd thought they were amazing, but now I doubted it. A perfect stranger was now marked as my other half . . . my meant to be . . . my eternity and destiny . . . all before we'd spoken a single word to each other.

It wasn't that I disliked this guy, I just didn't know him. At all. Sure, he was handsome, but was I supposed to feel some intense emotions already? I wasn't sure. I hadn't actually asked any of the soulmate pairings how this went down for them, and now I desperately wished I had. But Cooper *was* handsome. Very much so. He was tall, probably about six-foot-two, with muscles cut in all the right places, especially in that gray long-sleeved shirt he wore. His profile was beautiful too. I wanted to like him, I wanted to have that instant crush feeling, but it hadn't happened. But he smelled like Irish Spring soap, and to my surprise I liked it.

"See, this is the part where you say something out loud so I don't feel as crazy as I do right now." Cooper chuckled and looked down to meet my stare with bright-green eyes. "A sound effect could work too?"

I closed my eyes and sighed. "Sorry, Cooper. Was I silent this whole time?"

"Yeah, but in your defense, I think I was too." When he laughed, I opened my eyes again and stared up at him. He had a warm, gorgeous smile with perfect teeth. "I don't even know how long we've been standing here silently staring at the shack."

"Why are we here again?" I grimaced. "I may not have been processing words when we left."

"That's fair." He gestured to the wooden shack. "This is where all Sword students come to get their talisman. I think . . . I think this was Tenn and Tegan's way of giving us a moment alone while also knowing we'd need something to do with our hands because we'd be too awkward to sit still."

That did it. I snort-laughed.

He chuckled.

"So, no big deal. Just going to pick out my one super special weapon with the soulmate I just met a few minutes ago." I nodded. "No big deal at all."

"It is, though, isn't it?" He cursed, then pointed to a picnic table under the oak tree. "Let's sit over here for a second?"

I let him lead the way to the table, then we both sat on the same side with our backs pressed against the tabletop. We continued to stare at the building.

"We should probably start by actually looking at each other."

I snort-laughed again. "I think that's how we got into this."

He threw his back and laughed. "Fucking fair."

"You're funnier than I expected," I said before I could stop myself.

He looked over to me with a sparkle in his green eyes. "You mean when I'm not basically the parent of The Coven despite both my parents being in The Coven."

I snickered. "Does anything get your dad ruffled?"

"No, and honestly, thank Goddess, because Tegan would've been a lot more of a menace."

"Tenn called her a chaos demon—"

"Tenn did? When?" He sighed and threw his hands up. "He finally admits it out loud and I missed it."

"You two seem close."

He nodded and his cheeks flushed a soft pink. "We were raised together, it's a whole long story, but he's always been like a brother to me."

"And now he's shagging your sister over lunch."

He sighed. "That's unsanitary."

I threw my head back and laughed.

He smirked. "You should probably know that I have this long running joke where I pretend that their relationship bothers me and I make a big deal about their PDA. It'll probably come back to bite me in the ass here."

"Let me guess, you freaked out when it first happened, and no one lets you live it down?"

"I could have handled it better." He hung his head. "I'm just glad it wasn't me who caught them in Lookout Tower—"

I gasped. "That's right! He told me about that. Well, *Archie* did."

"You know, I'm sorry you've been through everything you have since Halloween but . . . but I'm glad he got to be Archie for a week or so. I think he needed that."

"Oh? He seems to handle stress pretty well."

"He does, but when your whole existence has been stress, you learn how to manage early on. He's been real tense these last few months."

"Does Tegan help or make it worse?"

"Both, definitely both." He grinned. "My sister is a force to be reckoned with, and you put Bettina with her? Chaos. Poor Tenn, soulmate and sister are bat shit crazy evil villains."

"What about Bentley?"

"I try to avoid eye contact most days."

I snort-laughed. *Again.* "Stop it. He's your brother—"

"And I love him. But dude just stares at you and these orange crescents flash inside his eyes, and you know he's seeing your future, but like you don't want to know and yet you can't help but dissect his facial expressions."

"So we need to buy him some mirrored sunglasses."

He laughed and his shoulders bounced. "We should. Yes. Bentley is great, but he was nine years old in January—"

"Excuse me, *what?*"

"You heard me. He was nine. He was kidnapped by the Seelies and thrown into the Wild Night . . . four days later he emerged as a sixteen-year-old."

I whistled and shook my head. "Let me guess, another long story?"

"Oh, and none of our long stories are happy, feel-good. They're all horrible and sad and traumatic."

"So I'll fit in." I rubbed my hand over my chest. "This whole soul-mate thing is a bit crazy to me. You don't seem as freaked out."

"Bentley has been warning me my soulmate was coming for months. Hard to be surprised when it then does." He wrung his hands together. "I've also been in The Coven since before my memories stuck, so my normal is a little skewed."

"I just feel like . . . I don't even know you and you're my soulmate. That's wild. Couldn't we get a second? I didn't even get to introduce myself first."

"That's how it works for arcana. It's at first sight." He turned to look at me and held his left hand out. "But it's nice to meet you. I'm Cooper Bishop."

"Frankie Proctor." I smiled and took his hand. "Enchanté."

His skin was warm and surprisingly soft, but there was no electricity, no buzz. My thoughts went immediately to Everest, so I had to look away from Cooper. Every moment with Everest was intense and electric, a moth to a flame. But maybe that wasn't how soulmates were supposed to feel. Maybe him feeling like a warm cozy blanket to cuddle up with on the couch was the right feeling, not the *I've just been struck by lightning* feelings I got from Everest.

"I know what you're feeling right now . . ." he said suddenly, very softly.

I sighed. "I don't know about that."

He nodded. "You feel like this can't possibly be right when your heart lies elsewhere. Like being near me may be comfortable and peaceful, but it's not that all-consuming, *cannot breathe without me* kind of feeling."

I blinked up at him with my heart in my throat. I nodded.

"And I want you to know I get that. You're not alone in that feeling." He scrubbed his face with his hands. "We can't help the circumstances under which we met. We can only be a part of them now that we have. Whatever we . . . experienced before this—"

"Oh my God. Did you have a girlfriend?"

His face fell. "No. I knew better. The saying *never date a Bishop* is a real thing in our world."

"What, why?"

"Because every single Bishop on record has had a soulmate. Or died young before they could meet them. So dating is just asking for heartbreak." He stared at the ground with eyes that seemed far away. "It's a blessing and a curse."

"So, no matter what our hearts might feel for someone else, we are each other's fated destiny?"

"Soulmates are one soul that was split into two, then sent out into the world to find its literal other half—"

I cursed.

"You Proctors all have such pirate mouths." He chuckled, then to my surprise, he stood up and faced me. "Look, why don't we just focus on being friends right now? Give our hearts a chance to mend."

"Okay. Friends. I can do that." I smiled even though I wasn't sure how I was supposed to get over Everest quickly. It was properly unfair that I didn't just suddenly have that instant-love with my own soulmate. "Why did we stand?"

"We're going inside to get your talisman." He walked backwards toward the door. "C'mon, this is the fun part."

When I got inside, I froze. My jaw dropped. It had to be three stories high. Each of the four walls was lined with swords of every size and shape. The bronze color of the metal glistened in the sunlight pouring through the glass ceiling. On each wall, there were two ladders that slid up and down so people could climb to the weapons higher up.

It was a library of swords.

It took my breath away.

I took a few steps farther in, then spun in a circle. I shook my head. There was a serene energy floating around us that I didn't want to disturb. Then I noticed the pedestal in the center. It was beautiful, sitting in the brightest ray of sunlight. On top, the pedestal was a bowl, holding inside it the deepest, darkest royal blue I'd ever seen. I walked over to get a closer look but stopped short. There was a ring of what looked like salt surrounding the pedestal. Over to my left, the little circle was open, though I got the distinct impression we weren't supposed to step inside until told to do so.

I cleared my throat and backed up until I stood beside him. "What now?"

"This talisman you're about to make should be your most sacred possession. It will be a sword to use in combat, but it will have specific qualities made only for you. This weapon will aid you in more ways than one. You'll find every single type of sword imaginable." He smirked. "That's the spiel we're all taught to give."

"Cool. So I just pick one?" I looked around. "How? And then what?"

"Think of them like blank keys. You're going to walk around, hold them, and swing them around until you find one that calls to you."

*Walk around. Got it.* I just needed to try some weapons on until one clicked. I moved down the right wall, but all of the weapons there were types of daggers. But I had a dagger courtesy of my aunt and uncle—*and my cellphone.* I moved on to the next wall but found the opposite problem. These were all ridiculously long for my short body. There were also curved swords and serrated blades.

"Try closing your eyes." He squeezed his shut, then held his hands out. "That helped some of us focus in on where our magic was leading us."

I shrugged and closed my eyes. I had nothing to lose. *Okay, magic. Let's do our thing here?* At first I saw nothing, but then I lifted my hands and my neon-blue flames shot out of me. They swirled around the entire room without landing on one specific thing. Little pink flames dripped down like raindrops on my blue sea. But then my waves merged into one at the back wall. I opened my eyes and hurried over there.

And then I just stared.

My pink flames were dancing around a pair of sais.

They were silver and about the length of my forearm. With a

shaky hand, I reached out and grabbed the hilts. I gasped. The second my skin touched the metal, warmth rushed up my arm. It tingled a little, but not uncomfortably. Something in the air around me shimmered. I felt light on my feet. I smiled and gave the sword a test swing. When I pulled it back, my eyes widened. Pink mist wrapped around my hands and around the three-pronged sai in my hand.

I felt like Raphael the Ninja Turtle.

"Holy shit! I didn't know there were sais in here." Cooper reached out and ran his finger along the long middle prong. "Your cousins are gonna be so jealous."

I snort-laughed. "You have a knack for making me laugh."

"Well, then, we're off to a better start than Em and D, where Em basically hated him for existing." Cooper chuckled, then turned and waved for me to follow. "Bring those over here, Raphael."

I grinned. I'd just called myself the same name. Perhaps the universe knew something we didn't. I was so caught up in my own head about soulmates and what we are *supposed* to feel and show that I didn't realize we'd stopped in front of that pedestal. Or that Cooper was chanting something in the ancient language, which I now recognized the sound of. When he was done, light flashed above the water. Six lines of words in perfect, elegant script were written in the air, glowing a bright white. I couldn't read them from my angle, but something told me I'd be able to once I got up there.

"When you're ready, step inside the circle, recite the spell, then place your sais in the holy water." Cooper moved to stand by the opening of the circle. "You go in here."

"Got it." I took a deep breath, then stepped inside the circle. The words of the spell glittered in front of me. I licked my lips, then read them out loud, *"I call thee Goddess for this sacred bond, Blessings of power from the ancient beyond. With magic and valor, honor and creed, Transform this blade to what I need. Dipped in the water of thy holy well, See sword and soul in parallel."*

The air shimmered, and a little white arrow appeared, pointing down to the pedestal. With my heart in my throat and my breath trapped in my lungs, I gently laid the blades of my sais inside the holy water. That royal blue water rolled like waves crashing on a beach, like waves in a riptide splashing and crashing into each other. Pink flames moved around the edge of the bowl, then slid over the water. My eyes widened. The hilts warmed in my hand.

When my magic settled and the water went back to normal, I lifted my sais up off the pedestal and gasped. They were *red*. Every single inch of them were bloodred. They were *gorgeous*. For a few moments all I could do was stare at them.

Cooper stepped up beside me. "And to think, some people have *that* reaction to meeting their soulmates."

The evil cackle that came out of me might've embarrassed me in front of other people. But Cooper Bishop was actually, surprisingly, one of the easiest people to be around. So maybe the universe hadn't quite lost its mind . . . Maybe him being my soulmate made perfect sense.

Or maybe that was what I was telling myself.

# CHAPTER FORTY-TWO

## FRANKIE

"DID YOU KISS HIM?"

I gasped. "No, I didn't kiss him! I just met him!"

"Didn't stop you with Everest—"

"*ESTHER.*"

Mei-Ling cackled.

"Really, bestie? REALLY?"

She shrugged. "I mean, she sounds like she has a point."

"No." I pointed my cracker at her. "*I* didn't kiss Everest. He kissed me and that was a few days after he showed up in Tampa. And might I remind you, dear bestie, I had not just met him."

"Right, you'd already climbed that mountain—"

I groaned and shoved my apple slice into her mouth. "Whose side are you on?"

She bit the apple and chewed, looking totally unbothered.

Birdie reached over the plate of crackers to grab the tray of cheese slices. "I think it's a good thing you left out all the saucy details at lunch today."

"Poor Tomás." Jo snickered. "*Il ne s'en remettra jamais.*"

Madge rolled her eyes. "Pretty sure he was recovering just fine with Whitney last night. He told Seamus all the dirty details, right, Ava?"

Ava froze with her hand hovering over the bowl of watermelon. "I

435

wasn't aware we had secrets. Wait, was I not supposed to say anything—"

"I'm the one who told him to ask Whitney to the dance." I leaned forward and stole some watermelon from her bowl. "I have never had any romantic feelings for Tomás, so I genuinely hope Whitney does."

"Right, right. No one help her change the subject." Esther narrowed her eyes on me. "Cooper is your soulmate. For real?"

I pulled the front of my shirt down to show off the green heart-shaped crystal on my chest. "I don't know why mine is green, but I know what it is."

"Yeah, what's with the colors?" Mei-Ling gestured to me and then to Madge and Jo. "I've now seen pink, lavender, and red—"

"RED?"

"*Rouge? Qui?*"

I frowned. "Do the colors mean something?"

"*Oui, bien sûr. Les couleurs signifient tout.*"

Madge nodded. "So, the color indicates the emotional state of the relationship. There's always, like, a default color. Then once the glyph completes like ours, it'll change colors to reflect moods."

"Like a mood ring." Birdie grinned and popped open another soda. "It can be quite convenient."

"But there's always a default color." Esther pointed to the girls. "Go on, tell her. You're the soulmates here."

"Tenn and Tegan's is pink—"

"Pink means profound mutual love." Madge pressed her hand to her chest and sighed. "The only reason I'm not offended is because it's super rare. Light blue means new love, which is the color most glyphs are to start."

"Not ours." Jo ran her fingers over the yellow heart on the back of her right hand. "Yellow means peace and harmony."

Madge smiled at her. "And lavender means true love that comes after light-blue after the couple has gotten to know each other."

Esther pointed to me. "And emerald-green?"

"Nervous." Madge grimaced. "But given the way this has all gone down, I am not that surprised. Give it some time and I'm sure it'll change."

"*Le rouge signifie le danger.*" Jo shuddered.

"Red means danger?" I frowned. "Whose is red?"

Mei-Ling's face fell. "Hunter Bishop. Most of the time it's green like Frankie's, but sometimes it turns red."

We all fell silent as that information settled in. That was my soulmate's parents and one of them was clinging to life. I didn't know how to handle that, how to feel about that. Obviously I felt horrible for them, but they were still such strangers to me that I felt hopeless. I wanted to feel something for my own soulmate. And knowing that everyone else knew I was nervous about it just made me want to puke.

That was how we'd gotten out here in the first place. I'd called Esther in a bit of a panic after I'd gone to get my talisman with him. She'd called an emergency girls' night picnic. Mei-Ling wasn't allowed to wander off too far since humans weren't supposed to be in Eden, so we'd set up our little picnic at the edge of the courtyard between Edenburg's campus and Coven Headquarters. I could see the front door to the house, which meant they could see me.

"Okay, I'm gonna say something controversial here." Ava leaned forward and the golden glow from the lamp post above us made her brown skin shimmer. "Maybe you *should* kiss Cooper."

"He *is* your soulmate." Birdie's cheeks flushed. "Maybe it'll help?"

Mei-Ling narrowed her eyes on me. "Could go either way. I mean, I saw you with Everest. I saw that chemistry—"

"Yeah, we did too," Esther said with a chuckle. "But just because you have a soulmate doesn't mean you were never allowed to be attracted to someone else."

I bit my lip and nodded. "Besides, I shouldn't want a vampire anyway. I've seen Twilight."

We all laughed. But then Mei-Ling's face fell.

My heart sank as I realized what I'd said. "Mei-Ling—"

"It's okay, Frankie. Really. Malik . . ." she cleared her throat and shook her head. "I'd only known him a few months. I'm grateful for the time we had together. It . . . saved me. After everything. Sometimes people come into our lives but they aren't meant to be there permanently."

"Amen to that," Esther said softly.

Ava sat up straight. "Oh, shit, there he is."

*Everest?* I glanced over my shoulder and my stomach sank. It wasn't Everest. Of course it wasn't. He was a vampire lord. He wouldn't be in Eden. But my reaction to seeing my own soulmate and being disappointed it wasn't the guy I was crushing on was a blow to the heart.

"What's he doing?" Birdie whispered.

He'd stomped out the front door to the left and marched straight into the forest, right where Sweyn had been standing when she'd lured me out of bed.

Mei-Ling sighed but it sounded like a swoon. "He's super-hot."

The girls giggled. I waited to be jealous, but it didn't happen.

"He's not hot?"

Esther shrugged. "We've all known Cooper for twelve years. I've never used the word hot to describe him—"

"*Why not?*"

"Because he's like everyone's older brother." Birdie grimaced. "He's a great guy and obviously conventionally handsome—anyone with eyes would tell you he's good looking. But . . ."

"He gives big brother vibes." Esther nodded in agreement. "You have a big brother, Mei-Ling. You get that, right?"

"I do." I smiled. "I tried to have a crush on Tai so many times growing up, but no. He is my brother."

She chuckled. "Ruined all of our plans."

"Yeah. Though earlier Bettina was complaining that *her* best friend is dating her brother and then torments her by talking about their sexy times." I frowned at my bestie. "I don't think either of us would handle that well."

She snickered. "Fair."

"Now, Everest on the other hand? No brother vibes." Ava fanned herself and whistled. "Like damn."

"That is not helping, Ava." I groaned and tugged on my hair. "I need some kind of spell or potion or something to remove these feelings for Everest so that I have a fair chance of falling for my own soulmate."

Esther pursed her lips. "Generally speaking, spells and potions for love are frowned upon but your Coven gift is potion making, so maybe *you* can make one."

I sighed. "Maybe I'll talk to Tegan. I don't know if she can empathize, but I'd trust her knowledge of magic."

A rush of tense, sharp energy rushed through the trees a split second before Savannah came stomping out of the woods barefoot with jars of dirt. Her blue and white hair was tied up in messy space buns, and there was dirt smeared on her face. Her blue eyes were red and a little bloodshot. Pink symbols flashed above her head for potions I needed to make her, and it reminded me of the Sims game.

Cooper emerged from the forest hot on her heels. "Kiwi."

Savannah gasped and whirled around on him. Black magic was swirling around her hands as she used one of the jars to point at his face. "You don't get to say that to me anymore."

*What is happening here?*

"Savannah, please—"

"No, ma'am. No," she drawled in that thick accent of hers that gave the word *no* at least two syllables. "Not yet. No. Lea'me'lone."

Cooper stopped in his tracks and just watched her stomp up the steps and inside the house. He sighed and rubbed his chest, then frowned and looked around until he spotted me. I should've felt embarrassed that he'd just caught me watching him, but I didn't. So instead I just gave him a small smile and waved.

The girls must've waved behind me because his smile widened and he waved back while shaking his head in amusement. Then he started toward us.

I turned back to the girls. "Be cool. Don't say anything about it. He said we could just be friends for now, so be cool or there will be ramifications."

They nodded just as Cooper walked up to us. "Hello, ladies."

"Hey, Coop!"

"Hi, Cooper!"

"*Salut!*"

"Wanna join us?" I patted the grass beside me.

He sat on the red brick wall that I was leaning against, which was only about a foot and a half tall. "Nice night for a picnic."

"Want some?" Esther held up the plate of cheese slices.

He shook his head. "I don't have much of an appetite right now, but thank you."

"Is everything okay?" I nodded toward the house, knowing he'd know what I was asking. "Are you okay?"

He sighed and I felt the pain in his aura. Pink symbols floated above his head. "She's going through a lot. I'm , , , I'm trying to help, but I think I am making it worse."

"It is not your job to save everyone, Coop," Esther shook her finger in the air. "Or even to protect them."

He smirked. "I don't know. This Mark on my arm says I must protect them—"

"From demons and monsters." Ava threw a stalk of celery at his face. "Not daily emotions."

"*ATTENTION, COVENLINGS, GET YOUR ASSES IN HERE NOW*," Tegan's voice yelled in my mind so loud I jumped.

The girls frowned and looked at me weird.

Cooper just chuckled. "That's Tegan."

I rubbed my temples. "Does she do that a lot?"

"Yes." He smirked. "She can be quite demanding."

"She's calling all of us home?" I eyed the house. "Why?"

Cooper stood and stretched his legs. "Yeah, and . . . I'm afraid of the why as well. But that tone in her voice means something has happened and our Coven Leaders are calling an emergency meeting." He held his hand out to me.

I put my hand in his and let him pull me up to my feet. There were no sparks, no electricity, no desperate desire to kiss him. It took everything in me not to compare him to Everest on every aspect. I cleared my throat and turned to the girls. "Sorry, I have to bounce—"

"Nah, we're used to Coven business." Esther waved me off. "Just text us later."

I started to walk away, then paused. "Can Mei-Ling stay out here with them?"

"Um, yeah, that's probably fine." Cooper pointed to Esther. "Bring her back to the house when y'all are done here?"

Esther gave him a salute.

"Mei-Ling, that okay with you?"

"Are you kidding? I need to get away from Tai for a second, wherever he is."

"Oh, Tai is playing video games with Warner and Lancelot." Cooper smiled. "Tegan may ask you to return sooner, but until then just hang with them."

"I got bestie." Esther gave us a thumbs-up. "You guys better go before Tegan comes looking."

I waved and turned toward the house. For a few seconds we

walked in silence, but then I had to ask what was on my mind before I lost my chance. "Cooper?"

"Yeah?"

"Um . . . am I making things worse . . . for Savannah?"

He let out a gutted sigh. "It's not your fault."

*Ouch. Poor Savannah.* I knew that moment had been more than just friends talking. There was too much pain in their eyes.

*"It's not your fault either, Coop."* I whispered.

He nodded and smiled down at me. *"Neither is Everest your fault."*

"We're one hell of a match."

He snort-laughed. "C'mon, let's see what our chaos demon wants."

We hurried up the steps and through the front door to find the entire Coven already in the living room. My gaze shot straight to Savannah who was sitting curled up in the chair by the window with both of her black cats in her lap while she stared at the flames in the fireplace. I did not miss the fact that Hunter sat on the stone ledge in front of the fireplace. Bentley, Emersyn, and Deacon sat in a row down the line from him. Easton and Lily were in the chair next to Savannah. On the other side of the fireplace, Tennessee was sprawled in the big recliner with his long legs stretched out and Tegan curled in his lap. They were both looking in the Book of Shadows silently, probably talking to each other telepathically.

On the couch to their left, Bettina, Jackson, Royce, and Thiago sat silently with tense expressions like they knew they weren't going to like whatever was about to happen. Across from them on the other sofa were Willow and Chutney sat on either side of Constance with two little blonde girls sound asleep in their laps. A man with tortoise-shell glasses and tired eyes was perched on the back of the sofa behind Constance, running his hand through her hair.

Kessler and Timothy sat at the dining table sharing a bag of chips while their ladies, Mona and Katherine, were reading some other big book. There was another woman I didn't know with black hair and blue eyes standing and looking over their shoulders at the book. She kept reaching over and pointing to something on the page. I liked her vibe, dressed in all-black with a ton of silver jewelry, she looked like she ran a witch shop. A guy with long silver hair walked out of the kitchen with a big glass bowl of what looked like marshmallows, which made me have questions.

Weirdo and Waldo were sprawled on their backs on the fluffy white rug in the middle of the room with all of the house's dogs between them in one giant cuddle puddle. I grinned and shook my head. Bubba, Houdini, and Bobokins seemed to have forgotten I existed since we arrived. They apparently had taken to Olli's mission to cheer Albert up constantly. Squishy's fire tail still made me nervous, but none of the other dogs seemed to care.

No one paid us any attention, which was a relief. Cooper winked down at me, then walked over to sit next to his uncle at the table. I wasn't sure where to go but I took a step forward and Bubba's head snapped in my direction. A white-tipped tail flicked back and forth from within the pile which made all of the others lift their heads to look at me. They almost looked like a hydra, just one giant dog with all different heads. I chuckled and plopped down on the carpet between Lennox and Warner's heads. They nodded in my direction but said nothing.

After a few seconds, the door on the stair wall opened and Bentley hurried out into the room. He glanced around, then nodded. "Good, we're all here."

Deacon whistled so loud I cringed and covered my ears.

Tenn nodded. "Thanks, D. All right we're all here now, so let's focus. Tegan, you called this meeting. Why don't you start us off?"

She looked around the room with pale-green eyes the same exact color of my soulmate's. Except her eyes held a sharpness unlike anyone else's. "Right, so Bentley has something to show us—"

The whole room groaned and cursed.

Royce scrubbed his face with his hands. "Tegan, my heart can't handle it. Just give it to us straight."

"I haven't seen it yet—"

"That's a bloody lie, you little shit."

She rolled her eyes. "You know, a little white lie wasn't gonna hurt them."

Jackson shook his head and laughed.

Bentley cleared his throat. "Brace yourselves—"

Everyone groaned again. I was lost.

Then Bentley pulled the long sleeve of his shirt up to his elbow and my eyes widened. Written in an elegant black scroll beneath the black *V* had to be nearly two dozen lines of words on his skin. They had not been there when I left the house for the picnic.

I raised my hand. "Excuse me, what the shit is that? Why's everyone freaking out?"

"When the Goddess sends us a prophecy or a quest, it appears on my skin like this." He held his arm out to show me. "*This* one is a quest."

Savannah cursed. "Ma'am, can you just skip to the part where you read it out loud for us?"

"That's a long one. The last time we had one that long, some of us wound up in 1692." Royce eyed Bentley's arm like it was going to attack. "I have a very bad feeling about this."

Deacon pointed to him. "That's my line."

Tennessee cursed. "Just read it, Bentley. Give it to us once as a whole, then you and chaos demon can dissect it."

"It's too long. My ears won't listen that long," Warner grumbled.

Tegan wiggled her fingers. "For what I seek is deep and dire, I see my words etched in fire."

All at once the lines written in black on Bentley's arm hovered in the air as little orange embers that sparkled and flickered.

"*Shadows hunger, thirsted calls, Beyond our land in ancient halls. Through the lines in thy wall, Is where the darkness made their fall. To find the answers that you seek, Make thy move like a sneak. But scattered are the tools demanded, So one by one they'll be commanded,*" Bentley read the words out loud. "*For if she hears thy sliding close, His secrets will fly among the crows. Recover his book that tells the tale, To part two worlds on forever's scale. Thy first stop comes with ease, That price was paid in family trees. By hand of magic, strength in deed, Honor's Court can play with speed. Buried deep, lost to the rubble, A Tower's stone calls to trouble.*"

Tennessee let out the most vulgar string of obscenities I'd ever heard.

I snort-laughed.

Deacon cringed. "I do not like that."

"So y'all just usually figure out what these mean?" I pointed to the words floating in the air in little embers. "This isn't gibberish to you?"

Everyone looked to Tegan.

"Feels like mutiny, but okay." She grinned, then jumped to her feet and walked over to stand in front of the spell words. "Does anyone want to weigh in here?"

"Do you not know?" Thiago's eyes were wide.

"It feels too obvious and easy—"

"*WHOA,*" everyone yelled.

"No, that's fair." Bettina snapped her fingers. "The first two lines are about the Unseelie, followed by two lines of them sneaking through the holes in our walls—"

"Not just anywhere." Cooper pointed to the words. "It says *through the lines*, I bet that means on the fey lines. When Tegan fought those Unseelie in Salem, they were on the fey lines."

Everyone nodded.

"So there are holes in the dimensional wall along the fey lines, which is why it's not the same as the Gap. Whatever tools we need to use to close those up have been spread out, probably stolen with time. And she wants us to search for them quietly so we don't alert our enemies, which tells me our enemies will want this same object." Tegan began pacing and tugging on her bottom lip. "The rest is . . ."

"Are we going to Seelie?" Tenn looked to his soulmate. "This sounds like Seelie."

Tegan let out a deep breath and nodded. "It means Seelie."

# CHAPTER FORTY-THREE

## FRANKIE

"WELL, YOU'RE GOING TO SEELIE." Tegan pointed to herself. "*I* cannot."

Tenn paled. "Why not?"

"Babe, you were there last time—"

"But it's not the same now," Tenn said in a rush, jumping to his feet. "Fuckface is dead—"

"It's still Seelie regardless of who runs it—"

"Babe—"

"*Babe.*" She put her hand on his chest. "Seelie may now be connected to Earth, but once inside, it's still *Seelie*. The tunnels alone were too painful for me. I fear full Seelie would take me down."

He groaned and scrubbed his face with his hands. For the first time I noticed he wore silver rings on both hands. I wasn't sure how I'd missed that. The gold bands on his arm flashed like they wanted attention.

"It's safe there now, Babe. And it's as safe as possible here." Tegan gently pulled his arms down, then tapped one finger on his forehead. "I'll stay right here in Eden, and you can relay everything happening."

"*Fine,*" he growled but it did not sound fine to him at all.

Tegan smirked and turned to everyone else. "It says, *thy first stop comes with ease,* so I don't expect any problems. Y'all just get in there and find this book."

"Yeah, no big deal. Totally." I shook my head. "Who is going and where?"

"Into Seelie."

"Yeah, y'all keep saying that as if I'm supposed to know—"

"Oh. Right." Tegan grimaced. "So, there are two types of fae: Seelie and Unseelie. They have their own realms separate from ours, but in February we were forced to merge Seelie with Earth. It's very complicated to explain."

Bentley cracked his knuckles. "We concealed the opening into Seelie for safety reasons, but it is right here in Eden."

"Out front, to be exact," Thiago mumbled.

Everyone grumbled.

"Oh." I nodded. "Okay. So you know how to get there? And where to go once we're inside?"

"I lived in Seelie for seven years," Bentley said with a rough voice. "I know Seelie. More importantly, we are now allies with what's left of Seelie. One of our own is the Seelie Princess—"

"Our cousin, actually." Tenn frowned. "Wait, was it cousin? Uncle Kenneth?"

The man with long silver hair looked up from his bowl of marshmallows and smirked. "The three centuries between Cyrus and me does muddy the water on what to call each other, doesn't it?"

I held my hand up. "Wait, you're a Proctor too?"

He smiled at me. "Kenneth Proctor. Descended from Myrtle Proctor and her son, Cyrus. My nephew was Micah Proctor, Haven and Hope's father."

"Obviously I know you're our uncle. I meant what do we call Saffie?"

Bettina sighed. "Can we just call her Saffie? Like I think the three centuries nullify the need for a family title?"

"You've been around my family too much." Jackson shook his head. "*Nullify.*"

Kenneth frowned like he had to think about it. "I also think Saffie would prefer to just be Saffie. Any other name just makes her sad, for obvious reasons."

Everyone nodded.

"I need to make some family trees," Savannah said suddenly. "All y'all are getting hard to follow, especially when you throw in angels and reincarnation."

I opened my mouth to ask questions, then sighed. "You know what? No. I don't want to know that yet. I just know I'm a Proctor, but my aunt and uncle always said I didn't have family left besides us three—"

"That is because your magic crawled into the dark crevices of your soul and refused to come back out." Kenneth smiled sadly at me. "The loss of your parents was a blow, but they weren't exactly lying. The extent of our family lies in this room, and in Seelie, but you could not know that while you thought yourself human. The fragility of the mind required total separation."

Jackson chuckled. "I nullify my previous comment. You've just been with your family too much."

Kenneth and Bettina grinned.

Tenn pinched the bridge of his nose. "For the fragility of *my* mind, let's nullify the other options and just say we're cousins, 'kay, Franks?"

"You got it, boss."

"What about her other question? The *who* is going?" Easton pointed to the words still floating in the air. "Nothing in there about who. You gonna read the tarot?"

Bentley stared at the ground.

Everyone groaned.

I looked around. "What? He didn't say anything?"

"The Goddess, also known as Valathame—*that's her name*—talks to Bentley," Warner said from the ground right beside me with his eyes closed. "That's the role of the Hierophant. He talks to Her. So sometimes She gives out these riddles for them to solve but then slides a little note for the B-man on the side."

Everyone pointed to Warner and nodded.

I chuckled. "This group is quite entertaining, I gotta say."

"Glad you think that since you didn't take my warning and get out before a soulmate trapped you here." Deacon grinned. "But alas, you're stuck with hothead over there."

We all glanced to Cooper, who I never would have labeled as a hothead. Cooper just nodded as he grabbed a giant marshmallow out of Kenneth's bowl, licked the bottom, then chucked it right at Deacon. It slammed into D's forehead with a *thud*. And stuck there.

Everyone laughed.

"Sure, but *I'm* the chaos demon." Tegan crossed her arms over her chest.

Tenn grinned.

Timothy cleared his throat and stood up. "Right, so Coven Leaders or Bentley, who is going on this first part of our quest to Seelie to find the book?"

Tegan and Tenn both looked to Bentley.

He shrugged. "Look, this quest is going to get ugly. But this step isn't, so whoever wants to go can go. If you wanna see what Seelie looks like, then this is a good chance to do so. If you wanna sit this one out, then stay."

"Except for me and Tegan," I said and then everyone's gazes snapped to me. "Because she cannot go, and I have to go."

Bentley and Tegan smiled, so they saw what I did. Tenn looked to his sister who was gesturing to me with a nod.

Chutney raised her hand. "Why do you have to go, Frankie?"

"It says Tower in the last line. It's capitalized, so it's referring to a person."

"*Ohhh,*" most of the group said under their breath.

Lily stood up. "Well, I'm going. I think my PTSD needs some closure."

"Same," Willow and Savannah said at the same time and stood.

"Right, so if you are going to Seelie, please line up at the door." Tegan gestured to the front door. "I'd rather not have any civilians watching all y'all march up to the gate thinking they can do the same to get in. While it may be safe there, we don't want to open the doors. So, I'll portal y'all to the gate, then you can go in."

Lily, Easton, Savannah, Willow, Chutney, and Royce all jumped up and hurried to the door. Timothy and Kessler exchanged glances, then slowly stood and headed over. Hunter stopped at the door to the stairs, then nodded to his children before going down to his wife.

Constance shook her head. "For obvious reasons, I'm going to stay."

"Thiago?" Royce cleared his throat. "You don't want to see?"

He opened his mouth, then closed it. Then cursed. "You know what? Life is short. Let's go."

I pet all the dogs, then got up and walked over to the door with the others. As soon as I stopped and turned back, I found Cooper right behind me. He gave me a small smile and a nod, so I smiled in return. Bentley strolled over to the front of our line to lean against the door.

"You know what? I think I'll stay." Emersyn pointed to us. "Go on, D. We both know you want to. Just don't die."

He grinned and then kissed her forehead before rushing over to stand with us. "If I die, she's gonna kill all y'all."

The others laughed.

"Babe, *go*." Tegan pushed at him. "You too, bestie."

Bettina jumped up and wrapped her arm around her brother's, then dragged him over to the line with us. She looked over her shoulder. "Lancelot, the fuck are you doing still sitting there?"

He sighed. "Fine."

Once Jackson was standing with us, Tegan held her hand up. "Go get that book." She snapped her fingers.

Bentley opened the door and Tegan's white portal box was all we could see. He nodded. "Follow me."

All at once, we turned and followed Bentley into that white unknown. It was as fast as a blink of the eye. When the light faded, we stood just before a wooden gate—like an actual gate. But that wasn't the part that surprised me. Two massive trees bordered a circular opening made of stones stacked carefully. The forest stretched out from both sides of the trees. Within the stone circle, a wooden gate blocked a faint, glowing blue light that peeked around the edges.

Bentley waved his hand and spoke in a language I didn't know. Orange lightning bolts streaked across his arm. The wooden gate slid into the stones, vanishing from sight. That blue glow washed over Bentley and seeped onto us. It was a spectacular turquoise and blue combination that I'd only ever seen in the ocean. Bentley nodded and waved for everyone to follow him through the stone circle and into the light.

"Frankie—"

I cursed and about jumped out of my skin.

Tegan chuckled. "Sorry."

"Dammit, woman." I pushed my hair back and turned to face her. "I thought you weren't going?"

"I'm not." She held up a bracelet. "You need this."

Before I could ask a single question, she grabbed my wrist and wrapped the bracelet around it. Her magic flashed against my skin, fastening the clasp with ease. I frowned. It was made of two rows of white crystals all the way around.

"Babe?"

"I just forgot something—"

He reached out and grabbed her by the back of her neck, then dragged her mouth up to his. I hadn't intended to watch them kiss, but the passion between them just came out of nowhere. I looked away only to have my eyes meet Cooper's. My heart sank. He stood ten feet ahead by the stone circle waiting for me. He glanced to his sister, still locked in her embrace with my cousin, then he rolled his eyes.

"Okay, that's enough. Damn." Cooper shook his head. He held his hand out to me. "C'mon, Frankie."

*Frankie, not Francelina.*

*Shut up, brain. You told everyone to call you Frankie. Don't be upset when he listens.*

Everest was the only one who ever ignored my request, so hearing my full name just made me think of him. But apparently hearing Cooper call me by my nickname also made me think of Everest. It was super helpful. I shook those thoughts away and placed my hand in my soulmate's, letting him pull me up to the open gate.

"Seriously, are we gonna have to start all over with the honeymoon phase?" Cooper sighed, but his gaze was locked above my head. "You were gone like two weeks. Max. We're starting all over with the face-sucking all the time?"

Tenn stopped beside us just before the opening into Seelie. "I saw your dead body, Coop. I had to watch Savannah and Riah fight to bring you back to life. You're gonna have to suffer through watching me live mine to the fullest every second I get." Then he smiled and leapt backwards into the light.

I looked up to Cooper. "You died?"

"And I'm never going to hear the end of it," he said with a sigh.

"You don't like PDA, do you?"

He gestured to where they'd been kissing. "It's PDF with them far too often. Like, just close the door. She can portal anywhere. Just snap your fingers and bring yourselves to privacy."

Braison had told me about their PDF too, but I wasn't going to bring that up. Instead, I just chuckled and tugged on his hand. "Come on. Let's not keep them waiting."

Together, we stepped into the glowing light and cold air washed over me. But the moment the light faded, warmth wrapped around me like I'd gone back home to Florida. Cooper looked around and whistled under his breath. I nodded. The rest of The Coven was standing a little ways ahead of us, also looking around at the fantasy we'd just stepped into.

Just through the gate there was a lush meadow full of gorgeous plants and flowers of every color imaginable. Colors that I'd never seen on Earth. They were almost neon and glowing. The meadow was wide, giving plenty of space to walk around and get situated. At the edge of the meadow sat a large bay that glistened like starlight. It was evening in Seelie, so the waters were a silver color, but I couldn't help wondering what color the sun made it. The silver of the water at night was like liquid moonlight. I was mesmerized by it. The meadow stretched out to the left, then dipped into a forest that even from here looked equally as magical as the meadow.

The trees to the left of the gate rustled and swayed and shadows filled the space between them. But then a massive black dragon emerged from the dark with glowing red eyes. My jaw dropped. I backed away several feet, pulling Cooper with me.

"LONAN!" Chutney squealed and raced over to him to give him a hug. "What are you doing over here?"

The black dragon gently lowered into the lush turquoise grass. He blinked his red eyes slowly, then huffed and little flames burst from his nostrils.

"Oh, he lets you guard the gate, eh?" Chutney giggled. "Are you healing well?"

He grumbled.

Her face fell. "Well, maybe you need to actually behave and do as they say?"

He snorted.

"Boys." She rolled her eyes. "You know they'd let you stay if you wanted to. You don't have to stall your injuries."

The dragon narrowed his eyes, then turned to Tenn.

"I don't see why that *wouldn't* be true." Tenn smiled. "It's nice to see you, Lonan. It'd be better to see you healed."

Savannah walked right up to him and pointed her finger at the Death Mark on her arm. "Don't make me put you on blast, you hear?"

"She makes a good point." Deacon cleared his throat. "You're gonna need your strength for what you want."

The dragon named Lonan huffed and sank into the grass like a puppy pouting.

"Of course I'm gonna agree with them!" Chutney threw her hands up. "It makes no sense just to allow yourself to remain injured to avoid going back to the Old Lands—"

"Lonan." Tenn stepped up in front of him. "I promise I will not force you back to the Old Lands. Please, heal. Then we'll help you. Okay?"

Lonan let out a big sigh, then pushed up off the grass and spun around. He vanished into the shadows as fast as he appeared. Tenn just shook his head. Savannah and Deacon turned to Bentley.

"He's just scared," Chutney said softly. "Whatever caused his banishment has really messed with him."

Tenn wrapped his arm around Chutney's shoulders. "And we'll help him any way we can. I mean, we're good friends with the others now. We just are waiting for Bentley to give us the green light."

"I know that feeling well."

We all jumped and turned toward the sound of a feminine voice. The others all relaxed and smiled at her. She was a pretty little thing with warm hazel eyes and hair like liquid gold. The chains of diamonds wrapped around her body really sparkled against her dark skin. Her clothes left little to the imagination and looked exactly like image results I would've gotten on Pinterest had I searched the word *fae princess*.

"Ziva," Bentley whispered her name on a sigh.

"It's about time you returned." She put her hands on her hips and arched one eyebrow.

He chuckled and pulled her in for a hug. They held on tight to each other for a long moment before stepping back. Then she went around to the others, giving them hugs.

"I like your hair this gold color," Willow said softly with a blush on her cheeks.

"Thank you, Willow." Ziva's smile widened. Then she looked around and frowned. "Where's Squishy?"

"In a cuddle puddle on the living room floor," I said with a laugh. When she looked to me, I waved. "Hi, I'm Frankie."

She shook my hand. "Ziva. Nice to meet you. Welcome to Seelie, the new and improved Seelie."

Water rippled on the bay and then at least a dozen heads popped up through the water. One after another, the women pushed up on rocks and small boulders at the edge of the shore and flicked their tails out of the water. My eyes widened. *Tails. They have tails. Oh my God. Mermaids. Those are real-life mermaids.* In the blink of an eye, the bay was full of them.

They had bright sparkling eyes and long hair that fell in waves to their hips. The scales on their tails looked like liquid metal. They were a shade darker than the water itself, and I wondered if that was some evolutionary trait for a reason. They waved and batted their eyelashes at Bentley.

He cleared his throat and turned to us. "Go ahead, find them. Find the book. I need to . . . handle something."

Tenn pursed his lips and nodded. "Sure thing, dude."

Cooper scowled and watched his little brother turn away and walk into the water in the middle of all the mermaids with Ziva right on his heels.

"Come on, guys, we need to find them so we can find the book." Tenn marched away from the bay and onto a trail that led up the middle of the meadow.

Though, after seeing *this* meadow, I'd never look at another one the same way. The forest all around it had these little golden twinkling lights that were almost like swarms of fireflies. The flowers themselves were completely foreign to me. Some were close to Earth's roses and tulips and such but in neon colors with dots. The meadow was wild in its growth. The bushes weren't in any kind of order. It was like they were planted and set free to grow as they pleased. A narrow stone pathway cut through the middle of wildflowers.

I looked up and did a double take. Up ahead there was a massive tree, some kind of mix between a weeping willow and banyan tree. I'd never seen a tree that big in my life. Its huge branches stretched out to create a serene little canopy beneath its leaves. Little lanterns dangled from chains on the long branches. At the base of the tree, beneath a canopy of roses and vines, was a round bed. It had white blankets and white drapes covering the sides. It was straight out of a fairytale.

Then I saw the people.

A beautiful woman with long black hair was draped over the bare chest of a man with long, vibrant red hair. She was propped up on her elbows, her thin fingers tracing his skin. He curled her hair around his fingers. Little flickering golden orbs danced all around them as they seemed to be lost in each other's eyes.

Tenn choked on a gasp. *"Grandmother?"*

The woman lifted her head from the man's chest and grinned. "Grandson!"

*Grandson? What? HOW?* The woman rushing toward Tennessee didn't look much older than me, so I wasn't sure how she was his grandmother. Sure, I now knew immortal beings existed, but Tenn wasn't one of them. His grandfather may have been an angel, but I thought the rest of his family was very, very mortal. Yet those were the words they'd said.

*Wait a second. Tenn's family is MY family. Or at least part of it.* I pushed through my Coven-mates who'd all frozen in their tracks to gawk at the woman. I needed to see her better. When I did, my confusion deepened. The woman all but tackled Tennessee in a hug that he returned without hesitation. So far, they looked alike, but that was only going by the long black hair and tan skin.

When she pulled back, she looked up at him with silver eyes that sparkled. She reached up and cupped his cheek, and that was when I saw the gold, glowing lines on her face and all the way down her right arm. *"Haven.* Where is your sister?"

"I'm here," Bettina said as she pushed through to her. "Sorry, I was a little distracted by the way you look."

She blushed and looked down at herself. She wore strips of silky white material bound together by shiny silver rope of some kind. In the center of her chest, in the same spot as mine was, she had a heart-shaped crystal that shined a bright aquamarine color. Golden, swirly lines spread across her right shoulder and down her arm to where it covered each of her fingers. A silver diadem sat across the middle of her forehead.

"My little Hope, I am also now constantly distracted by the way I look." She chuckled and stepped back, then turned her attention to the rest of us. "Ah, my darling Coven. How fare thee this night?"

"Who *are* you?" I heard myself whisper.

Her silver eyes shot right to me, then widened. "Francelina Proctor. *Finally.*"

Before I knew it, I was in her arms. It was the warmest, cuddliest hug I'd ever gotten. I found myself wishing she wouldn't let go. When she eventually did, those silver eyes seemed to peer right into my soul. I wanted to sit and talk to her forever. I didn't even know who she was.

"Daughter of mine." She reached up and smoothed my hair back. "I am Myrtle Proctor. We share the same blood."

My eyes burned like they wanted to cry. I'd known she was related to me. Yet *she* knew without asking. I cleared my throat. "How did you know who I was?"

She smiled, then with one hand, tapped on the silver diadem on her forehead. "I am the Lead Crone. It is my job to know things . . . and I have been watching you since the day you were born. I cannot tell you how happy I am to see you finally back where you belong."

A hot lump of emotion formed in my throat. "You . . . you knew my parents?"

"Wonderful people, even if I am a little biased." She winked to me. "Now, I suspect I know why you are here, but perhaps you'd like to tell us?"

Tenn leaned around her and cleared his throat. "Thorne?"

The man with the long red hair, who was still lying in bed where Myrtle left him, sighed dramatically. "I am busy."

Light flashed in front of my face. I gasped and threw my hands up —and felt my magic rush out of me. My neon-blue flames shot across the meadow straight for the bed Thorne was lying in. When my magic rolled across his bare stomach, his eyes flew open. He threw his hand up and caught my flames around his fingers.

Eyes like hot embers met mine in an instant. He smirked. "Well, this is interesting."

# CHAPTER FORTY-FOUR

## FRANKIE

YOU'VE SAID *that to me before.* The moment his eyes met mine, I knew I'd seen this man before. I saw the memory vividly in my mind. He had long, wild red hair with metallic beads wrapped around some of the strands. His glowing orange eyes had an energy that felt like pure wildness. I remembered the sharp jawline and cheekbones . . . and the pointed ears. He wore the same crown made of tree branches with dark-pink flowers on it and strings of turquoise leaves and glowing twinkle lights. Only his outfit was different, but seeing as he wore no shirt or shoes, all I had to go on was the olive-green pair of pants that cut off above the knee.

*I know you.*

*And you know that.*

"What is interesting?" a female voice said from *right* behind me, so close I felt her breath on my neck.

I gasped and spun around, and my magic shot right at her. "Sorry—"

"That's fun." She giggled and caught my blue flames just like he had. "I like the way it tingles a bit."

My pulse quickened. It was *her,* the same woman from my vision that first night in the infirmary. There was no forgetting their faces, not as beautiful as they were, but there was something particularly mesmerizing about *her.* Yet again, I could only stare. She still had wild hair that varied in shades of blue, purple, and turquoise. Her skin was still lusciously tan. Her eyes met mine, and I heard myself gasp. Again. They were unlike anything I'd ever seen. Her eyes held a galaxy of colors that glittered just like the Milky Way. Her outfit was basically giant green leaves that covered her lady bits that were connected by flowered vines, which were strapped all around her torso, chest, and limbs.

"Francelina, I'd like you to meet the new rulers of Seelie." Myrtle gestured to the intoxicating woman. "This is Princess Sage."

*SAGE. Dammit. I knew that. I knew that name.*

*What is happening?*

"And this is Prince Thorne, my soulmate." Her voice had softened when she said his name.

A massive wolf lunged from behind that bed. It was blacker than night itself and seemed to be made of smoke and shadow. My heart stopped. I knew that dog. It wasn't a wolf at all. I'd seen it. Its paws and tail weren't solid in form. That wasn't something a person forgot. Nor were the creepy eyes. One was glowing gold, the other sparkling red. *I know you!*

"*You're Spot,*" I whispered. Those mismatched eyes snapped right to me. His tail of smoke swished back and forth. He lunged for me, melting into a puddle of shadow and smoke at my feet. But when I reached down, I found his body to be solid and furry like a normal dog. I was so confused. "What the hell is happening here, Spot? Can you explain it?" I said to the dog as I rubbed his spooky smoky ears.

"Spooky Clifford!" Savannah yelled in a high-pitched voice that only an animal lover could make.

Spot's face snapped in every direction until he spotted Savannah. When he did, he let out a little howl and then vanished into thin air— reappearing *on top* of Savannah and pinning her to the ground. Everyone moved toward her, but she threw her hands up.

"If this the hill I'm gon' die on, then I'm gon' die on it," she yelled. "Lea'me'lone!"

We all chuckled. Cooper closed his eyes and shook his head.

Thorne looked around our group. "My, my, so many of you. Hold on." He flicked his wrist.

Vines shot up from the ground and swirled together until they formed not one, but two, grand-looking thrones. Thorne and Sage sat immediately.

"Thorne—"

"Give it a second, my love," he said with a wicked sparkle in his eyes.

Sage rolled her purple eyes. "Must we always humor you?"

Thorne arched one fiery eyebrow at her. "The kraken? The giant paralyzing snail you told Henry about—"

"Really, brother, shall we list *your* track record?"

Jackson raised his hand. "Wait a bloody minute! That wanker of a snail was *your* idea?"

"I KNEW IT!" a girl yelled from above us.

By the time I looked up, I spotted a girl with hair an even brighter-red than Thorne's floating down to us on wings that seemed to be made of stars. She was a tiny little thing with huge lavender eyes and a wide grin. Like Myrtle, she had gold lines on her face, and the lines of her soulmate mark were also gold instead of black. The crystal on her chest and hand were aquamarine. I was fairly certain Madge explained that color to mean old love, which I did not understand for this girl who definitely looked my age.

"SAFFIE!" everyone in my group yelled in chorus.

She landed with a squeal and a clap of her hands. "YOU'RE HERE!"

And then they tackled her. I couldn't see her, but I heard her giggles. My pulse quickened. I recognized her too. In my vision, she'd called Thorne her father. I closed my eyes. *This is fine. Everything is cool. You know more now than you did that night. You know Everest and his tricks. You know that vision wasn't just a dream.*

"Francelina?"

I jumped and opened my eyes to find the petite redhead right in front of me. I blinked. "You're Saraphina, his daughter?" I pointed to Thorne.

She grinned. "Yes, and Myrtle is my mother. You can call me Saffie."

I exhaled in a rush. "This is too much."

"Spot, for the love of all that is holy, you're a damned *hellhound* not a golden retriever. Get off of Savannah's face."

My stomach tightened into knots. I knew that voice. I wasn't even surprised to be hearing it since the others were here. Yet still, seeing the two gorgeous blond guys from the vision tipped my sanity toward the edge.

"Francelina?"

"Frankie," I whispered back automatically. "They're . . . you're . . . you have all the names—"

"That is true. We do have many names." The guy with the long hair smiled, his golden eyes sparkling. "I am Riah *and* Zabkiel—"

"Your hair was blond? Now it's white?"

"Ah, I see." Riah walked over and pressed his palm to my forehead. Silver mist swirled around me and then my thoughts became lighter and smoother. "Is that better?"

I licked my lips and nodded. "Yes? Thank you?"

"My hair is whiter when I am in Seelie," he answered, which I was impressed he remembered. "And this is my brother, Malachi, or Raziel."

The other one walked up, the one with the short hair but the same gold eyes. He gave me a small smile. "You shouldn't be here, *lita toah*."

That did it. My patience snapped. I pointed to Riah. "That was HIS line."

Malachi chuckled. "Teamwork makes the dreamwork, *lita toah*—"

"What does that mean?" I shouted and pushed my hair back. "*Lita toah*. That's what you called me. What does it mean?"

Riah pursed his lips. "Perhaps you dreamed that part?"

I crossed my arms over my chest. "Perhaps you're gaslighting me in an attempt to not answer me."

Malachi threw his head back and cackled. When his brother looked to him, he lost it even more, bending over to rest his hands on his knees.

Riah looked to me and blinked. "I've never been accused of gaslighting before. It feels weird—"

"Oh, THAT feels weird?" I gestured to each of the people I'd seen before. "You were all in my dream, and I want to know why. Or, *vision*, whatever you wanna call it. How were you in my head?"

"We weren't," Riah said softly.

"Excuse you—"

"Okay, okay. Riah, may I?" Thorne gestured to me. "I can see she has rattled your poor, innocent little golden heart with the gaslighting comment, so let someone whose heart is colder handle this?"

"I wasn't gaslighting—"

"Intentionally." Malachi walked over and gripped his brother's shoulder. "What Thorne means to say is, perhaps let someone less inclined to follow the rules handle this?"

Sage snickered.

Saffie shrugged up at him. "He has a point?"

Riah threw his hands up. "Where's Tegan? She'd understand this mutiny."

Tenn snort-laughed.

I narrowed my eyes on Thorne. "Well? Someone start talking."

Thorne cocked his head to the side like a confused puppy. "What did Everest say about it?"

I gasped. My eyes widened. "I never said Everest was there. How did you know—"

"Because *we* were there, darling." Thorne crossed one knee over the other and leaned back in his throne made of vines. "That was no dream or vision. We were all there that night in the park."

"What? No. How?" I turned to my friends but none of them had been there except for Tenn, who'd been around the next day and after. "*Archie?*"

He grimaced. "Some of what you were experiencing were dreams of some sort. That is not a lie. Whether they were clairvoyant dreams as Esther thinks or just dreams, I don't know. But that night . . . that was different—"

"They said I was lucid dreaming!"

"You are capable of doing such," Malachi said with a chuckle. "Ten out of ten do not recommend though."

"I don't know. Sometimes it's fun." Deacon shrugged.

Cooper chuckled softly. "I would have to concur with the *father of the year* over there and *not* Deacon."

I frowned and looked to Thorne.

He gasped like I'd offended him. "He was not referring to me."

"Yeah, don't throw rocks in a glass house, Father." Saffie winked to him.

Riah threw his head back and laughed. "That is the gift that keeps on giving, my brother."

Malachi crossed his arms over his chest and scoffed. "Whatever, you're welcome. You'd all still be in 1692—"

"I'm never going to live *that* down," Thorne said with a grimace.

Tenn, Cooper, Deacon, and Royce all pointed to him with warnings in their eyes.

"Seeing as it nearly killed me, I would say not." Deacon wrapped his arm around Myrtle's shoulders. "Your soulmate and your daughter, on the other hand, get all the credit for spending three centuries fixing your shit."

"This is fun." Sage leaned back and grinned. "You should come visit more often."

"CAN WE FOCUS?" I groaned. "I'm at my wit's end here."

"You were astral projecting, my dear Francelina," Thorne said gently. "So, you weren't fully there, but you were there."

My face fell. I had no idea what to say to that. I just shook my head. There were too many questions.

Riah turned his golden eyes to me. "That is what I meant by *you shouldn't be here*, because astral projection is too dangerous for the untrained."

"Right, darkling?" Malachi arched one eyebrow in Savannah's direction.

"Ma'am, this ain't 'bout me."

He shrugged. "You need to be careful."

"Look, I Googled *who gives a shit* and my name didn't pop up in the results." She gestured to herself. "I'm new here, ma'am. Pick on the regulars."

"Speaking of . . ." Jackson cleared his throat. "Where's Chloe?"

Malachi was still shaking his head and laughing at Savannah. "Your sister is investigating the hall of doors at Oxford with your father and Millie-Anne. Your mother and Cassandra are with them."

"So . . . uh . . ." Lily looked around. "Where is your mother?"

"Out looking for her sisters with my ex-girlfriend."

Myrtle gave Thorne the side-eye. "Who happens to be your mother's soulmate."

"See, this is why I said I need to make some family trees," Savannah grumbled.

"I'm with Savannah, *this ain't 'bout me*." Thorne grinned and drew a halo over his head. "All my schemes are acted out."

"Which is how you forgot to release those spirits you stationed in Hidden Kingdom to protect your daughter." Sage stared at him.

Thorne sighed. "Fine, that one might be on me."

I cursed. "This is like wrangling five-year-olds. What's the deal with this astral projection that I did without knowing I could do it?"

Myrtle walked over and squeezed my shoulders. "Devon Bishop would be the one to talk to about it, that is her specialty, but she is not yet conscious. However, you *and* Savannah could get some help from the dreamwalker behind you. And if Cooper is not comfortable with that, Tegan fears nothing. Have her look in the Book of Shadows."

I nodded.

"And when you're ready, come to me on Crone Island and I will help you." She tucked my hair behind my ears, and it was such a maternal, loving gesture that I almost cried. "These four are angels, bound by the laws of Heaven on what they are, and are not, permitted to reveal to you. They are just too old to remember empathy for the anxiety of a mortal mind."

"Oh." I frowned. "They're not just being asshats?"

"They are, for sure, but not without reason. Luckily, *I* am mortal and arcana, so I am not bound by the same bindings." She smiled. "I'm sure by now Haven has informed Tegan that you will be asking for her assistance, and she is already looking for answers for you. In this Coven, you just have to ask, and help will be there."

I glanced around to my Coven-mates and found nothing but warm, encouraging smiles. Tenn nodded. I smiled, then looked back to this relative of mine. "Thank you, Myrtle."

"Thank you, my love," Thorne beamed down at her. But then he turned his gaze back to us and all the joking vanished in his eyes. "Now, I suspect you are here on Coven business, or you would not have brought everyone without warning."

"Well, you never did have that ball we discussed."

"Sage, please." His face turned sharp. "When Sweyn is dead, I shall celebrate. Not a day sooner."

"Well, at least we can agree on that." I wrapped my arms around my waist.

Tennessee nodded. "You're right. We are here on Coven business. It's about the Unseelie."

Thorne, Sage, Malachi, Riah, and Saffie all snarled.

Tenn smirked. "I do not disagree, but I do believe we've got our hands full with this one, and we do not know as much as we need to know to destroy them."

Saffie twirled her long red hair around her fingers. "Aunt Sage did say they were going to be your next battle."

When Tenn turned wide eyes to her, she just shrugged. "Don't blame me for praying we'd have more time. We've all been looking for answers to the same questions."

"Yes, but you lured Tegan to a squadron of them in Salem before Samhain."

"I did not think crazy pants would follow me *alone*." Sage rolled her eyes. "You were all with her. But I digress, I merely saw they came through, and because we had not yet revealed our true allegiance, I was not at liberty to vocalize. So, I had to make it look like a trap."

Tenn nodded. "Fair. What else can you tell us about your counterparts?"

"Well . . ." Saffie took a deep breath. "Unseelies have black eyes and purple blood. They CAN come out in the sunlight but only if they are on the fey lines and only for a few minutes. Otherwise, it kills them as it does vampires. They wear fake hair with their helmets to make themselves look Seelie."

Thorne nodded. His gaze was sharp and pensive. "Do not use all your tricks at the same time. They will learn how to protect themselves from it by the time you next see them."

Riah looked to Tenn. "Meaning your glorious work drowning them will no longer be a strategy you should hope to use again. You will now never be able to drown them. I assure you that."

"Survival is their main skill," Sage added. She gripped the armrests of her throne like she wished she was fighting something. "They will always evolve."

Malachi scratched his jaw, then his eyes turned to me. "Oh, and that mostly only worked because Everest put holy water in those potions Frankie made."

Myrtle shook her head. "*Malachi.*"

He shrugged.

"*That's* what that was?" I rubbed my temples as I saw that memory with new light.

Myrtle frowned at nothing, then refocused on Tenn. "Haven, was there a new prophecy given? Is that why you're here?"

"Bentley did come through with you before abandoning you." Thorne looked to Sage. "Did you—"

"Yes, I did. Bentley knows what he's doing."

"Right, so, Valathame sent us a quest. We know it's referring to the Unseelie and how they've been getting through the holes in the fey lines." Tenn glanced around to us. "We also know we're going to be collecting tools, but we have to do so secretly so Sweyn does not beat us to them."

"That is a crucial part of this quest," Sage said with a snarl.

"As is the part you're not telling us," Bentley said as he stepped out from behind some trees. He walked over and held his arm out so they could see the lines of the prophecy. *"Recover his book that tells the tale, to part two worlds on forever's scale."*

Thorne grimaced. "Seelie and Unseelie used to be one. A long, long time ago—before Sage and I were born—our father managed to win the civil war between our kinds and locked them out of Seelie. Permanently."

"Well, apparently there's a book that'll tell us how to do this, and it should be here."

Thorne frowned at me. "Here? Are you sure?"

"Brother, *Thy first stop comes with ease, That price was paid in family trees*—that's definitely us." Sage tapped on her chin as she thought. *"By hand of magic, strength in deed, Honor's Court can play with speed* . . . This suggests that this book is something we can use our magic to retrieve quickly."

"But where is it? What were the final lines?" Thorne snapped his fingers in Bentley's direction. "Your arm?"

*"Buried deep, lost to the rubble,"* Myrtle read softly. *"A Tower's stone calls to trouble.* Daughter of mine, what might you know about a stone?"

My eyes widened. "You know."

She grinned. "I am Lead Crone."

"And like four hundred years old."

"Yes." She shrugged. "And the Irit family is special, so I have been aware of this treasure for centuries."

"So you know for real." I scrubbed my face with my hands.

"This is why I said to come to Crone Island so I can help you. Seelie is not a place for the magic you're using." Myrtle glanced to the angels, and when they all nodded, she looked back to me. "Those are an angel's tool."

"Well, they're how I did the astral projection. I was just holding them in my hands when suddenly they were flashing and stuff—then I was there." I pointed to the long-haired angel. "Riah told me not to use them until I spoke with Tegan, and I haven't had a chance yet."

"*Buried deep, lost to the rubble,* suggests this book was here and buried in the destruction that was Seelie before father died." Thorne pursed his lips and glanced around. "Though the use of the word *rubble* would suggest the palace ruins."

The others nodded.

"*A Tower's stone calls to trouble,*" Bettina whispered. She'd been quiet this whole time but now she turned to me. "Calls to trouble. I think your rune stones may act as a magical beacon to where this book is now hidden."

"Like George," Tenn said softly, his eyes distant.

My jaw dropped. "Oh. *Oh.* Shit. I don't have them, they're back in my room—"

"Your hand." Tenn held his wrist up and pointed to it. He shrugged. "Tegan."

*Tegan? OH!* I lifted my wrist to look at the bracelet she'd put on my wrist. When I reached up to unhook the clasp, the stones flashed that neon-blue I recognized so well. Golden, glittery symbols appeared in the middle of each stone. Tegan had realized we'd need these and then found a way to give them to me discreetly.

"Incredible." I frowned. "But wait, will this affect how I use them? Was it safe to transform them like this?

"Tegan would not have transformed them if it altered their state in any way." Myrtle gave me a reassuring smile. "But carrying them around in that velvet bag is inconvenient and cumbersome, so she gave you a way to always have them."

"She's so convenient." Malachi chuckled.

"Which is why we ignore the chaos demon side of her," Cooper said with a chuckle. He turned to me. "Go ahead. Use them."

My gaze shot right to Riah because he'd told me not to use them until I spoke with Tegan. "Is that safe?"

He inclined his head. "We will not allow harm to fall upon our home or our friends."

"That means yes." Malachi rolled his eyes. "Have at it, kid."

I nodded and looked to my bracelet. My pulse quickened, and my chest grew tight. Knots formed in my stomach. They were all watching. This was super important. And I had no idea what I was doing. In the few times I'd used my rune stones, I'd been holding them in my hands and they just acted without me provoking them. Or at least without me realizing I'd provoked them. But as I stared at them . . . nothing happened.

"Frankie?"

"I'm trying. I just . . . I've never intentionally used them like this."

"She's also new here, y'all," Savannah grumbled.

Riah sighed. "We are not supposed to help."

"*Use your magic*," Saffie whispered.

Myrtle nodded. "And your intention."

My magic and intention. Right. That helped. *Not.* I bit my bottom lip and stared at them. *Okay, stones. Show me the book? Go get it— they're not a dog, Frankie.*

"*Meh, fuck it,*" Malachi said under his breath and then he was right beside me. He reached out and took my right hand in his, then forced my hand to wrap around the bracelet. When I looked up into his golden eyes, he nodded and gave me a wink. "Close your eyes. Think about what we need. Recite the last lines of the prophecy if that helps you focus your intentions. Then push your magic into the stones. You should feel it happen. When you do, open your eyes. Okay?"

I nodded.

"*I'm telling Chloe,*" Jackson whispered with a chuckle.

"It's best if she gets used to me quickly." Malachi shrugged. Then he looked down to me and lifted his hand off mine. His golden eyes were calm and steady, like the moonlight reflecting off the flat ocean's surface. "At one point or another, we were all new at this, so no one is judging. Just breathe and let it rip."

"Yeah, like batting demon gnats in the school gym." Tenn grinned.

"Okay. I've got this." I took a deep breath, then closed my eyes as Malachi instructed.

He'd said to think about what I needed, and reciting the prophecy would help me focus, so that was what I did. *Buried deep, lost to the rubble, A Tower's stone calls to trouble. Buried deep, lost to the rubble,*

*A Tower's stone calls to trouble. Buried deep, lost to the rubble, A Tower's stone calls to trouble.* The stones warmed beneath my touch. Excitement tingled through my veins. *Recover his book that tells the tale, To part two worlds on forever's scale. Buried deep, lost to the rubble, A Tower's stone calls to trouble.*

One by one, I felt each stone awaken with power. They pulsed with electricity in a line like someone was walking by flipping on switches. It was working. Next, I had to push my magic into them, so I took a deep breath and pictured those neon-blue and pink flames curling under like a wave pulling off the shore. I held my magic and my breath.

*Recover his book that tells the tale, To part two worlds on forever's scale. Buried deep, lost to the rubble, A Tower's stone calls to trouble.*

I exhaled and pushed, picturing my magic leaving my hands like waves crashing back onto the sand. Those pulses grew hot and sharp as they slid down my palms, into my fingers, then out the tips of my nails. I opened my eyes just as my magic did exactly what I'd pictured in my head. Neon-blue waves with sparkling pink flames rolled out of me in every direction. Everywhere it touched, the colors of the meadow grew bright like they'd been plugged into a socket. Malachi and Riah's gold eyes flashed white as their white angel wings popped out of their backs. Thorne and Sage's hair sparkled with color, their own white angel wings coming out.

My flames hit Bettina and gold bands sparkled from her fingers. The bands on Tenn's arm flashed so bright everyone cringed. Riah reached over and covered them with his hand and a shake of his head. White wings that matched the angels' flapped behind Tenn's back.

"*Malachi,*" Bentley and Myrtle said at the exact same time.

"What? Fine. I gave it a little jump start." He rolled his shoulders and his wings vanished. "Whatever, Val knew I'd be here. She knew we'd help, hence the words she used. Let's just carry on and get this damn book."

I smiled up at him. "Thank you."

"Do you see anything?" Bettina hurried over, taking my wrist in her hand which made the gold bands wrapped around each of her fingers sparkle again. That was when I realized they weren't mid-rings but actual lines on her skin. Just like on Tenn's arm. "Shit, I can't see it. Can you?"

I looked down and frowned. "The stones are flashing pink one row at a time from the bottom to the top, but not all the way around. Just does that over and over."

Tenn cocked his head to the side and tapped on his chest. "When Tegan and I were in the Garden of Eden, we were guided by a pink light that flashed almost like a wave from one side to the other. It was telling us which way to go."

My eyes widened. I looked down at them with new eyes. "Okay, so we walk straight? It's kind of ambiguous in these stones though."

Bettina chanted something in the ancient language. As her words finished, pink flames billowed up from my stones and into the air above them—*and formed an arrow.*

I gasped. "That worked. It's an actual arrow now. Can you see it?"

They all shook their heads. Well, except the angels who were avoiding eye contact.

Sage leapt off her throne and hurried over to me. With a flick of her wrist, I lifted into the air. "All right, *you* just watch that arrow and tell us where to go."

A giggle slipped through my lips as I wobbled in the air. I folded my legs under me and held my arm out in front. That glowing pink arrow pointed straight ahead. "I'm only gonna watch the arrow because otherwise imma be hella distracted."

"That's fair," Saffie chuckled.

"Right, so it says to go straight." I mimicked the arrow's point.

"You know what?" Cooper held his hands up, bringing my attention up to him. "Why don't those of you who fly just follow the yellow brick road and then meet us back here?"

"Yeah, we just wanted to see this place." Royce flopped down on the turquoise grass with all the flowers surrounding him. "You don't need us."

"Yeah, we're just emotional-support Covenlings." Deacon wagged his eyebrows as he sat down beside his cousin.

"I shall stay with them, Father." Saffie skipped over to them and sat down. She patted the grass beside her. "Sit, friends. Tell me everything while they're busy."

"Fine, but someone is carrying me 'cause I wanna go." Bettina looked around to the winged people. "Who'll it be?"

Tenn rolled his eyes. "As if it's not always been me. Shut up and climb on."

She giggled and hopped onto his back, his wings sticking out on each side. "Okay, Franks. Lead us."

When I pointed straight ahead again, a warm breeze carried me forward. Nearly every part of me wanted to just look around, because everything here seemed to glow or sparkle. I wanted to see it in all its glory, but everyone was counting on *me,* and over my dead body would I be the one to screw this up. So, I kept my head down and my eyes locked on the glowing pink arrow. Whenever it changed direction, I called it out to the others.

Luckily, from The Coven, only Tenn and Bettina had come along, and they were my family. I was comfortable around them. It was like my magic knew their magic. I was also secretly glad the others had chosen to stay back. That was a lot of pressure to be under.

I made a mental note to return to Seelie when I could walk around and explore, because in my peripheral vision it was gorgeous. We seemed to be walking through a forest where the light of the moon did not quite travel. Everything was cast in dark shades of blue and green. The only light came from the little glowing, golden orbs that were *everywhere.*

Sage told me they were fairyflies, which were similar to fireflies but from Seelie.

All of a sudden, the arrow pointed straight down. I gasped. "STOP!"

Everyone froze.

The arrow blinked like it was really trying to make a point. "It's here. Arrow is pointing straight down."

"Interesting." Thorne walked up beside me and Sage and looked down at the ground. "Actually, I do believe this makes sense for Father."

"Every time you call him that, I want to be sick," Tenn grumbled.

"What would you like me to call him, little Michael?"

He sighed. "King Assface was thrown around before he died. We've taken to King Fuckface lately—"

"I prefer the latter," Bettina added as she hopped off Tenn's back.

Sage snort-laughed. Riah and Malachi snickered.

Thorne pursed his lips and nodded. "I can fully support both of those."

Sage finally sat me down on my feet, so I stretched my legs and glanced around. We were still deep in a forest, but instead of grass and soil, it was stone slabs and rubble—I gasped. *RUBBLE.*

"*Buried deep, lost to the rubble,*" Bettina whispered. She pointed to the stone slabs. "Was this part of his palace?"

Thorne and Sage nodded, their expressions grim. Riah and Malachi went over and put a hand on their shoulders for support. I looked to my cousins and frowned. They just shook their heads.

"*Later,*" Tenn signed. I hadn't even realized he'd been learning sign language, but it made me happy to know he at least knew some. I nodded.

"*By hand of magic, strength in deed, Honor's Court can play with speed.*" Riah looked to Thorne and squeezed his shoulder. "Last time Val sent them to you, she referred to you as a twisted Court. The verbiage change is quite sweet."

Malachi nodded, his eyes locked on the stone ruins of the palace. "I played with speed once. In the 70's. Ten out of ten do not recommend."

I wasn't sure who started it, but suddenly we were all laughing.

Riah wiped his eyes. "What is wrong with you?"

"What? I was lightening the mood. You're welcome."

"I really am disappointed I never saw the connection." Riah shook his head. "Your son is just like you."

"Yeah, but is that the chicken or the egg?" When we all frowned, he shrugged. "I mean, nature versus nurture? C'mon, we knew him before he died, and he was just a goofy—"

"Perhaps we should focus on the task at hand so our little mortal friends can be on their way?" Sage gestured to the three of us. "They have a quest to finish before she catches on."

"Thank you, Sage." I pointed to the ground. "Which one of you two has earth magic?"

"You're a quick study, Frankie." Thorne smirked. He held his hands out in front of him. A neon-green glow billowed from his palms and shot down to the stones. "Let's get us a book that holds crucial information that would've been useful to us."

"Sometimes I wish there was a video of him dying that we could rewatch over and over."

Riah smiled. "I agree, Sage. I died before he did, so I missed the glorious moment."

The ground rumbled and vibrated through my feet. The others weren't even remotely concerned. That green glow billowed all around us, casting the trees and plants in its light.

"Just ask Tegan." Bettina tapped on Tenn's arm beside her. "She has this trick where she can make a hologram of something that went down."

"Yeah, except watching your father die will be a much different viewing experience than watching my mother die," Tenn said with a lopsided smile that did not match the words he'd said.

My eyes widened. "This is that fucked-up sense of humor we were talking about before."

Everyone else just nodded.

Finally, the stones flew up into the air and over our heads. The broken rubble slid out of the way as the dirt began to break apart. It was a miniature earthquake glowing in green. A golden cube shot through the crevice straight into the air between us. It glowed like pure sunshine. Thorne reached out and snatched it, wrapping his fingers all the way around it. The thing couldn't have been more than two inches tall, so I was definitely confused about where the book was. Sage placed her hand over her brother's, and a wave of water coiled around their hands, chased by a purple-ish smoke. Dirt and fire joined the others until it was a ball of elements swirling together.

After a few moments, those elements vanished.

And a book sat in Thorne's hand.

We all leaned forward to get a look. It was larger than a normal hardcover book or journal and had to be three inches thick. The book itself was black but it almost looked like wood that had been intricately carved. I'd just never seen wood that color. There was some kind of design etched across the entire front, back, and spine. Symbols were burned into the wood. The edges of the pages were as black as the cover, but as Thorne moved the book, they shimmered and reflected the green magic.

"It's locked." Thorne cursed. "Of course it is."

"You cannot have expected otherwise from him," Sage grumbled and took the book into her hands. "How dare this be so beautiful."

She wasn't wrong. It was breathtaking. Now that it was right next to me, I saw that some of the carvings and etchings were actually gold metal embellishments. I leaned over Sage's shoulder to see better. On the front cover, there was an eight-pointed star shape made from the gold metal. There were bars that stretched from the star all the way around the book. It was a cage. A metal cage. And the way to open it was through the middle.

"We need the key," Bettina grumbled with a curse.

Bentley stepped out from between the trees. His gold eyes flickered with orange crescents. "It's funny you should say that."

# CHAPTER FORTY-FIVE

## FRANKIE

"C'MON, Bentley, just let us have it already."

Lily covered Easton's mouth. "You have to stop setting him up so easily."

Easton wagged his eyebrows and his blue eyes sparkled.

We were back in Coven Headquarters. I didn't even know how we got back here so fast. It'd all gone by in a blur. Bentley had shown up to say there was more to the prophecy and we'd made a mad dash out of there so we could do as the prophecy demanded and move quickly. For all I knew, we'd left by portal. I'd been a bit too preoccupied by the growing sensation of dread. Like something bad was coming for me. I couldn't shake it.

Bentley rolled his eyes. "*Make thy move like a sneak,* remember? We are dealing with the Unseelie. I'd rather not speak of our quest publicly."

Timothy reached over the back of the chair and used his hand to turn Tegan's head away from the book in her lap to Bentley. "Trouble, can you pay attention so he'll show us?"

Her eyes shot up to us. "I'm listening. Go ahead, Bentley."

Tenn leaned his hip against her chair and crossed one leg over the other, his arms already crossed over his chest. It was interesting that I'd never seen Archie stand like that but Tennessee was like that often. It had to be a stress or nervous tick thing. He nodded to Bentley.

Bentley lifted his long-sleeved shirt up to his elbow.

"I've never been so relieved to find it shorter."

Easton threw his hands up and covered Lily's mouth in the most dramatic ways. "I can't believe it's my turn. I can't believe *you* said something dirty."

Everyone chuckled but their attention snapped right back to Bentley.

"This one is interesting. Parts of it feel too obvious, which makes me nervous. But here we go . . ." He cleared his throat. "*To find the key to the lock, Take a walk down the block. When hiding treasures becomes vital, Seek the line with trust in title. For secrets are always in plenty, An angel relies on one in twenty.*"

Silence.

"My man, how is that too obvious?" Thiago ran his hands through his dark hair. "That is entirely vague."

Then the words clicked. *That must be the sense of dread.* "Ah, fuck. Me again?"

Tegan, Bentley, Tennessee, and Bettina all looked to me at the same time with tight smiles and knowing expressions in their eyes.

"*You should expect to play a significant role in this quest, given who our enemy is,*" Tegan said into my mind.

Constance raised her hand from where she had not moved on the couch. "Frankie, why do you think *you* again?"

"*An angel relies on one in twenty.*" I held my wrist up to display my rune stones turned bracelet. "An angel gave these stones to one of the founding twenty families. *Seek the line with trust in title.* Line being bloodline. Title being founding family. I don't know. Maybe I'm seeing me because—"

"It is you." Tenn held his hand up. "Or should I say, it's Esther. Her bloodline was trusted with those stones. That clue cannot be a coincidence."

"Agreed," Tegan and Bettina said in unison.

I stared at Bentley's arm. "It says, *Take a walk down the block.* Do you think that's literal?"

"You did evacuate all of Tampa here." Kessler turned away from the fireplace he'd been staring at. "The Irit family house is in Eden, close by."

Tegan stood, wrapping one arm tight around the book so it was flush against her body. "Uncle Kessler, I'm going to use you to portal us to their house."

He nodded. "Are we all going again?"

"No," Tegan's voice was low and sharp, a tone she didn't usually use. "Bentley, I want you here. There's too much Seelie in your veins still. They'll be on guard. I want them to make their mistakes early so we can learn from them."

Bentley nodded.

"Deacon, can you do me a favor and go down to my mother . . . See if you have better luck getting in touch with her?" Tegan snapped her fingers to the left. "Savannah, you too, ma'am. You and Mom connected in that battle. There's something to that . . . I just don't know it yet."

Emersyn scowled and it scrunched her face up. "What's happening with Mom, twin?"

"I'm not sure," she said softly. "Katherine, I need you to watch Dad. I . . . have concerns."

"I'm one step ahead of you on that one."

"Mona, you, Daniel, and Kenneth get to school." Tenn turned to look at them. "Please confirm for me the teachers are adjusting well to the new curriculum. I have a bad feeling."

"Landreia, Lennox, and Warner?" Tegan waited until all three of them were looking at her. "Go to the library on campus. Find me everything and anything that mentions vampires, Unseelie, and Nephilim. And take Mei-Ling and Tai with you. They're good around a library."

"Actually, Bentley?" Tenn glanced to Royce, then back to our Hierophant. "It's time for you to try your new trick on Henley. See if there's anything we can use to try and get her awake."

Royce whimpered.

"Royce, would you like to go with Bentley?"

He closed his eyes and nodded.

Jackson raised his hand. "Perhaps I should put a call in to my sister and my mother? I suspect they're aware but . . ."

Tenn let out a deep sigh. "Thanks, Lancaster. Yes, please."

"Everyone else with me." Tegan marched to the front door. "Uncle Kessler, at the front, big guy."

The rest of us huddled together by the front door, again.

Tennessee and Cooper stood behind me where I could just barely make out Cooper asking Tenn if he was okay.

"I don't know. Since I stepped foot in Seelie, I just have this overwhelming sense of dread." Tenn shook his arms and legs out. "Like I'm waiting for the other shoe to drop."

"That's how I feel too," I whispered, and Bettina nodded.

Tegan pressed one palm to Kessler's back, rainbow mist swirling around her fingers. "Open the door."

He opened the door, and just like last time, the white portal box sat waiting. We all took a step forward and then the cold air of the portal washed over me. When the light faded, we stood outside of a front door. A purple front door. It made me smile. Kessler reached up and knocked.

The door opened and Esther's dad was standing there with an apron covered in flour. He pushed his glasses up high on his nose. "Oh, hello, Coven."

"Hey, Elijah." Tenn smiled and held his left hand out to shake. "I am sorry to bother you—"

"Anything for The Coven. Come in, come in." Elijah stepped back but smiled at me as everyone went inside. "Esther will be happy to see you."

We walked into a cozy living room with lower ceilings than in Headquarters. The fireplace was roaring and crackling. The sofa was brown suede that looked lived-in in the best ways and had cozy fluffy blankets thrown across the armrests and back. The television was paused on an Adam Sandler movie. To my right were rows of boxes like they'd just moved, and then I remembered they'd been evacuated.

Elijah hurried to the far side of the living room and leaned through an open doorway. "Ladies, The Coven is here."

"*What?*" Leah hissed.

"*Really?!*" Esther's voice was excited. I heard hurried footsteps and then Esther slid around the corner wearing a baggy sweater, leggings, and fuzzy socks. Her gray eyes widened when she saw us. "Hi—wait. You're like all here. Why? What happened?"

Tenn glanced around at us before turning back to her. "Short answer, we're on a quest from the Goddess. You're familiar with us doing those—"

"Yes," Esther said with a nod. "What do you need from us?"

"Well, we're collecting special tools we'll need for our mission, and that has brought us to your doorstep—"

"*Why?*" She glanced to me. "Wait, is it because of her stones?"

"No." I walked up to the front and stopped. "Because this quest quite specifically mentioned you."

Her face paled. Behind her, her parents held on to each other. "What did it say?"

"*To find the key to the lock, Take a walk down the block. When hiding treasures becomes vital, Seek the line with trust in title. For secrets are always in plenty, An angel relies on one in twenty.*"

Esther shuddered. "So there's a key somewhere in my house."

Leah wrapped her arms around her daughter. "We don't want to hinder you. Just tell us what you need us to do."

"Right now, just stand here." Tegan stepped up and cracked her knuckles. Then she flung her arms out and a rainbow-colored fog covered every inch of the house, seeping through doorways and around corners. "Spread out, y'all. See if anything signals us."

We scattered like cockroaches on a summer night after a rainstorm. Each of us went in a different direction, but we were all doing the same thing: touching everything and hoping it was the clue. We were ransacking this poor house, but I had to give my Coven-mates credit, everything they touched they made sure was put right back where they'd found it.

"*When hiding treasures becomes vital* and *For secrets are always in plenty . . .*" Leah rubbed her hands together and pursed her lips as she thought. Then she turned to Esther. "Could it be the box the rune stones were held in?"

"Why do you ask that?" Tegan's voice was soft but intense.

"Well, I was just thinking that *hiding treasures* and *secrets in plenty* suggest this is an important item, not just any object around the house. But more importantly, an item that had more than one secret attached to it." She turned to Esther. "The box?'"

Esther flinched. "I thought that was just a random box?"

Leah shook her head. "Why would it be random?"

Esther grimaced. "I don't know?"

"Where is it?" Leah stared blankly at her. "Esther, where is it?"

Esther threw her hands up. "I told you it was heavy!"

"*Esther*," Leah all but growled. Her hands gripped the edge of the couch.

"Gram said I was to always carry the rune stones on me. At all times. But that box was heavy and cumbersome. How am I gonna keep *that* in my pocket?" Both of her eyebrows were arched to the sky. "So, I left the box at Gram's house, where it would be safe."

My stomach rolled. "Esther, please tell me you didn't trash it."

"No, no, of course not! The stones came from an *angel*." She curled her black hair around her fingers. "I just . . . it's heavy."

"Tegan. The book." I pointed to them. "Show them. It's a specific shape."

She pulled the book out from where she'd stashed it in her leather jacket pocket. The moment she lowered the front cover for Esther and her mom Leah to see, both women gasped and gripped each other.

"It *is* the box." Esther pretended to put the key into the lock. "It's the same shape and has the same metal and symbols on it."

Hope rushed through me. "Okay, where'd you last see it?"

"At my grandmother's house—"

"More specifically?"

She pushed her hands into her hair, her gray eyes wild. "I don't know, it's been years. It was in the purple room—no, maybe the green room? Gram moves stuff around all the time—"

"She wouldn't have thrown it out," Elijah said softly. "Right, Leah? I mean, this box was passed down to her before you two—"

"He's right. My mother definitely wouldn't have thrown it out. It's in that house."

Tenn nodded. "Babe, get us there."

Tegan cleared her throat. "Leah, I need you to picture your mother's house in your mind and not let it go until I tell you, okay?"

Leah licked her lips and closed her eyes. She frowned. "Okay, I see it."

Tegan snapped her fingers and that white light flashed all around me. We stood out front of a massive white house that looked like it was trying to imitate the White House. The front lawn was massive and even included a lake. The forest that brushed up against the back of the house was definitely not otherworldly. If I had to guess, I would've said this was central Florida somewhere.

"I didn't want to startle my mother into a heart attack," Leah whispered, "by just appearing there."

"That's fair." Tenn gestured to the elegant glass front doors. "Why don't you lead the way? We'll give you a head start so we're not all standing there when she opens it."

"Thanks, Tenn. I'll wave when we're ready." Esther took her parents' arms and dragged them to the front door at a quick pace.

"Babe, what's the plan when we get in there?" Tenn fidgeted with his silver rings. "I just have such a bad feeling right now."

"I know. Me too." She exhaled roughly. "Tenn, B, and I will search the upstairs with Esther. Y'all look around the downstairs. Keep your heads on a swivel."

"And if we see any Unseelie, don't throw all your tricks at them," Timothy grumbled. "We should not ignore that warning."

"We're not getting attacked by Unseelie though, so that's fine. Right?" Willow glanced around to us. "Right?"

"GUYS!"

We looked up just as Esther waved us forward. White light flashed and then we were in a grand living room. My eyes widened. Granny Irit's house was *niiiice*. The floors were a gorgeous cherry hardwood, and the grand staircase was also that same wood. It was open, too, so the wooden railings all the way up still left the house feeling open and airy. The upstairs was open in the middle with a walkway that stretched around in a big square, continuing the wooden railing right from the stairs. There were at least four bedrooms up there. The wall directly behind us, the front wall, was made mostly of glass on both floors, so during the day, natural light would've spilled in gloriously.

"I have moved it around over the years, for different reasons." Esther's grandmother curled her silver hair around her fingers, the same nervous tick Esther had. "I think it's upstairs in one of the bedrooms."

"Esther, come with us." Tenn headed for the stairs.

"Frankie, hold this." Tegan shoved the book into my chest, then sprinted for the stairs. "Split up."

"Why did she give me the book instead of putting it back in her pocket?"

"It's best to not always try to decipher her antics." Timothy chuckled as he turned to scan a large bookshelf on the far-left wall. "However, I would wager this has something to do with the magic radiating off that book preventing the key from being found, like clouding her vision."

"Oh. That makes sense." I looked down at the book in my hands and swallowed nervously. It was heavy enough that I needed both hands. I wasn't sure how Tegan had it in her pocket.

"She doesn't entrust a lot of people with her toys," Cooper whispered. "Feel honored."

My face flushed. Cooper stood by my side. His eyes were watching the front lawn through the windows, though he wouldn't see much with how dark it was. It had to be getting late at this point. I looked around to the others and found they were all searching for the box. Emersyn was *in* the fireplace, with a fire raging against her skin. Willow and Chutney were checking the shelves of decorations and picture frames. Kessler was lifting furniture with one hand to check underneath.

Thiago opened the front door. "I do not like the darkness that lingers here."

"Mom, let's check your bedroom just in case," Leah said gently, then took her mother and husband's hands and led them to what I assumed was the master bedroom on the first floor.

"Easton, let's check the kitchen."

I exhaled and started pacing the carpet. That sense of dread was growing with every second. My stomach was in knots. My pulse kept sending these little flutters through my body. I couldn't stand still. I hugged the book to my chest and gnawed on my bottom lip.

Thirty minutes, or maybe thirty seconds later, Esther came running out of the bedroom in the corner with her hand held high in the air. "GOT IT!"

She sprinted across the balcony to the stairs, then flew down them before Tenn, Tegan, and Bettina even made it there. I rushed over to the base of the stairs and lowered the book cover so we could confirm. Esther raced straight up to me with a gold, circular metal object that looked more like a sundial than anything else. It matched the book perfectly, both in color and in shape. Esther slammed the key into the lock, and the click sound it made when the key was inserted was very satisfying. She turned the key. The gold metal pieces slid up and into the star like snakes slithering away.

"DON'T OPEN THE BOOK!"

But it was too late, Esther had already lifted the front cover. I cursed and slammed my hand down to close it when magic exploded from inside of it, throwing me, Esther, and Cooper apart like a bomb had detonated. The book flew straight up in the air.

"Tegan!"

"BABE!"

"T!"

A cloud of bubbles appeared above me, swallowing the book before shooting back down toward the ground. When the bubbles hit the floor, it was Tegan, but smoke billowed beneath her hands everywhere her skin touched the book. She hissed and tried to keep it closed like it took a lot of effort.

I dove, shoving her to the side and forcing her hands off it. "TENN!"

Tenn was already there, sliding in to catch her before she whacked her head into the stairs. He cursed violently and took her hands in his, holding them up with horror on his face. Her palms were bloody and raw.

"THE BOOK!" Bettina shouted.

The book had landed on its spine, but gravity was pulling it down on its back. I scrambled for it with my hand outstretched but not fast enough. It landed with a *thud* and the front cover wide open. Black smoke shot up from the dark pages. It swirled around, then morphed to take the shape of three black dragons that were only about six inches long. I slammed the book shut, but it was too late. We all just stared in horror as the smoke-dragons flapped their smoky wings and shot like rockets out the front door and vanished.

Thiago threw the door shut and locked it.

We all just stared out the glass in silence.

Kessler's face blanched at something over my shoulder. "Are her hands—"

"I'll heal," Tegan whispered, but her voice was strained from pain.

I cursed. "That's not gonna be good."

"Are we about to be attacked?" Easton asked with a tight voice.

Tegan sighed. "I think that's a safe assumption."

"This is my fault. I'm sorry. I didn't *think*." Esther squeezed her eyes shut and shook her head. "I'm sorry—"

Cooper gasped and dove for the windows. "The stars—MOVE—"

The glass windows and doors exploded into a million pieces. Smoke and shadow flew inside faster than a rushing tide. Ice-cold air coiled around my ankles and dragged me toward the open windows.

# CHAPTER FORTY-SIX

## FRANKIE

I SCREAMED and tried to kick my legs, but whatever held me had a firm grip. It was ice-cold but was burning my skin. Sharp shards of glass sliced into my arms and legs where my clothes weren't covering my body. I hugged the book tighter to my chest and looked for help, but everyone was being dragged across the house with me. We all struggled and cursed, throwing magic into the smoke gripping our legs, but nothing was working.

We flew up and out the windows only to slam into the concrete patio before being dragged again. My whole body burned. I couldn't release my grip on the book to grab ahold of anything. Grass and dirt slid up my jeans and up my back. Esther screamed. I looked up and choked on a gasp. Unseelie fae were hovering in the night sky above us, looking like dementors in silver body armor.

It was all happening too fast, yet somehow in slow motion.

Golden light flashed to my right as Tenn summoned Archangel Michael's sword to his hands. Even while being dragged across the lawn, he sat up and swung the glowing blade through the smoke dragging us. He shot straight up into the sky with his white angel wings. The Unseelie swarmed all at once. But there were too many of them. Even with dozens attacking him, *we* were still being dragged—we lifted into the air.

Tegan screamed and threw her arms out. White magic shot out of her in every direction. The grip on my legs vanished, and we crashed back onto the lawn. We all scrambled back to our feet. The others pulled out weapons and charged into battle. I needed a weapon. My dagger was on my phone in my pocket, but my sais were back in my room. I was such a stupid rookie. I hadn't brought them with me. My dagger would have to do. I reached for my phone when five Unseelies dove for me at once.

I somersaulted, then leapt back to my feet. *Shit, shit, shit.* Cooper lunged in front of me and swung his sword. The clash of metal on metal made a sharp hissing sound that hurt my ears.

*"Get to Holy Ground, Francelina,"* Everest's voice growled in my mind.

I gasped and froze, looking for him in the chaos of the night. *Everest. EVEREST. Where are you?* I spun in a circle, looking for that head of white-blond hair. I searched every shadow, but he wasn't there. *EVEREST! WHERE ARE YOU?*

Kessler jumped in front of me and plucked one of the Unseelie right out of the sky and then ripped his head clean off. Purple blood splashed all over us as Kessler tossed his body aside.

"They want the book!" Cooper shouted and swung his sword again. "TIM!"

Tim raced over with a gnarly sword covered in ice, the three of them surrounding me in a protective bubble. But it wasn't going to hold them off long. I tried to look for Tenn or Tegan, but they were just glowing spotlights shooting across the sky.

*"NOW, FRANCELINA!"* Everest shouted in my head as if he were right next to me. *"PROTECT THE BOOK!"*

I cursed and looked around, but nothing screamed Holy Ground. No one had told me this was even a thing or what it would look like —wait. HOLY. As in Heaven, as in angels . . . *like Angelic rune stones!* I stretched my arm to press one hand to my rune stones still wrapped around my wrist in the bracelet. The blue stones glowed to life, instantly answering my call. My heart was pounding.

*Show me Holy Ground!*

The glittery gold runes flashed and then my pink flames flickered out of the stones and into the air above them. At first they were a tornado, then an arrow formed, pointing diagonally to my left. I cursed.

"*Come with me!*" I whisper-shouted to them. *Nothing new to them.* "*No new tricks!*"

We ran full speed, following the compass that was my arrow. The others didn't even question me. They just followed me and attacked every Unseelie that came near. But they just kept coming. They swooped down like seagulls trying to steal food off my plate at the beach. We weren't making any headway.

An Unseelie dropped down right in front of me, his silver body armor sparkling under the glow of Tenn and Tegan. I saw his black eyes through the opening in his helmet—and the world changed around me. Gone was Granny Irit's front lawn. I was suddenly in a desert with the sun still clinging to the dark-red sky behind me. But the Unseelie was still coming for me at full speed. My heart stopped. I dropped and slid under the Unseelie's feet, then jumped back to mine.

I was on the front lawn again.

*What is happening?* I looked around, but everything was the same. Still a dark navy-blue sky with Unseelies dive-bombing us. Granny Irit's house shone like a beacon.

"*Keep moving, Francelina,*" Everest shouted. "*MOVE.*"

The arrow was flashing to the left. I cursed and sprinted the way it said, but I was flying blind. Everything in front of me was just dark— the sky turned dark-red again. The lawn was now mounds of sand and clay. Tears burned the backs of my eyes. I glanced down at my arrow but it was gone. I held no book. There were no rune stones. Just two red, blood-covered hands and gold armor splattered in purple and black blood.

Two Unseelies flew up in front of me.

Magic flashed in my palms. Neon-blue and pink flames looked like little orbs in my hands. I charged straight ahead, then at the last second, as I was within inches from the tips of their swords, I threw my magic orbs into the Unseelie's faces. I didn't look back as they dropped to the sand. But I did glance around the desert. My heart sank. My friends were outnumbered five to one, and the sun had not yet fully set. Once it did, we would be ambushed. Magic flashed in every direction as my friends fought back. Their gold armor was dented and falling apart. We had to end this. Now.

I slid to a stop and summoned my magic to my palms, then shot it out of me like rushing rivers. It moved across the sand and clay, pulling Unseelie beneath its waves.

"*FRANCELINA!*"

I looked up and spotted Everest standing in the middle of a glowing pink circle. But he looked weird. He wore a white suit and no armor. I frowned.

"*HERE! NOW! MOVE!*" he shouted *in* my head.

My legs answered, sprinting right for him. The battle raged on all around me, but Everest was there. I raced for him and tried to ignore the fear in his eyes or the way his gaze bounced left and right and back again. I had to get to him.

His eyes widened. "*DIVE!*"

I dove for him and that strange glowing pink circle—my knees slammed into cold grass, but gravity had me crash face-first because I refused to let go of the book for even a second. *THE BOOK!* I cursed and flipped onto my back, then pushed up on my knees. The book was still clutched in my arms, pressed to my chest. The sky was dark. I was on the lawn again.

"*—CELINA . . .*"

I gasped and looked up with my heart in my throat. The desert sky had turned purple. Night was upon us. A sea of Unseelie flew up from behind the mountain on the horizon. They would be upon us in mere moments. Everest was nowhere in sight—

A warm shadow wrapped around my eyes. I froze. But then it faded, and my breath left me in a rush. The vision was gone. I was back on the front lawn of the house with my Coven-mates, not on some mountain desert at sunset.

Cooper slid up beside me. "What are we doing here? We're out in the open—"

"Holy Ground!" I pressed my palm to the cold, damp grass, and my rune stones glowed like spotlights.

Cooper's green eyes widened. He turned to the fight raging in-between us and the house and whistled. The others all looked in his direction, then their gazes dropped to my palm on the ground.

"*HOLY GROUND, GO!*" Tegan screamed into our minds.

The others bolted for us. Kessler grabbed Timothy by the shirt and threw him. He landed and rolled into a crouch like he'd practiced that move a million times. Kessler leapt to the side and grabbed Thiago, throwing him onto Holy Ground, except *he* was not trained for this so he rolled so hard Cooper had to catch him. Then Kessler turned and ran *into* the fight in the opposite direction. But I knew what he was doing. He was going back for the others. They were fighting without magic against an enemy that was just playing with its food. They were faster and stronger. The only reason we were alive was because of whatever Tenn and Tegan were doing—and because they wanted the book in my hands.

"*DOWN!*" Thiago yelled.

I dropped to the grass, but hands gripped my hair and pulled, lifting me off the ground. Tim swung his blade, slicing the Unseelie's hand off in one clean move. It dropped to the ground and burst into ash. But we didn't get a chance to celebrate as more dove for me and then dodged Tim's ice-blade at the last second. Thiago pushed me down onto the grass, my body weight pinning the book beneath me. He shouted something, but it was definitely Portuguese and I had no idea what he'd said. I craned my neck back to watch what was happening with my heart pounding like a runaway freight train.

Esther, her parents, and her grandmother emerged from the chaos with Emersyn hot on their heels. Three Unseelies went flying—*no, wait. PIECES of Unseelie.* My stomach rolled just as Kessler reappeared in a dead sprint for us. He had Willow and Chutney thrown over his shoulders, but he was dragging Easton and Lily on the ground, one in each hand. Tim and Cooper cursed and leapt off our glowing pink circle to help Kessler get the others.

The Unseelie dove for me one after another.

The others wouldn't let me up. They wanted me protecting the book, so I was helpless to do anything but watch. I hated it. Every muscle in my body yearned with the need to pull my weapons and fight. We were all on Holy Ground now except for Tegan and the power siblings.

Tegan's hair was snow-white.

I didn't quite know what that meant, but I knew it was bad news. She'd gone all white that one night, and that was why she'd been unable to prevent us from getting kidnapped by vampires the next day. This was bad news for us. We needed her strong.

"DOWN!"

I braced myself for pain, but none came, only pressure from my friends pushing me down and the splash of purple blood around me. I cursed. "Why doesn't Holy Ground have a roof!?"

"BETTINA!" the rest of them shouted in perfect unison.

I looked up just in time to see Tenn swoop down and grab Bettina. He dove for us, dropping Bettina at our feet and shooting back up into the sky faster than my eyes could even track. He was too fast. Not human fast.

Bettina slid to her knees in front of me. She swung her arm in a perfect arc, then slammed her gold-hilted sword into the grass two inches from my face. A glowing, light-pink dome spread over our heads, enclosing everyone inside and on Holy Ground. Two Unseelies slammed into her dome and burst into dust and ash. She jumped to her feet and held her right hand out to her side. A second later, Tenn's long black sword slammed into her palm. She nodded to us, then spun on her toes and raced back into the fight.

"We have to do something."

"We can't just leave them out there—"

"But we can't stay in here all night—"

"We won't last the night, look!"

I looked up and my stomach sank. More and more Unseelie were flying in from somewhere out of sight. I didn't understand where they were coming from. I didn't understand enough of anything yet. But they were right. We couldn't sit here in this bubble until dawn. That was too far away. There were too many of them, and we weren't one-hundred-percent sure it wouldn't fail and leave us exposed. And the three of them couldn't keep fighting at the speed they were.

Tegan dropped to her knees and threw her arms out. White lightning slammed into Tenn's back, but it was like he didn't even feel it. Michael's sword lit up like a supernova, glowing too bright to even look at. Not that I could see him, Tenn moving faster than he had been a moment ago. Now he was literally just a blur of white against a dark sky. Unseelie bodies were bursting into dust in his wake. Tegan turned and threw lightning into Bettina. The golden bands on her fingers glowed like Michael's sword, then white lightning coiled around Tenn's black sword.

Timothy cursed and dropped to his knees beside me. "She turned it into a Holy weapon. *How?*"

Unseelie were dropping into glowing, severed pieces on the lawn.

Suddenly I was flipped onto my back, like the book itself had thrown me. The book was shaking and trying to wiggle out of my hands. It lifted off my chest and pushed against my arms. I screamed as my fingers were slipping—Kessler slammed his hands into the book, forcing it back down against me. My breath was knocked from my lungs, but I still had the book. And then my whole body lifted off the ground, taking Kessler with me. The others tackled us, piling on top to keep us down.

"Oh my God." Esther paled from the top of the pile. "Someone has to get her."

"We can't. We can't get through the dome—"

"TEGAN!" Esther screamed. "NO!"

We all jumped and craned our necks around to search for her, then all cursed in chorus. I felt everyone's panic building right along with mine. Tegan was on her knees facing us, facing *away* from most of the fight, throwing magic into Tenn and Bettina. Her eyes were open but definitely unseeing. It was almost like she was in a trance.

And a few Unseelie were charging for her.

"TEGAN!"

"TWIN!"

Everyone around me was shouting. Emersyn tried to get off the pile, but Cooper and Thiago were above her and not budging. The fear in Cooper's eyes would haunt me forever. And then Esther leapt off the pile and ran.

"NO!"

Esther charged right through the dome which made the others gasp. Tegan was only about ten feet away from us, but the Unseelie were moving in *fast.* They swung their swords—Esther dove and tackled Tegan, lifting her off her knees and slamming into the grass. The Unseelie drove their swords right into Esther's back. She screamed and her back arched, blood pouring out of her wounds instantly. Tegan's body flopped lifelessly beneath her, that white lightning streaking across the sky like it was waiting for her to call it again.

Cooper gagged. "*No, no, no! TEGAN!*"

"Did they get her too?!" Emersyn screamed.

Tennessee was panicked. He tried to fly to them, but Unseelie kept crashing into him and grabbing him. He was totally and entirely surrounded. His mismatched eyes were wide with fear fifty feet above his soulmate.

Bettina reached up with those glowing bands on her fingers and *grabbed the lightning* out of the air. The others cheered as her long fingers wrapped around a literal lightning bolt and pulled. She swung her arm and flicked that lightning bolt around like it was a whip. It sliced through the Unseelies surrounding Tenn. He tucked his wings and dove headfirst for his soulmate and our friend. Esther hadn't moved but her body was twitching. Her parents were wailing. Granny Irit was praying.

Tenn swooped down in a blur of light and scooped Tegan and Esther off the ground—and then they were suddenly on the ground beside me. Tenn's hands were shaking as he reached for Tegan's throat to check for a pulse.

"She's alive. Go!" Timothy hauled his nephew to his feet and shoved him out of the dome. "HOPE!"

Tenn cursed violently but stormed in the direction of his sister who was still holding on to the lightning bolt.

"No, no—don't pull!" Tim shouted.

I looked over as Leah's hands froze on the Unseelie swords protruding from her daughter's back. "Why not!"

"That'll kill her too fast." Tim peeled her hands off the hilts. "We just need to get her to Eden, to Katherine—"

"HOW?" Thiago pointed to our High Priestess. "She's out!"

"We need the sun," I said between labored breaths.

Lily groaned. "I can't. It hits their armor. I was trying."

"So get their armor off!"

Thiago scoffed at me. "How?"

"Cooper! You have sleep magic, right? Can't you use that here?"

He scrubbed his face with his hands, his green eyes wild as he watched Tenn and Bettina fight. "Yeah, but how can dreams help right now—"

Emersyn gasped. She gripped the front of her brother's shirt and shook him. "PUT THEM TO SLEEP! Like you did Bettina that night the plane crashed!"

Cooper's face fell. His eyes widened. He nodded, then closed his eyes and frowned. His arms trembled. I felt his magic building. The ground vibrated beneath me. He took a deep breath, then opened his eyes and threw his hands out. Magic that twinkled like stars shot out of him.

"TENN!" I screamed.

Unseelie dropped to the ground all around us. Unmoving.

Cooper swayed but someone caught him.

Tenn landed right in front of me with Bettina draped in his arms. "Coop? Please?"

He cursed and flicked his wrists—Bettina gasped and leapt out of Tenn's arms, then relaxed when she saw it was him. She blinked over to Coop and then nodded in approval. Tenn spun around to face the lawn. Then I realized the pressure from the book had vanished. It wasn't trying to fly away from me anymore.

"Did it work?" Cooper asked softly.

Tenn nodded. "For now. Let's pounce on it."

Bettina dropped to her knees and yanked her sword out of the ground. The dome vanished. Without another word, everyone jumped off of me and raced to the lawn. Easton and Thiago were pulling helmets off and running while Lily followed them with beams of sunlight streaming from her palms.

Tenn was on his knees beside me, his hands shaking, his eyes locked on Tegan still under Esther. "Lift her off."

"Tenn, we don't know—"

"I said *lift her off*," Tenn snarled.

"I'll do it. Let me." Kessler cursed. He crouched down and slid his arms under Esther's body. "In three . . . two . . . one—"

He lifted Esther up and she screamed. I winced and pushed up onto my hands and knees as blood spilled over the side of her body. Leah and Elijah wailed. Esther's face was contorted in pain. Her body began to shake.

"Hold on, Kiddo. Just breathe," Kessler said softly. "I've got you. We're going to get you help."

"Tegan?" Tenn checked her body for wounds, but there didn't appear to be any. Esther had blocked *all* of them. Tenn swayed, then pulled Tegan into his lap. He pressed his hands to her chest, right over their soulmate glyph that was still pink when I would've expected it to be red. "Babe, can you hear me?"

For a moment, we all just stared at her unmoving, unconscious body.

Then, for reasons I could not explain, I took one of Tegan's hands and pressed it to my bracelet. My pink flames wrapped around her wrist instantly. Tegan's other hand lifted just enough off her stomach to snap her fingers.

Everything went white.

# CHAPTER FORTY-SEVEN

## MORGAN

"Honey, I'm home."

My cheeks flushed with heat. I placed the dinner plates on the table as he kicked his shoes off at the door like he always did. I bit my bottom lip. It was our anniversary, our seven month anniversary, so it was a big night. We'd been so busy building our dream life that I hadn't had time to cook for him but we'd have forever to do that. Instead I'd gotten take-out from his favorite Italian place and set the dining room table all fancy.

"In here, my love," I called out to him.

"It smells like..." He prowled into the room with his eyes closed. His nostrils flared. Then his eyes flew open and that gorgeous green gaze landed on my body. "Dinner *and* dessert."

I arched my back and did a little stretch just to let him see just what his gift was going to be. But I was a bit of tease lately, so I turned and leaned over the table to light the candles in the centerpiece. The cold air swept over my bare skin as I angled my hips for him to get a better look.

He growled and it made my body tingle in all the right places.

"Hungry, my love?" I glanced over my shoulder and bit my lip. "You can have whichever you'd like first, Azazel."

He yanked his black silky shirt off in one clean pull, revealing all that chiseled muscle I loved running my nails over. I planted both hands on the table, spread my legs *just* enough, and arched for him. Just like every time, his body rose to the occasion while confined by his black leather pants.

He walked up behind me and slid his finger into my body from behind. When I moaned, he whispered, "*I can't wait for you to see my plans for us, Morgan.*"

"*Show me,*" I breathed as I rocked my hips against his finger.

I heard the sound of his zipper and my body flushed with heat. He gripped my hips and slammed *all* the way into me. I gasped and my eyes rolled as he filled me deeper than anyone else had. Sometimes it was like our first time and I was instantly lost to my passion for him. I braced my hands on the table and arched my back for him. The whimpered moans that came out of my mouth were raw and primal. I couldn't get enough of him.

Then he pulled out and flipped me around before shoving my legs apart and sliding right back in until his hips crashed into me. He liked dinner and a show so I laid back on my elbows. He leaned forward and dragged my bra down until my bare breasts were on display. When he sucked my nipple into his mouth I screamed his name and the world exploded around me. And as we both rode that high, I wondered how I ever got so lucky to find a lover like *mine.*

I was just getting ready for more when he slid out. So I sat up and wrapped my arms around his neck. "I wasn't done with you yet."

"But are you ready for the next phase of our plan?" Azazel wrapped his arms around my waist and pulled me back onto his cock, making me gasp. His breath brushed over my ear as he slid in and out of me, his hips slamming into my body hard enough to bruise. "The *big* step?"

I gripped his shoulders and moaned. "Yes, Azazel, *please.*"

He rolled his body into me without slowing until we both hit that high again together, moaning each others' names until are breaths were ragged.

"Now, I'll ask you again, Morgan..." He stepped back, pulling his body out of mine far too soon. He reached down and pulled my bra back up to cover my breasts, the slid my dress back over my body and tied it closed. His hands gripped my knees and forced my legs closed. "Are you ready for the next phase of our plan?"

I grinned as butterflies danced in my stomach. I reached up and took his face in my hands. "The one we've been waiting on?"

"That's the one."

I squealed and did a little shimmy dance. I'd never felt so happy in my life. Our happily ever after was right around the corner. "Yes, Azazel, yes. I am so ready."

"Excellent." He grinned and raised his hand then flicked his wrist. "Because tonight is the night."

The front door opened. A man I'd never seen before walked into our home. I gasped and sat up straight but Azazel kept me in place with his hands on my thighs. My pulse quickened. I wasn't aware we were having a guest. It was our anniversary. But I trusted Azazel, he'd never hurt me in any way.

"Welcome," Azazel purred. He waved for the man to join us. "Please, come in."

I watched as the man stepped into the dim glow of the candlelit room. He was tall like Azazel but thinner, even with toned muscles in his arms he was much slimmer than my love. His hair was sandy blonde on top, long enough to fall into his face, but the side were buzzed short to his scalp. His skin was fair and smooth but covered in tattoos. The muscle shirt he wore showed off his arms and the full black and white sleeves that ran from shoulders to wrists. It was too dim to see what the details were though. He looked to the left at the table set up for a romantic dinner and I spotted some kind of bird tattooed on the side of his throat.

"Morgan, I'd like you to meet Liam Elira." Azazel gestured to the man. "Liam, this is Morgan. The one I've told you so much about."

Liam's blue eyes locked on my face and there was obvious, blatant hunger in them even before he looked me up and down like I was a buffet he was about to devour. He stopped right beside Azazel and his thin lips curved into a smirk. "The one you've been promising me I'd meet when the time is right?"

Azazel chuckled. He reached forward and grabbed the silk ribbon that tied my dress together and yanked it clear off my body. I sat up a little and my dress slid apart, revealing some of my body to this stranger. My heart pounded.

"What are we doing, Azazel?"

"You'll see..." Azazel purred.

He gripped my knees and dragged me to the edge of the dinner table then threw my legs wide open. Cold air swept over my bare body and my dress slid down my arms, leaving me sitting there with only a red lace bra on with my legs spread in front of this man.

I frowned up at the love of my life. "Azazel?"

He stepped aside and slid Liam in front of me, right where he had just been standing when he fucked me. To my absolute horror, Azazel reached down and unzipped Liam's jeans, freeing is *very* eager body from its confines. The tip of Liam brushed against my thigh. I tried to move but Azazel caressed my thigh and my whole body warmed until I let out a little moan.

Azazel gestured to my body. "She's officially yours, Liam."

I gasped and sat up. "What did you say? What do you mean? Azazel, what's happ-"

He snapped his fingers and light flashed all around me.

"*Mine,*" Liam purred as he pushed my legs wider so he could step in between them. I felt the tip of him slide over me. "*All mine, Morgan.*"

"Please, Liam, I've waited all day for this." I moaned and gripped his shirt. batted my eyelashes at him and rolled my hips. "Happy anniversary, my love."

Liam let out a deep chuckle as I dragged his mouth down to mine. He devoured me with his kiss and his tongue until I was squirming. His hands gripped my thighs and pulled until my back hit the table then he leaned down over me. I gasped and my eyes rolled as he filled me over and over. My pulse quickened and heat broke out across my body, and pooled in my stomach. I screamed his name and the world exploded around me. And as we both rode that high, I wondered how I ever got so lucky to find a lover like *mine.*

As my pleasure sang through my body I heard someone clapping.

I frowned and looked toward the sound. It was Liam's good friend Azazel, I had no idea how long he'd been standing there but he definitely had just gotten one hell of a show. My face flushed with heat except I wasn't embarrassed. Liam was the love of my life, there was nothing to be ashamed of.

"Liam, you didn't tell me we were having a guest for dinner."

"Well I didn't want to ruin the surprise," Liam purred. "I can't wait for you to see Azazel's plans for us, Morgan."

I smiled. "What are they?"

"I am so glad you asked." Azazel grinned and snapped his fingers. Light flashed all around us.

We stood at the front stoop of a mountainside home, tucked between the trees and hidden from the world. Golden light spilled from the windows. It was so romantic. I squeezed Liam's hand and leaned into him. He had some surprise for us. Something huge he said would change our lives forever. I'd never felt so happy in my life. This man right here was my end game, and I knew it—but I wasn't going to admit that to him already.

Liam looked down and smiled, his blue eyes twinkling in the moonlight. "You're going to love my surprise. I've been planning it just for you for months."

I bit my lip to try and not smile too much. "As long as we're together, I am going to love it."

The front door of the house opened. His good friend Azazel stood just inside. He smiled. "Welcome home, love birds, please come in."

Liam pressed his palm to the small of my back and led us inside where it was warm and cozy and smelled like chocolate. Soft music played in the background. I heard the soft whisper of voices like perhaps there was a party happening.

"What's going on here, Liam? Is this a party?"

He tucked my hair behind my ears. "No, my love, this is your surprise."

"I love surprises," I mumbled to myself as anticipation rushed through me.

"I'm so glad you do, Morgan." Azazel waved for us to follow him into a massive living room. "Because you two will see *this* through together. Surprise!"

I gasped. My jaw dropped. There *were* other people here. But not just people. Women. There had to be dozens of them, sitting on furniture and the floor. Each and every one of them was pregnant. They all seemed to be about six or seven months pregnant, if not more.

The women all looked up to me and Liam with warm, bright smiles.

"Are...are those..." I blinked. "Are these for...for..."

Azazel wrapped his arms around mine and Liam's shoulders. "It's time we prepare you for your children. I've been hard at work making them for you."

# CHAPTER FORTY-EIGHT

## FRANKIE

*\*\*HI about that TW\*\** *So if you skipped chapter 47 let me recap what ol' Zazzy is up to...Azazel kidnapped the human Morgan in book one, used his angel magic to make her think she's in love with him but NOW he's made her think she's in love with a guy named Liam. Oh, and there's a part about her and Liam arriving at a house full of all of Azazel's former conquests who are pregnant - the last page of ch 47 is safe if you wanted to read that. Hope this helps!*

I KNOCKED on the door and braced myself.

When it opened, I was not expecting to find Malachi on the other side. He gave me a small smile and stepped aside so I could enter. Inside the healing room were Thorne, Sage, Esther's parents, and Granny Irit. Standing around the bed were Mona, Katherine, Myrtle, and Riah.

Esther was on her stomach with gnarly, raw wounds on her back.

I shuddered and looked away. "How is she?"

Malachi sighed. "Stable. Unseelie wounds are a bitch. But she should make a full recovery in due time."

"Thanks." I wanted to trust his word but the looks on their faces were too tense. Too silent. It felt like a lie, like they just didn't want me to know the truth. I looked over to her parents and my eyes burned. "I'm so sorry—"

"Don't be. This was out of your control." Leah gave me a hug, then ushered me back out the door. "Go. The Coven has important things to do right now. She'd want you out there doing them, not sitting by her bed. Promise."

I groaned and nodded. "Okay. If anything changes, please text me. And if she wakes—"

"I'll tell her you were here." She winked and stepped back inside. "Thank you, Frankie."

The door clicked shut. Something was not right in there. They weren't telling me stuff.

I wanted to scream.

Instead, I turned and walked back up the stairs to the living room where my Coven-mates were already gathered for a Coven meeting. We had to discuss the new lines of our prophecy. This whole thing was a crash course on being a part of this group. I nodded to Tenn as I walked over and sat in the chair by the front window near the fireplace. Everyone looked drained and exhausted. I knew it was sometime in the afternoon, but after our late night, I wasn't surprised.

"*BABE,*" Tegan called into our minds.

Tenn gasped and turned to the stairs. "Tegan?" And then he was racing up and out of sight.

"You know, we should build him like a chute or something." Bettina gestured to the ceiling. "That way he can just fly straight up into their penthouse without rounding the stairs."

Lennox perked up. "I can do that."

Everyone looked to her.

She frowned. "Maybe I'll talk to Landreia first so I don't bring the whole house down."

Everyone nodded.

I chuckled.

Tenn came down carrying Tegan in his arms. Deacon held his hand out. Thiago, Warner, and Jackson cursed and put money in his hand. Everyone else rolled their eyes.

"That was dirty play," Royce said with a smirk. "They weren't here last time."

Deacon looked him in the eye. "I'm the Devil, Royce. Why are you always surprised by this?"

Tenn sighed but the smile on his face couldn't be hidden. "Where would you like me to sit you, babe?"

She leaned her head against his chest, the long white strands sliding over his arm. "Closest to the food."

Warner groaned. "Dammit."

"You've got to be bloody killing me." Jackson threw a wad of cash at Deacon. "This is bollocks."

Thiago shook his head. "We fell for his tricks."

Deacon threw his head back and laughed.

Tegan grinned. "Where's Dad?"

"I'm here," Hunter said from the door to downstairs. He looked at Tegan in Tenn's arms and shook his head. "Again?"

"Here, take my spot. I'm gonna get her some food." Emersyn jumped off the couch, then rushed to the kitchen.

Hunter walked over and sat in the spot his daughter had just vacated, but he'd left the spot on the end open enough for his other daughter. He patted the seat. "Put her here, Tenn."

Tenn carefully sat her next to her father, whom she immediately leaned into with a smile. His golden magic wrapped around her like a blanket. When Tenn tried to walk away, Tegan's leg shot out and hooked around his knee. She frowned at him. He hung his head and smiled, then sat on the coffee table in front of her.

Everyone stared at her, waiting.

She closed her eyes and seemed like she was falling back asleep against her dad's arm but then she whispered, *"How's Esther?"*

"Katherine called in reinforcements. Thorne, Sage, Riah, and Malachi are all downstairs with her. Oh, and Myrtle." I looked to the stairs and my heart hurt. "They're confident she'll heal, but I just do not like the expressions on their faces."

Tegan cringed. "I owe her one."

Everyone nodded, their faces grim.

Tenn reached out and squeezed her knee. "Babe, I think everyone is wondering how you're full white witch but awake—"

*"Valathame,"* she said with a sigh, like it took all her strength to say it. Her eyes were only open a crack, but they were that white and gold combo I remembered from the first time I woke up. She stared at him for a long moment, then closed her eyes. *"Takes too much energy to talk out loud."*

*"We can hear you,"* Tenn whispered back. *"Are you about to go down for days again?"*

"*Valathame taught me trick.*" Even her mental voice was weakening.

Hunter groaned.

The stair door opened, and Riah rushed out. He frowned and looked over the room until he got to Tegan. His face fell. "She said to ease into that trick, Tegan, not dive into the deep end."

Tegan smirked but didn't open her eyes.

Riah rolled his eyes and made his way over to her. He pressed his palm to her forehead and silver magic coiled around her body. She sucked in a deep breath, then exhaled. She opened her eyes. They weren't green yet, but they were fully open. Her skin had a little more color to it.

"Thanks, Riah," she said with a voice that was a little stronger.

"That's all you're getting for now." He pulled his hand back and shook his head. Then he pointed at her and she looked up at him. "No magic—"

"Well—"

"Fine, Bentley. But one." Riah arched his eyebrow to our psychic. "We need her for emergencies."

He nodded his head once.

Then Riah turned and went back down the stairs.

"*I got in trouble,*" Tegan whispered with a little snicker.

Bettina walked over and handed her a steaming cup of what looked like hot chocolate. "You *are* Trouble, bestie."

"What about you two angel freaks—I mean, children?" Easton gestured between Tenn and Bettina. "That was intense last night. You okay?"

"Well, I have no recollection of getting home or getting in my bed, so . . ."

"I carried you, Son." Kessler laughed. "You're a lot harder to carry than you used to be. Long ass legs now."

Bettina climbed into Jackson's lap and curled her legs up. "I don't think I've ever slept that hard."

"There was drool." Jackson grinned.

Easton frowned. "None of that answered my question. Where's Savannah, our new soul checker?"

"Downstairs with Devon," Hunter said softly.

Emersyn strolled out of the kitchen with a plate of fried chicken.

"You, eat. Y'all, the non-humans look and feel fine. I don't think we'll know what side effects come with what Trouble did until Trouble is back on her feet more."

"So, Benny, did we get another prophecy?"

I gasped and sat up straight. "Fuck, where's the book? Where's the key?"

Bentley held his hands up. "In a safe place, a secure place that will prevent magic from getting out and ambushing us with another attack."

I groaned. "I'm sorry, guys. I should have stopped Esther from turning the key—"

"Don't." Tenn shook his head, but he didn't look at me. "We don't do that here. None of us are perfect. We're going to make mistakes. We all trust each other, so we cannot start with blame, or it will tear us all apart."

"How did you know there was Holy Ground there?" Cooper asked softly from the stone ledge by the fireplace.

*Everest told me . . . in my mind.* My cheeks warmed. I should have told them the truth, one of them might've been able to help me figure things out. But I couldn't get myself to say the words, so I just held my wrist up. "I asked the stones."

Everyone nodded like the answer was sufficient.

"*Liar,*" Tegan whispered in my mind.

I looked up to her and found her smirking with her eyes closed. My cheeks were on fire now, so I looked down and ran my fingers over the stones.

"*Everest told you, didn't he?*" Tegan asked in my mind.

I nodded slightly.

"*The plot thickens.*" She even chuckled in my mind.

Cooper cleared his throat and leaned forward to rest his elbows on his knees. "Tenn?"

Tenn flinched and looked up, but his eyes seemed a little dazed and unfocused. He cursed and pinched the bridge of his nose. "Uncle Tim, can you . . . just for right now—"

"I've got you, Nephew." Tim walked over and squeezed Tenn's shoulder. "Let's keep moving. Bentley, please read us the next prophecy."

Bentley nodded and slid his shirt up. There were only six lines on his arm this time and that felt like a relief. He cleared his throat. *"This is where thy path gets tricky, Before you go we must be picky. By cloud of storm and winds divine, Seek the friend to trade in swine. In his wake you will be tested, Who sees the magic uncontested."*

I scowled. That meant nothing to me. But as I looked around the room, I saw more than a few smirks and chuckles, so some of them knew something about those lines.

Timothy shook his head. "I don't know about all of those lines, but it sounds like we're going to pay Leyka a visit."

"Sounds like Leyka is going to tell us who all is going on the *next* step of this quest." Royce closed his eyes and shook his head. "Why do I feel like this guy is always bad news for us?"

"Maybe he's the angel of omens?" Cooper shrugged like he wasn't joking.

I looked around but everyone was deep in thought. "Who are we talking about? Who is Leyka?"

"My brother." We all jumped at the sound of Myrtle's voice. She stood just outside the door on the stairs wearing a ceremonial white sheath dress and her long black hair in pigtail braids. *"By cloud of storm and winds divine.* He is the Angel of Storms."

"Your brother's a—you know what? Nah. I'm putting myself on a need-to-know basis." I shook my head. "Do y'all know where and how to find this angel Leyka?"

Emersyn pursed her lips and stared at Myrtle. "Is he on his beach?"

Myrtle laughed and walked toward Tenn, but then she crouched down beside Tegan and put her fingers to her forehead. "I think given the word *swine*'s inclusion in the spell, it's a likelihood. He has a strange sense of humor, and Valathame enables him."

"So how can we get there without Tegan?" Willow asked softly.

"You don't." Myrtle lifted her silver diadem off her head and slid it onto Tegan's.

Tegan gasped and sat up straight, her eyes going wide. She held her hands up and looked at them like they weren't hers. "Whoa. Wicked."

"Portal everyone down to Leyka, then return that to me." Myrtle stood up straight.

Tenn hung his head. "Does she have to go?"

"Yes. We all have to go." Bentley held his hands up to stop questions. "Except for Devon, Henley, and Constance."

Tim nodded. "Myrtle, if you're going down, can you send Savannah up?"

Myrtle squeezed Tegan and Tenn's shoulders, then turned back for the stairs. "She'll be up momentarily."

"Right. Everyone else, let's get moving. We can't afford to lose any more daylight." Tim gestured for the front door. "You've got five minutes. Be dressed, armed, and ready for anything at that door in five. Our lovely pets, sorry, but you'll need to stay here. We already have one down. We don't need more."

I remembered Archie telling me that Tim had been Coven Leader for over a decade until Tenn was given the job. It was funny to think back to those conversations now knowing Tenn was talking about himself. If I hadn't gotten to know him as Archie, I may not have entirely believed that he didn't want to be the Leader because it was such a natural position for him to be in. Though I could see how Tim was good at it too. It was obvious he'd slipped back into the roll at his nephew's request.

Everyone else hurried up the stairs and out of sight, leaving me, Cooper, Tenn, and Tegan sitting there with Timothy. But after a moment, Tim strolled over and leaned against the front door.

Cooper reached out and touched my arm. "You okay?"

I nodded. "That feels like a loaded question."

He smirked. "Welcome to Coven life. But do you need to get ready?"

"After last night? I slept in my clothes." I gestured to my outfit which consisted of my Vans sneakers, jeans, and white sweater. Granted, white wasn't the best battle option, but apparently I didn't own dark colors. My rune stones were still in bracelet form. My phone still had my sticker with my bat-dagger. I reached down to the ground and lifted up my sais for him to see. "Though if someone has a magical trick for me to carry these around—"

"I got you, girl." Lennox pulled her wand out. "Thigh strap okay?"

"Badass, yeah."

She flicked her wand a few times, then sparkly magic scooped my weapons out of my hands. By the time I looked down at my legs, I had one sai strapped to the outside of each thigh. My eyes widened. She giggled and winked at me, then went down the stairs.

"Well, I guess I am ready. You?"

"Ready."

I glanced up and found Tegan leaning against Tenn's chest with her eyes closed. They were still sitting. It actually reminded me of toddlers who played until they passed out. I leaned closer to Cooper. "*Is Tenn okay?*" I whispered.

He grimaced and leaned close enough that our heads were nearly touching. "*When she goes down, it's hard for him to concentrate. The soulmate connection is too intense.*"

The door opened under the stairs and Savannah stepped out. Her blue eyes landed on me and Cooper huddled close together so fast that I didn't have a chance of moving away. She swallowed roughly and marched over to the front door, careful not to look in our direction at all. My heart sank. I was hurting her, and I couldn't do anything about it. I stole a glance up at Cooper but found him staring at the ground with flushed cheeks. I was hurting him too.

I rubbed my hands over my chest, over the mark that claimed us as soulmates. I kept trying to ignore it, to not think about it so it wouldn't hurt me so much. But that was silly. It wasn't going anywhere. Cooper was my soulmate. We just had to find our way to being in love like all the other soulmates we knew. As I looked up and watched Tenn and Tegan, I wondered what that had to feel like, to feel so consumed by your love for someone and to know they felt every ounce of that back.

But hell, I would've settled for being more in love with Cooper than him with me if it meant my heart didn't keep throwing Everest at me. It was so stupid. It was hopeless, and yet every time I let my mind wander, it went right to him.

Hunter, Bentley, and Emersyn were the first to come down the stairs and join Savannah at the door. Granted, their eyes were all locked on Tegan in the living room. Deacon, Kessler, Easton, and Lily came down together and while they were normally the jovial type, their expressions were grim and tense. Royce and Thiago were holding on to each other as they got in line at the door. Willow was pulling Chutney down the stairs, who was yelling up to Warner about the dogs. I couldn't remember who had warned me that my dogs would abandon me for her, but they'd been right. Sure, the boys slept in my bed with me, but as soon as I was up, they wanted Chutney.

Jackson and Bettina were the last to join us. When they did, Cooper and I went over and got in line. But Bettina was staring at her brother and best friend. After a moment, she walked over and tapped their arms. Both of them jumped like they'd fallen asleep.

Tenn scooped her up and walked over to us at the door. "Okay, babe, I'm going to picture Leyka's island. Bring us there."

Tegan took a deep breath, then snapped her fingers. "Go."

Tim spun and opened the door. Just like before, the white portal box was right there waiting for us to step through. No one seemed worried about this trip. They were just overall nervous. Though the line itself said, *seek the friend,* so that probably put everyone at ease.

Cooper reached down and squeezed my hand. "Leyka's a goof, but he's with us. We trust him."

I smiled and nodded. I was nervous, though I wasn't sure why. Perhaps it was the unknown. Perhaps it was the weird verbiage of this prophecy. Or perhaps it was knowing one of my best friends had nearly died because I acted too impulsively. Cooper's hand was the only thing keeping me anchored to my sanity. The warmth in his skin felt like lying on the beach. His hand was tight in my grip when we stepped into the portal.

White light washed over me.

When it faded, I was standing at the front of the Great Hall in Edenburg. I scowled and reached for Cooper, but my hand found only empty, cold air. My eyes widened and my pulse quickened. Cooper wasn't next to me. I spun in a circle. None of them were. Not a single Coven-mate stood by me. *Where the hell did they go? Why am I here? Was there a glitch in Tegan's magic?*

My stomach tightened into knots. I gnawed on my bottom lip and looked around. The Great Hall was full of students eating their lunches like a normal day at school. Except it was way past lunchtime. *Wait a second. Is that Mei-Ling?* It was Mei-Ling. That was my best friend sitting next to Birdie and Ava. I started toward them and spotted Tai sitting next to Tomás. *What are they doing here? They're not supposed to be out of Headquarters.*

Seamus lifted his arms, and I spotted big glass vials in his hands. One was full of a foamy green substance while the other was pink and swirling with bubbles. I hurried closer just as he started to pour both into a third, empty mason jar. My heart skipped. That wasn't right. He had to stop before he hurt himself and our friends. I didn't know how I knew this, but I knew it like I knew my own name. I ran over but when I opened my mouth to yell out for them, I spotted a reflection in the windows I hadn't expected to see.

I spun around to face her.

Vanessa.

The random friend of my aunt and uncles who'd rented us that house in Tampa. She stood there in black jeans and a black tank top just watching students do potions in front of her. *This is wrong. This is very wrong. Why is she here?* Sure, I knew Tampa had been evacuated to Eden, but none of the adults were attending school here. And Vanessa hadn't been a teacher.

I headed for her with a frown. "Vanessa!"

Silence.

I was only about five feet away now. "Vanessa!"

More silence.

*What is happening?* I reached out and touched her arm and white light flashed all around her. I gasped and jumped back just as her hair turned snow-white and her skin paled. Her green eyes turned white and gold. The all-black jeans and tank top outfit changed into this ethereal white gown that sparkled.

"Who-who are you?"

"I am Valathame."

"What happened to Vanessa? What did you do—"

"I *am* Vanessa." She looked down at me with those creepy white and gold eyes and grinned. "I knew you'd do well in this."

I flinched. "What?"

Vanessa, or Valathame, tapped under my chin with her finger. "Remember, if it feels too easy, it is. But that doesn't always mean you've made a mistake."

"What's happening here? Where is everyone else?" I shook my head. "That is gibberish."

She shrugged one shoulder. "To you, perhaps."

"Wait, *Valathame?* Isn't that our Goddess?"

"Yes, *I am.*" She chuckled. "It's nice to officially meet you. Brace yourself."

I opened my mouth to speak when light flashed all around me. One second I was in the Great Hall of Edenburg, the next I stood on a beach with the sun shining down on me. A man was reclining in a hammock, wearing a pink pair of swim trunks and drinking from a fancy coconut that even had an umbrella. His curly blond hair was wildly disheveled. I wanted to push his black sunglasses up so I could see his face, but I didn't.

He looked up at me with a wide grin and a laugh. "I knew you'd be second."

I flinched. "What? You did? Wait, second?"

That was when I spotted Savannah hiding behind a palm tree. She wasn't looking at me, but I knew she saw me. I wanted to go up to her and tell her I had no say in this. That I didn't want to be the cause of her pain, but I knew it was probably no use. She knew that already.

One by one, all of my Coven-mates appeared on the beach with me. Everyone wore matching scowls as they looked around. The guy in the hammock laughed harder, then tipped his head back to tap more juice out of the coconut. Everyone had appeared except Tegan and Tenn. They were nowhere in sight.

The man held his hand up and a box hovered next to him. But then I saw Tegan and Tenn in the box, just lying in a field of flowers.

Tenn looked up and sighed. "Can we come out now?"

He laughed and snapped his fingers. Tegan and Tenn appeared, standing in the sand with Tegan leaning her weight into him.

The guy sat up to get a better look at Tegan. Then he tapped on his forehead. "Borrowing from my sister?"

I gasped. "*You're* Leyka?"

He grinned and looked right at me. "And *you're* Francelina Proctor. Look at us! We're so good at this game."

"How do you know who I am?"

He shrugged. "How could I not?"

I scrubbed my face with my hands. "I am so confused. What just happened?"

"*In his wake you will be tested, Who sees the magic uncontested.*" He grinned and pulled the orange slice off the side of his coconut and ate it. "You were all tested. Congrats."

"So, we all passed the test?" Bettina narrowed her eyes on him. "What *was* that?"

Leyka pursed his lips. "I have no idea—at least not specifically. Each of you saw something different, something catered to *you*. It wasn't so much a test you could pass or fail, more of a *who gets to participate*."

"*Before you go we must be picky,*" Tenn said with a curse. "Why weren't Tegan and I tested?"

Leyka snapped his fingers. "Bentley, if you'd be so kind as to hold your arm up."

We all groaned.

"Read it aloud for us, dearie," Leyka purred as he licked orange juice off his tanned fingers.

Bentley glared at the angel and shook his head. But then he held his arm up and read the words, "*The book holds words vast unknown, Seek the tool to read the stone. Those claimed by his chosen token, Your fate lies on the broken. Between the shadows, whispers call, You know the drill, you've seen the fall. Mind the trail to danger's end, Within their tricks the cipher blends.*"

I just stared at Bentley as the words echoed in my head. They were bad. They made my stomach turn just hearing them, and I didn't even know what they meant. But I knew it was bad. Especially as everyone else's faces fell and their eyes glazed over. Their skin all looked paler than a moment ago.

They knew something I didn't.

"Okay, speak up. Share with the class, please?" I looked around but no one would meet my stare. "What the hell is going on?"

"*You know the drill, you've seen the fall,*" Easton whispered. His face was scrunched up like it hurt him.

Lily closed her eyes and leaned into him.

"I cannot believe you're gonna say this to us right now." Savannah put her hands on her hips. "Ma'am, we basically didn't survive last time, and you wanna send us again? You out ya' dam'mind."

"What is it? Where are we going?"

"The Land of the fucking Lore." Savannah cursed. "Ain't it? *Ain't it, Leyka?*"

He chuckled and shrugged one shoulder. "It's the Unseelie. You shouldn't be surprised you have to go back—"

Everyone groaned and started pacing around like the panic meant they couldn't stand still. I didn't understand. I had no idea what they were talking about. But I felt what they were feeling, and I didn't like it. I felt like I was caught in a riptide and was drowning in the panic rolling off my friends.

"*Mind the trail to danger's end, Within their tricks the cipher blends.*" Savannah kicked sand. "We almost all died, ma'am. What in the—"

"I know, and that is why Heaven has taken certain . . . liberties to try and see you through your next trip there. Valathame is back on Earth now, and she's ready to play dirty. There's a reason the Aether Witch's magic mirrors her own. She's the OG Queen of Darkness." Leyka sat his coconut down and stretched his arms, that shit-eating grin plastered on his face. "The Land of the Lore is a product of Unseelie. It is *their* magic. Some of you have felt that firsthand. We could not help you last time without betraying Thorne and Sage's cover. *This* time, we're pushing the boundaries. Well, perhaps not *we*."

"Leyka . . ." Bettina growled.

"What does that even mean? Must you speak in riddles?"

"I *could* speak in riddles. That would be fun for me. But you've already got a riddle you're working on, so I won't." He wagged his eyebrows. "Now, look, Lucifer has decided to help you—"

We all gasped.

*The Lucifer?*

"The one and only Lucifer, yes." Leyka grinned at me. Then he snapped his fingers and eight gold medallions appeared out of nowhere. They just dangled in the air as if they were on hooks. "Here's the deal: eight of you will take one medallion each. Think of this as your express pass. The idea is to get you in and out. A token, so to speak."

Hunter bent over and rested his hands on his knees. "Who . . . who must return—"

"I am so glad you asked, Hunter." Leyka cleared his throat. "Let me start by informing you that Tennessee and Tegan are NOT allowed to go back in there—"

"WHAT?"

"HE'S HOW WE GOT OUT!"

"HOW DO WE FIGHT THEM WITHOUT HIM?"

"So, no one objects to Tegan being benched here?" Leyka smirked. Everyone shook their heads.

"Feels kinda like mutiny, but okay," Tegan said softly with a laugh.

"The eight venturing through the Land of the Lore to find your next tool are . . ." Leyka rubbed his hands together, then used his fingers to count each person off. "Frankie, Lily, Easton, Chutney, Kessler, Willow, Royce, and Thiago."

There was a lot of panicking and groaning.

I pressed my hands to my stomach. "How do these medallions work? Why do we have them?"

"Lucifer's magic cannot just be handed out to anybody. You have to earn that honor. The eight of you passed the test. You were able to connect enough with Lucifer's magic to withstand his tricks." Leyka shrugged. "Or should I say, you were able to see through his tricks."

Cooper huffed. "I'm going."

"Starboy," Leyka frowned, "you didn't get a medallion—"

"I don't care. She's not going in there without me."

Leyka looked around. "I'm sure your soulmate is capable of taking care of herself. I do believe she's proven that to be true by now."

Cooper put his hands on his hips. "I'm going."

Leyka scoffed. "Look, the medallions can get multiple people in but only get *one* out. So, while we all admire your effort, Mr. Bishop, you cannot go unless you plan to stay there."

"I don't like it—"

"Well, la de fucking da, my dude. Since when is that new for us?" Leyka laughed a deep belly laugh. Then he gestured to the gold medallions just floating there. "Look, we're even on the white lies, right? I didn't tell y'all about the time travel and y'all didn't tell *me* I wound up an angel. Tit for that and all that jazz. Keltie is my soulmate. You know where my allegiance lies. We're bending Heaven's rules to help you, so grab your medallions before Lucifer changes his mind. You'll want to catch the Unseelie with the element of surprise, so you have to hurry."

All at once the eight of us reached forward and grabbed one of the medallions.

And everything went dark.

# CHAPTER FORTY-NINE

## FRANKIE

THE SECOND I wrapped my hand around that medallion, everything went dark. The warm, salty breeze was gone. The sound of the lapping waves faded away. Everything was just silent. My body jerked for a split second, and suddenly I was surrounded by a damp forest, and the deep, earthy scent of dirt and trees invaded my senses. Fog crept over the ground toward us and the shadows almost seemed to move around me.

Alarms went off in my mind. I needed to move. I felt this intrinsic panic to run for my life. But my body was frozen in place. I wasn't even sure if the others were here with me because they weren't in my peripheral vision—*wait. What's that?* Slowly, as if their magic was slow to kick in, I felt their auras click into place and tingle against my spine. Relief washed through me. I wasn't *here* alone. I'd never been afraid of the forest, day or night, but something about this place was wrong.

Around us, pine trees towered into the night sky. Each of their trunks and branches were solid black shadows against the light of the moon shining through. The air was a foggy, faint blue—almost silvery. It glittered in the distance just beyond our reach. I looked straight up, but there was no end in sight for the trees.

A cold chill slid down my spine, like fingertips tracing my skin. I shivered. "Where the hell are we?"

"The Land of the Lore," Bentley said softly behind me.

Silence.

*WAIT.* "BENTLEY?" I spun around and gasped.

"NO!" Easton threw his hands up in the air, then tugged his short hair. His blue eyes were wide. "No, no, no, no! You shouldn't be here!"

Lily whipped her head back and forth like she was looking for the exit sign. "How the hell did you get here?"

I opened my mouth, but no words came out. Fear gripped my soul. This part of the quest was supposed to be crazy dangerous. That was the whole point of being tested for Lucifer's medallions. We weren't all supposed to go. Only eight of us had been selected. I glanced around. Only eight of us held the round, gold discs in our hands. Me, Lily, Easton, Chutney, Kessler, Willow, Royce, and Thiago.

But standing in front of us were Bentley, Bettina, Deacon, Savannah, *and Cooper.*

My breath left me in a rush.

Kessler's face was pale as he reached out and gripped both Bentley and Cooper's shirts. "Tell me right now, did you touch the medallions?"

"No," they said at the same time.

Savannah squeezed her eyes shut and wrapped her arms around her waist as she rocked back and forth. "I don't wanna be here again. I don't wanna do this again."

Bettina's eyes were wide as she stared at the forest behind me. "*So, this is it.*"

"This is where half The Coven almost died." Royce reached out and grabbed Thiago's shirt. "Stay close to me."

Thiago swallowed nervously, his dark eyes bouncing around. "The darkness is thick here. We should not linger."

"They should not be here," Easton basically cried. "How are we getting them out? We only have eight medallions."

"By now Tegan and my brother have realized that I am not there. They'll be working on a plan already." Bettina pulled her sword out, the golden hilt sparkling in the moonlight. "But we aren't safe *now*—"

"No, we're not. We have to move. Those of you new to this place, you need to stay on the damn trail. Do not leave it. Stay together. Keep an eye on each other—"

"And know this forest is going to try and kill you. It's the land of the forest sirens." Deacon twirled his wrists and red magic flashed in his hands. "Trust nothing but *us* standing on the trail with you . . . or you will die."

Bentley sighed and pointed ahead, forcing us all to turn and look ahead of us. "These blue flames will lead us to the archway. Everyone *stay on the trail.* I cannot stress this enough."

"Just do what Bentley says, whatever he says." Willow bounced on the balls of her feet. "Don't fight him."

Deacon cursed under his breath. "Lead the way, Bentley, again, before we're picked off for lunch right here."

Bentley nodded and waved for us to follow him. We moved as a unit, each of our steps hitting the ground in perfect unison like we'd rehearsed for it.

"Do *not* slow down," Bentley said as we approached the first flame. "Or stop. And if we say run, you run."

"Where do we run *to?*"

"There's an archway. You won't miss it." Lily pointed ahead with her dagger, but her violet eyes glanced left and right as we walked. "Follow the flames and get to the arch."

"But do *not* go through the arch." Bentley cursed. "Nod if you understand that."

We all nodded.

Up ahead, the air shimmered blue around the flame, casting us all in a silvery-blue haze. My magic *burned* to come out and fight, like it knew the danger we were in more than I did. Dirt as black as shadows flew up all around my body. The air pulsed like a shockwave, moving away from us and into the forest. My pulse skipped.

Deacon's violet eyes bounced around the forest. "I can *feel* it again—"

"*Faster. Move,*" Bentley said with a growl. He rolled his wrists, and his skin turned black from the elbows down. Those orange lightning bolts streaked through the charred black parts and into his palms. Flames flickered between his fingers and then two fire-covered swords appeared in his hands. "*We cannot stop—*"

I gasped. Ice-cold air brushed over my feet and coiled around my ankles. Fingers clawed at my legs and tugged at my jeans. With each silent plea, their hands pulled at my body. I looked down to find a thick white fog covering our feet like we stood in a creek.

"Move. *Go. GO, GO, GO!*" Savannah leapt forward and shoved me forward. "*Go, go, go. MOVE!*"

Bentley leapt around and got back in front of me with his flaming swords raised. "*WE HAVE TO KEEP MOVING! NO STOPPING!*"

"*Whoa, whoa, whoa.*" Easton hopped around and swung his blade. "Not again!"

Arms made of white fog reached up, swaying unnaturally as their ghostly hands tried to grab anyone in their path. The hands pulled on us, gripping our clothes and weapons and tugging.

"Faster, y'all. FASTER, DAMMIT!" Savannah hissed and shoved at us again. She kept glancing over her shoulder. "*Pick 'em up an' put 'em down!*"

In front of me, Bentley was speed-walking confidently into the night. Ahead of him, floating blue flames glistened in the distance, marking the trail. I cursed and skipped to catch up and keep pace with him. Every few steps something moved from within the trees, but I knew not to look. We weren't running but almost. I'd never walked this fast. My hips were starting to burn. Figures made of white fog danced between the trees. They twirled in big puffy skirts of smoke, spinning and skipping alongside us.

"Keep moving!" Bentley shouted over his shoulder without slowing. "Join them and you die."

Something cracked under my boots. I ignored it and kept walking, pretending the crunching of every step was twigs and branches.

"Don't look down, my dudes," Deacon said softly. "You know what's down there!"

I hadn't meant to look, but I was a sucker for temptation and Deacon's threat just made me need to. I looked down and my heart skipped beats. Skulls and bones covered the ground. They smashed under our feet, shattering like eggshells. Light flashed through the trees. Little glowing turquoise orbs floated up from the ground and into the air, rising up to the sky.

"*They are coming!*" a female voice shouted in my mind.

"Who said that—"

A loud, cheerful whistle rang through the forest. It sounded like music—

"*DON'T LOOK!*" Bentley shouted. "*Do not look.*"

I squeezed my eyes shut without hesitation.

"RUN!" Savannah screamed. "RUN!"

All at once, we sprinted forward. The whistling grew louder, like it was moving closer to us, but we were running full speed now with Bentley at the front and Savannah in the back screaming at us to run.

"HELP!" A women's shrill voice ripped through the whistling. "HELP ME!"

"*DON'T LOOK!*" Bentley screamed. "*TRAP!*"

Royce threw up vines to stretch between the trees to block us from getting off the trail. "NOW I CAN'T! RUN PEOPLE!"

A woman's broken sob echoed between the trees. "Please, PLEASE! Is someone out there?"

My stomach tightened into knots. Every single part of me wanted to run to this woman's voice.

"HELP ME! I BEG YOU! HELP!"

"RUN, RUN, RUN! DO NOT WALK! RUN!" Savannah yelled. "THIS AIN'T LIKE BEFORE. MOVE!"

One of Royce's vines whipped out and wrapped around his throat. He choked on a gasp, reaching for the vines with his hands. We screamed his name and slid to a stop, scrambling to get back to him but the vines had him lifted three feet in the air. It was like something out of an alien movie. Even with all of us hitting the vines with our blades, the grip on Royce's throat was getting *tighter*.

Royce's face turned blue. His sapphire eyes bugged out.

"LEAVE! NOW!" Deacon fired red mist into his face, his own voice breaking. "GO!"

Royce's hand flew up and slammed the medallion. White light flashed from within his body. The vines hissed in protest. And then he shot straight up into the clouds like a rocket.

The vines he'd summoned attacked. This place had just used Royce's own magic against him and nearly killed him.

"RUN!"

We leapt into a sprint again. I pushed my legs to move faster, praying I wasn't walking off the path because I wasn't looking down, I kept my eyes on Bentley in front of me.

"COME HERE, PLEASE! HELP ME! I'M RIGHT HERE!"

A cool gust of wind brushed over my back and swept through my hair like someone was running their fingers through it. But there was no one there. Bettina was hot on my heels, but her hand gripped my sweater, not my hair.

Ice-cold hands made of smoke grabbed me by the arms and then threw me straight up into the trees. I heard myself scream as it dragged me higher and higher. *THINK, FRANKIE!* It was stealing me, pulling me up into the darkness.

Thiago slid under me and threw his hands up. The shadows of the trees vanished, like he'd shined a spotlight up at us. I spotted Bettina, Willow, and Chutney floating up with me, tethered only by shadow-vines with hands. *HELL NO.* I threw my hands out and shot my magic. Blue and pink flames spread like a wildfire around us. Bettina roared and shot ice into the shadow-vines. There was a crack and then we dropped to the ground in a pile on top of Thiago. We scrambled to get back up.

"*They are coming.*"

"*They are coming.*"

"Who said that?" Chutney shouted. "That's not the same voice—"

*SAM.* That was Sam's voice. I recognized it in an instant. That sultry southern voice of Everest's betrothed haunted me in Avolire. I turned to Bentley with wide eyes and mouthed *SAM*.

He cursed and we charged forward. "MOVE!"

A soft, faint humming sound whispered through the trees. It sounded like a softer version of a church's organ. I felt the rumble of the tone in my bones. My gaze locked on the blue flame in front of us. It flickered and swayed in the opposite direction, like it was urging us on, like it knew something we didn't.

"Not that noise again," Willow cried, her head whipping back and forth. "NO!"

Savannah ran in front of us and threw her arms out, black smoke shot in every direction. "RUN!"

Willow dropped to her knees, clutching her ears. Blood ran like rivers out of her ears and down the side of her neck. She screamed so loud her voice cracked.

"*RUN!*" Bentley flung fire from his swords into the trees. "GET HER!"

Kessler scooped Willow up and ran after him. The others were already running. I fell into step behind Kessler, wanting to watch his back. But then I heard talking. The voices were soft at first, but with every step we took, they grew stronger and louder. They were feminine and high. The voices sang but not in words, just this range of notes that seemed to move around us and tickle one ear at a time.

"*Frankie,*" Everest called to me.

My legs stopped short like he had some hold on my body. My heart pounded. That was Everest's voice. He always spoke to my mind, the same way Tegan did. My heart did weird flips in my chest. I hadn't seen him since he left me in the tower that night, since before my memories came back.

"*Frankie, over here.*"

I gasped and spun toward the sound of his voice and spotted him thirty feet away between the trees. *Everest.* I took a step forward, then froze. He was off the trail. They'd said not to leave the trail. Bentley had been emphatic about that. But Everest was off the trail. I stared down at the ground trying to find exactly where the trail was going.

"*Frankie, come here.*"

His voice was moving. I frowned and spun around to find him behind me now, but when I glanced back, he was still in the first spot. My pulse quickened. Everest was all around me, stepping out from behind trees in every direction I looked.

My eyes widened. He was everywhere. Beckoning me to come to him. I wanted to. I wanted to run to him with every fiber of my being. And then there was just one of him, standing just five feet off the trail in his pristine white suit.

He held his hand out to me and licked his lips. "Come, Frankie. You're safe with me."

I lifted my hand out toward him and took a step. *Everest.*

"*STOP, FRANCELINA,*" Everest growled in my mind. "*STOP.*"

I gasped and leapt backwards, my feet slipping on a tree root and sending me crashing to the ground on my back. Sharp pain shot up and down my spine. I screamed a curse.

"*GET UP, FRANCELINA. NOW. GET UP,*" Everest yelled in my mind.

Then it hit me. *Francelina.* Everest always called me Francelina. Always. Never, ever, not even once did he call me Frankie. I licked my lips and looked around. "*Everest?*" I heard myself whisper out loud.

"*That is NOT me, Francelina.*"

My heart stopped. I licked my lips and nodded. *"You don't call me Frankie."*

*"Never, Francelina. Do you understand what's happening?"*

I nodded again. My arms were trembling now. *"Forest sirens."*

*"GET UP, Francelina. NOW."*

I pushed up to my knees, then all the way to standing, but my body was sluggish. It was taking all of my energy to move. My breaths were short and tight. And then the drums started. Butterflies danced in my stomach. The hairs on my arms stood tall. Each beat sent vibrations up my legs and into my bones. The ground rumbled. Every muscle in my body tensed. The drums pounded feverishly, and my pulse mimicked.

My fingers tingled and I felt myself grow weaker.

*"Come dance with me, Frankie,"* Everest's voice whispered from my right.

My gaze snapped toward it, helpless to resist.

*"Close your eyes, Francelina."*

I squeezed my eyes shut.

*"Good girl,"* he purred, and it sent heat rushing through my body. *"Take a deep breath, open your eyes, THEN RUN."*

I took a deep breath, then opened my eyes and ran just like he'd said. About thirty feet up the path, I spotted my Coven-mates sprinting back to find me with panicked expressions on their faces.

*"THEY'RE COMING NOW!"*

The branches hanging low over the trail dropped to the ground *and landed on four legs.* They didn't have hands or feet. Their arms and legs were made of solid white and tapered down to points. Their backs were curved like a humpback's but had sharp spikes along the spine. These creatures had tiny round heads with big, gaping black holes where eyes should have been.

"FRANKIE!" Bettina shouted up ahead.

The creature lunged for me, but muscle memory kicked in, over-riding the shock and fear. I pushed off the ground and leapt over it like it was a hurdle at the Olympics. I managed to jump over it but another one swooped down and slammed into my side. I cursed and crashed to the ground. The creature loomed over me.

Red lightning pierced its head, pulling its attention away from me.

It turned and lunged forward, tackling Deacon to the ground. Red lightning flashed left and right.

"FRANKIE!"

I scrambled to my feet when another creature lunged right for me. My breath caught in my throat. Chutney dove in front of me just as the creature swung all four of its legs at me. All four pierced through her shoulders and legs. She wailed as her blood splashed all around her. The monster just stood there on top of her. I crawled over to her, but Bettina got there first. White lightning coiled around Bettina's opal-bladed sword as she swung it through the creature's limbs, severing them all off in the beat of a second.

"CHUTNEY!" I slid over, pulling her head into my lap so I could press my hands to her chest. "Breathe. Just breathe. Nothing vital was hit. Just breathe—"

She screamed, her eyes wide and locked on something over my head. Red lightning flashed left and right in my peripheral vision. I heard my Coven-mates shouting and fighting these monsters. Bettina spun and sliced her sword through another creature.

I had to get Chutney out of here. I yanked her sweater back and dove for the gold medallion tucked under her clothes. At the last second, I remembered to grab her hands and pressed them to the metal. Her eyes widened the second her fingers grazed it—white light shined bright and then shot straight up into the sky, taking Chutney with it. I watched until the light faded. And then the oak trees above me *moved*.

What I thought were thick trunks were tall humanoid figures that were the same texture as trees. My eyes widened. I glanced left and right, and my stomach dropped. We were surrounded. It was an ambush, and we fell for it. These weren't the same creatures we'd just been fighting. These were taller, more human-like. They stood on two legs and had long arms with three branch-like fingers.

And they were charging right for my friends up ahead.

I cursed and leapt into a sprint.

Bentley leapt over the creatures, slicing his fiery swords through their necks and then flipping mid-air and rolling across the ground. The monsters lunged onto the trail from within the trees. One grabbed Cooper by the throat and lifted him up, but its long, weird fingers tore his shirt torn down the front and blood splattered.

"NO! COOPER!" I dug my toes into the ground, but I wasn't moving fast enough, it was like my body was moving in slow-motion.

A humanoid-tree-monster swung its long arm and collided with Kessler's back, causing him to fly forward and roll across the trail with Willow still in his arms. Another monster scooped Lily and Easton up in each hand, pulled their arms wide, and then slammed them into each other as hard as it could. They bellowed in pain as their bodies made horrible crunching sounds. Metal popped and rained to the ground in pieces.

Savannah dropped to her knees and started screaming words in a weird language. Black smoke swirled around her body. Something was wrong, very wrong. I raced for her because everyone else was thick in battle and fighting for their lives. But before I could even get to Savannah, Bettina was thrown over my head. I dove and caught her, but her body was encased in *ice*. I hissed and rolled her onto the ground—my heart sank.

The ice covered her entire body except for her face,

But fresh, red blood was filling her little sarcophagus and drowning her. She coughed and spit up the blood, but it was too much. I pressed my hands to the ice and pushed my magic out, but the blue and pink flames just danced along the ice's edge. I rolled her onto her side so the blood poured out and she could breathe.

"BENTLEY!"

He slid in a split-second later and pressed his fiery, lava-covered hands to her ice-covered chest. It melted away—and Bentley was gone. She was bleeding but I didn't know where from. Only her face and chest were free of the ice.

"FRANKS!"

I glanced over my shoulder and spotted Kessler's medallion flying toward me. I reached out to grab it when a creature sliced it in half. Kessler screamed. Bettina coughed and my body went cold. Her skin was losing color. I cursed and yanked my own medallion off and slid it into her mouth. She closed her mismatched eyes and then bright white light sucked her up into the sky and out of sight.

Just as I jumped up, I watched as a monster clawed Deacon from head to toe. I screamed and threw my magic into the monster before it could sink its teeth into him. I pulled my sai off my thigh and pounced. Adrenaline had me killing the beast and turning for Deacon before I even registered what I'd just done. Deacon was groaning and trying to get up. My eyes stung. His soulmate glyph was shining bright-red, and I knew it wasn't from Emersyn.

There was so much blood. I yanked my sweater off and ripped it into long strips. "MEDALLION!" I screamed as loud as I could without looking away from our Devil.

"I've had worse," Deacon groaned through clenched teeth, but then I tied a tourniquet around his arms and he hissed.

I pushed the rest of my sweater into the main wound on his chest, then ripped his belt off his hips. Somehow, I managed to slide it under his waist, then tightened it around his stomach, pinning my sweater in place to hopefully stop the bleeding.

Kessler ran by me, dropping a medallion onto Deacon's chest. I pressed it to his bare skin, then forced his hand to touch it. I sent a prayer to Valathame as that white light stole him right out from under me.

Savannah screeched and lifted off the ground. Smoke was shooting out of her body like it was coming from her pores. She screamed and threw black magic out of her palms. With one swish of her hand, she drew a symbol in the air. But then her eyes rolled backwards, and weird noises left her mouth.

Cooper gasped and reached for her, but two monsters leapt in front of him. "SAVANNAH!"

Her eyes cleared. She looked right at him. "Run," she said in a calm, stone-cold voice.

"SAVANNAH!" Cooper's voice broke. "NO!"

We couldn't get to her. We were surrounded. Each of us was fighting off at least two monsters. I wasn't even watching what I was doing, my gaze kept shooting around looking for injured people.

Savannah lunged for the broken medallions on the trail. Words left her lips in a weird whisper. She drew that symbol in the air over the medallion, then light flashed around her. Those big blue eyes of hers locked on my soulmate and she whispered, *"Please run."*

Then she was gone.

"MOM?" Bentley's voice cracked.

We all gasped and froze.

A woman who looked scarily like Tegan was on her knees between two trees. Her entire body trembled. Her head jerked left and right, up and down, making her dark hair swish around. She mumbled a stream of words, but they weren't coherent. Her eyes rolled in different directions. She gasped and her back arched. Her whole body convulsed and twitched. She collapsed and flopped on her back like a fish out of water. Her arms and legs thrashed. She swung her head back and forth. Even from here I heard her teeth rattling against each other.

"Just like before," Bentley whispered. He swayed and staggered. "That's what she was doing last time!"

"Devon?" Kessler stumbled toward her.

*That's Devon?*

"No, no, Mom is NOT here." Cooper grabbed his uncle's shirt and yanked him backwards so hard they both crashed to the ground.

"Then why is she HERE?" Bentley's voice was breaking.

I turned toward him just as a monster lunged from behind a tree. "MOVE!"

But it was too late. Those three-pronged finger things burst through his skin on his shoulder. I threw my sai and it impaled the monster's face at the same time Cooper's sword slammed into its gut. Kessler got to his nephew first, scooping him up off the ground.

"GET HIM GONE!" a woman yelled.

I looked toward the unknown voice and gasped. It was Devon. She stood just behind us with a sword gripped tight in her hand. "Devon? H-how?"

"Never mind that. Get him gone, Kessler!"

Kessler paled and blinked up at her.

Cooper looked around in a panic. "Mom, we need a medallion."

"Who has one? There should be one left!" I shouted, but another round of monsters were seconds away.

A dozen Devons appeared behind her. It was like someone hit copy and paste over and over. Her entire body shimmered and sparkled. Then it clicked. Astral projection was her gift. She wasn't really here at all.

"I HAVE IT! COMING!" Thiago shouted.

One of the Devon forms in the back sprinted over to Thiago and took the medallion he held and flew over to him, dropping to her knees. Bentley began convulsing. His arms turned jet-black and those orange lightning bolts streaked across his skin. Cooper cursed and pressed the medallion into his brother's chest, using Bentley's non-injured hand.

Bright light flashed and took Bentley with it.

"LOOK!" Lily shouted. "THERE IT IS!"

"You need to go," Devon yelled. Another dozen copies of her filled in the space so it was just a wall of her. "I can hold them. Get to the circle—"

"Mom—" Cooper's voice broke.

"I'm not dead. Not yet," one of her bodies said while three others used their swords to point at the arch. "GO. NOW!"

Kessler and Cooper spun on their toes, grabbing my arm and dragging me into a sprint. Thiago had his arm around Willow's waist. They were running with us. Lily and Easton were limping and bleeding from somewhere, but they were booking it.

And then I saw it.

The archway.

It wasn't at all what I was expecting. My steps faltered. It wasn't just an archway. It was half of a wall made of old gray stones. It looked like maybe there was once a full structure there. Or part of a wall. The stones were broken off on one side of the archway, but on the other it stretched out to even include a little window. *Who's looking through that and why?* Because it was not an accident.

The forest was full of towering pine trees rowed up one after another, yet in this ring around the stone archway, all of the trees were *oaks*. Massive oaks with branches thicker than my body. The trees' branches stretched out at angles, some of them hanging low over the trail that led to the archway—like they were protecting it. Moss and flowered-vines clung to the stones and hung down through the opening of the archway. The air was lighter in this ring of trees. It was a pale blue-green color and seemed to carry a bit of a haze in it.

"We did it," I breathed as my legs burned and begged to stop running. I pointed at it like they could've somehow missed it. "There it is!"

"*I remember the spell for Seelie, get inside the circle!*" Lily whispered. "*We can get out that way!*"

Together we leapt over the stone circle and sprinted for the archway.

*"Within their tricks the cipher blends,"* I quoted the prophecy. "It's gonna be hidden right in front of us somewhere."

Cooper crouched beside me. "Use your stones."

I lifted my wrist and pressed my fingers to the stones. They lit up, glowing blue instantly. *Please guide me to the cipher we're here to find.*

*"What the hell is THAT?"* Thiago backed into the archway with a grunt. He pointed straight behind me. "WHAT IS THAT?"

"I don't see anything," Cooper cursed.

*"Oh meu Deus,"* Thiago whispered.

The glowing pink arrow lifted off my stones and pointed for me to go around the other side. I hurried over, then froze. A wall of darkness was moving toward us. A cold chill slid down my spine.

Queen Sweyn stepped out from behind the trees and darkness. She was every bit as awful and beautiful as I remembered. I hid behind the stone wall of the archway but peeked around as Sweyn lunged for Easton. There was a crunch and a scream—and Lily collapsed ten feet away from them. Sweyn's eyes lit up.

Thiago jumped in front of her to shield Easton, but Sweyn just licked her lips. "Another Hanged Man, my favorite snack."

She threw Easton aside, caught Thiago by the shoulders, then sank her fangs into his tanned skin. Thiago's back arched as he gasped. Black lines covered his mouth—Cooper tackled Sweyn like it was Superbowl Sunday, but she got right back on her feet. She reached down and threw Cooper into a tree.

*"Frankie,"* Willow whispered beside me.

I cursed and looked back down to my arrow. It was pointing to a narrow spot between two stones. Willow and I began digging for it, but we were both watching the fight.

Kessler pulled a tree out of the ground, then threw it like a javelin right into Sweyn's chest. She flew back into the forest with a growl that made the trees vibrate. Cooper was already on his feet and racing back toward us, so Kessler hurried over to Easton and Lily, who hadn't yet moved. With a quick whip of his wrist, they flew like baseballs into the circle. Thiago coughed and tried to crawl, but Kessler made quick work of scooping him up and carrying him into the circle with us. Thiago's bite wound was still bleeding, so Kessler held his hand over it.

Willow threw her hands up and a shimmery wall of iridescent blue surrounded us. "Find the damn cipher. That won't last."

I was barely paying attention to the arrow. My soulmate was out there alone, but I couldn't help him if I didn't find what we were here for. Willow and I discovered the object must have been between two massive boulders. I pried one of the stones on the edge loose, dirt caking under my fingernails.

"COOPER!" Kessler shouted. "RETREAT!"

"There it is!"

But I didn't look. My eyes landed on Queen Sweyn, Everest, and the wall of vampires emerging from the tree line without a worry in the world. Those red eyes glowed in the dark and made my stomach roll.

"*Kessler, grab that stone!*" Willow whisper-shouted.

I was frozen in place, watching in horror as five vampire sentinels dressed in their white trench coats lunged from the trees and attacked Cooper. *NO!* I pulled both of my sais out and charged for them. Cooper was holding them off with expert moves, but I knew they were just toying with him. I'd seen their speed firsthand.

I really didn't know what my plan was, but over my dead body was I going to sit back and watch these vampires kill my soulmate. I didn't let myself look at Everest. I couldn't afford even a moment's distraction. Two of the Sentinels saw me coming and abandoned their attack on Cooper. But they underestimated me. This was the single moment where a decade of martial arts training paid off. Despite their hyper-speed, I took them by surprise by dropping into a slide through their legs and then flipping over. I didn't actually know what my body was doing. I just knew I was doing it.

Both Sentinels flew into the air and crashed in a heap at Sweyn's feet. I jumped up and ran for Cooper as the vampires charged for us again.

Sweyn gasped. Her red eyes widened. She shouted something in a weird language and the vampires all froze in place. Her jaw dropped. She pointed to Cooper. "He's your soulmate."

I arched one eyebrow.

She shouted in that language, and the vampires pulled back. I saw the fear in her eyes. It wasn't a look she wore often. But as she looked from me, to Cooper, to Kessler behind us, I saw the math adding up.

She was afraid. I didn't understand *why,* but she'd called off the Sentinels when she saw *Cooper* was my soulmate.

And then I made the mistake of looking to Everest. His white and blue eyes were glowing with rage—and narrowed on Cooper. He snarled and his upper lip curled up to reveal two sets of fangs. He balled his hands into fists at his sides as his body trembled.

Sweyn's eyes widened.

A pale arm shot into my peripheral vision, gripped me around the waist, and dragged me into a sea of darkness.

# CHAPTER FIFTY

## FRANKIE

AT FIRST ALL I saw was vibrant blue light and little golden orbs floating everywhere. I tried to fight against whatever held me, but then I looked up and spotted Thorne's face hovering above mine.

I gasped. *THORNE!*

I tried to sit up and see where we were, but we were moving too fast. The neon-colored flowers beneath me looked like the ones we'd seen in Seelie by those thrones made of vines. *We are in Seelie!* My heart pounded as that relief hit hard. I craned my neck around to look for the others and wanted to cry when I saw them. Kessler still had his hand around Thiago's throat, but they were both alive and that was what mattered.

"Out of your damned minds going back in there—"

"Sage, it was hardly any choice of theirs." Thorne swiftly carried us straight for the gate that led back to Eden. "Look, those of you injured just now, your injuries may not heal as fast as they should once you leave Seelie. You can always return to us to correct that."

And then everything went dark.

*NO, NO, NO!* I gasped and jumped—*and landed on all fours inside Coven Headquarters.* I had no idea how we'd gotten here. I hadn't seen us leave Seelie, but I *did* see Thorne crouched down with his hands stretched out and magic billowing from his palms. I couldn't quite see what was going on. My senses were slow, the room was blurry on the edges and the sound was like I was in a fishbowl or underwater.

I blinked and shook my head, then looked around again. My heart dropped. It was *chaos*. There were rivers of fresh blood in every direction. The living room was not the infirmary. They had a whole set up downstairs. I'd seen it myself. Yet the living room had turned into a battlefield triage. Chutney was sprawled on the wooden coffee table with blood dripping over the edges onto the carpet. Saffie was hovering above her on little wings made of stars, sprinkling golden pixie dust onto Chutney's wounds.

"She's up!" Mei-Ling shouted, suddenly right in front of me.

Everything went dark again.

"NO!" I screamed and my eyes flew open. I saw the ceiling of Headquarters for a split second before Mei-Ling leaned over me. Something was wrong with me. It didn't make sense. "*Why—*"

"She's up again!" my best friend shouted to someone.

I rolled onto my side and choked on a scream. Tennessee was on the ground in front of the fireplace with his sister in between his legs. He was pinning her down with his arms and legs. She was lying mostly on top of him and convulsing. Tenn had her arms pinned up over her head, but they flopped like a fish out of water. His face was scrunched like holding her down was actually a struggle. He kicked his legs up and hooked them over hers to trap them against the ground while she shook. Blood poured out of her, but there was so much of it, I couldn't tell from *where*. She kept covering him in ice, but when it touched the golden bands on his arm, it would evaporate. The cycle continued over and over. Jackson held her face in his hands, trying to keep her eyes focused on him while he whispered to her. Timothy was on his knees pouring colorful potions into her eyes and mouth while Thorne did *something*.

My stomach rolled like I was going to puke—and everything was dark again.

I woke with another gasp, this time on my stomach. There was no vomit beneath me, so that was a good sign. But when I craned my neck back to look up, I found the chairs by the front window thrown aside. Emersyn held Deacon's face in her blood-stained hands. She was yelling at him, warning him not to die on her again. I hated the *again* part. Deacon was on the ground, the gouges down the front of his body were gaping and—bile shot up my throat. This time I did puke, but there was nothing in my stomach to evacuate, so it was mostly clear liquid.

"FRANKIE!"

My eyes rolled and I felt myself slipping again, but large hands gripped my shoulders and flipped me over. *Cooper.* It was Cooper. He pulled me into his lap to prop me up. My whole body was numb and tingling. I felt Cooper's chest rumble like he was yelling but I couldn't hear it. Every sound was distant.

"She's up again —why is this happening?" Mei-Ling leaned into my view, her gaze scanning my body. "I don't see *anything.*"

I knew she was talking about me, but I couldn't focus on myself, not when this carnage was unfolding around me. Bentley was propped up against the wall by the door that led down to the infirmary. There was a smeared streak of blood from a few feet up down to where he was sitting as if he'd crashed into the wall and slid to the ground. Mona was tending to the gory wound on his shoulder.

The door flew open. Katherine, Myrtle, and Lennox sprinted into the living room with trays of vials and stuff. Myrtle went to Chutney. Katherine straddled Bettina's legs and was splashing her. Lennox went over to Deacon. Hunter was in the middle of a couch gripping Royce with one arm and Willow with the other. Royce's throat was dark-purple and blue. Willow's eyes were wide, and the blood still stained the side of her neck from her ears. Both of them were staring at nothing, just shaking their heads. Hunter's golden glow of magic coiled around them.

Savannah sat on the bottom step of the stairs with her black cats clutched to her chest. Her eyes were closed, and her lips moved like she was talking, probably a prayer or chant. I scanned the room until I found Thiago on the dining room table with the young healer Gin from Tampa working on the wound in his throat.

"JUST SNAP IT BACK IN!" Easton bellowed. "DO IT, KESSLER!"

Kessler leaned over and pushed on Easton's arm—Easton roared and then cursed obscenities.

Lily covered her mouth with her hand that was swollen and *definitely* broken. Actually, her whole arm looked like a marshmallow. I looked to her other hand and found four of her fingers purple.

The lights went out, sending me back to darkness.

"Frankie!" Cooper and Mei-Ling shouted.

I woke with a gasp. I tried to speak but my mouth was dry and not moving.

"THORNE!" Cooper snapped. "WHAT'S WRONG WITH HER?"

Thorne slid in front of me, his green clothes drenched in blood. His fiery gaze scanned me up and down and back again. He shook his head and held his hands up. His magic slammed into my face, making me cough.

"I don't see any injuries—"

"This is not physical, Cooper." Thorne tipped my chin up, forcing my eyes to look at his. He narrowed his eyes. "Did you see Everest in the Land of the Lore?"

"No, Everest wasn't there—"

"*You wouldn't have seen him,*" Thorne whispered. His narrowed gaze seemed to re-inspect me before returning to my face. "Francelina, tell me right now, did you see Everest in the Land of the Lore? Yes or no."

"*Yes,*" I whispered, but it was barely visible.

Thorne cursed. "Foolish, risky child," he grumbled and pressed his hands to my temples.

Mei-Ling scowled. "I don't think Everest is a child—"

"He is to *me,*" Thorne said, but he was focused on me. "Don't fight the darkness this time. Let it take you. I'm right here—"

And it took me.

Everything went dark.

Rainbow mist swirled through the dark and then my eyes flew open. Tegan was leaning over me, her hair still snow-white. Her eyes were still that creepy gold and white. The diadem was gone, but I knew she had to give it back to Myrtle.

Thorne leaned over beside Tegan. "Blink twice if you can hear me." His voice sounded like gravel.

I blinked. Twice.

Thorne nodded, then vanished.

"Good. Coop's gonna sit you up again. Tell me if everything is still off." Tegan gestured for her brother. "Slowly."

I braced myself for the room to spin and my stomach to roll, but it didn't happen. The room was clear, unfortunately so. The sight before me was haunting. I must have been out for a little bit because Chutney wasn't on the coffee table. Tennessee was sitting in the same spot, but Bettina was no longer in his lap, though her blood *was*. He stared at the floor with a pale face, looking traumatized. Timothy was gripping his shoulder, but I wasn't sure which one of them it was supporting. Over by the window, only the tossed-aside chairs and blood stains showed evidence of Deacon being there.

"Where . . . where are they?" I pointed. "Deacon. Chutney. Bettina—"

"They're downstairs in the infirmary now. They're stable." Tegan pressed her hand to my forehead. "Thorne is down there with them."

"*We need Riah*," Savannah whispered, still sitting on the stairs.

The silence clung to the air like a rotten egg.

"Thorne said he called for them, but they'd gone down to see Lucifer—"

Everyone shuddered.

Tegan sighed. "Sage had to stay by the archway. Grabbing y'all weakened the barrier. She had to make sure no one *else* came through. Thorne is doing his best right now."

"*We are lucky to have him then*," I whispered and pushed up out of Cooper's lap because I needed to feel my body functioning properly. "Where's Bentley and Thiago?"

"Over here," Bentley said with a softer voice than I'd ever heard him use.

Once Tegan leaned to the side, I spotted Bentley and Thiago sitting at the dining room table with bandages wrapped around their injuries. I looked to the couch. Willow, Hunter, and Royce hadn't moved, but they weren't shaking anymore. Easton's arm was in a sling. Lily's right arm was strapped straight down against her body. Four of her fingers on her left hand were in those little braces. Kessler sat in the big chair behind Tenn, his eyes distant and dark, but I didn't see any injuries.

Only Kessler and I had made it out uninjured. At least physically. Mentally and emotionally, I would be forever changed.

I licked my lips. "What happened to *me*?"

Tegan rubbed her face with her hands, and I realized they, too, were covered in blood. She shook her head like she didn't know the answer. But then I heard her voice in my mind say, *"Everest did some-thing to you in there. Something to block your senses from being taken over by the Unseelie. It was crazy dangerous but likely the reason you are uninjured and quite possibly the reason y'all got out alive."*

I swallowed nervously and nodded.

She pushed to her feet, then walked over to sit on the stone ledge in front of the fireplace, right next to her soulmate. She ran her fingers through his hair. He squeezed his eyes shut and cringed.

"Where's the cipher? Who did I hand it to? Where is it—"

"Here." Bentley held it up in the air, then stood up and walked over to sit on the coffee table. "We have it. But that's not all we have—"

Everyone groaned.

"I know, *I know.* This next part of the prophecy—well, tonight only proved even more that we have to move quickly."

"Especially now that Sweyn found us in there," Easton grumbled. "She was furious."

"What happened in there . . . with Cooper?" Thiago raised his hand in the air. "She was ready to have her bloodsucker army take us out, then like . . . froze."

"She's afraid of the Bishop family."

Everyone looked to me with frowns. Except Tegan, who smirked.

"That night she lured me out here in Eden, she was spooked by the Bishops." I reached up and tapped on Cooper's bicep. "Tonight she stopped when he ran out—"

"No." Willow shook her head. "She froze when she saw your soul-mate marks. She's afraid of the Bishops, but seeing that your soulmate is one? It made her pause. She was trying to decide if she wanted to provoke your terrifying family."

Everyone was just staring at us. I could see their brains working.

Bentley handed the cipher to Tegan. "That's gonna suck to decode."

"I'm just glad we have it. I was looking at that book and the entire thing must be written in Unseelie. No one speaks Unseelie—not even Thorne or Sage . . . or the angels."

Tenn hung his head. "Or the angels aren't allowed to tell us they speak it. Either way, same result."

"Once we decode this, we'll be able to read the book." She slid the cipher into the inside pocket of her leather jacket. "The book is missing a page. I think we can all assume that's the page we need. We must have to decode it first to know our next step—"

"Actually, not quite." Bentley raised arm with the new prophecy written on it.

Willow cursed. Everyone looked to her with wide eyes because she never cursed. "What? Look how long that one is!"

Tenn nodded. "Babe, read it."

Tegan cleared her throat. "*Beyond the arch of magic's lane, Lies a shadow of Coven's bane. Rouse the spirits of their rage, By word of magic, set thy stage. For what you seek is deep and dire, Paint their lawn in dragon's fire. And when they come to slay your trust, Give to them the one she lust. With blood and bone, pain to borrow, A crown upon a seat of sorrow. From the marble within her lair, Retrieve the stolen without flair.*"

"Avolire." I nodded. I'd suspected it already. "Our magic is restricted by that archway."

"By word of magic, set thy stage." Timothy looked to Tegan. "Time for your tricks?"

"Time for *mine*." Willow rubbed her hands together, but her face was a mask of rage. "It says *paint their lawn*. If I've learned anything from Tegan, it's that word choice is everything. Valathame isn't saying to bring the dragons, she's telling me to make the vampires think we did."

Tegan smiled.

"Which means you'll need my fire." Emersyn looked at her hands. "Maybe Tegan can fly me around so I can shoot fire from Willow's dragons?"

Tegan *grinned*. "Keep going, y'all."

Kessler pursed his lips. "*And when they come to slay your trust, Give to them the one she lust.* We think she wants Frankie—if her actions prove anything. So, we need Willow and Tegan to make Sweyn think Frankie is ripe for the taking."

"Hey, Cooper, how'd you like to be bait this time?" I looked up to my soulmate and arched one eyebrow.

Tegan chuckled. "I am so proud of y'all."

Cooper frowned. "Bait? What do you mean? Why—oh, because she's afraid of the Bishops and I'm your soulmate."

I nodded. "If we can distract her with *you* and the dragons, then I can get inside to her throne. Because that's where this leads us. *A seat of sorrow within a lair of marble.*"

Tegan jumped to her feet, her eyes sparkling mischievously. "Let's go. Now. She won't expect us to attack after the Land of the Lore, so it's our best opportunity. We have to go now."

Tenn leapt to his feet. "She's right. The injured are in as good of hands as possible. We can't let their sacrifice be in vain. That being said, Em and Lancaster, we'll understand if you need to stay—"

"No." Jackson turned away from the front window he'd been staring out. "How many times have you or Tegan been near death and down and the other has had to fight? My soulmate might be *my* whole world, but my job in this Coven means I have to save the actual world. So, we're with you."

Emersyn nodded. "Just tell us what you want us to do."

Tenn's eyes glistened as he turned to Tegan. "What's your plan, babe? We all know you have one."

Her lips curved up in a crooked smile. It was almost in slow motion, like I was watching the Grinch about to steal Christmas. She snapped her fingers, and all of our clothing turned as white as the snow that'd be on Avolire's front lawn. "Now we'll blend."

Tim shook his head and chuckled. "Is that your whole plan, Trouble?"

Hunter raised his hand. "Do we get to know your whole plan?"

Tegan shrugged. "I'm gonna portal us to just outside that arch so we can use our magic freely. The second we hit that snow, it's game on. We need to lure them out as fast as possible. We're the distraction, the decoys. The second Frankie gets her shot, she's going in. Cooper, Lily, and Bentley, you're going with her."

All three of them nodded.

"I want Willow to stay by my side so we can work together. We'll remain outside the arch as long as possible. Emersyn, stay by me until her illusions are going so Sweyn won't figure it out. Also, Thiago, your magic may be of good service to us, so you'll hang back with us too." Tegan waited until those three nodded, then she continued, "Now, because Frankie is who she wants, I'm going to make the real Frankie invisible, then have Willow send an illusion-Frankie out into the lawn. This won't fool her for long, so . . . Frankie, be ready to move."

I nodded. "The second they go for the illusion, I'll slide inside, especially if I'm invisible. I'll be at the door and ready to go."

"Perfect. I assume you remember your way around?"

"It haunts my waking thoughts, yes." I smiled and gave a thumbs-up.

"As soon as we get there, I'm going to attack the castle. The rest of you . . . fight. Easton, wait until they come for us, then cover everyone with armor." She turned and pressed her hand to Tenn's chest. "I need you to be doing what you do so arrogantly that they'll be unable to resist the urge to go for you."

He smirked. "Arrogant bait. Got it."

"Be my eyes out there. I care more about all of us coming home than how many fangers we take out. They are *fast*." Tegan turned to Cooper. "You. I'm going to have you walk out with the illusion-Frankie, but as soon as the real Frankie makes her run—"

"I'm ready." He cracked his knuckles and bounced on the balls of his feet. "Let's get in there before all of our vengeful rage subsides."

Tegan marched to the front door, and we all hurried after her with Tenn at the back. There was no joking, no laughter. We were all tense and pissed. Marching into Avolire with the intention of ambushing them was brazen and potentially suicidal.

None of us were hesitating.

Death had no room in here.

Tegan threw the front door open, and we all leapt into that white box. My sneakers sank in the snow. The air was bitterly ice-cold and stung my bare skin. I looked down and realized I'd taken my sweater off to be a tourniquet, so I was only in my sports bra. I'd never been more thankful for high-rise jeans. We'd portaled into the forest just beyond the border of Avolire, which made sense. They wouldn't have seen us arrive this way. But that arch was just up ahead in perfect sight.

Heat washed over my back.

We all jumped and spun around—my jaw dropped. A massive dragon was crouched in the shadow of the trees. The white snow landing on him had already camouflaged his light-gray scales. Despite his size, he was only visible by the glow of his yellow eyes.

"*Hey Silas, thanks for coming,*" Tegan said into our minds. "*Chutney is injured, but I trust you'll be okay without her?*"

He puffed little smoke balls out of his nose.

"*I don't want you to fight. You are backup. You are the escape plan if something happens to me.*" She pointed her finger at him. "*Get them out of here if I can't.*"

Silas closed his eyes, then opened them. It looked like a nod, so we all nodded back.

Then we turned to face the white castle standing like a glacier in the blizzard of the arctic circle. Everyone pulled out their weapons and rolled to the balls of their feet. We were waiting for Tegan's signal.

Willow wiggled her fingers and I saw myself with Cooper at the front of the group. A chill ran down my spine. Tenn tapped on those gold bands and summoned Michael's sword to his hands, the glow radiating light like the actual sun.

Tegan held up her fingers and counted down from three . . . two . . . . one . . .

We charged.

Tegan flew up ahead of us and launched flaming orange balls of fire right into the castle's exterior wall. Smoke and flame shot up into the dark sky. The castle rocked under her attacks. Willow threw one hand up and a dozen dragons circled the air above the castle.

I wanted to sit and watch the magic these incredible witches were about to display, but I had a job to do. They were risking themselves as my distraction, so I needed to be ready to run for the throne. She'd only made me invisible so that if a vampire spotted us inside, they wouldn't see *me,* they'd see the others. When we passed under the arch, I wanted to vomit. We'd gone to such lengths to get me out of this place, and now I was voluntarily running back in.

Tegan and Emersyn launched fire-bombs into the castle walls from every angle. Lightning struck the towers and windows exploded. Golden light spilled onto the snow.

Sweyn screamed from somewhere inside her icy castle.

Tennessee stood in the middle of their front lawn with Michael's sword out. Hunter, Kessler, and Emersyn stood right behind him with Timothy and Jackson a few feet away. Easton, Royce, and Savannah were close to the arch.

Then there was me and Cooper. We stood just a few feet from the front door, which was only a couple feet away from us.

Vampires rushed out in their white trench coats with their long swords drawn. They moved in a blur, leaving only a flurry of snow in their wake to know where they were. Just as they made it to Tenn, he threw wind into the front line and sent them flying into the air where a purple dragon drenched their bodies in flames.

Sweyn leapt out of the shattered windows of her ballroom with Everest, Saber, and Sam hot on her heels. They ran out in a dead sprint, blending in with the snow. Our friends were surrounded by vampires in the blink of an eye. Willow had dragons dive-bombing and raining fire on them—which was sent by Emersyn who was flying around with them. The ground rocked and the castle rumbled. I couldn't watch the fight. I had to watch my target. Hunter glanced to us subtly, then spun and shot golden magic.

Sweyn shrieked and her face turned red. She pointed at my illusion. "YOU!" Then she charged for me.

I cursed. We were too close to the door *and* the illusion. If Sweyn got to it, she'd know it was a fake and we'd be screwed. I realized this part of the plan may have been faulty. But then Tenn swooped and scooped Sweyn right off the snow. They struggled in the air as she tried to snap his wings off.

"EVEREST!"

Everest lunged like a snow leopard on the hunt. He leapt over the other lines of the Sentinels and raced right for me. My heart skipped. I froze in place. He pulled a silver sword the length of his arm out of nowhere. My eyes widened. The look on his face was lethal. Stone-cold predator. This was the moment, the chance to sneak inside while everyone was focused on Everest, but I couldn't move. I'd never seen *that* look on his face. It shook me to my core.

"KILL!" Sweyn screamed.

Everest landed right in front of my illusion and Cooper. He pulled his arm back, then swung his sword—*right through Cooper's neck, severing his head from his body.*

"NOOOO!" My Coven-mates screamed as Cooper's head hit the snow.

I couldn't move. I couldn't scream. I was frozen. There was nothing to do. There was no saving him. Our plan had gone horribly, horribly wrong. My chest was burning.

Sweyn threw her head back and cackled. She clapped her hands and danced.

The Sentinels pounced on my Coven-mates, taking advantage of their distraction. But they couldn't fight. They were frozen in horror as Cooper's body crashed to the snow.

But then sparkling light-blue magic slammed into the faces of the vampires nearest my Coven-mates. Everyone it touched dropped to the ground, instantly sound asleep. Rainbow mist shot across the lawn at the exact same time and crashed into something invisible a few feet in front of me. The magic faded in the blink of an eye.

Cooper stood there twenty feet behind his severed head with his magic coiled in his palm. He fired his magic into another dozen vampires. "Try again, bloodsucker."

I gasped so hard I staggered backwards.

It was fake. That was FAKE. That Cooper next to the illusion of me had also been an illusion. Cooper was alive and well right in front of me and putting vampires to sleep while our enemy gawked.

Savannah dropped to her knees and puked.

"No." Sweyn's eyes were wider than a full moon. Her face was pale, and those red eyes were *seething*. "NO!"

Tegan appeared at the edge of the snowy lawn, her white hair flapping in the breeze. Her gold and white eyes sparkled. She let out a deep laugh and held her arms out to the side. "Taste my rainbow, bitch."

"YOU!"

"Yeah, ME." She waved her arms. "Come and get me."

Sweyn, Everest, and all the vampires charged for her.

Cooper, the *real* Cooper, spun and raced over to me. He grabbed my arm and dragged me to the front door. Bentley and Lily were hot on our heels. "This is our chance! Let's get this page and get the hell out before I lose my head for real."

# CHAPTER FIFTY-ONE

## FRANKIE

WE STOPPED at the end of a grand hallway where the wall behind us was made of limestone instead of marble. The ceiling was vaulted with wooden beams. My focus went to the wall in front of us, which was a row of massive stained-glass windows running the entire stretch of the hallway. Each window held a different image. They were Sweyn's lie, images to literally teach vampires an incorrect version of history where the vampires were the victims. My stomach rolled.

But I remembered standing right here with Everest. I didn't want to go back to those days, to those memories, yet my mind and heart had a different idea. Suddenly I was right back there with him, begging him to run away with me.

*"And I'm the enemy in disguise."*

*He reached up and tucked my hair behind my ear, then traced the backs of his fingers across my jaw. "No, Gali, that would be me."*

*My heart sank. I looked up at him, and my chest felt tight. I wondered just how long he'd been playing this game. Hiding. Scheming. I wondered if he was as lonely as I suspected. My heart hurt for him. This palace was a ruthless, cold place. I reached out and took his hand. "Run with me."*

*He closed his eyes and cringed. With a sigh, he leaned into me and pressed his forehead to mine. His breath swept over my face. For a brief moment we stayed like that, just breathing each other in. Then he* pulled back, his eyes dark and distant and refusing to meet mine. "One day."

I wanted to scream. "Why? What's stopping you? Be on the side where your heart lies."

He cleared his throat and stepped back. A cold draft filled the space between us. "My heart died a long time ago."

"No, it didn't." I glanced left and right, then reclaimed the spot right beside him. "Your heart shines through the darkness brighter than a full moon's reflection on the snow. Just because this palace is too cold to recognize the warmth, it does not mean it's not there."

He looked up at me with the most unreadable expression I'd ever seen. It broke my heart, and I couldn't even explain why. I had no idea where these emotions or these words in me were coming from. I barely knew him. But I knew him.

"Run with me, Everest."

He gave me a soft smile that melted my heart a little. "I shall meet you there and count the hours between."

My eyes burned. A hot lump formed in my throat.

"Come, we can't get caught out here," Cooper whispered in my ear as he squeezed my hand.

I gasped and shook myself out of that moment. I may have been invisible, but Cooper, Bentley, and Lily were not. We'd gone to Sweyn's throne room first, but her throne had not been there, which meant it had to be in the ballroom. I tugged on Cooper's hand to get us moving. The others couldn't see me, so we had to improvise. I led them down a flight of stairs made of stone to a grand wooden door that had to be twenty feet tall. When I pulled the door open just enough to slide through, my pulse quickened and my palms got sweaty.

Like Sweyn's throne room, this room's ceiling was made entirely of glass, as were three of the four walls. The stars twinkled in a navy-blue sky beside a crescent moon. The wall of windows were all shattered, so not only was snow pouring inside but we would be visible to the battle raging outside. We were going to be on full display.

All four of us froze with our backs to the closed wooden door.

Straight ahead, sitting in the middle of the room, was Sweyn's throne—a throne that was a smaller and more polished version of the one in the other room. *This* throne was made of marble. *From the marble within her lair, Retrieve the stolen without flair.* I'm such an idiot.

"*Can any of you make yourselves invisible?*" I whispered.

They shook their heads.

"*Okay, stay here. Watch my back,*" I whispered. "*If I need help, I'll shoot my magic out.*"

"I've never been able to sneak up on any of you," a voice said from *right* behind us.

We all gasped and spun around. My eyes widened. Braison stood in the open doorway. We hadn't heard him approach. Hadn't even heard the door open. Cooper, Lily, and Bentley all breathed his name. They were statues beside me. I glanced up and saw the tears in their eyes as they stared at their friend, their former family member.

Braison stepped inside the ballroom, silently closing the door behind him. He wiggled his fingers and thick gray smoke shot out of his palms. He strolled forward, whistling softly as his magic blocked the view of the throne from the outside. Then he stopped and leaned against the window frame at the far end of the room and looked at us. "This will not hold them, it may even make them more curious, but it *will* act as a speed bump."

"Braison," Cooper whispered.

He held his hand up and shook his head. "Now is not the time for our emotions. I can feel her in here, which means *they* can too. Whatever you're doing, do it *fast* or I fear that little Headless Horseman act out front may make a repeat."

"Braison—"

"Be fast." He nodded once, then leapt through his gray smoke and out of sight.

Lily whimpered. Cooper let out a shaky breath.

"Go, Frankie," Bentley whispered.

I cursed and raced for the throne, dropping to my knees at the base. And then I realized I hadn't asked anyone for advice on finding a hidden compartment. The pages of the book were dark in color but this whole throne was white—so it wasn't part of the throne, which meant it had to be inside of a drawer or something.

"*The window,*" Bentley whispered.

A moment later a handful of vampires leapt through Braison's smoke and landed inside the ballroom. Their eyes spotted my friends instantly. Cooper threw out his magic and put them to sleep. Lily drenched them in sunlight, burning them to ash in seconds.

"Frankie, hurry," Bentley said in a rush.

"Any tips how to find a drawer or something?" I cursed. "I'm still new here—"

"Push your magic into the throne, like pouring water. Follow it to where it pools. That'll be the compartment."

I pressed my palms flat to the seat of the throne and pushed my magic out just like Bentley said, imagining it was water. The neon-blue flames slid over the seat and down the sides. The magic flowed to the bottom left, at the base of the armrest that went all the way to the ground. I glanced up and realized Sweyn's staff was usually propped right here, so that would be a great way to hide a secret drawer.

It took me a moment or two, but finally I managed to pry open a tall, narrow door in the armrest. Relief washed through me. But it was short-lived because the compartment was *empty*. Nothing but empty, cold air greeted me. I stuck my hand into the dark crevice, yet found nothing.

"It's empty." I shook my head and turned on my knees to face my friends. "It's gone."

Cooper scowled. "What do you mean?"

"Are you sure?" Lily asked with panic in her eyes.

Bentley cursed and lifted up his left arm that was covered in a white sleeve. "Pull my sleeve up. Pull it up."

His other arm was in a sling so he couldn't, but Cooper was quick to yank that sleeve up—he cursed violently. "You cannot be serious."

"Read it," I whisper-shouted but didn't move in case it had a clue for me.

"*Remember where thy forsaken, A ruse we now must awaken. To play with rules that can't be broken, For only one can claim the spoken. But drop thy sword, flee the scene, This quest becomes evergreen. For upon the dawn my word shall come—*" Cooper gasped, his face paling. He licked his lips and looked up to meet Bentley's eyes. "*The Angel of Tides must ring his drum.*"

Bentley squeezed his eyes shut. Lily grabbed his wrist and re-read it.

The last line meant something to them, but not to me.

The lines *flee the scene, This quest becomes evergreen* meant something to me though. It meant Valathame knew the missing page wasn't here. She knew we *had* to come here for some reason, but we weren't going to find this missing page.

Black smoke billowed all around me. My skin sparkled and I knew Tegan's spell wore off because my friends cursed. Before I could even scramble away from whatever this was, Everest emerged from within the darkness.

He reached down and grabbed me by the jaw, his fingers digging into my skin. I hated how much I loved it. He lifted me up to his eye level. "Cooper is *not* your soulmate," he snarled.

My heart was pounding in my chest. I frowned. "What—"

Everest shot black magic into my chest, then blasted it across the room toward Cooper. He turned my face to watch as the green heart-shaped crystal on his chest *vanished.* My eyes widened. He dragged me over to a column a few feet away, then dropped me to my feet and spun me around to face my own reflection in a mirror. The soulmate glyph on me was *gone.*

My pulse was flying. He gripped my hair, tipped my head back, then sank his fangs into my throat. I gasped and my whole body flinched. My body lit on fire inside. I watched my reflection as my blue eyes changed to pink . . . as those lines slid down my throat to my shoulder.

"*You're mine,*" Everest growled. "Not *his.* MINE."

An explosion rocked the castle so hard dust rained down on us. Everest tossed me to my knees on the ground, then vanished into darkness and completely out of sight.

# CHAPTER FIFTY-TWO

## FRANKIE

EVEREST WAS MY SOULMATE.

*Everest . . . was my soulmate.*

I wanted to cry, scream, and throw up. We were running through the snow to the battle, to our Coven-mates. But I saw nothing. My entire soul was locked on this revelation. Everest was my soulmate. Everything suddenly made so much more sense. In hindsight, it was painfully obvious. In the back of my mind, I registered the sharp chill of the snow hitting my skin and the sounds of the war happening up ahead.

*Everest is my soulmate.*

I had so many questions.

Bright light flashed in front of me, snapping me out of my mental spiral. Lily was in front of me shining thick streams of golden sunshine from her palms into the battle up ahead. Vampires burst to dust and ash like fireworks left and right. Cooper knocked a dozen vampires out. With one flick of his wrist, they were all asleep.

I looked ahead and my heart sank. Willow had dragons of all colors flying around and shooting flames, which were really being sent by Emersyn. It was incredible. I saw rainbow mist light up the tree line. Tennessee was a *monster* zooming through the battle.

Sweyn was up there, I saw her white hair and heard her hideous cackle. Saber and Everest were fighting by her side.

Green flames shot up in front of me, causing me to make a sharp right turn. Sam charged for me, her long blonde hair flying behind her like a cape. My soulmate's betrothed. She tackled me into the snow. I tried to push her off, but she had that vampire strength I couldn't overpower. But she wasn't hurting me. Instead, she pressed her palms to my right shoulder and neck and screamed.

*Oh no, she knows what this mark means*—warmth covered my upper body all the way up to my jaw. I stopped fighting her and looked down. Sam had somehow used magic to cover me up. I looked up to her with wide eyes.

She snarled and dove for the other side of my throat. I gasped.

*'I'm not gonna hurt you, Frankie. Stop fighting me or it WILL hurt.'*

I froze with my hands on my shoulders as her voice echoed in my mind.

*'Sweyn CANNOT see that soulmate mark on your shoulder. Everest's cover cannot be blown yet,'* she yelled through my mind. *'You have to get out of here. Take The Coven and GO. You can't win this tonight, not like this.'*

Then I remembered Sam's voice warning us something was coming in the Land of the Lore.

*'The Unseelie and demons are coming. She made me call for them. The fallen angels are coming, and there's SIX of them now.'* Her voice wasn't screaming anymore, like she was new to this trick. *'On the count of three, I need you to blast me with as much magic as you can, then run for the arches.'*

I nodded enough for her to feel it.

*'Three . . . two . . . one—NOW!'*

I pushed my magic out and into her chest. I threw it with everything I had. Sam screamed and flew up in the air. I scrambled to my feet just as Cooper lunged through the green flames. He reached down and lifted me off the snow and into a sprint.

We made it around to the rest of our Coven-mates. Tenn and Tegan weren't there. Our Coven Leaders were thick in battle, surrounded by Sentinels and Sweyn. Everest was fighting Tennessee but I could tell neither one of them were trying that hard to kill the other. The rest of us were just trying to work through the vampires between us and the arch. But Lily and Cooper were weak from the Land of the Lore. Their magic was flickering.

"BEYOND THE ARCH OF MAGIC'S LANE!" Bentley yelled as he fought off a vampire. "We're weaker here! Conserve your strength!"

"Get to the arch!" Tim shouted. "GO!"

Tegan screamed and rainbow magic exploded out of her. Sweyn shot into the air and crashed into the snow back by the ballroom's shattered windows. But Tegan slid backwards and slammed into the arch.

Everest threw his hand up and the ground shook like an earthquake, throwing us all to the snow. Only Tenn and Everest stood still. We kept trying to get up, but the world trembled too hard. Gravity kept us down. All we could do was watch.

Black liquid bubbled up from beneath the snow. He flexed his fingers and twisted his hand. The liquid looked like tar. He'd summoned pillars made of tar all around Tennessee. The tar moved and pulsed.

And then the tar took the shape of *people*.

"*What the fuck is that?*" Easton breathed.

The tar kept morphing until it was shaped like people with weapons. The tar monsters lunged for Tenn. It was twenty on one. They attacked him with expert moves and skill. Tenn was Tenn though. He moved with speed even the vampires didn't have. Michael's sword sliced clean through the tar people, chopping them into pieces. But the second they hit the snow, they just began reforming.

And then Tennessee froze.

His sword *lowered*.

Cooper and Timothy were crawling in the snow to try and get to him. Kessler was leaping ahead but kept crashing again. Everyone was yelling. Tennessee had just stopped fighting. He'd lowered his sword until the tip of the blade hit the snow. He staggered backwards. The tar monsters he'd already sliced up were reforming already. They were going to ambush him at once.

Tenn just stared at one of them. His face was pale and a little green. His mismatched eyes were wide. "*Libby?*

My Coven-mates froze.

The tar monster in front of him shined with a red glow from within the tar until the tar was gone, leaving a very human-looking girl standing in its place—a girl with light-brown hair tied in a side braid and hazel eyes . . . a girl with the Roman numerals *XV* written in faded gray on her left forearm.

Tenn dropped Michael's sword in the snow. "*Libby*."

Libby grinned and raised her sword up above her head and grinned. "Did ya miss me?"

LIBBY. *Insert evil cackle.* Are y'all surviving that Twilight-inspired moment for Cooper's beheading? *More evil cackling.* There's more where all that torture came from so buckle up for the rest of The Coven Saga - we're only halfway through! For now, Frankie has *finally* joined The Coven officially and is ready to take on her enemies...*and her true soulmate Everest.* Season Four **The Coven: Vampire Magic** is just getting started so make sure you CLICK HERE to preorder book 3, *The Scarlet Witch!* Then also swing over to my FB group or subscribe to my Newsletter to read a bonus scene for The Potion Witch!

IF YOU HAVE a young reader who is a fan of this series that reads with you (like a kid/grandkid/sibling), OR you're just not a fan of spice then I have some good news for you...I have an ebook version that is PG13. no spice. only like 2 F-bombs. To get this version you MUST be subscribed to my NL and purchase the real version on amazon. If you email me with proof of purchase of The Potion Witch (chandelle@chandellelavaun.com) I will send you the download link for the PG13 version. KU does not count for this, must be an actual purchase. (I also provide PG13 versions of *The Blood Witch, The Rose Witch, and The Wolf Witch* - also my non-Coven book *Of Blood & Nightmares*)

. . .

STILL CRAVING THE COVEN **RIGHT NOW**? WELL GREAT NEWS, CLICK HERE AND GO TO MY FACEBOOK GROUP AND READ BONUS SCENES POSTED IN THE FEATURED POSTS!

Become a Chandwitch and connect with me and other fans of The Coven! We're totally weird and crazy in there, but it's a whole lot of fun! Just CLICK HERE to join my Facebook group!

---

Most of The Coven is Saga prior to now is fairly clean, but it's growing up and growing with the characters and who they are. So expect the spice to continue if it fits the story. **BUT DO YOU WANT MORE SPICY BOOKS RIGHT NOW? Because I've got TWO within The Coven Saga.** *The Rose Witch* and *The Wolf Witch,* both of these are standalone stories about new characters in the Coven universe that you can read right now without reading any of the rest of the saga!

Read below to find out just how wild those stories are!

**HIS MAGIC LURKS in the shadows...**

I feel his eyes on my back with every step I take. He's following me. Chasing me. There's nowhere for me to go, nowhere to hide that he won't find me. He moves in smoke and shadows. He *is* the darkness. He tracks my every move like a predator with gold glowing eyes in the night. I know he's going to catch me, the only question is...why do I want him to?

I have no idea who he is or what he wants. I know I should be terrified...but I'm not.

There are things happening to me...things I can't control or explain...things that only I can see. Magic pours from me like a scarlet river and this locket around my neck pulses with dark, electric energy. I think it's what *he* wants...but he isn't the only thing on the hunt for it. Demons hide around every corner, they attack mercilessly and relentlessly - the only thing they seem to be afraid of is *him*.

That should be a warning, except there's something inside me that begs to be near him. I feel it like a magnet, drawing me closer and I'm running out of reasons to fight it.

He is the Prince of Hell...and he's either my savior or my damnation...

**The Rose Witch is a novel set in The Coven saga but is designed to be read as a stand-alone.**

**CLICK HERE** to read **The Rose Witch** now!

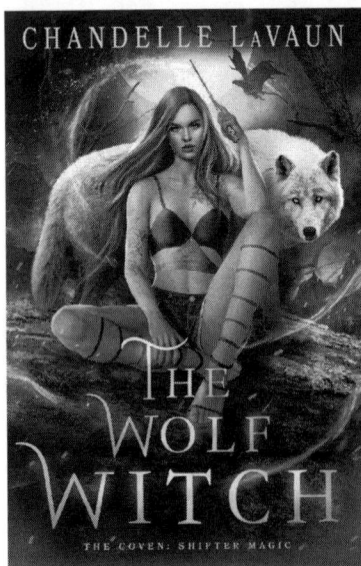

**SOMETIMES MAGIC THROWS A CURVEBALL...**

I thought I had everything figured out. I'd gone to the academy for witches and mastered my magic. I'd opened my own witchy occult store, just as I always wanted. And my family was as close as ever. Everything was going according to plan.

Until the wolves showed up and dragged me back to their land. It was all a misunderstanding. They had the wrong girl, the wrong idea. I was just a witch.

And then I *shifted*.

But nothing is as it appears...and now my life is in danger.

***This is a stand-alone story with an HEA and no cliffhanger! You don't have to have read the rest of The Coven Saga!***

CLICK HERE TO READ THE WOLF WITCH NOW!

VAMPIRE MAGIC IS *season four* in The Coven Saga, if you haven't read Season One (*Elemental Magic*), Season Two (*Academy Magic*), or Season Three (*Fae Magic*) then check out my website to read all about them so you can get caught up before The Scarlet Witch releases in 2025!

BUT IF YOU wanna know where it all got started...check out Season One: Elemental Magic

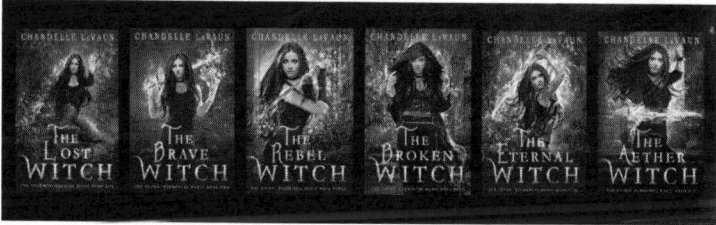

**CLICK HERE** to read Season One: **Elemental Magic Series** now!

# CHANDELLE LaVAUN

# THE POTION WITCH

THE COVEN: VAMPIRE MAGIC BOOK TWO

**This one is for content creators on Tiktok and Reels, y'all keep my adhd squirrels happy when the anxiety goes into chokehold mode...**

*Some people survive chaos,*
*And that is how they grow.*
*And some people thrive in chaos,*
*Because chaos is all they know*

*-unknown*

# THE COVEN

## AS OF THE START OF POTION WITCH

**0 : The Fool : Chutney Burroughs** – Cups Suit – Communicates with animals.

**I : The Magician : Willow Walcot** – Wands Suit – Illusion magic

**II : The High Priestess : Tegan Bishop** – *Aether Witch* – All Suits – All elemental Magic

**III : The Empress : Emersyn Bishop** – Wands Suit – Fire, smoke, & metal magic

**IV : The Emperor : Tennessee Wildes** – Swords Suit – Wind, water, & earth magic

**V : The Hierophant : Bentley Bishop** – Cups Suit – Divination

**VI : The Lovers : Easton Corey** – Swords Suit – Magical armor

**VII : The Chariot : Devon Howe Bishop** – Swords Suit – Astral projection

**VIII : Strength : Kessler Bishop** – Swords Suit – Super strength

**IX : The Hermit : Timothy Roth**– Swords Suit – Speaks & reads all languages

**X : Wheel of Fortune : Royce Redd** – Wands Suit – Nature magic

**XI : Justice : Constance Bell – Wands Suit – Crystal magic**

**XII : The Hanged Man : Thiago Diaz– Suit Unknown – Light & shadow magic**

**XIII : Death : Savannah Grace– Wands Suit – Communicates with the dead**

**XIV : Temperance : Hunter Bishop – Cups Suit – Emotions magic**

**XV : The Devil : Deacon English – Pentacles Suit – Persuasion magic**

**XVI : The Tower : Frankie Proctor – Suit Unknown – Potion magic**

**XVII : The Star : Cooper Bishop – Swords Suit – Dream magic**

**XVIII : The Moon : Henley Redd – Wands Suit – Moon magic**

**XIX : The Sun : Lily Warren– Pentacles Suit – Sun magic**

**XX : Judgement : Bettina Blair – Swords Suit – Ice magic**

**XXI : The World : Jackson Lancaster – Swords Suit – Truth magic**

# THE COVEN READING ORDER

THE CHOSEN WITCH

THE LOST WITCH

THE BRAVE WITCH

THE REBEL WITCH

THE BROKEN WITCH

THE ETERNAL WITCH

THE AETHER WITCH

THE FIRE WITCH

THE HIDDEN WITCH

THE FALLEN WITCH

THE CITY WITCH

THE WILD WITCH

THE FROZEN WITCH

THE SECRET WITCH

THE UPTOWN WITCH

THE EMPIRE WITCH

THE ROSE WITCH

THE CURSED WITCH

THE ROGUE WITCH

THE ROTTEN WITCH

THE DEATH WITCH

THE WOLF WITCH

THE BLOOD WITCH

THE POTION WITCH

# ALSO BY CHANDELLE LAVAUN

The Coven: Elemental Magic Complete Series

The Coven: Academy Magic Complete Series

The Coven: School of Magical Arts NYC Series

The Coven: Fae Magic Complete Series

The Night Realm: Magic Marked Trilogy

The Night Realm: Christmas Marked Series

Fatal Fae (The Night Realm)

Fiery Fae (The Night Realm)

Final Fae (The Night Realm)

Trick My Treat (The Night Realm) - coming soon

Of Blood & Nightmares (Forgotten Kingdoms)

Queen of Death (Gods Reborn Series Prequel)

# ABOUT THE AUTHOR

Chandelle LaVaun was born and raised on the beach in sunny South Florida. Her love of The Mortal Instruments, Percy Jackson, and The Black Dagger Brotherhood inspired her to go from fangirl to author. She follows her muse across many genres, writing in urban fantasy, paranormal, high fantasy, contemporary, and hopefully one day a murder mystery to make Agatha Christie proud. Her favorite things in life are dogs, pizza, slurpees, and anything nerdy. She suffers from wanderlust and hopes to travel to every country in the world one day...just as soon as they let her big dogs buy a seat.

**The Potion Witch**

Published by Wanderlost Publishing

Copyright © 2024 by Chandelle LaVaun

Cover designed by Lori Grundy @ Cover Reveal Designs

Pentacle art & portraits by Samaiya Beaumont

❀ Created with Vellum

Made in the USA
Middletown, DE
24 August 2024